# WEST OF
# SHERIDAN

Dean Ross

ISBN: 1469919524
ISBN 13: 9781469919522

*For my wonderful wife.*

*You truly are my better half. Thank you for making me a better man, for showing me a living example of patience and kindness, and for allowing me the freedom to explore crazy ideas like trying to write a book.*

For more information, reviews, interviews with the author, an in-depth look into the inspiration behind this story, and much more, please visit:
www.westofsheridan.com

*It is a man's own mind, not his enemy or foe, that lures him to evil ways.*

**—Siddhartha Budda**

*Before man is life and death, good and evil; that which he shall choose be given him.*

**—Ecclesiastes**

*The small man thinks that small acts of goodness are of no benefit, and does not do them; and that small deeds of evil do no harm, and does not refrain from them. Hence his wickedness becomes so great that it cannot be concealed and his guilt so great that it cannot be pardoned.*

**—Confucius**

# 1.

"Martha, I don't know what kind of magic you are workin' in that kitchen, but I swear I've never had trout taste any better." Jack set his fork on the corner of the plate and wiped his mouth with the edge of his napkin

Frank rolled his eyes. "Here we go."

She smiled as a slight blush rose in her cheeks. "Jack, you are the sweetest man, but you know, you say the same thing every time you have dinner with us."

Jack grinned at her. "And every time it gets a little better. Thank you. That was truly somethin' special."

Her smile blossomed even further. "I don't know how you manage to stay single when you sweet talk like you do. There has to be someone special out there for you. A man has needs after all."

He squirmed a little in his chair, surprised by her comment.

Frank noticed his friend's unease at the remark and quickly interjected, "Honey, is that coffee I smell?"

Martha slid her chair back as she stood, saying, "Yes, it is. I figured if this stubborn old goat is insisting on driving home

tonight, the least I could do was fill him full of coffee before he left."

Jack handed his plate to her outstretched hand and said, "It'll keep me up all right. I'll have to pull over every fifteen miles to get rid of it. Probably won't see home till Monday with all the stops."

Frank leaned over the table and said, "You know, you could just stay here. We have plenty of room, and I might be able to find a cribbage board. It'd give me a chance to win back a little of the money you took last time."

"Thanks, but I can't. Miguel wants to brand colts in the mornin', and he's been makin' noise about tryin' to fill his elk tag in the afternoon. I need to get back. Besides, it's an easy drive."

"What is it over there —a hundred miles?"

"'Bout a hundred fifty. Usually takes me three hours with the trailer."

"Yeah, but didn't they get a little snow in the Bighorns the other night?"

"They did, but when I came through this mornin', the roads weren't bad at all. I can't imagine it'll be much different on the way home."

Frank took another drink of his wine. "Say, I hope you don't mind my asking, but how are you guys doing over there?"

"Don't mind at all. So far, we've been pretty lucky. Cattle prices have followed the rest of the commodities, and we've been able to hold 'em and sell late, which has helped a bit. Other guys weren't so lucky or had early contracts. They had to deliver at prices not much better'n rustlin'. We're also still movin' a few of the better horses, but the rest of the horse market is terrible. We couldn't give away a regular horse if we had to."

"You're still selling a few out West?"

"A few. When we get home, Miguel is gonna spend a couple a weeks with Dingo, and then he's off to Arizona."

Frank leaned back. "Ah man, I love that horse. I don't even wanna know what they're gonna pay for him. I know I can't afford it."

Martha stepped back into the dining room with two cups hanging from one hand and a coffee pot in the other. Frank said, "Get this, honey, Jack just told me Dingo is already sold."

"Oh, I'm so sorry," she said, looking at her husband with a disappointed frown, as she put the cups in front of the men. "I know you really liked him, but wasn't that the plan?"

Frank shook his head, "Yeah, it's the damn plan."

"Well, shoot," Jack said. "I'm the one who's sorry. I didn't know you were interested. We might be able to work somethin' out."

Frank sighed. "No no. I'm sorry. I don't need a horse and I can't afford one. This is all just a combination of things. I was supposed to retire this year, and I guess I had a picture in my head of riding off into the sunset. I found out a couple of weeks ago I can't retire. They won't let me. I have to work another three years before I'm eligible for my pension, which, by the way, they've reduced, and now they tell me I can't collect Social Security since I have a government pension."

Jack's eyebrows rose. "Wow. That's a little rough."

"You're damn right it is. The part that gets my gall is these assholes in Congress just wasted it. When I started with the Park Service thirty-two years ago, they told me what the retirement deal was. I didn't ask for it. They told me what Social Security would pay and when. Then they went and pissed it all away. They lined the pockets of the bankers on Wall Street, and it comes out of what they promised to me."

Martha stood next to her husband and put a hand on his shoulder. "We'll be okay."

Frank looked up at her. "We won't starve. It's just—well, goddamn it—we had plans."

"'Course you did," Jack said. "Nobody can blame you for that. This whole economy has everybody in a world of hurt. Annie wanted to come home for Christmas this year. Do you know how much a round trip ticket from St. Louis to Sheridan is? Would you believe over twenty-eight hundred dollars?"

"You've got to be shittin' me," Frank said in amazement.

"No, sir, I am not. There's not but two flights to choose from either. What's more is I had to give almost nine dollars a gallon for diesel when I filled up this morning."

"Have you been to the grocery store lately?" Martha asked. "I think this is the first year I'm going to be glad when Frank gets his elk."

"Hey!" Frank said incredulously as he turned to face her. "You like elk."

She winked at Jack. "Yes, dear. Of course, dear. Whatever you say, dear."

Jack winked back at her and said, "Tell you what, Martha. Maybe we could talk the ol' boy here into huntin' for one of those short, squatty black elk that stand around eatin' grass on my ranch."

She said, "That would be nice. I wouldn't have to hear about how sore he is from carrying that rifle up and down all those hills and hauling his elk out."

"Sure. We could put a lawn chair in the back of the truck and drive him right on out to where they're standin'. Hell, he might even be able to hit one if I get him in close enough."

Frank said, "I think it must be about time for you to head home. I take you up to my fishing spot, I feed you at my table, and this is how you treat me?"

Jack laughed. "Yep. What are friends for?"

"And 'old boy'? You're not that far behind me."

"I'll be fifty next fall."

Martha said, "Jack, you're not that old. You should start thinking about meeting someone and settling down again."

Frank laughed and added, "Yeah. Maybe one of them high-maintenance trophy wives. That's what you need."

"Whoa," Jack said, putting both hands in the air as if to signal a truck to stop. "On that note, you're right. I do need to be gettin' down the road."

Frank leaned forward and smiled, "Not so much fun when it's on the other foot, huh?" He winked. "We're just teasin'."

Jack grinned. "I know, I know. But, I should get goin'. Even if I pulled out right now, I won't see home much before two in the morning."

Once the horses were loaded and secure, Jack walked along the trailer toward the truck. He heard the familiar *shunck* sound as the driver's door automatically unlocked, and the interior lights came on. He shook his head and opened the door, leaning his back against the post, as Frank walked around the front of the pickup.

Jack said, "I'm never going to get used to this keyless bullshit. In my opinion every truck needs a key. Worked just fine for a long damn time. Now all they give me is a card for my wallet, and the goddamn truck acts like it's possessed. Do you know all I do is press a button and it starts itself? Damnedest thing I ever saw. There's not a single button or knob on the radio or the heater; it's all controlled by a computer screen."

"I'm afraid the world is moving on without us, buddy," Frank said with a note of resignation.

Jack smiled, "They think they are, but when those young techno-hikers and -campers with their GPS, their 4G cell phones, and their fuel cell stoves get lost, they hit the button on their satellite watches, and your boys ride in on technology that ain't changed in two hundred years to save their sorry asses."

Frank laughed. "Yep. That's about the size of it. Thanks again for bringing up the new horses. Of course, you do realize we are perfectly willing to come and get 'em. You're not that far away."

Jack smiled and said, "Did you ever wonder why I always bring the horses myself and just happen to arrive about nine in the morning? That ride in the mountains and the afternoon with a fly rod, not to mention your beer, is well worth the price of the fuel."

"Here I thought I was doin' you a favor. You were just taking advantage of my hospitality," Frank said, grinning back at him.

"Oh hell. You enjoy these days as much as I do. It's the closest thing to a day off you'll ever take."

"That's about the size of it. By the way, I was just curious, why do you drag Marlena all the way over here and back?

You could just ride one of these?" He nodded toward a small pasture. "They're all yours."

"It's kinda hard to explain. She and I don't get to spend much time together these days, and I guess I just prefer to spend nice days like this with her."

"No explanation needed. When you own the dealership, you get to drive the Cadillac. By the way, can I ask, where is Dingo headed?"

"There's a guest ranch in Arizona that has their eyes on him. After a couple years with us and half a year with your boys in the park, these horses are about as sure-footed and dead-broke as they'll ever be. If they don't spook in the middle of Yellowstone with grizzlies and wolves, they won't spook any-where. When you have bankers, corporate execs, and movie stars payin' to ride, their lawyers want 'em to be safe."

"So if I was thinking about getting a horse, we might be able to work something out?"

"You bet, Frank. Keep your eye on the little filly in the bunch I dropped off this mornin'. She's gonna be a really good horse, and I'll make you a hell of a deal if you're interested."

"A hell of a deal is still more than what your new fancy truck is worth," Frank said, shaking his head.

"Naw. You'll get the good buddy discount. But the next time I come up here, you better convince the fish to bite a little better than what they gave us today."

Frank smiled. "They will, or I'll jump in and hook them on the end of your line myself."

"Somehow I don't doubt you would. I better get goin'. I'd like to get these horses out of the trailer before I have to dig 'em out of all the shit. Say thanks to Martha again for dinner. That was somethin' special." Jack stuck out his hand and Frank shook it hard.

"Sorry about Martha pushing you on the dating thing. I know you don't like to talk about it."

"I don't mind. She just wants everybody to be happy."

"And you don't have to wait until you bring horses up. Give us a call or just drop by. We're always around."

"I might just do that," Jack said, as he climbed into the seat. "Maybe when things slow down a bit."

"Sounds like a plan. Take care."

"Thanks. You too."

Jack slammed the door and pressed the start button on the right of the steering column. The dash lit up, and he heard the compressor whine before the big diesel barked to life. The center screen flashed a welcome message and then revealed the environmental controls for the truck. He touched the lower left-hand corner of the screen, and the page switched to the GPS navigation. Another press of the screen revealed the cameras inside the trailer, and he could see the three horses standing quietly. He pressed the back button, and the screen returned to navigation. He pressed "Home," and the screen quickly showed "calculating," before returning to the map showing him the route. A hundred fifty-five miles, two hours, fifty minutes.

Jack put the truck in gear and gave a quick wave to Frank as he pulled out of the ranger station drive at the entrance to Yellowstone National Park. As he turned east on Highway 14, he thought, *Damn, I shouldn't have stayed that late. Two in the morning before I get home. Two thirty before the horses are unloaded, and three before I get to bed. Got to be at the Sheridan airport by eight to pick up those buyers. It's gonna be a short night.*

As the truck pulled onto the road, he pressed the upper right-hand corner of the screen, and a woman's voice said, "Say the name of the person you wish to call."

Jack said, "Barn."

After two rings, a deep voice with a slight Hispanic accent said, "D-bar-D. This is Miguel."

"Caballero! What the hell are you still doin' there?"

"Hello, boss. I was just finishing a few things."

"It's Friday night for God's sake. You have a wife at home. Get the hell out of there."

"If you are still working, I am still working."

"I'm not workin', hell, I've been fishing."

Miguel laughed. "I wasn't working either. Julie is here. We just got back from a ride in the canyon. She is brushing down horses right now."

"That sounds better. How'd you guys do today?"

"I got the colts rounded up and picked up the nitrogen. Oh, and I noticed the windmill quit on the number three water tank again."

"Yeah, but the creek is full. We won't need to fix it till spring."

"The secretary of Fox Point Polo Club called today. She say that they will be a little delayed tomorrow morning, and you should not expect them until nine or ten. They will call you when they are about an hour away."

"From the plane? How the hell are they gonna call me from the plane?"

"She did not tell me that. She just say that they will call you. And she ask about security. She say that a very important person will be here, but she did not say who."

"Did you give her the usual story?"

"Yeah. When she heard that we have kept an ex–vice president safe for a week, she seemed to relax."

"Good. Hell, that's great. I can sleep in a little bit. I still have three hours before I get home."

"How was Marlena today?"

"Fine. Why?"

"Tony told me he thought her near front shoe was getting loose when he picked her feet yesterday. I told him he should have said something. We could have fixed it for you."

Jack rolled his eyes and said, "She didn't have any trouble with it, but we better get it looked at tomorrow."

"Yes, sir. First thing."

"Did the stock from Kansas get there?"

"Oh, yes they did. We put them in the end paddock, away from everything else. They all look good, but one is very good."

"Lemme guess. The black one with the white star?"

"Yes, sir! He has very good conformation and a good eye. Maybe we should wait to cut him."

Jack smiled as he thought about how similar he and Miguel thought about horses. "I was thinkin' the same thing."

"What did you say? The phone is breaking up."

"I agree with you. Go home. I'll see you in the mornin'."

"Good night, sir. Drive careful."

"Good night." Jack reached over and pushed the "End Call" button on the screen. As he looked around, he thought it was odd the call should be breaking up. Cell service had always worked fine for another ten or twelve miles. That's when the computer screen blinked.

# 2.

"Hey, you about done in there?" the manager asked from behind the counter.

Mark could hear the closing music of a *Jersey Shore* rerun behind the techno being pumped through the house speakers. He thought, must be nine. "Yeah, just cooling down."

Devin stepped from behind the desk. "Dude, it's Friday night, and you're like in here every Friday night. Don't you have anything better to do?"

Mark set the dumbbells back in the rack, sat down on a bench, and started wiping his face with a towel. "Yeah, I got plenty to do. But since they put me on days, I can't get in here until late. Besides, you're supposed to be open till ten."

"Yeah, well, the owner said we are going to start closing early on Friday, Saturday, and Sunday. There's not enough people at night to keep the lights on. I was supposed to close at eight, but I figured you hadn't heard about the new hours yet."

"Fuck! I hate Gillette. Back in Denver—"

"Yeah, yeah, yeah," Devin interrupted. "Back in Denver, back in Denver. If things are so great back in Denver, why are you still here?"

"'Cause I gotta have a job, dickweed!"

"Dude, you're only like—what—twenty-five? Live with your folks."

Mark shot him a severe look and said, "I'm twenty-eight, and livin' with my folks is not an option."

"Whatever, man. Don't get all bent out of shape. I'm just sayin'."

"I know. I'm gettin' sick and tired of working all the time, you know? Lisa is all over my ass saying we never do anything, but she has no problem spending my money. I got all these fuckin' bills."

"Dude, you should just declare bankruptcy. It's what everybody is doing. Then you can tell the credit card companies to shove it up their ass."

"Yeah, and then they'll take my truck."

"Oh, wow. Yeah, that would suck." Devin thought for a minute and said, "Looks like you're screwed. Sorry, man."

Mark looked up. "Thanks. Hey, did you score any T?"

A huge smile lit up Devin's face. "I did better than that. I got andro and HGH."

"No fuckin' way!"

"Oh yeah. I gotta meet the dude tomorrow in Casper, but I'm gonna need a little of the green."

"No sweat. What do you need?"

"A grand."

Mark's eyes widened. "What? You gotta be fuckin' kidding?"

"No, man. The price of everything is going up. The guy said it was the best he could do. I got other stuff from him in the past. He always has good shit, total brand name, and his prices are reasonable."

"Fuck. All right. I'll give you half now, and then I have to meet you in the morning with the rest."

"Cool," Devin said, relaxing a little. "I knew I could count on you. Hey, you wanna meet at Buckers later. There was a bunch of hotties in here earlier talking about going."

"Fuck yeah. I need some fresh."

Mark opened the door of his apartment about a foot and felt the door hit something. He pushed a little harder and watched

as the door pushed a large brown box away. He stepped in, closing the door behind him, and looked at the box. It was addressed to Lisa and was sent from 'bebe.'

Lisa stomped into the living room with her arms crossed in front of her and said, "Where the fuck you been?"

Mark looked up at her, surprised by her attitude. "I was at the gym. I told you."

She dropped her left hand to her hip and started shaking her right index finger at him. "You most certainly did not. I thought we were supposed to go out to eat tonight."

"What's this?" he asked, pointing at the box.

"Don't try to change the subject. I thought we were going out."

"What's 'bebe'?"

"It's clothes, asshole. Are we still going out? 'Cause I'm starving."

"Clothes! You bought more fuckin' clothes! We talked about this. How the hell am I going to pay for this stuff? Where's the receipt?"

"It's called an invoice, dumbass. You only get a receipt when you buy something at the store."

"Whatever the fuck it is, show it to me."

"No."

"Lisa, goddamn it. Show it to me!"

"No."

"Fine," Mark said, as he marched across the floor toward the living room.

"What are you doing? You still haven't answered my question about dinner."

He opened the lid of the laptop and waited for the screen to come to life. "I'm going to check the credit card."

"Fine! I'll get you the fucking invoice." She started walking toward the bedroom, adding, "But you have to understand, I had to buy a couple of new sweaters and things for winter. I'm not going to sit around and freeze my ass off in this godforsaken shit hole while you're gone all day."

Mark thought about closing the lid again and waiting for the invoice, but instead hit a shift key making the screensaver disappear. In the middle of the screen was a small window that read:

```
Cowboy69: u don't know what screemin is yet. u
          thought last time was good? Hell, I'll
          make u beg for it.
Sassy_L89: Last time was gr8, but ul b the 1
          beggin for air when I grind my sweet
          pussy on your face.
Cowboy69: Same place? Noon on Mon?
Sassy_L89: u got it, or should I say, ur gonna
          get it.
Cowboy69: ur gonna get it. All of it. See Ya.
Sassy_L89: l8tr
```

"Here's your fucking invoice," Lisa said, marching back into the room. She looked over Mark's shoulder at the computer and said, "Oh shit."

"What the fuck?" Mark said in nearly a whisper.

"Mark. It's not what it seems," she said quickly. "I never meant for you to see that. I can explain."

"You fuckin' *whore!*" He stood up fast enough to make the chair fall over behind him and started walking toward her. "You fuckin' cunt! I work all day trying to make money for us to live on, and you sit here on your ass wasting it on shit you don't need when you're not out fucking some cowboy!"

She just stared at him for a second and said, "Fuck you, Mark. This is all your fault!"

"*My* fault? How is spending all this money and fucking around my fault?"

She paused for a split second trying to decide what to say. Her eyes narrowed and defiantly said, "Because you don't satisfy me!"

For Mark it was as if time slowed down. Without thinking, his right hand curled into a fist and it rose. It wasn't a full-force

roundhouse, but rather just rose from his side from where his hand had been. As it flew through the air toward Lisa, she turned her head slightly, and he connected with the side of her face in front of her left ear. He watched as she fell to the floor, raising her arms to protect herself from another blow. "Fuck you!" he roared.

She started crying.

He walked over to the desk and picked up the laptop. Lisa looked up just in time to see it crash to the floor exploding in pieces. "I'm leaving! When I get back, you better have all your shit packed up and outta my fucking apartment."

"Where am I gonna go?" she said between sobs.

"I don't fuckin' care. Just get the hell outta here, you fucking stupid pig! And if you take one thing that belongs to me, I'll take everything that I have paid for and leave you with nothing!"

"I'm gonna call the cops!"

"Call 'em. See if I care. There isn't a judge in the country that would convict me of anything once I tell them what you've done, you fucking whore!"

An hour later, Mark sat thinking in his truck near the shore of the Gillette Fishing Lake in Dalbey Park. He thought about hitting Lisa. He had never hit a girl before, although there had been times when he wanted to. In one way he felt bad—no, terrible. It was like there was an aching in his gut he couldn't quite get rid of. It was like he was now infected with some incurable virus. He was now a woman beater. He wanted to take it back and wished he could do the whole evening over again. But in another way it felt good. Damn good. The fucking cunt deserved what she got and a whole lot more. He wondered how long she had been fucking around on him. Was this the first guy or were there others? Images flashed through his mind of things he should have done to her. He should have stuffed that computer in her lying mouth or, better yet, shoved the invoice up her ass.

In the past he had always lost arguments to girls. He didn't know why. He knew he was right some of the times, but still it

pissed him off that they were *always* right. Yeah, he had did-dled a couple of girls while he was living with Lisa, but that was different. That bitch always wanted him to feel like he wasn't quite good enough. A little win every now and then reminded him that she was lucky as hell to have him.

The night air was cool. Not cold—that would come soon enough—but still cool enough to make him wish he had grabbed his jacket. He rolled up the window, started the truck, and decided to head to Buckers. It was almost eleven, but that's when things started happening. As he was about to pull out of the parking lot, the radio faded, and the screen flashed "incoming call" and then "Lady Love." He pushed answer.

"Mark, listen, I am *sooo* sorry. You were totally right tonight and I was wrong. I don't know what I was thinking. Could we talk about this a little?"

"Ah, I don't know."

"Oh, come on. We both said some terrible things, and, like I said, I am so sorry. I want to make it up to you. You can cut up the credit cards, and I will get a job. I promise. If I could just stay here tonight, maybe we can talk about it."

"I gotta think about it."

"Where're you at? Maybe I could come down there, and we could talk about it now?"

"No. I'm gonna meet Devin at Buckers. We can talk about this later."

"Are you coming home tonight?"

"I don't know yet."

"We can work this out. Couples have rough spots all the time. I just don't want to do anything rash, you know, 'cause I can't live without you."

That did it. The bitch finally realized who was the man. Maybe he would think about it. Maybe they both had overre-acted a little.

"Mark?"

"Yeah, I'm still here. So, you can't live without me, huh?"

"You're the best, baby. I've never met anyone else that even comes close to you."

He smiled. "Okay, you can stay the night, but the rules are gonna change."

"You're awesome. If you come home tonight, I'll let you do *anything* you want."

"Anything?"

"You got it."

"Maybe I will come home tonight."

"What? The call was kinda breakin' up."

"Maybe I will come home tonight."

"I'll see you later you big—" The call cut off.

That was weird, Mark thought, as he drove through town. Cell service was usually pretty good. It's never done that before. As he drove down Main Street, he noticed the traffic lights start flashing yellow and then turn green. That's weird. He pulled the truck into a spot at the end of the lot across the street from Buckers and shifted into park. He was just about to shut the truck off when it quit by itself. Nice timing. He got out and pressed the button on the key fob, but nothing happened. He opened the door and pressed the lock button, but again, nothing happened. Damn. Now I have to get the truck fixed. What else is going to go to hell? He pressed the lock stem next to the window, slammed the door, and started walking across the street to the bar.

# 3.

It was the change in the computer display that first caught Jack's eye. The screen switched by itself to a view of the horses in the trailer. As he turned his head briefly, he noticed the horses were on high alert with their ears standing at attention. The screen then switched again to the GPS display and then switched to the environmental controls.

"Goddamn thing." He reached to switch the screen back to the horses when the display went black. His mind had just enough time to register total darkness, the complete lack of lights anywhere on the truck, when the engine died and a bluish white electric arc jumped across the hood in front of him. Without hesitation he grabbed the shift lever and shifted the truck into neutral. About one hundred feet ahead, he could just make out a light-colored gravel pull-off on the right side of the road and started to steer for it. A second brighter arc of white fire danced on the windshield between the hood and the top of the truck, and he felt the trailer pull hard to the right. Jack held the wheel tightly with both hands and turned the truck toward the left to counter the pull. Thoughts raced through his mind, but few of them made any sense. He shouldn't be close enough to the side of the road for the trailer wheels to have

hit the gravel shoulder, but that's what it felt like. Suddenly the truck began bouncing in a rapid, heavy, rhythmic up-and-down motion. Although the headlights weren't on, he could still see enough of the pavement to know it was smooth. He pushed hard on the brakes, but the truck lurched forward with tires squealing on the pavement. As it did, the trailer pulled hard to the right, let up, and then pulled toward the left with enough force to twist the entire trailer and truck. As Jack glanced out of the driver's window, he saw almost the entire length of the trailer and realized that he was moving down the road jack-knifed, with the tires still squealing on the pavement. One clear thought ran through his mind: something's got ahold of me. Jack felt pain in his left wrist and looked down to see his watch ringed with the white fire. He glanced back up toward the window to see the window frame, the mirror, and the trailer glowing in the electric blue light. Then his world went black.

# 4.

Mark had just reached the center of the street when he heard a loud sizzling sound and felt a strong tug at his waist. He stopped and glanced down as a hard, sharp wrenching at his belt threw him off balance. Thinking one of his friends was messing around, he was about to say something, when he saw his belt buckle and cell phone tear loose and smash violently into the ground. The sizzling sound grew in intensity, and the world around him lit up in dazzling bluish white light that was so bright it hurt his eyes. Guys at the coal mine had warned him never to look at an arc welder, and he reflexively shielded his face with both hands. The white light was bright enough to filter between his fingers, making them glow bright red. Feeling a little dizzy and disoriented by the sound, he knelt on the ground and wrapped his arm over his eyes.

A series of rapid-fire, deafening explosions with thunderous concussions he could feel in the pit of his stomach knocked him flat to the pavement as glass, dirt, and debris started landing all around him. He pulled his head up just far enough to see the world around him on fire. "We're being bombed" was the last thought that went through his mind before the world went black.

# 5.

When Jack's eyes opened, he was still sitting in the driver's seat of the pick-up. His hat had slid forward, covering most of his vision, and his head ached. As he lifted his hat back onto his head, he began to remember what had happened. He asked aloud, "What the fuck was that?"

Wondering how long he had been out, he looked at his watch. The little luminescent marks on the hands and face glowed brightly, showing him it was 11:10 p.m. He couldn't have been out for more than a minute or two.

He unlatched the seatbelt and opened the door. As he was about to slide out, it struck him that the dome light hadn't come on. Stepping out onto the ground and leaning against the truck for support, he tried to figure out what had happened. Nothing made sense. One minute he was driving and everything was fine, and the next, everything had quit and seemed to be on fire with electricity. Had he really passed out? He thought he had, but that didn't make any sense either. Nothing had hit him. Although he had a dull headache, he didn't have any sore spots and didn't seem to be bleeding. He didn't crash—or did he? He stepped away and looked back at the pick-up. No big dents that he could see. As he started

to move toward the front of the truck, it struck him that it was too bright outside. He could see more detail in the truck and the gravel than he should have been able to. Although there was a moon, it wasn't supposed to be this bright. He looked up.

The sky was like nothing he had ever seen before. Ribbons and clouds of color pulsated and filled the night sky. Toward the north he couldn't see much of the sky due to the mountain and trees along the road, but toward the south he could see all the way to the horizon—and the entire sky was filled with moving streams of silver, red, yellow, blue, gold, and orange. As a child he had seen the northern lights while on vacation in Alaska with his parents. This was similar, but there was so much more. The entire expanse of sky was filled with color. He could still see the moon in the southeast, and a few stars twinkled in the brief gaps between the ribbons of light. The streams seemed to move from north to south as though they were flowing around the entire planet.

Jack leaned against the front of the truck and slid to his knees. The moving vista was incredible and the enormity of the motion was disorienting. The sheer magnitude was hard to grasp. He felt lightheaded. The last few minutes of his life were like nothing he had ever experienced in his forty-nine years. First the bizarre "accident," and now this sky—the whole thing seemed to be too much to wrap his mind around.

A horse chuffed in the trailer. The sound pulled him back to reality and the issues at hand. He stood up and started walking around the front of the truck again. No dents in the bumper or grill. On the passenger side, the front fender had an odd, almost speckled look in the strange light. He reached over and ran his hand over the side. The metal fender was rippled like frozen little waves of steel. As he looked down the side of the truck, he could tell that all of the steel on the fender and passenger door of the truck had the same rippled appearance. The back fender was smoothly caved in. Not dented as if he had hit something, rather it looked as though the entire fender had been made inside out. Walking toward the back, he

couldn't see any scratches in the paint, just the majority of the fender smoothly caved in.

"What the hell?" he said to nobody in particular.

Looking at the top of the gooseneck, Jack noticed the top of the trailer was pushed down, with a crease running along the side and around the front. Inside the truck bed, the gooseneck hitch had been pushed down through the bed and the frame below. As he walked the length of the trailer toward the back, most of the windows along the side had broken outward as the top was compressed down. Did something land on the trailer? he thought. And then, I have to get those horses out of there and see if anybody got hurt. At the back of the trailer were two doors that opened outward. He could see the top of the trailer was crushed down, bowing both doors slightly outward, yet the latches remained solidly hooked. Trying to get a better look at the problem, he reached over and lifted the small plastic cover and flipped the switch. The trailer's load lights remained dark.

"Dammit."

As he walked back up to the driver's door to get a flashlight, he realized the front of the truck was in the gravel on the right-hand side of the road, but the back half of the truck and the entire trailer was positioned across both lanes of the highway. I need to get some flares out, he thought, before somebody makes this a whole lot worse than it already is. Reaching the driver's door, he tried the handle and found the truck locked. The doors automatically lock when I'm driving. They let you out, but not in. Terrific. The little card in his wallet should have unlocked the door as he approached. Remembering the electrical problems before the crash explained the doors and the lights on the truck, but shouldn't have explained the trailer lights since they were on their own power system.

He patted his pockets and then remembered the keys lying in the ashtray. He thought about the situation for a minute and remembered the open moonroof. He climbed into the bed of the truck and then up onto the toolbox behind the cab. He could see the moonroof was only open about halfway, not nearly far enough for him to crawl through. A few minutes

later he returned with a long, straight stick. Lying on the roof of the cab, he used the stick to push down the unlock button on door's armrest.

"Dumbshit! Why would that work?" he said aloud as nothing happened. He withdrew the stick and fished his pocketknife out of his jeans. He cleanly cut the end of the stick at a forty-five-degree angle and whittled a small V into the end of it. He hooked the V around the lock stem and lifted slowly. He could hear the stick beginning to break, but finally the lock lifted.

"'Bout time I caught a break."

Inside the truck he found the flashlight under the driver's seat and switched it on. Nothing happened. I just put new batteries in this goddamn thing not three weeks ago, he thought. He unscrewed the back of the flashlight and found the spare bulb in the butt piece. He inserted the new bulb and tried again. Nothing happened.

Exasperated, he threw the flashlight on the floor of the passenger's side and reached around back to unlock the rear door. He noticed his cell phone sitting in the cup holder of the center console. He tried several times to turn it on, but the screen remained black. "Cheap piece of shit." He stepped out, opened the back door, flipped the seat forward, and began digging in the little compartment looking for flares. He slammed the seat back down in frustration when the compartment came up empty except for a small toolkit. He was about to give up on the flares when it occurred to him that they were in the big toolbox behind the cab. As he reached for the latch on the side of the box, he realized for the first time that the lid, or at least a foot of it, had been neatly folded up and stood at ninety degrees to the rest of the box. When he opened the lid, it only allowed about three inches before the bent lid hit the back window of the pickup.

"I swear. If it's not one thing, it's another."

He climbed back into the bed of the truck and tried to bend the lid back down. It moved only a little with his hands, but when he stood on it and jumped, it bent nearly straight.

Lifting the lid, he found six flares and two reflective caution triangles. He picked up all of the flares and the caution signs, but before he got down, something made him think. Without realizing exactly why, he threw two of the flares back into the box and walked out on the highway.

With the flares lit and the signs set up, he returned to the back of the trailer. He lifted the left latch and turned it easily. When he pulled on the door, it refused to move. In the tool-box he found a two-foot pry bar and a five-pound mallet. After working on the door for about a half hour, he managed to pop the left door open. The small tack closet had a light that was supposed to come on when the door was opened, but by this time Jack wasn't surprised to find that it didn't work. He could hear the horses inside the trailer, and they sounded fine, despite the crazy way they had come to a stop. He had looked through the windows and found three sets of eyes staring back at him. Everybody seemed to be breathing normally, and although sounding like they wanted out of the trailer, none of them was fussing.

It took him almost two hours to get the other door open. The smell of horseshit and hay greeted him as the door finally swung open. Before getting the horses, he sat on the edge of the trailer and rested. It occurred to him that nobody had stopped to help. In fact, nobody had even driven by. He looked around. A few night birds sang their songs in the distance, and he had heard a coyote earlier, but he hadn't heard or seen a single car. That was odd. This stretch wasn't usually busy on Friday night, but there were always a few cars or trucks. This was a highway for crying out loud. People were always using this road.

Jack looked at the sky again and scratched his head. The ribbons and swirls of color continued to cover the entire expanse of sky just as before. The half-moon was now straight south of him. He listened as intently as he could and scanned the sky.

"No airplanes," he said out loud. "Not a single goddamn one. What the hell is going on?"

A horse chuffed as if in reply.

"Yes, dear. I'm coming." He stood slowly and picked up a lead rope from the hook in the tack closet. Marlena was the first one out of the trailer. As she stepped onto the ground, she looked up and spooked a little, hunkering down and stabilizing her legs.

"Weird, ain't it?" Jack asked her.

She settled quickly but continued to gaze upward at the unusual sky. Jack tied her to the side of the trailer and went after the rest of the horses. When all of them were out, he carefully checked them. They all seemed to be unhurt and healthy, except Lucy, who had a cut on her right hip. Jack examined the cut and found it was superficial, and the bleeding had stopped long ago.

He led the horses to a small stream in a grassy meadow that ran along the road about fifty yards to the south. He felt exhausted. He looked at his watch: 2:45 a.m.

"Good thing it don't run on batteries, I guess." Considering his options, he said aloud, "You're all hungry and I'm tired. Whadaya say we set out in the morning?"

He walked to the back of the trailer and dug a pair of hobbles from his saddlebag. He walked back to Marlena and put the hobbles on her. "Stay close, now." He fashioned hobbles for the other horses with their lead ropes.

Jack climbed into the back seat of the truck and lay down with his jacket and a saddle pad over the top of him. Thinking, he sat up and opened both back doors and then lay down again. It might be a little cooler, he thought, but at least I'll hear someone coming.

Sleep didn't come easy, despite how tired he felt. As he lay on the leather seat, he looked up through the open door and watched the fantastic colors in the night sky.

# 6.

Mark didn't awake, so much, as he suddenly became aware of things going on around him. A faint burning pain was increasing along the outside of his lower right leg, and his head hurt. He rolled over and looked toward his feet to see an orange smooth flame and smoke rising from the outside of his pant leg. He quickly beat the flames, sending a shower of sparks and black shreds of his jeans to the pavement. The flames went out quickly, and the pain stopped almost immediately, so he sat up. The world around him—everything—was on fire.

He spun his head trying to take in everything. In front of him, the parking lot where he had just sat in his truck a few minutes ago was now piles of twisted metal with thick fat flames leaping and jumping into the sky puking pillars of black smoke. There was nothing that resembled his new Ford F250 4x4. Just beyond the parking lot was a two-story building with its roof on fire, and a car, maybe a Corvette, sticking out of it. To the west an auto parts store stood leaning at an extreme angle with at least one of its walls missing. Mark spun around. Buckers bar was behind him. The tall brick wall that faced him looked okay, but Mark could see a car parked on the side of the street near the front end of the building with orange flames leaping

skyward. No words formed in his mind. He couldn't think. All he could do was turn his head and try to take in the incredible devastation around him. Slowly, he stood. Around him the roar of hundreds of fires and occasional explosions filled his head. Open-mouthed, he turned slowly, trying to comprehend.

A whistling sound above him quickly grew louder. He looked up just in time to see half of a propane tank similar to the one in his gas grill crash into the street and bounce toward him. He tried to move, but the hunk of flying metal just clipped his left shoulder as it sailed by.

Pain and danger suddenly registered in his mind. *I've got to move.* He ran toward the front of the bar and the safety of the brick wall. On the sidewalk, he checked his shoulder and found nothing but a bruise. He began moving toward the entrance around the corner. A ragged length of twisted pipe stuck out of the brick at the same level as his head. He could see a sticker on the side in the shape of an arrow with the word "potable." He ducked below and ran to the front of the bar. The flames coming from the car were dying down a little, but the black smoke continued to billow into the sky. As he rounded the corner, he could see somebody's truck, a dually, laying on its side and pushed up against the front of the building. As he moved around the pickup, he saw the bottom half of a girl sticking out from under the truck. Mark stopped.

He had never seen a dead body before, and there was no way this girl could be anything but dead. There was no blood, just bare legs, a short denim skirt, and part of her bare midriff showing. Her shoes were missing, and he could see that she had painted her toenails red. He looked away and thought, oh my God!

He passed the truck and tried to look into the building. The truck blocked most of the windows, but a few panes of glass behind the truck were dark. I've got to get in there, he thought. He looked around to see if there was anyone he could call to for help. Up and down the street, cars and buildings were burning everywhere, but there was nobody he could call to. He stepped up on the side of the bumper hitch sticking out of the back of

the truck and tried again to look inside. He could see flames in a building behind the bar. What the hell? Mark jumped down and ran around to the back of the bar. The back wall was reduced to a pile of bricks where it had once stood. Beyond it, throughout the entire inside of the bar, it looked as though somebody had covered everything with aluminum foil. Mark remembered the roof and ceiling were made of steel with steel trusses supporting a low-peaked roof. When it rained, it would get so loud inside you couldn't hear somebody talking next to you. Now the entire thing had been neatly pressed into the building and covered everything. Mark could tell where the bar itself was, and where the pool tables in the back were, although they were now much shorter than they used to be. Several of the tables and booths were reduced to small lumps under the steel plating. Mark could see no people. Maybe they all got out before the roof caved in. Fucking terrorists! I have to get to Lisa!

The walk home should have taken him about thirty minutes. As he started moving south, it became obvious the devastation was not limited to the downtown area. These fuckers bombed the entire town, he thought. The whole damn thing is gone. Everywhere he looked, fires raged and homes were wrecked. Several train cars had slid off their tracks and wiped out an entire block as they slid north. He saw a few people standing out in their yards or in the street. Some were crying; some were just wandering. One older man ran up to him and begged for help finding his wife. Mark helped him lift a twisted refrigerator off an older woman that was completely squished. Mark gagged when he saw her chest was flattened and the side of her abdomen had split open to reveal a glimpse of her intestines. The man sat on the floor and sobbed.

As he walked he realized there were no lights anywhere, yet it wasn't quite dark out. He looked up and almost fell when he saw the brilliant, dazzling display of color throughout the night sky. Ribbons of color pulsed, twisted, and turned, covering the entire sky. He couldn't make out any stars at all, only the weird colors. He stopped and just stared at it for a while.

The movement of the entire sky made him feel dizzy, and he had to look away. *What the fuck could do that?*

He walked past the police station, which was dark. A few of the windows had blown out, showering glass on the sidewalk, and all of the rails leading up the stairs to the entrance were gone. Trying to find out what happened, he walked up to the main doors and saw glass strewn over the sidewalk. He stuck his head in and called. "Hey! Hello? Anybody in there?"

Nobody answered.

He stepped through one of the broken doors. He thought maybe everybody was out trying to help people, but there should still be somebody here. They had to have a radio dispatcher or someone who would coordinate things from the cop shop. "Hey! Anybody here?"

He walked farther into the building and saw a flashlight lying on the floor. He picked it up and tried to turn it on. Nothing. "Hey! We need some help out here. Anybody around?"

As his eyes adjusted slightly to the darkness, he could make out shapes deeper in the building. On his right a lady slumped over a desk that seemed to be too low. He moved toward her. "Hey, lady!" She didn't move. "Hey, lady! I'm talking to you." He stepped toward her and felt something slippery and kind of sticky on the floor. The floor was too dark to make out any details. He reached over and put his hand on the desk, but it seemed way too low—like somebody had cut the legs off. He touched her shoulder, and it felt cold.

"Oh fuck! She's dead," he said and backed up.

He turned and started making his way back toward the front of the building when he saw a wooden desk in the corner with something lying on it. He walked over and saw a gun, holster, handcuffs, and an extra magazine sitting on the corner. I bet with all the excitement tonight nobody will miss these. I could just say I found them. He picked up the gun and the extra magazine and stuffed them into his pockets.

Outside the weird sky continued unchanged. If anything, it might have gotten a little brighter. He kept glancing up as he

walked, amazed by the crazy sky. When he finally reached his building, he felt exhausted. It wasn't the walk; that was easy. It was the freak-show roller coaster he had been on all night. First the fight with Lisa, then the end of the fucking world. All of the cars in the parking lot were still burning or had burned themselves out, but the building still looked okay. A blackened hunk of twisted metal sat smoking where Lisa's Camry had been parked earlier. He shook his head and walked to the front door, reaching in his pocket for his keys. Inside his pocket was nothing but a hole. The keys were gone. He tried the door anyway and found it open. Sometimes it wouldn't lock when the power was out. Inside, the building was pitch dark. He felt along the wall to the stairs and made his way to the second floor. He ran his hand along the wall and counted three doors before he found his own. The door stood open.

He walked in and called, "Lis?"

No answer.

He walked into the living room and could see the broken laptop still on the floor, where he had thrown it earlier. A little light filtered in from the sliding glass door, casting an eerie greenish glow throughout the room. He walked into the kitchen and pulled open the utility drawer. He rummaged around until his hand felt the smooth sides of the lighter he kept for special occasions when he could score a little weed. He flicked the lighter and walked over to the dining room. Lisa had always left candles in the middle of the table. They never used them, but they had to have them. Whatever. He lit one of the candles.

Lying on the table was a note from Lisa. The top line read, "From the Desk of Lisa Griffith." He always got a kick out of that. Yeah, like she needed a desk for anything except holding the computer so she could shop online.

*Dear Mark,*

*Actually, I thought about things again, and I realize that I was right, and you are a asshole. The asshole part I can almost*

*deal with but the worst thing is that you are a looser. A huge fucking looser and you will never amount to any thing. I've decided to leave afterall. I need somebody who can provide me with the things I deserve. Have fun jerking off your boyfriends at the gym.*

*Fuck You Very much!*
*Lisa*

Mark stared at the note for a moment and then roared, "That fucking bitch! I'll kill her!"

He took the candle and walked into the bedroom to see what she had taken. The door to the bathroom stood open. He pushed it open and found Lisa lying face down on the floor in a pool of dark blood with her curling iron sticking out of her neck.

"Serves you right, bitch," he said aloud, as he turned and walked back into the bedroom. As he sat on the edge of the bed, an idea came to mind. He smiled and thought about it some more. The smile broadened and then became a laugh. He laughed even harder and then said, "Why the fuck not?"

He did indeed stuff the invoice up her ass.

# 7.

Jack awoke suddenly. His eyes flew open and registered giant fuzzy lips and whiskers above his face. As he jerked his head away, Marlena jumped back from the open door of the truck.

He laughed. "Good mornin', darlin'. Sorry I gave you a start, but you kinda surprised me." He sat up and looked at his watch: 7:15 a.m. "We got to sleep in a bit today. Probably needed it." Jack put his coat and hat on and stepped out of the truck. The day seemed like any other. No weird colors in the sky and a faint breeze from the west with a tangy hint of woodsmoke in the air. In the daylight he could better appreciate the truck and trailer. The trailer was still stretched across both lanes of the road, and the truck was parked in the gravel side lot along the south end of the road. Not a single car or truck, he thought, all night long? That ain't right. He looked up and saw a clear blue sky. Not a single contrail either. This must be serious.

The truck had more damage than what he had seen in the dark. A huge bump in the middle of the hood stuck up like a tumor. Jack popped open the hood to see what could have pushed up on it and found the motor had been twisted inside the engine compartment and the exhaust manifold and turbo

charger had pressed into the hood creating the bump. "What the hell?" he said, looking at the big engine. "Good thing it's still under warranty." He slammed the hood.

Jack retrieved all three horses and tied them to the trailer. He checked all of them again and like last night found them to be healthy. The cut on Lucy's hip was even more superficial than what he had previously thought. He checked the shoes on Marlena and found all of them to be tight. Her feet probably needed to be trimmed, but otherwise everything seemed fine. As Jack walked around the corner of the trailer to get his saddle, a small gust of wind smelled heavy with smoke. He looked west down the road and saw nothing out the ordinary. He picked up the saddle off the rack and heard the left stirrup fall off onto the ground.

"What the hell?" Jack said, as he looked at the stirrup. He walked to the horses and put the pad and saddle on Marlena. He checked the stirrup strap and found the buckle missing. He had just used the saddle yesterday, and everything had been in perfect order. Now the stirrup buckle was completely missing. Jack walked back, picked up the stirrup, and found the buckle embedded into the aluminum floor of the tack closet. Even kicking it with the toe of his boot failed to move the flat steel part.

Over the next forty-five minutes, Jack found several plastic zip ties in the toolbox, cut several holes in the stirrup leathers, and fixed the stirrup. He found a small bag of beef jerky he had meant to eat on the way to Yellowstone yesterday and a half-bottle of Diet Coke in the truck. He put these, the extra flares, and a small pair of binoculars in the saddlebags along with the hobbles. Back in the truck, he found two extra cans of Copenhagen and then reached for the big 460 Smith & Wesson magnum revolver from where it had been sitting on the passenger seat. He had brought the gun with them fishing in case they had run into any of Yellowstone's less agreeable residents. The gun had slid into the footwell in front of the passenger seat but still rested comfortably in the leather shoulder holster. When he checked it, everything seemed to be in order.

Since he was going to leave the truck, he decided to take the compact .45 he kept in the center console as well. He slid the holster inside his waistband behind his right hip and clipped it to his belt. Last, he picked up the rawhide rope from its hanger above the back window and tied it onto the saddle.

He tied a short rope from Dingo's headstall to Lucy's and picked up Dingo's lead rope. After hoisting himself up into the saddle on Marlena, he said, "All right, everybody listen up. We have a long way to go to get to Cody, so I don't want any of you horsin' around. I'll call Miguel, and he'll come get us. If you all behave yourselves, you'll get a little extra grain tonight. Everybody ready?"

He was just about to set out when it occurred to him that sunglasses might not be a bad idea. He stepped down from the horse and opened the driver's door. He found the glasses mangled on the dash and tossed them aside. He pulled two photos from the visor, looked at them briefly and slipped them into his shirt pocket. As he closed the door, he had a vague, strange feeling he wouldn't see the truck again. Back in the saddle, he held Marlena's reins in his left hand and Dingo's lead rope in his right and set off toward the east.

# 8.

As they walked along the road, a light breeze blew straight out of the west. The smell of smoke seemed to grow stronger even in the last half hour since they left. Occasionally Jack would look back, but he couldn't see anything out of place—other than the empty highway. On Saturday morning this road should be busy. Even though it was late in the season, lots of cars would be making their way to the park for an overnight weekend stay, and trucks, especially the loggers, should barreling down the road, pushing everyone out of their way. As they walked along, the smell of smoke wafted up to him again. An idea occurred to Jack. Maybe part of the park had caught fire again. There were so many dead pine trees due to the beetle infestation that any spark or flame would cover hundreds or thousands of acres in no time. The feds would close down Highway 14 at Cody—that would explain both the smell and the lack of cars. But, if that were the case, there should have been a parade of emergency vehicles headed into the park.

He had covered about five miles moving at a good pace when he rounded a bend and saw somebody walking the same

direction he was headed along the road about a half mile in front of him. He bumped the horses up to a trot.

When he was about an eighth of a mile behind, he could tell that the person walking was a young man. He called, "Hey, buddy! Wait up!"

The kid paid no attention but continued to walk with his hands in the front pocket of a hooded sweatshirt. Two small, white wires hung down from under a knit cap and a big, nearly empty, frameless backpack hung from one shoulder.

Jack rode straight up behind the kid and said, "Hey, buddy!"

Again, no response.

Jack pulled Dingo up close behind on his right and then moved Marlena past the boy, close to his shoulder. Dingo, without anywhere else to go, pushed the young man onto the shoulder of the road.

"Hey! What the fuck? There's a lot of road here. Get your own!"

Jack turned Marlena toward the shoulder of the road in front of the boy and pulled her up to a stop. "Why didn't you answer me?"

The kid looked up, and Jack could see his eyes were deeply bloodshot and swollen. "I couldn't hear you," the young man said, pulling the white plugs out of his ears by the cord.

Jack just looked at him for a moment. The kid appeared to be about twenty and was wearing a sweatshirt with "MIZZOU" on the front. His jeans looked to be about four sizes too big, with several rips in them, and his tennis shoes were muddy and had no laces. He stared at the boy for a moment and said, "I have two brand new one hundred dollar bills in my wallet. I'll give 'em both to you if you prove that thing works."

"What thing?"

"You know what thing."

"My iPod? You wouldn't like what's playing."

"If it's playin' anything, I'd say it would be the sweetest damn thing I ever heard. Prove it's workin'."

"Fuck you!" the kid said and started moving toward the front of the horse.

Jack bumped Marlena ahead and then stopped her, only using his legs. He leaned forward on the pommel and said, "Son, it looks to me like you had a long night." He paused and looked down the road to the east. He added, "It's a hell of a long way to Cody. We might be able to help each other out. What do you say we start over? My name is John Neumann. Most people call me Jack."

"Were you in that truck back there a few miles?"

"Yep. I had a weird accident last night and then spent half the night gettin' horses out of the trailer. I slept on the back seat."

"I thought you were dead."

"Dead?" Jack asked surprised. "Now why would you think I was dead? Generally you don't come across many dead people alongside the road."

"If you had the night that I did, you would have thought you were dead too."

"Did you start out in the park?"

"Yeah, but I don't really want to talk about it."

Jack climbed down from Marlena and walked around the front of the horse as she blew and shook her head. He stuck out his hand to the boy and said, "Again, I'm Jack Neumann."

The man that stood in front of Ryan was tall, at least six-foot, thin, and wore a black cowboy hat slightly downturned on the front brim. He wore a denim jacket over a once pressed but now wrinkled red shirt and jeans. His boots were worn and had black and silver spurs that hung from the back. A little salt-and-pepper hair stuck out around his ears from beneath the hat. His face showed a few creases near the corner of his blue eyes and a warm, genuine smile.

The kid stuck out his hand and shook Jack's. "I'm Ryan Miller."

Jack shook the boy's hand, thinking it felt like a dead fish. He said, "Let's walk and talk." They started moving east on the road, as Jack held Marlena's reins and Dingo's lead rope, with Lucy following easily. "I'm headed to Cody this morning to see if I can get a lift home. Yesterday, I was at the main ranger

station with a friend of mine. I dropped off a couple of horses and picked these up. Everything seemed fine when I left at about eleven or so last night."

"Everything is not fine now. That's for sure."

"Care to tell me what happened?"

Ryan shook his head. "It's a long story."

"We have a long walk."

"I was camped at the top of Grizzly Peak."

"Grizzly Peak? There's no campsite up there. Hell, I don't think there is even a trail up that way."

"Look, do you want to hear this or not?"

"Sure I do. I'm just wonderin' why you're up on Grizzly."

"Last year at school, some of the guys were talking and made a bet that nobody could stay at the top of Grizzly Peak all night by themselves. There was a bunch of us that threw some money into a pot. By the time school was out, it was like two grand. When school started back this year, nobody had collected the cash, and a few more people got in on it. So, the total went even higher. It was like five grand at the end of September. I was like, 'Fuck it. I can do this.' I borrowed some gear and bought a plane ticket to Cody."

"If you were alone, how would you prove you stayed there?"

"I had set my phone up to Tweet my GPS coordinates every five minutes. At about five last night, my cell phone rang, and the guys were like, 'No fuckin' way, dude!' I was like, 'Way.' They wanted some pics, so I emailed them. That just blew their fuckin' minds, ya know?"

"Sure."

"So, I got the tent set up. That totally sucked. There was no instructions or anything. It took me a while, but I got it. After that it was really kind of boring. I sat there and listened to a few tunes. Then I watched a movie on my phone. That kind of sucked since the picture is so small, but it helped pass the time. After it was dark, it got kind of freaky, ya know? Like there's totally a lot of bears around there. So, anyway, I was sitting in the tent just thinkin' about stuff. I was going to go to bed when my girlfriend called. I talked to her for a while and then my phone

just went dead. The call broke up once and then just dropped out. I tried to redial, but it didn't work. Then the flashlight shut off, and it was totally dark. That's when the freaky shit started happening. At first the tent started shaking a little. Then it stopped and then it started up again even harder. The zipper on the front was shaking really, really hard. I thought it was a bear trying to get in, so I grabbed the can of pepper spray. I read the thing that Yellowstone has on the web, so I made sure to bring like a huge can of bear spray. All of a sudden, the tent just collapsed. Everything came down on top of me. I could see this weird bluish light glowing on the zipper of the tent and on my pack. I was like freakin'. Then everything went black again, and then my hand with the pepper spray started moving by itself. I was like, 'Fuck, man! A bear has got me!' So I started spraying the pepper spray."

"In the tent?"

"Yeah. The blue light came again, and I could just make out where the zipper was, but it didn't do any good. It was like the zipper was welded shut. Eventually, I just tore my way out of the tent, but by that time the pepper spray was in my eyes, nose, and mouth. Everything was burning like hell, and I couldn't see anything. I started pukin' my guts out, and my heart was like pounding so hard I thought I was going to die—or maybe I wanted to. That's some wicked shit."

"I've heard that," Jack said, as Dingo blew for the third time behind them.

"So anyway. Now it's dark, my tent is totally wrecked, I'm sick, and I just want to get the hell out of there. I found the flashlight, but it's a complete piece of shit. I don't really want to hike through the woods in the dark, but like, I don't have any other choice, right? So I found as much stuff as I could find and started walkin'. The weird thing was I could see pretty good for the middle of the fuckin' night. That's when I looked up. The sky was unbelievable. It was totally trippin'. Here I was standing on this mountaintop in the middle of Yellowstone, and the sky was all these wild colors, and it was like flowin' and poppin' and movin'. I've never seen anything like that before.

At first I thought it was the pepper spray that was making me like trip."

"You fell?"

"No. Not like trip as in 'fall down.' Like trip as in acid. It was crazy. The good thing was that I could see a little bit. I used the GPS to get to the top of the mountain, but now, I like got nothing but gravity to get me down. I kept trying to watch the moon and keep it behind my right shoulder. I think I did fall a couple of times, but eventually I came out on the road. When I hit the road, I started walking east. I parked my car by the trailhead to Avalanche Peak, so the rangers wouldn't get suspicious. When I finally got back to my car, it was totally burned."

"Burned? It was on fire?"

"Yeah, like it was on fire, but by the time I saw it, it was almost burned out. There was nothing but a smoking heap of steel. One of the tires was still burning a little. I kept walking. I knew it wasn't that far to the ranger station. I was like, fuck it. I'll tell them everything. Let 'em fine me. I just want to go home. So I kept walking along, you know? Well, pretty soon I came to a car in the middle of the road. I think it had been driving when everything went nuts, and it burned up too. The worst part of it was this guy was hanging out of the window that was totally burned. His mouth was open, like he was yellin' for help. It was awful."

"I'm sure it was," Jack said in a consoling tone.

"I walked along this area where there was a long guardrail. It was like the thing was ripped out of the ground and thrown all over the place. Just before the sun came up, I made it to the ranger station. The whole place was on fire, and it had spread to the forest behind it. There was a guy that looked like he was leaning against the fence at the entrance station. Well, he wasn't sleeping there. He was dead."

Jack wanted to ask what he looked like, but just now didn't seem to be the right time, or maybe he didn't want to know. It was probably the young guard that had been manning the station when he came out last night. He made mental note to call Frank when he got to Cody.

"So anyway, I kept walking. When I saw your truck, I was sure you were dead in the back of it. This whole thing's been a fuckin' nightmare, ya know?"

"Sounds like it. How's your eyes now?"

"They're not too bad. Every once in a while I forget and rub them. It makes everything start burning again."

"Well, I guess that'll teach you not to rub 'em." Jack stopped in the middle of the road. "Ryan, this walkin' is fine for the heart, but it does slow things down a bit. Do you know how to ride?"

"Ride what?"

Jack looked over at the young man, not quite believing the question. "Horses."

"Never been on one."

"Can you ride a bike?"

"Sure. Can't everybody?"

"Then you can ride a horse. I don't suppose you have a change of clothes in that bag of yours?"

"Yeah, one. Why?"

"'Cause your bear spray is botherin' the horses. Tell you what, why don't you change, and we'll ride instead of walk."

"Where should I change at?"

"Here's about as good a place as any."

"Here? I can't change here. There's no place to change."

"Son, there's nobody around. Just go ahead and strip off. Personally I'd pitch them clothes you have on. You'll never get the spray out of 'em."

"Whoa. Wait just a minute. First of all, you might be a freak and just want to see me half-naked. Secondly, these are a hundred and eighty dollar Abercrombie jeans. I am not pitching them."

"I don't care what you have or don't have, and the horses will never tell. Those jeans look like they are about played out anyway. You can stuff 'em back in the bag if you want. Just make sure the zipper is closed tight."

"If by 'played out' you mean worn, they are supposed to look like that. That's why they cost so much. My mom always

told me never to take a ride with strangers. Now here I am in the middle of nowhere and a stranger comes riding up and wants me to strip and then go for a ride. Somehow this sounds like a bad idea."

"Suit yourself. I'm ridin' out of here in about five minutes. I don't mind leavin' you if you want."

"Fine. Just wait a minute." Ryan walked back behind the horses and pulled the sweatshirt over his head. When the breeze wafted past Marlena and Lucy, they stomped and snorted.

"See there?" Jack called. "You're aftershave don't sit well with them."

"Like I give a shit about horses."

"You will," Jack said smiling.

# 9.

Mark awoke lying in the middle of his bed. There was something very comfortable about the familiar feel of the comforter and the smell of his pillow. He opened his eyes to bright sun streaming in through the windows. He looked over at the clock on the bed stand. It was black. The events of last night came flooding back to mind. He sat up quickly and looked around the room. The door to the bathroom stood open, and he could see the lower half of Lisa, lying face down with her bare ass and legs on the carpet in the bedroom and the rest of her still inside the bathroom. A small tuft of paper protruded from between her legs. He smiled.

"You got what you had coming, bitch," he said aloud as he looked her over. He thought the curve of her bare skin kinda looked a little hot. He sat up. When he could see further into the bathroom, the site of the huge pool of dark congealed blood covering most of the bathroom floor was revolting.

He turned way and stood up, looking out the window. From the second floor, they could usually see a good portion of town. The site before him was completely alien. The water tower was missing. Many buildings were no longer standing or appeared different, parts were missing. Pillars of smoke seemed to be

coming from everywhere, and a haze seemed to blanket the entire town. He couldn't see a single normal-looking car. The main road behind his apartment had several burned-out hunks of metal that once might have been cars.

He rubbed his face. He said, "Fuck. It's worse in the daylight than it was last night."

He turned back toward Lisa. Seeing the little piece of paper again, he thought, damn, somebody is going to think I did this to her. He walked over and knelt next to her legs. He reached for the paper, and his fingers touched her butt cheek. The skin was different than it was last night. Now it was cold and harder than it should have been, and the sensation made him pull his hand back quickly. He reached carefully and pinched the edge of the paper and began to pull. It ripped, leaving him with only a small piece. "Oh man! That is so nasty!"

He sat back and thought about it. The paper had to go all the way in, or it had to come out. Both options seemed disgusting. An idea came to him. Maybe there was another option.

He got up and stripped off the clothes he was wearing last night, leaving them in a pile on the carpet next to Lisa. He briefly turned toward the bathroom and then thought differently, heading out to the living room and bathroom in the hall. He reached into the tub and turned on the shower. Nothing came out. "Fuck."

He tried the sink in the kitchen, with the same result. In the utility closet, he found a small bucket and stuck it under the valve at the bottom of the hot water heater. Opening the valve he filled the bucket with lukewarm water.

He bathed, standing in the middle of the kitchen on the tile floor. He didn't care where the water splashed; it wouldn't make any difference. He spit the used toothpaste into the sink and left it. He dressed in jeans, a heavy flannel shirt, and his Doc Martens and then packed a change of clothes and some travel things into a small backpack. He noticed the gun he had found last night, laying on the table. He looked it over, able to really see it for the first time in the daylight. It was a Colt 1911 and read *Gold Cup Trophy* on the side. He ejected the magazine

and worked the action, ejecting a round. He smiled and re-loaded the weapon. It felt good in his hands: comfortable, natural, and powerful. He put the extra magazine in his back pocket and the pistol in his waistband and then noticed Lisa's cell phone lying on the table. He put it in his pocket and set the bag and his leather coat by the door.

Taking a candle and the lighter he had found last night, he walked down the hall to the stairs. He could hear people talking loudly and quickly in one of the other apartments. He ignored them and quietly opened the door to the stairwell. In the basement he lit the candle and found what he was looking for. Two five-gallon plastic containers of gas stood in the corner next to the lawnmower the maintenance guy used. He blew out the candle and took both of them with him.

Back in the apartment, he piled as many of Lisa's clothes as he could find on top of her body. He poured the entire contents of one of the containers onto the pile and placed the empty can on top. He poured the rest of the gas over every-thing—the bed, the couch, the dressers—and then poured a little line down the hallway to the front door. The fumes in the apartment made his eyes water. Knowing that any spark would cause an explosion, he filled a plastic soda bottle with gas and set it next to his bag by the door.

He looked around the apartment one last time and decid-ed to open the window a little. A little air might just help things along. Mark put on his coat, threw the bag over his shoulder, and used the little bottle to extend his line of gas to the edge of the door. He opened the door and then continued the line as far down the hallway as he could.

With a flick of the lighter, the line of gasoline jumped into flame. It raced down the hall and under the door. He started to run down the stairs as he heard a huge *wump*, and the air in the stairwell sucked past him. He opened the outside door to sunshine and started walking.

As Mark walked toward downtown, a thick column of black smoke gained strength behind him. He never looked back.

# 10.

After Ryan changed and stuffed everything into the backpack, he walked up to the side of Marlena and asked, "Am I riding this one?"

"Nah. I don't think you want to ride her. She's kinda particular about who is on her back. I'm afraid she'd have you on the ground in a whole lot less than eight seconds."

"I bet she wouldn't."

Jack turned to look at the kid. "Son, you just told me you've never been on a horse before. What makes you think you could ride her?"

"I bet I can. That's all."

"You've got guts. I'll give you that. Not much in the way of brains, but you do have guts. That's usually a dangerous combination."

"I can outthink you any day of the week, old man, and I bet I can outride you in no time."

Jack smiled and decided to let the challenge go unanswered. "Tell you what, let's put you up on that one." He pointed to the Buckskin gelding standing beside Marlena. "That's Dingo. He's a damn good horse and easy to get along with. He'll put up with just about anything you try."

"Where's my saddle?"

"You don't have a saddle."

"Well, what am I supposed to sit on?"

"The horse."

"Where do my feet go?"

"On the sides."

"But, don't I need those little hangy-thingies?"

"Stirrups? No. It's called riding bareback. You'll get the hang of it."

"What do I hang on to?"

"I'll show you." Jack tied his reins in a loose knot and dropped them in front of Marlena. He walked back to Dingo with the lead rope. He clipped one end to the side of Dingo's halter and then tied the other end to the opposite side of the halter. He tossed the loop over the horse's head and onto his neck.

Ryan asked, "Is my horse a boy or a girl?"

"Girl horses are called mares. Dingo used to be a boy, now he's a gelding."

"Gelding? What's that?"

"You know, a boy horse that's been castrated."

"Castrated? You mean someone cut his dick off?"

Jack started laughing. "No. Nobody cut his dick off. His penis is still where it's supposed to be. When he was a colt, we removed his testicles."

"You cut his *nuts off?* Jesus! Why did you do that?"

"If he was an intact male, he'd only have one thing on his mind, namely, breedin' these mares. As a gelding, he's happier and much more user-friendly."

"Happier? I don't think he's happier at all. How would you like to have your nuts cut off?"

"He was gelded long before he was sexually mature. He's never had any sexual impulse and never will. He's never known the difference. Very few stallions actually get to breed. The rest of 'em would be fightin' and frustrated all the time. This way, they're a lot happier."

Ryan was shaking his head. "I don't know, man. Seems a bit rough."

"Not at all. In general geldings make the best horses. Just think, they get to go on all the adventures while the stallions stay home."

"Yeah, but the stallions get some once in a while."

"Yep, they sure do. But ask yourself this: would you rather stay home and 'get some' for about three or four months outta the year and be frustrated the rest of the time, or go on an adventure and ride all year long?"

"I don't know. I'd have to think about that one."

"Well, while you're thinkin' about it, get up on this horse."

"How?"

"Just climb up, boy. Here, let me show you," Jack said. He stood next to the horse with his left shoulder next to the left foreleg and his hand on the horse's withers. With a smooth, seemingly effortless motion, he swung his right leg up and over the horse and sat squarely on his back. He slid off easily and said, "Now, you try."

Ryan stood exactly like Jack had done and placed his hand on the horse's withers. He swung his right leg and jumped with the left and went up and over. Jack saw Ryan's left leg straight up in the air as the kid hit the ground on the other side. Dingo turned his head slowly and looked down at the boy on the ground.

Without smiling Jack said, "Maybe not quite so much push this time. Do it again."

"I don't know about this. He's kind of slippery. Maybe I could use your saddle on this horse and you could ride your horse bareback."

"Nope. Not with them shoes you got on. They're bad in stirrups. Get a foot hung up and it could break your leg or worse. Besides, it's my saddle and my horses. Get up there, son."

Ryan swung again, this time being very conservative in the push. He almost made it, but started to slide back off as Jack caught him and pushed him up onto the horse.

"There you go!"

"Oh, dude! This is so weird. I can feel him breathing."

"Yep, they do that. Here," Jack said and handed him the rope. "You don't want to pull on this. Dingo will think you want him to stop. If you keep pullin', he's gonna back up. If you need to hang on to something, hold this." Jack took a large hank of Dingo's mane and held it up to show Ryan. "Horses have no nerves in the roots of their mane. You can pull on this till the cows come home, and he won't care a bit. If you want him to turn, just lay the rein across his neck like this, or this." Jack showed him how to lay the rope on the horse's neck. "Just that little bit of pressure is all he needs, to know where you want him to go. You shouldn't have to tell him to go or stop. He'll follow me just fine. But if you do, just give him a little squeeze with your legs. That means go. Remember, the harder you squeeze, the faster he'll go. If he's walking and you squeeze, it's like shifting him up to second gear, and he'll start to trot. If you squeeze again, he'll start to lope."

"Is that like galloping?"

"It's like a slow gallop, yes." Jack smiled at the thought and said, "You probably don't want to do that just yet. Oh, and don't slide your feet very far back. If you kick him in the flank, he won't like it. A lot of horses would buck, but I doubt Dingo will. I don't think he has much buck in him."

"What do I do if he bucks?"

"You'll fall off," Jack said, with a big grin on his face.

"You sound pretty confident of that."

"I watched you get up, remember?"

Ryan didn't answer him but sat there looking forward. Jack broke the silence. "We'll start out slow and just see how things go for a while. Let you get your balance." Jack handed Ryan his pack.

"Maybe you could carry it."

"What? No, no. I have my own things. This here is yours."

The kid slipped a little as he put the pack on. Lucy, who was standing next to Dingo and directly downwind, snorted.

"The horses don't care for your pepper spray. We'll have to see how things go."

As Jack walked back to his own horse, Ryan said, "Or what? What will we do if it's a problem?" Jack ignored him. He dug around in one of his saddlebags and found another lead rope. He clipped one to the front of Dingo's halter and took Lucy's in hand. Holding both ropes, he climbed up on Marlena. "Ready?"

"I guess."

"Let's go." Jack made a little kissing sound with his mouth, and the horses started walking down the road at a slow pace. Twice within the first one hundred yards, Ryan almost slipped off the side of the horse but managed to right himself again at the last second.

# 11.

After about a mile or so, Jack picked up the pace to a normal walk. Ryan appeared to be doing a little better maintaining his balance, and Dingo wasn't complaining about him. They continued to ride along quietly with just the sounds of the horses' feet and a slight breeze in the trees.

"Hey," Ryan said, breaking the peace and quiet.

"Yeah?"

"Is that a gun under your arm?"

"Yep." Jack reached with his right hand and pulled the huge, stainless steel revolver out of the leather holster under his left arm and held it out to the side."

"Oh my God! That thing is huge!"

"I get that a lot," Jack said, putting the weapon away.

"What's it for?"

"Mouthy kids."

After a minute Jack looked back over his shoulder, grinning. Ryan's eyes were wide.

"You're kidding me, right?"

"Yep. I was fishin' yesterday with a good friend of mine up near where you were camped. I had this along in case we ran

into a bear. They can get a little ornery this time of year. Pepper spray don't work for shit."

Ryan didn't say a word.

After another mile or so, they passed a minivan on the shoulder of the road. The blackened shell of the vehicle stood in stark contrast to the golden Aspen trees on the hill behind it. As they passed Jack noticed two dead bodies in the ditch alongside the van. The occupants had obviously tried to escape the fire that had engulfed their vehicle. A little further down the road, Jack noticed the back bumper and the right rear wheel. Further yet, he saw a big black spot on the pavement with fresh scrapings and a small chunk of twisted metal.

"Gas tank blew," Jack said.

"How do you know that?"

"The van was driving at the time. That spot is where it let go. It blew the bumper and the right rear wheel off. The parts landed over there, and the van coasted to a stop back there."

"Why do you think it blew?"

"I been thinkin' about that. Remember that weird white-blue fire? Well, I bet it was an electric spark. I saw it all over my truck last night when things went nuts. If that spark had happened inside a gas tank, the fuel vapors would explode."

"Why didn't your truck go up?"

"It's diesel, not gas. Diesel won't go up with just a spark. It takes a lot more heat to ignite."

"Is that why my car burned up?"

"Probably."

"So what caused all of this?"

"I'm working on that."

"Do you think the rental company is going to understand what happened? I mean, I didn't call the police or anything."

"You haven't gotten to a working phone yet."

"I know, but sometimes they're like, 'It's totally your fault, and you have to pay for it.'"

"I wouldn't worry about that just yet," Jack said.

"How far do we have to go? My butt is getting tired."

"Oh, we have a ways yet. We'll stop after a bit and rest, but I'd like to get a few more miles behind us first. By the way, notice anything weird about the sky?"

"Last night? Yeah, I told you. That was fuckin' weird."

"No, today."

Ryan looked up and scanned the clear blue sky. "Nope. I don't see anything."

"Exactly."

"Like what? There's no clouds—is that what you're getting at?"

"Nope. We just had a little cold front go through a day or so ago. There shouldn't be any clouds. Notice anything else missing?"

"There's no skyscrapers."

"Anything else?"

"Nope."

"Airplanes. There's not one contrail, and we haven't seen one light plane go by all mornin'. Not a one."

"Wow, you're right. There isn't one line across the sky. But sometimes they don't always make those lines."

"Right," Jack said. "But when they're at altitude, there's always a bit of contrail, even if it fades out quickly. I ain't seen a one, and I've been watchin' for 'em."

"So what's that supposed to mean?"

"I don't know for sure. Let's just wait and see."

They rode on in silence for another hour. Jack could tell Ryan was thinking hard about what he had said and what they had seen. He was thinking about it as well, and he didn't like what he was coming up with.

Ryan broke the silence. "Hey. You know that weird sky last night?"

"Yeah."

"Do you think that could have been an Aurora?"

"Aurora? I'm not so sure what that is."

"You know. Like the Aurora borealis. The northern lights."

Jack said, "Years ago we could see the northern lights a little bit, but they didn't look anything like that."

"Yeah, but what if something messed up the ionosphere."

"Like what?"

"Like a solar storm."

"How do you know about this kind of stuff?"

"I'm doing physics and astronomy at Mizzou."

"Well, then I guess you would know better than I would."

As they reached Buffalo Bill Reservoir, they rounded a corner and could see a tanker truck sideways across both lanes of the highway. The trailer was lying on its side and slowly burning, with thick, dark clouds of smoke rising into the clear sky.

Jack pulled Marlena to a stop. "We're gonna need to detour. That crude oil truck has the entire road cut off." They turned right on a little gravel road and headed south for a quarter mile before turning right on another road, which would lead along the south side of the reservoir. For the next hour, they wound around various roads and then dirt paths until Ryan had no idea what direction they were headed in.

"Where are we going?"

"Round the south side of the lake and then up to Cody. A friend of mine has a ranch back there, and we can ride across it. I know the ground pretty well."

"Good. My flight is supposed to leave at five fifty tonight."

"We should be in Cody in plenty of time for you to catch your flight. But I have a feeling your flight has been cancelled."

Ryan sighed audibly. "You think this thing is bigger than just Yellowstone Park."

"Yep, I do."

"Maybe the whole area?"

"Maybe."

Ryan rode quietly again for a few minutes.

Jack said, "It looks like you two are gettin' on just fine. You can drive. I'm tired of draggin' your sorry ass around." He pulled Dingo up behind him and reached around and unclipped the lead rope. "You shouldn't have to turn him much. He'll just follow along."

Ryan asked, "So, this is a really good horse?"

"Yep, he's a really good horse."

"So, say I wanted to buy him. How much would he cost?"

"Dingo's already sold. He was supposed to be on his way to Arizona next week."

"If he's a good horse, why did you sell him?"

"That's one of the things we do. We train really good horses."

"How much did you sell him for?"

"Dingo there, he sold for fifty-two five."

"Five hundred twenty-five dollars doesn't sound like too much for a horse."

"No, no, son. Fifty-two *thousand* five hundred."

"You are shittin' me!"

"Nope. Lucy brought more than forty-four thousand."

"So these two horses are worth almost a hundred thousand dollars?"

"Yep."

"Why?"

"They're special. We go through lots of horses before we start trainin' any. They have to have the right mind before we invest any time into 'em. Then we spend a lot of time and train 'em very specifically. Over the years we have developed a reputation for selling only the best. The ranch that bought them has some very wealthy people as clients. They need to make sure that those clients are as safe as they can be. We sell only the best stock."

"What about your horse?"

"Marlena? She's special. She's the best horse I've ever owned. She's my horse and she's not for sale at any price."

"What if I offered you a million for her?"

"Some things are not for sale."

"Sure they are. Everything has a price."

"Nope. That's not true. Some things are just not for sale."

"What if I gave you two million and put her in a movie and made her famous? Would you sell her then?"

"Nope. First of all, although I think she's the best horse I've ever owned, my lead man Miguel doesn't like her a bit. I'm the

only one she'll let ride her. She bucks everybody else off. If she can't get 'em off with a buck, she'll bite 'em."

"She sounds like a bitch."

"Maybe. She's just particular. But if I asked her to run all the way home, she would. Even if it'd kill her. She'd give me anything I asked and then some. But, she also knows that I won't ask for anything unless I have a reason. She trusts me."

"Why you? I mean why does she trust you and only let you ride her?"

Jack smiled to himself. "That's a long story that'll cost you a drink to get. How you doin' back there?"

"We're okay."

"As we crest this next rise, there's a pretty view. When we start downhill, you're gonna slide forward on that horse. Keep a hand on his withers to hold you back. You'll be up on his neck if you don't."

"Will he get sore with me riding on his back like this?"

"You can't weigh more'n a buck-fifty. That horse is twelve hundred pounds. He hardly even knows you're back there 'cept for you're kickin' him in the ribs all the time."

As Jack came up over the rise, he pulled Marlena to a stop, staring at something in the distance. "Oh shit!"

Ryan rode up alongside and said, "What is it?"

"Look there," Jack said as he pointed to a long dark strip in the middle of a brownish green valley. Jack pulled the pair of binoculars out from his saddlebag and scanned the area.

"What is it?"

"Trouble." Jack looked back at Ryan sitting on top of Dingo. "Listen, I'm gonna ride down there fast. You won't be able to stay on top of that horse at my speed. I want you to get down and hold your rope and Lucy's rope. The horses will stay with you. After I've been gone for ten minutes, then you can get back up and walk down there. There's a trail that goes right to where we are headed. Don't try to steer the horse. He knows the way. Just walk 'em. Got it?"

"No. Wait. I can keep up. Really."

"No, you can't, and this is not up for debate. Get down."

Ryan looked a little scared. "I'll get lost."

"No, you won't. I know where you're at. Remember, don't try to drive, just let 'em take you there. Even if it seems wrong to you, trust the horses. They know the way. Get down."

Ryan slid reluctantly off the horse and stood sullenly holding the rope. Jack handed him Lucy's lead rope and said, "When I leave, they're gonna want to follow. Don't you let 'em go."

"What if Lucy goes?"

"She won't. She'll stay with Dingo. He's the boss. Make sure you hold 'em. I'll see you a little later. C'mon, girl. Heyaw!"

Jack rode off at a hard gallop. At first, Dingo tried to follow and danced a little at the end of the rope but soon stood quietly. Ryan watched Jack disappear and then reappear down the side of the mountain and across the plain in front of them. He followed a dry river gulch and then popped out through the brush on the north side. Ryan watched until all he could see of Jack was just a dark speck moving fast across the green-brown sage toward the dark slash in the earth. As Ryan looked closer at the slash, he noticed a hint of something shining. He looked closer and saw what appeared to be a silver rectangle—no, that wasn't quite right. It was a wing. An airplane had crash-landed in the middle of the sage.

# 12.

As Ryan stood on the top of the crest looking down at the crash site, all he could think of was home. The summer had been great. Once school was out in the spring, he had moved back home, and his parents again took care of everything. There was always food in the fridge, the video games were awesome, the computer always had unlimited access, and he could hang out with friends whenever he felt like it. He wanted to be there now. Dad could take care of this. He always knew what to do. Mom would make sure that his burning eyes got fixed right away. She sometimes got on his case about things, but she always took care of him. He wouldn't have to stand on a mountaintop in the middle of bum-fuck-Egypt with two horses and wonder how he was going to get down.

Horses? What the hell was he doing with horses anyway? He briefly thought about just letting them go and then walking down by himself, but it would be a lot easier to ride and let the horse do the work. What was he going to do when he got down there anyway? If he just waited here long enough, that old cowboy would come back up and get him, if for no other reason than to get his expensive horses back. Did he really want that old crotchety fart to come back? He seemed to know

about horses, but he was sure stupid about a lot of other things. Like jeans—how could anyone possibly think of throwing his Abercrombie jeans away? What a complete moron. Why the hell did he ride down to that crash? What was he going to do? If there was anybody still alive, which there probably wasn't, he wasn't going to change anything by riding down there like a freakin' maniac. They could have both walked down there and not changed a fucking thing. The guy was a complete idiot.

What was it he had said? Something like guts, but no brains? What a fucking idiot! That just showed how ignorant he was.

Ryan looked over at Dingo. The horse stood quietly but intently looking where the old fart had gone down the hillside. "All right, you old nag. I don't care what that old asshole says, you're not worth much more than dog food to me. If you so much as think about bucking me, I'll make sure that you become glue before I fly out of here." He stood next to the horse the way Jack had done and placed his hand on the horse's back. As he swung his leg up and over, the horse stood perfectly still waiting patiently for him to get situated.

"You're lucky you didn't move. I would have decked you. I saw it in a movie once." He held the looped rein in his left hand and the lead rope to Lucy in his right. He was going to squeeze with his legs, but even before he could generate much pressure, the horse started walking down the trail in the direction Jack had left. Lucy trailed to his right, keeping the lead rope just a little bit slack.

"Wow. I'm doing it! I knew I could. I told that old fucker I could outride him in a couple of days!"

As the horse stepped carefully down the slope, Ryan slid forward. He tried to keep his right hand on the horse's bump, holding himself back, but despite his constant push, he continued to slide forward. The bump—what was it the old guy called it? His winters? Anyway, it did stop him from sliding forward, but only because it hit him square in the nuts. With every step the horse made, his testicles smashed against the horse's bump.

"Oh, shit. Stop. Stop!" He pulled back on the looped lead rope, and the horse stopped immediately. The quick halt to the

forward motion smashed him even harder. He pushed himself back onto the flat of the horse's back, relieving the pressure on his man-gear.

"Oh, man. We have got to do something different." Realizing he couldn't hold himself back on the horse and hold Lucy's lead rope at the same time, he reached over and unclipped the lead from Lucy's halter. At once, the horse walked in front of Dingo, and he started following her.

"Hey, I didn't say go. Stop! *Stop*, you stupid flea bag!" The horse not only continued forward but sped up to get closer to Lucy. Ryan dropped the looped rope and pushed back on the horse's bump with both hands. That seemed to work a little better, but he had no control over the horse. Then again, the rope was draped over the horse's neck right in front of him. How hard could it be to grab it if he needed to? About halfway down the hill, Lucy came to a log that Jack must have jumped. He watched as Lucy walked up to the log and then half-stepped, half-jumped over it. Dingo approached the log as if it was no barrier at all and jumped over. As the front legs of Dingo hit the ground, Ryan felt a little off balance. He squeezed the horse with his legs to hold on. At this, the horse sped up. This must be what Jack called a trot, because it was rough as hell. The horse was bouncing him all over the place, and Ryan was afraid he was going to fall. He placed both hands on the back of the horse's neck and held on. Dingo trotted right up to the back of Lucy, and she also sped up to a trot.

They continued down the hill at what Ryan considered to be breakneck speed. He kept sliding around on the horse until he was leaning down with his arms wrapped around the horse's neck. As the horse moved up and down with the trot, Ryan felt out of sync. He seemed to be coming down when the bump of the horse was going up. With each step of the horse, most of Ryan's weight was coming down on his nuts.

"Oh-oh G-God, s-s-st-op. P-l-ea-se s-s-t-op. F-r th-e l-o-ve of G-G-G-od, p-p-l-ea-se s-s-t-op!" he chanted, as the horses continued to make their way downhill. By the bottom of the hill, Ryan held on by nothing more than the wrap of his arms around the

base of the horse's neck, with the side of his face pressed hard against the warm fur at the base of his dark mane. His body flopped behind him atop the horse, slightly off to one side and then the other. When the trees opened to flat sage, Lucy broke into a slow lope and Dingo followed suit. To Ryan, the speed was blindingly fast. He dared not let go for fear he would be trampled by the thundering hooves, but at least this was much smoother than the bone-jarring trot. A dull ache blossomed up from his belly, accompanied by a sick, almost nauseating feeling of pain. Ryan felt, rather than saw, the horses drop into the dry creek bed. The pace was smooth, but the speed was still unimaginable. He held his eyes tightly shut and held the horse with both hands for dear life. He made no sound. Please let it end, he thought. Please God, let this end. Don't let me die. He briefly heard Lucy's pace change and felt Dingo jump up out of the creek bed. As the horse leaped, Ryan felt his legs fly up above and behind him and for a split second knew what was coming before it happened, but was powerless to stop it. When his legs came back down, they fell on both sides of the horse, and his testicles landed under him, squarely on the horse's back just as Dingo's back was rising. The blow was almost more than he could bear. He felt his hands loosen on the neck of the horse and just as he was about to let go, the horse slowed to a walk. The walk continued for a minute, and then the horse stopped. He loosened his grip and allowed himself to slide off to the right, onto the ground. He hit the ground hard, but it was still way better than the pummeling he had taken on the horse's back. He lay still for a moment and then slowly opened his eyes.

Jack was standing over the top of him, smiling. "Have a nice ride?"

"Fuck you" was all he could manage, in a squeaky voice.

# 13.

Jack had heard the horses coming down the hill. When he looked over to see what was happening, he couldn't help but smile at the strange position of the boy on Dingo's back. He watched the horses lope slowly across the flats. It was interesting how Dingo kept changing his lead to keep the kid on his back. With the right lead, he would lean a little to the right, on the left lead he would lean a little farther to the left. The swaying motion of his back managed to keep the kid on board. Good horse, he thought. Damn good horse.

The devastation at the crash site was a lot to take in all at once. The impact of the plane had certainly taken its toll on the precious lives it had once held, but it was also clear that wolves or coyotes had been at several of the victims in the night. There were no obvious signs of life.

The site of the idiot kid flopping on the back of the horse was a welcome break to the destruction all around him. Jack needed a break and walked out to where Marlena stood grazing as the kid rode in. On any other day, he would have laughed himself into tears. In all the years that Jack had spent with people and horses, he had never seen anything quite like this display. It hurt him just watching the kid bounce along.

He had finished checking the cockpit and the forward part of the cabin. There was no sign of any survivors. The aft part of the cabin and the tail were left about eight hundred yards to the east in a deep groove the plane had cut into the soil. Jack had planned to get Marlena and walk along the crash site, checking things along the way, when the kid made his ride and stopped in front of him. As he thought about the situation, he figured he might have just one little job to do before leaving. He stood next to Marlena and the kid.

The boy rolled over and then got to his knees. "I think I might puke."

"Go ahead if you need to."

"Aren't you going to help me?"

"Help you puke? No, I reckon you can manage that on your own."

"Help me to my feet, asshole."

"Careful, son," Jack said and offered a hand.

The kid stared at him with a look of contempt, took his hand, and stood up. "Careful? Careful about what, you fucking *fuck*! You knew they would do that."

Jack stared coldly at the kid. "I've had just about enough of your name-callin'."

"Oh, and what are you going to do? I'll call you anything I fuckin' want to."

Quicker than Ryan could have imagined, Jack's right hand snapped out and slapped him hard across the cheek. "No, son, you won't. Believe it or not, I am try'n to help you. I let you ride my horses, and I tried to tell you how to get down here. You chose to do it differently. I told you before, I won't have any problem ridin' off and leavin' you behind."

Ryan's face stung. He was so surprised by Jack's slap he didn't know what to do. At first he just stood looking at the older man, but as anger and embarrassment welled up within him, he felt he had to do something. He turned back toward the horses and took several steps, so he was standing directly in front of the Dingo. "I told you, you sack of shit. Now you're gonna get it." As he clenched his right fist, he heard

a tick-tick-click-tick and turned to face Jack with the large revolver in his hand pointed at his head. The hole in the end of
the barrel looked as big as a sewer pipe, and it didn't move.

Jack's voice was low and steady. "Son, if you have a problem
with me, I'd invite you to give it a shot. But if you so much as
swing at that horse, I promise you, it'll be your last act in this
life."

"You wouldn't shoot me over this horse."

"Try me."

The two of them stood looking at each other for a full minute. Jack finally broke the silence and said, "I know this is an
awkward situation. On the one hand, you're pissed off and you
want to get it out. You don't really think I'll shoot, but you
don't know me very well, and I just might. The fact is: you're
becoming more convinced I will with every second that passes.
On the other hand, you don't want me to ride off and leave
you out here by yourself. We're a lot farther from the road than
we used to be, and you're not sure how to get back. You'd also
like to try to kick my ass, but you're a little sore from that ride,
so you don't really want to try it right now. So here's a plan
for you: Take two steps back from that horse, open your right
hand, drop your head, and say, 'Sorry.' Then add, 'What can
I do to help?' I'll take this gun off you. You can either try me
now, or save it for later."

There was absolutely no doubt in Ryan's mind that Jack
would shoot him. There was something about the calm way
the man talked, held the gun, and his steady piercing blue eyes
that was very convincing. The weirdest thing was he called it.
He knew the situation exactly, and he offered a way out. Ryan
opened his hand, stepped back, and said, "Sorry. I got a little
carried away."

Jack uncocked the pistol and slid it back into the holster.
"There. That was easy. Let's walk down to the other end of the
crash."

Ryan felt a huge rush of relief. It was like the air came back
at once. "What about this end?"

"I checked it. Believe me; you don't want to go over there. There's no use in seeing that mess."

"Don't I need a rope to lead this horse?"

"Naw. Let him go. He'll follow along."

As Jack led Marlena, the other horses fell into a line behind her. They walked in silence for a few minutes. Finally Ryan couldn't stand it any longer. "You wouldn't have shot me, would you?"

"Rule number one: never pull a gun unless you intend to use it."

"Over a stupid horse?"

Jack stopped and turned toward Ryan, "I watched those horses lope slowly for you. Dingo kept changing his gait and lead, so you'd stay on top. There's nothin' wrong with not knowin' how to ride, but there is somethin' wrong with not bein' able to admit it. A man who would hit a horse that just helped him out isn't trustworthy; he ain't worth havin' around."

"So now you don't trust me?"

"No further than what I can throw ya."

"So how do I get you to trust me again?"

"Trust is earned. Besides, who said I ever trusted you to begin with?"

"You know, I didn't ask for any of this. This wasn't part of the vacation extravaganza I had planned. I didn't exactly wake up this morning and say, 'Gee, what can I do for fun? Oh, I know. How about busting my nuts on the back of a fuckin horse!'"

Jack laughed. "Son, I know you're out of your element. You're a city boy from a suburban, upper-middle-class family. Probably a suburb of St. Louis. You go to college in a town that's smaller than what you thought it was gonna be. You thought this was gonna be a quick trip to prove you're a man to your buddies, and it turned into somethin' a whole lot more. The horses and I know this area, and we're offering help if you want it. But you gotta cut us some slack."

"Okay," Ryan said, looking at the ground in front of him. "How do you know all that stuff about me?"

"It's easy. You've been tellin' me all mornin'. All I got to do is listen."

Ryan thought about this for a minute. "When do we get to your friend's place?"

"You been on it for the last hour."

"You are shitting me!"

"Nope."

"Then where's the house?"

They passed a twisted engine with an arm sticking out from underneath it. "About another hour or so ahead."

"How big is this place?"

"Big enough. But not too big by some western standards. Some other friends of mine ranch almost four hundred eighty sections."

"Sections? What's a section?"

"Section is a mile square: 'bout six hundred forty acres."

"So that's like, what?"

"A little over three hundred thousand acres."

"You gotta be fucking kidding, right?"

"Nope. Serious as a heart attack."

"What do they do with all that?"

"Cattle."

# 14.

When they came to the tail section of the airplane, Jack could see it was a Delta commuter jet that had gone down. It was evident from how the plane came in the pilot had tried to find a flat spot of earth to get it on the ground in one piece. If he was trying to land at the same time everything went crazy last night, he probably couldn't see much and had no power to control anything. On the other hand, if he did see the mountains in front of him, he would have tried to get the plane on the ground before running smack into them, which would cause a faster crash landing than he would have wanted, but it still might be better than plowing into the side of a mountain. Looking at the gash in the earth and the scattered sections of the plane, Jack thought the pilot must have glimpsed the hills in front of him and put the plane on the ground fast.

The main cabin of the airplane had broken into three pieces. The front half had continued to slide west and was the portion Jack had already checked. The back half had split in two, with the bulk of the cabin destroyed and spread over a wide area of ground. The tail section had broken off cleanly and stood upright with the rudder pointed at the sky. Both wings had sheared off, and the left one lay upside down in front of

them. Jack bent down, ran two fingers through the sparse grass next to the wing, and smelled his fingers.

"Jet A. We know she didn't run out of gas."

"Do you think it was that weird thing last night?" Ryan asked, with a tone Jack recognized as fear in his voice.

"Yep."

"Then whatever happened might have affected this whole area!"

Jack stood up. "Maybe more'n that."

"Hello? Is someone there?" A woman's voice called from the direction of the tail section. The rear door of the airplane hung down from the upright tail cone, and a young dark haired woman appeared in the opening. "Hello! Help!"

Jack dropped Marlena's reins and ran for the tail section as Ryan stood motionless. He yelled back over his shoulder as he ran, "C'mon, boy! Let's help!" Ryan started walking slowly, following Jack toward the tail.

When he reached the open door, Jack could see the young lady was standing on the ground inside the upright tail section amid a jungle of broken wires, insulation, cables, and tubing. As he leaned through the opening, she looked as though she might start crying and said, "Oh, thank God! I am so glad to see you. Can you please call for help?"

"Is there anyone else?" Jack asked, ignoring her question.

"Yes. Well, there was. One of the flight attendants and a passenger left when the sun came up this morning to find help. They promised to send someone for me, as I seem to have a bit of a gash on my leg and injured my ankle. Excuse me, sir, but could I ask you to call for help? As you can see, there has been a terrible disaster."

"I'm afraid we're all the help that's comin'. Cell phones don't seem to work at the moment. Which way did they go?"

"They left in that direction," she said, pointing toward the southwest. "I watched them walk for what seemed like an hour."

"Uh-oh," Jack said.

"What is it?" The girl asked.

"There isn't much help that way. They'll run directly into the Shoshone National Forest. There isn't even a decent road for a hundred miles. Besides your leg and ankle, are you okay?"

"I am otherwise unharmed."

"I bet you had a long night. We'll get you out of here in no time." He lifted himself up onto the edge of the door and jumped down inside the tail section with her.

The young lady was medium height, athletically proportioned, and very pretty, with big, dark brown eyes and straight, dark hair that hung to her shoulders. The right sleeve of her shirt was missing, and she had a small airline blanket wrapped over her shoulders. She stood on her right leg and held a small airline pillow against her left thigh, but he could see the surrounding jeans were stained with blood.

As Ryan walked up, the young woman asked, "I realize we are in the western United States, but specifically, may I ask, where we are?"

Ryan answered, "Wyoming. From what I've seen, it's pretty close to bum-fuck-Egypt." He pointed at Jack and added, "He said it's about an hour or so just to get to Cody."

"Ryan," Jack said from inside the tail section. "Come over here and help me."

The kid took a few steps, looked inside, and said, "What?"

"We're gonna get her outta here. Okay, darlin', I'm gonna lift you up. Just have a seat on the edge of that there door." She wrapped an arm around his neck as he lifted the young lady in his arms and set her on the edge of the door. "Here, Ryan. Help her down. Careful with her left leg and ankle."

"I can't carry her!"

"I'm not askin' you to carry her; I'm tellin' you to help set her on the ground."

Ryan awkwardly put an arm behind her back and another under her legs and lifted her off the edge of the door. As he swung her around, her left foot hit the doorframe.

"Ouch! Oh God, it hurts!" She cried.

"I said careful! Dammit!" Jack said, looking disgusted.

"Sorry," Ryan said, looking away.

Jack climbed out of the tail section and helped Ryan set her carefully on the ground, so she could lean against the plane. He knelt in front of her. "My name is John Neumann, but most people call me Jack."

"Hello, Mr. Neumann. It is a pleasure to meet you. My name is Nicole Meredith." She smiled at him and stuck out her hand. He shook it. Her grip was firm and confident. He liked that.

"Well, it's nice to meet you too, Nicole Meredith. I need to get a look at that cut on your leg. Is that okay?"

She pulled the pillow off her leg, and both Jack and Ryan could see a rip in her jeans and a long vertical cut in the top of her thigh. "Can I see your pillow?"

"Certainly." She handed it to him.

Jack turned the pillow over, examining it, and then set it aside. "There's not much blood on it, and the wound hasn't been bleeding for some time. Ryan, can you see if you can find the first aid kit from the airplane? They usually keep it in one of the overhead compartments in the middle of the plane. It's usually red and looks like a small tackle box."

"How am I going to find something like that in all this mess?"

Jack looked up at him. "Son, I could use a little help."

"Oh, all right," Ryan said with resignation and walked toward the other section of the plane.

Jack pulled a knife out of his pocket and flicked it open. "What are you going to do with that?" Nicole asked with apprehension in her voice.

"I'm just gonna get rid of some of the material so I can get a look at that cut you've got. I promise I won't hurt you. Do you know what you cut your leg on?"

"No. Everything happened very quickly. The flight was completely uneventful until the lights went out. The pilot made no announcements at all. It was as though one minute we were flying, and the next we were crashing. It was incredibly frightening."

"I bet it was. How many passengers do you think were on that flight?"

"It was really quite empty. Perhaps seven or eight of us at the most."

"I hope you don't mind my askin', but your accent...I can't quite place it. Where're you from?"

Nicole smiled. "I was born and spent the first few years of life in Glasgow. My family then moved to Sydney. We lived there for several years before returning to Scotland. For the last ten years I have been living in England, where I was attending university."

"Well, that explains it."

"I'm sorry. Does it bother you?"

"Not at all. In fact, it sounds kinda nice. I was just wonderin' is all."

"Hey! I found it!" Ryan called, as he ran back to where Jack knelt beside Nicole. "It was just lying right over there."

"Good job, son," Jack said, as he took the little case from the kid.

Ryan asked, "How's her leg? Is it serious?"

"The cut is clean and straight. For the most part, it's just superficial. She might use a stitch or two, but it's really not too bad." He found a small bottle of Betadine and started to clean the wound. "This might sting a little bit. Where were ya headed?"

"I had arrived in New York the other day with the intention of meeting someone. I guess he had to leave on business unexpectedly. I found myself with little to do, so I thought I would visit an old friend in San Francisco."

"And then things started goin' haywire. I'd kinda like to hear what you experienced up there."

Nicole took a deep breath and exhaled. "I'll tell you what I can remember, but it seems I might have passed out, or fell asleep. I know that truly makes no sense, but it is the best I can recall."

"I guess it'll have to do," Jack said as he worked.

"We departed from St. Louis on schedule, and everything seemed quite ordinary. The flight attendants had given us a snack, and I had enjoyed a cocktail, so I was feeling really rather

sleepy. I seem to recall the pilot announced over the intercom they were experiencing a few technical problems, and we were being rerouted for our approach into Salt Lake City and would be arriving late. I was holding my iPod and listening to some American music when the lights went out. I couldn't help but notice my music stopped at the same instant. I pulled the phones out of my ears and could hear the airplane's engines slowing down, and it felt as though we had begun to descend. I thought, 'How odd, he just mentioned we were going to be delayed, and now we are beginning the descent.' I recall the plane shaking violently and a bright flash of light, as though lightning had struck us; yet there were no clouds. I could see the ground quite clearly. That was the last I remember until I awoke, still belted into my seat, on the ground with wreckage all around me."

Jack looked up again. "So you passed out last night at some point. Ain't that different? I did the same thing."

"Is that significant?"

"I'm not sure. It might be. I need to think on it a bit. Nicole, your cut here isn't terrible, but it does need a stitch. Do you mind if I fix it up before we head out? I don't want you to start bleeding again."

"Wouldn't it be better to call an ambulance?"

Jack pointed with his thumb behind him. "Do you see that brown horse over there?"

"Yes."

"That's your ambulance. Her name is Lucy."

"Surely you are joking?"

"No, ma'am. I'm afraid it's the best we got."

"Well then...I believe I'm out of options. Have you ever done anything like this before?"

"Once or twice." He winked at her.

She sighed, "If you think it's best."

"Ryan, would you go get the little red case out of my left saddlebag?"

"Jesus. What am I? A fucking gopher?"

Jack turned quickly toward him. "Son, there's a lady here. I'm only gonna tell you once to quit that cussin'."

Ryan looked embarrassed. "All right. All right. Jesus." He walked off slowly toward the horses.

"Is he a friend of yours?"

"Ryan?" Jack smiled as he continued to clean the wound. "I wouldn't say we're friends. No. I had a little trouble with my truck last night, and he and I met this morning on the road out of Yellowstone. He was walkin', and I had horses, so I offered him a lift."

"That's very kind of you."

"Thanks."

"You two don't really see eye to eye, do you?"

"That's a nice way to put it. No, we don't."

Ryan came back with the bag.

"Thank you," Jack said as the kid handed him the kit. "Have a seat, son. I need your expertise."

"Mine?" Ryan asked, surprised.

Jack arranged a few instruments and laid a folded paper containing a sterile pair of gloves open on the ground. He took a bottle with a blue label and filled a syringe with the contents.

Nicole asked, "I can't imagine that many people ride horseback with all of this medical equipment. Why do you have this?"

"This stuff? Oh, well, sometimes when we're out in the sticks, somebody gets cut. It's easier to just fix it on the spot."

"I see."

Jack changed the subject as he continued to work. "Ryan, this morning you said something had to disrupt the ionosphere to cause that display we saw in the sky last night, right?"

"Yeah. Something big."

"Would a nuclear burst do it?"

Nicole interrupted, "Oh my. Do you think there was an attack on the United States?"

Ryan shook his head and said. "Back in nineteen sixty-two the U.S. conducted a test where they exploded a high-altitude nuclear weapon over the South Pacific. They called it Starfish

Prime. It caused an aurora, but it was nothing like what we saw last night."

Jack said, "Nicole, I have to inject that wound with a little numbing medicine. I ain't gonna lie to ya. This'll hurt, but it'll get numb very quickly. Are you okay with that?"

She had a worried look on her face, but said, "That will be fine."

Jack started injecting and occasionally glanced up at her face. He could tell it hurt as he watched her bite her lip, but she refused to utter a sound.

"So you don't think this could have been a nuke?"

Ryan said. "No way. It was way too big for that. A nuke would have disrupted the magnetosphere and the ionosphere locally, and the aurora would be small. It would travel in the lines of magnetic polarization, but…" He trailed off and sat staring at nothing for a moment. All at once he jumped up. "Holy Shit! I know what it was! I know! Oh my God!"

"Care to share it with us?" Jack asked, as he clicked a shiny metal clamp on a tiny needle and pulled a long, thin, clear thread out of a package.

Ryan paced, tapping a finger to his nose. "I gotta think about it a minute."

Nicole said to Jack, "If you don't mind my asking, what is that?"

"This? This here is Monocryl. Works good for little cuts like this."

Ryan paced some more and then said, "Okay, okay. I got it. One of the important things they learned from Starfish Prime was the effect of EMP. That stands for electromagnetic pulse. If you run electricity through a wire, any wire, you create a small magnetic field around the wire. That's how an electromagnet and a motor works. But also, if you move a magnetic field around a wire, you move electrons and can create electricity. That's how a generator works. When they set the high-altitude nuke off, it created a magnetic pulse big enough that it moved electrons in wires all the way over in Hawaii, about twelve hundred miles away. The electric surge in those wires shorted out

TVs, blew out streetlights, and stopped a few cars. I think we had an EMP last night. A huge one. That's what all the sparks were from. When they set off that nuke in sixty-two, you could see an arc of aurora almost two thousand miles away, and they say it lasted for about seven minutes. Whatever happened last night was big enough to cover the whole sky, and it lasted all night long!"

"How do you know this?" Nicole asked.

"We talked about it in one of my physics classes." Ryan went on, "When Starfish Prime went off, the magnetic pulse lasted only a couple of nanoseconds. The event last night lasted at least several whole seconds! That's like billions or trillions of times bigger! The only thing that could do it would be a star… Wait." He paused, thinking. "Oh man! I got it. This was a huge solar flare! Coronal mass ejection. It had to be. It's the only thing big enough and close enough to do something like this. If the flare was big enough and the pulse was long enough, the moving magnetic field could be huge. That would make sparks jump out of anything ferrous."

Jack was carefully working, but said, "I think you lost me."

"The magnetic field also wasn't uniform, that's why…Oh my God. I get it! Okay. It's like this. A huge solar flare jumps off the sun's surface and is directed at the earth. Since light travels faster than the pulse, we could see it before it actually hit us, but only by a couple of minutes. This thing happened in the middle of the night, so our side of the earth was facing away from the sun. When the magnetic field washed over us, it wasn't like one big wave, but rather like hundreds of thousands or millions of smaller waves going every which way. So it would depend on whether a big wave hit a spot where you were or a small wave. That's why some of the guardrails we saw looked fine and others were all twisted in all kinds of directions. That tells us the field wasn't even uniformly polarized. There was just all these crazy waves pushing things in all kinds of directions. That means the flare came very close to us and didn't have time to polarize. Wow. Shit. That must have been freakin' huge."

Jack stopped what he was doing and looked over at Ryan. "So what you're tellin' us is that this is global."

"Oh yeah. It would have to be. Also, there's no telling what the other side of the planet is like. It could have been cooked."

Nicole looked pale. "What you are saying is that the United Kingdom is gone?"

"Not necessarily," Ryan said. "It wouldn't be directly opposite us, but more like toward one side. China would be on the opposite side. And I'm just guessing here. A flare doesn't have to be hot. It can be just particles, or other parts of the spectrum, you know, like radio waves and stuff."

Jack said, "If the magnetic field was as strong as you say, could it affect the earth's magnetic field?"

"Wow. That's a good question. I don't know. Maybe."

"I'm sorry, but what does all this mean?" Nicole asked, looking very worried.

Jack concentrated as he continued to work on her leg but said, "Well, darlin', I'm not sure we know yet. Judgin' by what Ryan here told us, we might've gotten the least of the damage, since we'd be the most sheltered by the planet. Isn't that right, son?"

"Yeah. Maybe. At least I think so."

Nicole looked very serious. "Mr. Neumann, exactly how bad are things?"

Jack stopped what he was doing and looked directly into her eyes. "We don't know yet. I had quite an experience with my truck last night, and you know what it did to an airplane. We'll need to get to town to learn more, but I have a feelin' it might be bad."

Tears immediately welled up in her eyes and rolled down her cheeks. "I'm frightened."

"I am too."

"Will you help me?"

Jack smiled at her. "Don't worry. I'll take care of you."

# 15.

Mark put his right hand in the pocket of his leather jacket and felt the grip of the Colt. The thought of the barrel pointing at his junk made him a little nervous, but having the gun made him feel a lot stronger—maybe even dangerous. But the damn thing jammed under his belt wasn't very comfortable. He hadn't walked very far, but it kept digging into his side. He'd have to find a better way to carry it, maybe something that would allow him to get to it fast. The shiny, black leather duty holster would have worked, but it was too obvious where it had come from. It had history. He didn't need anything with history. He seemed to recall a gun shop on the west end of town. They might have something, but it was a long walk.

The devastation was indescribable. When he left the apartment, it became apparent that although things last night looked bad, he had no idea how bad. The sunshine revealed utter chaos. Every house and building he passed was damaged in some way. Many were completely destroyed. He noticed that most, if not all, of the light poles were bent or missing. He had passed one house where an old lady lay in the front yard with what looked like a washing machine lid sticking out of her back. He also noticed every car appeared to be burned—most

were even flipped over or on their sides. Even most of the garages that had held cars were burned. How could terrorists do that? It must be some new kind of technology. He passed a burned SUV lying on its roof in the middle of the street. The hulk of black steel still held what was left of four passengers. Somebody was going to have to get that mess cleaned up in a hurry.

There was also a bunch of weird stuff. On one corner he passed a wooden telephone pole that was peppered with drywall screws. Most were embedded into the wood sideways, and some were even stuck in the wood headfirst. A couple of the manhole covers were missing, and he saw one bent in half. Along one block several fire hydrants with the big steel pipe connecting them had been ripped out of the ground and thrown up against some houses.

When he reached the business district, he saw a small crowd of people in front of the police station. Some stood and talked in small groups; others sat alone on the steps or sidewalk. Mark walked up to an older guy standing by himself wearing a Carhartt jacket and cowboy hat. "Hey. Does anybody know what happened?"

"Goddamndest thing. Some folks here say it was the Iranians, but I think it was the Chinese. Goddamned sneaky bastards."

"Were we bombed?"

"I don't know anything else that could have done this much damage. Do you?"

"No, I suppose not."

"I'll tell you what it was," a guy wearing a denim jacket said, as he limped toward them. "It was CERN. You know, that big test facility in Switzerland. People said they shouldn't mess around with that kind of stuff, and now look where it's got us."

The guy in the hat shook his head. "If that place is in Switzerland, why would it have blown everything to hell over here. That just don't make sense. Besides, I heard that everything in Buffalo was fine. We were the only ones in this state

that got bombed. The terrorists wanted to shut down the coal mine."

"This is the wrath of God," a loud voice boomed from behind them. The three of them turned to see a middle-aged man walk toward the front of the building with a book in his hand. He continued to make his way up the steps as he said, "This was foretold from the beginning and has now come to pass. As told by John the Prophet, 'I looked and there before me was a pale horse. Its rider was death, and hell was following close behind him.' Ladies and gentlemen, welcome to the apocalypse. Decide you this day who you will serve."

A heavyset man with no neck and a sweat-stained button-down shirt walked up the stairs waving his arms and said, "Now now now. Reverend, you may be right, but we don't need to go scaring everybody half to death. They're already scared."

"As well they should be!"

Mark leaned toward the guy with the hat and asked, "Who is that?"

"That's Frank Paulson. He's one of the city councilmen."

The heavyset guy continued, "Everybody, let's just calm down a minute here. Ladies and gentlemen, I'm sure you're all wondering what happened. As I have spoken with some of you, I have heard all kinds of theories and ideas, but the truth of the matter is that we just don't know yet. We must have faith that our government will find those people that have committed this terrible tragedy and bring them to justice, but first we must help ourselves. I'll be straight with you. We're in kind of a pickle here. We don't seem to have any working phones, every radio we can find is no longer functioning, and all computer services are down. As you know, we have no electricity and no water in any part of the city. We have only been able to find two police officers, and one of them is injured. Our firefighters aren't in much better shape. I can tell you, I have learned from a reliable source that our mayor was fatally wounded last night, and, as such, I am assuming his responsibilities.

"First, we must attend to the injured. I am asking that each of you organize a team of two people and start a house-to-house

search for the wounded. When you search a house, I'd ask that you make a big X on a sign or, heck, even on the front door of the house to let people know that it's been searched. If there are bodies inside, just write the number you find on the door as well. That might help things in the days to come. If you do find somebody hurt, help them get outside, and we'll get them to the hospital."

A tall man in the back yelled, "Can't do that. Hospital's burned."

"Okay. Well, we are going to set up medical service in the schools then. I also need some people to help get that started. I expect everyone to help. It's in these terrible times that we find our strength and pull together to overcome. Together we can succeed. We are Americans. We will always overcome."

The self-appointed mayor continued his speech, but Mark had lost interest. There was no way he was going to get tied up with one of these little gruesome-twosome, house-to-house search parties. Seriously, what was he going to do? Check old ladies with washing machine lids sticking out of their backs? Yep. She's dead. Nope. There was no way he was having any of that. It was time to get out of Dodge.

He made his way toward the back of a crowd that seemed to have grown during the speech. As he slowly backed up, he noticed people nodding their heads in agreement with the speaker. When he got to the back edge of the gathering, he casually slipped around a corner into a small side street and started walking away fast.

At first Mark wasn't sure where to go; it looked like everything was burned or at least damaged. When the Colt dug into his side again, he decided to walk west. Seemed like as good of an idea as any. Maybe he could find the gun shop. He couldn't remember what it was called, but he did seem to recall it was on Echeta Road near I-90.

As the blocks passed, he noticed an incredible amount of destruction, but it didn't look like the old movies of World War II where cities had been bombed. There weren't any blast holes in

the ground or buildings that had exploded, rather most of the cars and trucks had exploded and buildings burned. The more he looked, the more he realized that the damage seemed to be mostly things made out of metal. He passed a truck sitting sideways on the sidewalk that had been flattened. The whole thing wasn't more than a foot high. It looked like a giant's foot had smashed it into the ground. But twenty feet away, a four-wheeler seemed fine except for the pipe sticking through the gas tank.

He started thinking about what the councilman had said: virtually no cops and no radios. Wasn't that interesting? Even if one cop was out, who could he call for backup? How would he call? Mark stopped suddenly with a thought and pulled Lisa's cell phone from his pocket. He pressed the power button and held it, but the little apple never lit up. He checked his watch. Stuck at 11:02. "Holy shit!" Mark said aloud. This is just like *StarCraft*, he thought, or even *Modern Warfare II*. You could get a leg up on the enemy by setting off an EMP over their base and taking out their technology. They did the same thing in *The Matrix*. I bet this was a fucking EMP! He laughed aloud and threw the phone as far as he could. The thing was useless.

Ahead on the right, he saw a huge crater in the ground with dirt and debris showered over everything in the surrounding block. The sight of this large raw hole in the earth made him think again about a terrorist bombing. Maybe they did it after all. As he walked closer, he could make out the only remaining corner of a red and white plastic sign. He recognized it as a Conoco gas station. Most of the store front was missing, and the remainder burned nearly to the ground, but he could see where the top of the building looked as though it had been blown back and away from the crater. The hole itself was almost L-shaped. The tanks. It had to be the underground gasoline tanks that blew. All morning long he'd seen nothing but burned cars, and now the underground tanks were blown. Maybe the EMP had something to do with gas, but that didn't really make much sense.

A couple of blocks farther, he noticed a Kum & Go convenience store. The front windows of the building were broken,

and several of the large metal shelves appeared crumpled and thrown out on the parking lot. His stomach rumbled, and he walked toward the building. Sticking his head inside, he said, "Hello? Anybody here?" With no reply he stepped over the remnant of the window ledge and into the store. In the past he had lifted a few things now and then. Everybody did, and it was never anything big. Just some small stuff. Now he began filling his bag with as much beef jerky as he could stuff inside. He grabbed a few other things as well, but if he wanted to stay in shape, protein was the name of the game. He found a couple of bottles of water and a huge can of Lo-Carb Monster. A little pick-me-up in the morning might sound good. He hoisted the bag on his shoulder and was about to stand up when he heard a thickly accented Indian man say, "Hey. What are you doing in here?"

Mark thought quickly. He stood slowly as he turned toward the sound of the voice. He hoped he might look a little intimidating. Mark stood almost six-feet tall, but this morning he was wearing his black Docs, which added a little more height to him. He was also wearing a thick, black leather motorcycle jacket, dark t-shirt, jeans, and, of course, he had the gun. He stared unblinking at the little man. "I was just fixing breakfast. What are you doing in here?"

"This is my store. Get out of here. I will call the police."

"Call 'em," Mark said, surprised at how calm he felt, and started walking toward the man.

"You are stealing from me! Get out. Get out now!" he yelled, as he continued backing away.

"This is now a free country. I'm free to take whatever I want, and you are free to try and stop me."

"Get out, get out, get out!" the little guy yelled, as Mark slowly made his way toward the window. He walked past the man and was about to step over the ledge when out of the corner of his eye he happened to see the guy swing something toward his back. He spun, sticking his hand out, and just happened to perfectly catch a broomstick with his left hand. With his right he pulled the Colt from his belt. He jerked hard on

the broomstick bringing the man closer and pressed the barrel against his forehead.

"Bad idea, buddy. Do you want to die here?"

The man blinked and started shaking. After a couple of seconds, he managed, "No."

Mark said, "I ought to shove that broom up your ass. Maybe it would teach you a lesson. Never fuck with somebody who's a lot bigger than you."

The man was shaking violently now and managed a little nod.

Mark pulled the gun away and heard what sounded like water dripping. He looked down to see water dripping from the man's pant leg and spreading on the floor. "I think you sprang a leak, you pathetic fuck." He stepped over the ledge and started walking again.

After he had gotten a couple of blocks from the store, Mark's heart started racing, and a wave of nervous energy washed over him. At first he laughed. The picture of the guy pissing his pants was awesome, but he had to consider the possibilities. What might have happened? The guy might have had a gun of his own. He was stupid to have gone into that store without checking things out better. The guy also could have had a knife, in which case sticking his hand out would have left him with a bad wound. Lastly, the guy could have had a couple of buddies outside. That would have gone bad. But on the other hand, what he had told the guy was right. He was bigger. In fact, he was bigger than most guys. Although he wasn't sure how far the destruction reached, at least in this little part of the world, he was completely free.

# 16.

As he made his way west, Mark continued to think about the implications of no police, no communications, no electricity, and no transportation. If he could get the last issue worked out, the other problems might become opportunities. Ahead he saw what looked like a large upside down L standing in the middle of the road. Even as he drew nearer, it didn't look at all familiar. Only when he got close could he understand what he was looking at. A huge, steel bank vault door had bent in half and was standing imbedded in the asphalt. Even the locking wheel was bent but still in place. He looked around and spotted Security Bank a block away.

As he walked toward the building, he constructed a plausible story in his mind. If anybody asked, he would say he simply had an account with the bank and wanted to make a withdrawal so he could buy something to eat, since his debit card wasn't working. Without a working computer, nobody would be able to prove him wrong. He decided before walking inside he should walk around the outside to have a better idea what might be in store for him. Always better to rule out any surprises. The damage to the building was incredible. Several

walls were partially knocked down or broken out, with bricks and glass scattered everywhere. Nobody was around.

Inside the building he could see the huge safe standing wide open, since the door was about a block and a half away in the middle of the road. Sun shone inside the safe, and he could see the ceiling peeled back like a tuna can. Money was blowing around the floor. Lots of it. He smiled. He stepped into the safe and helped himself to several stacks of one hundred dollar bills, tucking them into a pocket of his backpack. As he turned and was about to leave, he noticed a wall of safe deposit boxes with several of the little metal doors missing. He pulled on one of the steel drawers inside and found it stuck. He tried another and found a bunch of worthless documents. In the third he found a stack of gold coins. He quickly snapped up all twelve of them. He started to feel nervous. It was one thing to explain why he was in the bank, but quite another to explain why he was digging through a bunch of safe deposit boxes. Besides, from where he stood, he couldn't see the entrance, and some-body could easily sneak in behind him. He stuffed the coins in his pocket and then hustled outside. Nobody had seen a thing. This was too easy!

An hour later Mark walked up to the front of Wild West Weapons. A man with thin, gray hair who looked to be in his sixties sat on a stool under the shade of a small canopy in front of the store. A large black military rifle lay across his lap. Mark said, "Morning. I don't suppose you're open for business."

"Yep. I'm open. Guys are gonna need me now more than ever."

"You think so?"

"Yep. How else are they gonna protect themselves?"

"You make a good point."

"Can you pay?"

"Mark pulled several hundred dollars out of his back pack. I got money."

The guy shook his head. "That ain't gonna get it. That's fine to wipe your ass with, but it won't buy anything in here."

"Dude. It's money."

"Nope. It's fiat. We used to call it money, but I reckon I could pick up a wheelbarrow of that shit in a couple hours. It's worthless."

"So how do I buy something?"

"Got anything to trade?" The older guy asked.

Mark reached into his right front pocket and pulled out one of the gold coins.

"There you go!" the guy said and stood up from his chair. "Come inside, son. Let's see what we can do for you." They walked through the door into a dark room lit by three kerosene lanterns hanging from the ceiling. "My name's Red Burton. I've been trying to clean things up since last night. It was a hell of a mess. There's a pile of guns over there that are wrecked. They're bent to hell by whatever happened, but I still got more than a few that are just fine. What is it you're looking for?"

"I got this," Mark said as he pulled the Colt. "I need a holster for it."

Red picked up the pistol and said, "I hope you don't mind," as he unloaded it. "This is a nice weapon. Been well cared for. You like 1911s?"

"Yeah, I guess."

Red looked at the pistol carefully, narrowed his eyes, and said, "Did you recently come across this?"

Mark knew he was busted. "Yeah. I found it."

"Thought so. This one belonged to a cop and a good friend of mine. I found him and his wife dead in their home last night. I put the competition sights on and did the trigger work myself."

"Sorry. You can have it back."

"He won't need it anymore. It's yours if you want it."

"Maybe we could trade?"

"Sure. I'll trade you for it. What are you looking for?"

Mark thought for a minute and said, "I want something fast and easy. It's gotta be powerful enough to actually work, and I don't want to mess with it."

Red walked behind the counter and pulled out a black and silver handgun. "This here is what you want. This is a Springfield XD(m). This one is in .45 but I also have one in 9 mm if that's too big. It's lightweight, so you can carry it without breaking your back, and it'll hold thirteen in the mag and one in the pipe. Best thing about it is that it'll eat anything that says .45 ACP, and it's always ready to go."

Marked picked up the weapon, and it felt good in his hands. Very good. "That's awesome. The 9 is smaller?"

"Yep." He pulled out another pistol that was all black. "This is the compact. They both come with a paddle holster, but this one works best in a belt rig that fits in the small of your back. Out of sight and out of mind."

"Cool. How much?"

"With that Colt and the gold, we are well within your price range."

"What else do you have?"

"What else do you want?"

Mark grinned. "What I really want is a machine gun."

"I've never carried any NFA weapons. There's just not much call for 'em over here. In my opinion they don't do much more than turn money into noise. Pete Christensen in Buffalo has a few. They're expensive though."

"Like how much?"

"Depends on what you want, but I would figure on at least twelve or fifteen thousand for something usable."

"Whoa."

"Yep. Like I said, they're expensive. Probably even more now. They really aren't all that useful either unless you got a squad of soldiers headed your way. They're just not very accurate. These are not the days to be wasting ammo."

Mark thought that was an interesting comment. "Why do you think that?"

"Look around! Do you think this was the only place damaged? I bet the whole damn country looks just like this."

"A bunch of guys downtown said that terrorists bombed us."

"Bombed? You think we got bombed? Hell no. I've seen bombing—did three tours in 'Nam. First of all, why in the hell would anybody decide to bomb Gillette, Wyoming? There's nothing here except the coal mine and taking that out would not be high on anybody's priority list. Second, did you hear any planes or missiles last night? I sure the hell didn't. Third, did you happen to see the sky? There weren't no terrorist did that. Whatever it was, we just happened to be in the blast zone, and if we were in it, so was a big fuckin' part of what used to be the United States of America. Here, let me prove it to you." Red walked behind the counter to where the cash register should sit. Mark hadn't realized it was missing until now. When Red came back, he placed a clear plastic square on the counter about six feet away. He placed another in front of Mark and then set two more, farther down along the counter. "See for yourself."

Mark looked at the Silva compass in front of him. The red end of the needle pointed directly away from him. He walked over to the first compass and noticed that it was pointing ninety degrees to the right of the first. When he checked the other two, he found they were pointing in different directions as well. "Whoa. What's up with that?"

"I'm not sure," Red said. "Now watch this." He picked up the other three compasses and brought them next to the one in front of Mark. The needles rotated and then all faced the same direction, away from Mark, but all three were moving slowly toward the right. "Trouble is, north is that way." He pointed to the door.

"So compasses don't work anymore? Is that what you are saying?"

Red sighed. "No, son. What I'm telling you is that whatever happened last night, it was big enough to mess up the entire earth's magnetic field. This thing might be worldwide."

Mark felt like all the air in the room suddenly disappeared. It was hard to breath. He stood for a moment with his mouth open and then bolted for the doorway. He had to get out. He had to breathe. Standing in the sunshine, he gulped air. He

put both hands on his thighs and bent over, breathing in and out deeply. Red came out and stood next to him. "Slow down. Don't want to hyperventilate. I know it's a lot to get your head around. I damn near did the same thing myself. You listen; I'll talk. If this thing is widespread, then what we got is what we got. You strike me as somebody with a brain, that's why you have gold and you are trying to buy some weapons. If you're willing to part with some of that gold, I'll give you some advice. Come on. Let's go back inside."

Inside the store, Red pulled two plastic chairs away from a plastic table. "Have a seat." Mark sat down, dug a gold coin from his pocket, and laid it on the table. Red picked it up, saying, "Maple Leaf. That'll work. Okay, here's the thing. I'm not gonna sell you that 9 mm. You don't want two pistols of different calibers. You only want to carry one caliber for your pistol and one for your rifle. That brings me to the second point. Don't worry about all that full-auto bullshit. You need one, solid, good shooting rifle that will reach out and touch somebody if you need to. I'm gonna fix you up with a .308. It will also eat anything that says 7.62 NATO on it. Did you grow up around here?"

"No, Denver."

"Got any family or ties to this area?"

"Just my job."

"Well, that's over. Get the hell out of here while the weather is still reasonable. If I were you, I'd head west. Buffalo would be a good start, but it would be better to get to the other side of the Bighorns before the cold sets in. Better yet if you could get to the Pacific Northwest. More food and better weather. When the wind starts blowin' and the temperature drops, we'll have coal to keep warm, but not much else. I'm not sure how many people are still around, but I bet there won't be enough food for 'em all to get through winter. It's gonna be bad. You want to get set up where you can eat, sleep, shit, shower, and stay warm without worrying that someone is going to take it from you. You follow me?"

"Yeah, I think so."

"Now, you sit here, and I'm gonna get you set up. I'll show you what you need and give you a rough idea how to use it."

An hour and a half later, Mark walked out the door carrying a new pack with some new gear, a new pistol, and a black rifle. At the edge of the parking lot, he stepped into the road and turned west.

# 17.

"Wow, that is really quite impressive," Nicole said, looking at a straight, single, fine line down the front of her thigh. "The incision is beautiful. I suspect you have practiced that before," Nicole said.

Jack looked up quickly at her. "Why do you say that?"

"I expected a result quite different than this. Do you sew often?"

He looked back down at his work. "Horses mostly. The occasional cowhand every now and then."

"How many stitches do I have?"

"Two."

"Two? I must have more than two. That slice was at least eight inches long."

"That cut is no more than five inches. There's only two stitches, but they run back and forth inside the wound." He broke a little glass vial with some cotton in the end and dabbed a little blue liquid along the incision.

"What's that?"

"Glue."

"Glue? What? You're gluing me together?"

"It's special glue that's made for this kind of thing. Don't worry; you'll be good as new. I want you to keep this elevated as much as you can and I want you to take some ibuprofen every four hours. It'll help with the pain and keep the swelling down. "

"I will. Will it hurt when the numbing medication wears off?"

"It might be a little sore, but we'll keep you fixed up."

Jack and Ryan searched through the wreckage trying to find Nicole's bags. Something about a passenger, still belted into her seat, caught Jack's eye. An elderly woman, he guessed to be in her late-seventies, looked as though she was sleeping, with her head tipped forward. It was the unusual brown spot on the right upper corner of her white blouse by her collarbone that caught his attention. He stepped toward her for a closer look. The woman didn't appear to have any cuts or discernible traumatic injuries anywhere, but the brown spot appeared odd and out of place. He lifted the collar of her shirt, but couldn't quite see, so he unfastened the top two buttons of her blouse and pulled it forward.

"You're a sick fuck," Ryan said from behind him.

"Not really. This is odd. Take a look."

Ryan walked up from behind Jack to see a round spot of blackened skin on the woman's upper chest and what appeared to be a burned line that ran up the skin to her collarbone and then disappeared. "What the hell did that?"

Jack touched the woman's burn and said, "Her pacemaker."

"Oh shit! My grandma has one of those. Do you think it was the flare that did that?"

"Yep. I do."

"Oh man. I don't want to think about that. Cover it up, and for God's sake, quit looking down old ladies' shirts." Ryan walked away and started looking through a pile of luggage, insulation, and twisted aluminum.

In the seat next to the woman sat a man about Jack's age. He also looked peaceful, and Jack could see no big cuts and no obvious fractures. Jack pulled his shirt forward and looked.

No obvious burns. As he walked away, he took his hat off and scratched his head, thinking about what he had seen.

"I think I found one!" Ryan yelled. "Wait a minute—here's the other one!"

Jack walked over and found Ryan trying to roll a large brown bag with a gold nameplate by the extended handle through the sagebrush. The bag tipped and twisted as he pulled. "Might be easier just to carry it," Jack said.

"Try and lift it. I bet the damn thing weighs a hundred pounds!"

Jack picked it up easily by the side handle and said, "More like fifty. Don't worry about it, son. I've got it."

Ryan dragged the smaller bag as Jack carried the larger to where Nicole sat. Jack asked, "Both of these yours?"

"Yes, and I'm so pleased you've found them."

"I don't s'pose there's any way to make one small bag out of these two?"

"Not unless I leave quite a few things behind. They are packed quite tightly."

"The reason I'm askin' is that we have about five miles of country just like this to cover before we get out of this mess. I can probably strap one bag on a horse, but I don't think we can carry much more than that."

"I see. Well, I will just have to make do, won't I."

He smiled, "If you could, it would sure make things easier."

"Do you think that I would be able to carry a small tote on my back, Mr. Neumann?

"I think that would be fine."

"Wait! What about my stuff," Ryan said. "I forgot my bag! We have to go back and get it."

Jack said, "As I recall, there isn't anything worth savin' anyway."

"My iPhone, GPS, some clothes, and my plane ticket are in that bag."

"The phone and GPS are shot. The clothes are full of pepper spray and the ticket is electronic. You don't need any of that stuff."

"Yeah, but it's my stuff."

"You'll get more," Jack said and then walked on ahead.

Thirty minutes later, Jack had fashioned a saddle pad out of several layered airline blankets and tied a small bag over Lucy's back using the lead ropes and one of Marlena's reins. Nicole had lightened the bag considerably, taking only the bare necessities for the next couple of days.

"Darlin', have you ever ridden a horse before?"

"Yes, I have. I took lessons as a child."

"Good. Ryan, you're back on Dingo."

"Aww man, what about her?" Ryan asked, pointing at Nicole.

"She's going to ride Marlena."

"Why does she get the saddle? I thought you said nobody could ride Marlena but you."

"I'm gonna ask Marlena for a favor," Jack said casually and walked over to his horse. He stood by her head and scratched her neck. He whispered something into the horse's left ear and then walked over to Nicole.

Jack scooped her up off the ground and walked over to the front of his horse. "I wanna introduce you two. Marlena, this is Nicole. This is the girl I told you about. Nicole, this is Marlena. Just reach up and scratch her forehead. She likes that." Nicole scratched the horse. Jack walked over and, lifting her a little higher, helped her into the saddle. Marlena stood motionless. "There you go. Just let your legs hang down. You don't need to put 'em in the stirrups. Hang on to the horn."

"What a fuckin' load of crap!" Ryan said. "You had me going with that mean horse story. That was such a crock of—"

"Son. What I tell you about that cussin?"

"Whatever!"

Jack took the single rein and walked out in front of Marlena.

"Hey! Aren't you going to ride? This is going to take all day!"

Jack ignored him and started walking at the best pace he could manage through the sage.

# 18.

It was late afternoon when Jack, Nicole, and Ryan reached Diamond Basin Road on the southwest outskirts of Cody. As they moved along the east side of the Buffalo Bill Reservoir, they began to see houses and barns. All of them appeared damaged. Many were burned nearly to the ground, while others were missing roofs, partially collapsed, or damaged in some other way, with broken windows and doors, or scorched on the outside. One house had both the tractor and trailer of an eighteen-wheeler embedded into the side. As they walked down Southfork Road, a middle-aged man came out to talk with them. He hadn't been into Cody but had seen a large amount of smoke coming from that direction last night and this morning. Otherwise, he knew less about the disaster than they did. Finally, the road made a steep grade downward along the side of a steep hill and merged with Yellowstone Avenue, the main street in Cody.

The devastation in town was unimaginable. Nothing seemed to be untouched from the disaster. Many buildings were little more than smoking piles of rubble, and in some places a few small fires still burned. Scattered in the road and in the parking lots alongside were the blackened, burned-out hulks of

cars and trucks. The fire that raged here last night must have wiped out most of the town. They walked the horses east along Yellowstone in silence. Finally Jack said, "Before we moved to Wyoming 'bout ten years ago, we came here for a visit. I liked Cody. Wanted to move here. In fact, I think I liked Cody better than just about any other place I had ever been. There was somethin' about the people. They say every town has a personality. Well, Cody feels like your best friend. Honest and solid."

"Do you live here now?" Nicole asked from atop Marlena.

"Nope. We found a place outside of Dayton, just west of Sheridan. It's east of here 'bout a hundred twenty miles or so. We found a nice ranch with good water and more'n a few trees."

"So you are a long way from home as well. Did you grow up in Wyoming?"

"No, ma'am. I was born and raised in Texas. Odessa early on and then Austin; a bit in Houston and San Antonio."

"Do you have family there?"

"In Texas? Yep. I got a few. How 'bout you? All your family still on the other side of the pond?"

"So to speak, yes. I have a sister in Italy at the moment, and my mother is in Glasgow. My father is…well…he is a long story."

"I see."

"Hey," Ryan yelled from behind. "Where are we going? You said we were headed for town. Well, this is town."

"I'm not sure yet, but we'll find somethin'," Jack called back to him.

"We gotta find something soon," Ryan said. "I'm starving and I'm tired. Unlike you, I was up all night."

"A little patience son. I'm workin' on it."

"Patience? I've been patient all day. Now, I'm fucking hungry, thirsty, and tired. I'm sick and tired of sitting on this goddamn horse and my ass hurts."

Jack stopped suddenly. He dropped the rein he had been using to lead Marlena. The horse dropped her head and stood still as he walked back to where the boy sat on Dingo. Standing

next to the horse and looking up at the kid, he said in a quiet voice, "What did I tell you about that cussin'?"

"Oh, for Christ's sake," Ryan said, rolling his head. "Grow up. I'm sure she's heard a lot worse."

Nicole interrupted, "It is true. I grew up in Scotland. Really, this is no trouble at all."

Jack's face was turning red as he stared at the kid. "It don't matter what she's heard before or what she hasn't. A man's got to have some self-control. If you can't find any, I'm gonna help you."

"Fuck you, old man. I'm gettin' sick—" He never finished.

Quick as a flash, Jack had reached out and held the front of the kid's knee with his left hand as he grabbed the young man's foot with his right. A quick lift was all that was needed to unbalance him sending him over the other side of the horse. Ryan landed with a hard thump. "Ow!" he said, scrambling to his feet. "Goddammit!" he screamed, as he made his way around the back of the horse. "What the fuck?"

Jack stood motionless, looking at him.

"You're pretty fuckin' tough with that goddamn bazooka hanging under your arm!"

Jack slowly unbuckled the strap in front and lifted the pistol and holster from around his neck. He laid it on the middle of Dingo's back. "Go Ahead. Make your move."

"Maybe I would if I wasn't so fuckin' hungry and tired."

Jack's right hand moved in a blur. He slapped Ryan across the cheek and mouth, hard enough to spin the kid's head to the right. The boy staggered but managed to stay on his feet. Tears welled in his eyes. "Ouch!" He took a deep breath. "That...hurt."

"It was designed that way."

"Why'd you hit me?"

"You know why."

"Yeah, but you didn't have to hit me."

"Apparently I did. So far it seems to be the only thing you listen to. I told you before to quit that cussin', and I mean what I say. You are welcome to stay with us or not. It's up to you. If you

stay, there will be rules." Jack put the pistol back on and swung up onto Dingo. "You're walkin'. It'll help with your sore parts."

Ryan was going to complain, but then thought better of it.

Jack put his heel to Dingo's side, and they walked up to the front of Marlena. As he reached out to grab the rein, Marlena flattened her ears and tipped her head toward Dingo. Jack pointed at her and said, "Knock it off! What I told him goes for you too." She immediately relaxed.

Nicole asked, "What was she upset about?"

"Marlena is the boss. She don't like me ridin' Dingo, and she really don't like him leadin' the way. It'll be okay now."

There was an uncomfortable silence as they set off walking again. Several minutes later they approached a large, log framed wooden building on the right with most of the roof missing. Jack said, "I know the folks who own this place. Let's pull in here. They might know where we can find a spot to stay." Jack looked around for a moment and then added, "Better idea. Let's pasture these horses over there." Directly across the street, a large, well-tended lawn that encompassed several acres was surrounded by a split rail wood fence that appeared to be completely intact. A decorative tepee stood on the corner, seemingly unaware of the devastation surrounding it.

Jack pulled the saddle and bridle from Marlena and fastened the hobbles the same way he had last night. He then untied the luggage from Lucy and turned her out as well. He fastened hobbles to Dingo's front legs and let him go in the lawn after Lucy.

Watching the horses graze, Nicole asked, "Won't they trip with those ropes on their legs?"

"Nope. They've been trained. They know how to get around just fine. Let's go see if we can find some help." Jack turned and stepped off the curb toward the large store across the street.

When they walked up to the door, Ryan asked, "What's RMES?"

Jack said, "Rocky Mountain Extreme Sports. David and his wife have run this shop for the last seven or eight years. They

bring clients into Yellowstone for everything from mountaineering and ice climbing to whitewater and fly-fishing. They know their stuff." Jack was about to pull on the door when he noticed it off the hinges and leaning against the frame. He pulled it aside and leaned it against the entryway. "Dave? Hey, Dave?"

"Who's there?" a voice asked from the shadows of the building.

"It's me. Jack Neumann. I've got a couple of friends with me."

A tall, lanky man with a neatly trimmed white beard appeared from behind a wooden counter holding a shotgun. "Jack? Is that really you? What in the hell are you doing here?"

"I was fishing in the park yesterday. Had a heck of time with the truck and had to hoof it out. I picked up a couple of strays along the way."

Dave walked up to the three of them and stuck out his hand first to Nicole and then Ryan. "Hello, I'm David Swenson. Normally I'd put on some coffee for you, but things have been a little interesting around here."

"What's with the scattergun?" Jack asked, lifting his head toward the tightly held weapon.

"Had a little trouble earlier. Actually, I was just sitting back there wondering why I was bothering to protect this stuff with the roof gone and part of the back wall missing."

"Could be worse. Could've burnt to ground."

"Don't I know it?"

"Where's Kathy?" Jack asked, looking around the store. A pause made him look back at Dave.

He shook his head and choked up. "We were just sitting on the deck last night having a glass of wine went things went nuts. She was sitting in the Adirondack chair, her favorite. I think I might have passed out. I remember lightning jumping all over and then waking up in my chair. She just lay there. I tried to wake her up, but nothing I did worked. Finally I realized...she wasn't breathing. I tried...I mean I tried...but the fire..."

Jack put an arm over his friend's shoulder. "That's all right. You don't have to tell it. I know you tried."

"I didn't know what to do."

"There wasn't anything you could do. She was gone."

Dave's head was down, and he cried silently for a moment. "Why?"

"It's not fair. I know. She died peacefully. You can take comfort in that."

Dave stood quietly for another minute or two, collecting himself, and then asked, "Do you guys have any idea what happened?"

"Ryan here's got it about figured out," Jack said, pointing at him. "The kid's pretty bright. Go ahead and tell him what you know."

Ryan looked at Jack, surprised, and then said, "Well, I think it was a huge solar flare. Since we were on the dark side of the earth, we were facing away from the sun. The magnetic field from the flare caused a huge EMP and made the sparks jump off of everything metallic. The sparks, or lightning as you called it, started all the fires."

Dave looked surprised. "A solar flare could do all of this? I've heard of them before, but I thought they just messed up radio waves and could wreck a satellite or two."

"Yeah, but if it was a lot bigger—like orders of magnitude bigger—it could easily do all this."

"So what you're telling me is that this thing is widespread."

"We think it's probably global," Jack added.

"Oh. Oh my. I need to sit down," Dave said. "This is too much." He walked back a few steps and then sat down hard in a folding canvas chair. "Global? Holy cow."

"That's what we think anyway."

"I tried several of the emergency beacons. They don't work anymore. In fact, I can't find anything electronic that works. Hell, even my watch quit." He looked up at Jack. "How are you going to get home?"

"I've got three good horses with me. I figured I would ride out in a couple of days."

"Ride? You're going to ride all the way to Sheridan?"

"Sure. We'll just take it easy is all. I might need a little gear though."

"You are welcome to anything and everything in the store. You know that. I owe you everything."

"No, you don't. We've been over this."

"Well, I at least owe you for the saddle you got for me last spring"

"All right. I'll bite on that one. If you don't mind, I'd like to borrow a camp tent with a couple rooms, stove if you got one, a little food, and some gear for me and my friends."

"That won't even come to ten percent of what I owe you."

"Today the price of everything in your store just went way up, my friend."

# 19.

Four hours later Dave, Nicole, and Jack sat around a campfire in the middle of the lawn where the horses grazed. Ryan was sound asleep in a sleeping bag on a cot inside a small tent joined to the big wall tent by a canvas walkway. The four of them had finished a meal of Mountain House spaghetti and meatballs and blueberry cobbler. Ryan had exclaimed it was the best meal he had ever eaten in his entire life and then quietly headed to bed. The three of them talked for a while about what they had seen and experienced in the last day, and possibilities in the near future, while the sky boiled with ribbons and blossoms of spectacular color. Finally Dave said, "I should get back to the store. I'll be staying there for the foreseeable future. I need to keep an eye on things." Jack and Nicole thanked him and wished him goodnight.

Jack pulled a small, leather-wrapped flask from the saddlebag that lay near his chair, unscrewed the cap, and took a drink. Nicole said, "May I ask what you are drinking?"

"This here is Bulliet bourbon. My particular brand of poison."

"May I have some?"

"You drink whiskey?"

"I am from Scotland. Of course I drink whiskey."

He passed her the flask. She took a long drink. "Are you married, Mr. Neumann?"

"Let's get this straight right from the get-go. I am not Mr. Neumann. Please call me Jack."

"All right then. Are you married, Jack?"

"I was."

"Any children?"

"I've a daughter who's away at college. She's in vet school in Illinois."

"Have you been a rancher your entire life?"

"No, no I haven't. I came out here ten years, two months ago. I bought the D-bar-D from a couple who were third generation ranchers. By the time I got it, they'd lost most of it to the bank. The following spring I met Miguel. He's the ranch foreman and my right-hand man. At the time he was only twenty-three and still wet behind the ears, if you know what I mean."

"No, I am not sure that I do."

"He was illegal. I needed somebody to help out, and he was available. I wasn't crazy about hirin' an illegal alien, but when I saw what he could do with a horse, I changed my mind. We made a deal, though. He had to get legal or get the hell out.

"I'd picked up a couple of horses at auction. I knew a few things about horses, and I knew the ones I bought looked good, but they were young and full of piss and vinegar. There was one day when I thought I would break one of those horses. Miguel was workin' in a lot behind the round pen and started watchin' me. He didn't speak much English at the time. I guess he just couldn't stand watchin' me get thrown to the ground anymore, so he jumped in. An hour later, he was ridin' the worst of the bunch. He understands horses better than anybody else I've ever known. It's a gift—pure and simple."

"So he is still an illegal resident?"

"Nope. I helped him become a citizen about two years after I met him. He's proud of being American, too. He won't speak a word in Spanish. He's become a hell of a businessman too. Smart guy."

"And a friend?"

"Probably my best friend. In all honesty, I consider him more of a partner than an employee. He knows it too. There was a time when he ran it all. Had to. He did a fine job of it."

"May I ask why your ranch is called 'D-bar-D'?"

"I don't know where it started, but it worked out for us. We changed the brand when I bought the place. Now, if you look at that brand"—he pointed to the white mark on Marlena's back leg—"the first *D* is backward, there's the bar, and then the second *D*, so it looks like a snaffle bit. We get a lot of recognition from it."

"I see. So you primarily raise horses?"

"We mostly raise cattle, but the majority of our income used to come from horses. It's run a little dry lately with the economy. We supply horses to a wide variety of places who demand high-end, well-trained, smart horses. We have contracts with several guest ranches that cater to high-dollar clients. We also supply horses to the forest service, the border patrol, the national park system, the Canadian Mounties, and a few police departments. Those clients want mounts they can rely on, so we supply only the best."

"That's very interesting. How long does it take to train a horse for that type of environment?"

"It mostly depends on the horse but also on where they're going. For example, if I'm sending a horse to a guest ranch in Arizona, that horse will be at least eight or nine years old, and they will have spent time in a variety of situations first. I just picked those two up from Yellowstone on Friday," he said, pointing at Lucy and Dingo. "They were s'posed to be going to Arizona. After a year in the park, they are sure-footed and spook-free."

"Spook-free?"

"They won't jump away from somethin' if they're scared."

"Oh, I see. Horses like that must be very expensive."

"Depends on what you consider expensive. My buyers feel like they are gettin' a hell of a deal."

"What was the most expensive horse you have ever sold?"

"Five hundred fifty thousand."

Nicole's mouth hung open as she looked up at Jack. "Surely, you must be kidding me?"

"No, ma'am. It was a horse that was used in a movie. The actor wanted him more than I did."

"That's extraordinary!"

"No, what was extraordinary was that I was paid three thousand a day plus expenses while he was on set. The movie company kept him for six months. Then I sold him."

"So, that's another—what?"

"A little over five hundred thousand."

"My God, man!"

"He's a good horse."

"I should think so," she said emphatically and then added, "but that is certainly a rarity."

"Not as rare as you might think. There's lots of people who want a horse that's sound, reliable, and smart. Some of them have the money to buy 'em. For a few years, D-bar-D was becoming a brand that certain people who want to be seen with the 'right' brand were looking for. I was startin' to have trouble keepin' up with the demand."

"So all of your horses are branded. That must be painful."

"Not all the horses get branded: only the good ones we sell. It's not a bit painful. We use a freeze brand. The iron is soaked in liquid nitrogen and then applied. The hair grows back white, so the brand stands out."

"May I ask what you did before you were a horse rancher?"

"You may, but I don't usually talk about those days. The past is the past."

"I'm sorry to have pried. Please excuse me."

"You can ask me anything you like. Believe me, your questions don't bother me. If I don't want to answer, I won't. How's that?"

"Sounds quite fair. You may also ask anything you like. I have no secrets."

"Fair enough. I am kinda curious. You said you were in school in England. What were you studyin'?"

"I recently graduated with a dual master's in social anthropology and economics."

"Good Lord!" Jack laughed. "That's an interesting combination. Must've had a career lined up?"

"That is wherein my problem lies. You see, I had thought I wanted to be an international economist. I truly loved the material I studied, but now I find myself at an existential moment."

"A bit of angst, huh?"

She smiled broadly, "You are educated!"

"Just 'cause I ride a horse and wear a funny hat don't make me stupid."

"I never thought it did. *Où êtes-vous allé à l'université?*"

Jack smiled. "*Je n'ai pas dit que j'ai fait.*"

Nicole sat up straight and exclaimed. "Oh, my God! *Usted es mucho más que un vaquero.*"

"*Qué usted ve es todo allí es.*"

"Mr. Neumann, there is much more to you than meets the eye."

"Not necessarily. It depends on what you're lookin' at, I guess." He smiled at her. "I believe I was interviewin' you. So now you got this big, fancy education, and you're not sure what to do with it?"

"It is perhaps more correct to say that I am not sure if I want to do anything at all with it, but I suspect that despite what I want, my plans have changed."

"They may have at that."

"My father is in international banking specializing in developing markets. I had hoped to work with him."

Jack took another drink of the whiskey. "Oh. So you flew over here with a new sheepskin or two in your pocket and hoped to connect with Daddy?"

He passed the flask to her as she thought for a moment about his words. "What an interesting way to phrase your question. Would you care to explain?"

"You mentioned you had lived in various places all over the world when I asked about your accent. Then you said you were goin' to school in Oxford. It takes more than a couple of years

to get two master's degrees. If your daddy was in international banking, he was probably in New York. It just seems to me it would be hard to get to know somebody when they're half a world away for a long period of time. I'm guessin' when you showed up in New York, Dad was gone. Nobody flies that far without tellin' somebody else they are comin' for a visit. So, your pa either forgot, or somethin' more important came up. Either way, I bet it feels pretty chilly from where you're sittin'. Do you want me to go on?"

"Please do," she said and drank from the flask.

"Well, I guess you found yourself alone in New York with nothin' to do but think, so you started thinkin' about the whole thing. Like what *you* want out of life. So you decide to go talk it over with some friends and then spend a little more time by yourself in San Francisco thinkin' things through. That's where you're at now. Thinkin' things through."

"You are very good. I am not sure whether to be insulted that I am superficial and simple, or impressed that you are amazingly insightful."

"You're not superficial. You're normal, that's all. Understandin' you really want somethin' other than what you've spent the last bunch of years trainin' for is hard. Makin' the choice to change is even harder. Trust me, I know."

"I have such a difficult time throwing away all of those years and all the work I have done."

"You're not throwin' anything away. Education can't ever hurt you."

"Doesn't it seem a bit wasteful for a wife and mother to have two master's degrees?"

"Not at all, if it's what *you* want. My guess is you've either had a bad string of boyfriends or not many at all. Am I right?"

"Whatever would cause you to make such an accusation such as that?"

He smiled. "You didn't answer my question."

"I shouldn't have to."

"Somebody plannin' on becomin' a wife and mother usually has a man lined up. I don't see a ring on your finger."

"That's a bit over the line, don't you think?"

"You're right. I'm sorry. Probably the whiskey talkin'. I made the comment 'cause women tend to look for someone just like their pa, if they look up to him, or somebody exactly the opposite, if they think he wasn't so good. I s'pect you don't know your pa very well."

"I don't know him at all. My father has always concentrated on his work. He has become quite successful."

"There's a big difference between rich and successful."

"You're quite right. He has become extraordinarily wealthy, but as a family man, he is an ass."

Jack looked over at her with a sly grin on his face. "How'd that feel?"

"How did what feel?"

"Callin' your pa an ass. I bet it felt good. Probably the first time you done it."

She smiled back at him. "It did feel kinda good." She took another drink.

"There you go. That's a step in the right direction."

"May I change the topic?"

"Of course."

"I would like to try to guess your particular history."

"Be my guest."

"I think you were most likely living in a large city, probably Dallas, when you met and married your wife. The two of you were quite successful and lived in a large home on top of a hill. You became bored with the dull drudgery of business and decided to move to Wyoming and start raising cattle. After several years your wife got entirely fed up with ranch living and left you to move back to the city with her mother. Now your daughter lives miles away, and you don't see her very often, except when she needs money. How am I doing?"

Jack laughed. "You're off a little."

"Would you care to correct me?"

"You're right. I was living in a big city before I moved here, but I started out in a small town. I grew up in Odessa, Texas. My folks are good people who worked hard for a livin'. I was

a good student, and yes, I did go to college, but I got married beforehand. My wife worked and paid the bills while I went to school. I did have a job in a big city, but it wasn't Dallas, it was San Antonio. We only had one child, my daughter. The one I told you was in school. We couldn't have any more, although both of us wanted to have a big family. After a while the job was gettin' to me. It was my wife who decided we should do somethin' different. She just couldn't stand seein' what that job was doin' to me and our family. I had a…"—he paused—"friend who suggested we take a look at Wyoming. They had a little property up here. My wife and I decided together to move up here. She loved Wyoming. She was busy with the horses, the house, and things in Dayton and Sheridan. By the time she was diagnosed with cancer, it was already too late. It had spread to her liver and her lungs. She only lived about six months after the diagnosis was made. She's buried on the ranch, like she wanted. She loved it that much." He took a long drink from the flask.

"I am so sorry. I have completely underestimated you all day. I didn't mean to pry, and I certainly didn't mean for you to bring up all those memories. Please forgive me."

"Oh, that's all right. Most people see a cowboy hat, and they think 'idiot with six legs.'"

"You didn't mention how you were employed."

"Didn't I? That's odd. Must've forgot."

"What did you do?"

"I'm gonna let you figure that one out. You can work on your insightfulness. We talked about your pa. What about your history?"

"Oh, it's really not at all exciting. As I might have mentioned, we started out in Glasgow, Scotland. My grandfather owned a large shipping company and was a member of parliament. I have an uncle who now runs the company and all its subsidiaries. My father, on the other hand, became interested in banking, and we relocated several times for his work. Ultimately it was my mother who had enough of the instability. She put her foot down and demanded we settle. They purchased a home

in Scotland, and it is where she lives today. My father, however, continues to follow his work. They are still married and probably always will be, but I doubt they have spent more than an hour or two together in the last ten years. He still calls her on occasion but mostly to discuss financial matters. I know he has had at least two girlfriends in the past, and probably has another now."

"That's your folks. What about you?"

"I have always been the good girl, while my sister has been a little more unorthodox. I went to a catholic school and then off to university. My mother made sure I was enrolled in the acceptable extracurricular activities of the Scottish aristocracy. That is how I learned to ride. Equestrianism is only for the elite. I also was involved with dance, choir, and I play the piano."

"What do you like to do?"

"Whatever do you mean?"

"I mean, if you had a couple of days off, what would you do, or where would you go?" Jack took another drink and passed the flask back.

"I enjoy reading."

"That's good. What do you read?"

"Mostly textbooks."

"That's not readin'—that's studyin'."

"I love the beach."

"There you go. Do you honestly like horses?"

"There was one I used to like when I was little."

Jack said, "Really? Tell me about him."

Nicole took another drink. "I was probably thirteen or fourteen, and I was taking dressage lessons with three other girls. They had paired me an older Dutch Warmblood named Zelfdegeest. I called him Jimmy. When the other girls would ride, we were required stand in front of our horses quietly and watch. He used to tickle my neck with the big whiskers on his lips and make me laugh. Once I got yelled at because he did it so often. His nose was so soft, and he had these big blue eyes that could look right through me. I would swear he actually liked me. I think he preferred me to other girls who would ride

him. When we would practice our routines, I would often make a mistake in my cues, but he knew what the correct maneuver would be, and he would ignore my mistakes. I used to dream he was once a prince and an evil witch had turned him into a horse. One day at lesson, I kissed him on the nose, hoping he would turn back into a prince..." Her voice trailed off.

"And then what?"

"Oh, it's not worth mentioning."

"Sure it is. What happened?"

"He remained a horse, naturally. One of the other girls saw me kiss him and started to make fun of me. It was shortly thereafter that I quit dressage all together."

"Now that is a cryin' shame."

"Why do you say that?"

"Somebody forgot to tell you the rest about the magic."

"What in heaven's name are you talking about?"

"The magic. When a princess kisses a prince who's been turned into a horse, it takes a while before the spell gets reversed."

"I believe you've had enough of the bourbon."

"And you have to believe. You can't ever quit believin'. That's part of it."

"I believe you have gone stark raving mad. That is what I believe."

"Nope. I'm as sane as a judge. You quit believin'."

"I grew up."

"That's too bad. We all get older, that's a fact. But too many of us grow up. In some ways it's good to get older and more mature, but all too often we lose our dreams along the way, and that's nothin' but a damn shame. I always wanted to be a cowboy, but I grew up and forgot my own dreams. Thought I had to be something impressive. Took me a while, but I got it straightened out. I think we need to help you find out what it is that makes you tick."

"I know what makes me tick, and I'm learning what makes me ticked off."

"What do you dream about now?"

"I'm an adult. I don't need to dream."

"Oh, that's where you're wrong, darlin'. You do need to dream. You need a reason to jump out of bed in the mornin' and a direction to face when you leave the house." He looked up at the sky full of color. "I think the world has just changed, and it's brand spankin' new. You can do anything you want. You just gotta want it."

They sat quietly at the fire for a while, passing the flask back and forth. Finally Nicole said, "You were a bit hard on Ryan today."

"It may have seemed that way, but believe me, the boy was beggin' me to whack him."

"That makes no sense whatsoever. Why would someone want you to hit them?"

"He wanted me to care enough to do something. The worst thing I could have done was to let him get away with it and do nothin'. He and I had a little conversation earlier about the cussin'. He was gettin' tired of ridin' in the back, and he wanted to know if I gave a damn about him. If you listen to what he says, you can tell he has been spoiled his entire life. Probably his folks way of makin' up for the fact they weren't around much. Now he's alone out here except for us, and he wants to know somebody cares."

"There certainly are no secrets around you."

"Oh, sure there are."

"You are a bloody mind-reader."

"Nope. Not at all. For example, right now I have no idea what you're thinkin'."

Nicole giggled. "That's because my mind switched off with the last swallow of your bourbon."

"Hell, maybe I am a mind-reader," Jack said, laughing a little.

"Just as I said."

Jack stood up, stretched, and checked his watch. "I have to call it a night. I'm about dead on my feet."

"Do we have a plan for tomorrow?"

"Not just yet. Feel free to sleep in as long as you like. I'm goin' to bed. You can let that fire burn itself out if you want. There's no wind and not much of it left."

"Thank you."

"No trouble. It's just about out anyway."

"That's not what I meant. Thank you for helping me today. I am very glad I met you."

"You're very welcome, ma'am. It's been my pleasure."

"Good night, Mr. Neumann."

"Good night, Miss Meredith."

She watched him walk into his tent and then sat staring at the fire, with the sky dancing in brilliant color overhead. An eerie glow lit the ground around her, and she could see the horses grazing in the grass beyond the tents. A green glow intensified behind her, and she turned to look.

"Sorry," Jack said from behind her. He held a small glow stick in his hand. "I forgot; you might need a little help gettin' to your tent."

"Oh, yes. I forgot as well. Thank you. That would be very helpful." She stood on one leg.

Instead of letting her lean on his shoulder, he swooped her up in his arms. "There's no sense in hobblin'. It's not that far, and you ain't all that big."

She wrapped her arms around him as he held her and started walking toward the tent. She pressed herself close to him and smelled the faint scents of horses, leather, and woodsmoke. Suddenly she felt an overwhelming sense of safety and security. She didn't want him to put her down.

Jack walked into the tent that had been set up for her and carefully set Nicole on the edge of a small army cot Dave had given them. He stuck out his hand, which held two small paper packets of Advil. "Here. Make sure you take these. They'll help with your ankle and the hangover you'll have in the mornin'."

"I can assure you I will not have a hangover. You didn't have nearly enough whiskey in that little flask for either of us to have a hangover."

"I'm just teasin' you a bit. I set your stuff over there, and you can keep this little light. If you need anything, I'm just on the other side of that canvas wall."

"Thank you again, Mr. Neumann. It appears that I will never be able to repay you for your kindness."

"You already have, ma'am."

# 20.

Throughout the afternoon Mark had made his way through the west part of town. It hadn't taken him long to decide to follow Red's advice and head west. Buffalo was about seventy miles west of Gillette on I-90. He figured it would take him at least four days if he walked hard and fast, but there had to be a better way.

He had seen a few people as he made his way through the last few neighborhoods before the edge of town, but people seemed to keep their distance from him. That was good. He missed his iPod, but in his head he sounded like Kid Rock.

*I'm an American badass, Watch me kick*
*You can roll with rock, or you can suck my dick*
*I'm a porno flick, I'm like Amazing Grace*
*I'm gonna fuck some hos after I rock this place.*
*They call me Cowboy, I'm the singer in black*
*So throw a finger in the air and let me see where you're at*
*Say, hey, hey, let me hear where you're at and say, hey,*
*hey, hey, hey...*

The afternoon wore on into evening. Mark kept an eye on the sky, and so far there weren't many clouds. He wondered if the crazy colors would be back tonight and guessed they

probably would. Along the freeway were endless miles of grass and slow-rolling hills with scattered outcroppings of rock. He shook his head slowly as he thought that only yesterday he could have made the drive to Buffalo in an hour, sitting in a heated or air-conditioned truck, listening to satellite radio or his iPod. Man, what a difference a day made. He had a small two-man tent in his pack, but Red had told him to find shelter wherever he could. He would almost always be more comfortable in a building than in a tent, and comfort translated to security and rest. Sunset was still an hour or more away, but he should start looking for somewhere to spend the night. He had enough water to get him until midday tomorrow, but more was always better.

As he crested the next rise, he spotted a small ranch house with a couple of outbuildings sitting in a small grove of trees about a mile from the freeway. No-brainer. He turned toward the ranch house. Twenty minutes later he was lying very still in the tall grass on a small rise to the east of the ranch. The place looked quiet. He spent the next twenty minutes watching the house through the scope on his rifle. No movement. Maybe the place was vacant. The house looked fairly intact. He could tell the gutters had been ripped away and part of the chimney was missing, but the walls seemed to be up and the roof looked tight. Go time. He stood and casually walked toward the house. In his right hand, the XD(m) was out of sight, slightly behind his back, but it was also ready for anything. He walked into the yard and called, "Hello? Anybody home?"

No answer.

He walked up the step and banged on the door. Again, no answer. He opened the door, fully expecting to be met by some crazy guy with a shotgun, but the house looked empty. He walked in carefully and quietly with both hands on the pistol guiding the way. No one in the living room and no one in the kitchen. In the hallway he carefully opened a door and found a made bed. He opened the next door in the hallway and found two people sleeping in bed.

He jumped back suddenly, banging his boot against the doorjamb and nearly tripping in the hallway. Neither person moved. Pistol raised, he carefully walked closer. As he drew near, he realized by their pale gray color they were dead. "Holy shit! You guys scared me," he said, looking at the bodies. They were older, probably in their seventies. The man lay on his back, and Mark could see the edges of a big, black and purple burn mark on the upper left corner of his chest, like he had been struck by lightning. The lady had no marks at all. Probably got scared to death when the old guy got zapped, he thought. He stepped out of the bedroom and closed the door.

In the kitchen he made himself at home. Digging through the cabinets, he found a couple cans of stew and set them on the table. Looking around through a few drawers, he found a can opener, but also candles, a lighter, a bowl, and a spoon. He set up the camp stove the way Red had showed him but couldn't manage to get the fire started. After resorting to the instruction manual, he lit the fire and warmed the stew.

The hot food probably had too many preservatives and more carbs than he really wanted, but the taste was wonderful, and the ability to sit, relax, and eat made him tired. He found yesterday's newspaper lying on the counter by the backdoor and decided to read while he ate. He noticed an article comparing the price of several fitness centers in the area and a smaller article touting the benefits of a personal trainer. At once an overwhelming sadness came over him, and he pushed the newspaper aside. Life was over. Everything had changed. Now, instead of working out, bullshitting with Devin, hanging out at the bar, and arguing with Lisa, he was sitting at the table of a dead couple, who were still in the bedroom, and eating stew out of a can.

Lisa was dead. The realization hit him like a baseball bat in the chest. He felt a huge, deep, hollow pain. How could things have changed so much, so fast? She could be a complete bitch sometimes, and she spent money like water, but still, Lisa was dead.

He set the can down, turned off the burner, and then leaned back in the chair. He rubbed his face, but the stark realization remained. He got up and went outside. The air was cool, and a slight breeze rose out of the west. He breathed deep and felt a little better. The setting sun and clear air made the grass, the fence, the old barn, and even the blackened hulk of what used to be a pickup stand out with rich color and clarity. He sat on the step, and his mind started to drift back to Lisa, and the hollow feeling in his chest came with it. He pushed it away and instead started thinking about the present. He was going to survive.

If everything Red had said was true, then this was only the beginning. He would have to learn quickly not only how to survive, but to come out on top. Someday things would settle down. They had to. He was going to be one of the "haves" and not one of the "have-nots." It seemed to him that since everything was different, the rules had to change as well. Today, right now, in this moment, there is no federal government, no state government, no army, no police, no game wardens, no boss, nobody who could say what the law was and tell him what he could or could not do. Hell, there was no law. It was now survival of the fittest and only the strongest survive.

A determination rose in him. He was not going to just survive, he was going to thrive. He was going to have everything he deserved and more. Hell, he was going to have everything he wanted and the *way* he fucking wanted it. His twenty-inch arms could out-press and out-curl anybody at the gym. He was fucking cut and had the abs, pecs, and quads to prove it. He hadn't worked this hard for nothing. All the pain at the gym was about to pay. He was strong enough to take what he wanted and smart enough to keep it. The days of busting his ass for some soft old man to get rich were over. If one of the guys from the mine ever called him "Pussy" or "Pussyman" again, he would take the Bobcat he used to spend ten hours a day in and crush their sorry ass. Fuck that shit. It's my turn to drive.

He stood up and walked back into the house. Inside, he peeled off his shirt and stood bare-chested, flexing a little in

jeans and his boots. He walked into the unoccupied bedroom and stared at himself in the mirror on the dresser. Damn, he looked good. The butt of the pistol stood at attention on his right hip; the black contrasted nicely by his tan side. He turned and looked at the pistol on his back. The weapon waited upside down, held in its holster for use in a second's notice. Above it rose the inverted triangle of his back, perfectly proportioned and well defined. The tribal armband tats completed the picture, adding just the right amount of contrast and further defining his arms. He gave himself one more glance and walked back out into the living room.

Since the sun was starting to set, he decided to go through the house quickly to find anything that might be useable. He could give it another quick once-over in the morning, but he had to be on his way early. Too many miles to cover in too little time. Rummaging through the kitchen drawers, he found a bunch of knives, but they were of little use compared to the tactical knife he got from Red. He found a roll of duct tape. That might come in handy. Above the stove he found a box of strike-anywhere matches. Those were definitely keepers. The living room held nothing of value to him, but he did find a blanket in one of the closets. No sense unpacking the sleeping bag if he didn't need to. He lit one of the candles and went downstairs. In the basement a small family room held a nice TV, but that was worthless. A gun rack hung on one wall. The shotgun and two rifles were designed for hunting. His own tactical rifle was much better.

Back upstairs it was nearly dark. He would check the barn in the morning on the way out. He stepped outside and could see the sky was dancing with color again. Nothing had changed since last night. He wondered how long this crazy sky would go on. Back inside the house, he decided to get ready for the evening. Even though it was early, he might as well sleep since there was little else he could do in the dark. Besides, he was exhausted. He moved the couch under the picture window at the front of the house. If he heard something in the middle of the night, he could just sit up and see what was going on over

a large part of the yard. He stripped down to his underwear, pulled the blanket over him, and closed his eyes.

As soon as his eyes closed, he started thinking about Lisa again. His mind went to the time when they had first met. She had sucked him off in the bathroom at Buckers. Goddamn, she was hot. That heavy feeling started to weigh on him again, and so he let his mind go back to yesterday's fight. He still couldn't believe she was fucking somebody else. He might have married her if she hadn't spent so damn much money all the time. He started drifting off to sleep.

# 21.

A sound in the yard made his eyes snap open. He didn't think he had fallen asleep yet. What was it he had been thinking about? Oh yeah, Lisa putting on her makeup in the bathroom, wearing nothing but a little thong. He heard another noise outside, and a sudden fear rose up in him. Carefully he sat up and peered through the bottom of the window. A light bobbed in the front yard and was moving toward the house.

*Holy shit! Somebody's coming!*

He crawled to the far end of the couch and carefully snuck his head up far enough to see out the window again, and yes, the light was definitely closer. It was close enough now he could tell it was a lantern held out in front of somebody. He had to think, but there was no time. They would be at the door any second. He wished he hadn't gotten undressed, but at least he had a pistol. He slipped down and crawled on the floor around the end of the couch, to the door, and slowly, silently stood, with the pistol held tight in his right hand. Maybe whoever it was would just go away.

"Hello? Henry? Maggie? Are you home?" a female voice said from the other side of the door. "Hey. It's Megan. I didn't

see you today, so I thought I might walk over and check on you. Hello? Anybody home?"

Mark wanted to shout. They're dead. Please get the fuck out of here. But instead, he stood stock-still, pressing his back to the wall, and held his breath. He heard the handle turn, and the door slowly started to open. As it moved inward, the door covered him from the entryway. He stood motionless.

"Henry? Maggie? Are you here?" The lantern light flooded the room as a young woman stepped inside holding the light out in front of her.

Without thinking, Mark stepped forward and grabbed the handle of the lantern with his left hand as he pressed the barrel of the pistol against the girl's head with his right. "Not a fucking sound."

She screamed. In a fluid motion, he quickly set the lantern on the floor and slammed his left hand over her mouth. Her eyes were wide with terror, and she sucked air through her nose as he pulled her head close with the gun still pointed at her. "Shut the fuck up!" He could feel her mouth moving under his hand and the warm breath from her nose over his fingers. Muffled, unintelligible sounds came from his hand. With the back of his foot, he kicked the door shut. She was breathing hard. "Are you going to shut up?"

She nodded weakly.

He held his hand in place. "Is anybody with you?"

She looked terrified but shook her head.

"If you scream, I'm going to shoot you. Do you understand?"

She slightly nodded beneath his hand.

He held the barrel of the gun directly in front of her face as he slowly removed his hand. She took a quick deep breath, and for a second he thought she was going to scream again, but she held it. Her eyes were wide with terror. The girl appeared to be in her mid-twenties. She had long, brownish red hair that hung loose around her face and wore a lined denim jacket and jeans.

"Megan. Is that your name?"

She nodded.

"Where did you come from?"

"I…" She hesitated. "Two farms down the road. About a mile and a half from here."

"Did you walk here?"

"No. I rode."

"Rode? What did you ride?"

"Horse."

"Is there anybody at your house waiting for you?"

She hesitated.

"If you lie, you die."

"No."

"Where's the horse?"

"Tied by the barn."

"Who do you live with?"

"I'm staying at my parents."

"Where are they?"

"My dad had an angiogram of his heart yesterday, and the doctors wanted him to stay overnight. So he's still at the hospital."

"Both of them?"

"Yes."

Mark thought for a moment and then said, "Sit on the floor in the middle of the room. Don't make any sudden, fast moves, or I will shoot you. If you scream, I will shoot you. If you try to run, I will shoot you. Do you understand?"

Megan nodded and moved carefully to the middle of the living room. She sat with her legs crossed, never taking her eyes off him. Mark picked up the lantern and walked toward the kitchen, keeping the gun pointed at her. He set the lantern on the floor in front of her, so he could watch her as he went into the kitchen. He came back with the roll of duct tape.

"Take off your shoes and put your legs out."

She hesitated and asked, "Why?"

"Just do it."

She wrestled with one of her boots a little but did as she was told. He wrapped the duct tape tightly around her ankles. She sat motionless.

"Take off your jacket."

"What are you going to do?"

"Just take it off."

She took the jacket off and asked, "Are you going to hurt me?"

"I don't know yet."

"What happened to Henry and Maggie?"

"They're dead."

Her eyes widened with panic. "Oh my God! You killed them?"

He knelt in front of her with a mildly angry, confused expression. "No. They were dead when I got here. Put your hands behind your back."

She did and asked, "What happened to them. Why are you doing this to me?"

He moved behind her and wound the tape around her wrists tightly in a figure eight. He was glad she couldn't see his hands shaking. "You're sure full of questions."

"I just want to know what's going on."

He ripped the edge of the duct tape with his teeth and then scooted on the floor so he was sitting in front of her. He relaxed a little and said, "I'll tell you what. I'll answer a few questions if you answer a few questions."

"Okay."

"You said you were home alone. Did you talk to anyone today?"

She shook her head and said, "No. My cell doesn't work; the house phone is out; my laptop doesn't work. Nothing. What happened to Henry and Maggie?"

"They died in that thing last night. They're still in bed if you want to go say hi."

"What happened last night?"

"No. My turn. Did you leave the house today?"

"No, not until I came over here. Okay. So, what was that?"

"I'm not sure, but it was huge. Probably planetwide. Everything is completely fucked up. The town is completely trashed. Almost everything is burned. I haven't seen a single car that hasn't been burned or blown up."

"What? You have to be kidding?"

"You really haven't been out of the house, have you? Everything is wasted. The whole freakin' city looks like a disaster movie. There's dead people everywhere."

"Oh my God!" Megan said, as tears started rolling out of her eyes.

"I'm not lying. It's unbelievable. I would've never even dreamed something like this could happen. It's crazy."

"I had just gotten home from the hospital last night. I went out to feed the horses when the lights went out. I saw these weird electric sparks start jumping all over the place. The next thing I knew I was lying in the middle of the yard and my rental car was burning. It's a good thing I parked away from the barn. Oh, I saw our windmill was twisted up and thrown up against the garage, and the tractor was standing in the middle of the front yard! I thought it was just something that happened to us. You know, like a freak tornado or something. I tried to call my dad, but the phones were out. I even tried my cell, but it was dead. I thought that was weird. I waited for the electricity to come back on, but it never did. I thought somebody would stop by today and help me, but no one ever came."

As she talked Mark looked her over. The girl was pretty. Prettier than he originally thought. She wore a dark blue sweater that looked like it would be soft if he touched it. She had started to relax as she spoke. He also noticed her eyes drift over him. He asked, "Why did you come here?"

"The Carvers are good friends of ours. They said they would stop by today to find out how Dad was doing, but they never showed up. I thought maybe they might need help if all that crazy stuff happened here too." She paused and then added, "Are you sure they're, you know, dead?"

"Oh yeah. I've seen enough dead people in the last day to know what they look like. They're dead all right. Like I said, you can check them out for yourself if you want."

"No. Really. That's okay. I believe you. I just can't believe all this stuff is going on, you know. I was supposed to go back to New York on Monday."

"You live in New York?"

"Yeah. I work for Marigold & Thorneberg as a public relations and media consultant. I also do event planning for some special functions. I came home to be with my dad for this angiogram. I also volunteered to plan a small charity appearance in Sheridan for one of our clients. That way the company picked up my expenses." She sat quiet again, thinking. Finally she asked, "Why am I tied up? Are you going to rape me?"

"I'm thinking about it," he said matter-of-factly.

"Seriously?"

"Yeah. Why not?"

"Well, can you at least untie my arms?" she responded in the same flat tone. "This is really uncomfortable."

"I guess. As long as you promise not to do anything stupid."

"What am I gonna do? You're the one with the gun."

Mark slid around behind her and unwound the duct tape. Megan rubbed her wrists and asked, "Why are you sitting in your underwear?"

Marked smiled. "'Cause you came barging in here while I was trying to sleep."

"Sleep? It's like nine thirty?"

"What else is there to do? It's not like I'm gonna watch TV. Besides, I have to get out of here early in the morning."

"Why? Where are you going?"

"West. I gotta get someplace better before winter gets here."

"Wait. What? I don't understand this at all."

For the next twenty minutes, Mark told her in detail about the devastation in town and explained what Red had shown him with the compasses. He explained what an EMP was and why nothing electric or electronic would ever work again. When she insisted the government would come to help, he said, "You just don't get it. There is no government. Even if there's a part of it left, there's no way they are coming to Wyoming before trying to help out a thousand other places. As of last night, there is no fire department, no cops, no state—nothing. We are on our own. I'm headed west in the morning."

Megan stared at him, considering what he had said. Suddenly her face changed, and the panicked look returned. "Did you see the hospital? Tell me. Did you see it? Is everything okay?"

Mark looked at the carpet in front of him. "I saw where it used to be. The whole thing burned to the ground last night."

Her face twisted into anger and sorrow. "You knew my parents were there! Why didn't you tell me? Goddammit!" She buried her face in her hands and sobbed with big ragged breaths.

Mark had no idea what to do. Yeah, she had told him her parents were there, but he also knew how she would react. He felt bad for her. She looked so sad. He decided to give her some time, so he stood up, got his jeans from the floor by the couch, and put them on. He walked into the kitchen, found the candles, and lit one. He remembered seeing a couple bottles of wine in one of the cabinets. He found one and a couple of glasses and went back out to the living room. Megan still sat on the floor crying into her hands. He sat down and started twisting the top, but nothing happened. He started peeling the metal stuff off the top and saw a cork stuck in the neck of the bottle. Fuck. How do I get this stupid thing out? He went back to the kitchen, looking for a corkscrew, whatever the hell that was supposed to look like. He found something with a twisted metal prong and two flapper ears in one of the drawers and went back to the living room. He fumbled with the bottle for a while when Megan said with ragged soft breaths, "Here. Give me that."

He handed her the bottle and the corkscrew thingy. She deftly popped the little cork out as her breath hitched occasionally. She poured herself a big glass of the dark red liquid and handed the bottle to him. He poured the same amount into his own glass and took a drink. Eww, the stuff tasted weird. Not terrible, but not good either.

She sighed deeply. "So I guess you don't drink wine."

He looked at her. She was looking at him with a hint of a smile. "Not usually. No. This stuff tastes a little nasty."

"Actually, it's very good. Thanks for getting it. Why didn't you tell me?"

Mark sighed. "Sorry. I should have. I just knew…I knew you would be sad."

"Of course I'm sad, but you should've told me."

"I know. Sorry."

"So you saw it yourself? Maybe some people got out?"

"Yeah, I saw it. I don't really think anybody got out. There was no way. You saw how fast it hit last night. The hospital was bad. All of the buildings in the whole area were burned. The parking lot looked like a bomb went off."

Megan looked like she was going to start crying again but instead took another big swallow of the wine. She spoke quietly, "I knew the answer before you even told me. All that oxygen and stuff…I just wanted to hope. You know, maybe somebody got out. Did you lose anybody?"

"Yeah. My girlfriend."

"I bet she was pretty."

"Yeah."

"Did you love her?"

"We lived together for the last year or so. I kinda did, but it was complicated." A mental image of Lisa shaking her finger at him flashed through his mind.

"It always is. Let's change the subject, huh? You were saying something about heading west? Why?"

"Because winter is coming. Red explained that Gillette's winter is bad, which is mostly due to the open prairie that surrounds it. Even if we have plenty of coal to burn for heat, there won't be enough food for everybody. Even if I only make it to Buffalo, that's a lot better in winter than Gillette. At least there's plenty of beef there. I want to try to get further west and find someplace to, you know, set up. I'll get some food stocked up, get some cattle, get a lot of guns, plant a garden. I'll get things set up, so I don't have to depend on anybody. I'll learn how to hunt and fish. Maybe I can even get some solar stuff set up. You know—something sustainable."

"How are you going to get all that stuff?"

Mark raised his hands palms out. "Here's a ranch that's up for grabs. Nobody would give a damn if I moved in here. Hell, there's nobody to give a damn. There's gonna be lots of places just like this all over." He raised the pistol. "The rest I'll just take."

"You're just going to steal it?"

"Who's gonna stop me? Besides, who fucking cares? I bet three-quarters of the people in Gillette are dead, and it's probably the same everywhere. Their stuff is just lying there, up for grabs. I don't think it's stealing if nobody cares."

She thought about what he had said for a minute and then asked, "What's your name?"

"Mark."

"Hi, Mark. I'm Megan Bennett." She stuck out her hand. He shook it. "Are you from Gillette?"

"Not originally, no. But I've been living here for the last two years."

"Where are you from?"

"I grew up in Denver. I came up here for a job."

"So you must work at the mine."

"Yeah."

"And you obviously like to work out a lot."

He unconsciously swelled with pride. "Yeah."

"Mark, I'll tell you what. I'll make you a deal. If you don't hurt me, I'll teach you how to ride a horse. You could get to Buffalo or anywhere else you want to go a lot easier."

Mark thought about what she said for a moment. "I could just take your horse."

"Yes, you could. But do you know how to make him go or stop or turn or anything else? It would be a lot easier if you had somebody to teach you."

"How do I know I can trust you?"

"You're the one with the gun."

# 22.

Nicole awoke drenched in sweat. The sun had obviously been shining for some time, and the inside of the canvas tent was sweltering. Worse yet, she was twisted up in the sleeping bag. The thin nylon had stuck to her skin as she started to sweat, and instead of slipping past her legs as she rolled in her sleep, it twisted around her, wrapping her tight and making her even warmer. She twisted around, trying to get loose, and momentarily forgot she was on a narrow cot. As her behind slipped off the edge, she tried to grab the opposite side of the cot, and her arm stuck to the material. She hit the ground with a thump. The reality of the whole situation came flooding back to her. She wasn't hurt, but she started to cry. All the emotions she had tried to keep bottled up for the last thirty-six hours came pouring out all at once. She thought about her sister and her mother. She had no idea if they were alive, and even if they were, she would probably never see them again. They would undoubtedly worry about her, yet there was no way for her to tell them she was alive and well. She thought about her friends in Scotland, London, Sydney, and Dubai. People she used to talk to almost every day on the phone or Facebook. If what Ryan and Jack had said were true, she would never see them

again. She thought about her favorite restaurants, the ballet, the nightlife in London and New York. All of it—gone.

After fifteen or twenty minutes, she pulled herself together and untangled herself from the sleeping bag. She sat on the edge of the cot in her soaked t-shirt, with her wet hair stuck to her face, neck, and back. She looked down at her thigh. The bandage Jack had applied had come loose with her sweat, and the laceration was now no more than a thin vertical line. She had to admit, the man did a very nice job, especially considering the circumstances. She stood carefully, testing the ankle. It was sore, but much improved since the previous day. She hobbled over to where Jack had set her suitcase. She found a clean pair of jeans and a simple shirt. She longed for a shower; it didn't have to be anything fancy, just some way to wash the sweat and grime off. A new wave of tears came over her. Something as simple as running water was now a luxury she didn't have.

She pulled herself together and changed. She pulled her hair back and fixed it into a ponytail. She found her toothbrush and went outside to look for one of the bottles of water they had filtered last evening.

Ryan sat by the fire with a stick. He looked over when he heard her and said, "Wow. You finally got up. I started thinking you might be dead in there. Nice hair by the way."

Nicole smoothed her hair, finding several strands that had escaped the ponytail. She walked to the fire where he stood. "What time is it? Oh, wait. Forget I asked that?"

"It's probably close to noon. I'm getting hungry. Jack left early this morning, just after the sun was coming up. He said we could just hang out, and he would be back later."

"Where did he go?"

"Don't know. He just started walking. Oh yeah. He left one of those things for you." Ryan pointed at two big, black bags hanging from a tree with a long tube sticking out of the end.

"Whatever is that?"

"It's a shower."

"Oh, please tell me you are not joking."

"No. Seriously. You can hang it from one of the big poles in Jack's tent. He's got it all set up in there. It works pretty good. I bet yours is really hot by now. Mine was a little cold."

Nicole limped over to where the bag hung in the tree. On the end of the little black hose was a small, red shower nozzle and a small valve. She tried to lift it, but her ankle complained. "Ryan. I don't suppose I could beg you to put this in there for me?"

"Beg me? Sure. Tell you what. I'll put it in there if you let me watch."

"Forget it. I'll do it myself."

"Relax, I'll do it. I was just joking." He lifted the bag out of the tree and started walking toward the tent. "Seriously. I was just joking. You don't have to mention that to Jack."

Nicole followed slowly. Inside the tent Jack had scraped a shallow hole from the grass and a trench that led under the tent wall. He had put a wooden pallet over the hole to stand on without having your feet get muddy. A small bag with soap and shampoo hung from the tent wall near the pallet. After Ryan had hung the bag, she thanked him and agreed not to say anything, although she did find it interesting that Ryan was worried.

She undressed and stood on the pallet. Opening the valve released a shower of very warm water that felt glorious on her skin. Despite how crude and primitive this arrangement was she felt wonderful. It was amazing how the simple act of taking a shower could improve her outlook.

When Jack walked back into their small camp in the middle of the park, Ryan sat on a folding chair near the fire poking it with a stick. The boy didn't look up, and Jack was in no mood for conversation anyway. He was tired. He dropped a small bag by the gear and walked past the boy and into his tent. In front of him stood the most beautiful woman he had ever seen, completely naked and glistening with water and soap. "Oh my gosh!" He turned away quickly. "I'm so sorry. I didn't know you were in here."

Behind him he heard Nicole say, "I'm sorry. I didn't realize you would be back. I'll be done in a minute."

Jack stood facing the tent flap with his back toward Nicole. "No no. You take all the time you need. I'll be outside. I got plenty to do." He left quickly.

Jack walked over to where Ryan still sat by the fire. He was about to say something when Ryan said, grinning, "You're welcome."

"You knew she was in there."

"I helped her put up the shower bag, like you said. You never asked."

"You should've said somethin'."

"What? You didn't like it?"

Jack, still stunned by what he had seen, said, "Son, that wasn't right. It wasn't very polite for either one of us."

"So you didn't like it?"

"That's not the point. The point is: this ain't college. That kind of bullshit stops now. Understand?"

"Fine."

Jack found one of his saddlebags and pulled out a brush. "Here. You got somethin' to do while you think about it. Take this and one of those lead ropes and go brush down Lucy and Dingo. You better leave Marlena alone. I don't think she'll take to you brushin' her just yet."

"What's she gonna do?"

"I've been around horses a long time. You've been around 'em one whole day. Those are my horses over there, so I probably know 'em better'n you. You should trust me on this."

"Fine. Whatever," Ryan said, as he took the brush and a lead rope and stomped out to the horses.

Later Nicole came out of the tent, looking radiant. She wore a nice pair of jeans and a button-down shirt that clung to her in all the right places. Her hair was pulled back into a smooth, glossy, dark ponytail, and she was smiling.

"Mr. Neumann, I can't thank you enough for that wonderful gift this morning."

Jack sat quietly, not entirely sure what she was talking about. "The shower, of course."

"Oh, that. Oh, that ain't nothin'. I just got some water from the creek in one of those shower bags and hung it in the sun. I told that boy to set it all up for you. Did he do it?"

"Yes, he did," Nicole said, keeping everything else to herself.

"I am sorry for walkin' in there like that. Ryan didn't say a word to me, and I didn't know you were in there."

A slight blush rose in her cheeks, which made her all the more beautiful. "It's no big deal, really. Where were you off to so early this morning?"

"Did I wake you? I'm sorry if I did."

"I was dead to the world. I only woke just before you returned."

"That's good. You needed the rest. I met with a couple local guys I know and helped out a bit. We're gonna have a meeting tonight of everybody we can round up in town. Try to get things organized a bit. This afternoon we got a couple things to do, and we gotta get the word out about this meeting. Interested in helpin'?"

"Of course. I'll gladly help any way I can."

Jack picked up the small bag he had carried into camp. "I got a stack of paper and some markers. If you could make a few signs for us, Ryan and I will go paste 'em up this afternoon. There might be a couple of things around here to do while we're gone."

"Of course. I'll start working on them now."

A scream came from the other side of the park. Jack and Nicole both looked up just in time to see Ryan hanging by his butt from Marlena's mouth.

"Goddamn kid!" Jack said, as he jumped up and started running toward the horse. Marlena dropped him and then dipped her head for another bite. Jack yelled, "Ah," and waved his arms at the horse as he ran. The big black horse looked at him and backed up a couple of steps. As Jack arrived, Ryan stood up. "Are you hurt, son?"

Ryan was visibly shaking. "I think I'm okay."

"Drop them pants. Lemme take a look."

"It's okay."

"Drop them damn pants, boy! If she broke the skin, we'll have to get it cleaned out."

Ryan turned and unbuckled his pants. He pushed them down.

"Now, you're shorts."

Ryan started to protest but decided against it and dropped them.

"Bend over," Jack said, as he looked at Ryan's bare, white backside. He then looked back over his shoulder at Nicole and pointed at the white butt while he grinned. "Pull 'em up. You're lucky you wear them loose britches. If she'd a got ahold of your ass, you'd be in a world of hurt. What'd I tell you about her?"

Ryan just stood there fastening his pants.

"What'd I tell you?"

"I know, I know."

"You obviously don't know, and you just proved it. Next time I'm gonna let her have her way with you."

Anger was rising in Ryan. "I ought to…" He didn't finish.

Jack's voice was low, stern, and just above a whisper. "If you lay a hand on that horse or cause harm to come to them, Nicole, or me, I'll bury you in them hills over there. Are we clear?"

Ryan was holding back his rage. "Yes."

Jack turned to leave. "By the way, I think you could use a little sun on that ass. Nicole nearly went blind from the glare." He paused and then added, "Payback's a bitch, ain't it?"

# 23.

Mark awoke lying on the couch with bright sunlight streaming in through the windows. His head pounded with every beat of his heart, and a thick, sweet, terrible taste filled his mouth. He didn't move but just lay there. He remembered talking and even laughing with Megan and finishing the first and second bottles of wine. He vaguely remembered opening a third bottle of something and drinking that one too. He thought they went outside for something, maybe the horse, but there weren't many details to piece together.

He slowly sat up and looked around the room. There was no sign of Megan except her sweater balled up in a corner by the door. He pulled the blanket back and found her pants in a wad next to his thigh. What did I do? He stood slowly and noticed that he was still wearing the jeans he put on last night. He looked around the room again and saw his bag lying in the kitchen where he had left it, and next to it his rifle still sat propped against the wall. He couldn't see his handguns anywhere, and there was still no sign of Megan.

He walked slowly and carefully to the hallway and opened the door to the guest bedroom. Megan lay face down on the bed, wearing nothing but thin yellow panties, his XD(m) next

to her, and there was blood everywhere. "Ah! Oh shit!" he said out loud and involuntarily backed toward the door. A low moan came from the bed. Sheer panic grabbed him, and Mark was unable to move. As he looked at the grotesque scene, bile rose in the back of his throat. Mark's first impulse was to get the hell out of there as fast as he could, but another sound came from the bed, and Megan's arm slowly started moving. Panic rose even further. She's gonna come back and get me. He stepped back once more and bumped the door into the wall with a thud.

"Oh my head," Megan moaned and rolled over.

Relief washed over Mark like a bucket of cold water. He went to the bed. "Oh my God. Are you okay?"

She squinted up at him. "I feel like shit."

Mark's relief was so deep he lost himself. He stood for a second, not knowing what to do, and then he wrapped his arms around her and hugged her tight.

She croaked, "Wow. Good morning to you too."

Without letting her go, he said, "Oh fuck. I thought you were dead. I thought I might have killed you."

"Killed me? Last night you said you might be in love with me."

He pulled back from her. "I did?"

"Yeah. You also took my pants, so I couldn't run away. I took your gun, so you couldn't run away and leave me. Don't you remember?"

"No. I don't remember much at all." He looked at her, lying on the bed in front of him. She was naked except for the panties, and they didn't cover much. The side of her face was streaked with red, and her hair was matted with the stuff. Her breasts and belly were also streaked red, but looked nice. Very nice.

"Why did you think I was dead?"

"Look around."

She sat up and pulled the blanket over her as she looked around the room. "Oh shit. I guess I must have gotten a little sick."

"What were we drinking?"

"You remember the wine."

"Yeah."

"Do you remember the bottle of Bloody Marys from the fridge?"

Mark started laughing. His head pounded every time he breathed, but he didn't care. "No, but that explains it."

"How are we gonna clean this up?"

Mark laughed again. "We're not."


Three hours later they were ready to leave. Mark had run the last of the water out into the bathtub, and they used a bucket to wash up in the sink. He had made them breakfast over his little stove while Megan washed her hair and cleaned up. The hot greasy food, a little coffee, and some ibuprofen made them both feel better. He stood in the yard as she got the horse out of a little, wooden paddock. He watched closely as she showed him how to saddle the horse. Just as he was thinking about climbing up in the saddle, she took it off and said, "You do it."

"Oh, man."

"The only way to learn is to do it."

He did what she had shown him, and with a few slight adjustments, she said he had done a good job. "Here's what we're gonna do. I don't really feel like chasing you and Fred around right now, and I'm not going to ride at anything other than a walk. I had to throw my bra away."

"I thought you looked good. Really natural."

"Very funny. We're gonna walk back to my place. I'll lead Fred while you sit in the saddle. It will help you learn to balance."

"I thought we were headed west."

"First of all, I haven't decided if I'm going with you. Secondly, we'd need at least two horses, and lastly, I'm not going anywhere looking like this, without anything else to wear. So we are at least spending tonight at my place."

"Okay. Fair enough."

"Oh yeah. One more thing. I want a gun."

"What?"

"You heard me."

"What if I say no?"

"Then I'm leaving."

"It wasn't part of the deal."

"It is now."

"What do you need a gun for?"

"The same thing you need a gun for."

Mark thought about it for a minute and said, "What the fuck." He pulled the Springfield and holster from his belt and handed them to her. He watched as she pulled the slide back just enough to see a round in the chamber. Then, she slid the gun back into its holster and attached it to her belt.

"Okay. Climb on up."

Mark was a little surprised. "You know about guns?"

"Yeah. A little."

"Why'd you pull that slide thingy back?"

"To make sure it's loaded. If I need it, I want to make sure it's ready to go."

She looked at him for a moment. "Have you ever shot one of these?"

"Well, not actually shot one of these, but I've shot guns lots of times."

"Right. Well, I can see we need to work on that at my place as well. Get on up there."

Mark climbed up and sat in the saddle as Megan adjusted the stirrups for him and then handed him his rifle. "Just sit tight and hang on if you need to. Try to keep your legs off him."

"Okay."

She took the reins and started walking toward the gate.

# 24.

Jack and Ryan set off walking toward the center of town. It had taken Ryan a little while to cool down, but he came around. Jack was beginning to wonder if the boy could be taught after all. As they walked, they talked.

Jack said, "Now, you understand where to go, right?"

"Yeah. I'm supposed to follow Sheridan Road to Highway Fourteen and then turn north. Then, I'm supposed to follow that for quite a ways and then make my way through the residential areas to the south on the way back."

"You got it."

"I should have a gun."

"Do you know how to use one?"

"Sure. You just point it at the bad guy and pull the trigger. How hard can that be?"

"There's a little more to it than that. I'll show you how to shoot, and then we'll get you set up."

"That would be cool."

"Don't forget to paste them signs up or hand 'em out. We need to get as many people at the meeting as we can."

"What's this meeting about anyway?"

"We gotta get people organized a little, so they can help each other out. Times are gonna get pretty rough, I think." Jack pulled the little round tin out of his back pocket and put a little in his mouth.

"I've seen you do that before. What is that stuff?"

"Copenhagen. It's tobacco."

"Can I have some?"

"Ever had it before?"

"No, but I have friends that use it."

"The first time can be a little excitin'. You might want to go easy." He handed the tin to Ryan.

Ryan opened the lid and pinched some of the black gritty stuff between his fingers and lifted it to his mouth. He popped the lid back on and handed the tin back to Jack as though he'd done it a thousand times. He said, "It kinda floats all over the place."

"You learn to get a hold of it. Just tuck it between your lip and gum."

Jack watched as Ryan worked his tongue around his mouth. Finally he spit a big black wad. A little string of brown spit flipped down onto his lower lip and chin. He wiped it off with the back of his hand. They continued to walk as Ryan kept working the stuff around in his mouth. Jack noticed when Ryan stepped a little wide with his left foot and then stumbled a little.

"There's the exciting part I was tellin' you about. How you doin'?"

Ryan was very pale.

Jack said, "Whoa. Let's take a little break here for a minute." He grabbed the young man's shoulder and pulled him to a stop. "You look like a ghost. You sure you're okay?"

"Ah, I don't know. I feel a little, you know, lightheaded. Maybe I could just sit down for a minute." He sat down hard on the curb in front of the remains of the Irma Hotel.

Jack looked at him. "You might want to spit all that out. The next step is pukin'."

Ryan leaned over and spit everything out of his mouth. He took a little water from the bottle he brought with him and rinsed his mouth out. "That stuff burns."

"Yep. It'll do that."

"How can you chew that all the time?"

"Don't know. Been doin' it so long, I forgot how I started."

After a minute Ryan got to his feet. "I feel better. Thanks, but I might not take that up."

"Probably a good—"

He was cut off as a gunshot rang through the air. Jack stood up and turned as he listened. "On the south end of town. Probably nothin'."

"Do you hear a lot of guns around here?"

"Not usually. No."

They started walking. Ryan noticed their pace was significantly faster. A few minutes later, a second shot rang out.

"That's a shotgun. You can tell from the sound."

"Really? How?"

"Hard to describe. More of a boom than a bang. I'm gonna turn here; you know where you're headed, right?"

"You're going to where the gunshots are coming from, aren't you? Can I go with you?"

Jack thought for a moment and decided there might be a lesson in this. He said, "Sure. Just watch your head, get down quick if it's necessary, and do exactly what I tell you."

A few minutes later, they turned east on Stampede when they heard another shot—this time much closer. Jack said, "You keep an eye on me. If I start movin' fast, you'd best do the same."

"I will," Ryan said with excitement in his voice.

Ahead they could see a parking lot on the right and a bigger road beyond. Jack said, "That's a grocery store parkin' lot. I bet that's where the trouble is. That shotgun doesn't have a very long range, but you'd be surprised how far it really can reach out there and touch you. I want you to keep back."

Ryan nodded in agreement.

They stayed away from the front of the store as they crossed the street and walked through the parking lot of the Boot Barn to get a better look at what was going on. From the corner of Seventeenth Street and Stampede, Jack could see twenty

or thirty people standing in the parking lot amid a couple of burned-out vehicles. Three bodies lay on the ground in front of the Piggly Wiggly store, and a man sat on a lawn chair in front of the main door with a shotgun across his lap. He turned to Ryan and said, "You stay right here no matter what happens. You got that?"

"Yeah."

"Nope. That ain't good enough. You got it?"

"Yes! I got it already. I'll stay back."

"No matter what, right?"

"Yes. No matter what."

Jack walked over to where the group of people stood. He asked a tall man in a big straw hat what was going on.

"That bastard pulled his chair up there this morning and said he staked a claim over the place. If anybody wants anything, they gotta pay for it."

"Is he the owner?"

"Naw. One of the guys over there says he's just some local guy."

Jack shook his head. "What's he askin' for?"

"Gold mostly. He's makin' some pretty crude remarks to some of the women."

"I see," Jack said. He took his hat off in an exaggerated motion and then scratched his head. He started walking toward the front of the store, slow and steady, approaching the man from just to the right of straight on.

When the man picked up his shotgun, Jack said, "So, what's the deal here, buddy?"

"I ain't your buddy. If you want to come in this store, you're gonna have to pay."

Jack kept his hands in plain sight and kept moving forward. "Pay? Hell, there's money blowin' all over the streets. The doors to the bank are busted wide open. You can walk in and take all you want. I doubt there's anybody who would give a damn."

"Nope. You gotta have gold or pussy to get in here."

Jack gave a little laugh. "Well, as you can see, I'm completely out of the latter, but we might work somethin' out with the

former. What kinda gold are you lookin' for?" He was getting close now.

The man gripped the shotgun tight. "Eighteen-karat or better. A full ounce gets you half a cart. Two ounces and you can fill it."

Jack kept moving forward slowly. He was now about fifteen yards in front of the man. "Two ounces for a cart full of groceries? Seems a little spendy. What would you say to a half ounce for a full cart?"

"No, sir. But I will meet you halfway. One ounce will get you a cart, but only half with cans."

Jack was about to speak when he noticed someone move fast on his left in his peripheral vision. The man in the chair started to raise the shotgun. In a flash, a shot rang out, a third eye opened in the seated man's forehead, and a brass case tinkled on the ground behind and to the right of Jack. He lowered the Kimber and turned to his left to see the man in the white hat finish his run to the front of the store. "Goddammit!"

The crowd of people moved toward him. They started patting him on the back, saying thanks. A man with a big beer belly and a bollo tie shook his hand and said, "That was the bravest goddamn thing I ever saw. Helluva shot, too!" A lady who looked to be in her sixties came up and gave him a big hug. "Thank you, sir. Thank you." Another younger lady pushing a stroller with a toddler told him he was wonderful. They all offered their thanks and then walked toward the front of the store.

A thought suddenly struck Jack. He yelled, "Ladies and gentlemen, if I could have your attention for a moment." A few people who had already made it into the store came back out, and everybody else stopped. He continued, "I know you all need something to eat. My name is John Neumann, and I been talkin' to a couple of the city council members this morning. There's gonna be a meetin' at the high school this evenin' at about what you figure to be seven o'clock. We are all gonna need to work together to get through this, and part of that means we're gonna have to divide up the food in the grocery

stores so *everybody* gets some. I'm gonna ask that if you don't have anything at home, go ahead and get something to eat, but please use the perishable food first. If you need medicines, please talk to somebody at the hospital. They can help you."

A guy in the back said, "What if I don't want to wait?"

Jack shook his head. "You see this gal over there with her kid, or that young couple over there? Do you really want to take food for yourself they might need? We all gotta eat and we will. But we need to be smart about it. We need to do the right thing. That's all I'm askin'."

Jack watched as most of the crowd started nodding their heads. Some started walking back toward where they came from. One guy approached Jack and said, "You all need help?"

"Yes, sir, we do."

About a half hour later, Jack and Ryan set off again. Jack had recruited the guy who asked to help to watch the store. The guy had said he would just repeat what Jack had told everybody, but he wouldn't stand in anybody's way if they were determined. Another couple had volunteered to distribute some of the flyers and pass the word about the meeting at the high school.

When they were out of earshot of the store, Ryan said, "That was un-fucking-believable! Holy shit! You totally smoked that guy."

"That was nothin' to be proud of. I wanted to talk some reason into him."

"Seriously. You're a total hero. That was cool. It was an awesome shot. Right between the eyes! You must be like a ninja-master with that gun."

Jack stopped walking and looked directly at Ryan. "Son, a man just lost his life, and I took it from him. There's nothin' cool about it. Just a couple of days ago, all them people back there would have been screamin' and runnin' away at the sound of a gunshot. Today, they're pattin' me on the back as they just walk on past a dead man into that store. I feel terrible. Not only for that guy and everybody else who died in the

last few days, but also for all of us. Look how far we've already changed. A couple of days ago, that man would have never dreamed of pullin' up a chair in front of a store with a shotgun, demandin' payment for somethin' that wasn't his. Today, people are happy as hell I killed him. I'm afraid for where we are headed."

"Oh, it's probably not that bad. It was like a one-time thing."

"Nope. I think it's the beginning of what things are gonna be like for a while. You watch yourself carefully when you are handin' those flyers out. Don't let anybody catch you off guard. And for cryin' out loud, don't let yourself get pulled into anything. Walk away. We'll get you fixed up with a gun sooner rather than later. Okay?"

"Yes, sir."

"All right. I'll see you back at our camp a little later. Be careful."

"Thanks. I will."

The two parted. Jack walked west toward a residential section of town south of the main business area while Ryan went north. Jack thought more about what he had said to Ryan. The more he thought about it, the more he was sure he was right: This was just the beginning. It was gonna get worse.

# 25.

The walk to Megan's place wasn't that far, maybe two or three miles at most, but it took them nearly an hour and a half. Neither of them talked much along the way. Both felt like hell. Mark's head still throbbed despite the Tylenol and ibuprofen. Megan had stopped for a couple of minutes along the road, and Mark thought she was going to puke. A couple of hours of fun had left them both severely incapacitated for hours. At another point along the way, he thought he heard her crying and happened to notice her shoulders hitch a little.

Riding the horse seemed easy enough. Mark had no trouble staying in the saddle and even tried rocking back and forth a couple of times to make sure he was comfortable and could stay balanced. When they pulled in the yard, Megan simply said, "Okay. Get down." He did, and she pulled the saddle and pad from the horse and then turned Fred out in a wood-fenced pasture with three other horses. She half carried and half dragged the saddle to the barn and left it by the door to a little inside room. "Here. Put this away." Mark came over, and she showed him a rack to lift the saddle onto.

He followed her into the house. She pointed to a big leather couch and said, "Make yourself at home. I'm going to take

a nap." She walked out of the room into a hallway without another word.

He looked around a bit. Nice place. Not over-the-top, but not inexpensive either. The home was casual and comfortable but also reflected owners who had a little extra money. The TV was huge and built into the wall. A very nice stereo system accompanied it, but would forever remain quiet. Nice art pieces and decorations tastefully accented the room.

Mark walked into the kitchen and found a warm diet Mountain Dew in the fridge. He downed it, not realizing how thirsty he was. The kitchen, like the living room, was clean, simple, and very nice. The appliances were all stainless steel and looked new. The huge dent in the door of the dishwasher had probably come from the event the other night. As he walked back into the living room, he thought he heard Megan crying down the hall. She obviously didn't want to be disturbed, so he lay down on the couch and closed his eyes.

When his eyes opened, he could tell the sun had shifted in the sky. It now streamed in at an angle through the windows to the west. He stretched and looked over to see Megan sitting quietly in a chair, watching him.

"Hey," he said, sitting up. "How are you doing?"

"Fine."

"Did you sleep?"

"Yeah. A little bit. I've been thinking."

He leaned back into the leather of the couch. "About what?"

"You and what you said, mostly. Tell me what your plan is again."

Mark said, "I've been thinking about that too. I want to go west. I figure at first I'll just head over to Buffalo and see what is going on, and then I'll come up with a plan to get me farther west. Maybe Idaho or eastern Oregon. It depends on what I come up with. If I can't move very fast, then I'll have to find somewhere to spend the winter before I move west next spring."

"And then what?"

"Well, like I said, I want to find a place where I can survive long term. I'm not sure what that is yet. Maybe it's a farm or ranch; maybe it's a town."

"A town?"

"Sure. As long as it's sustainable. Why not?"

She sat quietly, staring at the rug on the wooden floor, for several minutes. Mark started to get uncomfortable with the awkward silence. Without looking up, she said, "When I was seventeen, I hooked up with a young cowboy. He was pretty good looking and tough as hell. I left home and went with him on the rodeo circuit. My dad wanted to kill me. I know he would have killed that cowboy if he would have caught him. I spent about nine months with him chasing a dream. We got into some crazy shit. Seriously crazy shit. In the end I realized he was taking the road to nowhere on meth, and the dreams were over. I came back home, got my shit together, and went to college. I started chasing my own dreams."

She looked at him and continued, "So things are going pretty good for me. I gotta six-figure career, my own place in New York near Central Park, and I'm looking at a promotion and a big raise. I came back home to be here for my dad, and now everything goes to hell. If what you told me is true, and I think it is, my dreams are over. When I listen to you, it feels a lot like it did with that cowboy. You have dreams, and you might just have the fire to make it happen.

"So now I am stuck with a choice. I can stay here and try to figure out what to do on my own, or I can go with you. If I stay, I obviously won't last here at the house very long. There's not much food, so I'll end up in some kind of shelter in Gillette. If I go with you, I'll be riding west into God only knows what.

"I'll tell you what, cowboy. I'll ride with you, and I'll teach you how to shoot and ride a horse, but I'm not gonna be some arm candy for you—a little plaything to have around when it's convenient and then thrown out when it's not. I'll buy into your dreams, but I'm making the decisions *with* you. You are not—and *will* not—be the boss over me. If you start making a bunch of decisions without talking to me, I'll ride off and leave

your ass. If you start treating me like shit, I'll kill you in your sleep. Any questions?"

Mark was grinning. He liked this girl. "Yeah. One. I gotta take a shit. Is that okay?"

She smiled back at him. "Take a bucket of water with you to flush with. Save the clean stuff in the tank for drinking."

"One more question. I'm a man, and men have certain needs."

She cut him off. "Don't give me that sorry shit. If you play your cards right, things might work out just fine for you. If you don't, well, I guess that's why God made your arms long enough to reach your dick."

They spent the next two hours in back of the house. Megan decided to start with the rifle. After Mark made the first couple of shots, she said, "Let me see that," and took a couple of shots. "The damn thing isn't sighted in. How do you expect to hit anything with this?"

Mark stammered a weak response of something to the effect it was Red's fault.

She shot again, this time at something Mark couldn't see, and then adjusted the scope. She shot again and turned the knobs a little more. Three shots later she handed him the rifle, and said, "Here. Take those bottles and start walking. I'll yell at you when to stop."

Mark left with three empty beer bottles in his arms. After he had walked quite a ways, he turned to see her waving him farther on. He kept walking, occasionally looking over his shoulder. Finally he stopped and yelled, "Here?"

She waved him on farther. This was crazy. Nobody could shoot a beer bottle this far away. He kept walking. When he looked back, she was lying on her stomach in the grass, bent over the rifle with her eye to the scope. She waved him on farther. He kept walking until he heard her whistle. He set the bottles in a line on an old prairie dog hill and started back.

When he got back, he said, "No way. There's no way you can hit those from here."

She put her eye to the scope, breathed out slowly, and squeezed the trigger. The shot rang out as the first bottle exploded.

"That's pretty close to three hundred yards. If you can't hit that target with this rifle, then you should just find a nice little shelter in Gillette. Do you even know anything about this gun?"

"Yeah. I know it's a 38."

"Nice. It's a .308. This one is an Ultimate Match by Les Baer. They are probably one of the best gun-makers in the world. That's a hell of a scope on it too. Did you get this from Red?"

"Yeah."

"Well, he set you up right. I bet he charged you an arm and a leg for it too."

"I paid in gold."

"Gold?" She turned toward him.

"Yeah. He said paper money wasn't worth anything anymore. The stuff is just lying all over the place. I traded twelve gold coins for all the stuff I have with me."

"What did the coins look like?"

"He described them and held his finger and thumb together to show her how big they were."

"So each one was an ounce?"

"Yeah, that's what they said on them."

"Do you know how much they are worth?"

"I don't know. Enough to buy all this stuff."

She laughed. "Oh yeah. Each one of those coins was about thirty-two hundred dollars. That means you gave him almost forty thousand dollars for three guns, some ammo, and some camping gear. Nice going. This is a nice rifle, but it's not a thirty thousand dollar rifle."

Now Mark laughed. "First of all, I had those coins for about twenty minutes. I found them in a bank vault with some cash. Red was willing to trade for them, and so was I. It's probably going to be easy to find some more. Secondly, I don't think the company that made that rifle is in business since the event the other night. I think that makes it just about priceless."

She smiled at him. "Good point."

She made him shoot the rifle over and over again. He started to get close to the bottle on the third shot and hit it with his fourth. When both of the remaining bottles were destroyed, she made him shoot at the pieces, critiquing his technique and helping him fix little problems. By the end of the second box of ammo, he could reliably hit what he was aiming at.

"Okay. Let's try handguns." She traced the outline of a person on a big sheet of cardboard and leaned it up against a tree about fifty feet away. She nodded her head toward the target and said, "Let me see what you got."

Mark picked up the XD(m) and held it in front of him with his right hand. He was just about to squeeze the trigger when Megan said, "Whoa! Stop right there. What the hell are you doing?"

"I'm gonna shoot the target, like you said."

"No no no!" she said as she walked up to him. "You're holding the gun all wrong. What do you think you are? Some kind of a badass gangster?"

"No, it's just that this is the way I've seen it done before."

"Yeah, in the movies. It doesn't work."

"Sure it does."

"Okay. Fine. Go ahead and try it. I bet you can't hit the cardboard."

"Anywhere on it? Sure I can."

"What do you want to bet?"

Mark though for a moment and grinned deviously. "A blowjob."

Megan didn't even blink. "Fine. You have three shots. But if you don't hit it, you owe me a hot bath."

"Where am I gonna get that?"

"I don't know and I don't care. That's up to you to figure out. But I want it tonight, otherwise I'm going to charge you interest."

Mark felt pretty confident. How hard could it be? It was a big piece of cardboard and it wasn't very far away. "Okay. You're on." Quickly he pulled up the pistol and fired three rapid shots. Without looking he said, "I'm thinking maybe after we eat. Yeah, that would be good."

Megan started walking toward the target. "Come on, gangsta. Let's see what you did."

The cardboard stood perfectly intact. No holes.

Megan said, "Why is it every guy thinks he has to know everything? You obviously have never shot anything before. I have. My dad used to shoot competitively, and I have been around guns my entire life. Will you trust me now?"

"You could have told me that before."

"It wouldn't have made any difference. You had to prove it to yourself. Now here's the thing, Mark. Guys tend to fall into one of two categories: those big enough to admit a girl might know something and be willing to learn, and those whose ego just can't handle it. Which one are you?"

"I'll learn. Hell, I don't care."

They started walking back to the spot he had shot from. Mark said, "You knew I was gonna bet a blowjob, didn't you?"

"Yep."

"How did you know?"

"Because you say what's on your mind, and you're a guy. It was pretty obvious."

"Would you have done it?"

She smiled at him. "I was sure you weren't going to hit that target."

"But what if I would have gotten lucky?"

"I guess you didn't get lucky." She winked.

For the next hour, she made him shoot both pistols. She showed him how to stand, how to place his hands on the weapons, and how to line up the sights. After practice and Megan's coaching, he started getting better.

As they walked back to the house, Mark said, "Thanks."

"For what?"

"For teaching me. You're a good teacher."

She smiled. "You're welcome. You'll be a good shot if you practice. I'll tell you what. I'll make dinner while you start working on my bath."

"You're gonna hold me to that?"

"Of course I am. You would have held me to it. Besides, I still smell like wine and Bloody Marys."

"You know, you scared the hell out of me this morning. I thought you were dead."

"I wondered why you were hugging me so tight this morning."

Mark grinned. "That was part of it. The other part is that you were almost naked."

She hit him in the shoulder. "For a second there, you were almost sweet. Good luck with my bath."

# 26.

It was late afternoon when Jack got back to camp. As he walked down the street, he rounded a corner and could see Nicole sitting at a picnic table that had been pulled into camp. She spotted him and stood immediately. When he walked into camp, Nicole limped toward him and wrapped her arms tightly around him. "Wow," he said, holding his arms out to the side. "Musta missed me. What's all this?"

She pulled away to look up at him. "Earlier a young man came into camp. He said you sent him to help with the meeting tonight. He told us all about the terrible shooting. I am so glad you are unharmed." She hugged him again.

"I'm fine. It was no big deal."

"John Neumann! You simply cannot walk up to an armed man and demand he put his gun down. You could have been killed."

He smiled. "That's not exactly what happened. Let's sit down, and I'll tell you about it."

For the next several minutes, he relayed the details of the shooting. "See, I told you I was never in danger."

"That is not entirely true. The man was armed, and it was clear he had violent intentions. I'm afraid there will be much more of this."

"Funny you should say that. I was kinda thinkin' the same thing myself. Didn't you say you had a degree in social anthropology?"

"I did."

"A master's, right?"

"Yes."

"I hate to put you on the spot, but do you think you could talk to some of the community leaders before the meetin' tonight? You know, kinda give us an idea what to expect."

"Well, I'm not sure my opinion on the matter is much better than anyone else's. My subject of study was slightly different, but I could think about it a little."

"I'm sure anything you have to offer would be a help. Right now everything is just chaos. Three-quarters of this town is gone. People are walkin' around lost, and it's the middle of October. We're lucky the weather has been as nice as it has. It's gonna get cold soon. Damn cold. If people don't get organized and ready now, they aren't gonna make it through the winter. Enough people have died as a result of this…this solar flare. I can't abide with more people starvin' to death just 'cause they don't know what to do."

Nicole sat quietly next to him. She could hear his throat tighten with emotion. He continued. "There's food around. Plenty of it. It's still in houses with no living occupants; it's on the shelves in the grocery stores; hell, there's silos full of corn just north of town. We just need to get everybody on the same damn page."

"Jack." She leaned forward and looked at him very seriously. "I want you to listen to me very carefully. You are not responsible for these people. For that matter, you are not responsible for Ryan or me. It was very kind of you to rescue me yesterday, and for that I am eternally grateful, but you must understand that my safety and my well-being are my own responsibility. The same is true for everyone left here in Cody. It is wonderful

that you and others would be so kind to offer help, but people are ultimately responsible for themselves.

"I know you are exhausted. You simply must be. I've no idea what time you awoke this morning, but you must have done a hundred things even before you left. If I might give you a small piece of advice: you should go take a nap. Get some rest. I'll wake you in plenty of time for the meeting."

Jack sat quietly for a moment and then looked at his watch. "It's three thirty. Here." He unsnapped and handed her his watch. "If you could make sure I don't sleep past five, I might take you up on that offer."

Nicole looked at the watch. "Rolex. I was curious why your watch still functioned when everyone else's has seemed to fail. It would be my pleasure. Please, go get some rest."

A hand gently touched his shoulder. "Jack?"

His eyes opened to see Nicole kneeling next to him. "It's five o'clock. I brought a shower bag for you if you'd like."

He rubbed his face. "You didn't have to do that. I coulda come out and got it."

"It was no trouble, really."

"Well, thank you. That was very nice. I kinda hate to get all cleaned up and then put these dirty clothes back on, but for the time bein', it's all I got."

"Actually, I picked up a couple of things for you at Mr. Swenson's store. He said it was no trouble at all. In fact, he tried to give me more. I am sorry, but I did notice the size of your jeans the other day. It was printed on the back label. I had to guess at your shirt size and some of the other things. Mr. Swenson helped me pick things out."

"You did all that?"

"I'm sorry if I've overstepped my bounds."

"Not at all. I'm just a little surprised. I should have thought of it myself. Thank you."

"You are very welcome." She stood to leave.

"I don't have to worry about you bustin' in here while I'm takin' a shower, do I?"

She looked back over her shoulder, smiling. "Paybacks are a bitch, isn't that right?"

Jack laughed. "Yes, ma'am, they are indeed."

# 27.

Jack walked out of his tent feeling much better. He was rested and clean. It was amazing how much small luxuries could make a difference. Three men stood near the fire. "Neil, Mike, Bobby. Glad you could make it." He looked around and saw Nicole limping toward camp from the pasture.

She noticed Jack looking in her direction and the three men, and hurried. "Sorry I'm late. I was watering the horses."

"No trouble. What happened to Ryan?"

"I haven't seen him yet."

Jack's eyebrows bunched momentarily in concern. He said, "Nicole, I'd like you to meet Judge Neil Williams, Dr. Michael Henry, and Mayor Robert Stark. We call him Bobby. Gentlemen, I'd you to meet Miss Nicole Meredith. I helped her out of an airplane wreck yesterday. She has a hell of an education and may be able to give us a little insight."

As they shook her hand, all three said, "Ma'am."

"Let's have a seat," Jack said, as he motioned toward the picnic table.

As they all sat, Mike said, "Thanks again for helping us out this morning, Jack. It would have been altogether different if

you wouldn't have been there. I know Mrs. Meyers will thank you with every step she takes."

Jack could feel Nicole's gaze on him but ignored it. "No trouble at all. I'll swing back by from time to time. Just give a yell if there's anything else I can do."

"Thanks. I will. By the way, I brought a little something for you." He handed Jack a small brown bag.

Jack opened it and pulled a bottle of Bulliet out far enough to see it. "You have a good memory. Thank you."

"You're welcome. I figured you could use a little sip to take the edge off in the evening."

Judge Williams spoke next. "Hell, we all could. So, I heard you had a little trouble today."

Jack smiled. "Word sure gets around fast, even without phones. Yeah, we did, but we got it under control. I had plans for a different outcome."

"That's what I heard," the judge added.

"What else did you see out there?" the mayor asked.

Jack went on to describe the details of the town as best he could. He added, "I think we got the grocery stores pretty well taken care of for now, but it won't last. We need a community plan and as many volunteers as possible. Tonight."

"That's my plan," the mayor said.

"We also need a plan for clean water tonight," the doctor added. "If we don't there's going to be a bunch of sick folks around here."

"I have some ideas about that as well," the mayor said.

The judge said, "If I'm hearing you right, we need to come up with a three-fold outline for things. First we have to address the immediate concerns of the population: food, water, and safety. Sounds like we have some ideas there to get us started. Secondly, we need to figure out what to do with the upcoming winter. Lastly, we need to figure out what the hell we are going to do in the long-term. If what you say is true, Jack, we are on our own. Trouble is—what the hell are we planning for? It'd sure be nice to have a crystal ball about now."

Jack said, "That's why I asked Nicole to join us. Her education is, in part, social anthropology. If anybody can give us an idea what to expect, I think she'd be the one."

"Hmm," Nicole said, "well, it seems to me the best starting point for a discussion of this nature is to start with the culture we have known. I would like to set politics and particular political ideas aside and simply speak in generalities. As you know, and as you all hold so dear here in America, government is a representation of the people. Therefore, it has at least four major functions for the benefit of those people. It sets laws—which protect society as a whole, as well as individuals—it facilitates communication, it regulates portions of society to ensure safety and fairness, and it establishes a medium of currency, which facilitates trade and commerce.

"The other night, the society we have known our entire lives winked out of existence, or perhaps I should say, it was zapped out of existence. We have been thrust into a state of anarchy. By the way, *anarchy* simply means 'no ruler,' or 'absence of government.' Today there is no communication, no laws, nobody to enforce the laws if there were any, no way to inform someone we designate to be an authority that another person is breaking the law, and no medium of currency to exchange for goods and services. If you haven't yet noticed, there are dollar bills quite literally blowing in the street, and anyone can pick them up; therefore, they have no value.

"So, the real question at hand is: what is to become of us? What happens now? A recent example is Somalia. In the early nineteen nineties, the Somali government fell. The country had essentially no formal government until two thousand six. Certain aspects of the country did, in fact, prosper, but there was also widespread brutality and warfare, as several warlords controlled various regions. In short, there was nothing less than utter chaos throughout the country for years. There is a problem with this example, in that communication remained intact, and goods and technologies could flow into the country from other countries, which remained very functional and could profit from the trade.

"Perhaps a more appropriate example is the aftermath of Hurricane Katrina. With the breakdown of communications and absence of law, and doors to every store and home standing open, a small portion of the population went absolutely mad. They shot people for no reason, stole anything they could carry, exploited women, and lawlessness became the rule. The man with the biggest gun was in charge until a functional, well-trained, well-equipped police force—a bigger gun—could restore order.

"Since Jack came back from the incident at the grocery store, I have been thinking about the situation we now face. This is so unique that I daresay there is no example we can look to in order for us to understand what is to happen. However, there are several constants that pervade every instance of anarchy in the past. There will be violence. There are always members of the population who will exploit their newfound freedoms to their own advantage. If I want something, I can just take it, because there is no one to stop me. If you try, I will shoot you, and again, there is no one to stop me. Secondly, the weaker members of the population will suffer the most. It is normally the job of government, which is to say, society en masse, to care for those who cannot care for themselves. Without government, they have no protection. Women and children are almost always the victims and pay the highest price in a lawless society. Traditionally, power is preceded by strength. In other words, those with the biggest army win.

"The key to end the anarchy and establish a new government will be organization and a strong, compassionate leader who truly cares about the wellbeing of the people. Throughout history we have seen time and again that it is far better to be ruled by an all-powerful benevolent king, than it is to be ruled by an unaccountable committee.

"If you would be so kind as to indulge me, I should try to make some predictions. However, please understand that I have absolutely no fact on which to base these hypotheses.

"First, I should think there would be a time of quiet shock. Our very existence has changed so drastically, people will

require a period of time just to comprehend what has happened. At this point, where we are today, very few will realize there is no government, no police, no military—there is nobody coming to help. However, this will be short-lived. Generally speaking, there are people who are hiding in our present society and have been abiding by the law strictly because they fear the repercussions of their heinous desires. They will be the first to appear. They are the worst and must be dealt with firmly, because indulging in their fantasy will only serve to make it stronger. Later, if others realize there is, in fact, no penalty for any wrongdoing, a larger number of the population will indulge themselves. I believe it is this larger group that can be influenced. You see, they understand what the 'right thing' to do is and why; but without a leader to bring this quality out in them, they will regress into a more primitive state.

"One last prediction, and I am sure that you will think me absolutely mad for even suggesting such an outrageous and preposterous idea. I would have been laughed out of the university for even dreaming up such a daring notion, because I have nothing to base this on whatsoever. If you consider our society is new as of yesterday, then it will evolve into something different, as this current state is unstable. Understanding the geography and culture of the United States of America, as it existed two days ago, the evolution will take one of two forms. Either it will generally evolve from the rural society toward the urban society and will therefore have a strong moral ethic, or it will evolve from an urban society toward a rural society and have a power-based, warlord type of regional division. The reason I suggest this is quite simple. Although we know, in fact, there is a heterogeneous population, the predominant mindset in rural areas is moral and rather conservative. The ideas of 'earning' something and 'working to build something' are deeply ingrained. However, the real unrestrained strength in urban areas is not the intellectual liberal base, which previously held power by appeasing the masses, but rather it is the fight-to-survive, urban poor—the gangs and thugs, in other words. They already know the value of a weapon and how to use it.

They are very well trained in the practice of 'take-what-you-want,' and the only thing they respect is power.

"Actually, as I think about it now, both will evolve for a time, but only one form of rule will eventually survive. The two ideologies are polar extremes and cannot coexist and tolerate one another. Ultimately, unless a strong government is instituted and order restored, I believe there will be a war."

It was very quiet around the table when Nicole finished.

It was the judge who spoke first. "May I ask where you went to school, ma'am?"

"Certainly. I was at Oxford."

The judge looked at Jack. "Dr. Neumann, you have your hands full. Not only is she beautiful, she's a hell of a lot smarter than you."

Jack felt Nicole's eyes again. He grinned. "Ain't that the truth?"

The mayor spoke next. "Ma'am, where are you from?"

She turned toward him. "I was born and have family in Scotland. But I lived for a while in Australia and then England."

"So you are a long way from home?"

"I am indeed."

"Do you have any plans?"

"For the foreseeable future, travel is out of the question. It is for that reason, among others, I choose to stay here. I prefer to cast my lot with the moral. It is not only logical and obvious for me as a woman, but also because it is the manner in which I would prefer society to ultimately thrive. I believe what Jack told me to be solidly true. We have an opportunity to make things better, but we must work together to make it happen, and time is of the essence."

Mike said, "Ma'am, what you're suggesting is that we arm ourselves and prepare for war?"

"I am not suggesting anything. I am merely attempting to predict the future in a very general sense, and that, of course, is extraordinarily difficult. If we examine the same problems on a more local basis, I should think that you will see more individuals such as the man at the grocery store today. If you

organize quickly and turn the majority toward their moral roots, I should think you could see an extended time of relative peace. Cody is somewhat unique in that it is isolated by distance from any major metropolitan area. If the rest of the country has seen the same depopulation we have witnessed here, I should think there might be individuals or small bands of brigands who challenge you in the near future, but nothing significant for some time."

The mayor said, "A determined individual or a small group could still pose one hell of a threat. I think we need to recruit a security leader tonight as well. I hadn't planned on that this soon, but it makes sense. They'll need time to get ready."

Mike turned to Jack. "What are your plans, cowboy?"

"I figured I'd make sure you all got things off the ground, and then I need to get home."

"That's a long ride."

"It is, but it's probably easier now than a month from now."

"That's a good point." The mayor started to get up and said, "We should get to this meeting before they start without us."

# 28.

"Supper," Megan yelled from the back of the house.

"Be right there," Mark yelled back to her, as he looked over his project. He wondered if she had taken her time making dinner to give him more time to get things ready. He thought she probably had. He looked things over again, trying to think of anything he forgot. He smiled. If this worked, she was going to be very surprised, and he was going to be a superhero. He lit the burner and adjusted the gas so it roared. He needed as much heat as possible.

"You've been busy," Megan said, as Mark came into the kitchen through the back door.

"Yeah," he said, grinning sheepishly, looking proud.

"Have you been working on my bath?"

"Yeah."

"And?"

"And what? I owe you a hot bath. It's warming up right now."

"Really?"

He tried to play this off as no big deal, but inside he was bubbling with excitement. He couldn't wait for her to see his creation. "Sure."

She looked at him suspiciously. "Wash your hands and have a seat."

"It smells great."

"It's no big deal. I made a casserole with some ground beef in the freezer. The stuff was thawed, but it wasn't bad. I hope it tastes all right."

He rinsed his hands. "If it tastes as good as it smells, it'll be terrific." He thought for a moment. "Where did you cook that at?"

"On the stove, silly."

Mark sat down at the table with a puzzled look on his face. "Okay. Explain this to me. Why is it every car we've seen is burned or blown to bits, and the entire town burned down, but you can still cook in here, and I found a propane tank outside that's just fine?"

"That is weird. We have a propane tank for the house. It's the big white thing out back. My dad used to call it the hippo."

They started eating in silence, both thinking. Finally Mark said, "Ah-ha! I think I know what the deal is."

"What?"

"Air. The gas tank on a car is half full of air, so when the sparks hit it, they ignited the gas fumes; but a propane tank has no air in it at all. The space above the liquid is just propane, no air. Sparks alone wouldn't do anything. It would need the air to start on fire."

Megan smiled. "You're pretty smart. Is that what you're using to heat my bath?"

"Yep."

She looked at him smiling. "Huh."

He said, "By the way, where does the water in that big, black, plastic pipe come from?"

She made a circle with her fingers about three inches in diameter. "About that big? Valve on the end of it?"

"Yeah. That's the one."

"It's an irrigation line. Dad had it run to the back of the barn when we put the tank in. He used it for a lot of different things. Why?"

"Is the water clean?"

"Oh yeah. It's great water. He even thought about hooking it up to the house. It freezes in winter, but otherwise we have water all year. There's a well and a big tank on top of the hill to the north of us. I think it holds like a couple of thousand gallons. Why?"

"I used some of the water from that line to fill your bath. I wanted to make sure that you weren't going to be soaking in swamp water or cow pee or something like that."

She laughed. "No. There's no cow pee in it. You can drink the water." She paused and then asked, "You filled my bath? But I didn't see you coming in and out of the house."

"No. Sorry, your bath isn't in the house. You didn't say it had to be."

"Where, exactly, is my bath at? If you dug a hole and are going to fill it with muddy water, I'm gonna be pissed."

"I owe you a bath, and a bath you'll get. You asked me to trust you; now you have to trust me."

"Okay. Fair enough, but if this is some kind of a joke, I'm not gonna be happy. I'm actually looking forward to this."

"You said bath, and I am going to deliver a bath."

Mark helped Megan clean up after supper. She kept asking questions about what he had in store, but he gave her no specific information, enjoying the torment. He made her sit in the living room while he went to check the temperature. When he got back, he said, "Almost ready. If you take your time, you can start getting ready. Better grab everything you're going to need. I have a couple more things to do, so if I'm not here when you come out, you have to wait for me."

She looked at him suspiciously. "Okay, but it's almost dark out. Do I need the lantern?"

"I'll take care of all that. Don't worry."

"I am worried. I don't know what you are up to."

"That's true." He smiled.

When Megan came back downstairs, she was wearing a white bathrobe and slippers. She held a pink bag and had a big bath towel draped over her arm. Mark stood in the living room, waiting. He could hardly contain himself. "Ready?"

"I think so. If you are going to play a trick on me, this is going to end badly for you. I have lots of guns, and I know where you sleep."

Mark just smiled. He led the way out the back door and toward the barn.

"The barn? We're going to the barn? I can't imagine what you have cooked up in there."

Mark said nothing. He just kept walking. Overhead the last of the sun was setting fire to the evening sky. Red, purple, and orange clouds seemed to point the way to the back of the barn. He opened the front door, and they stepped into darkness. Mark picked up the lantern he had already lit and standing just outside the door. The light danced on the old wooden stalls and posts as he led Megan to the back door. He positioned her in the middle of the barn's main aisle and said, "Wait here."

"Where's the bath?"

He smiled at her. "Patience."

He walked to the double doors at the back of the building and turned the lantern lower and lower, making the old barn dark. When it finally went out, Megan could hear him set it on the floor and unhook the door latch.

As the double doors opened, Megan gasped and held her breath. About ten feet beyond the door, in the drive, Mark had built her bath. He had taken an old steel stock tank about eight feet in diameter and three feet high, cleaned it, and put it up on concrete blocks he had taken from a pile her dad had made when he tore down an old building. He had used more blocks and some boards to make stairs up to the edge of the tank. Just beyond the tank, three ladders held two long boards at angles to one another surrounding the back edge and held what appeared to be fifty or sixty candles. A low fire was glowing between blocks under the tank. To complete the picture,

the sun was setting behind the tank, creating a red and purple silhouette.

"Your bath, ma'am."

"Oh my God! You did all this?"

"I owed you a bath."

"Is it warm?"

"Check it yourself."

Megan walked to the edge of the huge tank. She dipped her hand into perfect bath water. "It's not going to fall over is it?"

"I jumped around in there before I filled it. It's steady as a rock."

"How did you get it warm so fast? I mean, you haven't been working out here all that long."

"The water in the black pipe was already very warm to start. I just had to heat it up the rest of the way."

She laughed. "This is the craziest thing I have ever seen. It's beautiful."

"Thanks," he said. "There's a couple of features I'd like to point out to you. First of all, on the other side of the back edge is a small shelf where you can put your things and still be able to reach them when you are in the water. Second, you will notice a small plate on the shelf with the candles. I found a couple Dove chocolates. Every girl likes chocolate, right? Last, you will notice an old, beat-up cowbell I found sitting next to the chocolates. If you need anything, just give it a ring."

"Where are you going to be?"

"I thought I would sit on the deck. I can hear you if you need anything, but I'll still be far enough away that you will have some privacy."

"Wow. I gotta say…I'm completely blown away by this. You did an awesome job."

"Oh, a couple more things. I put a couple of clean blocks in the water to help you get in, and remember that the burner is right under the middle of the tank. It might be warm if you sit there."

She smiled. "Thanks. I will." She turned toward him and kissed him on the cheek. "Thank you. This is incredible."

He smiled, but in the red light of twilight, she couldn't see the blush rise on his cheeks. "You're welcome. Enjoy." He turned and walked around the edge of the barn toward the house.

She ran her hand around the water of the tank again. Not too warm, but warm enough to be relaxing. She waited for a few minutes and then climbed the stairs. They felt solid. She stood on the last stair and removed her bathrobe, laying it on the step beside her. She took the scrunchie out of her ponytail and slowly stepped into the water. It felt glorious. Wet, warm, and wonderful, the water seemed to pull all of the stress and sorrow she had been feeling for the last two days away from her. She sat near one of the edges with the water almost up to her shoulders and closed her eyes. The back of the tank above the water line was a little chilly compared to the water, but it felt good. She let herself slide down into the water, and silence washed over her. In this moment, everything was all right again.

Mark had walked around the barn to the window near the front door. From here he could see through the barn and the open doors to the bath beyond. He watched Megan climb the stairs and take off her bathrobe. He froze the image in his mind. She was the most beautiful woman he had ever known. She stood naked with her entire body dark in silhouette against the red Wyoming sky and candles beyond. When she let her hair spill free, it hung just past her shoulders and burned with the red and yellow fire behind her. He watched her step into the tank and sit down. Even the shape of her head seemed beautiful. His knees felt weak, and there didn't seem to be enough air. When he watched her slip under the water, he left the window and walked quietly to the deck behind the house.

Mark sat for what was probably ten minutes but felt like ten hours. It was hard to simply sit and wait when a beautiful naked woman was only a couple of seconds' walk away. He heard the cowbell ring. A voice in his head screamed *YES!*

Although he wanted to run, he walked casually around the barn. Megan leaned on both arms on the edge of the tank. He

could tell she was smiling and could see her wet hair smooth and glistening in the candlelight. In an emoted accent, she said, "Oh pool-boy. Could you be a dear and fetch the bottle of Champagne I placed in the freezer. You might bring the glasses on the counter as well. Oh, and please bring me another towel. This one might be wet."

"Champagne? Really?"

Megan was still smiling. "Run along now. Don't dawdle."

Mark did run. The bath was awesome, but a little alcohol was only gonna make things better. With Champagne in hand, he ran back until he was almost around the barn and then slowed to a walk. She was leaning on the edge again. He held the bottle over his arm and said, "Your Champagne, ma'am." He looked past her face over her shoulder and could see the outline of her back, her butt, and her legs floating in the water. His mind went blank. Part of him wanted to think of something clever, maybe some way to talk his way into the bath with her, but there was nothing.

Megan was smiling devilishly. "You can set them over there, by my bell."

He turned and set them down. His mind was still blank. Finally he managed, "Will that be all, ma'am?"

"No. No, it's not." She turned away from him and let her legs float. "This bath is entirely too big, and it's lonely out here all by myself. Besides, I need someone to wash my back. Why don't you get in here with me?"

Mark felt like a kid on Christmas morning. "Yes, ma'am." He pulled his shirt over the top of his head as he made his way around to the stairs. He sat on the top stair and took off his shoes and socks. He stood up, facing away from her, unhooked his belt, and took off his pants, tossing them on the ground next to the stairs. He turned and smiled at her. Facing away again he pulled down his underwear and stepped backward out of them. As his right foot came down, he missed the back of the wooden stair and instead stepped on the edge of the tank. He almost caught himself, but his foot slipped off the edge of the tank, and he fell backward, arms flailing, into

the tank. A huge splash and wave from the center of the tank rolled over Megan. When Mark came up from underwater, he heard her coughing. Quickly he turned to her. "Oh my God. I'm so sorry. Are you okay?"

Megan was coughing and laughing at the same time. She tried to get air, but the combination of laughter and water in her nose, throat, and lungs made everything worse. She coughed between laughter and then snorted, which made her laugh even harder. The sight of Megan struggling while laughing made Mark a little worried at first. Her snort and then intense uncontrollable laughter pushed him over the edge, and he started laughing with her. When they started to calm down and almost quit, Megan started giggling again. The giggling blossomed into a deep belly laugh, and they started all over. Finally, after several minutes Megan managed, "Smooth."

# 29.

Nicole sat next to Jack in the first row of high school bleachers far on the edge near the east side. She was surprised at the number of people who showed up for the meeting. The far west end of the stands were damaged and looked unsafe, but the remainder appeared to be fine and were nearly full. People also sat on the ground on what was left of the running track and football field.

Mayor Stark stood in the middle of the crowd and yelled for everybody to quiet down. When they did, he explained that, like everything else, the PA system no longer functioned. He would do his best to make sure everyone could hear, but it would be easier if everyone was as quiet as possible. He introduced himself to those who didn't know him and laid out the plan for the meeting. First he would explain what they knew, and then he would explain the plan they had come up with to try to help. He also reassured everybody they would answer as many questions as possible, and all comments and suggestions would be considered. As Nicole listened to what he said, she was impressed by how comfortable he made the crowd in such a short time. This man was an experienced politician and a very good speaker. If he truly believed what he said, he just

might be able to lead these people into a working, functional community again.

After a few minutes, the mayor said, "Ladies and gentleman, I'd like to introduce you to Dr. Jack Neumann. Although Jack lives on the other side of the Bighorns, many of you may recognize him as a board member of the Buffalo Bill Historical Center and a strong supporter of our community. Jack has some information on what might have happened to us."

Jack stood up and walked to where the mayor stood. Nicole heard whispering voices throughout the crowd. She wondered if they were talking about the shooting earlier today.

"Good evening. Like many of you, I had an accident the other night. I was drivin' out of the park when everything went a little crazy. The next mornin' I ran into a young man from Missouri who happens to be studyin' physics. I was hopin' he was gonna be here tonight to explain what he knows, but since he ain't, you're stuck with me." His voice was deep and rich, and although she knew he was raising his voice to be heard, it didn't sound that way. He sounded as though he was talking directly to each member of the audience.

"The man can capture your attention, can't he?" a voice said to her left. Nicole turned to see Judge Williams standing alongside the bleachers. The judge was a tall, handsome man with gray hair and a neatly trimmed mustache.

"Yes, he certainly does."

"You're a lucky gal to have found him. If you stick with him, he'll keep you out of trouble. Have you talked with him much?"

"A little. I know he's from Texas, and a few other details, but he doesn't really talk much about himself."

"That is true. I've known Jack since he came up here looking for a place to call home. We tried like hell to find a place near Cody, but it didn't work out that way. Did he tell you about his wife?"

"Very little."

"She was a wonderful person, and they were very much in love. You could tell every time they looked at each other. She had a passion for the western art museum, and Jack made it

happen for her. He sold one of his favorite horses, so she could donate a piece of art she wanted. She said she wanted as many people as possible to enjoy it. When she died, he took it hard. Real hard. I didn't see him for almost two years. Then one day he started coming back around. Jack and I have talked about everything. I know things about that man his wife didn't even know." He smiled and winked at her. "Oh, nothing bad, just typical guy stuff. But to this day, I have no idea what happened with his wife. I know she died from cancer, but that's about it. He doesn't talk about it."

"Do you happen to know what he did for a living before moving to Wyoming?"

"Didn't he tell you?"

"No. He said I should figure it out. Earlier someone re-ferred to him as doctor, and now the mayor just introduced him the same way. Do you know what field his PhD is in?"

The judge smiled, "Oh, I can't give away Jack's secrets, now can I?"

"Oh please, Mr. Williams. Don't make me beg."

"Nope. I can't tell you that. But you're pretty bright. I bet you'll figure it out in no time. If you don't mind, I'd like to ask you for a favor."

"Of course. Anything."

"I suspect Jack is already thinking about heading home. Dayton is nearly one hundred fifty miles east of here. The first hundred miles are no big deal. It's the Bighorn basin and it's flat and wide open. But that last fifty miles is up and over the Bighorn Mountains. They're gonna be treacherous this time of year when they start getting snow, especially on horseback. If I pleaded with Jack to stay and help us, he would. He is the kind of man who will give you the shirt off his back or take a bullet for a friend, without thinking about it. That little episode at the grocery store today doesn't surprise me a bit. It's just the way he is. But it might be awkward. You know, he'd feel obligated to helping us out. On the other hand, if you asked him, he might just stick around."

"Why would he consider staying if I asked him?"

The judge smiled again. "Oh, I don't know. Men are sometimes funny that way." He leaned in closer to her. "I'll give you a little tip. I think Jack is a little taken with you. He's got a new little spring in his step I haven't seen in a while. I know he's been talking a lot about you. I'm not telling you what to do; it's just that, in times like these, we need as many good men as we can get."

"Oh my. That's quite a great deal to consider. Thank you. I will think about what you have said very carefully."

"If there's anything I can do to help, or if you need to know something about Jack, other than what he did for a living, just come find me."

"Thank you. That's very nice of you to offer."

"Take care, Miss Meredith."

"You too, Judge Williams." She watched as the man walked away. Nicole leaned back and put her hand to her head. Her thoughts were racing.

Jack was answering a question from the audience when Dr. Henry approached him as he stood in front of the crowd. The doctor whispered something in his ear and then left, with Jack nodding in agreement. "Ladies and gentlemen, I would love to stay and answer as many questions as I can, but in all honesty you now know as much as I do. Everything else is just a guess on my part. If you'd like to talk about this further, just come find me tomorrow. Unfortunately, I need to run. Thank you for your time and attention." He left the front of the crowd as the mayor stood up again and began speaking. He walked directly over to Nicole.

"I saw you talkin' to the judge. Don't believe a word that man says."

"He was saying a few very nice things about you."

"See. I told you he was a liar. You haven't seen Ryan yet, have you?"

"No. I'm beginning to worry about him."

"Me too. Listen, I need to run for a bit. Can you get back to camp by yourself?"

"Yes, of course. It's just down the street."

"I wish I could help. Here. I want you to take this and keep it with you." He handed her his compact .45.

"A gun. Oh my."

"It's ready to go if you need it. Just click this little safety off and pull the trigger. It'll shoot every time you want it to."

"Oh, I don't think I need a gun."

"I hope you're right, but it's better to have it and not need it, than need it and not have it. Tomorrow we're gonna get you set up with one, and I'll show you how to use it. I got to go."

"When will you be back?"

"As soon as I can." Jack paused for a second, like there was something he wanted to say or do, but turned and left.

Nicole sat on the bleacher and listened to the rest of the mayor's talk and a speech by a young man who stated he was an EMT and spoke about health concerns and medications. An older fat man then stood up and talked about obtaining drinking water and the dangers of drinking unfiltered river water. Finally a retired army colonel stood up and asked for volunteers for a security detail. The mayor got back up at the end and asked people to volunteer for various things. Nicole watched them speak, but she heard few of their words. Her mind was thinking about what the judge had said.

She sat alone by the fire, watching the ribbons of color play in the cool night sky. She felt so very alone. All her friends and family weren't even on the same continent and were most likely dead. She was thousands of miles from anyone she even knew or any place she had ever been, and now even the new people she had met had left her alone. Silent tears welled in her eyes and spilled quietly down her cheeks.

Jack's voice came out of the darkness. "If it wasn't for those tears, I'd think this was about the coziest little campfire I could imagine."

Nicole wiped her cheeks with her hand. "Hello. Sorry, I was waxing nostalgic."

Jack pulled another folding chair close to her and sat down. "Don't apologize to me. I should apologize to you."

"Whatever for?"

"Wyoming is my home. I know lots of people around here. I should never have left you on your own like that. Wasn't right. It was inconsiderate and I'm sorry."

"It is not your responsibility to entertain me. You have already done far more than enough."

"That's nice of you to say, but I respectfully disagree. Could I offer you a taste of whiskey as a token of my humble regret?"

Nicole laughed. "Good Lord, I thought you'd never ask."

Jack came back from his tent with the bottle in hand. "I should've picked up a couple of glasses today."

"There are plastic cups on the table. I'm not particular if you're not."

Jack grabbed the cups. "I was gonna just drink from the bottle, so these are high class by comparison." He sat down, poured two glasses, and handed one to her. He sighed and then held up his cup. "Here's to day number two. Let's hope the rest get a hell of a lot better." They drank.

He asked, "I don't s'pose you've seen Ryan?"

"No. Nothing yet. Do you think he is in trouble?"

"I'm worried about him, but there's nothin' we can do till it's light."

"Then what?"

"We'll take a couple of horses and go look for him. I know a place on the other end of town that has saddles. We'll get one of the other horses outfitted for you over there."

"You don't suppose they would have an English saddle?"

Jack smiled. "There's a place over near Sheridan with a polo field and a handful of ponies. I think they own the only four English saddles in the entire state. I'm sorry, but we're gonna have to get you ridin' western."

"I really don't mind at all. It's just the large knob on the front of a western saddle that bothers me. Seems a bit dangerous."

Jack raised his eyebrows at her. "Dangerous for you? Think about that from a man's perspective."

"Oh dear." She laughed. "Yes, I can see where that might be a bit of trouble."

"The horn is actually pretty useful. It's not as dangerous as it seems."

Nicole let a moment of silence pass and then said, "May I change the subject?"

"Of course."

"It's none of my business, I know, but might I ask where you went tonight?"

Jack sighed. "I went up to the hospital."

"May I ask why?"

"There was a young lady who was havin' trouble deliverin' her baby."

"And they asked for your experience?"

"They did."

"Are delivering baby horses similar to delivering baby people?"

Jack chuckled quietly and then started laughing. His laughter continued to build until he was laughing deeply from his belly. He waved his arms. "I'm sorry."

"What? Did I say something amusing?"

His laughter intensified, and now he was holding his sides as the laughter continued to roll out of him.

Nicole was becoming annoyed. "What is so funny?"

He tried to control himself but continued to laugh. "It's not you. It's this whole stupid situation. I need to let you in on somethin'."

"What? What is it that could possibly be so amusing?"

"Nicole, darlin'. My previous job? Well, I was a surgeon."

"Oh my God. I feel like such a fool."

"Oh, honey, don't. You only know me as a cowboy. I told you I raise horses and cattle. I didn't tell you what I did before."

She sat with her mouth open. Finally she hit him hard on the shoulder. "You were a fucking surgeon? Why didn't you tell me?"

"I don't tell anybody. That part of my life is over."

She looked at the top of her leg. "Well, it certainly explains things a bit. And just what kind of surgeon were you, *Dr. Neumann?*"

"I did trauma and cardio-thoracic."

"I'm not sure whether to be angry or amused."

Jack tapped her cup with the back of his finger. "Here. This'll make it more amusing. Don't be angry. It's not your fault. It's mine. I could've said somethin'."

"You certainly could have. Is there anything else I should know?"

Jack looked at her seriously for a moment and then said, "Sometimes I fart while I sleep."

Nicole started laughing. "Oh, lovely. You are a wealth of surprises, aren't you?"

"Yes, ma'am. I aim to keep you on your toes."

She laughed a bit and was about to say something when Jack turned quickly and became serious with a finger held up and said, "Shhh. Listen."

They sat in silence for several minutes. Nicole said, "I don't hear anything."

Jack whispered, "Where's the gun I gave you?"

Nicole leaned over and pulled it from beneath her. Jack pulled it out of the holster, checked it, and slid it back into place. He hooked the holster on the right side of his belt. "It's probably nothin', but better safe than sorry."

"What did you hear?"

"There's somebody out there. Maybe three or four of 'em. They're walkin' this way. We'll find out soon enough."

"What should we do?"

"Sit and wait for 'em."

"Do you think they mean to harm us?"

"No. Probably not."

Off in the distance, they could both hear laughter. Jack stood up. "Oh shit."

"What? What is it?"

"It's Ryan, and he has company."

A few minutes later Ryan walked up to the edge of camp, leading a horse with a girl sitting on top. "Hey, everybody!"

Jack stood up and said, "Where the hell you been?"

"I was out giving away the flyers and telling people about the meeting like you said."

"The meeting was over hours ago."

"Yeah, that's why I came back." He laughed. "This is Brooke. She's a friend of mine, and this is Penny. She's also a friend of mine. Penny is a horse."

"Are you drunk?" Jack asked.

"I don't know if I would call it drunk, we mighta had a little to drink."

Brooke said, "Oh yeah, we're drunk." She leaned to the side as she sat on the horse.

"Guess what?" Ryan asked. "Brooke is from Jefferson City. That's right by where I was at school. We were like neighbors."

Jack felt a hand on his arm. He looked over to see Nicole standing next to him. She quietly said, "Go easy. He's been through an ordeal as well."

Jack walked over to the side of the horse. The girl sitting on top was blond with long hair, about medium height, and wore a short, little black skirt that was hiked up around the top of her thighs showing her panties. A rhinestone-studded denim jacket covered a tight, white t-shirt. "Come on down, darlin'. I'll help you out. I don't want you to get hurt." He held out his arms, and the young lady slid off as he helped her to the ground.

"Hey, Brooke, these are the people I was telling you about. This is Jack—he's kind of a hardass—and this is Nicole. She's nice."

Jack shook the young lady's hand. "Pleased to meet you."

"It's nice to meet you too. Do you guys have anything to eat? I'm like, kind of starving?"

Ryan said, "Yeah! Eating drunk is the best!"

Jack looked over at Nicole. She held out a hand and gently patted the air. He shook his head and, pointing at the horse with his thumb, said, "What's the story with this?"

"Oh! Yeah. That's Penny. Isn't she awesome? I got her today."

"She's somethin' all right. Where'd you get her?"

"A guy rode into town on her from some place called Meezee."

"You mean Meeteetse?"

"Yeah, that might be it. Anyway, he saw me walking and said if I wanted her, I could have her. How awesome is that? He told me I should give her something to drink and then left. I was in the parking lot of a 7-11 so I found a foam cooler and dumped a bunch of Gatorade in there. She drank everything. It was crazy. I bet she went through something like twenty bottles!"

"Son, I'm gonna tie her over in the grass by the museum. We need to keep her away from the other horses till we know she ain't sick."

"She ain't sick—she's awesome. But okay. That's cool. Whatever you say, man."

Jack took off the saddle and bridle and led the horse away.

Nicole said, "Let's see if we can find something for you two to eat."

When Jack got back, Nicole was stirring something in a pot over the fire. "Are you hungry?"

"As a matter of fact, I am. I haven't had a thing all day."

"Why didn't you say something earlier?"

Jack said, "Frankly, I was too lazy to get up and make it."

"I would have made something for you."

"Thanks, but I'm not your worry."

"It's the least I can do to help. Please, next time say something."

"Okay. Deal. What happened to Ding and Dong?"

She looked at him with a crooked smile. "Stop it. They are in Ryan's tent. I believe they have probably passed out."

"So has that girl just joined our little posse?"

Nicole started scooping a plate of chicken and rice out for Jack. "Most likely, yes. I spoke with her a bit. She's very nice. She was here visiting a friend and was planning to fly home yesterday. She is completely alone and ran into Ryan. He helped her out, and now she's a bit taken with him."

"Marvelous."

"What is the horse like?"

"As funny as it may be, I think Ryan might have saved the damn thing's life. The Gatorade was actually a very good idea few people know about. My guess is somebody rode that horse hard all the way from Meeteetse. That's at least thirty miles. He probably thought the thing was dead on its feet, and so he just walked away. Funny he left the saddle, but it ain't exactly the best piece of leather I've ever seen. Anyway, she's hasn't had the best care. Feet are rough, coat is matted, and she's thin. Too thin. Probably full of worms."

"Lovely."

"We'll see how she does over the next couple of days. Maybe a project is what that boy needs."

# 30.

Megan opened her eyes to bright sunlight streaming through her bedroom window. For a few brief seconds, in the fog of morning, she was a teenager again. Dad was probably already outside working on something, and Mom was downstairs reading the paper and drinking her second or third cup of coffee. She started to stretch, and the moment was gone as reality came flooding back to her. She turned onto her back and looked over at Mark as he slept. She remembered the events from last night. The bath, the splash, both times they had sex in the water, the walk back to the house, and both times they had sex in the house. Actually, the last time felt different— more like making love. It was slow, gentle, and thoughtful. The other times were great, but she liked the last one the best. It felt like it meant something. She turned back onto her left side and pushed herself back into him. In response, he turned to his left and wrapped his arm around her. As weird and fucked up as the whole situation was, this was not bad. In fact, it was pretty damn good.

She put her right hand over his as they lay there. She didn't say anything; there was no sense complicating this; she just wanted to enjoy the moment. She thought about him. When

they had first met, he had scared the hell out of her. But it didn't really take long to figure out he wasn't a bad guy; he just needed a little reassurance. At first she had wondered if he wasn't very smart, but after talking to him and spending time together, she realized he was very intelligent, he just didn't know anything. He seemed kind of naive when it came to anything about the outdoors, the farm, hunting, or shooting. But, he could be taught. She was very surprised how quickly he had learned to shoot both the rifle and the pistols. And the bath? That had to be one of the most amazing things she had ever experienced. How in the world had he figured out how to do all that, and in such a short time? That was amazing. He was a little into himself. It was obvious he liked the way he looked, but then again, so did she.

It was his plan, though, that had really started her interest in him. She remembered seeing the possibilities when he mentioned it the other night when they met. If everything was as fucked up as he said it was, and she had no reason to doubt him, then a man with a plan was a good thing. A hot man with a plan was a goddamn gold mine. The way he talked about "taking what he wanted" and "getting everything he deserved" kind of took her back to those times with Billy on the rodeo circuit. Maybe that's why she had fallen so hard for the cowboy. He had promised her the world on a platter. She didn't want to fall for this guy, at least not yet, but you never know.

She felt something growing against her butt cheek as Mark's hand moved up and gently squeezed her breast. Guys were so simple. Let them see a little, say something a little suggestive, or even the right smile, and they would do just about anything. Women, on the other hand, were nothing but a pain. They were always so catty, trying to compete with each other and outdo each other. There was always a hierarchy with women, and you had to know your role. God, she hated that. She reached back with her right hand and let it follow the contour of his side and hip. There was no hierarchy here. She was the woman, this was her man, and she was on top. Come to think of it, that wasn't a

bad idea. She pushed the blankets down, rolled him over onto his back and climbed on top.

Megan looked over the horse's back to see Mark walk out with one of the bags. She asked, "Did you get everything?"

"Yeah. I had to get a little creative, but I think I got it all."

"Are they close to the same weight?"

"About as close as I can get them."

"Good. It's much easier on the horse. If you go get the other one, I'll finish this britchen, and we can start loading."

"What's bitchin'?"

She laughed. "No. Not bitchin', britchen. It's this leather strap that goes behind the horse. I have to adjust it so it fits him right."

"That horse kinda looks like he has the mange or something. Is that normal?"

She laughed again. "Yes that's normal. Hunter is a Red Roan, and he's supposed to look that way. I've got a lot to teach you, don't I?"

"Probably, but I can already tell you that he's a Red Roan, and he has totally bitchin' straps!"

She shook her head. "Just get the other bag."

When Mark returned, he set the bag down and said, "I don't know about these boots."

She asked, "Don't they fit?"

"Yeah, I guess so. They feel weird. You know?"

"When we get to Buffalo, you can find a new pair that fit. You only have to wear them when we are riding, and if it wasn't important, I wouldn't make you do it."

"So, what's the deal with the boots again?"

"If something would happen and you fell off the horse, your foot needs to slip out of the stirrup. You wouldn't want the horse to drag you by your leg, would you?"

"Might be better than wearing somebody else's shoes. What's up with the weird saddle? It looks uncomfortable."

She talked as she continued to work. "This one is called a sawbuck. This is what we attach the panniers to. My dad bought

this stuff a few years ago to use elk hunting. These are really nice. My mom was mad because he spent so much money. If he knew I was using them now, he'd…" She trailed off.

Mark didn't want her to start feeling bad, so he quickly changed the subject. "So which one am I going to be riding?"

"You'll be on Fred, the one you rode the other day. He's pretty laid back."

"So you get the brown one with the black hair?"

"She's chestnut colored. That's Chic."

"What's up with the saddle on Fred? Why doesn't it have the bumps in the front like yours does?"

"That's my dad's saddle. It will probably fit you better. It's called a Wade. I can put some bumps on there if you want?"

"What are they for?"

"They help you stay on if the horse bucks."

"Is he gonna buck?"

"Fred? No way. He'd probably die before he bucked."

"Then I guess I don't need 'em. Hey, weren't you gonna get a gun?"

"Yeah," she said, finishing up. "I'm gonna go get it now. Did you remember the bags with the handy stuff?"

"They're sitting right next to my rifle. Ready to go. Is that stuff for the saddlebags?"

"Yep. It goes in here," she said, pointing to the bags behind his saddle. "Easy to get to."

Mark stood by the horses, waiting. Megan came out of the house wearing a jacket and a red belt with a pistol in a futuristic holster and three magazines pointed back at an angle. "Whoa. That looks awesome! What kind of gun is that?"

"I had to find one that would be fast to use if I need it and in the same caliber as what you have. We don't want to carry fourteen different kinds of ammo around with us. This is one of my dad's race guns." She pulled the pistol out of the holster and handed it to him. "This one is an STI Legend."

"That is the coolest thing I've ever seen! You are totally badass!"

"You think?"

"Oh yeah. Why is the grip so big?"

"It's a double stack. This one holds twelve rounds in the magazine and one in the barrel."

"What's up with that holster?"

"It's for competition. It's very fast."

"I bet it is! Wanna trade?"

"No."

"I had to ask."

"I know."

Mark lifted the bags as Megan tied them onto the sawbuck. She checked everything over and then checked it again. She set Mark's rifle on top of the sawbuck frame and tied it in place. "We can get to this pretty quick if we have to."

"So you think we are going to have to pull guns and start blasting?"

"I hope not. I just don't want to get caught needing something in a hurry and not being able to get it. Are you ready to go?"

"Yeah, I think so."

Megan climbed up on her horse and looked at the pasture. Joey, an old gray, stood by the gate starring at them. "I feel so bad for him. I wish there was a way to let him out, but he would just follow us."

Mark looked over at the horse. "Why would he follow?"

"Because we are taking his herd away. Everybody is losing their herd these days."

"So, if he could get out in a day or so, that would be cool?"

"Yeah. He could get to the barn, where there is enough hay to last him for the next three winters."

Mark thought for a moment. "Hang on. I got an idea." He ran into the house and then came out a few seconds later. Megan watched as he removed the pin holding the gate closed and then cut something with a small knife. He jammed the object into the slot where the pin normally sat from the bottom. He walked back, grinning. "That ought to work."

"What did you do?"

"I took a slice of apple and put it in place of the pin. If the mice or birds don't get it, it will just dry out and fall out. That's why I stuck it in the bottom."

"An apple? Joey will just try to get it himself."

"Yeah, but he can't reach it. He might keep trying for it. When it falls out, we'll be long gone."

Megan smiled from the top of her horse. "That's a terrific idea. I'd kiss you if I could reach you."

"I'll take a rain check."

As they rode out of the yard and turned west onto the gravel road, Megan looked back over her shoulder. She was leaving home again. When she was young, she couldn't wait to leave. In the last few years, it was good to be home once in a while, but it was nice to be on her own in the city too. Now, leaving felt terrible. She felt as though she was leaving everything she had ever cared about—her life—behind her. She told Mark, "Just ride. Don't try to steer him. He'll just follow behind. If you see anything come loose on Hunter, yell at me."

Mark knew she felt bad. He could hear it in her voice and decided to give her some space. He let his horse follow.

Megan pushed Chic out front and set a nice pace for them. She looked back to make sure Mark was doing okay and then let the emotions have her.

# 31.

Nicole walked out of her tent into bright sunshine. She saw Jack sitting at the picnic table with a cup of coffee and a pad of paper next to him and said, "Are there no clouds in Wyoming?"

Jack turned and said, "Mornin'. Not much like England, is it?"

"No, and thank God. I certainly do not miss the dreariness. It's dreadful nearly all the time. This, on the other hand, is wonderful."

"You like Wyoming?"

She poured herself a cup of coffee from the pot hanging over the fire. "I must confess that if it were not for the flare, I don't think I ever would have visited. I would have never had a reason." She sat down across from him. "Tell me, have you ever had an experience when it was as though your eyes were opened all at once? The first time something like that happened to me I was taking a scuba diving lesson on the Great Barrier Reef. I couldn't believe the color and beauty of all the fish and life on the reef. It was as though I had lived my entire life with this vastly different and beautiful world right next door, and I had never known it was there."

"Yep, I know what you're talkin' about. Same thing happened to me the first time I came to Yellowstone."

"I feel that same way now, but it's different. It's much slower and interspersed with this awful tragedy. I feel a bit robbed. I wish I would have known this was here beforehand. I would have liked to have seen this area before things went so badly."

"If you like it now, you would have loved it before."

"It's difficult to describe. Things here seem so—I don't know—real. Perhaps it is nothing more than the clear air."

"No. I think you're right. Things here are very real. Life is different. There is none of the falseness of the urban and suburban areas I have ever lived in. It's the people that make it this way. They're more relaxed and laid back, but they work hard and earn what they have. In general, they don't give a damn about the car you drive, what kind of clothes you're wearin', or whether or not you happened to shave this mornin'. But they do care if your word is worth somethin'. I have seen million dollar deals happen on nothin' more than a man's handshake."

"Is that why you moved here?"

"Yes, ma'am, it is. I prefer life this way."

Nicole though about what he had said while she sipped coffee, holding her hands around the cup for the warmth. "I interrupted you when I came out. May I ask what you were doing?"

"You may. I was plannin' out the next day or so. Makin' a couple lists."

"Anything exciting on our agenda for the day?"

"This mornin' we need to run by the hospital quick. I should check on the C-section patient from last night. Then we'll head over to the museum. I need to talk to a man about a wagon."

"Is that a code for something?"

Jack looked confused. "Code?"

"Well, I have heard someone say they 'need to talk to a man about a horse,' and it was code for using the bathroom."

Jack laughed. "Nope. I do, in fact, need to talk to a man about a wagon."

"What is the wagon for?"

"My horses are also taught how to pull. Since I have about a hundred fifty miles to go before I get home, I figured it would be a lot easier going if I could use a wagon. Easier to haul all this gear."

"That is interesting. Have you considered staying here?"

"Oh, I probably need to get home."

"This is a very nice area. You realize they could use a man with your talents around here."

"Ahh. Now I know why Neil was talkin' to you last night. He wants you to convince me to stay."

"He already asked you?"

"Twice. I turned him down both times."

"He did make several points that seemed really quite reasonable."

"I bet he did. I've known Neil a long time. He's a long-range thinker and always has somethin' planned for the future. This particular plan is to turn Cody into a regional medical center. He thinks he needs me to do it. Problem is, it's not part of my plan."

"He said the trip would be quite dangerous."

"Not if I get out of here before the snow hits the Bighorns. A hundred fifty miles is no big deal in a pickup, but it's gonna take me the better part of a week with horses. The earlier I get going, the easier the trip will be."

"I thought you liked Cody?"

"I do."

"Then why wouldn't you stay?"

Jack sighed. "Two major reasons and a smaller third. First, as sure as I know I'm sittin' here now, I know if Annie made it through this disaster, she'll be headed home. She's smart enough and tough enough to make it too. I have to be there when she gets home. The second reason is Miguel. I can't leave him hangin' out in the breeze. If he's dead, he deserves a proper burial. If he's alive, it'll take both of us to keep the ranch goin'."

"You said there was a third reason."

"I did. I guess it's 'cause it's home. It's where my good boots are at, where my favorite readin' chair is, and where my pillow feels just right. It's where my wife is buried, and I kinda had plans to lie next to her."

Nicole quietly said, "I see."

"I know it's not fair. You're home is thousands of miles away across an entire ocean. If it was closer, I'd do about anything to get you there."

"No. It's not that."

"Well, what is it?"

Nicole sat quietly, not knowing how to answer him. "Let's discuss something else."

"No. You have somethin' on your mind, and it appears we need to get this cleared up."

She stared at the cup in her hands as she began to speak. "All right. I will tell you. The other night I was deposited into this strange world with absolutely no way to get home. In fact, my home is most likely gone. The people who were stranded with me after the crash left without me, leaving me completely alone. But then, a wonderful, caring man rescued me, took care of my injuries, and walked several miles so that I might ride his horse. He brought me to a town that has been largely destroyed, but found a place for me to sleep, fed me, made sure that I was safe, and he talked with me. He cares about the things I have to say. You see, I have never met a man like him before. He is courageous and confident, yet he is warm and sensitive. He cares about the same things that I care about, and he understands me better than nearly anyone I have ever known. The problem is, I've grown quite fond of this man, and now he is telling me he is going to leave."

Jack tipped his coffee cup back and drained the last swallow. Without saying a word, he stood up, refilled his cup, and, as he came back to the table, he said, "I guess if we're truth-tellin', then I better come clean as well." He sat back down across from her.

"A long time ago, I met a woman. She was the one. She put up with a lot of my shit and stuck with me through some of

the roughest times anyone should ever have to deal with. She damn near forced me to leave Texas and move up here, and in so doing gave me the life I always wanted. She died a few years ago, and it was my fault. I was left alone and deserved to be. I decided to keep it that way.

"So, the other day I met a young lady by chance. I didn't go lookin' for anything. She's very intelligent. Keeps me on my toes. She has a grace and peace about her that I haven't seen in a long time. She is funny and warm and caring. Her beauty is simply astounding. It takes my breath away. When she smiles, the whole world around her lights up, and I swear the angels start to sing. A Wyoming sunset pales by comparison. Trouble is, she's young. She has her whole life ahead of her, and she needs some young man who can provide the adventure, the fun, the passion, and the excitement she deserves. She needs somebody who will be there to hold her hand when she's old, not some old goat who she has to help out of a rockin' chair when she is still in her prime.

"Nicole, I have to go home. I'll make sure you're squared away before I leave. If you have to be stuck someplace, it's best to be somewhere that's gonna make it through the rough days ahead. There're some good leaders here. They're gonna get things going again, and Cody will come out of all this just fine. This is a good place to be stuck."

"Shouldn't I be the judge of that?"

"Of course. But I want you to make a wise decision."

"And a wise decision in your estimation is to stay here, the first place I have seen since the flare."

"It is."

"And what if I disagree? What if I decide that I simply do not have enough information to decide to stay here and would like to see something else before I decide where I should stay?"

"I understand you're upset..."

She stood. "No, Dr. Neumann, I am not upset, as you delicately put it. I am angry as hell. I do not appreciate someone making enormous decisions on my behalf without asking my opinion." She threw the remaining contents of her cup on the

ground, slammed the metal cup on the table, and stormed back to her tent.

Jack sat alone at the table, thinking about the conversation. From behind him he heard, "Whoa, is she pissed. What'd you do, call her the wrong name? I did that once." The kid sat down at the table where Nicole had been.

"Mornin', Ryan. How's your head?"

"Eh. You know."

"There's coffee on the fire."

"Thanks. Maybe in a bit."

Jack smiled. "Did you hear that bear last night?"

"Bear?" Ryan asked with a surprised look.

"Yeah. I think it was about three or so in the mornin'. I heard an awful growlin' just outside the tent."

Ryan's head sank. "Shut up."

"You might want to clean that barf up or put somethin' over it before somebody steps in it."

"All right."

Jack stood. "I have to go to the hospital. Tell Nicole I'll be back in a bit. I think she wanted to go with me on a couple of errands."

"The hospital? Are you okay?"

"Yep. I'm just fine. Just tell her, will ya?"

"Yeah." He groaned, laying his head on the table.

# 32.

Jack came back to camp about an hour later. Nicole had Dingo and Marlena tied to the fence, and she was brushing them down. He asked, "Are we talkin'?"

"Yes, of course we are talking. I don't believe in the silent treatment. There is no sense in it."

"Sometimes people need a little space to figure things out."

She stopped brushing and turned toward him. "Of course they do, and I need some time to think about this situation and our disagreement, but that does not mean we shouldn't talk about anything at all. Nor does it mean that I don't want to go with you today."

"Good. Looks like you're gettin' around better."

"My ankle is much better. Thank you. How is your patient?"

"Considering it's the first time I have ever done anything like that before, I'd say she's doin' just fine."

"And her child?"

"Bouncin' baby girl. Just a squallerin' and hollerin' like they do." He winked at her. She reluctantly smiled.

An hour later they pulled up to a stop in front of a small store on the main street in town. A red awning said Custom

Cowboy and hung as it always had. The broken windows and missing door were the only signs anything was unusual. As Jack walked through the door, a pretty, middle-aged woman came out of a back room. She wore a beaded western blouse, jeans with boots, and her hair was fixed perfectly. She said, "Jack Neumann. I guess miracles never cease."

Jack said, "Donna. How ya doin'?"

"I heard you were in town. Some say you shot a man in front of the Piggly Wiggly yesterday."

"It wasn't quite as simple as all that."

"So I heard. They're callin' you a hero. Say you saved at least one man's life."

"Again, it wasn't quite that simple."

"Not the way I heard it. They say the old guy pulled up on a man runnin' toward the store, and you shot the bastard right between the eyes from fifty feet away. Dropped him deader than disco."

"More like twenty feet."

"Makes no difference to me, so long as he's dead. Who's this with you?"

"This is Nicole Meredith." He hesitated and then added, "She's with me."

Donna stuck out her hand to Nicole. "It's very nice to meet you. Any friend of Jack's is always welcome here."

Nicole said, "Thank you. It's very nice to meet you too."

Donna turned to Jack and gave him a wry smile. "And they told me you were off the market. Hell, I woulda thrown Bill out years ago if I knew you were shoppin'."

He asked, "How's Bill doin'?"

Donna's expression changed suddenly. In an instant, the smile was gone and sadness filled her. Her hand came to her mouth as she said, "I lost him."

"My God, Donna. I am so sorry to hear that."

"I can't talk about it," she said as tears filled her eyes. "I keep forgettin' that everything's changed and he's gone. It was quick. He didn't know a thing. I just miss him so much."

Jack walked to her and held her tight. "It's okay. You have a lot of friends here. He was a good friend and a good man."

"Thank you, thank you." After a moment she let go of him and said, "Okay. Enough of that foolishness. You two came in here for somethin'." She sniffed. "What can I do for you?"

Jack said, "I need to get Nicole set up from head to toe. Trouble is I don't have any way to pay you right off."

Donna waved her hand. "We can worry about that later, or never. Makes no difference to me."

"It makes a difference to me. I *will* make it right with you."

She waved her hand at him again as she took Nicole's hand. "Come on, darlin'. We got some shoppin' to do."

An hour later Jack still sat on a bench in the small, wood, hat-fitting room, leafing through a book on the history of Yellowstone. He could hear the women laughing and carrying on in the back of the store. He smiled and turned another page. From the front of the store, he heard the quiet sound of crunching glass. He set the book down next to him, took off his hat, and leaned forward to peer around the corner of the door. A young man was walking in carefully and quietly with a single-action revolver held out in front of him.

Jack stood slowly and quietly as he slid the big revolver out of the leather holster from under his left arm. He was careful to stay behind the frame of the doorway. The kid was focused on the sound of the women in back as he stepped quietly around a display case of bracelets and pendants. As he passed the hat-fitting room, Jack stepped out behind him and pressed the barrel of the big gun against the back of his neck as he cocked the hammer.

In nearly a whisper, he said, "Son, what you feel is the barrel of a 460 Smith & Wesson XVR revolver. I've killed a grizzly with this before, so I know it works. It takes just a hair over two pounds of pressure from my finger to kick this off. If I do, it will completely separate your head from the rest of your body. Now, you have a choice. You can either set that peashooter on the ground and live another day, or try somethin' stupid, and I will liberate your soul. What's it gonna be?"

207

The young man slowly put his hands out to the sides and bent down very slowly. Jack moved with him, keeping the barrel pressed tightly against his neck. The kid set the pistol on the ground and slowly stood. Jack said, "Good choice. I wasn't exactly lookin' forward to cleanin' your brains off the walls today, but I'd'a done it. Now, let's take a little walk outside." As they walked out the front door, Jack could again hear Nicole and Donna laughing in the back room.

On the sidewalk Jack pressed the kid up against the brick wall and searched his pockets. He found a big knife attached to the kid's belt and threw it on the ground. From behind him he heard, "Hey, Jack! Whatcha got there?"

He turned to see Colonel Robert McNeilus with three other men walking toward him. Jack said, "Mornin', Robby. This idiot was fixin' to loot the place with people still in it. I reckon he figured it'd be a lot easier than how she turned out."

"Want us to take him for ya?"

"Sure."

"What happened?"

"He came in with a gun. It's still on the floor inside. He didn't see me waiting in the hat room."

"Is Donna in there?"

"Yep."

"Did she see everything?"

"Nope. She's still helping a customer."

"So I have your word on it."

"Yep."

"Good enough for me. I guess we're done. This is the second one today. Thanks for doin' the heavy lifting for us."

"No problem. I'll see you later." Jack walked back into the store and sat down in the hat room again. He picked up the book. Things have certainly changed, he thought.

A few minutes later, Donna called for Jack to come down to the basement. She said, "I want to show you somethin'. Bill was working on this when he...well, when everything changed."

A saddle sat on a stand in the middle of the room with the right fender out and resting on a small, portable, marble table. The saddle looked nearly new and was made of rich, well-oiled, dark leather with flowered tooling covering almost all of it. A light buckskin padded seat was pattern stitched and accented the rich leather. Donna said, "This is a fifteen-inch A-fork Bill made and sold last summer to a customer in California. They sent it back and wanted some initials on the fenders. I don't know where Bill was gonna put 'em. The thing of it is, they don't have the saddle paid off yet, and I have no way to collect on it or send it back for that matter. Nicole can have it if you think it'll work."

"I think it's beautiful." He turned to Nicole. "But, it's up to her. What do you think?"

"I think it is positively incredible, a work of art, but I don't know the first thing about saddles."

"An A-fork like this will fit about any of our horses just fine. A lot of riders in Wyoming use 'em because you can sit in it all day and still be comfortable. Next thing is you need to find out if it fits you. Jump up on it."

Nicole sat in the saddle as Donna and Jack adjusted the stirrups for her. She said, "This is wonderful."

Jack watched as she bounced up and down a little and then sat and rocked her hips back and forth. He stepped back, eyes wide. "Yep. That'll do."

Jack put a new saddle pad, the saddle, saddlebags, and bridle on Dingo while Nicole and Donna bagged the rest of the items. When he walked back inside, Donna pointed to a gun on the counter and said, "What's this?"

"It's a gun—a .357. Some kid dropped it off. It's yours now."

"I don't need this."

"Yes, you do. Trust me. Keep it with you. Better yet, get one of Bill's holsters, strap it on, and don't take it off."

Nicole studied him and said, "There seems to be a bit more here than what we are being told. Am I right?"

Jack smiled a little. "You might be."

Nicole said, "Donna, if I were you, I believe I would take this advice to heart."

"I think I will. Nicole, it's been a pleasure."

"No, no. The pleasure has been all mine."

Donna smiled and turned to Jack. "I could just listen to her talk all day. Jack, you take care of that girl. She's a keeper."

Jack shot a look and a half smile at Nicole, who just shrugged her shoulders and smiled back at him. He stuck out his hand to Donna. "Thanks. I got a rough idea what I'm into you for."

"You don't owe me a thing. Just bring that girl back, so I can tell her how to get the upper hand with you."

"I think she's already got that figured out."

# 33.

Jack and Nicole walked the horses through the main street of Cody, carefully guiding them around the burned-out remains of cars and random debris that littered the town.

"Where are we off to now?" Nicole asked.

"We have to head back and unload. The trunk is full," Jack said as he patted the overfilled bag tied to the back of his saddle. "Then, off on another errand."

"Will this be as much fun as the last?"

"Depends on what you consider fun."

She smiled. "Shopping was fun."

"Judgin' by the size of these bags, I'd say it was."

As they rounded the next bend, they could see camp in the little park across from the high school. Jack mumbled, "What the hell," as he looked.

"What is it?" Nicole asked, sensing Jack's concern.

"Is that a body on the picnic table?"

Nicole looked and said. "Yes, it is. That's Brooke."

"Why's she on the table?"

"I'm not sure. Listen, Jack, she is a young girl who has been through quite an ordeal. She is alone, and, like many of us, she is completely out of her element."

"I gathered that last night. Why are you tellin' me this?"

"I'm simply asking that you go easy on her. Oh, and another thing. I believe she is really quite enamored with Ryan, so you might want to, you know, give him some space."

Jack said, "So, you don't think I can handle this."

"I think you can handle it just fine. In fact, I'm sure of it. I just think things might go a bit easier if you consider my suggestions, is all."

Jack smiled and shook his head.

"What? Do you think this is amusing?"

"You kinda of remind me of somebody I used to know."

"So am I to assume that someone has made a suggestion to you like this before?"

"You might." He pulled Marlena to a stop and climbed down. Nicole pulled Dingo alongside him and did the same. Jack tied both horses to the fence and began untying the packages.

The girl sat up on the table. "Hey!"

Jacked glanced at Nicole and then said hello to the girl. He filled his arms and walked into camp.

Brooke got down from the table and said, "Hi. I'm Brooke. Are you Jack? I don't think we've met. Ryan told me all about you yesterday. He said that you helped him out the other day. Oh my God. Is that a gun under your arm? Wow. That thing is huge. A friend of mine at school has one too, but it's a lot smaller. I was out here visiting another friend of mine from college when everything went like totally freaky. Well, actually Jenna was more like a friend of a friend, but it's not like that's important, right? I knew her pretty good too. She was actually two years ahead of me at school. She was out here doing an internship with the Western Art Museum. Have you been there? It's not really my thing, but I thought it was pretty cool anyway. So, are you like a real cowboy?"

Jack stood looking at her with his arms full. He didn't know where to start. After a few uncomfortable seconds, he said, "It's nice to meet you." He started walking toward the tent again. From behind him Brook said, "Ryan went to go look at his

horse. He asked me if I wanted to go, but I was like, eh, I kinda don't feel so good, you know? I mighta had a little bit too much to drink last night." Jack pushed the flap aside and walked inside the tent.

A few minutes later, Nicole came in carrying the rest of the bags, smiling. "So, what do you think?"

"Is she gonna be like that all the time?"

"She's a bit nervous."

"She makes me dizzy."

Nicole laughed. "Oh, stop."

"Last night she called me a hardass."

"I'm sure she doesn't remember a thing."

"I'm not surprised. Where do you want all this stuff?"

"Oh. So sorry. Just put it down anywhere. I'll sort it all out later."

Jack set everything down and headed back to the tent door. "I'll wait for you out here, and we can leave when you're ready." He paused. "Please don't let me wait too long," he said and winked at her.

Outside, Ryan was walking back as Jack came out of Nicole's tent. He said, "Hey, hey! Did you get some?"

Jack looked at him, confused. "We got some clothes and gear for Nicole. I just helped her carry it in. How's your horse?"

Ryan rolled his eyes and then brightened. "Penny? She's awesome! She's like going to town on that grass over there!"

"That's what they do. By the way, I want to let you know you probably saved that horse's life yesterday."

Ryan looked shocked. "I did?"

Brooke said, "He did? Really? Like, how'd he do that?"

"Gatorade. That feller you got the horse from probably rode her into the ground comin' up here from Meeteetse. Left her for dead with you. The Gatorade not only rehydrated her but gave her some salt and a little sugar. That was smart. Just don't do it again, unless she's severely dehydrated."

"I saved her? Wow. Cool."

Brooke said, "That's totally cool. You're like that rescue guy on *Animal Planet.*"

Ryan smiled.

Jack noticed Nicole coming out of her tent. He said, "Ryan, we're gonna run a few more errands. I gotta couple of things for you to do this afternoon, if you have time."

"Maybe. What?"

"If you're gonna ride that horse, you need a pair of boots. Brooke, you'll need some as well. Can't ride with those shoes. You might get hung up. There's a place in town where you should be able to find some."

"How do I pay? All the credit card machines don't work anymore."

"Trade if you can. If not, tell 'em you're with me. They know me in there. You might want to find some more clothes too. Warm ones. It's been unseasonably warm lately, but I bet it'll cool off again before long."

Brooke said, "Ooh, I want to find some boots with rhinestones on them."

Ryan asked, "Is that what you guys are doing?"

Jack started walking to his horse. "Among other things, yes. We should be back by dinnertime." He stopped and said, "I'd appreciate it if you two were here tonight. There's a few things we need to talk about."

"Uh-oh," Brooke said.

"Nope. Nothin' bad. We just need to get some plans made."

# 34.

It was late afternoon, and they had been following I-90 west for the last five hours. It seemed like an eternity to Mark. His ass was sore, he was tired of riding, and he was tired of literally looking at a horse's ass in front of him. The only excitement was when Hunter, who plodded along in front of him with all their gear, took a shit, which he seemed to do with exceptional regularity. He squeezed his legs a little, and Fred's head came up as if he suddenly remembered something. The horse sped up, pulled to the left, and walked past Hunter. Awesome! When he was alongside Megan, he pulled back on the reins just a little, and the horse slowed to match the pace of Chic. "Hey. How are you doing?" He had watched her carefully when they first left and could tell she had been crying. He had given her plenty of space.

"I'm okay. How are you doing?"

"My ass is killing me. How far do you think we've gone?"

"I don't know. Maybe twenty miles. Maybe."

"Twenty miles is all? I can't believe people used to get around this way."

"That's why they didn't go very far."

"I saw a sign back there for Barber Creek Road. What do you think about stopping for the night?"

"If there's actually a creek, yeah, it's probably a good idea. We need to water these horses."

"Maybe we can find a house or a ranch or something."

"Sure. Sounds good."

"Red told me it's always better to stay inside a building when you can. It's easier to defend. He also said that I should scout the place out before I go in. Got to know if there is somebody there, where the exits are, and where trouble might come from."

"Wow. You're pretty serious about this aren't you?"

"Hey, I busted you, didn't I?"

She smiled at him. "Yeah, I guess you did. I seem to recall that you were thinking about raping me."

"I still am."

"Isn't it better with a willing participant?"

"I don't know. I haven't tried it the other way yet." Mark grinned at her.

She gave him a devilish look. "Maybe I will tie you up and have my way with you."

"Maybe you will."

A half hour later, they rode down the Barber Creek Road exit to find an old, abandoned gas station. Twisted metal lay everywhere, and the remaining building was about to fall over. Megan suggested they follow a small gravel road to the west that seemed to parallel the interstate. A few minutes later, they spotted a group of buildings ahead. Mark insisted she stay back with the horses while he checked the place out. After another half hour, he waved her up to him.

"I can see a house and a bunch of other buildings. Probably a cattle ranch. The place looks quiet. There's no movement at all. I can see water near the back of the house. I'm not sure if it's a creek or a pond."

"Sounds perfect. Let's go."

"Let me go in first with the rifle. You can tie up the horses, and I'll come and get you when I know it's safe."

"Seems like overkill to me, but whatever." She watched as Mark held the assault rifle in both hands to his chest. He ran low with his head held down toward the house and quickly pressed his back up against the building. He maneuvered along the wall like a commando in a bad action movie. When he made it to the door, he held the rifle in his right arm pointed forward and with his left, carefully opened the door. He disappeared inside.

Megan tied the horses to a section of welded pipe fence that appeared to be intact. She followed the fence with her eyes and was interested to see how the fence appeared normal in some areas and in others was twisted, upturned, and bent. In a few areas, it was completely missing. She walked to the side of Hunter and started to loosen the rigging that held the bag on the right side. She hadn't mentioned anything to Mark, but her ass was sore too. She hadn't ridden much in a long time. These days her butt was more used to the soft leather office chair behind her desk overlooking West 55th Street in Manhattan than it was a to a hard leather saddle. When the bag was loose, she let it slide into her arms as she pulled it away from the sawbuck. It wasn't terribly heavy, but it would have been a lot easier to let some doorman carry it in. She carried it behind the horses and set it down hard. She stepped between Chic and Hunter to loosen the other side. As she started working on the straps, Chic stepped to the side, squishing Megan between her and the bag. "Ouch, dammit!" She elbowed the mare, convincing her to step back. As she pulled on the buckle and tried to dig the clasp out of the strap, it caught her nail and broke it. "Fuck!" She pulled her hand away and sucked on the fingernail. Megan never had great nails, but these weren't bad for the first time in a long time, and besides, she had spent nearly seventy-five dollars on the French manicure in Manhattan. Now they were broke, and she would probably never have nice nails again. Damn it! Why does everything have to be so hard

all the time? She started working on the strap again and just managed to get it loose when she heard Mark.

"Hey! Megan? Where are you?"

She pulled the bag off the sawbuck and hoisted it in her arms over to where the other one lay. "I'm right here. What do you want?"

Mark jogged over to her. "You better come see this."

"What? Can't you just tell me?"

"There's a guy in there."

She stopped and looked at him in surprise. "What?"

"You heard me. I'm not sure what to do. You better come see this."

She followed him as he led the way to the house. "This better be important."

He looked back at her but continued leading the way into the house.

They walked through a living room that smelled a little stale but looked pretty much average, with the required, dated couch, recliner, and TV in the typical spots. Mark continued on through a small dining room and into the kitchen. An older man sat on the floor, leaning up against the cabinets under the sink. A huge piece of spiraled, partially painted steel was wrapped around and partially through his abdomen. Blood covered his pants and the floor.

"Oh shit!" Megan gasped, as she saw the man. She instinctively put a hand to her mouth.

"He's still alive," Mark said. "I think that's part of the fridge wrapped around him."

She looked carefully and could see that, yes, he did appear to be breathing. "What do you want me to do?"

"I don't know," Mark said, shrugging his shoulders. "What do you want me to do?"

She motioned him to follow her as she made her way back out of the house. Once they were on the step, she said in a low voice, "What are we gonna do with him?"

Mark shrugged again. "Hell if I know."

"Is there anybody else around?"

"No. And I checked everything. Know any first aid?"

"First aid? Fuck, this guy needs a hospital. I don't think first aide is gonna help anything. Shit. Well, we can't take him with us."

"Yeah, I kinda figured that too."

"Besides, there is no hospital in Gillette anymore."

"Yeah."

"And there is no way to get him to Buffalo. We have at least two solid days of riding. Maybe three."

"That's what I thought."

"We gotta put him out of his misery. You gotta shoot him."

Mark was shocked. "What?"

"You heard me. Just shoot him. It's what we would do to a sick cow or a horse that broke its leg. The guy is just lying there suffering."

"Why me?"

"Because you are the man. Besides, you were the one who was so tough saying how he was just going to take what he wanted."

"Yeah, but...," he trailed off.

"You're not going to puss out on me?"

Mark paused for a second and then said, "No. Fuck. This is no big deal, right? Like you said, the guy is suffering. I'm doing him a favor."

Mark walked back into the house, this time with his pistol in hand. Megan waited outside on the step, quietly listening.

A shot rang out. Then she heard Mark saying, "Oh. Oh, fuck. Oh." A second shot then slammed through the late afternoon. Megan walked back into the house. In the kitchen she could see the man's legs twitching, and he was no longer leaning against the cabinet. Blood, hair, and some other stuff were sprayed over the floor and cabinets to the side of where he had sat. She looked at Mark, who looked pale, and asked, "What happened?"

"After the first shot, he started flopping all over the place and doing this weird gasping thing, so I shot him again."

"That did it?"

"I guess. The whole thing didn't last too long, but it was fuckin' weird. Kinda sicked me out."

"Wow. That sounds bad. Sorry. Are you going to drag him outside?"

"Yeah. I guess. I'll take him out the kitchen door if you hold it."

"Okay."

Mark grabbed the man by his well-worn boots and started pulling him across the linoleum floor toward the door. The twisted metal caught on one of the cabinets and pushed open the slice in the man's abdomen a little. Mark looked away quickly. The metal then slid free as he continued to pull. He tried not to look at the man's face and noticed Megan looking away as he pulled the man through the door and out into the back yard.

That night they pulled a mattress from one of the bedrooms and laid it on the living room floor. Megan had found a clean sheet and a couple of blankets in a closet and made the bed for them. The lantern sat on a coffee table behind them and shed a warm light as they passed a bottle of sherry back and forth. They had both been quiet all evening.

Mark said, "You know, killing that guy wasn't such a big deal. I mean it was gross, and I didn't expect him to start flopping like that, but otherwise, you know, it wasn't so hard."

Megan looked at him. "You did the right thing. He was just going to suffer until he died anyway. You just shortened the suffering part. That's all."

"Did you ever see anybody die before?"

"I saw a guy get trampled by a bull at a rodeo. Later we heard that he died."

"Man, I have seen a lot of dead bodies in the last couple of days. I never saw one before everything went nuts. This was the first time I actually saw somebody die, you know?"

"Yeah."

"I saw a guy shoot his dog once. It was kinda like that."

Megan asked, "Why did he shoot the dog?"

"It had cancer, and he couldn't afford the vet bills, so we took it way out of town, and he shot it. I had to bury it 'cause he was so torn up."

Megan took a drink from the bottle and asked, "Did you see your girlfriend die?"

"No. She was dead when I got there."

"How did she die?"

"Curling iron."

"Curling iron? I can see getting burned, but not killing somebody."

"It was sticking out of her neck."

"Oh. Shit. Sorry."

"Yeah, it was bad. I saw a bunch of people that looked like nothing was wrong with them. You know? They were just lying there dead. It's like they just fell over. I know I passed out for a while, but I woke up again."

"So did I. I told you I woke up in the grass."

"I remember."

"So, like, what did you do when you saw your girlfriend?"

Mark took a drink. "Ah, I don't know. It was complicated."

Megan sat up a little more. "What do you mean, *complicated*?"

"Well, we had this huge fight. She had bought a bunch of stuff again, and we started fighting about that."

"Why did you fight about that? I mean she should be able to go shopping if she wants?"

"She didn't have a job. Once in a while would have been fine, but we had these huge credit card bills, and she just kept on buying stuff she didn't need. Anyway, I asked her for the receipt. I wanted to know how much she had spent, and she wouldn't show it to me. So, I was going to get on the computer and see how much the credit card was charged. That's when I found out she was cheating on me. She had left a chat window open."

"Oh shit. What did you do?"

"We argued for a while, and I told her to get out. Then I left. She called me later and told me how sorry she was and on and on and on. So I told her she could stay. That's when

everything went crazy. I had to walk home. When I finally got there, I found her on the floor, and she had written me a note. She changed her mind and wrote some pretty mean things."

"Really? Like what did she say?"

"I don't really want to talk about it. Let's just say it sounded like her new boyfriend decided to let her move in, and she was pretty cruel. She called me a bunch of names and things like that."

"Oh my God. What did you do?"

"Nothing."

Megan whacked him playfully on the shoulder. "Oh bullshit. You did something."

After a few seconds he said, "I stuffed the note up her ass."

"Really?"

Mark smiled. "Yeah, really."

"You mean you pulled down her pants and literally stuffed the note in her butt hole?"

"Yeah."

Megan leaned back and started laughing. "That's awesome!" She laughed even harder. "That's totally awesome! I wish I could have been there to see that."

"You think so?"

"I totally think so!" Megan said, still laughing a little. "After what she did to you, she deserved it."

They lay there quietly for a few minutes, and then Megan said, "I got something for you, but you have to close your eyes."

"What?"

"Just sit up, close your eyes, and do what I say."

Mark sat straight up and closed his eyes.

Megan wrapped something around his head and tied it in the back. He opened his eyes but could see nothing but blackness. He heard her say, "Put your arms together in front of you." He did and felt her wrap a length of duct tape around them. A few seconds later, she wrapped duct tape around his ankles. "Okay, big boy. You're mine now. You are going to do what I want, when I want it, and you're going to love every second of it."

# 35.

Everybody had finished eating as the sun was starting to set on the western horizon. After the dishes were cleaned up, Jack called a meeting. They had all sat down when Ryan asked, "So what's the big meeting about?"

Jack said, "I have a few things for ya, and we all need to be on the same page about a few things. First, how'd your shoppin' go today?"

Brooke said, "I got like four new pairs of jeans. They're really kind of blah. Not something I would normally wear, but I think they fit okay. I got a couple of tops too. The selection was like unbelievably limited. Do you know that almost everything in town is like, Western wear? Seriously. What am I going to do with that? What if I want something, you know, a little more hip?"

Jack cut in, "How 'bout the boots?"

"Oh my God!" Brooke said. "I found the cutest pair of boots today. They are kinda purple and snakeskin; only they were a little bit too big. I had the lady even try to find some in the back, but she said they were special order. I asked how long it would take to get some in, but she didn't know, so I had to go

with a different pair that are zebra-striped. See?" She held a foot in the air with a wild black-and-white pattern.

"Those are sure somethin'," Jack said. "Ryan, how 'bout you?"

"Yeah, I found some. The lady said they were made of python skin. They are pretty comfortable."

Brooke said, "Nicole, what did you get?"

Nicole held up her foot. She wore a brown boot that was stitched with little flowers and beads across the toe, and the pattern then repeated on the shaft. The boots looked as though they had been carefully broken in, but also looked new.

"Oh my God!" Brooke said, "Those are awesome. I want some like that. Where did you find them?"

"They were at a small store downtown. Jack found them for me."

"Okay, okay," Jack interrupted. "We do need to move along. Tomorrow morning a couple of the guys from town and I are going to pull an old wagon out of the museum. Ryan, I could use your help with that."

Nicole said, "Good Lord. Certainly you don't intend to sacrifice a museum piece. That's a part of history."

Jack said, "It is, but it's not. This is an old one that a friend of mine restored to working condition. He didn't make it pretty; it was somethin' they wanted on display to show people what things were like in the old days."

Ryan smiled. "Hell, if people wanted to know what it was like in the old days, they could have just asked you."

"Funny. They are pulling a bunch of wagons out. It's the only way to get around anymore. That brings me to my next point."

Ryan's horse whinnied off in the distance.

Jack stopped and listened for a minute. "Ryan, did you check on your horse this evening?"

"Yeah."

"What did you think?"

"Everything looked fine."

"Was she grazin'?"

"No. She was just standing there."

"Hmm," Jack said, narrowing his eyes.

"What?"

"Let's go have a look at her. I didn't much care for that sound. Ryan, grab that bucket of water. Nicole, could you bring that lantern and would you please find us some soap."

Brooke asked, "What do you want me to do?"

"Darlin', I just want you to look pretty."

She smiled. "Okay. That's easy."

Jack found a small brown bag in his saddlebag and started walking toward the horse. As they walked up to the wooden fence, Nicole held up the lantern as high as she could. A few feet away, the mare was lying down. "Oh, look. She's in for a bit of a nap," Nicole said, sounding motherly.

"I don't think so," Jack said. "Can I have your lantern?"

She handed it to him, and he climbed over the fence. The mare was lying down but held her head upright. Sweat soaked her face, neck, and sides. Occasionally she would bite at her side. "Oh shit!" Jack said. "I thought this might be the case. She's colicking. Ryan, grab that rope and get in here. We've got to get this horse on her feet."

"What's a colic?" Ryan said, as he made his way to where Jack stood next to the horse.

He took the rope from Ryan and clipped it on the horse's halter. "Colic is when a horse's intestines get twisted or impacted. If we don't get her guts movin', she'll die before mornin'."

"There has to be something we can do for her. Is this my fault?"

"No. It's probably the long grass in here. It's awfully rich for a horse that ain't seen much of it before. She was probably half starved and gorged herself on it. Now she's twisted up tighter than little sister's tennis shoes. Here, take this rope. You pull as I try to convince her backside to get up. Pull!"

Ryan pulled hard as Jack first lifted the backside of the mare and then waved his hat behind her. Reluctantly, she rose.

"There you go son! That's twenty-five percent of the battle right there. Now get her walkin'. The more she moves, the better chance we got."

Jack walked back over to the fence, where Nicole and Brooke stood. "I think Ryan's gonna get a hell of an education in horsemanship tonight. We need to get things ready for him."

As Ryan brought the mare back to the fence where they stood, Jack asked, "Did she shit?"

"I don't think so."

"That's what you want to see. Make sure you pay close attention to her. She needs to move her bowels, and when she does, you want to look at the pile closely. Make sure there's no blood in it."

"What happens if there's blood in it?" Nicole asked.

"If there's just a little, we'll watch her. If there's a lot, we'll have to put her down."

"Oh my. So this is really quite serious?"

"About as serious as it gets for a horse."

"Does it happen very often?"

"Not too often, but every now and again. Mostly with horses like this one, where things got changed too much, too fast."

"I'm gonna need the bucket with water," Jack said.

Nicole lifted it over the fence.

"What's the water for?" Ryan asked.

"You'll see in a few minutes."

Jack said, "Brooke, I need you to do me a favor." He handed her his knife. "Take this and go cut about five feet of the garden hose on that reel over there by the building. Can you do that?"

"Yeah, I guess."

"Now what?" Ryan asked.

Jack picked up his little brown case. "First, I need to give her a couple injections."

"What are those?"

"I need to give her something for the pain. If it gets any worse, you won't be able to help her, and she'll get dangerous

to be around. The next one is a strong anti-inflammatory drug. It will help prevent her gut from swelling up and makin' things worse. The last one is a light sedative. I don't want to put her out; I just need her to be very calm. Hold her tight."

Jack gave all three injections into a big vein in her neck. The mare looked visibly relieved with the pain medication and then started to relax after the third drug started to take effect.

Jack said, "Nicole, could you hand us that bar of soap."

"What's that for?" Ryan asked.

"It's for you," Jim said, smiling. "You wanted to be a horse owner, and now you are. You might want to take off your jacket."

"Why? What's going on?"

"Don't worry. I'll talk you through it. Get your right hand and arm wet in that bucket and really soapy."

"My hand?"

"No, both your hand and your arm, all the way up past your elbow."

"Past my elbow?"

"Yep."

Ryan knelt by one of the buckets and began to wash his hand. He splashed water up his arm and rubbed the soap on it into a lather.

"There you go. That's good. Nicole, can you come in here and hold this horse for us?"

"Certainly."

"Now what?" Ryan asked.

"Now, you and this mare are going to get real cozy. Come over here." Jack stood just to the right of the horse's hindquarters. He lifted the tail.

"Whoa. Wait just a minute," Ryan said and took a step back.

"All kidding aside," Jack said in a more serious tone, "she's your horse, and she needs your help. Her bowel is twisted or impacted. What you're gonna do is hold your hand like this." Jack made a fist with his right hand, the fingers curled under and inward with the palm of his hand covering the nails. "In this position your fingernails can't scratch her. You are going to push your hand slowly though her anus and up inside her,

about halfway up your arm. If you meet any resistance, or she pushes against you, stop. Inside there you are going to extend your finger and push around a bit. If you feel a lump or a mass, let me know where. Okay?"

"Oh, I don't know about this."

"I just told you what you need to know. I'm standin' right here next to you. You'll do fine. Now, stand next to her back left leg, not right behind it. Ready?"

"Yeah, I guess."

Jim lifted her tail again as Ryan closed his eyes and put his hand back behind the mare. All at once his hand disappeared inside the mare.

"Ah, son. I think you probably need to watch what you're doin'."

"No. I think I got it."

"Nope, no you don't. That's not her anus, son."

Nicole started to giggle, and Ryan turned bright red in embarrassment. He pulled his hand out, and this time watched what he was doing.

"There you go. That's the right hole. Nice and slow, you don't want to hurt her."

"Oh, this feels so gross. I can't believe I'm actually doing this."

"Yep, you're a sick fuck now. Isn't that what you called me?"

Ryan's head dropped so that he was looking at the ground in front of him. "Yeah, about that, I'm like really sorry."

Brooke came back with the section of garden hose and looked over the fence. "Oh my God! What are you doing?"

Jack smiled. There were several inappropriate comments he wanted to make, but he said, "Ryan's tryin' to get his horse fixed up. Did you find the hose?"

"Yeah—but like—what the hell?"

Ryan said, "I think I feel something."

"What?"

"It's like a big hard ball right in front of my finger."

"Slowly and very carefully try to move it."

As he did this, Ryan felt a vibration course along his arm, and a loud horse fart erupted from the back of the mare around his elbow. He grimaced, "Oh God! This is so nasty."

From the other side of the fence, Brooke said, "I think I'm gonna puke."

"No no. That's good. You're decompressing her. She's impacted, and that'll be easier to fix than if she had a twist. See if you can decompress her some more."

He did and another loud fart erupted.

"Okay," Jack said, "you can pull your hand out now. Nice and easy."

Ryan removed his arm from the horse and looked to see it covered with shit.

"That stuff washes right off," Jack said, smiling. "But don't wash it just yet. We aren't quite done."

Jack said, "Okay, Brooke, now we need your help."

"There is *no way* I am doing that."

"Nope. You don't have to. What I need you to do is stand up here on the fence and hold that bucket of water as high as you can. You will also need to hold one end of the hose in the water. Can you do that?"

"As long as I don't have to stick my hand up that horse's ass, I think I can."

"We have a deal. Ryan, take the other end of this hose with your clean hand, and when Brooke gets ready, I want you to start a siphon. Make sure you plug the hose with your finger until you get it inside that mare, understand?"

"Yeah, I guess so."

Jack handed Ryan the end of the garden hose as Brook held everything as high as she could. "Here. Take this in there with you all the way up to that ball; then let your finger go. With your fingers, I want you to see if you can start breakin' up that impaction. Careful though, don't let her splash you."

Ryan held the tube in his hand while he reinserted it into the horse's rectum. As before, he pushed very slowly forward. "Okay, I'm there."

"Go ahead and start breakin' that up."

"It feels gritty."

"Sand. She's been grazing in a sandy pasture without much grass on top. I bet all that trotting yesterday and this good grass has got it stirred up."

"This is really very interesting," Nicole said. "I didn't realize that horses could have a problem with sand."

"They sure can. This is a textbook case. She was probably kept in a poor pasture and ate a lot of sand with a little bit of grass. The trip to Cody got it moving, but it was the dehydration that made it stick."

"So the Gatorade didn't hurt her?" Ryan said.

"Probably saved her life. How you doin' in there?"

"It's breaking up slowly, but it feels like it's starting to fall apart into chucks."

"Okay, son, pull your hand out again."

As he did, a huge rush of liquid stool squirted out of the back end of the horse. The mare bore down, and a broken lump the size of a softball shot out of her and bounced off Ryan's chest.

"Oh, fuck!"

"There we go!" Jack said, as the mare strained again and started to shit on the ground behind her. "Congratulations, Ryan, you have saved your horse's life again."

Everybody except Jack was shocked by the quantity of shit that started to pile up on the ground behind the mare.

"Wow," Nicole said, staring at the horse.

"Yep, it's surprising how much can be stuck behind the dam," Jack said, as he leaned against the fence.

"Now what?" Ryan asked.

"Walk her for about thirty minutes or an hour. She should be fine, but you might check on her later tonight. We'll give her a good once-over tomorrow. Oh, yeah, don't pick your teeth."

"We'll see you back at camp," Jack said, as he and Nicole left.

Brooke stood by the fence. "I'll tell you one thing. You're not touching me with those hands."

"Why not? It's kinda the same."

"The fuck it is. Seriously, make sure you wash good. You smell like shit."

"Thanks."

"I'll see you back at camp." She turned and left.

Ryan was left alone with his horse. He washed his hands and arm with the little bit of water that remained in the bucket. He walked to the front of the little mare and rubbed her neck. Her eyes were closed but opened slightly as he touched her. She looked exhausted. "You've had a big day today. I guess I have too. Sorry about the...well, you know. I'm not weird or anything, it's just that I had to help you. I don't want you to die. There's been too much of that lately. I'll make you a promise: I'll take care of you if you take care of me. How about that?" He rubbed her forehead. "We can take care of each other."

# 36.

Mark opened his eyes to gray, diffuse light coming in through the living room window. He had no idea what time it was or how long they had been sleeping. Megan lay still sleeping against his left side with her arm over his chest. He thought about the things they had done last night, and a smile came over his face. When she had blindfolded him and tied him up, he had initially started freaking out a little. The loss of control and the helplessness were frightening. But she had turned the whole thing into an incredible erotic experience. The things she said and did made him feel powerful and wonderful. It was as though she wanted to tie him down, so she could have all of him—all to herself in any way she wanted. The whole experience was amazing.

He began to think about their experiences together over the last couple of days. They hadn't known each other very long, but he was starting to have very deep feelings for her. He looked down at her as she slept. Maybe he was falling in love with her. He remembered the sight of her stepping into the bath, the look on her face when he had fallen into the water, the look on her face when she laughed about what he had

done to Lisa. Yeah, he could fall in love with her very easily, and probably already was.

He glanced around the room. In the cool, gray light, he could see a couple of photographs that hung on the wall near the entryway and an old painting of cows crossing a river behind the couch. A sense of reality opened in his mind like a light switched on in a dark room. Today was Tuesday. He was somewhere between Gillette and Buffalo, lying on a mattress on the living room floor in somebody's house, whose owner he had shot. Lying next to him was a girl he had only known since Saturday, but who he was undoubtedly in love with. They were traveling by horseback, and everything he had ever known was gone. They now existed in a completely different world: one where all the technology that had been part of everything was gone and the law of survival of the fittest now prevailed.

He smiled. This was good. No, this was great. He fucking loved it! In a flash a couple of days ago, not only had all the technology disappeared, everything that had sucked about the world disappeared as well. Everything was new. There were no credit scores to worry about, no bills, no asshole bill collectors calling on the phone every damn day. Hell, there were no phones! There was no boss breathing down your neck, and no asshole guys with more seniority calling you "Pussy" because you drove a little Bobcat. Now, in this world, the most beautiful woman you could imagine wanted to be with you because you could give her a hot bath, a sense of safety, and the dream of something better.

This world was much better. In this world the smartest, the strongest, and the most daring not only survive, but thrive. In the old world, he had been just another guy struggling to get along, but this world was his. This is where he would be at home.

Megan stretched and looked up at him. She smiled. "Hi."

He smiled back at her. "Good morning."

She looked at him closely and said, "You look like the cat who just ate the mouse."

"More like the dog who just ate the pussy." He grinned at her.

She playfully whacked him. "You're terrible."

"That's not what you said last night."

"You're right. You were awesome. That was fun."

"Wanna do it again?"

"No. I gotta pee. Besides, we need to get going. We have a long way to go today." She pushed the blankets back and stood up in front of him. "What? What are you looking at?"

"You. Do you know how beautiful you are?"

"That kind of talk will get you everywhere."

An hour later Mark had collected the horses while Megan packed the bags. He helped her put their saddles on but managed to get the bridles and bits by himself. He had watched her closely enough yesterday to put the packs back on Hunter, but she needed to help him with the straps.

They took a last quick look around to see if there was anything that might be useful. Just as Mark was about to follow Megan out of the bedroom, he stopped. Something didn't look quite right. He turned and noticed a framed picture of some ducks sticking out too far from the wall. He lifted the corner, and it pivoted outward on hinges. Behind it the door of a wall safe was twisted in its frame. "Hey, Megan, take a look at this."

She stepped back into the room. "What's up?"

"A safe." He pulled on the door, and it moved a little. "I can't quite see inside."

"Hang on a second. I might be able to find something to help with that."

Mark tugged on the door a few more times, and each time the door gave a little more. Megan returned with a broom. "Here. See if you can use this to pry the door open."

Mark stuck the wooden pole in the door and pried. The door gave a little more and then popped about a quarter of the way open. On the top shelf, there was a stack of papers and a revolver. Mark pulled it out and looked at the gun. "Python .357."

"Really? She took it from him and checked it out herself. She swung the cylinder out and found it loaded. "This is really nice. Maybe we should take it. We might be able to trade it for something."

"Hey, look at these?" From the bottom shelf, he pulled out a stack of round silver coins. Each was marked with Walking Liberty on one side and an eagle on the other. "There's a bunch of them in here."

"Those are silver eagles. Each one was worth about a hundred and fifty dollars. Grab them all!" Megan grabbed a pillow from the bed and took the pillowcase off. She collected the coins as Mark pulled them out of the safe. She counted roughly a hundred of them.

"That's it for those, but look at what else I found." He pulled out two gold coins marked the same way.

"Oh my God! How many are there?"

"I don't know yet. I can't see too good. It's dark in there." When he had finished, he had removed twenty of them."

Megan said, "Let's see…that's sixty-four and fifteen. Wow. We just got almost eighty thousand dollars. Is there anything else in there?"

"I don't think so. You can check if you want. Your hands might fit better than mine."

She ran her hand around the safe and came out with an old Crown Royal bag. "We can keep the gold in this. The silver can go in the saddlebags. Wow, I'm glad you spotted that. You know what, cowboy? You might just make my dreams come true after all."

Mark smiled proudly. "I'm just getting started."

He started to follow her out of the bedroom when he noticed an oddly shaped box in the closet. He reached up on the shelf and pulled it down. The box was somewhat conical in shape, had a handle on the top, and little snaps on the sides. "What's this?"

Megan looked at it. "That's a hat box. Open it up."

He did and found a black cowboy hat.

Megan said, "Wow. This guy was for real." She picked it up and turned it over. "This is a Stetson El Patron. I bet he didn't wear this very often."

"Why not?"

"It's probably a five or six hundred dollar hat. You don't wear this shoveling shit; maybe to something formal or a cattle sale, but definitely not every day. Try it on."

Mark put the hat on, and it fit a little snug.

"Oh yeah! That's you, my big, badass cowboy." She gave him a look that told him she did indeed like the hat. He decided to keep it.

# 37.

It was a little cooler, but the weather was still unseasonably warm for the middle of October. Jack sat at the table, drinking coffee and making a few notes under a flat gray sky, when Nicole came out of her tent.

"I'm beginning to develop a complex," Nicole said, as she walked toward the fire. "I was determined to get up and have coffee ready for you when you awoke this morning, but now I am starting to feel as though I am as lazy as a Frenchman."

Jack laughed. "I do my best thinkin' in the mornin'. On the other hand, I do my best talkin' in the evenin'. You might see where I run into a little trouble."

Now Nicole laughed. She poured herself some coffee and sat down across from him. "I am sorry about the direction our conversation ran off to yesterday. It wasn't my intent to quarrel with you."

"I know. I'm sorry about that too."

"I want to thank you for everything yesterday. I especially enjoyed talking with Donna. She had very nice things to say about you."

"Donna is a good egg. One of the best."

They both sat in silence for a few minutes, staring at the table. At the same instant, Jack said, "Listen...," and Nicole said, "When..." They both apologized and told the other to continue. Jack finally said, "Ladies first."

"I was going to ask if you knew when you thought you would be leaving?"

"Tomorrow mornin'."

Nicole sat up straight in surprise. "That soon? Oh my. I wasn't prepared for that. I suppose you want to beat the snow."

"I do."

"And I don't suppose you would reconsider?"

He shook his head. "I won't."

"Well then. I have spent a great deal of time thinking about this since we spoke yesterday morning. In fact, the very notion of you leaving pervades my every thought since that time. As I mentioned yesterday, I have grown quite fond of you, and I would like to get to know you much better. I'll only ask this once, and I will accept your answer as final." She hesitated and then asked, "May I go with you?"

"Yes."

"You see..." She stopped. "What did you say?"

"I said yes. I'd like it very much if you would come with me."

Nicole jumped up laughing and spilled her coffee across the table. She grabbed Jack's face with her hands, pulling him to her, knocking his hat off. She kissed him hard on the mouth and held it.

When she finally let go, he looked shocked and surprised. "Hell, if I'd'a known you were gonna do that, I would've invited you yesterday."

"Oh Jack! At this moment I believe I am the happiest girl in the world! This is going to be such an adventure!"

Jack was brushing spilled coffee from his pants and said, "Now, hold on a minute. There's a couple a things I'd like us to get straight right from the get-go."

"I am so sorry to have spilled on you. I'll take care of them later if you'll just leave them with me."

"Have a seat," Jack said, sitting back down at the table himself. "I've been thinkin' about this a bit, and I want you to know a few things before we leave. First, we'll be takin' a wall tent like those back there. You'll have your own space. I don't want you to think that I am expecting anything or...hell, I don't know...bein' inappropriate in any way. Along the way, we're gonna come across a couple of towns. None of 'em are very big. Greybull is the biggest. If you get tired of me and decide to head out on your own, I understand, but you can't just up and run off with a horse. We both will rely on them."

She interrupted him. "Are you thinking that I am going to grow weary of you and run off?"

"Well, let's just say I'm not so sure. I figured you might just come to your senses and realize you're hangin' out with a dusty old fart and get tired of it."

Nicole looked very serious, gazing at something behind him. "Hmm. I see. So, the walls of tent are made of nothing but canvas. Is that right?"

"They are."

"So in reality, they don't provide much in the way of security."

"They keep the wind out, but that's about it."

"So do you have any thoughts of additional security?"

"That's just the trouble. They—"

She cut him off. "Because as I see it, with such little protection, one little slice with a knife, and I could be in your side of the tent taking complete advantage of you." She gave him an evil smile.

Jack sat up straight with his eyes wide, then said, "Nicole, I think we should be serious."

"Actually, in a sense I am being quite serious. Jack, you have been nothing but a perfect gentleman since the moment I met you. Why should I expect anything different now or in the future? You know I am attracted to you. *Physically* attracted." She paused, letting her words sink in and then added, "You are now thinking something to the effect that this might be a Cinderella phenomena or even a Stockholm syndrome type of attraction.

You are incredibly perceptive about everyone around you. You often understand people better than they know themselves, but you cannot see yourself. I can assure you that this attraction is very real and not part of some psychological issue.

"Before I let you continue, I want you to think carefully about the words you choose. Previously you have said that I am intelligent. If you believe that to be true, then please give me the courtesy to make my own carefully considered decisions, as logical or illogical as they may appear to you. I believe I should be entitled to feel the way I feel regardless of what you might think is right for me."

Jack sat quietly thinking. "Fair enough. I'll give you a little insight about me. I live by a moral code that is kinda ingrained into me. Some people might think I'm old-fashioned, but I try hard to do what's right by others. I'm not sure what the right thing is here. I'm very fond of you, and I like spendin' time with you, but some people would say it's wrong for me to go traipsin' across the countryside with a beautiful young woman. The last thing I want to do is dishonor you."

Nicole grinned. "Fuck them."

In surprise Jack said, "Excuse me?"

"You heard me. Fuck them. Fuck them all! Jack, you are without a doubt the sweetest man I have ever met. But, I don't give a damn what anyone else might think. This is about you and me and perhaps the greatest disaster the entire human race has ever faced. We are both adults, both relatively bright, and both trying desperately to find a place to call home within this tragedy. At this moment you consider home to be a building on the other side of the mountains. I believe home is where your heart is. I understand that it is much too soon to know for certain, but I suspect that mine is with you."

Jack sat motionless at the table. Nicole's words had resonated inside him, seemingly amplified as they echoed off the cliffs and crags of old emotional baggage he carried.

"Jack, what I am trying to say is please continue to do what you believe to be right. It is what makes you the man you are and the reason so many people here love and respect you. All I

ask is that you let me help you determine what is right when it comes to the two of us."

He continued to sit quietly thinking.

After a few moments, Nicole said, "Please tell me what you are thinking?"

He hesitated and then said, "All right. I'm kinda thinkin' I'd like to kiss you again."

She smiled. "Now you're thinking straight. Get over here and kiss me before I change my mind."

They kissed long and slow and passionately. At one point Jack opened his eyes and saw Nicole's face so close. He couldn't believe this was happening to him. The warmth and wetness of her lips and the way her arms and hands held him so tight. It was all so fast and so unlike anything he would have ever imagined. It was wonderful.

An hour later Jack had rousted Ryan and Brooke. They sat on the chairs next to each other by the fire, drinking coffee.

"Ryan, did you check on that horse last night?"

"Yeah. Brooke made me get up. She was just eating like she always does."

"That's a good sign. While you're all here, I got somethin' for ya." He walked to his tent and came back to the picnic table with a bag. He reached in a pulled out a black plastic box. "Ryan, this one is for you."

"What is it?"

"Get over here and find out."

The kid got up slowly and meandered over to the table. He popped the latches on the front and opened the box to find a black handgun with black grips. "Whoa! Cool. This is for me?"

"Yep. But there's a few rules to go with it. This is a 1911. These kind of guns have been around since John Browning first dreamed 'em up and sent 'em to the military in nineteen eleven. This one is brand new. There's a holster and a mag pouch in the box. Now, here's the thing. We are going to spend a little time learning how to use this safely. If I see you

doing anything unsafe with this weapon, I'll take it from you. Understood?"

"Yeah, sure," Ryan said absentmindedly.

"Nope. Look at me, son. I'm dead serious about this."

The kid looked up.

"If I wasn't worried about your safety, there is no way I'd let you have this. You are going to leave it in the holster unless somebody is pointing a gun at you, right?"

"Like you?"

"I think I'm gonna change my mind."

"No no no. I promise."

"You promise what?"

"I promise I will leave it in the holster unless somebody pulls a gun on me."

"And if I catch you messin' around with it?"

"You'll take it away." Under his breath Ryan added, "Fat chance."

Jack stared at him intensely.

"Okay. I promise."

"Nicole, I got one for you too."

She walked over and stood next to Jack. He pulled a blue box out of the bag. "I want you to have this. This one is kinda special."

The lid of the box had a gold horse rearing up. She opened it to see a pistol in the same shape as the one he had given Ryan, but this one was very different. It was silver with a polished, chrome slide ornately covered in gold leaves, and gleamed as if it had a light of its own. The wooden grips were deeply engraved, with the word "Colt" standing proudly in the middle. "This is beautiful."

"Thanks. I think so too. This is a Diamond Grade. There were only a few of 'em made. I donated this one to the museum. Since everything went haywire, they decided to let me have it back. I'd like you to have it. As far as I know, there's only two of 'em in the state of Wyoming. This one and one a friend of mine in Buffalo owns. He and I bought 'em together at the factory."

"This is much too nice to carry about."

"Nope. I want you to have this. It's as polished on the inside as it is on the outside. I can't imagine a more reliable weapon. If you need it, I want it to go bang—every time."

"What about me?" Brooke said, as she made her way to the table. "I want one too."

"Yep, I got somethin' in here for ya." He pulled out a small black box. She opened the case and found a silver revolver with pink grips. "Oh my God! It's so cute! I love it! Is it real?"

"Of course it's real. Won't do you much good if it's not. This is the only one I could find in pink. It doesn't have the look the other ones do, but I think you'll make somebody think twice if they were comin' at you."

"When do I get to shoot it?"

"Right now."

They spent the next two hours behind the museum learning how to use the weapons. Jack showed them how to keep the gun safe until they needed it, how to hold it, how to aim, and finally how to fire it smoothly and accurately. They finished and were just about to walk back when Ryan said, "What about yours? How come you didn't shoot?"

Jack said, "I've done it once or twice before."

"Can I try it?"

"What?"

"That big fuckin' canon you carry around. I want to shoot it."

Jack thought for a minute, smiled, and said, "Okay. One shot. I'll set the target, but you have to pick up all this brass."

"Cool! Why do we have to pick this up? There's trash everywhere."

"We can reload it," Jack said, as he headed out toward the hillside they had been using as a backstop. He spotted a red plastic cup that had blown in by the wind and picked it up. He kept walking toward the hill.

"That's good," Ryan called from behind him. Jack kept walking.

When he came back, Ryan said, "That little thing is way out there. Nobody can hit that."

"This one's made for long range. Gotta have the right target to see if it works."

"Yeah, but that cup is like a mile from here."

"'Bout a hundred yards. Here you go. You can cock it like this." Jack thumbed the hammer back as the revolver clicked and turned the heavy cylinder. "Give it your best, but don't drop it."

Ryan took the heavy revolver and held it out in front of him with both hands. "This thing is freakin' huge!"

"Yep," Jack said.

Ryan pulled the hammer back like Jack had shown him. When he squeezed the trigger, the blast was incredible. The concussive wave slammed his chest and moved the hair on the side of his head. The flash that jumped from the muzzle was unlike anything he had ever seen before. The recoil slammed his hand, and he almost dropped the gun. "Holy shit!"

Nicole and Brooke had both jumped when the big gun went off. Brooke said, "Oh my God!" Nicole looked shocked as she held her arms over the front of her. Jack laughed.

Ryan said, "I thought the damn thing exploded! That was unbelievable. You actually shoot this thing? By choice?"

"Yep. It's the right tool for the job sometimes."

"There is no way you can hit that cup."

Jack took the big gun from Ryan and held it out in front of him with both hands. He breathed out slowly and squeezed the trigger. The gun roared again. Out against the hillside, the little, red cup exploded.

# 38.

Jack, Ryan, an acquaintance of Jack's who was now in charge
of the museum, and a young man working with him worked
for nearly two hours but finally managed to get the old, big,
green wagon out the front door of the building. Clearing
away the debris and removing the twisted metal that had once
been a doorframe had been the hardest part. With the wagon
now sitting on the concrete sidewalk, Jack shook the assistant
curator's hand, and he and Ryan began pulling the wagon
toward camp.

They stood side by side and pulled on the neck yoke at
the end of the tongue. As they slowly moved the wagon, Ryan
asked, "Couldn't we just use a horse for this?"

"I don't have the harness ready yet."

"Why did they give this to you?"

Jack said, "I helped 'em get this one and a couple others.
This one's not an antique. They were just usin' it for a display."

"So why do you want it?"

"So I can haul things around."

"Like what?"

"Like my ass back home."

"I thought you lived like a couple of hundred miles away."

"About a hundred and fifty."

"Yeah, so, you'll never get there."

"Sure I will. Take me about a week, maybe less with this wagon. How do you suppose people got around before we had cars?"

"Yeah, but that was like a long time ago."

"Still works."

"Maybe. So when are you gonna go?"

"In the mornin'."

Ryan stopped dead in his tracks, dropping his half of the yoke. "What? You're really leaving tomorrow?"

Jack continued to pull the wagon but it slowed considerably. "That's the plan."

The kid caught up with his half of the yoke and started helping again. "But wait. What about me and Brooke?"

"What about you?"

"Well, who's gonna help us?"

"You're—what?—twenty-two?"

"Twenty-three. I'll be twenty-four in a couple of months."

"You're an adult. What do you need help with?"

"Well, like everything. I mean, who's gonna show me how to shoot?"

"We did that this mornin'. You know how to shoot. Now you just need a little practice."

"Yeah, but what if the gun jams up?"

"Then I 'spect you'll figure out how to clear it."

"Okay, what about food? How am I gonna eat?"

"Just like you been doin' all your life."

"Yeah, but where am I gonna *get* the food?"

"Same place as everybody else."

"Okay. So, what about Penny? I don't know what to do with her."

"Son, you're in Wyoming. Just about everybody you've seen since you been here knows somethin' about horses. I reckon you'll have to ask."

"But this isn't fair!"

Now Jack stopped and let go of the yoke. "Tell me, what exactly is it that's not fair?"

Ryan stopped and dropped the yoke and tongue on the ground. "Everything!"

Jack looked at the boy with disgust. "The other day I stopped and helped you out along the road. I didn't know you, but you looked like you might need a hand. Since then, I dragged your ass back here, found you a place to get out of the weather, fed you, clothed you, tended to your horse, and provided you with a pistol and trained you how to use it. I also helped out your new girlfriend. Now you tell me things ain't fair?" He shook his head. "Ryan, you're an adult. It's high time you became a man. You should be takin' care of all this stuff on your own. Since you have started takin' your pleasure with that young lady, she is also your responsibility, and you need to take care of her."

"'Takin' my pleasure?' I'm not sure what that's supposed to mean?"

"You know exactly what I mean. The two of you ain't exactly quiet with your ruttin' around half the night."

"Yeah, but, how am I supposed to learn all this stuff?"

"What the hell you been doin' for the last twenty-three years, boy?"

"I didn't exactly know we were gonna end up living like the Flintstones."

"The flare and all the rest of this shit don't matter. Nobody expects you to know how to help that horse or shoot a gun, and they'll probably even cut you some slack not knowin' how to start a fire, but you need to be thinkin' how am *I* gonna get through this? I gotta find shelter, water, food, and safety. If you don't know how to find it, you gotta ask. While Nicole and I have been tryin' to get things organized the last couple of days, you haven't done a damn thing. Hell, you thought it would be more fun to go get drunk and laid than to sit and listen to the town meetin' and hear what they were plannin'. You ask me about food, but it was discussed at the meetin'. You ask me about shelter, and it too was discussed. The water situation, security, health care—all of it was talked about."

"So what am I supposed to do?"

"I don't know. It's really not my concern."

"I'm asking for a little help here."

Jack leaned against the wagon. He pointed to it with his thumb and said, "You see this? When this whole shit storm happened, I knew I had to get home. That means I have to travel about a hundred fifty miles on horseback. I can do it in the saddle, but if I had a wagon, I could bring more gear and make the trip a little easier. I asked myself where I could find a wagon. I know several sources, but the museum was closest, and they were happy to help, so I didn't have to look anywhere else. I knew when I saw this one I was gonna need a few things to make the harness complete, so I worked that out. I know I need water, feed for the horses, and food for myself. I need warm clothing in case it gets cold and a bunch of other things. Depending on what my needs were, I found the solutions. Now, what do you need?"

"A place to stay."

"Okay, good. How ya gonna find that?"

"I don't know."

Jack shook his head. "What kind of shelter do you want?"

"Anything."

"You could find another tent like the one we're using at camp."

"Yeah, I suppose that would work."

"But winter's comin', right?"

"Yeah."

"So a tent might not be the best solution. What about a house?"

"Yeah, sure, that would be better."

"Where're you gonna find one of those?"

"I don't know."

"Sure you do. Look around. There's hundreds of 'em. A lot of 'em don't have people livin' in 'em anymore. Maybe if you talked to the guys tryin' to get the town back on its feet, they might help you out. I heard they've been relocating people whose houses burned down."

"Okay, I could do that."

"What's next?"

"Food."

"Good. How are you gonna find that?"

"Maybe I could ask the same guys."

"Yep, that'll work. I bet they'd give you a hand, but, you know, they also need a lot of help around here. Would you be willin' to help them out?"

"Maybe. Depends on the job."

Jack shook his head again in exasperation. "Depends on the job? I thought you were tryin' to *survive* here. Now you're tellin' me you'll only take a job you like?"

Ryan looked uncomfortable. "I don't want to do anything gross."

"What is gross?"

"I don't know. You know, like picking up garbage or dealing with all these dead bodies or stuff like that."

"So you think those jobs are below you?"

"Not necessarily below me, but I do have a college degree."

"I thought you were still in school."

"I am. I mean, I'm almost ready to graduate."

"I bet they don't need a lot of physicists right now."

"Very funny."

"I'm bein' serious as a heart attack. This town desperately needs people to help clean up bodies, pick up trash, shovel horse shit, find and store food, help the older people out, sit on a security watch, and about a million other things. All those jobs are honorable, honest, and helpful. If you did any one of 'em, and the town helped you out by providin' a place to live and food to eat, I'd say it was a damn fair trade."

"Yeah, but what if I didn't want to do any of those things."

"Then I'd let you starve. Simple as that. The days of entitlement and soft livin' are over. They ended at about eleven o'clock Friday night. Now it's nothin' but hard work and tryin' to scrape by. There ain't gonna be one person in this town who will give a wet dog shit for your degree in physics. I ain't sayin' that to be mean; I'm sayin' it 'cause it's the truth. They don't

need that education; they need hard work and a team player. That's what they'll pay for."

"Yeah, but there's things I know."

"That is true. You do know stuff. If you can help 'em with the electricity, they might be interested. But, I bet they don't need a lot of theoretical physics right now."

"Okay, so what about you?"

"What about me?"

"What are you gonna do?"

Jack looked at him blankly for a moment. "Son, I own a ranch where I raise cattle and horses. I'm not exactly looking for work at the moment."

"Yeah, but maybe your house burned down."

"Maybe it did. I'll build another one."

"Okay, so what if all your cows and horses were dead. What would you do then?"

"Oh, I see where you're goin'. If I was in the same spot you are, in a town where I didn't know a soul, I'd be the first guy on the end of a shovel if that's what it took. And I'd make damn sure that somebody I cared about ate before I did."

"You're talking about Brooke."

"No. You are. I'm talkin' about bein' a man and doin' what's right. Let me ask you this: do you like her?"

"Yeah."

"I'm talkin' about more than just the physical thing."

"Yeah, I do. She's a lot of fun, and I like to talk to her."

"So what are you intentions?"

"I'm not sure I understand."

"Sure you do. Are you just hanging out with her for the sex, or are you thinkin' that you might consider marryin' her?"

"Marry? Whoa. Let's back the wagon train up a minute there, hoss. Who said anything about marrying her?"

"I asked what your intentions were. I guess I see it like this: if you're just hangin' out to get in her pants, then you're just gonna hurt her when you're done; and in my estimation, that's about as low as a man can stoop. On the other hand, if you really like this girl, and she might be the one, and you *honestly*

have no intention of hurtin' her, then you have a responsibility to her. Personally, I think it's a man's job to keep her safe, warm, and fed."

"Okay, so what if we were gay?"

"You're obviously not, and I'm not gonna talk about hypotheticals."

"What I mean is: why is it my job to provide for her? Why can't she provide for me?"

"Would you actually feel good about yourself if you let her provide for you? Besides, have you actually met Brooke?"

Ryan kicked the ground in frustration. "All this talk about being a man...this...This pisses me off. I mean seriously, why does everything have to be so fucking hard. You know? I didn't ask for any of this shit. Maybe I don't want to shovel shit or clean up dead bodies. Maybe I just want to hang out and have fun. I want to sit in a restaurant and have a nice meal and a couple of beers. Maybe I'll wake up and this whole fucking nightmare will be over."

"Son, that's exactly what's happenin' to you right now. You're wakin' up. Real life is hard. All the technology we had, all the comforts we had, we just took 'em for granted, and life became soft and easy. As a society we took away people's responsibility and gave 'em excuses. We stopped teachin' our young people what honor meant and how to live it. We stopped lettin' our kids get dirty and play outside, and we didn't let them get hurt once in a while. Instead we sat their ass on a couch, gave 'em video games, and expected they would somehow learn how to build somethin'. We taught 'em food was somethin' that came out of the microwave or a bag in the drive-through. Today all that stuff is gone, and I understand you're frustrated. You have a right to be. Nobody showed you anything different. All the lights and TV magic of the world has disappeared, and you are left with reality—and that is cold and hard.

"But, what you need to understand is that despite all the softness you have taken advantage of and been accustomed to, real life was always there in the background. It was waitin' for you. Real life got thrown in your lap with the flare, but

at some point you were gonna have to face it anyway. Maybe it would have been when you were married with a couple of kids and then lost your job. Or maybe it would have happened when your wife got sick, or one of your kids got sick. Maybe it might have been the economic collapse that people were always talkin' about. The cause of it don't matter. What matters is that at some point in your life you are going to wake up and have to face the fact that you—and you alone—are responsible for yourself and those you care about. You would have to make the tough decisions, come up with a plan, and then do the hard work that would be required. That's the moment it all comes down to, the moment when you either try your best and give everything you got without pride, without expecting anything in return, and without blame, or you don't. They give it all kinds of names like honor and self-respect, but the names don't matter. It's what you do that matters.

"Son, this is your moment. I'm sorry it got thrown in your lap when you didn't think you were ready for it, but life ain't fair. That's just the way it is. The only question on the table is what are you gonna do about it."

Jack picked up his end of the yoke. "What do you say we get this piece of reality back to camp?"

# 39.

By midmorning the flat, gray, overcast sky had broken into thousands of small, white, puffy clouds that seemed to be evaporating as the day wore on. Megan and Mark continued west, following the interstate through the grass-covered, rolling hills of northeast Wyoming.

Initially their conversation had been lively and brisk as they talked about the gold and silver they had found. As the miles passed, they continued to talk, but the conversation was more relaxed as they shared stories and experiences of their lives. Now, in the midafternoon, they walked quietly. The little sleep they had gotten in the last few days, along with the stress of the recent changes, the efforts they had made, and even the long miles in the saddle, were starting to take their toll.

"I don't know about you, but my ass is killing me," Mark said, shifting from one butt cheek to the other for the umpteenth time.

"You could take your coat off and sit on it. Better yet, use your t-shirt. It won't be so bulky."

"I have another one in my bag."

"And that is packed away on Hunter. Do you really want to go through everything to dig that out?"

"Not really."

"I didn't think so."

Mark handed Fred's reins to Megan. She held the horse as they continued to walk while Mark took his jacket and t-shirt off. He slipped the jacket back on and then folded the t-shirt before stuffing it underneath him. "Hey. That's better."

"I thought so. So, you used to work out a lot."

"Yeah. It was the only thing I was good at."

"I can't believe that."

"You might not believe it, but it was kinda the truth. It seemed like everything I used to touch would go to hell. Things never worked out for me."

"Really? Like what?"

"Well, I had a friend that used to race dirt bikes. He got me interested, and so I took out a small loan and bought one. We went out a couple of times, and it was a blast. My friend thought that I could be pretty good at it. Well, one day we went out, and I decided to take this jump. I landed wrong and completely trashed the bike. The guys at the repair shop said I bent the forks, the frame, and tore up a bunch of other things. So now I had a loan on a bike I couldn't use. I had to sell it for parts and take the hit."

"Oh, wow. That must have sucked."

"Sure did. That was only one thing too. It seemed like there was always something like that going on."

"Sorry. So you told me that you grew up in Denver and then moved here for the job, right?"

"Yep."

"So you never talk about your parents. Are they still in Denver?"

"You're right. I never talk about my parents. My dad left when I was a kid, or at least that's what my mom told me. Later I heard he was in prison. You know it has to be bad when your mom lies to you saying your dad ran off with another woman to protect you from the truth. When I was little, my mom worked all the time, and I was always with babysitters. She hooked up with a guy when I was in fifth grade, and she fell for him pretty

hard. She kept telling me that when he got divorced we would all live together, and then she wouldn't have to work so much. He dumped her a couple of years later. After that she started drinking a little. A little turned into a lot. I haven't talked to her in a couple of years."

"Wow. Jeez. Sorry."

"Don't be sorry; it's not your fault. It's just the way it was."

"You know, for all that, you turned out pretty normal."

"We had some neighbors that were nice. They used to watch me while my mom was at work. They kinda like adopted me, you know. I spent more time at their place than I did at home. They were pretty good people, helped me out a lot. They even gave me a guitar for my birthday when I turned twelve. I kinda fucked things up when I was in high school. You know, stupid kid shit. I still feel bad about it."

"So you never wanted to go to college?"

"It wasn't an option. I had no money for anything like that. I did go to tech school for a little while, but that didn't really work out either, so I got a job."

"What did you do?"

"What I didn't do would be easier to answer. I worked everywhere. I played in a band. I did drywall for a while, but the guys I worked with were just a bunch of drunks. I worked at a carwash, a grocery store; I tried to sell cars, but that completely sucked. I was a bouncer for a few years. That was kinda fun, and I met a lot of girls. That's what got me into the gym. I was working as a temp on a road crew when one of the guys told me about the jobs up here. I drove up here and applied. When I got to Gillette, they told me I could've just applied online. I think they were so impressed I would make the drive, they hired me."

"So you've been here ever since?"

"Yep. Exciting story, huh?"

She smiled at him. "Yeah. It is."

He smiled back at her. "You're lying, but that's okay. I've been thinking. Since this flare thing, everything has been going pretty good for me. In fact, it's been pretty damn awesome.

Here I am in the middle of nowhere with the most beautiful girl in the world, and she thinks I'm exciting. I got a killer hat, enough money to buy a house, some cool guns—hell, this is it!"

"You really think so?"

"What? That this is cool? Yeah, I do."

"No. That I am beautiful."

"Hell yes!"

"I always thought I was kind of, you know, plain."

"Anybody who ever said that ought to have their head examined. Babe, you are the most beautiful girl I have ever known. I'm constantly blown away by you."

"Aw. You are so sweet."

"It's the truth. Hell, I might as well hang it all out there. You amaze me. I don't know how else to describe it. I'm just blown away by everything you do. I want to hear everything you have to say, and I want to be with you constantly. You just...I don't know. Amaze me."

Megan leaned over toward him as they continued walking on horseback. He leaned toward her and they kissed.

When she sat up straight again, she said, "You're kind of scaring me, cowboy. You say all the right things. You're also doing all the right things. I could seriously fall for you. If I do and you let me drop, I'm gonna be pissed."

Mark smiled at her. "Go ahead and fall. Jump if you want to. I'll be there."

# 40.

Jack spent nearly two hours sorting out and repairing the harnesses and trying to get Dingo and Lucy hooked up. As he was finishing, Nicole asked, "What is your best estimate of the number of days it will take us to get where we are going?"

"You mean home?"

"For you, yes. For me, I am already there."

Jack smiled and said, "I'm not sure. We'll have to see how the horses do and take things at their pace. Even if we take it easy on 'em, it shouldn't be more'n a week."

"I'm afraid we don't have nearly enough clothing for that. I'll have to figure out some way to do laundry along the way. Also, would it be possible to hang the shower bags on the outside of the wagon as we travel?"

Jack put a hand on her arm. "Darlin', I think you might have the wrong idea about this kind of travelin'. Have you ever seen movies or heard stories about the pioneers as they made their way back in the old days?"

"Yes, I have."

"Well, the truth of it was that they didn't do much in the way of showerin' and laundry. I was kinda thinkin' we'd do pretty much the same."

"Nonsense. The simple fact we will be traveling by horse-drawn wagon does not mean we toss basic hygiene out the window. I can understand where a shower might be difficult, but a wet rag and a bar of soap is not too much to ask. Also, a change of clothing, especially under drawers, is by no means unreasonable."

He realized this was a lost argument. "Yes, ma'am. You do have a point."

"If you don't mind, I would like to give you a small list of things you could pick up today when you are about."

"You're not goin' with me?"

"I don't think so. I'd rather stay and get things organized, so we might be able to leave first thing in the morning."

"Fair enough. Maybe I'll take Ryan and Brooke with me."

"Brooke is napping in her tent. Ryan left a bit ago."

"He did? Where'd he head off to?"

"He said something to the effect that he wanted to find a job. Do you know anything about that?"

"I might."

"You can still take Brooke."

"I could…" He gave her a look, which said he'd rather not.

"She gets very nervous around you, and she compensates by talking. If you talk with her and make her feel at ease, I suspect she will settle down in no time at all."

"Or maybe she won't."

Nicole smiled. "That is a risk."

A half hour later, Jack sat next to Brooke on the seat of the wagon as the horses clopped their way around burned-out cars and trucks on the main street of town.

She asked, "Where are we going again?"

Jack said, "The first stop is to pick up a couple of things and see if we can find some parts to fix up the harnesses the horses are wearin'."

"What's wrong with the ones they are using?"

"Some of that old leather is just about wore out. I'd hate to get too far away from town and have the whole thing fall apart."

"Yeah. Nicole told me you were planning on leaving in the morning. She said it was like a really long ways."

"About a hundred fifty miles. Probably take us a week."

"So, like, where will you stay?"

"In a tent. Kinda like we're doin' now."

"Wait a minute. So if it takes like a week to go a hundred fifty miles, how long would it take to go to St. Louis?"

He thought about it for a moment. "Well, I reckon St. Louis is pretty close to thirteen hundred miles from here. If you could make twenty-five miles a day, it would take you close to two months."

"Two months!" The girl was shocked and quickly put a hand to her mouth. "Oh my God!" Jack could see tears start to form as she considered what he said. "How am I ever going to get home?" She started to cry.

Jack felt terrible. He didn't mean to upset the girl. He just answered her question as best he could, and now she was crying, with good reason. He knew he should try to comfort her, but how? He said, "There, there. It's not all as bad as it seems."

She looked up at him, still crying, with tears running down her cheeks and snot running from her nose. "Not bad? How can it be not bad? This is the worst. I'm stuck out here in the middle of nowhere, and you tell me it's gonna take, like, two *months* to get home. The only person I even knew out here died! It was awful!" She started crying even harder and buried her face in her hands again.

Jack put a hand on her back and rubbed for a while until she started to collect herself. He said, "Well, first off, you're healthy. You could've been hurt in the disaster the other night, but you weren't. Secondly, you got Ryan. I s'pect that boy thinks quite a lot of you. He's a good kid and he's smart."

She sniffed. "He's just another guy. They all want the same thing."

Jack subconsciously pulled his arm back. "That is a fact. Most guys do have one thing on their mind, and if they get it easy, they don't have to think about a girl any deeper'n that. On the other hand, if they have to marry a girl first, they get

to know her, find out what she's interested in, how she thinks, what she likes, what she doesn't like—all the things that are really important."

Brooke sat up and wiped her eyes with the back of the sleeve of her sweatshirt. "Oh. So you're the old-fashioned type. You gotta get married before you have sex. Well, I am a sexual person, and I don't want to be stuck with some guy who, like, completely sucks in bed."

"I am kinda the old-fashioned type in a lot of things. I'm not sayin' I think you have to get married before you have sex. You have to figure out what's right. All I'm sayin' is if you make 'em work for it a bit, you'll get to know 'em a whole lot better and maybe weed out the bad ones." Jack pulled the wagon to the curb and brought the horses to a stop. He pulled a long wooden handle on the side of the wagon.

"What's that?"

"Parkin' brake."

"Are we here?"

"First stop. SawBuck's."

Brooke decided to wait in the wagon while Jack went inside. A few minutes later, he came out leading a big man with a huge beard, and they talked while looking at the harnesses. After Jack had been back in the store for another fifteen or twenty minutes, he began carrying things out to the wagon.

After the fourth trip to the wagon, he climbed back up and sat next to Brooke. She smiled at him and said, "Who says guys don't like shopping? Do you think you got enough stuff?"

"Hope so, but we still got a few more stops to make." He let the parking brake off and snapped the reins as he made a kissing sound to the horses. They pulled away from the curb and headed down the road.

"So, it would really take, like, two full months to get to St. Louis from here?"

"Yep. That's if you did it on horseback. Longer if you had to walk."

"So, if I left right now, I wouldn't get home until just before Christmas?"

Jack thought for a moment before he answered, but decided that the truth was always best. "Probably take you longer than that. Weather is gonna be a problem. The goin' is pretty easy if it's nice, but if you get stuck in snow, well, you're gonna be laid up for a while. If you have trouble with a horse or some of your gear, it'll take time to get it sorted out. Worst thing is havin' to worry about bad guys along the way."

"Bad guys? What bad guys?"

"Did you hear about the man I shot at the grocery or the kid I had to straighten out tryin' to loot a store in town?"

"No. What happened?"

"Let's just say a few guys were tryin' to take advantage of the lack of law enforcement."

"You killed somebody?"

"Yep. Had to."

"Yeah, but I have a gun now."

"You'd need more gun than that. Darlin', you're a pretty girl, and some men would want to take advantage."

"Oh, I can handle myself with guys. That's no problem."

"Ever had a gun pointed at your head?"

"You mean, like, for real?"

"Yeah."

"No. Not for real. I had a boyfriend once who liked to play—"

Jack cut her off, not wanting to hear the rest. "These men wouldn't be playin'. This would be real, and it would probably end badly for you. Besides, you don't have a horse."

"Well, maybe I could borrow one of yours?"

"How would you get it back to me?"

"Oh. I didn't think about that. Maybe you could sell me one?"

"Sure. I'll sell you a horse, but, you know, money don't work anymore."

"I'll give you a blowjob."

"Whoa." The horses slowed. "No, not you two." He snapped the reins again, and the horses sped back up to a normal walk.

"You, stop that talk. I don't ever want you say somethin' like that again. Do you hear me?"

"What?" She sat up straight and slightly leaned away from him. "Jeez, like what's the big deal?"

"What's the big deal? You are. You're worth way too much to go offerin' somethin' like that."

"Well then, it should be a good deal for a horse. Besides, I'm pretty good at it."

"Brooke, darlin'. Stop that kinda talk. You ain't a whore, and you ain't gonna be one as long as I'm around. You should have a lot more pride in yourself than that. You're smart, you're pretty, you have a great sense of humor, and you have a whole lifetime ahead of you. I don't know who put all them crazy ideas in your head, but they were wrong. You're a nice young lady, and you have the potential to grow into a respectable, honorable woman, but you gotta change the way you think about a few things."

She sat quietly on the bench beside him as the horses continued to clop their way through the west side of town. "Do you really think all that?"

Jack looked over at her and smiled. "As sure as I'm sittin' on this bench."

"Then how am I gonna get home? I mean, if you were me, what would you do?"

"Well, if I were you, I wouldn't worry about gettin' home just yet." She started to protest, but he said, "Just hear me out. The same disaster that happened here also happened in St. Louis. As bad as things are here, I bet they're even worse in a city. Might be best to just let things cool off a bit. Let people kinda get sorted out a little. Before long I bet somebody will have a car or truck runnin'. That would sure make a difference tryin' to cover that kind of distance. If somebody gets some kind of communication workin' again, you might be able to find out if your folks are still in St. Louis. Maybe they got burned out like so many other people did. It would sure be heck to make that trip and find out they weren't even there. So, let's say nobody gets a car runnin', and there is no communications. At that

point I think I would wait until spring to leave. That way I know the weather is only gonna get better. If I got there and found out my folks were gone, I'd still have time to turn around and get back here or anywhere else I might want to go."

"Yeah, but spring is a long time from now."

"It's only a couple of months. It'll go faster than you think. Besides, it'll give you time to learn how to ride, shoot, survive on the prairie, and anything else you might need to know to get you there. A trip like that is gonna take some plannin'. You'd need some time for that as well."

"Ugh. It all seems so hard."

"It seems like it from this angle. A little plannin' might make it seem a bit easier."

"You think my parents are dead."

"Darlin', I have no way of knowin' anything like that. You're guess is as good as mine. I do know a lot of people lost their lives on the night of that flare. I 'spect more'll die this winter. Times are tough now, but they're gonna get a whole lot tougher before we see this thing through."

He pulled the wagon to a stop in front of Heart Mountain Feed & Supply. The main office building had burned to the ground, and two huge, steel grain silos had spilled their contents over the surrounding ground. A young man with a cloth tied to the end of a stick was trying to shoo a herd of cattle away from the grain. Jack pointed the young man out to Brooke and said, "That boy has his work cut out for him. It won't be long before those cows revolt and just run him down."

Jack ran over and spoke with the kid for a few minutes. Brooke watched as he fanned his hat at a couple of cows as they tried to sneak past him. A minute later she noticed him pull the big revolver out of its holster and fire it into the air. The boom echoed in the distance as the cows turned tail and ran back toward the pasture, away from the corn.

Jack then jogged over to a long building with a curved roof and came out carrying two big bags. When he got to the wagon, she asked, "What's that?"

"Horse feed. Buckle up; we got to move." He threw the bags in the back of the wagon and quickly climbed back up onto the bench. He snapped the reins twice, and the horses took off at a trot.

"Why are we goin' so fast?"

"We need to get that kid some help."

"Those cows can't eat all that stuff. There's way too much."

"The problem is that they'll eat till it kills 'em. He's tryin' to protect the cows, not the corn."

They rode about a mile farther east of town, and Jack came to a stop in front of an old, white house with a tractor leaning up against it. He set the brake, jumped down, and jogged around the back to a small outbuilding. A few minutes later, two men on horseback came riding out from around the building and headed back toward the feed store in a hurry.

As Jack climbed back into the wagon, he said, "There. A couple good men on horseback can keep those cows busy till they figure out somethin' to keep 'em out of that corn." He started his own horses moving again and turned the wagon around.

"Do you know those guys?"

"Nope. Just met 'em."

"So why did we come all the way out here?"

"'Cause that kid needed help."

"Yeah, but he could have got those guys."

"He'd'a had to walk. Take too long."

"So he traded the horse food for the help?"

"Nope. He said I could have the feed. I asked where I could find him some help."

"Really? That was nice."

"I was just bein' neighborly."

"But you live like a hundred fifty miles away."

Jack smiled at her. "We're all neighbors now. Besides, everybody needs a hand now and then."

# 41.

As the afternoon wore on, Mark wondered if it was possible to sleep while sitting in the saddle as the horses walked. They could now see the Bighorn Mountains in the west, but the landscape around them changed very little. He asked Megan, "How far do you think we've gone?"

"I don't know. A long ways."

"Getting tired?"

"I was kind of sick of this when we started. How are you doing?"

"I can't feel my ass anymore. I don't know if that's good or bad. My knees are killing me."

"I'm getting tired too. We'll stop before too long."

Way ahead in the distance, Mark spotted what appeared to be two small, black dots on the other side of the interstate. "Hey, Megan. Look up there. Do you see something?"

She looked where he pointed and said, "It's probably just more cars." Along the way they had passed dozens of burned-out cars and pickups. A few big semitrailers had been scattered along the road or tossed into the ditch. Most still held their drivers inside.

He looked again as carefully as he could. "Eh...I don't think so. I think that's some people riding toward us."

"Really?" She looked again. "Maybe. They're so far away."

"Yeah, but they'll be close soon. Is your gun ready?"

"Yes, but I highly doubt we'll need them. Just stay cool. It's probably people traveling just like us."

Fifteen minutes later Mark could clearly see two men on horseback as they rode. The men crossed the right lane and came over to the median as they approached. Megan led her horse toward the two men, and Mark followed.

"Howdy," the man sitting on a gray horse called as he waved his arm. "Where ya headed?"

Megan said, "We're trying to get to Buffalo. Where are you two going?"

The other man, a bit older and wearing a big black hat, said, "We got to get to Gillette. Our mom lives there, and we want to make sure she's all right."

"I'm Megan and this is Mark." Mark nodded at the two men. "We left Gillette a couple of days ago. It's a long ride."

"Yes, ma'am, it is," the younger said, smiling. "I'm Chuck and this here is my brother Willy. Since you two are on horseback, I suspect you had the same problems over there that we did in Buffalo. Hell of a mess. Half the damn town burned down."

Mark chimed in. "Pretty much the same thing in Gillette. Lots of dead people everywhere."

"All the cars and trucks burned up as well?" Chuck asked.

"Yep. That's why we're on horses like you."

Willy spoke in flat monotone. "There was a guy preachin' in the middle of town. He said it was the wrath of God. I don't know if I buy all that he was sellin'."

Mark agreed and then said, "Whatever it was, it was big. Have you seen a compass?"

The brothers looked at each other briefly. Chuck said, "A compass? No. Why?"

"They don't point north anymore. In fact, depending on where you set them, they point in all kinds of directions, or at least they did the other day."

"You gotta be shitting me," the younger brother said in astonishment.

"No, sir. Try it when you have a chance."

Willy looked them over carefully and said, "I don't suppose you got that pack saddle in Gillette?"

Megan answered. "No. My dad picked it up in Cody a few years ago. He used it for elk hunting. Sure comes in handy now."

"I bet it does. Wouldn't mind havin' one myself seein' as this is probably the normal method of travel for a while."

Willy paused and then added, "I'm just curious, are you two married?"

Megan answered quickly before Mark had a chance to say anything. "Yes. We're newlyweds. It's been—what?" She looked over at Mark. "Four months now?"

When Mark looked at her, there was something in her eyes he hadn't seen before, a look that was almost pleading. He said, "Yep. Four months on the twenty-eighth." He smiled at her and saw relief in her eyes.

"Well, congratulations. Heck of way to get started in life."

"One way or another, we're in this together," Megan said.

Willy took his hat off and ran his hand through his hair. "You two about done for the day or are you gonna push on?"

Megan answered quickly again. "We're doing good, and the horses are doing even better. I think it helps them to walk in the grass. We'll probably keep going until dark."

Chuck said, "Yeah, we should do the same. Probably got two more days to ride before we get to Gillette the way I figure it."

Mark said, "A solid two days, but the ride is easy. Take care."

Chuck said, "You too."

They rode their separate directions. When they were at least a mile away from the brothers, Mark asked quietly, "So we're married now?"

"Thanks. You were awesome back there. Did you see the way that Willy guy was looking at me? He was giving me the creeps. I think he was having some bad ideas."

Mark was a little surprised at her statement. He hadn't noticed anything, but Megan did seem to be more perceptive than he was. He decided to give her the benefit of doubt and just change the subject. "So we're really gonna ride until dark?"

"No. I didn't want them to think we were going to stop anywhere close. I want them to keep riding and not sneak up on us in the middle of the night."

"You seriously think they would do that?"

"Wouldn't you if they had something we really wanted or needed?"

"Maybe."

"Exactly. I have a plan."

"What do we need a plan for?"

"To make sure those guys don't come back. If they are going to follow us, they will wait until we are out of sight and then turn around. They'll tail us from a long ways back, so we can't see them. They think we are going to keep going for a while, but we are going to pull off the road right up here. You see how the road has this gentle bend to the right. Well, they can't see down the road very far. If we make camp behind those hills, they would never know we are there until they are past us. You can pick them off with your rifle as they come into view."

"Pick them off? Like, just shoot them?"

"Why would they come back?"

"I don't know."

"The only reason they would come back is to take the pack saddle. Or worse, that Willy guy wants me. I think that's a good reason to shoot somebody."

Mark couldn't argue with her logic. "Since you put it like that, I guess you're right."

They rode another quarter mile when Megan suddenly pulled her horse to the right and through the scrub alongside of the road. Mark followed as they cut behind a hill and followed a grassy draw between two steep hills to a flat area beyond. A small creek wound its way through the bottom of the draw, making the grass green and rich.

"This is perfect. Do you want to make camp or sit with the rifle?"

"The rifle, I guess."

"Okay. Climb up that hill and sit on this side of the crest. You should be able to just look over the top and see them if they are coming down the freeway. If you see them, wave at me, and I'll come up and help you. If I don't see you, make sure you let them both get real close, like the spot where we left the road. If you can't wave or you don't have time, make sure you shoot both of them. The second guy will try to run as fast as he can, so that second shot will be a lot harder. If you can't get him, shoot his horse. That will slow him down. Then kill him."

Mark was surprised. "How do you know all this stuff?"

She smiled. "I don't know…TV, movies, you know, stuff like that."

He grinned at her. "You're awesome!"

Mark had sat on the hill for almost an hour. After he had set up the rifle, he started watching the road closely. He saw nothing, but every once in a while, he looked back toward camp to see Megan stake the horses, set up the tent and the cook stove, unroll their sleeping bags, and finally sit down on the edge of her saddle. She smiled when she saw him looking at her and gave him a little wave. He was falling hard for her. He smiled back at her and turned back to watch the road.

He thought about this bizarre situation: sitting on a hill, waiting for the possibility that two potentially bad guys might come back. The more he thought about Megan's logic, the more he understood she was right. A fierce determination rose in him. Although he hadn't picked up on it, she was worried about these brothers. If she was worried, he was worried, and he would stay here all night long if that's what it took to make sure she was safe. If that Willy guy had given her a look, that fuckhead deserved to be shot. Actually, the slimeball deserved to be gutted and hung by his nut-sack. He almost wished they would come back.

About ten minutes later, his wish was granted. As he looked east along the road, he could see two horses moving at a fast walk. One rider wore a black hat, and the other was on a gray horse. Mark looked back over his shoulder. He couldn't see Megan anywhere. He thought she might be in the tent. He looked back at the road and could see the brothers more clearly. How had she known?

Mark felt a rising tide of nervous excitement building in him. He breathed carefully and slowly, trying to calm himself down. He looked back over his shoulder and still couldn't see Megan. He peeked carefully over the top of the hill just enough to see the riders. Now he could make them out very clearly. There was no doubt: it was the same men. He slid behind the rifle and clicked off the safety. Megan had said the scope was zeroed at two hundred yards. From what she had shown him the other day, the distance to the side of the road was pretty close to two hundred yards. He wondered what the difference of a couple of yards would make. Probably not much. He waited.

His heart was hammering in his chest, and his hands were sweating. Megan had told him about the first time she went hunting with her dad. She had a bad case of what she called "buck fever." She had explained it was all nerves. There was so much talk and preparation leading up to a hunt that the first time you get the chance to shoot you're so scared you can't. If he missed this shot, the brothers would know where they were and would probably come in with guns blazing. Now he was even more nervous. He wanted to look over his shoulder for Megan again, but didn't dare. He couldn't miss them as they walked by the relatively small window.

A horse's nose appeared in his scope. The magnification surprised him. He carefully watched as the riders came into full view. The brothers were riding side by side, and he was aiming at them from nearly the top of the hill. He thought about which one to shoot first. If he shot Chuck, who was riding on the inside, Willy might have to ride ahead to get around the spilled brother, giving him more time to make the second shot, but he would be riding crazy and irregular, making the shot

more difficult. Then again, he definitely wanted to kill Willy, so maybe he should be the first shot, and if Chuck got away, it wouldn't be such a big deal. As he watched the horses and men move, an idea struck him. He waited. As the two horses continued to move forward, the men were coming into alignment from his position. Megan had told him that if he had to shoot somebody, always aim for the center of mass: right in the middle of their chest. She was probably right, but this idea seemed like such a good one. He waited. Don't flinch. Hold steady. Let the rifle do the work. Aim small, miss small. Megan's words came rushing back to him as he felt the trigger on the pad of his finger.

As the brothers rode unaware, the crosshairs in Mark's scope held steady on Chuck's right ear. Behind him, Mark could see Willy's hat on either side of his brother's face. He slowly let his breath out and squeezed the trigger.

The rifle bucked, and the shot cracked in the clear Wyoming air, but Mark didn't notice. He watched through the scope as Chuck's head flipped violently hard to the right, and behind it Willy's neck opened with a bright, red torrent of blood. Both horses jumped, bucked, and began to run into the grass on the side of the road. Mark watched carefully as Chuck fell off his horse on the side of the road and Willy slid out of the saddle with his leg caught in the stirrup. The horse dragged him for about a hundred yards and then came to a stop. Neither man moved.

Mark sat up. "Holy fucking shit!" His entire body was shaking harder than it ever had before, and his heart was pounding in his chest. "Oh my God. I can't believe I just did that!" he said to no one in particular. He started to pick up the rifle but put it down again and sat back down. "Holy shit!" Finally, after a minute or two, he felt a little better and picked up the rifle. He clicked the safety back on, snapped the scope caps closed, and folded the legs of the bipod. He breathed deeply a couple of times and began walking down the hill. As he reached the bottom, Megan came running into camp from around the corner of a hill just beyond with her pistol in both hands out in front of her.

"What happened? What's going on?" she yelled to Mark as soon as she saw him.

He said, "It's okay. You can put that away."

When he reached her, she said, "I only heard one shot. What happened to the other guy?"

"They're both dead."

"Really?" She looked stunned.

"Yeah. Come on. Let's go check it out."

She remained standing still in amazement. "You got both of them with only one shot?"

"Yeah. What happened to you? I was looking for you."

"I was busy."

"Doing what? Where were you?"

"I was, you know, taking care of a couple of things."

"No. I don't know. I could've used your help up there. Where were you?"

She paused, not knowing how to answer him. Finally she said, "I was taking a shit. There. You made me say it. Can we stop talking about this now?"

Mark started laughing. It might have been the pent-up, nervous energy or just the humor in the situation, but he couldn't stop.

"Stop it. It's not funny."

He laughed even harder. "Yes, it is."

Soon she was laughing with him. "Yeah, I guess it kinda is."

When he had just about regained control, he asked, "So, when that rifle went off, did things go a little faster?"

She whacked him on the shoulder. "You are so disgusting. But, yeah, it kinda did."

Both of them were laughing hard enough for tears to come out of their eyes.

When they had finally regained their composure, they started walking toward the dead men. Mark looked at Chuck as he lay next to the road on his left side. The bullet entrance hole was barely noticeable inside his right ear. The pool of blood behind his head suggested the exit wound was much bigger.

He said, "It's hard to believe we were just talking to them a while ago."

"Yeah, but don't let that fool you. They were coming back here to hurt us."

"I know. I'm just sayin'."

"I'll go get Chuck's horse. We probably need to drag these guys away from the road. You can check his pockets if you want."

"Okay." Mark lifted the man's jacket to find a black Glock tucked into his belt. Mark took the gun and checked the rest of his pockets. They were all empty except for his wallet. Inside he found a driver's license, about three hundred dollars in bills, and a business card. It read: Chuck Hedstrom. Hedstrom & Hedstrom. Attorneys at Law.

"Get this. These guys are lawyers."

"Nice. Doesn't that just figure?" she said, as she led the horse. "I wonder if they stole these horses too. These guys don't really look the type to use a ranch rope."

"Ranch rope?"

"Yeah, this is a sixty-footer. This is a nice calf rope, and whoever used this saddle has spent some serious time with cows. See this?" She pointed to the horn. "This has been used and abused." She threw the loop to Mark, who put it around Chuck's legs. She climbed up in the saddle and wrapped the other end around the horn. She made a clucking sound, and the horse pulled the body away like he had done it a thousand times.

When Megan came back, Mark was checking Willy's body. The bullet had torn through his neck leaving the front of his spine exposed. "Oh man. This guy is nasty. I'm not too crazy about digging through his stuff."

"Just get his gun if he has one. We might be able to trade it for something we need."

Mark found a stainless steel 1911 pistol and two extra magazines. He put them in his pockets and then wrapped the rope around Willy's feet.

Megan jumped down from the horse. "There's one thing I want to do first." She swung her leg back and kicked the man

in the crotch with a sickening soft thud. "Asshole. Deserved everything he got." She climbed back in the saddle and dragged him away.

Mark grabbed the reins of Willy's horse and started leading him back toward camp. An idea struck him, and instead he climbed up in the saddle. It felt different. Kind of like the boots he was wearing. He made the same sound Megan had and rode the horse to camp.

That night they decided to pull the sleeping bags out of the tent and lie under the colors of the sky and the stars that shown through. Mark thought the crazy colors were starting to fade a little.

He turned toward Megan, who was starting to fall asleep. "We left your place two days ago, right?"

"Yeah."

"So, I was just thinking. I've shot three people in two days."

"Yeah."

"Does that seem a little weird to you?"

"Yeah, if you just say it like that. But if you think about what we've been through and what happened, it's not bad at all."

"Yeah, I was kinda thinkin' that too."

# 42.

Jack had parked the wagon next to camp. After they had unloaded everything, he had begun working on the harnesses. An hour later he proclaimed success and moved on to another project.

As he sat in the bed of the wagon working with a large sheet of canvas, Nicole stepped to the side and said, "So, how was your afternoon with Brooke? Did the two of you get along, or do I have to worry about a fight breaking out?"

Jack shrugged. "I don't know. We come from two different worlds and see things differently. I'm worried about that girl."

"Why is that?"

"She's got some funny ideas that are gonna lead her into trouble. Problem is I don't think she knows anything else."

"There is an old Scots saying. A wild goose never laid a tame egg."

"You may be right. But that don't mean I have to like it."

"No. I suppose not." She looked in the bed of the wagon, where Jack was trying to thread a long wooden plank through a piece of canvas. "May I ask what you are working on?"

"I'm fixin' to put the bonnet on this wagon, but to tell you the truth, I have no idea how it goes on."

"Bonnet? You mean like the wagons in those old western movies?"

"Yep. This is a covered wagon if you're smart enough to figure out how the cover goes on. At the moment this one has me beat."

"I'm sure you'll have it in no time. Is there anything I can do to help?"

"Nothin' right now. I have a couple of jobs for Ryan when he gets back."

"You have things that Ryan might be able to help you with, but not me?"

"It's heavy work."

"And I am not strong enough?"

Jack looked up from the wagon. "Oh, I didn't say that. I just meant that—"

"Perhaps you should let me be the judge of what I can and cannot do."

"You're right. I'll tell you what I got, and you decide if you want to take on the project. You see those barrels on the sides of the wagon?" He pointed to a worn, green wooden barrel attached to the wagon next to where she stood. "One of 'em has a spigot on the bottom. That's for water. The barrel needs to be rinsed out and filled. It's a lot of trips to the creek with a bucket."

"Can I not just take the barrel with me?"

"It'll weigh close to two hundred and fifty pounds when it's full. We couldn't get it back in that rack."

"I see. Easy enough. What is the other for?"

"It has a small chute on the bottom. We'll put the horse feed in there. It's in those fifty-pound bags, so s'pose I could get that."

"Fair enough. I am off for water."

Got to be careful what I say with a woman smarter than I am around. I could get myself into trouble, Jack thought as he watched her ponytail bounce as she walked.

Twenty minutes later he was trying to bend the wooden bows covered in white canvas over the wagon when he heard

Nicole scream. He dropped everything and leaped out of the wagon at a dead run. A panic rose in him as he thought about what might be happening to her. As he ran he pulled the little Kimber .45 from the hidden holster and carried it in his outstretched arm. His hat blew off, but he didn't notice. Ahead he could see the slight path they used to walk down the slight embankment. Weeds blocked any view of the creek. He tore down the path with the gun held out in front of him. When he came into the little clear area in front of the creek, he saw Nicole standing in the middle of the creek, soaking wet.

As Nicole stood up from the creek, she turned just in time to see a man running toward her. She screamed again in surprise.

Jack scanned the area with the pistol held in both hands. "What? What is it?"

"Good Lord, you nearly scared me to death!" She started to laugh.

"Are you all right?"

"Yes, of course. I am simply a bit wet and surprised by the cold is all."

He looked at her. The wet t-shirt clung tightly, revealing all the details beneath. He looked away. "Whoa. Ah. I heard you scream. I thought somethin' happened."

She continued to laugh. "It did, but it was my own clumsiness. Thank you so much for running to my rescue."

"Sure." He felt awkward and didn't quite know what to do or say. "Ah, would you like me to get you a jacket or somethin'?"

"That's quite all right. I'll walk back to camp with you. I need to get these wet clothes off and on the line, so they'll dry. Sorry to have frightened you."

"That's no problem. I'm just glad you're okay."

She looked up at his blue eyes as he kept his gaze fixed upward and smiled.

Dinner was chicken cooked in a Dutch oven over the fire with vegetables and dumplings made from buckwheat flour. Jack had told Nicole how he had prepared the meal when he was elk hunting, and she seemed to have improved his recipe.

As dinner was winding down, Jack looked across the table at Ryan and said, "Did you have any luck today?"

Ryan looked up and in a serious, almost somber tone said, "Mr. Neumann, may I have a word with you after dinner?"

Jack was shocked by the kid's words and the seriousness of his attitude. He glanced at Nicole, who wore the same expression. "Certainly. You wanna do it here, or do we need a little privacy?"

"No, sir. Here would be fine."

Nicole reached for the plates. "I'll get these out of your way."

Jack glanced at Brooke, who sat motionless next to him on the table bench. He looked back at Ryan and said, "What's on your mind, son?"

"Well, sir. Brooke and I were talking this afternoon. As you know, I went to talk to some of the guys who are trying to get things back in order around here. They said they could find me a house and some jobs for me to help out, but one of the guys, maybe you know him, a Mr. Stark..."

"Sure. He's the mayor."

"Yeah, well, he said that since I was new and nobody really knew me very well, they would put me on jobs that weren't *critical* to start. In other words, I'd have to work my way up."

"There's nothin' wrong with that. Everybody has to start somewhere."

"No. I told him it would be fine, but then Brooke and I started talking. She told me you said it would take at least two months to get to St. Louis, and we probably couldn't even leave until spring. She also told me there was, like, a lot to learn. You know, like horses, and things."

"That's true."

"Well, I was thinking. You have a ranch and probably need a lot of help. We would like to apply for jobs with you."

"With me?" The offer caught Jack off guard. "What would you do?"

"Well, I was thinking that you would probably need help with your horses and cows and stuff."

Brooke jumped in. "I can clean and help around the house. Really, I can. I can learn to cook too."

Jack sat up straight and glanced over at Nicole, who had begun washing the Dutch oven. She glanced up at him, winked, and ever so slightly nodded her head.

Jack said, "Nicole, why don't you come over here and join us. I think this discussion requires everybody."

When she sat down, Jack continued, "All right, I'm not gonna apologize for honesty, but I am gonna lay this on the line for ya. I've seen the way you two work around here, and quite frankly, based on what I've seen, I wouldn't hire either of you. Neither one of you has a work ethic worth a damn, and you don't have much of a sense of responsibility. You're askin' me for a job, but you have no idea what you are talkin' about." Jack scratched his head, thinking. "On the other hand, I can also see where workin' on a ranch might help both of you out. Hell, if nothin' else, you'd be a hundred fifty miles closer'n you are now. All right, we'll give this a shot if you want, but you need to hear what you're in for. If you still think it's a good idea, we'll talk."

"My ranch is medium-sized by western standards. It covers a hundred twenty-five sections. That's about eighty thousand acres. We have nearly five hundred cow-calf pairs and a bunch of ornery Black Angus bulls that all need tendin' to. That means days in the saddle from five thirty or six in the morning until well after dark. We also run about a hundred fifty head of horses. There is no such thing as a forty hour work week or vacation days. We run twenty-four–seven, three-sixty-five. You might be shoveling shit one day and cuttin' nuts the next. If we need to herd cattle and it happens to be rainin', we get wet. In fact, with all the changes that flare brought, I have no idea how hard things are gonna be, but I do know they'll be a hell of a lot tougher than they were. Some of the jobs are kinda fun, but most are just plain hard work. There's no such thing as a job that's too dirty or too disgustin'. They all need to get done."

He turned to Brooke. "Darlin', I don't have a full-time job cleanin'. In fact, I think I might put Nicole in charge of the

house. If you are lookin' for work, what I got is the same thing I was describin' a few minutes ago. You'd have to be in the saddle a good part of the time. I know right now I want to get a chicken coop set up. That means feedin' and cleanin' out the coop. I'll tell you right now that is a nasty job. You thought it was gross when Ryan here had his hand up the backend of his horse. Well, you ain't seen dirty yet. You'd be in charge of killin' and cleanin' chickens. You might also have to butcher a cow every now and then. That means diggin' the guts out.

"Miguel is my top hand. He runs everything. What he says goes, and if you have a problem with him, you'll have a problem with me 'cause I'll *always* back him up. Everybody works and every job is different. If you think somethin' isn't fair or it's too hard, take it up with Miguel, and he'll find somethin' harder for you.

"One other thing. It's my ranch, so it's my rules. And just so we're straight, right now I consider the two of you a couple, so what happens between you two is none of my business or anybody else's on the ranch so long as it doesn't affect the work. I've had other young ladies work as hands for me before, and everybody knows I will not tolerate sexual discrimination or intimidation. If somebody is botherin' you, I want to know about it, and it'll be their last day. Also, there is no abusing livestock. If I ever see somebody hitting or hurting a horse, cow, dog, or anything else, I will come down on you like a ton of bricks, and you'll be gone.

"Now, if you're thinkin' that it sounds like a hard, dirty job, you're startin' to get the picture. Here's what I'm offerin'. If you work for me from now until—let's say May fifteenth—I'll feed you, I'll put you up, I'll keep you warm, I'll make sure you have clothes and your own tack. You'll learn how to ride, how to use a rope, how to shoot, and on May fifteenth if you're still with us, I'll give you each a horse of my choosin'. If you decide to quit, I will take you to Sheridan and drop you off. There's no comin' back. I can't abide with quitters, can't trust 'em. With all that's gone on, I bet there's plenty of guys lined up lookin' for work.

"You'll find me to be tough but fair. I'll never ask anybody to do a job I wouldn't do myself. I understand that you both are brand spankin' new to all of this, and I don't expect perfect right off. I do expect you to try hard and do your best. Although there's days it won't seem like it, every job is important, and you should take pride in doin' every one of 'em to the best of your ability. I expect that everybody who works for me rides for the brand. What that means is that you do every job the best you possibly can, just like you were doin' it for yourself—and I expect loyalty.

"Now, with all that said, do you still want to apply for this job?"

Ryan looked at Brooke and then said, "Can we talk about it?"

"Of course you can."

Ryan and Brooke got up from the table and walked out beyond the fire. Jack watched as they both seemed to be talking at the same time. He quietly said to Nicole, "What do you think?"

"Is it really that hard? Your description is not far from a labor camp."

"It's better to set a high expectation and then let them fit in. When they start complainin', and they will, I can take 'em back to this little talk. To tell you the truth, I half expect 'em to use this as a ride to Sheridan and jump off."

"I don't think so. I'm not sure what to make of Brooke yet. She looks like a babe in a very big forest. But Ryan appears to be hanging on every word you say. I believe he takes this very seriously."

"Brooke is gonna be a problem."

"She might. Then again, she might surprise you. I was thinking while you were talking. What are your expectations of me?"

Jack turned to her. "You're not workin' for me. You're my guest. Besides, you've already exceeded any expectations I had."

"What if I hit a horse?"

He smiled. "You won't. It's not in you. But I'll say this, if you decide you want to leave, I will make sure that you have a safe place to go in Sheridan."

"I suspect that is an option I'll not likely exercise."

"You say that now, but you don't know me that well. I can be an ornery son of a bitch."

"So can I."

He smiled at her. "Fair enough."


Ryan and Brooke walked back to the table holding hands. Ryan said, "I have a couple of questions."

"Shoot."

"First, will we have any time off, you know, so like we could hang out and stuff?"

"Most days your evenings will be free unless there's somethin' important goin' on. In practice, we try not to work on Sundays. All the workin' horses get Sunday off."

"Oh. Okay. So, like, where would we live?"

"Most of the hands live in the bunkhouse. I 'spect the two of you will get a room in the basement of the house. There's a separate entrance for you."

Brooke said, "Do we get to pick out the clothes, or is it like a uniform?"

Jack laughed. "Nope. No uniforms. You can pick out your own clothes. I'll help you get started."

Brooke gave him an odd look. "What does that mean?"

"Well, for example, you're gonna need a few pairs of jeans. Wranglers work best 'cause the seam on the inside of the leg won't chafe you. We're headed toward winter, so your clothes are gonna need to be warm."

"Oh, okay."

Ryan said, "So, one last question. What about Penny, and do we get to name our new horses?"

Jack said, "We'll get to Penny when you decide what you are gonna do. As to namin' horses…well, they already have a registered name. You can pick any barn name you want."

"Barn name? What's a barn name?"

"It's what you call the horse every day."

"Oh. Okay. So, I guess we want the jobs."

"Ryan, Brooke, you both heard what I told you. I'm gonna hold you to it. When you shake my hand, we're a done deal, and you both are workin' for me. Are we clear?"

"Yes, sir." Ryan said.

"Brooke?"

"Yes, sir."

Jack stuck out his hand, and they both shook it in turn. "Okay. Here's the deal. You're both on clean-up tonight after dinner. Nicole and I have been doin' it since we got here. Ryan, when you're done, I want you to bring your horse over here and tie her to the fence. We're gonna worm her tonight and work on her feet a bit. Brooke, I'm gonna have you haul a bunch of stuff back over to Dave's place tonight. Nicole is going with you to pick out some winter coats, hats, gloves, and long johns for all of us. Then we're gonna get this wagon mostly loaded tonight."

Brooke asked, "What are you gonna do?"

"Supervise."

# 43.

Jack stood alone in front of the fire, sipping a cup of coffee. The sun was beginning to break the horizon, and the dark hues of night were fading. He knew he should start rousting everybody out of bed; it was going to take a while to get everything ready to leave, but the quietness and peace of the early morning held him.

For a moment he wondered what day it was. He looked at his watch and saw the little number on the side read seventeen. Wednesday, if he recalled correctly. It had been just over four days since everything changed.

*Changed?* The word didn't seem strong enough. Everything he had known, understood, and come to expect was now completely, totally, and irrevocably altered. Life—his life—would be divided. There would always be the before and the after. Life before the flare and life after the flare. He was now only beginning to understand how things would become.

Life before had been so easy. Both hot and cold water ran out of a pipe in the wall at the touch of a knob. Even better, you could mix the two to set the temperature just the way you like it. The temperature inside the house was seventy-two in the winter and seventy-seven in the summer. No sense in paying

those few extra dollars to run the heat or air conditioner any more than necessary. With the flick of a switch, the night would vanish, and he could easily sit and read. The push of a small button on the remote would ignite the sixty-inch LED TV, and he could just sit back and watch the news from anywhere in the world, watch a movie of his choice, or learn about dangerous snakes in Australia. Even though he chose to live on a ranch nestled into the foothills of the Bighorn Mountains in Wyoming, he could talk on his cell phone, home phone, or video chat with nearly anyone in the world at any time. Hell, he could sit in his office in the house and watch the horses in the barn, the round pen, or the foaling stalls—all on his computer. And food? Real food, good food was only as far as the fridge if he remembered to go to the grocery store, or he could just sit in the truck and drive to the Dayton Diner. All of this was everyday, and it was all so easy it had become part of the background noise of life.

Most of the people in America had lived like this. Okay, some didn't have all the luxuries he had, but they all had food, a clean place to live, air conditioning, heat, running water, a toilet, and a TV if they chose. Most had a hell of a lot more than that. It occurred to him that by far the majority of the people living in the United States had lives and luxuries that far exceeded the kings of the world only a hundred or so years ago. Today, four days after the flash, everything was different.

His mind drifted to Annie. She was so much like her mother. He had always thought about her a lot, but since Friday night she was nearly always on his mind. He sent up another silent prayer. He wondered where she was and what she was doing right now. He knew her well enough to know that if she was still alive, and he prayed to God she was, she would try to get home.

Despite his petitions and reassurances, she had determined it was her job to take care of him ever since Jenni died. Well, maybe it wasn't Jenni's death, maybe it was the depression that followed. He had gotten a little lost there for a while. But he had gotten past it, or at least most of it. Life had found a way to

evolve into a different kind of normal, and he was interacting with the world again. He wondered what Annie would think about Nicole.

Nicole. What about Nicole? A week ago they would have passed each other on the street a hundred times without a second glance. He wasn't looking, and she would have never been interested in an old cowboy. Today, only four days after the flare, four days after everything changed, she was insistent on leaving with him by horse-drawn wagon to his ranch nearly a week away. He wondered again if he was really attracted to her, the whole person, or was it simply a physical thing? She was physically beautiful—hell, stunning. There was no question of that. He was male. Enough said. But, yet, there was more. He had known plenty of beautiful women, some of them younger. But none of them had the same effect on him she did. There was something about her. Something about the way she thought, she moved, and she acted. Something about the way she laughed and the things she laughed at. It all coalesced into something he had never seen before and something that had touched him very deeply. Being practical, he wondered if there was something in her that reminded him of Jenni. Could be. The two women were very different, but in other respects they were somewhat similar. They both had a grace that pervaded every fiber of their being. It was present in their movements, in the tilt of their chin, in the flash of a smile, a sparkle in their eye, in the words they used, and the intent behind them. Both women had a soul of refinement. They were ladies on the outside, always polite, always confident, but also sometimes silly and ready to laugh. Both women also weren't afraid to round off his hard edges. He thought about Nicole's quick wink and nod last night when Ryan had asked for a job. Jenni would have done exactly the same thing. It wasn't that they were telling him what to do; it was more like their softness and caring perspective could help to round off his hard edges. They could help guide him to a better mental place to interact with somebody or make a decision. How did she know?

He could fall for this girl. She wasn't Jenni; she was Nicole and she was different. She was her own person. Although she shared some of the same qualities as Jenni, she was unique, and he was constantly reminded and surprised by her independence, her charm, her wit, the depth and breadth of her knowledge, and sometimes her boldness. When she had made the comment about slicing through the tent wall to get to him in the middle of the night, it had taken him by surprise. Yesterday when she had fallen in the creek, she knew the wet clothes were sticking to her, and she knew he was looking. There was nothing about her that was narcissistic, yet she knew she had a good body, and she wasn't afraid to show it to him. It wasn't done in pride, rather it was confidence. The boldness of her kiss had shocked him, but again it was her confidence, and he liked it.

He shouldn't have asked for the second kiss. That was too forward, and he had probably taken advantage of a token of gratitude in her excitement. In fact, the whole thing was moving way too fast. Hell, he had only known her a couple of days.

Marlena chuffed nearby, and Jack looked over to see her standing next to the picnic table. He quietly said, "Good mornin'. How's the love of my life?"

"I should hope I do not have to compete with a horse for that title."

Jack spun his head in surprise to see Nicole standing behind him with her own cup of coffee. "Good Lord. You nearly scared the boots right off me. How long you been standin' there?"

She said, "I'm not sure. Awhile. Long enough to drink half a cup of this awful swill."

"Why didn't you say somethin'?"

She walked toward him. "I was enjoying the view, and it appeared as though you were deep in thought. I didn't want to disturb you."

"The view? There ain't much you haven't seen before. Besides, it's still half dark out here."

She wrapped an arm around his waist. "I was watching you standing by the fire. You certainly cut a dashing figure."

"Dashing? Well, I don't—"

"I was paying you a compliment. The proper response is 'thank you.' If you wish to extend that, you could add something such as, 'that's very nice of you to say.'"

Jack smiled and said, "Thank you. That's very nice to say."

"You're quite welcome. But now then, back to my original question: the love of your life is this horse?"

"Shh. Not so loud. She thinks so, and yeah, I s'pose she's one of 'em. She's also a good listener."

"And I am not?"

"No, you're a good listener too. It's just that her advice is better." He winked at her.

She whacked him lightly on the arm. "If you keep this up, I can promise you more conversations with her instead of me." She winked back. "So, do we have a plan for this morning?"

"Yep. I was thinkin' about knockin' the help out of bed, packin' up the tent, loadin' everything up, and gettin' the hell out of Dodge."

Nicole smiled and then giggled a little. "Oh, I had a devious thought. Do you think it would be possible to remove the tent without waking them?"

Now Jack smiled. "I'd say it'd be worth a try. They'd think twice about sleepin' in again. You're right. You are devious."

"Oh sweetheart, you don't know the half of my thoughts."

Jack was now grinning. "I bet I'd find 'em interesting."

"I bet you would."


In less than half an hour, Jack and Nicole had completely removed all the sections of the large wall tent and the frame. When they carefully lifted the canvas from the frame surrounding Brooke and Ryan's room, Jack whispered, "That little army cot doesn't look very comfortable for two. I can hardly sleep on the thing by myself."

Nicole whispered back, "I don't think they do much sleeping."

Jack rolled his eyes and nodded in understanding. A few minutes later, they had carried the sections of the tent and the

frame across the street to Dave's store and had finished packing the wagon.

They leaned against the picnic table and had a little more coffee. In front of them, the park lawn was nearly empty except for the lone cot with two sleeping people. Nicole said, "I would have thought they would awaken by now."

Jack smiled. "You thought you were devious. Darlin', you ain't seen nothin' yet." He walked to the wagon and dug through a small bag for a minute. He came back lightly, tossing an apple in the air and catching it. He pulled a thin black knife from his pocket and with a flick opened it and began slicing the apple. "Watch this."

Jack casually walked over to where Brooke and Ryan still lay sound asleep. He carefully placed several slices of the apple near their chins and then walked off into the pasture. A few minutes later he came back, leading Ryan's horse. Nicole watched, giggling to herself, as he gave the horse a few slices of the apple. Once the mare got a smell of the apple, she gobbled it up greedily. Jack led her to where Ryan and Brooke lay and unclipped the lead rope. Just as he made it back to where Nicole stood, Penny found the apples. He said, "This ought to be interestin'."

At first the horse wasn't sure what to do. She could smell the apples and kept stretching her neck and head out to find them, but the sleeping people seemed to make her nervous. Finally, the smell was overpowering, and she plunged her nose in to find the source. Both Ryan and Brooke awoke, screaming at the giant, fuzzy monster that appeared to be attacking them. The horse jumped back as the cot fell over to the other side. Brooke landed mostly on top of Ryan and was the first to her feet. Jack watched in surprise to see that she was completely naked. "Whoa." He turned around quickly. "I didn't see that comin'."

Nicole turned him back around. "You must see this!"

Brooke kept screaming but started to realize what was going on and grabbed the blanket from where Ryan lay. She pulled hard, trying to cover herself up, and as the blanket unwound, it

spit Ryan out on the wet grass, also completely naked. He floun-
dered and flopped like a fish out of water. Finally he found the
sleeping bag that had been underneath them and covered himself. "What the fuck?" he yelled and struggled to his feet. Brooke
started to laugh and pointed at Jack and Nicole leaning against
the table. "What the fuck?" he said again, bunching the loose
bag around him. He started moving toward Jack and Nicole.

"Maybe I should have a talk with him," Jack said, as he started toward the kid.

"What the fuck was that all about, and where's my goddamn
tent?"

"Take it easy. It was just a little joke, and you got surprised
is all."

"Take it easy? You expect me to take it easy? What the fuck,
man?"

Jack continued to walk toward Ryan with his hand in the air,
palm out in a "settle down" manner. "This was nothin' more
than a little fun. You don't want to do anything you might regret when you cool down."

"Fun? You call this fun? I thought I was gone get eaten by
a bear!"

Jack reached Ryan and stood in front of him, trying not to
laugh. Both men could hear the girls laughing behind them.
"Wasn't nothin' but Penny comin' over to give you a good
mornin' kiss." He could see the kid starting to unwind. "Nicole
and I woke up early and thought we'd let you two sleep in while
we got things ready to go. All you need to do is saddle your
horse, and we'll be ready. Well, maybe you might want to get
dressed first."

Ryan started to laugh a little bit. "It was kinda funny, now
that I think about it."

"It was funny as hell. I sure didn't expect you to be in your
birthday suit."

"I didn't expect to wake up with a horse gobbling all over
me."

Jack stepped in closer and lowered his voice. "Ryan, you've
come a long way in the last couple of days, but I'm gonna give

you a little piece of advice. You need to get that temper of yours under control a little better. You got a hold of it here, and that's good, but it took a while, and you need to work on it. One of two things happens when you get surprised like that. Either everything speeds up, and you react without thinkin', or everything slows down, and you can make better decisions. The difference between the two is up to you. Reacting without thinking will always hurt you. Might even get you killed. Remember that."

"Yes, sir."

"Now, go over and laugh about this with your girlfriend. She's takin' your lead on all this. Get yourself dressed without showin' your ass to Nicole, and let's get these horses saddled."

When Jack got back to Nicole, she asked, "What were the two of you discussing over there?"

"Oh, just some guy stuff."

"I am glad he was laughing."

"Me too."

Jack started rounding up horses and putting the harnesses on Marlena and Lucy. Brooke came over to where he was working and asked, "Am I gonna be like, riding in the wagon? 'Cause if I am, I don't really want to wear boots, you know? They would be so uncomfortable if I was just sitting there."

"Nope. You're on horseback."

"But, like, I really don't know how yet."

"That's why you're gonna do it."

Once Jack had the harnesses on and the horses hooked to the wagon, he spent twenty minutes showing Ryan and Brooke how to saddle a horse. He explained the how and why of every step as he put the saddle on Penny. When he was all finished, he asked, "Any questions?" They both said no. He then took the saddle and bridle off, dumping them on the ground. "Okay. Saddle up." He stood back and watched as Ryan saddled the horse.

The kid did pretty good, only having a little trouble with the bridle. Jack watched as both of them grimaced when he

explained again how to put your thumb in the horse's mouth to get her to open it for the bit.

"What if she bites you?" Brooke asked.

"She won't bite. You're puttin' your thumb where there's no teeth."

"You mean like she has a big gap? Does she need a dentist or like a horse orthodontist?"

"Nope." Jack smiled at her. "They're all made that way."

When Ryan was done, Jack took everything off again and made Brooke saddle her. She got everything right on the first try. He said, "Good job." He checked the cinch, tightened it a little, and said, "Here's the plan. Ryan, I'm gonna put you up on Dingo."

"But..."

Jack shot him a look, and Ryan closed his mouth. "You're gonna ride bareback just till we get to a store on the way out of town. I want Brooke to ride in a saddle since she's never been on a horse before. You have. You and Dingo are here to help her. If she gets into trouble, help her out or holler at me."

"Oh, okay," Ryan said with a look Jack thought was relieved pride.

Jack and Nicole sat next to each other on the bench of the wagon. He looked back to see both Brooke and Ryan sitting comfortably on their horses. He gave them a little wave, and they waved back. He snapped the reins, and they pulled out of the park. Nicole said, "This is so exciting. I've never been on a carriage ride before." Jack smiled.

# 44.

Megan awoke to the sound of crows cawing nearby. The sound was sharp, incessant, and it sounded like a lot of them. She wondered what had them so occupied and argumentative nearby. A bunch of crows is a...oh yeah, a murder. She pictured them picking at the bodies they had dragged behind the next hill and smiled. Mark lay beside her with his arm flopped over his face keeping the sun out of his eyes. She had been right about those guys yesterday. She knew it. She *fucking* knew it. That Willy guy especially. He had a look that was just wrong. The best part of the whole thing was how Mark handled it. One shot. She still couldn't believe it. The way he explained it, it sounded like he knew what he was doing, but she couldn't help but wonder if there wasn't a little bit of luck involved.

She unzipped her sleeping bag quietly and slipped on her boots. As she stood up, she knew she must look silly wearing nothing but the boots, but she didn't care. She needed the boots on the rocky ground, and she might decide to crawl back in the bag until Mark woke up. There was nobody around for miles, except Mark, to see her. Besides, she kind of liked being naked. The cold air was a little chillier than she expected, but

she walked away from camp with a feeling of renewed energy that was better than a Starbucks grande ever gave her. It occurred to her that sleeping naked, especially in town, might not be such a good idea. Anything could happen at any time, and they would need to be ready to go in a moment's notice.

It had been awhile since she had made the drive between Gillette and Buffalo, but she seemed to think they weren't very far from town—maybe fifteen miles. They could be in town by noon if they got moving. She squatted to relive herself. It was so much easier without trying to negotiate pants and all the rest of the shit during the day. Guys had it so much easier. All they had to do was whip their thingy out and take a leak. It didn't matter what they were wearing. A thought struck her. What was she going to do when she got her fucking period? God, she hated that. What a pain in the ass that was during normal times. Now, out in the middle of nowhere on horseback, it was going to be a complete nightmare. She'd have to remember to pick up tampons in Buffalo. She let herself drip and then shook herself a little to let the last drop or two fall.

No matter where you lived, soon everybody would be pissing outside. She liked Mark's idea of heading west. A little less snow and cold would make things a hell of a lot easier without electricity and central heating. She started thinking of things they would need to make an extended trip. The guns they had were great. Red had set Mark up right, but the camping gear was really meant for one person, and it was mediocre quality at best. They would also need some cold weather gear, and sooner rather than later. Everybody in Buffalo would be trying to find that stuff as soon as it got cold.

As she walked back to camp, the chilly air worked its way into her, and she shivered a little. Layers. Making sure they had clothes in layers would be key. As they got into higher elevations it would be cold at night but warm up a lot during the day. They would need to be able to accommodate the change. Even during the day, layers would help. If they had to work hard at something for a while, they would start to sweat, but as soon as you quit, you would get cold. Speaking of cold, she was

either going to have to get dressed or get back in the sleeping bag. She looked over to check on the horses grazing nearby.

"Those have to be the best pair of…"—he paused—"boots I've ever seen."

Megan looked over to see Mark sitting up in his sleeping bag and grinning at her. "You like them?" She lifted a leg twisting the boot in the air. "I think they really go with my outfit."

"I've got an outfit that goes with your outfit." He grabbed his crotch through the sleeping bag.

"I kinda like your outfit, but I was thinking…I bet we are only about twelve or fifteen miles from Buffalo. If we get our shit together and get on the road, we could probably be there by noon."

"Noon? Really?"

"Yeah. And then we could find a place to stay, get cleaned up a little, maybe something to eat, and a nice bed to lie on when you rock my world."

"Deal. To tell you the truth, the inside of my sleeping bag is getting kind of funky."

"I noticed you were getting kind of fuzzy, too."

Marked rubbed the stubble on his chin. "Yeah, well, so are you."

She looked down at her crotch and then her legs. "I know, I know. I could use a shower or another bath." She started getting dressed in the same clothes she wore yesterday. "Why do you think I want to get to Buffalo so bad?"

Mark watched her from the sleeping bag. "You know they have no electricity or running water or anything like that."

"Yeah, I know, but it will be a lot easier to get cleaned up there than it is out here."

"What are you going to do if we are out riding for a week or two?"

"I'll get dirty, just like you."

"And you won't freak out about it?"

"Am I freaking out now?"

"Well, no. But we've only been out for a couple of days."

"Don't confuse me with any of your old girlfriends. I can make do just fine. In fact, as I recall, I was the one who taught

you how to ride and shoot. I can hang with you anytime, anywhere."

"Okay, okay. Don't get all defensive."

"You started this."

"I know." Mark sat quietly thinking. "You know what? I'm sorry. You're right. I shouldn't have been so, I don't know. Such a dick."

Megan looked at him in surprise. The argument, if you could even call it that, was no big deal. He had been a little up in her shit, but really, this was nothing. She was right and she knew it. And now here he was, apologizing? Could this guy be for real? Damn. She hoped so. She walked over to him and squatted down so that she could look into his face. "You're not a dick. You're awesome." She kissed him.

About five hours later, they rode down Main Street side by side, leading the other horses in a line behind them. They had come into town on Hart Street and passed a green road sign, which read Buffalo. Pop 4585. Elev 4645. It looked undamaged, other than it was sticking out of the middle of the road at an odd angle. Several gas stations and motels had been mostly leveled by the disaster. A huge pole had once held a McDonalds sign but was now twisted into the shape of a corkscrew. In some areas they had to weave around burned and twisted vehicles, and occasionally Megan could still see some of the occupants inside. She kept saying, "Oh my God," over and over as the real extent of the devastation became apparent to her. They had passed a small, brown building on the right with a sign that read Sub Shop. A huge bulldozer, which had been mostly flattened by some unseen force, stood on end from out of the center of the building. When they turned south on Main Street, Megan almost broke into tears. An old house she had remembered from trips with her dad had burned to the ground.

Mark pulled them to a stop in front of a liquor store where several men milled about in the parking lot. He chatted with them for a few minutes and then disappeared into the store. A few minutes later, he returned with several bottles and tucked

them into the saddlebags. "These are for later. Might help take the edge off."

As they drew closer to downtown, more buildings remained intact. Megan wondered if it was because they were constructed out of brick or the crazy randomness of the destruction. Mark pointed toward a long, two-story, brick building ahead on the right. A green stripe across the second floor bricks held white letters that read OCCIDENTAL HOTEL. He said, "Might as well see if we can find a room here. At least the building is still standing." They turned the horses toward the building.

Megan noticed two other horses tied to a No Parking sign in the median in front of the hotel. She pulled her horse between two burned-out cars and into an area on the far south end of the building that had once been an outdoor dining area. Most of the tables were gone, but a small, green, decorative wagon and two wooden benches stood seemingly undisturbed near the street. She said, "You go in and see if there is a room for us. I'll stay out here with the horses."

Mark looked at her, thinking she looked a little pale. "Are you okay?"

"No. Not really. I'm kinda blown away by all this. I mean, I know you tried to explain it to me, but the real thing is kind of overwhelming."

"I know. It's a lot to take in. Just stay here. I'll be back in a couple of minutes, and we'll have a plan." He rummaged through the saddlebags for a minute and then walked down the sidewalk toward the front door.

Megan sat down on a wooden bench. Her legs felt weak. It felt as though her mind was trying to make sense of everything around her, but it just couldn't quite grasp the enormity of it. She closed her eyes and leaned her head back against a tree behind the bench. Mark had told her what he had seen in Gillette, and on one level she believed him. She knew he was right, and somewhere deep inside her she knew her parents were dead. But now, the destruction and chaos, seeing the details of everything firsthand—it felt as though reality was crushing her. Along the way from Gillette, they had seen several dead

bodies. In fact, they had seen many. The first ones had shocked and repulsed her, but over the last few days, those feelings had worn off. She had quickly learned to simply not look if it could be avoided. But since they had come into town only a little while ago, she had seen probably fifty or sixty bodies. They seemed to be everywhere. Most of them, still sat inside the remains of vehicles, burned or charred; but a few were lying in the front yards of homes or parking lots, where it looked like they had fallen trying to run away from the flames. Some were not burned at all. They lay on the street or in lawns or on the sidewalk, creamy white and swollen, like grotesque caricatures of the people they once were. Her head felt light. She breathed in deeply, trying to clear her thoughts, when she detected a faintly sweet smell in the air. The smell of dead bodies? She bent over, putting her head between her knees, in an effort to stop the nausea and lightheadedness. After several minutes of sitting like this, and not feeling better, she felt a hand on her back.

"Hey, are you all right?" Mark said, gently rubbing.

"No. I'm probably gonna puke. You might want to stand back."

"I'm not going anywhere. I'll hold your hair."

She turned her head to the side, so she could see him, and gave a little smile. "You're all right, cowboy."

"You will be too."

"Do you smell that? Oh my God, what is that?"

Mark looked around. "You mean that kinda weird funk? It's probably that." He pointed to a large pile of cut flowers and brown, plastic vases that had spilled out the side of a box van and lay rotting in the sunshine. The delivery vehicle lay on its side and looked as though some unseen giant foot had crushed it.

"Rotten flowers? Is that what I have been smelling?"

"I think so."

She started to laugh. "Oh, wow. Thank God. I thought it was dead bodies."

"Eh, I don't think they smell like flowers."

She sat up, starting to feel better. "I haven't exactly smelled a lot of dead people."

"Yeah, but you've smelled dead things—like roadkill—before, right?"

"Sure."

"People are probably the same."

"Okay, I'll give you that. What did you find out?"

"There's a guy working in there trying to clean the place up. I think he's the manager or owner or something. Anyway, we worked out a deal. He said the inside of the hotel wasn't damaged too bad. At least most of the rooms are still usable. We have the biggest room in the place, which doesn't sound like it's all that big, and we can stay as long as we want for up to two weeks. No laundry, though. He will feed us breakfast and supper, but he gets to decide what we get. Oh, and he said that we could keep the horses in the park area behind the hotel along this creek. He said it goes back about two blocks or so."

"That's kind of handy."

"That's what I thought. Oh yeah, he also said that he would get us a kerosene lamp, and get this: they still have running water."

"Really? I thought without electricity everybody would be out of water."

"He said the city gets its water from someplace up in the mountains. The system always has pressure. A bunch of guys got together a couple of days ago and shut off areas that were broken or just spraying water all over the place. The only problem is they don't have any hot water. I guess some of the city guys are trying to get that worked out before winter. Something to do with the gas lines or something."

"No shit?" Megan thought about the implications of this. If the city still had running water and could get the natural gas flowing again, then cooking, hot water, and heat would be easy. Hell, if they could get a couple of generators working again, they might have electricity in no time. This place would be a boomtown. People would flock here from everywhere. "I wonder why the pipes didn't get all messed up in the event?"

"I asked him that. He said the city used the stimulus money a few years ago to replace all of the old water mains with new plastic stuff. Same thing with the natural gas lines. I guess they did both projects at the same time."

"So what does all this cost us?"

"Ten full ounces of silver, and I had to pay him today. Same price if we stay one night or two weeks."

"Wow. That's a little steep."

"Yeah, but he's probably the only game in town."

"We could go find an empty house."

"Yeah, I thought about that too, but then we have to worry somebody might come back or want it more than we do."

"Good point. So, I suppose we have to carry all this shit in."

"I can do it if you don't feel good."

"You'll be lucky to keep up with me, cowboy."

The room was nice, but not huge, and was carefully decorated to look as it had in the 1800s, with furniture from the period. A large, four-poster, king-sized bed made of beautiful cherry wood occupied the center of the room. A small couch sat across from it against the wall, and an antique table and chairs sat in a corner near the door. At first glance it appeared as though the disaster had completely missed this room. A second glance, however, revealed a floor lamp that was bent in two areas and almost reached back to the floor. The doorknob from the bathroom door was embedded in the ceiling, and a metal pipe stuck out of the wall near a dresser.

In the middle of the bathroom stood a huge claw-foot bathtub, with shiny chrome pipes standing perfectly from the wooden floor. Megan sat on the edge of the tub and tried the knob. Water ran from the tap. As she watched water run into the tub and down the drain, she thought how amazing it was to have this luxury. Running water inside the building. A week ago she would have complained there was no shower in the room, but today she was thrilled to simply have the cold water.

In the lobby she had read a small plaque that told the history of the hotel and listed some of its famous guests. She

wondered if some of the guests had been as thrilled with the running water as she was now. She looked over to see the toilet and smiled as she pictured some old cowboy, ecstatic he didn't have to go to the outhouse in the middle of the night. All of the technological advances society had made in the last one hundred years had been wiped out in a single freak accident. They were living in the Wild West.

# 45.

Jack was quietly thrilled with the progress they were making. Before leaving town they had stopped at SawBuck's and picked up a saddle and bridle for Brooke. He had found a nice, slightly used saddle that fit her and the horses well and seemed to have enough conchos and saddle strings to satisfy Brooke's sense of taste. He also picked up saddlebags and a pair of chinks for both of them. At first Ryan was a little hesitant and refused to try on what he called "short pants," but when the owner had explained how useful they were and that all of the cowboys wore them and relied on them, he changed his mind. Ryan had found a simple pair in brown leather, but Brooke found a pair in dazzling white leather with wild pink and purple embroidery across the top. She giggled as she kept looking at her butt in a mirror.

They followed Highway 14 south to the grocery store where Jack had shot the gunman. Now, two men with rifles sat in folding chairs near the door, and a third patrolled the inside. They picked up a little more food since Jack hadn't planned on Ryan and Brooke traveling with them.

As they pulled away and started making their way out of town, Jack made a few more notes on a little piece of paper and

then tucked it back into his shirt pocket. Nicole asked, "I have seen you jot things down on that little paper before. May I ask what that is?"

"It's my ledger."

"Ledger?"

"I'm keepin' track of what I owe all these folks. I'll need to get 'em paid."

"I thought money was no longer of much value."

"There's more'n one way to get somebody paid. Once we get home and situated, I'll come back and get these good folks taken care of."

She looked a little surprised. "You would ride all the way back here, some one hundred fifty miles, just to pay these people for those few items?"

"Of course, but it's not just them. I owe quite a few people in town. That stuff we picked up at SawBuck's don't come cheap. Normally, I don't believe much in credit. Doesn't sit well with me. But we're kind of in a bind right now."

"That is really quite remarkable. Not many people would do the same."

"Oh, I don't know. Maybe not in the cities, but out here a man is only as good as his word. I gave 'em my word I would make it right, and I will."

"Even though it would take you nearly two weeks and three hundred miles on horseback?"

"Don't matter. That's my problem, not theirs."

"Although I'm not advocating this, I could see where you might never meet these people again. A hundred fifty miles is quite a long distance today. You could simply never return."

Jack nodded his head. "That is true. I could do that, but I'd be the one who lost. I'd always know what I did. It takes a long time of doin' the right thing to earn a good reputation, and a reputation is nothin' more than other people knowin' what you already know about yourself. A little time and a few miles ain't much to keep it."

She put her hand on the top of his thigh and rubbed it a little. "You are an interesting man, Dr. Neumann."

As they left town, the highway bent gently to the east. Ahead on the right, a small lake with a white shoreline stood peacefully as though nothing had changed, but across a highway on their left, the large airport parking lot held nearly forty or fifty cars that were now nothing but burned, blackened ruins. Farther east, at least twenty small steel buildings, which had once been small hangers for personal aircraft, had completely disintegrated, with their contents strewn over a wide area. Twisted, contorted steel lay everywhere, and two small aircraft lay upside down and partially on top of each other in the middle of the westbound side of Highway 14. The walls of a brick building on the east side of the lot had partially fallen or exploded, with bricks strewn over the asphalt of the lot. As they passed the building, they could see the east side had been largely destroyed by fire.

"What is that?" Brooke asked from behind the wagon.

"The airport, or at least what's left of it." Jack looked over his shoulder back at Ryan, who sat motionless as Dingo slowly walked onward. The kid looked pale. From here they could see straight down the length of the runway, where a commuter jet had tried to land but had broken apart, scattering aluminum, parts, insulation, and passengers down the long, straight pavement. He wondered if Ryan had still held on to the false hope that the airport might not have been affected, that once they had gotten here, they might have found everything in its normal bustling state, with cars moving in and out, a jet sitting on the ramp, and crews getting it ready for the next flight. Instead, they found unimaginable devastation.

They continued east along the highway as it rose slightly and overlooked the airport and much of the town below. From this vantage point, the total destruction of Cody was apparent and overwhelming. Whole neighborhoods had been left in blackened ruins. Some city blocks had little or nothing still standing, and others appeared nearly untouched. They continued eastward as the city gave way to the flat scrub and grass that covered the Bighorn Basin.

For the next two hours, they walked the horses without much conversation, everybody lost in their own thoughts. Jack had kept them to a moderately fast walk, and the horses seemed to be doing fine. Around them the scenery was flat and largely barren, with small rolling hills in the distance and occasional rock outcroppings.

Nicole looked around at the view and said, "This is absolutely beautiful out here."

Jack said, "You like it?"

"Oh, yes. This is how I would have imaged the West to be. It conjures images of cowboys and Indians."

"We're not far from it."

"I suppose we're not. We have the horses, the covered wagon, and even the guns."

"Did I show you this little gem?" Jack pulled a short, double-barreled shotgun out from under the wooden bench they were sitting on.

"Oh, my. No, I don't think you did."

"This is called a coach gun. Back in the days of the stagecoach, the driver would keep one of these handy. It does wonders to discourage trouble."

"Good Lord, that thing must shoot an enormous bullet."

"Nope. No bullets. This one is loaded with buckshot. It a bunch of little pellets that spread out when they leave the barrel. Covers a wide area, so you don't have to aim carefully. Just be close."

"I see. Why are there two barrels?"

"Two shots. Then you have to reload."

"And is it deadly?"

"Yes, indeed. It just won't reach out very far. It's more for close work."

"I noticed that you put a rifle in the back this morning. The one with the loopy handle-thing hanging from the bottom."

"I did."

"I don't understand. Why do we need so many guns? Won't the ones we already have be enough?"

"Think of a gun like a tool. Each one is made for different kind of work. They all have their place and a specific use."

"That is one thing I have never understood about you Yanks. You all seem to love your guns. The impression of America from abroad is that you are all very well armed and very willing to use them."

"That's partially true. As a group, the citizens of the U.S.A. are well armed, but I think you'll find that we have lower crime rates than most of the rest of the developed world."

"Yes, but your standard of living is higher."

"Agreed. But wouldn't you say every society has certain members that are willin' to take from the more privileged?"

"Yes, of course."

"But we didn't have higher crimes rates."

"I see your point."

Jack continued, "I don't think guns ever had much of an impact in the way of committin' crime. Oh, they might embolden the occasional idiot, but that's more of an exception than a rule. Even if most criminals had no guns at all, they would still give their plan a try. Common criminals aren't exactly known for their intelligence. However, I think they do add a certain deterrence. Even the dumbest guy out there will think twice when his intended victim might shoot back. But, the real reason we have so many guns in America is freedom. The difference between an armed citizenry and an unarmed one is that the armed always have the ability to change the leadership. Our founding fathers thought the right to protect yourself and to protect your property was God-given. That applies to the individual, but it also applies to the group. If our leadership becomes a tyranny, then it's not only our right to protect ourselves, but it's our responsibility."

"I had never thought about it quite like that."

"Let's say I started makin' advances toward you, and you didn't like it. It's your right to tell me to get lost. If I keep pressin' the issue, it becomes your *responsibility* to protect yourself. Same thing goes for somebody tryin' to steal your cattle or steal

your freedom. Freedom is as much of a responsibility as it is a right."

"Well, I think you'd find very little in the way of resistance from me, most likely encouragement, but I do see your point." She smiled.

Jack smiled back. "In most of Europe, the ruling class had a long history of the people rising up against 'em. They don't want you armed in case you decide you don't like the way things are goin'. They've taken away the right to defend yourself against tyranny."

"Yes, but we could protest, much like you do here. It has always been effective in making the will of the people known to the rulers."

"What if they said no?"

"Well then, I suppose things would intensify."

"Yep. But only to a point. The rulers have the army, and they are the only ones with guns. As a ruler you generally pay a little closer attention when the citizens can revolt and shoot you."

"You make a very compelling argument."

"Thanks. I have spent some time thinkin' about this."

"I should say so."

Jack sat up straight and stretched his back. "What do you say we take a break?"

"Splendid. I could use a stretch."

Twenty minutes later Jack announced that break time was over, and they should all mount up. Brooke said, "I don't want to be tied up to the back of the wagon again. I'm ready to ride on my own."

Jack asked, "Do you know how to steer?"

"No."

"Here, let me show you." For the next ten minutes, he gave her a small lesson on the basics of riding. Each time he would show her something, she quickly said, "Okay, I got it." Finally he said, "Get up there and ride a couple of circles out in the grass."

"That's boring."

"If you been ridin' your entire life, it is. When you're just startin' out, it's a good way to find out what you know and what you don't."

Brooke climbed into the saddle like she had done it a thousand times. She held the reins the way Jack had shown her and made a clucking sound with her mouth. Penny walked out in the grass easily. Jack was surprised at how confident she was. She then made Penny walk in fairly small circles at first and then gradually widened the circle.

Nicole stood next to Jack and looked up to see his eyebrows raised in surprise. She said, "If I didn't know better, it would be difficult to realize she was a new rider."

"That's what I was thinkin'."

Brooke called to Jack, "How do I make her go faster?"

"You don't need to go any faster just yet."

Brooke ignored him and made the clucking sound again. Penny continued to walk. She then made a kissing sound, and the horse sped up into a trot. Jack watched as Brooke initially bounced in the seat. He was surprised to see her laughing. "This is fun!" Brooke yelled, as the horse continued to trot. Over the next few minutes, she changed the way she bounced with the horse by slightly pressing down into the stirrups with her legs and appeared to smooth out the bounce. She made the kissing sound again, but the horse didn't change speed. She leaned forward and pressed the sides of her heels into the horse, and Penny broke into an easy lope. Jack watched in utter amazement as the girl sat balanced and confident on the horse as though she had done it her entire life. She was smiling and laughing as Penny continued to make wider circles. Brooke pulled the reins gently to one side, and the horse straightened out. A few minutes later, she came back and stopped in front of Jack.

Jack shook his head. "Where in the hell did you learn to do that? You've been riding before."

Brooke was all smiles. "No, I haven't. I swear. It just kinda like made sense, and besides, everything was going so smooth

and it was so fun, I was like, wow, what else can we do. I kinda guessed that if I bounced before the horse did when she was all bumpy and stuff, it would get a lot smoother. It did. The last part was totally awesome. I want to do it again."

"Whoa. Hang on there. You'll have this horse wore out, and we still have a long way to go. How's your backside?"

"It's not too bad. I mean, I can like feel it and everything, but it's not too bad."

"Good. 'Cause you have a lot more time in that saddle in front of you."

As Jack climbed up into the wagon, he said, "You two stay close. This is a marathon, not a sprint. If you're too far out in front, I can't help you if you need it. Ryan, keep an eye on her."

"Okay."

Jack leaned toward Nicole. "I should have told Brooke to keep an eye on Ryan. I've never seen anyone pick it up that fast. The girl's a natural."

They continued east the rest of the morning and afternoon. Only twice they passed burned vehicles, and once they passed an older Chevy pickup that had been left abandoned along the road the same way Jack's Ford had. The bland, mostly flat sage and grass passed by slowly. They never saw any other people.

When Jack looked at his watch it was almost six thirty. They had just passed a sign that read Emblem, and several small buildings were scattered along the road. "We'll stop up here. I think I know a spot where we can set up camp off the road. Another mile farther east, he turned left onto a gravel road. The road continued north toward a small bluff.

Nicole could see a few trees scattered near the hill's base. "Why here?"

"There's a small creek up ahead where we can water the horses again. The trees will keep the wind out of our hair."

"Do you know this area?"

"Nope. Only seen it from the road."

"Why is it so green here and yet so brown only a few miles back?"

"Water. They irrigate. Folks around here produce a lot of hay and crops. This'll be all brown next year."

"Oh? Why is that?"

"No electricity to get the water out of the ground. Not a lot of rain on this side of the mountains."

It was nearly dark when the tent was set up, the horses fed and watered, and they finally sat down around a small campfire to a hot meal.

Ryan asked, "How far do you think we went today?"

Jack smiled. "We did good. Made it a lot farther than I would've guessed we would. I think Emblem is nearly thirty-five miles from Cody. We should be in Greybull tomorrow morning. If the horses are in good shape and we keep movin' like we have, we might just push on to Shell. After that the fun begins."

"Fun?" Brooke asked.

"The mountains."

"Hey, boss," Ryan said, "I was wondering. This tent is smaller than the one we had in Cody."

"Yep."

"Well, I noticed there is only one divider. It only has two rooms."

Jack realized with a sinking feeling where the kid was going with this. "Yep, I reckon it does."

"So, how is this gonna work tonight?"

"Generally we sleep at night."

"No. I know that. I was just wondering how the sleeping arrangements were going to work."

Jack glanced up to see Nicole looking at him, expecting an answer. He looked at Ryan and said, "I know what you're gettin' at, and it's really none of your damn business."

"Sorry."

# 46.

An hour later Brooke and Ryan said goodnight and disappeared into the tent. Jack and Nicole remained by the fire, comfortable in their folding camp chairs, watching the flames. Jack pulled the little, silver flask of whiskey out of a vest pocket and offered it to Nicole. "Good Lord, it's about time," she said as she accepted the flask from him.

She stuck her arm out as if to hand it back, but then pulled her arm close again. She said, "I'll only give this back when you tell me what the sleeping arrangements are."

Jack said, "That's evil trickery."

Her eyes danced in the firelight. "Yes, it is."

"Well," he hesitated, "you're gonna take the cot in the tent, and I'm gonna sleep in the wagon. It's my fault we only have the two cots and two rooms. I didn't think it through."

Nicole got up from her chair, walked over to Jack, and stood in front of him as he sat on the small folding chair. She sat down, straddling his legs, and looked at him closely for a moment. She handed him the flask and said, "All right then. I think we need to clarify a few things. For the last several days, I have made it painfully obvious I am more than attracted to you. In fact, the truth of the matter is that despite an awful

fear of being hurt, I am falling in love with you, and I am powerless to change my feelings. I have never felt quite like this before, and I have never tried to be so obvious. I realize I am awkward, but please understand that I don't know what else to do. Also, you said you were attracted to me, and I believe you. With the exception of two small kisses that I stole, you have done absolutely nothing to show you find me sexy or are romantically inclined. I need to know now, before I go mad, what the hell is going on. Are you attracted to me or not?"

Jack took a deep breath and looked deeply into her eyes. "Yes. I am attracted to you. Very attracted."

"Then why the hell don't you do something about it?"

"I'm not sure what to do."

"Oh, come on. It's not that bloody difficult. You are a man and I am a woman. The rest is really quite simple." She took his hand and guided it to her thigh.

Jack could feel the warmth of her leg through the material. In his mind he could picture her smooth skin just below his hand. An image of her standing nude in the rough shower in his tent flashed through his mind, and he could feel his heart quicken. "That's the trouble. It's not really simple. At least it's not simple for me. For you this is all new, but for me, well, I've got history. I had a life with somebody that I loved, and I lost her. I hurt her bad, and it was my fault, pure and simple. You might understand why I might be a little reluctant to hurt somebody I care about again."

Nicole thought about what he said. In a soft, caring, concerned voice she said, "Or care about somebody you might hurt?"

"Maybe."

From behind them the sound of quiet whispers and rustling in the tent turned into the sounds of Brooke gasping in a rhythmic, growing intensity. Nicole stood up and offered her hand to Jack. "Come on. Let's go for a walk. The sound of wildlife might be better suited to a conversation than the sound of wild life."

He took her hand, and the two of them walked slowly down the gravel road under the faded but still colorful sky. Marlena looked up and chuffed softly as Jack left camp.

Nicole said, "Twice now you have mentioned that your wife's death was your fault. I heard it was cancer. How can the two possibly be related?"

Jack sighed. "A man can't keep anything private." They walked quietly for a few minutes, and then Jack continued. "I've never told this to anyone. Hell, I can barely admit it to myself, but I'll tell you, and then you can decide if you still think I'm attractive.

"We had been here for a couple of years. Jenni was startin' to get involved with the museum and art scene in Cody. We got invited to a charity ball and award ceremony. Big, fancy, black tie event in Cody. It also happened to be her birthday. I knew she was gonna receive the award for Volunteer of the Year, so I surprised her with a gift and a little Champagne at a suite at the best hotel in town. Well, after the dinner, her award, and the dance, we went back to the suite and started doin' what couples in love generally do. Kind of in the middle of things, I thought I felt somethin' different in her left breast. It was one of those things, kinda lit up a light on my old doctor's warning panel; but with the evening and everything else, I wasn't about to ruin things by stoppin' and saying I felt somethin', so I ignored it. Time went by, and I felt it again. I rationalized it to myself; she's a low-risk person. There was no history of any type of cancer in her family, she was the wrong age, she never smoked—nothin'. Hell, she was healthy and could run circles around me. Since she was in her early-forties, she didn't even need a mammogram every year. When she finally went, almost two years after that charity dance, they found a mass. Of course the biopsy was positive. A CT scan showed the cancer had already spread everywhere."

Jack stopped talking and took a long drink from the flask. They kept walking, and Nicole kept a tight hold of his hand. "She did it all. She took the chemo until she damn near puked her guts out and she could barely stand up. She did the

radiation therapy—burned the hell out of her. She lost nearly thirty pounds, and at times the pain from the cancer in her bones would be so bad she would hallucinate. She kept sayin' she wanted to fight it. Wanted to beat it 'cause she wanted to be around to take care of me."

Nicole could hear his voice break a little. He took another drink of the whiskey.

"That woman spent her entire life takin' care of me. She worked while I was in school. She raised our daughter while I was workin'. When the job started takin' a toll on me, she was the one who gave up everything and moved us up here. That was for me, not her; she had a life and friends in San Antonio. I started gettin' the horse thing goin', and she would feed, water, shovel shit, or drive anywhere just to make my dreams come true.

"I stood by her side and did the best I could through all of her treatment. We went all over the country to see various specialists. They all said the same thing. In the end, I held her in my arms when she died. I heard that last breath and felt her finally relax. We buried her on the ranch, right where she wanted. It's a pretty spot behind the house on a hilltop where you can see forever. She said she wanted to be able to push her flowers up every spring."

Jack's voice had broken a little. He took another drink and walked quietly for a few minutes, collecting himself. "You see, if I would have said somethin', she would've gotten things checked out, and they would have found her cancer a lot earlier. Simple little surgery. Nothin' more than a lumpectomy and a little radiation. Everything would have been over and done with. Maybe I was too worried about what that little lump could be that I didn't want to know the truth. Maybe I was just worried about myself. No matter what excuse I try to put on it, the truth of the matter is that I knew somethin' was wrong and didn't do anything about it."

"Jack, I am so sorry, for *both* of you. That is terrible and tragic. In a perfect world, nobody should ever have to endure anything such as that, especially when it comes to the ones they

love. Your wife should not have had to endure everything she went through, but you should not have had to endure the pain you have been through either. But I have an important question for you. If you believe you are to blame, then what is your penance and when are *you* forgiven?"

She led him to a group of rocks along the creek and sat down on a large flat boulder. When he sat next to her, she continued, "I believe I told you that when I was small I went to a Catholic school. The nuns were harsh and swift to punish students for the slightest infraction, but they were also loving and caring and kind. They taught us the process of confessing our sins and receiving penance. They also taught about absolution and forgiveness. I remember one particular sister who told me that when I was forgiven I was as far removed from my sin as the east was from the west. She told me that God was love and *always* forgave us our sins no matter how grave *we* believed them to be. Understand, penance is not what you do in order to receive forgiveness, it is what you do for yourself to feel better about receiving the forgiveness you already have.

"So, here you are today. It has been years since your wife died. Donna at the Cowboy store told me that for several years you didn't leave the ranch. She also told me she has never known you to even so much as look at a woman other than your wife—that is why she was so surprised to see me with you. So, my question to you is: how much? How long do you have to be alone? How long do you have to carry this guilt with you? How much do you have to pay? Forgive me for being this forward, but it seems to me that your wife loved you as much as you loved her. How long would she have let you carry this around before she would have forgiven you? Jack, love forgives."

"This ain't about her."

"You're absolutely right. This is about you. Have you never made a mistake before or seen it happen to someone else? Life goes on. Your life goes on. You can remain in the past and dwell on what you cannot change, or you can move forward and live."

"Miguel told me the same thing."

"It sounds as though he is a brilliant man."

Jack smiled. "Did I ever tell you about Marlena?"

"No, I don't think so."

"She told me the same thing too."

"Oh, now this I simply must hear."

"We got Marlena when she was a three-year-old. I liked her conformation and her eye, but Miguel didn't care much for her. He thought there was somethin' wrong with her. We worked her for about three months and couldn't break her. Keep in mind, we usually get on a new horse's back in a week or two. She was mean. Kept tryin' all kinds of nasty tricks to bite us or throw us off. Finally we decided she wasn't worth the effort, so we'd put her to pasture as a broodmare. She tried to kill the stud when we had her bred, but we got it done. The followin' spring she foaled early. One of the guys made a mistake with a gate, and she and her foal ran out of the barn into a back pasture. We just let 'em go; the weather was supposed to be nice for a few days, and it would have been more dangerous to try and get 'em back in than just let 'em run—or so I thought. Well, a couple hours later, I heard this awful carryin'-on from out behind the barn. I looked out and saw that her foal had fallen through the ice in a little pond. Marlena was standin' on the shore pawin' at the ground and watchin' him struggle. I was the only one around, so I ran over there as fast as I could and after breakin' ice and strugglin' for forty-five minutes in that cold water, I managed to drag the foal out. He was long dead by that time, and there was nothin' anybody could have done differently. It was a damn shame. He was going to be a good horse. She kept nuzzling him, trying to get him up, and I could tell she kinda knew what was going on. I walked away and let her be with that foal overnight. The next mornin' she was standin' at the door to the paddock, so I let her in. I went back out and buried the foal. She watched me the entire time over the gate. When I came back to the barn, I walked through the paddock where she was standin', and she started followin' me. That's usually a sign a horse sees you as the boss. When I turned around, she came right up and let me scratch her head.

That was the first time since I bought that horse she actually let me touch her without tryin' to bite me. Two days later, I was ridin' her, and she never once offered to buck. To this day, she is the lead mare of our remuda, and I'm the only one she will let ride her. Oh, I can put you up there, but I better be close.

"Well, when we had the funeral for my wife, everything was done graveside. Right behind the grave is the east fence of our horse pasture. The entire time through that funeral, Marlena stood quietly all alone on the other side of the fence. I remember it was the strangest thing. She didn't graze, she didn't move. She just watched. It was like she knew. I sat in a chair alone by the grave for a long time after everyone else had left, and she just stood right there by the fence. She wouldn't leave as long as I sat there.

"I spent the next year and a half feelin' sorry for myself. In fact, it kept gettin' worse and worse. Miguel tried everything to get me out of that house. Toward the end of that stretch, I couldn't even get myself out of bed. I had quit eatin' and I didn't talk to anybody. One mornin' Miguel come in that house leadin' Marlena. He brought her right through the front door, down the hall, into my bedroom, unclipped her lead rope, and said, 'She won't eat either. The two of you can stay in here until you work this out.' Then he walked back out and shut the door behind him. I just laid there lookin' up at this giant horse. You don't really appreciate how big they are until they're in the house with you. Well, she come over and started pushin' me around with her nose. I had no choice. I had to get out of bed and start livin' again. After that, I still had a few bad days, but things started gettin' better. That was almost three years ago now."

"Smart horse. So you've gotten the same advice from me and your best friend, and even your horse seems to know that life goes on. Where does that leave you?"

"If you would have asked me a week ago, I would have said I was doin' just fine. Life was a routine; I was laughin' once in a while. Things were good."

"And you were alone."

"I was. Probably by design. I guess I figured it was the least I deserved."

"And is that okay with you?"

"I thought so, until you came around."

"And what are you going to do about it?"

"I'm not sure."

Nicole took a drink. "I understand. Things have changed considerably in the last few days. I want you to listen carefully because I am going to tell you where I stand, and I am going to make a promise to you as well.

"Thank you for sharing this with me tonight. I know this has been difficult for you. I understand you might need more time to sort all of this out and move on with your life; however, I am going to sleep next to you in that wagon tonight, and I will sit next to you on the bench tomorrow and the next day, and the next. I will hold your hand as we walk, and I will laugh at your stupid jokes, share your whiskey and your coffee, help you with lunch, dinner, laundry, and anything else I can find. The entire time I will crave the touch of your hands. I will dream of your arms wrapped around me, the taste of your kiss, and the day I will dig my nails into your back. I am not leaving you, Jack Neumann. I will wait for you as long as it takes or until you ask me to leave, but I will not leave you."

"You sound serious."

"You're damn straight." She smiled.

"You know, I was kinda feelin' bad that I took advantage of you the other day with that second kiss."

"Don't be silly."

"I'm serious."

She shook her head. "You realize, of course, that you are the one who is supposed to be chasing me?"

Jack smiled. "In a perfect world."

"What is your phrase? 'Cowboy up'? Well, my friend, I should say it's time to cowboy up."

"Now?"

"Hell yes, now. Why do you think I'm still sitting here?"

Jack pulled her into his arms and kissed her.

# 47.

Mark sat across a table draped in white linen from Megan as they sipped red wine. He was starting to like the taste of the stuff. The hotel manager's wife had served them, and two older gentlemen sitting at a similar table on the other side of the restaurant, grilled steak and canned corn for dinner. The taste was wonderful, and Mark had eaten until he felt as though he was going to bust. When dinner was finished and he didn't think he could eat another bite, she had brought out a bowl of strawberries and some chocolate sauce to dip them in. She had explained that these were the last strawberries they would see until next summer. Mark watched as Megan was in near ecstasy as she ate berry after berry.

As they were finishing dessert and about to leave and go back to their room, Mark could see two men in big black hats walk in the front door of the hotel and speak to the manager at the main desk in the lobby. The manager pointed at Mark and Megan. As the men approached the table, he continued his conversation casually with Megan but slipped the XD(m) out of its holster and held it in his lap.

"Excuse me," the taller of the men said. "I'm Cal Reynolds and this here is Art Bergman. We're with the Johnson County

Sheriff's Department. Do either of you know anything about a couple of the horses out back. One is a gray, and the other is a long-legged chestnut with two white socks."

Mark said, "Yeah, I know them. We brought them in. We rode into town this morning from Gillette. Found them wandering along the interstate about twenty miles or so out of town. Had their saddles on and everything."

"Did you happen to see who was riding them?"

"Nope. They were just wandering. Dragging their reins behind them. We figured it would be better to bring them along than just let them wander like that."

Megan added, "They seem like nice horses. One is a roper or a ranch horse."

Cal visibly relaxed. "You're right. They are nice horses. They belong to a ranch just north of here. A couple of nights ago two of their hands rode into town to find some supplies and were shot. They were left lying in the middle of road, and the horses were gone."

Mark said, "I took the saddles off and then put them back on again. Sorry if I messed up the fingerprints for you."

Cal shook his head. "No such thing as fingerprints anymore. All of the computers we used for that are toast. Same goes for ballistics, DNA, and just about everything else we used to have."

"Oh jeez. Sorry."

Art spoke up. "Same thing goes for the court as far as I'm concerned. If I find those guys, I'll deal out the justice myself."

Mark was a little surprised at the bold comment. "Yeah, I guess it's kind of like the Wild West again."

Art said, "Yep. Probably a good thing if you ask me."

Megan said, "We can help you get the horses and their tack. The saddles and stuff are in that little plastic shed by the back of the hotel."

Cal said, "If you could, that would be helpful. Thanks."

When they got back to their room, Megan lit the kerosene lamp, and said quietly, "You were awesome with those guys from the sheriff's department."

"Thanks. Once I found out what they were up to, I almost decided to tell them that we shot those guys."

"Probably better that you didn't."

"Yeah, probably." Mark walked around the room. "So, now what do we do. Can't exactly watch TV."

"Well, I was thinking I'd like to clean up, maybe wash my hair, shave my legs, you know, girl stuff."

Mark rolled his eyes. "Okay. Maybe I'll wander around downstairs for a little bit."

She smiled at him. "You're awesome."

He pointed at her. "No. You're awesome."

Mark talked with the manager of the hotel for a little while. The guy was nice enough, but most of the things he wanted to tell Mark about were his plans to make the hotel as famous as it used to be in the old days. Mark asked if he could check out the saloon. The manager explained that it wasn't quite open yet, but he didn't care if Mark helped himself to the bar and let him borrow a small lantern.

The saloon was a long rectangle with a checkered floor, moose and elk heads on the walls, and a huge wooden bar along the north side. At the far end, there was a small stage. A drum kit and two microphone stands were crumpled in the corner. A guitar stood on a little plastic stand in the corner of the stage next to a wooden stool.

Mark walked behind the bar and looked at all the various bottles. He decided that whiskey was the most appropriate and poured a little of the amber fluid into a glass. It burned as he swallowed. He took the glass with him as he walked up to the stage.

Almost two hours later, Megan came downstairs. She felt so much better being clean and wearing clean clothes. Her hair still hung wet on the back of her neck, but she didn't care. She looked around but didn't see Mark anywhere. She asked the manager, and he pointed toward the saloon. As she walked through the opening between the two sections of the

building, she heard rising notes on a guitar being handpicked. She thought she recognized the song and stood very quiet listening. After the intro Mark started to sing.

*This is my life, it's not what it was before*
*All these feelings I've shared*
*And these are my dreams*
*That I'd never lived before*
*Somebody shake me*
*Cause I, I must be sleeping*

*Now that we're here, so far away*
*All the struggle we thought was in vain*
*And all the mistakes one life contained*
*They all finally start to go away*

*And now that we're here, it's so far away*
*And I feel like I can face the day*
*And I can't forget that I'm not ashamed*
*To be the person that I am today*

*These are my words*
*That I've never said before*
*I think I'm doin' okay*
*And this is the smile*
*I've never shown before*
*Somebody shake me*
*'Cause I, I must be sleeping*

*And now that we're here, so far away*
*All the struggle we thought was in vain*
*And all the mistakes one life contained*
*They all finally start to go away*

*And now that we're here, so far away*
*And I feel like I can face the day*
*And I can't forget that I'm not ashamed*
*To be the person that I am today*

*I'm so afraid of waking, please don't shake me*
*Afraid of waking, please don't shake me*

*Now that we're here, it's so far away*
*All the struggle we thought was in vain*
*And all the mistakes one life contained*
*They all finally start to go away*

*And now that we're here, it's so far away*
*And I feel like I can face the day*
*And I can't forget that I'm not ashamed*
*To be the person that I am today*

It was obvious he was trying to be quiet, but his voice was rich and clear and carried the melody and the mood of the song perfectly. As Megan listened to him sing, emotions rose in her and spilled out in tears down her cheeks. As the last chords rang out in the empty saloon, she stepped out into the dim, flickering light. When Mark looked up and saw her, he smiled. She walked toward the stage and said, "Oh my God. I had no idea. That was amazing."

"No. Actually it was Staind."

"I mean you. You keep blowing me away, cowboy. I didn't know you could do anything like that."

"Thanks. I'm not really very good, but I like to play. It's always been kind of an escape."

"Did you mean it?"

"The escape? Yeah."

"No. The song. Did you mean what you sang?"

He smiled. "Yeah. I think it was the first song I played when I sat down. Just seemed right. I played a bunch of other stuff but kept coming back to it. If you had to hear something, I'm glad you heard that one."

"I just came down here to tell you that the bathroom is yours if you want it. I had no idea that you would be sitting in here playing like that. I would have been here all night."

"I kinda have trouble playing in front of people. I get nervous and then fuck everything up."

"If you play half as good as what I heard, it would be awesome."

"Thanks." He set the guitar back in its stand. "I suppose I should wash up and shave if I expect to get anywhere close to you tonight."

"If you keep playing like that, it won't matter."

He stepped off the stage and kissed her. "I hope this doesn't sound weird, but, Megan, I love you."

She hugged him tightly. "I love you too, Mark. I really do." She then pulled away again and added, "But, you do kind of need a bath."

# 48.

Mark stepped out of the bathroom looking good. Damn good. He was clean, shaven, trimmed up, hair fixed, and naked. He was also surprised to find Megan sound asleep on the bed. She was still dressed and lying on her side with her legs curled up and her right hand tucked under her chin. She looked so peaceful, so sweet. Something tugged deep within him as he watched her slowly breathing, lost in peaceful sleep. He thought briefly about waking her to see if she wanted to get undressed and maybe more comfortable sleeping, but she already looked so peaceful. He quietly blew out the lantern and slipped into bed next to her.

"Mark!" He was instantly awake at the sound of his name being shouted by Megan. She sounded scared. His heart was pounding, but he was disoriented in the dark. "Mark! Wake up! Somebody is stealing the horses!"

"What?"

"Somebody is trying to steal the *horses!* Let's go!" He vaguely saw the door to their room open in the dim light and heard Megan run out. He threw the blankets back and jumped out of bed. He had to think, but his head was in a fog. Pants. I need

pants. The only pair he could think of were the ones he had taken off in the bathroom. He ran into the little room, which was even darker than the main room of their suite, and fumbled through the pile of dirty clothes he had left near the sink. He finally found something that felt like jeans and struggled to feel for the top. After several seconds that felt like minutes, he managed to orient the pants and put them on as quickly as he could. Gun. I need my gun. He had to think. Where did I put it? A mental image of the XD(m) lying on the table finally came to him, and he ran back into the main room. He brushed his arm across the table, hoping to find the black pistol lying on the dark wood. At the last second, he felt it as he knocked it to the floor. Two of the little green tritium sights glowed under the table. He grabbed the gun and started running for the door. Just as he made it into the hallway, he could hear, the *pop-pop-pop* of Megan's pistol firing in rapid succession outside. He flew down the stairs and out the main door of the hotel. As he started to run down the sidewalk, he stepped on something small and hard, and pain shot through the bottom of his foot. Fuck! I'm barefoot! He slowed but continued to move toward the end of the building as fast as he dared. *Boom-Boom.* Two more rapid shots from Megan's gun, but this time much closer. He rounded the corner of the building near where they had sat in the afternoon. The darkness obscured everything except the biggest shapes. He carefully walked onto the patio. "Megan. Where are you?"

"Here. I'm okay. Get a light."

Mark ran back around the corner of the building and retraced his steps back to their room. He found the lantern but couldn't remember where they had put the little lighter. He patted the top of the table, the coffee table, and then the bedside table. Finally he found it on the top of the dresser. He lit the lantern and slipped his Doc Martens on before running back out to Megan.

As he came around the corner, she was leading Chic to the side of the building. "What happened?"

"I think they got Hunter and Fred, but it's hard to tell. I'm pretty sure I shot one of them. I might have hit another one, but it's so dark I can't see a damn thing."

"How did you know what was going on?"

"I woke up when I heard one of the horses fussing. Then I heard somebody say, 'Grab the other one.' That's when I knew."

"You're okay?"

"Yeah. What took you so long?"

"Sorry. I couldn't see anything. Couldn't find my pants, my gun, nothing."

"Don't worry about it now. Take the light and check the whole area back there. Maybe one of those assholes is still hiding back there."

"Okay."

"Oh, and Mark?"

"Yeah?"

"If you find one, kill him."

"Okay."

Mark stepped off the concrete pad of the patio onto the grass. The lantern cast a weak yellow-orange light over a small area around it. It sucked, but it was better than complete darkness. As he made his way farther away from the building, the brush became heavier and thicker and scratched his bare chest and arms as he tried to work his way through. As he made his way into the darkness, he kept the sound of the running water on his left to make sure he was heading in a straight line toward the back of the property. Seeing an easier path, he decided to climb a slight embankment and walk along the fence line on the north end of the lot, where there appeared to be fewer trees. As he came out of the weeds, he noticed a dark, rounded shadow in the grass in front of him. He walked up slowly and found Fred lying on his side. A huge wave of sadness washed over him, wrenching his heart. During all the miles they spent together on the trip form Gillette to Buffalo, Fred had been a constant companion. He had been patient and tolerated Mark's mistakes. He stood still when he was supposed

to and never danced around like the other horses did once in a while. A couple of times, he had even chuffed quietly when Mark walked up to him while he was grazing, as if to say hello. Mark held the light over him and saw a bullet hole in the big chest just behind his front leg. Fred's chest didn't move. He held the light over the horse's face and could see the horse staring blindly upward. Mark stroked the big animal's face, closing his eyes. He bent down and whispered into the horse's ear, "Thank you. I hope you find green pastures, buddy."

A part of him wanted to stay with the horse, but he knew he had to keep moving. He had never considered himself much of an "animal person," but the horses had kinda grown on him. Maybe it was the way Megan was when she was around them. She talked to them constantly and treated them as though they were just another person. Maybe that's kinda how he was beginning to think of them, like one of the gang. He stood up and started to walk away but heard a slight groan behind him. He turned and carefully made his way back. As he stepped around a tree, he saw a pair of legs wearing a pair of black-and-white Van's skate shoes. He held the light up and could see a kid who looked to be fifteen or sixteen lying on his back in the leaves and grass. Blood covered the front of his t-shirt, and he held a bloody hand over the lower right side of his chest. Mark held his gun in front of him on the kid and said, "Hey, fuckhead. Were you trying to steal our horses?"

The kid didn't move, but his mouth kept opening and closing like he was trying to get air.

"Hey, fuckhead. I'm talking to you." Mark kicked the kid's shoes.

The kid didn't try to move or say anything. His mouth just kept up the same fish-out-of-water gasping motion.

"That's right, you fucking asshole. That's what you get if you fuck with me, my woman, or my horses. I hope you die and rot in hell, you stupid little son of a bitch." He briefly considered popping a round into the little bastard's head but then decided not to. Better to let him suffer. He turned to leave and then turned back. He swung hard and connected the steel toe of his size-eleven Dr. Marten into the side of the kid's head.

He felt his foot hit hard and then give a little as the kid's skull caved in. "That's for my horse."

When he had finally made it all the way back to the fence at the far end of the property, he found Hunter. The horse was still somewhat frantic and paced back and forth along the fence line. "Whoa there, fella, whoa," Mark said in the most friendly voice he could manage. The horse stared at him in fear as though Mark was some kind of monster coming to eat him. It occurred to him the horse couldn't see him from the shadow cast by the top of the lantern. He held the lantern up so it illuminated his own face. The horse relaxed at once. Mark held the lantern high as he approached the horse slowly. "Whoa, buddy. It's okay. I'm just coming to help you back to the others. That's all. No big deal. Coming to bring you back home." When he was close enough, he held his hand out for the horse to smell him. As the horse continued to relax, Mark grabbed his halter and started leading him back.

When they arrived at the patio, Megan was standing next to Chic. She grabbed another lead rope for Hunter and then ran to where they stood. "Oh my God. I'm so glad you found Hunter. Did you see Fred?"

"Yeah."

"Where is he? Do we have to go get him?"

Mark looked at the ground. "No, we don't have to get him."

"Oh no. No no no. Please don't tell me I shot him. Please, no."

"I think he was standing behind one of the little bastards that tried to take him. He didn't suffer."

Megan sat down on the concrete, still holding the lead rope. She put her face in her hands and started to cry. "I can't take any more of this. I can't take any more death. Everybody I love… no more."

Mark sat down next to her and wrapped his arms around her. He held her that way for a long time.

The sun had been up for at least two hours when the manager came out of the hotel and brought Mark a cup of coffee.

"Your wife asked me to bring this out to you. I heard you had some trouble last night."

*Wife?* The word surprised Mark. "Yeah. A couple of kids tried to steal our horses. One of them and one of our horses is dead in the woods back there. I suppose the sheriff is going to come by and want to talk with us."

"Sheriff? No, I doubt that. He's dead."

"Yeah, but those guys at dinner. They said they were with the sheriff's department."

"They were. Cal Reynolds is married to the daughter of the rancher whose horses were stolen. The hand that got shot when their horses were stolen was his brother-in-law."

"Oh."

"I doubt anybody is going to care that you killed a horse thief. In the old days, they used to hang 'em."

"I've heard that."

"Back in the cowboy days, a horse was much more than just property. It was the way a man made a living and his only transportation. If you stole his horse, you most likely stole his livelihood and possibly sentenced him to death if you left him alone in the wilderness. From what I have seen, horses are a big deal again. Probably will be for quite some time."

"Yeah, I guess."

"Did you spend the night out here?"

"Just since the shooting. Maybe three or four hours."

"Sorry I didn't wake up. Gunfire isn't exactly rare anymore. I would have come out and helped you two."

Mark looked at him. "Sorry if I'm kinda getting in your face, but why are you bending over backward to help us?"

The manager smiled and then sat down on the bench next to Mark. "My dad bought the Occidental years ago and then handed it down to me. I was always a big history buff, and I especially love the Wild West days—you know, cowboys and Indians. I was the one who restored it. The hotel was famous back in the day because it was a nice place, but more importantly it was always a safe place. Guys could stay here and not have to worry who knew they were here or if their things would

still be there when they got back. I think there is a real opportunity here again. I want the Occidental to be everything it was and more. People are going to start moving around again, and I want them to stay here. I want Buffalo to be the center of the West. You two are helping me to figure out what I need to do to be ready when the time comes. I know now I need a place to board horses, and I'm working on that. Today I have to figure out how to provide better security. If you would be willing to part with a little more of your gold or silver, I'll hire a couple of guys to watch your horses and the hotel."

"You mean, like bouncers?"

"Doormen, and maybe a livery."

Mark said, "Two ounces of silver for the rest of the time we're here, and I won't charge you for the lost horse."

The manager looked as though he was going to say something and then simply said, "Deal. I'll have security here by this evening."

Megan came around the corner of the building as the two men shook hands. "Uh-oh. What did I miss?"

Mark said, "We now have security and someone to watch the horses for us."

"Oh, I'd shake on that too. I can't handle any more nights like last night."

The manager gave his best smile and said, "And you shouldn't have to, ma'am. I'll leave you two to your coffee."

When the manager was out of sight, Megan said, "Well, he's awfully accommodating."

"He wants to make the hotel as famous as it was in the past. We are his lab rats."

"Oh, I see. He should be paying us to stay here."

"Yeah, but I don't think that's gonna happen."

"I suppose. So, do you have any plans for the day?"

"I wouldn't mind getting a little sleep. My night was cut a little short."

"That's fine, but it reminds me, I meant to tell you about being ready for anything when you are sleeping."

Mark smiled at the double meaning of her comment. "I took a bath last night, a cold one by the way, shaved, and I thought I was ready for anything."

She smiled sheepishly at him. "Oh, yeah, sorry about that. I was just so tired, and I felt so good after everything—I just fell asleep. By the way, do you really?"

"Do I what?"

"You know."

"What?"

"Oh, come on. You said something to me last night. Did you mean it?"

"Do I love you?"

"Yes."

"Yes."

"Yes what?"

"Yes, Megan. I love you."

She squealed a little bit, bouncing in her chair and then hugged him. "I love you too, Mark." When she had settled back down again, she said, "If I didn't have to watch the horses, I would go with you upstairs and give you a reason to be tired."

"Oh, thanks a lot. That's like saying I've got a pizza and a movie, but you can't have any."

"Oh, sorry. Anyway, after you wake up, we'll go and start trying to find the stuff we need. I started a list. We are also going to need another horse. Maybe two. You go get some rest, and I'll figure out what the plan is. Deal?"

"Deal."

# 49.

Jack's eyes opened to nothing but pure white light. At first he was disoriented, but as he moved he felt something against him and looked down to see Nicole snuggled against him in her sleeping bag. He was in the back of the wagon, and the white canvas top was lit from above. The wood bed beneath him hadn't been as hard as he thought it might be, but a little padding would certainly help. He heard a soft rustling noise outside the wagon. A few seconds later, he heard one of the horses blow about two hundred yards to the north, near the creek. The sound outside couldn't be a horse; they wouldn't be that spread out. He slid from under Nicole's arm and reached for the big .460 Smith. He carefully and quietly made his way to the front of the wagon, occasionally hearing noises outside. In a single fluid motion, he stepped up onto the bench, cocked the big revolver, and said, "Freeze."

Brooke screamed. "Ah! Jesus! Don't shoot!"

Jack uncocked the gun and put it down. "I doubt very much Jesus would shoot you, but I would. What the hell are you doin'?"

The girl was breathing hard. "We we're trying to get everything ready to go before you guys got up. In case you don't

remember, we'd rather not have another little experience like we did yesterday. That was so totally embarrassing."

Ryan came running over at the sound of Brooke's scream. "What? What's going on?"

"Jack was going to shoot me."

"I was not gonna shoot you. Well, I was thinkin' about it. That ought to teach you to go messin' around a sleeping man with a gun. As a general rule, you don't want to surprise 'em."

From inside the wagon, Nicole said, "New rule. Nobody is to be shot before we've had coffee."

"Works for me," Jack said and disappeared into the wagon again. A few minutes later, he opened the back and climbed down with a small stack of clean clothes, a towel, and a bar of soap. "I bet that creek'll wake ya up."

As he was about to leave, Nicole asked, "Could you please bring back a bucket of water. I'd like to do the same, but I'll prefer the privacy of the wagon. I'll have coffee ready when you return."

"That's a deal."

An hour later they were almost finished loading the wagon and nearly ready to leave when Jack noticed Brooke standing behind the wagon with a hand held to the left side of her stomach. He casually walked over to her. "Sorry I scared you this morning.'"

She looked a little surprised but said, "It's okay."

Jack bunched his eyebrows. "How ya doin'?"

"Fine."

"Hmm." He looked at her for a minute. "Darlin', in the entire time I've known you, I have never ever heard you answer a question with a single word. Do you want to tell me what's goin' on, or do I have to guess?"

"Nothing. I'm fine."

"I don't think you are. When does your period start?"

"Oh my God! I'm not talking about this with you." She turned away from him.

Jack kept looking at her and yelled, "Nicole, could you come over here?"

As Nicole walked over to them, she said, "I was about to throw out the rest of the coffee when I realized we should have brought a thermos. Perhaps we could find one in Greybull. It would be nice to have a cup on the road. Tea would be even better."

Jack said, "Will you talk to Brooke. There's somethin' wrong, and she won't tell me what the problem is." He stepped a few feet away to give the two women some room.

Brooke looked over suspiciously at Jack and said to Nicole, "He's like asking me about my period and stuff. That is like so weird and *so* none of his business."

Nicole said, "Brooke, dear, you do know that Jack is a doctor?"

"No way. He's like a rancher, cattle, horse guy."

"He was a surgeon long before that. I know. I saw him at the hospital in Cody, and I heard from several people in town that he helped out from time to time. You should have seen the way he stitched up a laceration on my leg. It was quite simply amazing."

"You know, I did hear that guy at the saddle place keep calling him 'doc.' I thought that was some kind of weird cowboy talk or something. Oh yeah, and that Dave guy. He called him doc once or twice too."

"See. As I said, he is a physician. You can tell him what the trouble is. I can assure you he is not weird." She waved for Jack to come back to the conversation.

He said, "Will you tell me when your period is s'posed to start?"

"In about a week. Maybe a little more."

"I noticed you didn't eat much last night. Did you have anything for breakfast? You feel sick?"

"I just have a gut ache, okay. It's no big thing."

Jack thought for a minute and said, "When was the last time you moved your bowels?"

"Oh my God!" Brooke started walking away. "I can't believe we are talking about this. I mean, seriously, how much more disgusting can we get?"

"Bingo," Jack said and started following her toward the fire. He poured a cup of coffee and brought it to Brooke as she sat in one of the camp chairs. "Here. I want you to drink all of this. Then, I'm gonna give you another one, and you'll drink all of that. Maybe a couple more. If that don't work, we got another little trick or two. Don't you worry; we'll get you fixed up in no time."

Brooke looked annoyed and a little scared. "You know, I don't really want to do this now. Maybe we could find a little hotel or something in Greybull."

Jack squatted in front of her. "Darlin', you got no choice. It's the way things go. At this moment we are half a day's ride from Greybull. If you have a real problem out here, we're gonna be in a bad way."

Brooke started to cry. "Why does this have to happen to me? I mean, seriously."

In the most caring, understanding, quiet tone he could muster, Jack said, "You're shy. That's all. It ain't no crime, and it ain't nothin' to be ashamed of."

"But I'm not! That's just it. You saw me naked yesterday, and I didn't like freak out and everything."

"That's not what I mean, and you know it. You get started on that coffee. We'll get you fixed up."

Brook sat in one of the folding chairs and sipped the strong black brew. Jack walked over to the back of the wagon and started looking for something. Nicole came up alongside him and said, "I'm sorry. I didn't understand any of that conversation. What is the matter?"

"The girl probably ain't shit since the flare. She's constipated. Some people are just homebodies. It's more common than you might think and doin' your business outside is not exactly a common skill if you lived in a city your whole life. I have a three-fold plan for her. First, we'll let the coffee get her

gut workin' a little faster. Might be all she needs to get things movin'. If that don't work, I'll give her just a little touch of Copenhagen. That's like throwin' gas on a fire. If we still don't have any action, she'll need some soapy water. That will most definitely work."

"I don't understand. Why would drinking soapy water have any effect?"

"You don't drink it."

"Oh…Oh my."

"Yep. That's where you come into the picture."

"Me? Oh no. I don't think so. I am certainly no nurse."

"You're a friend. Right now she needs a friend. Besides, it's either you or me. I doubt Ryan would be able to help, and I don't think she'd want him to even if he could. She'd probably have a meltdown if I even tried to explain it."

"You are the only one who has done anything like this before; besides, you might be underestimating her. She seems to complain a great deal at first, but when she understands the situation, I think you'll find her to be more accepting."

"You think so?"

"I do."

"We'll ask her if the time comes. She can decide. By the way, do you know where Ryan ran off to?"

"No. Actually I haven't seen him in quite a while."

They heard whistling behind them and turned to see Ryan walking back to camp, tossing a roll of toilet paper in the air and catching it again.

Nicole watched from the back of the wagon as Jack pulled a chair next to Brooke. He sat down and handed her a roll of toilet paper. She dropped her head so that she was looking at her lap. She could see him quietly talking to her, and she imagined he was explaining the small procedure.

Earlier, she had watched fascinated as Jack had taken an empty soda bottle and cut a small hole in the top. He had taken a ballpoint pen, removed the insides, and forced the tip through the small hole. When she had asked him what the

apparatus was for, he squeezed it, and air blew through the tapered end. He explained that it was for the soapy water. She still felt a little embarrassed when she had asked if it needed to be sterilized. "Where this is goin', cleanliness don't really matter."

Nicole could see Brooke's shoulders hitch a little as Jack talked to her. The girl was crying, and she couldn't blame her. As the two of them stood up and started walking toward the grove of trees and rocks, Jack held an okay sign for Nicole behind Brooke's back. He put an arm around Brooke as they walked. Nicole felt bad. She could understand the medical reasons and even rationalize things in her mind, but the problem was still embarrassing, especially to a young woman.

On the other hand, she was impressed and even felt a little proud of Jack. She knew it would have been a lot easier for him to just let Brooke work out the problem herself. And he probably would have been justified insisting she help Brooke, but he didn't. He did the right thing. In fact, he always seemed to do the right thing. He could have ignored Ryan on the road from Yellowstone. He could have just dropped them off in town. He could have left quietly on horseback. He could have left Brooke and Ryan behind, but he didn't.

Her mind tried to picture what the procedure would be. As she started to construct a mental image, a new emotion came over her. She felt defensive and even a little angry. She should have been the one to help Brooke. Surprised at her own feelings, she stopped the thought process and tried to understand where this was coming from. *Jealousy.* She was feeling a little bit jealous. It didn't make sense. It didn't have to. The feeling was real. She knew that there was nothing sexual about what they were doing, and after all Jack was a doctor, but the fact of the matter was that Brooke was going to be baring everything to him, and Nicole didn't like it.

"Where are they going?" Ryan asked as he walked up to the wagon.

"Jack is going to help Brooke with that little situation I told you about."

"Really? How's he gonna help?"

"I think it's probably best if you don't know. If Brooke would like to tell you, I'm sure she will."

"Whatever. Are we gonna leave soon?"

"I believe that will depend on how things are progressing."

"I'm getting bored. I wish we would just get the fuck out of here."

"Ryan, you seem a bit angry. What's on your mind?"

"Nothin'. Well, it's just that old guy is out there helping my girlfriend, and I'm stuck back here with my thumb up my ass. I should be helping her."

"You do know that Jack is a doctor, right?"

"No way."

"Yes, it's true. I had to tell Brooke this morning as well. I thought you both knew."

"I thought he was a rancher."

"He is today, but he is actually a retired surgeon."

"No shit? He's not that old. I wonder why he retired."

"I don't know. He hasn't talked about it, and I didn't want to pry."

"Maybe he was really bad at it."

"Do you really think so?"

"No. Probably not."

"Me either." She turned and saw Jack walking back to camp. When he got close to the wagon, she asked, "How did things go?"

"Just fine. You might want to bring her a bucket of water, some soap, a change of clothes, and a towel. She might want to freshen up a bit."

"Was it that bad?"

"Oh, I doubt it. I didn't stick around. I was just thinkin' what I would want if I were in her shoes."

"Maybe I should go," Ryan said.

"You and I are gonna harness up the horses and get ready to leave. You're on the clock."

"But why does she get to go? Brooke is my girlfriend."

"It's a girl thing. Just let 'em be, son."

# 50.

An hour later they were on the road again. Ryan had wanted to ride his own horse, so Jack had put Brooke's saddle on Dingo. When she and Nicole had returned to camp, Brooke looked wonderful. Her hair was wet, but Nicole had done it in a French braid for her, and it seemed to glow in the morning light. She was clean, radiant, and had a spring in her step Jack couldn't help but notice. After she had climbed up into her saddle, she walked the horse over to the front of the wagon and said, "Thank you." Jack simply replied, "You're welcome."

Jack started them out a little slow, but as the horses seemed to find their rhythm, he sped them up to a fast walk. Brooke and Ryan rode ahead but were careful to stay in sight of the wagon and occasionally looked over their shoulders to make sure everything was okay. Nicole said, "So, how did things go back there?"

"Just fine."

"When I went to bring her those things you asked for, I did happen to notice that she wasn't wearing any pants."

"Nope. I told her it would probably be easier that way."

"Seemed to be lacking her underdrawers as well."

"I suppose."

"You know, Brooke is a rather pretty girl."

"Yep."

"I don't suppose you had a little peek?"

Jack turned toward her. "You're jealous."

"I am not jealous. It is simply that I...well, you know...I... All right! I might be a wee bit jealous. Can you blame me?"

Jack leaned toward her and said, "You don't have to worry. I didn't see a thing."

"How could you not have seen a thing? That makes no sense whatsoever. You had to have looked when you...were... you know."

Jack laughed. "I explained what the procedure was, and she thought she could do it on her own. I told her I would wait with my back turned a little ways away, and if she needed me, all she had to do was ask. She did fine on her own."

"So you really didn't see anything?"

He laughed again. "No."

"Well, that certainly makes me feel better." They rode for a few minutes in silence. Nicole then asked, "Did your wife ever feel jealous?"

"I don't think so. We talked about it once or twice, but I think she always understood the difference between a medical setting and a nonmedical one. You have to understand, there's a big difference when somebody is a patient and your responsibility."

"So in all the years that you practiced medicine, you never had a young, attractive patient, and if you did, you never looked or had nefarious thoughts?"

"Sure I had young female patients. Some of them were good lookin' too. Did I look? I don't know, maybe I did. I am a man, but I can honestly say that I never had any *thoughts*. It's a very different situation. Kinda hard to explain. Maybe the closest I could come to it would be to say that they were almost like your own kids. The *thoughts*, as you say, just never occur to you. Oh, I know, every once in a while you would read about some asshole doctor in the paper, but I knew a lot of docs, and

I think they would all say pretty much the same thing. It just never occurs to you."

"That's very interesting. May I ask you something else? I know this is rather personal and you don't have to discuss it if you would rather not, but why did you retire from medicine?"

Jack looked ahead at the road. "It's a long story, but I s'pose we got a long way to go. When I went to work, I joined a multi-specialty group in San Antonio. I made partner early, and over the years worked my way up through the ranks. It wasn't all that long before I was chairman of cardio-thoracic surgery at a major hospital and president of the group. That's when I got sued for the first time. I remember the case very well. There was this fairly young guy—I think he was in his mid-fifties—came into the ER with terrible chest pain. They did a CT scan on him and found out he had a thoracic aortic aneurysm. Do you know what that is?"

"I'm not really sure, no."

"The aorta is the biggest blood vessel in your body. It comes right out the top of the heart and gives out branches to everything else. He had an aneurysm, which means the wall had become weak, and it started to balloon up. It was so big it started to rupture or break open in the man's chest. If we didn't do anything, he'd bleed to death right there in front of us. I rushed him to the operatin' room, and we opened his chest. His aneurysm was worse than what the CT scan showed, and it was bleedin' bad. Before we could get him on bypass, he died—in a technical sense. His heart quit workin' altogether. I was squeezin' his heart, makin' blood pump through his body until we could get him on bypass. Well, after a bit we got it all fixed, and wouldn't you know it, but the guy got better. The only problem was that he had a small stroke during the operation. He could still get around, feed himself, and think, but he had trouble talkin'. We call it aphasia. His wasn't too bad, but it was real—there was no doubt about it. The family sued me for the stroke. I guess the guy was a motivational speaker, and after the stroke he couldn't work. The hospital and insurance company settled the case before we even went to trial. That

affected me pretty bad. I knew I didn't do anything wrong, but settling is the same as sayin' it was my fault.

"About a year later, my wife and I were out to dinner at a nice place in San Antonio one night. This ol' boy got to chokin' on a piece of meat. He was sittin' right behind me. I got him out of his chair, and we tried the Heimlich maneuver a couple of times, but he couldn't spit it up. He passed out and was turnin' blue, so I laid him down on the ground and decided to do a chrichotomy. That's makin' a small incision in his neck right below the larynx and puttin' in a little tube, so he could breathe. The whole time his wife was hollerin' at me, sayin' that I was killin' him. I kept tellin' her I was tryin' to save him, but she wouldn't have any part of it. A couple of other guys in the restaurant held her back, so I could work. I used a drinking straw as a tube in his neck. We had to do CPR and the whole bit. The funny thing is: the guy made it. Good as new. We got him to the ER, and they use a scope to fish out the hunk of meat. Damn thing was as big as my fist. They sewed up his neck, and he had no infection—nothin'. He was discharged from the hospital about three days later, walkin', talkin', and smilin'. His wife pressed battery charges against me since she didn't authorize the procedure. The state dropped the battery charges, but they let the personal lawsuit go through. They took a quarter-million dollars from me personally because of the emotional distress I put her through. I told the judge at the end of the trial that if faced with the same situation, I would do the same thing again. He agreed with me, but said the law was the law.

"The last one was a kid. I was in the emergency room late one night, lookin' in on another patient we were gonna operate on the next day, when this kid rolled in. A car pulled up outside and just pushed him out before they took off again. He was twelve years old and had a kitchen knife sticking out of his chest from a drug deal that had gone bad. Every time his heart would beat, you could see the handle of that knife wiggle. We got him to the OR and tried like hell to save him, but the knife had gone through his left ventricle. That's the real pumpin'

part of the heart. He died in front of me, and there wasn't a damn thing I could do about it. I looked into that child's face and wondered what he could have become and how things could go so wrong that a twelve-year-old would get killed in a goddamn drug deal. What a loss. His momma sued me for medical malpractice. Her attorneys said that a more competent surgeon could have saved him. We won the case, but I lost the war.

"I couldn't do it anymore. I was givin' everything to that job. I had spent years in school, residency, and fellowship. I was takin' time away from my own family to give to others, and what's worse is that I cared. I honestly gave a damn about each and every patient I worked on. To some docs patients are just cases—they're a procedure or a billing code—but to me they were always people. I never knew what I charged for anything, and never wanted to know. I tried to treat each one the best way I could. Each one of 'em had a family, friends, people that cared about 'em. They were people, and each had their own story, but in the end, too many of 'em wanted somethin' more, and I didn't have it to give.

"So, I was about all in. By this time I had quit as the president of the group and chair of the cardio-thoracic surgery department. I was doin' fewer and fewer cases, kept passin' 'em off to my partners, who were hungry. That's when Henrietta Landers-Lapham came in. She wasn't more'n five-foot-two and couldn't have weighed more than a hundred pounds soakin' wet. She was made of pure bull piss and vinegar and wrapped in a leather gunnysack. She'd been all over the city interviewing surgeons. Anyway, she tells me she heard I was the best, and she only wanted the best. I told her that was nothin' more than a rumor I spent a lot on money on. She grabbed my hand and said, 'You have soft hands. Bankers, insurance men, and cattle buyers have soft hands. You must not work for a living. I never trust a man with soft hands.'" Jack laughed to himself at the memory.

"She was from Wyoming. Lived just south of Cody and ranched nearly six hundred thirty sections scattered through

the northern part of the state. That's over four hundred thousand acres. She had family in San Antonio and decided to have a little lung cancer removed where family was around to help her. I guess she did trust me because she wanted me to do her surgery. Over the next year and a half, I got to know her very well. You could say we became close friends. She invited Jenni and I up to her ranch, said she wanted to show us somethin'. When we got here, we both fell in love with the area. She sat us down one night and looked me in the eye. She said, 'What the hell is wrong with you? You're in the misery business.' I asked what the hell she meant by that. She said, 'You are killin' yourself doin' a job you don't believe in anymore. What's worse is that you are draggin' your family into it as well. You need to get the hell out and start doin' what you were made for.' I asked her what she thought that was, and she said, 'Ranchin'. You were meant to be out in the middle of God's country chasin' cows, workin' with your hands, and takin' care of your family.' The next day a private helicopter flew in and picked the three of us up. She showed us a little ranch over near Dayton. That's where we're headed now."

Nicole said, "What a wonderful and terrible story. I simply can't believe the American people would stand for a legal climate that would hurt the medical community so badly."

"It was all about easy money. The people elected to office were all lawyers. They were going to make damn sure to protect their source of income. A few laws got passed that made it a little better, but the best docs got out when they could. That's why we had so many foreign medical graduates working here."

"So, do you still see Henrietta?"

"Two days after we moved into the ranch, four semis pulled up and started droppin' off cattle. A pickup with a stock trailer showed up last. They unloaded two of the meanest, nastiest, best-looking bulls I had ever seen. The driver handed me a note that said, 'This is a little housewarming gift for you. Welcome home, Dr. Neumann.' She died two days later at home on her ranch. The way I heard it, she just never woke up in the mornin'. Not a bad way to go, if you ask me."

"I should say not. What happened to her ranch?"

"Family fought over it for a couple of years. In fact, it still may not be settled."

Ahead Jack could see Ryan and Brooke had pulled to stop in the middle of the road. "I wonder what those two are up to?" As they rounded a slight bend in the road, they could see the huge B-29 bomber lying upside down with its wings spread across both lanes of the highway.

Jack pulled the wagon to a stop behind them. "Ryan, just go around it to the south. It's nice and flat."

Ryan said, "I don't think so, boss." He pointed at two men on the other side of the old airplane holding rifles.

# 51.

"Avery Johnson, what in *the* hell are you doin'?" Jack called from the bench in the wagon.

"Do you know these men?" Nicole asked quietly.

Jack whispered back, "The older guy on the right is Avery. I don't know him very well, but I do know about him. Used to do a lot of the Cowboy Action Shooting. Used to be pretty good from what I heard."

The older man stepped out from behind the engine of the big airplane. He was wearing a big black hat, tall leather boots, a white shirt, and wore a black leather belt high on his abdomen, studded with red shotgun shells and suspenders. He carried a lever action rifle. "Who goes there?"

Jack squinted at the older man as he studied him carefully. He said quietly to Nicole, "Don't do anything rash." He called to the man, "Avery, it's me, Jack Neumann. What are you boys up to?"

"I don't go by that name anymore. What's your business?"

Nicole whispered, "He doesn't use his name any longer? That's a bit daft."

"Shh. All them Cowboy Action guys use a handle or nickname. I can't quite recall his." A light bulb went on, and

he called back, "Mr. Friday. May I approach to discuss our intentions?"

"You may, but leave your weapons behind."

"I can't do that. You know me, and you know my intentions are honorable."

"Approach then, but keep your hands where I can see them."

Jack stood to climb down from the wagon. Nicole said, "Jack, I don't know about this. The man seems a bit mad."

"He is, but it'll be okay." He winked at her. As he passed Ryan and Brooke, he said quietly, "Just sit still, keep your hands on top of the pommel, and no quick movements."

Nicole watched as Jack walked out on the open road toward the airplane. As he passed the front of the plane, a third man stuck the barrel of a shotgun out of a window in the cockpit and followed him with it. As Jack came to the front edge of the wing, he stopped. The older man stepped up onto the wing and then over to Jack. Nicole was relieved to see them shake hands. The two men stood in the sunshine and talked for quite a while. Soon, the other men lowered their weapons. She became a little more nervous every time Jack would shake his head. She knew from his body language he was disagreeing with something the older man was asking. After several minutes both men started nodding in agreement. They shook hands again, and Jack began walking back.

He motioned for Ryan and Brooke to come close as he climbed up into the wagon. "We're gonna go around that plane to the south. Ryan, I want you to tie your horse and Brooke's horse to the back of this wagon. As we go through town, don't touch a gun and don't make any sudden moves. You don't want to scare anybody here."

"What is going on?" Nicole asked.

"I think half these boys went around the bend when the flare hit. The Bighorn County Regulators—that's the local Cowboy Shooters group—have taken control of the city. Avery

there, he's in charge. Goes by his handle 'Black Friday' full time. Nobody goes in or out without their permission. They were gonna charge us a tax to pass through, wanted to search the wagon and take what they thought was appropriate. I talked 'em out of it, but there's no stoppin' in town. If you have to pee, you'd best do it now."

Brooke asked, "So they are stopping everybody going through town? That's crazy."

"Explains why we haven't seen anybody, and you're right—it's crazy. But those guns are very real, and I don't doubt for a second they'd use 'em."

Ryan said, "But that guy is like—old."

"Son, a couple of years ago, he damn near won their national match out of fifty or sixty *thousand* participants. Don't you doubt for a second that he's not deadly, and I 'spect he's proved it in the last few days."

A young man on a black-and-white paint rode around the airplane and stood in the grass waiting for them. Jack said, "That's our guide. Get 'em tied up and sit still back there."

A few minutes later, Ryan had the horses tied by lead ropes to the back of the wagon. Jack waved at the rider and then started the wagon forward. They trailed the rider through the grass around the airplane and back onto the highway. They followed the road along a river down a gentle grade and around a gradual bend to the right into town. The devastation was similar to what they had seen in Cody. Burned buildings and cars lined the road, twisted metal and debris was scattered everywhere, and few things looked untouched by the destruction.

Jack leaned over to Nicole and said, "Notice anything different than Cody?"

"It's incredibly tragic. I was just thinking that it was all very similar."

"Anything missing?"

"Missing? No, I don't think so. I've not been here before, so I hardly think I would notice anything missing." Then it struck her. "There are no bodies lying about."

"Yep. Did you see the work crews? Looks like they have three-man teams tryin' to get things in order. They may be crazy, but they are efficient. Got to give 'em that."

In the middle of town, they turned to the left and followed Highway 14 east. Most of the brick buildings were still intact with little apparent damage. As the buildings started to spread out a little, they passed a group of long, red brick buildings with a twisted sign that read Yellowstone Motel in the parking lot. A line of people stood in the parking lot with plastic containers and buckets, waiting to get to the pool. Nicole said, "Oh my. Look at the queue to get water from the pool. Is that safe to drink?"

"Sure it is. Tastes like shit, but it won't hurt you. They must have a water problem."

"What about the river we passed?"

"That's the Bighorn. We're gonna cross it in a couple a minutes. Must not have worked out a way to filter it yet."

Ahead of them a concrete bridge spanned the river. On the far side, several burned cars, logs, a couple of old utility trailers, and a semitrailer were piled up as a roadblock. A single, narrow lane was left open on the far right side. The guide rode through the narrow lane, and Jack followed. As they passed the far edge, somebody yelled, "Jack! Hey, Jack!"

He turned to see a young man waving at him. Jack pulled the wagon to a stop on the other side of the roadblock and jumped down before Nicole could stop him. He walked back and spoke to the young man for a few minutes, shook his hand, and walked back to the wagon. Along the way he told Ryan and Brooke to untie their horses. When he climbed back up, sat down, and started the horses moving again, Nicole said, "Presumably you know that young man."

"That's Beans Weir. Good kid. Worked for me a couple of years ago. Said they had a town meeting like we did in Cody. Avery didn't care for what he thought was a weak approach to

town management. Shot the mayor and what was left of the city council. He and his boys been runnin' things ever since. Sounds like he don't put up with much. Everybody works and everybody eats. Nobody gets in and nobody gets out. A few people been sneakin' out in the middle of the night, but all of the food, fuel, and necessities have been confiscated. Makes it tough to get very far."

"Good lord. It sounds as though they are running a work camp."

"That's exactly what it is."

As they pulled away from town and the roadblock, they moved up a long slow grade. The scenery on both sides of the wagon was much the same as it had been: gentle, low-rolling hills, brown grass with scattered areas of sage, and occasional clumps of short trees. As they crested the grade, Nicole could see a jagged blue line just above the distant horizon. "Jack, are those the Bighorn Mountains?"

"They are."

"And we are going to cross them?"

"We are."

"Do you happen to know how tall they are?"

"Oh, I guess there's peaks that go over thirteen thousand."

"But we don't have to go that high, do we?"

"Nope. We'll go over Granite Pass. If I recall, I think the highest point we make is around nine."

"Nine thousand feet?" she asked nervously.

"Yep. Why?"

"That's awfully high."

"It's really not too bad. You sound worried."

"Oh, no. It's not that...well, now that you mention it, it does seem a bit high...don't you think?"

Jack thought about what she was asking and then said, "Darlin', how high do you think we are right now?"

"Now? At this moment?" She looked around. "Well, we certainly can't be all that high. I really have no idea, but I would guess something like two or three hundred feet."

Jack smiled. "Darlin', you're over four thousand right now."

"Four thousand feet in the air? That's not possible."

"Not in the air. On the ground. This ground is over four thousand feet above sea level. It'll be the same way when we cross the mountains. You'll be on the ground, but the ground will be about nine thousand feet above sea level. Haven't you ever been in the mountains before?"

"Well, now that you mention it, I really haven't spent any considerable time in the mountains. All the places I have lived were near the sea, and I spent holidays in Venice and Rome, of course, the Caribbean, the Maldives, Fiji, and various parts of Europe. My mother positively hated the cold, and so skiing was never an option. She preferred European culture, and my father preferred the beach. I believe it was so he could leer at young ladies."

"You certainly have been around the globe, haven't you?"

"Oh, a bit here and there. I can't say I was a travel enthusiast, and our family didn't go anywhere together after my father moved to New York. In college I would travel a bit with friends, but it was always at their insistence."

Jack sat up straight and looked around.

"What is it? You seem to be thinking about something."

"Did you feel that?"

"No. Nothing out of the ordinary."

"The wind just changed. Now it's blowin' from the south."

"Is that bad?"

"Not necessarily. Just somethin' we need to keep an eye on. I'm sorry I interrupted you."

"I was actually finished with my thought. Did you travel much?"

"Nope. We were always kind of homebodies. Oh, we did the family vacation once or twice a year, but nothin' to write home about. Once we moved up here, there was always somethin' keepin' us around."

"Yes, but didn't you spend quite a lot of time in Cody?"

"We did, but it's only a hundred and fifty miles."

"That is really quite a long ways."

Jack laughed. "Around here it's considered your backyard. I've heard it said in Europe you consider two hundred miles a long ways, and in America we consider two hundred years a long time."

Nicole laughed. "That's very true and quite *après peau.* Speaking of a long way, do you have a plan for a place to stay this evening?"

"Yep. I have some very good friends that live in Shell. Figured we'd stop in and see how they're doin'."

"I do hope they might have an extra bed. Although I would spend a hundred nights in the back of this wagon if I were next to you, I would much prefer something more comfortable. My back was not particularly fond of the arrangements last night."

"They have lots of extra beds, or at least did have. They run a high-end guest ranch."

"A guest ranch? I'm not sure what that is."

"Think of it like a vacation resort with a Western flair. Their guests can go trail riding or chase cattle during the day, but they are spoiled at night. Had some of the best chefs in Wyoming and ran a little four-star restaurant on the side."

"Four-star? Are you joking?"

"No, ma'am. They could start you out with a Boursin and then move you to a trout en papillote or a filet mignon that would melt in your mouth. Best part of it was you had the best accommodations, best service, and best food without the snotty attitude. They're good people. Down-to-earth."

"Out here in the middle of bloody nowhere?"

"Yep. When you're that good, word gets out, and people will come to you."

"I'm still not sure how this all works. Are they a ranch or a resort?"

"Yep. They're both. They actually started out as a ranch that has been around for over a hundred years. They started the resort on the side about twenty or twenty-five years ago. The

thing of it is, they don't do anything halfway. They built the resort right. Jenni and I used to stay there before we moved up here. We had friends from Texas who would come up every year and stay there and just hop over the mountains to see us."

"Although I am very excited to see this guest ranch, I believe I am more excited at the thought of sleeping in an actual bed."

# 52.

Mark was getting frustrated. For him, shopping was utilitarian. A job that needed to be done, but thankfully didn't come up very often, and when it did could usually be accomplished in a matter of a few minutes. Megan didn't share the same opinion. To her, shopping was a sport. It was about trying on as many articles of clothing as she could and checking each on in the mirror. Normally, Mark wouldn't care. Just let her do what she seemed to enjoy doing. But this was hell.

They had spent the entire day going through what was left of three different stores, looking for clothes. In all three places, they were alone, and the stores seemed abandoned. And in each of the three places, the devastation had taken its toll. Only a handful of clothes were still on shelves or hanging on a rack. Most were scattered everywhere, usually all in piles on the floor. Shopping wasn't a matter of going to the rack and browsing until you found something you liked and then finding the right size. Now it was digging through piles and piles of loose clothing on the floor, looking for the one thing that Megan held up as an example for him to find, making sure it was a size four—not a six for God's sake—and then making sure the

hanger hadn't ripped the top out of it or burned a couple of marks on it.

"Mark, help me find a cami. Something in white, preferably in a small-medium."

"Okay. First, what's a *cami*?"

"You know, it's like a sleeveless t-shirt for women, only cuter."

"Okay. What's a small-medium? I thought things were either in small or medium. I've never heard of a small-medium."

"It's the right size. Just check the label."

He started sorting through a large pile of women's underwear. After a few minutes, he said, "You realize we are looting."

"We are not looting," Megan snapped back from the other side of a mountain of loose clothes.

"There has been a disaster. We are in a store with nobody around, and we are stealing what we find. Looting—don't get me wrong—I have no problem with it. I'm just stating a fact, that's all."

"Mark, you're right. There has been a disaster, but things are in chaos, and we are just trying to survive. We need these things. It's not like we can run around naked. We have to stay warm."

"You need a cami to stay warm?"

"You know what I mean."

"I know exactly what you mean, and I agree with you, but I'm just calling it what it is. We are looting this store."

"Would you please stop saying that."

"Looting. Looting. Looting. We are looting this store. Hey, everybody, look. I'm looting a store."

"Looting implies that we are breaking the law. As you said the other day, there is no law any more. Therefore, we are not breaking any laws and not looting. We are surviving."

"Call it what you want. Hey, what's that on your hip? Is that a gun? Oh yeah, that's a gun all right. Maybe we could just call it armed robbery."

"Mark, would you just shut the fuck up."

"Like I said, I have no problems with it. There's a big bag of loot hanging on my saddle out there, and I'm thrilled to have it. I'm just calling it what it is."

"What do you think of this?" She held up a lacy thong.

"I'm calling that what it is too. That's damn sexy. Okay. New rule. The only thing you are allowed to wear under your new jeans is that or something similar."

"What if I told you I'm not wearing anything under my jeans."

"Okay. New rule. You're not allowed to wear anything under your jeans. Are you serious?"

"Maybe."

"Wow. You know that's dangerous. You must not have heard what happened the other day."

"No, I don't think I did."

Mark moved near her. "Yeah, so there was incredibly hot girl who was looting this store, and then some guy came along and raped her on a pile of clothes."

"Good thing I have a gun."

"Really? What gun?" He held her gun out behind him.

"Uh-oh. What's a poor girl to do?"

"You can start by letting me see what's under those jeans."

When they were finished, Mark looked out the windows toward the horses. The sun was fading fast. "Shit. We better get going. It's almost dark out."

"Really? It can't be that late."

"Check for yourself."

"Shit. We better get going, or we're gonna miss dinner. Get dressed and grab that stuff."

"Call me what you want, but don't call me late for dinner."

A few minutes later, they were tightening the cinches on their horses and getting ready to leave. Megan said, "Holy shit! Mark, look at that."

He looked up quickly but didn't see what had caught her attention. "What?"

"Watch." She was looking over the top of her horse and pointed down the street.

He looked in the direction she pointed but didn't see anything special. He could see a few buildings and a few burned cars and just make out a couple of people walking away from them several blocks away. "I don't see…" He stopped. One of them turned on a flashlight.

# 53.

During the last few hours, the temperature had slowly been rising, and it was becoming humid. Jack looked up and could see a layer of gray clouds moving in, obscuring the sky.

Nicole noticed him looking at the sky and asked, "Is it going to rain?"

"I don't know. They don't usually see much rain on this side of the mountains. Might get a little up higher."

"Do you think it will snow in the mountains?"

"Pretty warm for that. I bet this warm front is just bringin' moisture up from the gulf. Warm air comes with it. Usually just gives us a little rain is all. Probably do little more than make things sticky for a bit."

The road made a gentle bend to the left and then slowly dropped toward a grove of trees that spread out on either side. Jack whistled to get Ryan's attention and pointed to a small road on the right. They watched as the kid gently pulled his horse to the right and followed the road.

"Presumably we are getting close."

"Yep. Just down this road a bit." Jack pointed toward the trees. "That's the town of Shell. Population, fifty-two."

"Fifty-two total people?"

"Yep."

"From what I have learned in the last few days, It seems that is just about right."

Jack smiled at her and said, "You catch on pretty fast." He turned the horses to follow Ryan and Brooke up the hill.

The little road dropped down into a small, tree-filled hollow and then rose over a hill before bending to the left. Ryan and Brook waited at the bottom of the hill for the wagon to catch up before moving on ahead.

Up ahead on the left, the trees opened into a wide, green, grassy pasture surrounded by a beautifully stained, split-rail, wood fence. A driveway divided the fence with a tall, wood post entryway. A huge boulder in the center of a manicured rock garden to the left of the drive was inscribed, The Hideout.

Brooke pointed to the drive as she looked back at Jack. He nodded in agreement. Just as she and Ryan pulled into the drive, a young man who appeared to be in his early-twenties stepped out from behind a gatepost and racked the slide on a shotgun. He said with a German accent, "Please halt right dere."

As Jack pulled the wagon to a stop behind Ryan and Brooke, he said, "Few things will grab your attention faster than the sound of a pump shotgun." He looked at the young man with the gun and said, "I'm sorry; I don't know you. My name is Jack Neumann, and these are my friends. Is Luke around?"

The young man looked nervous. He shook his head. "Vhy do you all have guns?"

Jack smiled his best and warmest smile. "Probably for the same reason you got that one. Don't worry. We ain't here to cause any trouble. Just lookin' for a place to stay tonight. I've known Luke and everybody here for quite some time. If you could just ask…"

Brooke shifted in her saddle, and the young man whipped the shotgun around and aimed it at her. In the same instant, Jack pulled the big .460 revolver and leveled it at the man's head as he pulled the hammer back, causing the gun to speak

it's warning in a heavy *tick-tick-click-tick*. In a calm, steady, low voice he said, "Son, she's just tryin' to get comfortable. Been in that saddle all day long. Don't you go and try somethin' stupid, or you'll be dead long before you realize you left the safety on." The young man looked up at Jack. His eyes were wide and his face pale. Jack noticed the muzzle of his shotgun shaking. He continued in the same slow, careful voice, "Like I said, we're not here to cause trouble, but I can't let you get carried away with that thing. Why don't you just set that shotgun on the ground, nice and easy. Then I can put this thing away, and we can talk about this."

"I'm...I'm not supposed to do dat."

"I understand. Believe me, I do. But I want you to make the right decision here, and so I'm gonna help you out. You see, I can tell by the way you're handlin' that shotgun you don't have a lot of experience with one. When you racked that slide a few seconds ago, you didn't quite get her all the way forward, so even if you did have the safety off, she probably won't fire. On the other hand, you had to notice how fast I filled my hand with this revolver. That should tell you I've done it once or twice. In the very least, it should tell you that today is not my first day. Also, I bet you've never seen a gun like this one before. It's not really very common. Kind of a specialty gun. I use it for grizzly bear up in Yellowstone. A man carrying a special gun generally has a lot of experience with 'em. Last thing—and this is the big one. You're scared to death. I don't blame you. I would be too if I were in your shoes. But the trouble is: I'm not. You should be able to tell from my voice that I'm not a bit scared, so I must be pretty confident in my ability to walk away from all this. What I'm tryin' to tell you is that as you weigh your odds here you need to understand you are outmatched, outgunned, and your chances of survivin' are really pretty low. Everything comes down to benefit versus risk. If you try to pull that trigger, the gun won't even go off, but you'll die in the process—so you are riskin' everything. And the benefit—well unless you can see one I can't—there is none. So, why don't you just set that shotgun down on the ground."

The young man stepped back slightly and slowly bent down. He placed the gun on the ground and slowly stood back up, never taking his eyes off Jack. Jack noticed a dark stain on the black asphalt and several spent shotgun shells. He uncocked the revolver and slid it back into the leather holster hanging from his shoulder. "See. Now we can talk like gentlemen again. Looks like you had a bit of trouble here."

The young man nodded.

"I bet you weren't in the gunfight. Probably just heard about it."

He nodded again.

"Maybe lost somebody you got to know over the last couple of weeks?"

He nodded again.

"That explains why you're mannin' the gate and so nervous. I'm sorry to hear that. Now, I believe we were talkin' about Luke…"

From down the drive, the sound of a horse running at full gallop cut Jack off. He watched carefully as the rider flew toward them, hunkered low in the saddle, with a rifle in his right hand. The rider slowed and approached on the left side of the drive, keeping the big gateposts between him and the newcomers. A few seconds later, a sweat-stained, gray cowboy hat stuck out around the post.

Jack said, "Sean Bradley? Is that you? Get your ass out here, so I can see you."

The rider stepped out to take a better look. "Doc Neumann? Well cut off my legs and call me shorty. What the hell are you doing here?"

"Tryin' not to get shot at the moment. Your boy here is a little jumpy."

Sean climbed over the gate and walked over to the wagon. "Yeah, well if you had been through what we've been through, you'd be a little jumpy too."

Jack stuck out a hand. "I reckon we been close. Things are crazy all over. Goddamn, it's good to see you."

Sean shook his hand hard. "Even better to see you. I hope I can talk you into stayin' awhile. Nice wagon. Looks like you're about three hundred eighty-eight horses short of your old one."

"It hauls the load. If you got room, we wouldn't mind staying a day or so."

"Hell yes! Let's get you all up to the barn and off them horses, and we'll get introduced." Sean walked to the front of Jack's horses and said, "Grieg, open the gate for God's sake. These horses can't jump it with a wagon tied to 'em." The young man ran to the gate and pushed it open. Sean said, "I swear to God that guy is as worthless as a white crayon." Jack laughed and led the way to the barn with the wagon.

They had two of the big, sliding, wooden barn doors open. Jack drove the team inside and pulled them to a stop. Ryan and Brooke followed. As they started to take saddles and harnesses off, Sean came riding in on his horse. He said, "I let everybody know you're here. They should be comin' down in a minute to meet you. Okay, I gotta know. Why in the hell are you here?"

Jack said, "I was in Cody the other day. Tryin' to get back home. Figured this would be a nice place to stop."

"Well, we can sure put you up, but I don't know how nice it's gonna be. We've had a little trouble."

"I gathered that out at the gate. What's been goin' on?"

"A couple of nights ago, a guy showed up at the gate. Wanted somethin' to eat. We gave him a little food and sent him on his way. The next night he came back with two more guys. They didn't ask. They just started shooting. Luke had been standing at the gate at the time, and they just up and shot him. Scotty was standing behind him with a twelve-gauge and killed one of the guys. The other two rode off, saying they were comin' back. We've had the gate manned ever since."

Jack frowned. "They shot Luke? Damn. He was a good man and a good friend. They don't make 'em any better than that. The whole thing don't make sense. Food's pretty easy to come by. I bet they wanted somethin' else."

People started coming in through the open door. Sean said, "If you want to introduce your crew to us, I'll fill you in on who we are."

"Fair enough," Jack said and looked around. There were many faces in the small crowd he'd never seen before. "Well, I guess I better start with me. I'm Jack Neumann. I own a little spread on the other side of the Bighorns and have been friends with the owners and managers of this place for the last ten years or so. This here is Nicole Meredith: she is my significant other." Jack noticed Ryan's and Brooke's heads turn to look at each other as he said this. "The two on the end are Ryan Miller and Brooke...Darlin', I'm sorry, but for the life of me, I can't recall your last name."

"Bates."

"Ryan Miller and Brooke Bates. They are a couple from Missouri, and now they both work for me."

Sean said, "It's nice to meet you, and welcome to the Hideout. I'm Sean Bradley, and up until the other day, I was the head wrangler here. This is Scotty Walter and Jared Smith. They both work as wranglers here as well. Over there is Laurie Christopher: she's the head chef. And these folks are Jennifer, Kathleen, Steve and Sharon, Edgar and Silke, and that's Shari. They were all guests here when everything kinda went crazy."

Kathleen stepped a little forward and said, "Excuse me, but can I ask where you came from, and do you have any news from anywhere—like what happened and when is somebody going to come and help?"

Jack said, "All I can tell you is what we know today, and that ain't much. Ryan and I were in Yellowstone, or just outside of it, when everything went haywire. Nicole was in an airplane that crashed outside of Cody, and Brooke was visiting a friend in Cody. Ryan here worked out the details and has come up with about the best explanation we can find. In short, it looks like there has been a giant solar flare that caused a massive magnetic storm to pass over us. That's what caused all the lightning or sparks that set off explosions and killed every electrical device we have come across. I can tell you that Cody and

Greybull are devastated. There's nothing much of either town, but the few people left are tryin' to put things back together."

Sean said, "We were plannin' on riding into Greybull tomorrow."

Jack shook his head. "I don't think that'd be such a good idea. They have road blocks on either end of town and armed guards. They're not lettin' anyone in or out."

Sean said, "I guess that answers that question. Instead of standing around in the barn, let's get up to the lodge. I bet you folks haven't eaten yet. Scotty, Jared, you two feed and put their horses out. Everybody else, grab a bag, and let's get these folks moved in."

Jack said, "Brooke and Ryan, will you two show 'em how we feed, then come on up."

Ryan made a face and was about to say something but then thought better of it.

Jack and Nicole walked with Sean up to the lodge. Along the way Jack couldn't help but notice the huge piles of twisted steel pipe that used to be the turnouts, the round pen, and the arena. "So I heard what happened to Luke. What about everybody else?"

Sean shook his head. "Jesus. It's been terrible. On the night of hell, we lost Lila and the kids, Joseph and Rachel, and Marilyn. We also lost six guests. Three in a fire, one had a pacemaker that burned the hell out of him, and two others just died. We have no idea why."

"My God. You have been through hell. Sorry to hear about your losses. Those were good folks."

Nicole said, "May I ask who they were?"

Jack said, "Joseph and Rachel Howell owned the whole thing. Luke and Lila Koerner managed the guest ranch side of things for 'em. I was closest to Luke and Lila. Marilyn was Joseph and Rachel's daughter-in-law and married to James, their son. He runs the cattle and farm operation. All of 'em are salt-of-the-earth, hard-workin', good people. I think Joseph was a congressman at one point. Solid man with an honest reputation."

Sean said, "It's been rough. The part that sticks with me the most were the ones who just died. We checked on everybody the next morning and found 'em dead in their beds."

"I have a theory about that," Jack said. "Did you pass out when everything was goin' crazy?"

"Yeah. So did just about everybody else."

"The heart is electrical. There are fibers that run through it, called Purkinje fibers, that conduct the electrical impulse through the heart to coordinate each beat. If the EMP with that flare was strong enough, I don't know why it wouldn't cause an arrhythmia. Most people would recover from it just fine, but a few wouldn't."

"So in other words, some people were lucky and others weren't."

"I was driving a truck at the time. Just happened to be diesel and didn't flip over. Nicole was in an airplane. Yep, some of us were just plain lucky."

# 54.

After dinner was over, nearly everybody sat around the huge wooden table and told stories about their experiences after the event. Several bottles of wine passed around the table as everybody relaxed, but Jack noticed that Sean and Jared didn't touch the wine. As things wound down, Jack asked, "So, you boys headed out to the gate tonight?"

Sean said, "That's the plan."

"Need any help?"

"Nah, Not tonight. Your man Ryan is helpin' us out. Maybe tomorrow."

"Ryan? The kid that rode in with me?"

"Yeah. He and Jared were talking. Said he wanted to sit watch with us."

From behind Jack Ryan said, "Do you have a problem with it, boss?"

Jack turned around. "Not at all. In fact, I'm kinda impressed. Stop by my cabin, and I'll let you take my lever gun. Might be handy to be able to reach out and touch 'em if you have to."

An hour later Jack and Nicole walked back to their casita in the dark. Nicole put her arm around his and leaned toward

him as they walked. She said, "It is nice to have you to myself again."

"You and I were alone in the wagon all day. I thought you'd be tired of me by now."

"Not at all. I like having your undivided attention. When someone or something gets in the way, I start to get a bit jealous, and I want you all to myself again."

"I see. Well, now I'm all yours."

"Really? Do you mean that? Because if you are all mine, then I should be able to do anything I please with you." She gave him a particularly wicked smile that he could only just make out in the dark.

Jack was a little surprised and said, "Uh-oh."

She then added, "I do need one small point of clarification, though."

"Sure. Shoot."

"Earlier I heard you refer to me as your significant other. I suppose that could be the same thing as girlfriend, but it sounds rather sterile and doesn't quite have the same endearing quality. Although, I must say it is significantly better than 'she's with me.' I should add that I am not entirely versed with the region's vernacular, in which case the phrase could mean substantially more than how it would normally translate."

Jack looked at her and smiled. "How would you like me to refer to you?"

"I am not about to tell you what to say or when. I abhor women such as that. But, if it were completely up to my discretion, I should think that 'love of my life' or perhaps 'the woman I have dreamed of since the day I first drew breath' might be particularly good models on which to base your final description of my position."

"How much wine did you have?"

"Just enough to make the rest of your evening quite interesting."

"I gathered that much. Hell, I'm gonna have to dig out a dictionary to keep up with you."

"Wine does tend to make me rather verbose."

"Yes, ma'am. It does indeed."

They stepped up on the wooden deck that wrapped around to the front of the building and walked to the front porch of the casita. Jack could see a flickering candle through the window. "Look, someone's been nice enough to get our room ready for us."

Nicole turned quickly and pushed him away from the door and against the wooden rail. "Jack Neumann, you are absolutely not allowed into *my* room unless I get a kiss. A quick peck on the cheek will not suffice in this regard. This is to be a kiss of sufficient passionate quality and quantity that I—and I alone— deem you worthy to pass through *my* threshold." She stepped close to him and pressed her body against him.

"Your threshold?"

"Yes. *My* threshold. *My* door. *My* entryway."

"Hey Jack, are you up here?" Ryan said, as he stepped up onto the deck from the other side of building. "I came to get that rifle. I might need a quick lesson on how to use it as well, 'cause I've never used one before."

Jack could see Nicole roll her eyes as she whispered *fuck* under her breath. She shook her head as she pulled away from him and opened the door.

"Sure. Let me grab it," Jack said. A moment later he returned with the rifle. "This is a '94 Winchester. Probably one of the most popular and most useful rifles there ever was. It's very simple to operate. Shells go in here. You jack a round in the chamber by working the lever, and you make it safe by carefully letting the hammer fall like this."

Jack made Ryan work the rifle several times until he was sure the kid knew what he was doing and was safe with the weapon. He said, "Ryan, I want you to be careful out there tonight. Chances are you won't see anything at all. But if you do—if someone comes riding up to the gate in the middle of the night at a fast pace—you just blow' em right out of the saddle. Every damn one of 'em. There's no good reason anyone should be out there in the middle of the night other than

to make trouble for you. Make sure you stay behind good cover and don't forget your pistol. I don't want to see you get hurt."

"You're saying shoot first and ask questions later?"

"That's exactly what I'm sayin.'"

Ryan smiled. "You're worried about me, aren't you?"

"Nope. I think you can handle yourself just fine as long as you keep your head. But you have a tendency to lose it. Keep it cool, and you'll know what to do."

Ryan was grinning from ear to ear. "Thanks."

"You're welcome. Make me proud, boy."

"Yes, sir."

Jack watched the young man walk off into the darkness. He was amazed at the changes the kid had made in only a few days. It had been less than a week since they met, and the two young men—the kid Jack met on the road out of Yellowstone and this kid today—were very different. This kid was older, more mature, starting to take responsibility and step up to the role of being a man.

Jack opened the door and stepped into the casita. Several candles flickered, casting a warm yellow glow in the room. Nicole was standing with her back to him, leaning on the table. She appeared to be reading something by the light of a candle. The soft light on the other side of her created a silhouette, and a candle to her right shed just enough light to accent the image before him. He was captivated. For a moment he simply stood and looked at her. He turned away quickly as she started to turn toward him.

"Someone named Maria was here and prepared our room for us. She wants you to know she is very glad you are here. She also says they have checked things and have found the water functions normally, but the furnace doesn't work. Also, she apologizes profusely for the lack of extra towels and linen."

Jack took off the leather holster with the big revolver and hung it on the back of a chair. He hung his hat on a small, wire rack sticking out from the wall and then removed the holster

and pistol from his hip. He said, "If you hand me your gun, I'll take care of it."

Nicole removed the pistol and handed it to him. She watched as he walked into the bedroom and placed his gun on the bed stand on the right side of the bed and her gun on the bed stand on the left. She smiled. When he returned, she asked, "Do you suppose there is hot water? Maria wasn't specific."

Jack thought about it a little. "I saw a big propane tank behind the building when we walked over here. Might be a little hot water. "

"You have no idea what I would give for a hot shower. A bath might even be nicer. "

"Bathroom's all yours."

"Are you certain? I could be a while."

"By all means. Ladies first."

Jack could hear the shower running as he walked into the kitchenette. A bottle of wine and two glasses had been left on the counter for them. He looked at the wine and started thinking. He liked Nicole. No, it was much more than *like*. He had very strong feelings for her, but it was difficult to sort out simple infatuation from real feelings, especially in light of all that had gone on in the last week. He had told himself that no matter what he thought or felt about her, he was not going to complicate the situation with sex. If his feelings were real, they would grow stronger over time. He knew that every couple had differences. It would better to find out if those differences were enough they should go separate ways, or what they had together was strong enough they could work out. Ultimately, he had always thought that people should wait until they are married to have sex. Brooke had made a point, though. What if they were not sexually compatible? You'd hate to find that out only after you were married.

He looked at the wine. Neither of them had had that much to drink during dinner and after. Just enough to feel it, but adding more would only lower their inhibitions further. Nicole

had been obvious over the last few days. He knew where she stood on the situation. He thought about her standing at the table. Her long legs, the gentle curve of her hip, her slim waist, the lines of her back, her neck, her hair, the way her jeans fit... He picked up the bottle and was about to set it back down and then decided he could use a drink. He poured two glasses and set one on the corner of the desk in the living room where Nicole would see it when she came out of the bath.

He took his glass of wine and stepped out onto the deck. The night was still warm and humid. He was surprised to see how dark it was. There were no lights anywhere. He knew he should be able to see Highway 14 across the little Shell Creek valley, but there was nothing. No distant farm lights, no lights from the town of Shell. Nothing. Above him, the sky was black. He knew it must be overcast because even the stars were missing. To his right, a slight gray area appeared in the sky lighter than everything else. Must be the moon, he thought. Inside him the battle still raged. He thought about the wine again and then considered just going to bed. He was tired enough that sleep should come quickly. He also considered walking out to the gate and standing watch with Ryan and the others. But doing either of these things would undoubtedly hurt Nicole's feelings, and he couldn't stand the thought of hurting her.

"There you are. Did you pour this for me?"

He looked over and could see her standing in the doorway. Her hair was wet and hung down on her shoulders. She was wearing a t-shirt that barely made it to her thighs, and he could just make out the smooth skin of her legs. His heart skipped a beat or two. "I did."

She walked over to him. "You realize of course this will simply make me talk more and use bigger words?"

"I like the way you talk."

"Thank you. The water is splendid. I had no idea that such a simple luxury could become so rare. The bathroom is yours if you want it."

"Thanks. I think I will."

When Jack walked out of the bathroom, he was clean and had shaved for the first time in a week. He felt wonderful. The kitchen and the living room were dark. The soft, yellow glow now came only from the bedroom. He walked in, wearing nothing but a clean pair of jeans.

Nicole was standing at the dresser, removing new clothes from the packages in her bag. She glanced over to Jack and stopped. Her eyes widened a little, and she said, "Oh my."

"What?"

"I don't believe I have seen you clean-shaven before." She smiled. "And I know I haven't seen you without a shirt."

"I hope I didn't get rid of the good parts."

She stepped in front of him and studied him carefully. "Oh no. Not at all. In fact I should think you have been covering up the good parts. Are you still all mine?"

He looked into her big dark eyes and said, "Yes, ma'am, I believe I am."

She reached out, took his hand, and led him to the bed.

# 55.

Megan said, "Oh my God. We have to get that flashlight. That thing is worth its weight in gold."

"Holy shit! I thought everything electrical was ruined."

"Apparently not."

Mark thought about how much easier things would have been last night if they would have been able to see. His feet and chest still hurt from all of the scratches he received. Whoever controls the night, controls the day, he thought. "Take the horses and head back to the hotel. Save some dinner for me if you can. I'll meet you back there in a while."

"What are you gonna do?"

"I'm gonna see if I can work out a deal for that light."

Megan looked at him and smiled. "Okay, but be careful."

He winked at her. "Of course."

Before she had even left, he ran back inside the store and found a stack of black jeans. He carried them to the window and checked the tags in the fading light. He found a pair in his size, emptied his pockets, and changed pants. In another section of the store, he found a black hoodie that looked a little too big but put it on. As he reached the door, he saw a small

table of bandanas in a multitude of colors. An idea struck him, and he put a black one in his pocket. He stepped outside and checked both the pistol at his side and the concealed one in the small of his back.

Instead of running down the street in the direction he had seen the people with the flashlight, he ran around the side of the store and then jogged down a wide backstreet that paralleled the main street. The twilight was fading fast, and he looked up to see a gray, overcast sky. It was going to be very dark, very soon.

He jogged about five or six blocks and then cut over to the main street again. As he snuck out around a building, he could vaguely hear voices coming from farther down the road. He listened but couldn't quite make out what they were saying. He ran back behind the buildings and then paralleled them for another three blocks. As he was about to make the turn and cut over to the main street again, a bright bluish white light popped on in front of him and danced over the pavement. He quietly moved to the back of the building on his left and squatted next to a big piece of twisted metal. The light shut off.

A woman's voice said, "I don't care what you say, we are not having chili again for supper. I couldn't hardly stand it last night. That stuff must go right through you."

A man's voice said, "If I have to eat something that comes out of a can, I'd rather have chili than anything else. At least it tastes good."

Mark considered his options as he let them walk past. He tied the bandana around his head, covering his mouth and nose, and pulled the hood up over his head and stood up. As he quietly walked up behind them, the woman said, "There's a big can of stew. What about that?"

Mark stepped carefully and quietly as he walked up behind the woman. His heart was hammering in his chest so loud he was sure she could hear it. In a flash he stuck out his left hand and wrapped it around her face, over her mouth. He pulled her back against him as he pressed the barrel of the black XD(m) to her temple. "I'll take that flashlight." She writhed

in terror, and he tightened his grip on her. The man turned to his left, and in the darkness Mark could just see him move the light from his right hand to his left. As the man started to reach for the pistol on his belt, Mark said, "Don't do it, buddy. I'll kill you both."

He said, "What do you want?"

"I want that light."

"It's just a fucking flashlight."

"Then it won't be any trouble to give it up."

"Yeah, but I found it."

"And I found you." Mark could see the man weighing his options. He pressed the barrel of the gun hard into the side of the woman's head. She whined.

"Fine. Here. Take the damn thing." He held out his hand with the light.

Mark said to the woman. "Take the light in your left hand." She reached out and took the light from the man. "Good. Now hold it behind you." He moved the barrel of the gun to the face of the man and let go of her with his left. He quickly picked the light out of her hand. He put his right knee to her butt and pushed her forward. "Good. Now walk. Both of you. Don't turn around, or I'll shoot."

He watched for a few moments with his gun held on them as they walked away without looking back. The woman was crying a little, and part of him felt bad, but he knew it was just fear. He didn't hurt her and was glad he didn't have to fire a shot. He turned and quickly ran back down the backstreet the way he had come.

As he jogged past the store that he and Megan had been in, he decided to duck inside. He pressed the lens of the light against his hand and pressed the button on the back. A pink line around the lens lit up. He pressed the button again, and the light grew much stronger in intensity. One more click and it turned off. Goddamn! This was awesome!

When he made it back to the hotel, instead of going to the dining room to find Megan, he went directly upstairs. He quickly changed into regular blue jeans and a blue button-down shirt

she had picked out. Downstairs he found her in the dining room, almost finished with her meal. When he sat down, an older woman he hadn't seen before smiled at him and walked over to the table. "Your wife said you weren't going to make it. I'll fix you a plate."

"Thanks. Yep, I guess I made it just in time."

When she had left, Megan leaned toward him and said, "So?"

Mark said, "If you rub the front of my pants, you'll feel something long and hard, and it's not just that I'm happy to see you."

"You're shitting me?"

He smiled. "Nope."

"What kind is it?"

"It says SureFire on the side of it."

"Wow. That's a good one. I used to have one in New York, just in case the power went out. We might have to find special batteries for it. How did you get it?"

"We had a little talk. They gave it to me."

She looked at him with a knowing smile. "Gave it to you. Just like that?"

"Yep."

"Did you shoot anyone?"

"What if I did?"

She smiled and shrugged her shoulders.

"Nope. Nobody got shot."

"Good. Saves ammo."

"Seriously. What if I did?"

She leaned toward him even closer. "You were the one who said it was now survival of the fittest. That thing gives us a huge advantage. Think of what a difference it would have made last week when we were out in the middle of nowhere. Even last night—I could have shot those bastards right out the fucking window."

The woman brought Mark's plate and set it in front of him. "Is there anything else I can get you?"

"No, thanks. I should be fine."

Megan continued in a quiet voice, "I think there are a few things that improve our chances to not only survive, but to thrive. This is one of them. If somebody has to get shot, well, shit happens. Everything is all about the odds now. If there is any way we can improve our odds, we have to do it as long as the benefit outweighs the risk. Get it?"

"Yeah. Seems pretty clear when you put it like that."

"Mark, if there is one thing I know, it's that nobody is out there trying to make life better for you. They are all in it for themselves."

The hotel manager walked up to the table. "Excuse me, but I was wondering if you had a chance to meet Paul and Sidney yet?"

Megan said, "Yes, I did. They seem like they know what they're doing."

He smiled. "They do. Sidney has been around horses his entire life, and Paul used to be a military policeman. I think they should be able to provide adequate security for us."

Mark said, "Two guys working around the clock?"

The manager said, "For now, yes, and they are happy to do it. They are working in shifts. I suspect they'll hire additional people as needed."

Mark said, "Sounds like a lot, but, hey, if it works, it works."

The manager asked, "How's Rose doing?"

Megan asked, "Rose?"

"She's our new full-time chef and waitstaff."

Megan smiled. "She's very nice. I think she'll work out well for you."

"Excellent. Excellent. Is there anything else I can get for you?"

They both shook their heads. Mark added, "No. Thanks. We're pretty well set."

"I hope you aren't too full. We have dessert tonight."

"God, I hope it's something with chocolate."

"I think you'll be pleasantly surprised." He gave her his best smile. "Enjoy."

Mark leaned toward Megan and said, "Okay. What about that guy? He's trying to make things better."

"Yeah. For himself. Do you honestly think he's doing all this just for us? Get real. You said yourself he wants this place to grow, so he needs people out there spreading the word about how great it is. Besides, it's all about the money. He knows we have gold, and he wants it. You watch; he'll just *have* to ask for just a little bit more because of all the upgrades he's giving us. I bet he wants to talk with you tomorrow. All of this is all about him. He wants to own the best hotel in the West. He said so himself. He also wants to be the richest hotel owner in the West. That goes without saying."

Mark leaned back in his chair and thought about what Megan had said. She did have a point. He leaned forward again. "Okay, so what about before?"

"What about it? Same thing."

"What about churches?"

She laughed a little bit. "Yes, Mark. They were exactly the same. All in it for themselves. They want to grow, so they do all kinds of nice things because that's what a 'good church' does. More people join, and along with them comes more money. Have you ever heard of a church that doesn't ask for money? Better yet, have you ever heard of a church that says to all its members, 'Hey, you know, somebody just gave us a big contribution. All the rest of you can keep your money for a while.' No way. They don't do it. Instead they say, 'Hey, look what so-and-so gave us. You should all think about giving more as well."

Damn, she was right. Mark had done the church thing for a while with a girl he used to date. On Sundays she was a good girl, but the rest of the week she was a lot of fun. He had heard sermon after sermon about how people should give more. "Okay, so, you're right."

Rose brought two plates with big brownies covered in a caramel sauce. "Careful. These are still hot."

When Rose left, Mark leaned forward again, "You're right, but that doesn't mean we should go around shooting people."

"Of course not. But you can't live in the past. Times have changed. The rules of engagement have changed. It's now dog-eat-dog, and you have to take what you want. Besides, it's natural."

"Natural?"

She laughed. "Sure it is. Think about it this way; remember this afternoon when we were playing around in the piles of clothes? We we're just playing, but it was kind of hot when you were forcing me to have sex with you, wasn't it?"

"Yeah. It was hot as hell."

"Yeah, well, that's the natural thing. You were taking what you wanted, and it felt good. Damn good."

He leaned back in his chair again. He had never thought about things like this. It had never occurred to him. In fact, now that he thought about it, grabbing that woman in the street and taking the flashlight had felt good as well. There was a rush, a surge of adrenalin that jacked him up, and a sense of power that was amazing. Hell, even the feel of her ass against his knee felt hot. Maybe he had thought about things wrong his entire life and that was why he had been stuck in a low-paying, no-future job with a girlfriend who was cheating on him. Maybe this is what they had called the "winner's attitude." It was like Megan had just turned on a light for him—a flashlight—and he could see things clearly.

He leaned forward again. "Did I ever tell you that I love you?"

Her eyes flicked up to meet his, and she smiled. "Yeah, but I don't think I'll ever get tired of hearing it."

# 56.

Jack became aware that he was awake, but he didn't open his eyes. He had been dreaming, and he didn't want the dream to end. He had dreamed of making love to a beautiful woman with dark hair and big brown eyes. She had held him so tightly and told him she didn't want it to end, that he was hers and she was his. He could remember the smooth softness of her skin, the smell of her hair, the warmth of her breath, and the sweet taste of wine in her mouth.

When he opened his eyes, gray flat light filled the room around him. He turned his head to the left and looked straight into Nicole's sleeping face. Her dark hair was spread out on the pillow around her, and a single lock of hair fluttered gently in her breath. More details of the night rushed back to him. My God she is beautiful, he thought, as he studied her face.

He slowly turned his head back to the right to avoid waking her. He felt a new emotion rise within him—guilt. He had loved Jenni and had promised her to be faithful as long as they both should live. He had, but she hadn't lived. Was he supposed to be faithful as long as he lived? If that was the case, and he had always thought it was, he had broken the promise. It was bad enough to break a promise—something he told

himself he would never do—but this was a promise to Jenni, the only person other than his daughter that he cared more about than life itself.

A thought occurred to him. Where did Nicole fit in? Would he lay down his life for her? He thought he would. No, he *knew* he would and without a second's hesitation.

He remembered his conversation with Nicole. Life was supposed to go on. Maybe the promise was only for as long as the other person was alive. Maybe that's how it was supposed to be. Maybe life itself was about love. Maybe it wasn't about how much you made, or how many things you acquired, or how many people you helped, but in the end it was all about how much you loved—how much love you spread around. If God was love, it would seem that he wanted it spread around. He seemed to recall a preacher tellin' a story of Jesus being asked what command was the most important. He had said, "Love the Lord, your God, and love your neighbor as yourself." Made sense.

He stared at the light and ceiling fan, hanging inert in the middle of the room, and thought about Nicole. Even though it had only been a short time he had known her, in reality they had spent a lot of hours together. They had endured a lot of difficult hours together, and they had spent hours in the wagon with little to do but talk. He wondered how many dates people would have had to go on to spend the same amount of time together they already had. He knew he loved her. Although he had only ever loved one other woman, this felt similar and yet different. He turned his head back to the left and looked at her. She was beautiful, and the sight of her face tugged at something deep within him. He thought about her personality, her smile, and her laugh. He thought about the things she had said and how she impressed and amazed him with her insight and intellect.

Deep within him he could hear Jenni's voice. Why do you think *she* was sent to you? Let go, Jack. You can remember me and you can love me, but I want you to let go of me. My days on earth are over, but you have more. I want you to be happy. Let go.

He turned his head back toward the ceiling. Tears filled his eyes and ran down to the pillow as he stared at the fan. A soft hand and a delicate arm reached over his chest. Dark hair fell around him as soft lips alit on his cheek. She looked down at him, and a soft voice whispered, "Are you crying?"

"No, I'm not cryin'. I don't cry."

"Then why is it your eyes are leaking?"

"Must be dusty in here."

They made love again, but this time it was not the frenzied, passionate, erotic sex of new lovers, but slow, meaningful, and deeply intimate—the kind that only two people in love can share. When they were done, Nicole lay on top of him with her chin propped up on her hand, looking at him.

"It's the hat, isn't it?" Jack asked.

"What?"

"My hat. It's Black Gold, and I had it steamed special in Sheridan. Women can't resist it."

She started to laugh, and he felt her stomach move rhythmically on top of his own. "Oh God yes. It's that bloody hat of yours. Every time you wear it, I can barely contain myself."

"I knew it. I told Casey when he steamed the brim that my particular bend was dangerous. A lot of men can't wear a hat like that. They can't handle it." She laughed again, and he thought he could listen to the sound forever.

"How do you do that?" she asked.

"Do what?"

"Touch me so deeply. Even your silly sense of humor seems to penetrate deeper into me than anyone I have ever known."

He moved slightly, and his relaxing penis fell out of her. "There. Now I'm not touchin' you quite so deep."

She started laughing again, and this time she couldn't seem to stop. Every time she came close to stopping, another giggle would come over her, and she would start all over. She rolled off of him and lay on her back, still giggling.

"It wasn't that funny."

"It was rather funny, you have to admit, but that's not the entire reason I was laughing."

"What is it?"

"I was thinking about Ryan and his horse. I think perhaps Brooke is in for a bit of a surprise if he doesn't pay attention when they fool around."

Now Jack was laughing. "That was kinda funny, wasn't it?"

"Good lord. You should have seen his face."

"Speaking of Ryan, I guess things must have been pretty quiet last night. I didn't hear any shootin'."

"You didn't?"

"No. Did you?"

"I thought I might have. It was in the dead of night, and it sounded a long way off. I was sleeping very soundly. I may have been mistaken."

"Oh shit. I better get out there and find out what the hell was goin' on." He stood up.

"Shit. I should have lied and kept you all to myself for a while longer. Do you really have to go?"

"I should."

"Yes, I suppose so. But if I lie here like this, will you come back to me as quickly as possible?"

He looked at her naked body as she lay on her side on the bed.

"Darlin', you can lie there like that if you want, but I will always come back to you as quick as I can."

As Jack left the casita, he glanced at his watch. 10:40. He couldn't believe how late it was. All things considered, he probably needed the rest, but it wasn't like him not to wake up to sounds outside. He had known Ryan and the men were sitting watch, and there was a threat of trouble. In the past he could always tune in to certain sounds. He could listen for the sound of a mare having trouble foaling or the sound of coyotes too close to the yard during caving season. The sound of gunfire should have woken him up. As he walked toward the main lodge, he did console himself with the fact that the casita and the main gate were on two completely opposite ends of the property, and the distance was close to a mile.

He walked in the door and hung his hat on the rack in the entryway. As he walked into the main room, Sean said, "Hey, Doc. How ya doin'?"

"Not bad. Heard you had some trouble last night."

"We did, but your boy took care of most if it."

"Ryan?" Jack asked, as he poured himself a cup of coffee from the pot on a small propane stove and sat down across from Sean.

"Yeah. I had left and gone to bed. I didn't figure anything was going to happen. The way I heard it, it was along about four thirty or five in the morning when three guys come a blasting up the road to the gate on horseback. Your boy stood up and shot two of 'em right out of the saddle. Didn't flinch, didn't drop the rifle to jack another round in—nothin'. Just shot 'em dead. The third guy started to make a turn, and Scotty let him have both barrels from a side-by-side. That was the end of it."

"Did you figure out who they were?"

"Yep. One of 'em was a guy who used to work for James on the ranchin' side of things. I guess he got fired quite a while back and was pissed off. Carried a grudge."

"How's Ryan?"

"He came up for breakfast this mornin' with that girl of his. He didn't eat much and seemed pretty quiet. That girl sure can talk."

"Yes, she can," Jack said, smiling.

"I think Ryan went to his cabin. Probably needed some sleep. That girl is down at the barn fussin' with the horses. You still planning on sticking around today?"

"Yep. A day off would be a welcome break. But, I figure we gotta at least make it to Hunt Mountain Road tomorrow. It would be better if I could get all the way to Burgess Junction, but I don't know that I can push the horses that hard."

"Well, you're gonna be flat for the first five miles, until you get to the canyon. The next eighteen miles are gonna be the tough ones. If you take your time and let the horses rest a bit, you'll be okay. Hunt Mountain Road is just past Granite Pass. It's all downhill from there to Burgess. I'd be surprised if you couldn't get that far."

"You think?"

"Sure I do, especially since you're giving the horses a day off today. Does the breaker bar on your wagon cover both front wheels?"

"I'm not sure. Didn't look that close."

"I bet it does. If so, you can let the horses trot all the way down the other side. Just run that break enough it keeps the harness tight. You don't want the horses pulling, just enough to keep it in tension."

"I got two people on horseback."

"They'll be fine as long as the horses are in shape."

"Marlena is a little soft, but not too bad. She's been fine from Cody here. The other two I was bringin' back from Yellowstone. They're used to a couple of hills. Ryan has a little sorrel mare, though. I'm not so sure about her."

"Ryan has a horse? He seems like a city-boy."

"Somebody left it for dead. He's been takin' care of it, and she's come around pretty well, but I'm not so sure she can carry somebody up the mountains."

"If you want to take one of ours, I'd have no problem with it. Especially for Ryan. He helped us out a bunch last night. I might even go so far as to say he saved our ass."

"I'll talk to him about it and see what he wants to do."

"When you talk to him, tell him to look through the remuda. There's a couple out there I probably need to hang on to. There's some he can have outright, and a few others I'll trade him for. We can work it out."

"Thanks. That's mighty generous of you."

Nicole walked through the door and said, "Good morning." She poured herself a cup of coffee. The two men watched her. She sat down next to Jack.

Sean was smiling. He said, "So, I gather the two of you are a couple."

Jack said, "We are." He winked and said, "She's with me."

Nicole elbowed him.

Sean shook his head and said, "Well, butter my butt and call me a biscuit. Doc, I gotta tell you. This is good news and bad

news. It's great for you, but it's bad news for a whole bunch of women all over Wyoming that have been pining for you." He looked at Nicole. "Ma'am, you do know you have your hands full with him."

"Oh yes, I am quite aware of that, thank you."

"You know, Doc, the way she's lookin' at you, I'm beginning to wonder if you're not the one with your hands full."

"It goes both ways."

"You two enjoy your coffee. I can have Laurie whip up a little breakfast for you if you want?"

"No. Thanks. We're good. Lunch isn't all that far away."

"I gotta get down to the barn and keep things movin'. I got Grieg down there this morning shoveling horse feed back into the hopper. Sad thing is you gotta tell that boy when to stop. I think the wheel is still turnin', but the hamster's dead."

# 57.

Megan was cold enough that her teeth were nearly chattering. Having running water in the bathroom was nice, but warm water would be a lot better. She made up her mind; if the manager wanted any more money, the only way he would get it was to heat up the damn water. Still, it was worth the cold to feel clean.

They had two objectives for the day. They had to find good, warm winter clothes, and they needed at least one horse that could carry a pack—two would be better. She had an idea where to go for the first goal, but was unsure about the second.

Winter clothes and some better camping gear would be the easiest to find since she only had to rely on herself. As long as she could find a source, everything else would be easy. Pick out the clothes, read the label, try them on, and stuff them into a bag.

Horses would be another matter entirely. If you looked out at a herd of horses, there was no way to tell which ones were broke and which ones weren't unless you tried to saddle each one. Even some green broke horses would let you saddle them, but trying to ride would quickly turn into a rodeo. And a horse broke to ride and a horse broke to pack were two completely

different things. Well, not completely different, but different enough that it would have a severe impact on how they moved out of here.

The more she thought about it, the more discouraged she became. She needed to find a horse that was broke to pack, was healthy, had enough experience it would be calm and controlled for them, and could handle Mark. She had been impressed how quickly he learned to ride, but he was still new. The horse also had to get along with the other horses. She knew that any new horse she brought into the herd would have to go through the awkward adjustment phase when they all sorted out the dominance thing. She could picture Mark sitting on a horse who was dancing around and fighting him and also trying to pick on the other horses or was getting picked on. It would be a cluster-fuck.

The only way to find a decent horse was to talk to the owner. Of course, that meant the owner still had to be alive. A couple of weeks ago, it wouldn't even have been a consideration, but today it was probably the biggest obstacle in their way.

Okay, so, she needed to find the owner of a healthy horse broke to pack with an easygoing temperament, who was willing to sell, and she had to do it in a town she had only visited a couple of times, and that was mostly when she was younger. She stepped out of the bathroom and into the living room of their suite. She looked at the pile of clothes and gear they had amassed. They definitely needed two packhorses. Then it occurred to her they also needed a second pack. Fuck. We are going to be stuck here, she thought. She slid her pistol into its holster and decided to go downstairs to meet Mark for breakfast.

As she left the room, she could hear the low noise of many simultaneous conversations and people milling about. Walking down the stairs, she could see people, lots of them, mostly women, standing, drinking coffee, and talking in the lobby of the hotel. She wound her way through the crowd and into the restaurant. She spotted Mark sitting at a table alone eating breakfast and sat next to him. "What the hell is going on?"

"The hotel manager and some guy from the city put out word they were going to be hiring a few people. I guess all these people are looking for jobs."

"You're kidding. Where did they all come from?"

"All over, I guess."

An idea struck her. "Did they have a meeting this morning?"

"They were all here when I came down for breakfast. I didn't hear anything about a meeting."

"Hang on. I'll be right back." Megan stood up from the table and walked back into the lobby. She stepped up about three or four stairs and said, "Ladies. Excuse me, ladies and gentlemen, could I have your attention?"

The crowd became silent as everybody turned to look at the young lady who stood on the stairs.

Megan went on, "My husband and I were just talking a few minutes ago, and I had an idea. I heard that all of you came here in search of a job. It would have been nice to know what the job was before you got up early and came all the way here, wouldn't it? As you know we are all going to have to pull together to get through this terrible tragedy. It occurred to me that some of us have extra things, and some of us need a few things. Some of us have certain talents and abilities, and other need those talents. I believe if we work together, we can find a way to help each other out. I would like to propose that the hotel might donate a wall, either outside or maybe even inside, where we can all list things we need or list things we would like to trade. Think of it as a low-tech craigslist. If I'm looking for something in particular, I could post what I want and maybe propose a trade. If somebody had a job available, they could put it up there so everybody would know what they were looking for. Then, we could designate one day a week where everybody could get together, like a flea market, and trade. Does anybody have any thoughts about this?"

A man in the back of the room said, "How do you get in touch with somebody who has somethin' you need?"

Megan said, "Simple. You just spell out how somebody can get in touch with you in your ad. Maybe an address and a time when you are generally there."

A fat, dirty little woman said, "What about security? I ain't gonna bring anything valuable to town if it's just gonna get stole."

The manager of the hotel spoke up from behind the desk and said, "Let me worry about that for you, ma'am. The Occidental Hotel would be happy to provide space for such a bulletin board. We also have a large patio area around the side of the building that should serve nicely for a place to trade. We have already started to implement security for our guests, and we would be happy to extend the same courtesy to you every Saturday morning."

Megan could see several people in the crowd nodding in approval and starting to talk about the ideas. She said, "If you don't mind, I'd like to give things a try right now. My husband and I are looking for two horses. One of ours was shot the other day. We really need to find two sound packhorses and a pack-saddle and panniers. If possible, I'd like to find horses that are healthy, shod, and maybe a little older. We would be happy to negotiate a price, and we can pay."

A man in bib overalls standing in the middle of the crowd said, "Pay? Honey, maybe you haven't heard, but your money is pretty much worthless."

Megan shot back, "Yes, but gold and silver aren't. They always had value and they always will."

The man said, "Where'd you steal that from?"

Megan said, "First of all, anything I might have used to belong to my daddy before he..." She hesitated and tried to look a little emotional. "Before...you know...before he died. Secondly, what difference would it make to you where it came from? If you don't want to trade with me for gold or silver, don't."

Megan saw a hand shoot up in the back of the room. A pretty, blond-haired woman holding the hand of a little girl said, "I have exactly what you need."

# 58.

Mark was saddling the horses again. What a fucking pain in the ass job this was. Catch the horse, lead it back, tie it up, brush it out, put the pad on, put the saddle on, take the halter off, put the bridle on while jamming your thumb in its mouth, tightening the bridle, tightening the cinch, walking the horse around, and tightening the cinch again. Then do the whole fucking thing over again on Megan's horse! All this work just so they could ride across town. God he missed his truck. Just jump in, turn the key, and go. Winter, rain, summer—it didn't matter. He would always be warm and dry. He could sit and listen to the radio, talk on the phone, anything. This sucked.

Stacy was saddling her horse next to him. Megan had introduced her and her daughter, Sarah, after the meeting and had explained that the young woman had a couple of packhorses she wanted to trade.

Mark kept watching her out of the corner of his eye. She clearly had a lot of experience with horses and moved with ease and a conserved motion as she saddled the animal. Her horse was bizarre looking and appeared almost cartoon like. It was mostly white with big, round black spots all over it and

a black-and-white mane and tail. He said, "I've never seen a horse like that. What is it?"

She smiled and said, "This is Tony. He's a leopard appaloosa. My husband bought him for me after we were first married. He's kind of different looking, huh?"

"Yeah, I'll say. It looks like he was designed by a committee."

"The nice thing is I always know where he's at in the pasture. You can see him from a mile away."

Mark walked over to the horse and patted him on the side of the neck. "Wow. He feels like a horse."

Stacy laughed. "Of course he does."

He walked around the front of the horse to help her with the saddle. When he looked at the horse's face, he said, "Whoa. Oh man. That's so weird!"

"What?"

"He has one blue eye and one brown one."

"Yeah. It goes with his coloring. It's normal."

"Okay, but it looks kinda freaky."

She laughed.

"So Megan tells me you want to move into town?"

"Yeah, if I can find a place. Someone was telling me there are a bunch of vacant houses on the edge of town. I'd like to find one with enough room I could keep Tony, at least for a while. It's just too far for me to try to get to town, and it's too hard to take Sarah with me. If both of us are in the saddle, then I can't carry anything, and since she's only four, I can't leave her at home. Some good neighbors might be nice."

"Bet you kinda wish you had the minivan again, huh?"

"Oh no. I never had a minivan. I'm not that kind of mom. I had a pickup. Mine shared the same fate as everyone else's, but my husband's truck is still sitting there just like he parked it."

"Was it diesel?"

"Yeah. It was old, but it ran good. I tried to convince him to by a new one, but he wanted to keep it."

"Of course you tried to start it?"

"That was the first thing I tried. It's dead, just like the TV, radio, computer, and every other electrical thing we had."

Megan and Sarah came around the corner of the building. "Mommy!" the little girl yelled as she ran to Stacy.

"Hey, baby. Did you go potty like a big girl?"

The little girl nodded.

Megan said, "She's awesome. What a great kid. I wish they were all like that. Are we ready to go?"

"Yep," Mark said. He looked up at the gray, overcast sky and took off his jacket. The warm, humid air was starting to make him sweat under the leather. He bunched it up and tied it to the back of his saddle.

They walked the horses through town and west on Highway 16 for several miles. When it seemed like they were going to continue on into the Bighorns, they turned off onto a nondescript little gravel road and wound through the foothills of the mountains. After several miles they turned down a long gravel drive. Nestled into a small grove of trees, a nice, little, white country house and barn sat just on the other side of a small clear creek. As they crossed the wooden bridge, Mark could see Stacy trying to rein in Tony. He said, "Looks like he's glad to be home."

"Yes, and it pisses me off. He's supposed to listen, not think."

Mark was impressed at how deftly the young woman handled the horse, all the while balancing her daughter on her lap. He wondered how she had gotten Sarah up on her lap when they had left for town.

Stacy rode past them and into the barn. She pulled the weird-looking horse to the side and said, "Okay, monkey. Off you go." The little girl turned and grabbed a board of a section of stall divider and stepped off, so she was hanging onto the wood with her hands and her feet were standing on the next lower board. Stacy got off the horse, tied him, and plucked the little girl off the divider.

Sarah yelled, "No no no! I do it myself."

"Whatever," Stacy said and put the little girl back up where she had been.

Mark and Megan glanced at each other and smiled as the girl slowly worked her own way down.

When they had tied the horses and loosened the cinches, Stacy said, "Can I get you something to drink. I got iced tea."

"Works for me," Mark said.

Megan agreed, and they followed her toward the house. Megan said, "Can I ask why you have mules?"

"Mules?" Mark interrupted. "I didn't hear anything about mules. I thought we were coming to get packhorses."

Megan rolled her eyes a little and said, "Mules are better."

"How can they be better? I thought they were small and stubborn. I don't want to be fighting a stupid mule all day."

"Small?" Megan said, looking confused. "They're not small."

"Sure they are. I've seen them before. Big ears, gray colored, go hee-haw all the time. Jesus rode one."

Both Megan and Stacy started laughing. Megan pointed to a pasture to the west of the house. "Those are mules, dumbass. You're talking about donkeys. Big difference."

Mark looked in the pasture. He would have sworn those were horses out there grazing. He said, "No shit?"

Megan said. "No shit. A mule is a crossbreed between a horse and a donkey. The donkey is always the sire, and the horse is the mare. If it's the other way around, you get a hinny. They are pretty rare."

Stacy added, "Most people think mules are smarter than horses. They aren't as stubborn as a donkey, and they tend to be very surefooted and strong. You can ride ours, but we got them to pack, and they've been awesome. They can carry more weight than a horse, they can go further, they are better in the mountains, and they see better in the dark. You guys can go look at them if you want. I'll get the tea."

A half hour later, they sat at a round wooden picnic table beneath a big cottonwood. Megan asked, "What did your husband do Stacy?"

"He worked for the city. Did just about everything with the utilities. He got called when things started going wonky the night of the disaster. He took my truck and left for town." She

paused and then added, "We passed the truck on the highway back there. I had to get him out and bury him myself."

Megan was shocked. "Oh my God. That must have been horrible."

She nodded. "If he just would have stayed home, everything would have been fine for us. We bought this place a few years ago. Dave had always thought everything was going to fall apart with the economy. In the last few years, it started to look like he was right. We made some changes to the place to make it a little more self-sufficient and started putting things away. You know, things that would last for a long time. We have enough here to live on easily for a year or more. The creek runs all year long, and I can filter water. We also have a big garden every year, and we can smoke our own meat. It would have been easy."

Mark asked, "Why don't you stay now?"

"By myself? I thought about it, but then I thought, I have no way to defend myself, and if anything happened to me, what would happen to Sarah. I can't risk it."

Mark asked, "Don't you have any guns?"

"Oh, yeah. And if you can get them, you can have them. Come and see this." She stood and led them around to the back of the house.

A huge, gray, steel gun safe was lying face down on the door in the middle of the yard. Behind it, several sheets of plywood were nailed to the wall, obviously covering a large hole. "That safe weighs a little more than a ton when it's empty. There's no way to flip it over."

Mark looked at the safe for a moment and said, "Sure there is. You two can go back to talking about donkeys or mules or whatever the hell they are. Let me handle this."

An hour later he walked back around the side of the house. The two women still sat around the table talking. He said, "It's all yours."

Stacy spun her head toward him, "You got that thing flipped over? No way."

He smiled. "It's also open."

She almost ran to where the safe lay in the yard. It was now lying on its side with the door lying open in the grass next to it. "Oh my God! How did you do it?"

"Simple. I just used a car jack to get it most of the way up. Then I just heaved it over. The door was unlocked."

Stacy knelt on the door and started pulling guns out of the safe. Mark stood on the other side of the safe and couldn't help but look down the back of her pants as she bent over. She said, "This is so awesome! It looks like they're all just a little banged up." She knelt and looked up at him. "I could just kiss you."

"Not while I'm around," Megan said.

Mark thought of making a comment but decided it wasn't worth it. Instead he said, "Jesus. You got quite a few in there."

"Some of these were Dave's hunting rifles. Some were guns he picked up because he liked them or he got a good deal." She laid a big, silver revolver up on the safe. "That one is a Freedom Arms in 454 Casull. I think he bought that one 'cause he liked a character in a book." She pulled out a black, military-looking pistol and laid it down. "This one is mine."

Mark asked, "What is it?"

"Oh, that's a Beretta 92A1. It's weird. It feels a little big for my hand, but I can shoot it very well. Can't mess with what works." She pulled out another rifle.

Mark said, "Whoa. That's cool. What's that one?"

With her head stuck in the safe, she said, "FAL." She pulled another pistol out of the safe and stood up, "I can dig the rest of the stuff out of there later. Pick one or take them all."

Mark looked confused, "What?"

"Pick one, two, four, all of them. I told you that if you could get them out you could have them."

"Nope. No way. I already got what I need. Besides, they're yours. You need them if you want to stay around here. What we need are the mules. You two can work out the details while I go get them."

An hour later they were climbing back on their horses. Mark held the lead ropes for Gus and Ralph. He said, "I never

thought there would be a day when I was glad to be leading mules to town. Are you sure you won't need them?"

Stacy said, "Nope. With Tony and the other two horses, we have all we need. I'm glad this trade worked out well for all of us. Thanks again for the help with the safe. I think we might try and stay here."

"And we might come back and check on you," Megan said.

"If you do, I'll buy dinner. You're always welcome."

They waved goodbye and headed out down the drive.

About a mile down the road, Mark said, "You know, I never heard why Stacy and her husband had mules to begin with."

"Her husband was a big-time guide for deer, elk, and bear. He used them to pack hunters into the mountains and pack the elk out."

"Oh. Did you guys work out a good deal?"

"Yeah. Getting the safe open helped a lot. I offered two ounces of gold, but she only took one and a handful of silver."

"That's not bad, all things considered."

"I saw you looking at her ass."

Mark was surprised by the comment. "Yeah, well. It was kinda hard not to. I mean, it was hanging right out there."

"And it was nice too. Go ahead and say it."

Mark wondered if this was a trap. "Well, that's kind of subjective."

"Jesus, Mark. I thought she was hot. It's really not that big of a deal. She's gorgeous, and you're a guy. I'd be surprised if you didn't look."

Mark looked over at her. "You're either totally awesome, or you're trying to trap me. I'm not sure which."

Megan laughed. "I guess I must be awesome. I look at it this way. You are either going to stay with me because you love me, or you're not. If you leave, then you weren't the guy I thought you were. If you stay with me, you must love me."

"Looks like I'm stuck with you."

# 59.

Mark waited outside watching the horses as Megan tried to find the gear they needed inside Bighorn Mountain Adventure Supply. When they arrived at the store, four horses were tied to a fence surrounding the property, and several bicycles leaned against an old, large wooden house in need of a fresh coat of paint. Years ago the old house had been converted into a general store to serve the residents on the far west end of town. More recently the old general store had been converted into an Internet-based company that supplied camping, hiking, climbing, hunting, and fishing equipment to people all over the world. A small storefront served the local population and a few summer vacationers.

Nearly a dozen people were standing in a small group or sitting together, talking in the parking lot. The owner of the store was inside with Megan and a sawed-off, double barrel twelve-gauge. A man a few years older than Mark, wearing torn jeans and a black Metallica t-shirt, sat on the wooden stairs leading to the front door and leaned against a post with a black AR casually lying in his lap.

Megan had told Mark she would be a few minutes and walked right up the stairs past the man with the rifle. The

owner, an older man with a thin face and gray beard met her at the door, gun in hand. After a brief conversation, he lowered the shotgun, and she started shopping.

As he waited, Mark could hear brief snippets of multiple conversations going on around him. These people were not happy. Most seemed to be complaining about the store owner refusing to take credit cards or even cash for the items they wanted to purchase. By the looks of the guy on the step, relaxed and sitting with a bored expression, this was not their first group of unsatisfied customers. Megan's entrance into the store seemed to revive an earlier argument or confrontation, as the people in front of the store became more agitated.

A middle-aged guy with greasy hair, a dirty blue shirt, and an ugly, new, brown beard walked over to Mark. "Hey. Why did that girl you're with get to go in?"

He said, "I don't know. Go ask her."

"You go ask her."

"She's shopping. I'm watching the horses."

"Maybe she's in there suckin' that guy's cock."

Mark tipped his head slightly and shrugged his shoulders. "She might be. Maybe you should try it."

"Maybe when she comes out here I'll make her suck my cock."

"Tell you what, buddy, when she comes out here, why don't you ask her and see how that goes for you."

For a second it seemed like the guy was going to walk away and forget the whole thing. Mark had decided to let the whole thing go. Instead the guy said, "You're kind of an arrogant son of a bitch."

Mark said, "Confident. Not arrogant. Big difference."

The man stood for an awkward moment, thinking of what to say next. Finally he said, "I'm gettin' tired of your pussy mouth."

Mark moved fast. In a split second, he had his gun out with both hands at the ready and took two steps forward with the pistol held out in front of him pointed at the man's face. "I've had enough of your bullshit. I was standing here

minding my own business, and you had to start this. You just couldn't walk away, could you? Now, shut the fuck up; or try me, and I'll kill you. Either way, I'm done listening to your bullshit."

The man turned around and took a step away but muttered, "Fuckin' asshole."

Mark stepped forward, and with a short swing his right hand cracked the guy in the back of the head with the muzzle of the pistol. The man crumpled to the ground. Mark said, "I told you I was done." He turned and walked back to his horses. He watched the guy slowly get back up.

The guy on the step slowly stood, stretched his back, and walked over. "Wow, that was pretty cool. That guy has been here all day talkin' shit like that. I'm glad you whacked him. I thought I was gonna end up shooting him, and I was startin' to look forward to it."

Mark jokingly asked, "Have you had to shoot many?"

"A few, but not in the last couple of days. I think people are starting to get the message."

"A few?"

"Yeah. I needed a bunch of stuff, so I started helping out Mr. Thompson last Monday. He was having trouble with people trying to steal shit from him. He pays me by letting me have things I need from the store. The first day was easy. All I had to do was sit here and show people the gun. The next day a bunch of them tried to rush me. I shot three of them. One guy died right over there. The other ones were taken away by the people that was with 'em. The next day I killed two and shot another guy in the leg, but Mr. Thompson got one guy with his shotgun. It was pretty bad."

Mark was surprised. "Wow. I guess you guys are pretty serious."

"Oh yeah. Mr. Thompson says he can't stand looters. Says he'd kill 'em all."

Megan came bouncing out of the store and down the steps with a black jacket draped over her arm. She walked to Mark and said, "Here. I need you to try this on."

Mark tried on the coat while telling Megan what had just happened with the greasy guy. She spotted the man Mark described at the edge of a small group of people and glared at him. When she was sure he was looking at her, she made an exaggerated motion of wiping her mouth with the back of her hand. She turned back to Mark and said, "That ought to piss him off. How's it fit?"

"It fits good, but it's kind of light."

"This is just the liner. I wanted to make sure this fits before I found the shell. I think I have everything else." She took the canvas panniers off Gus and turned to go back into the store. She held the pannier out and said, "Reuse, recycle. I should only be a few minutes."

Mark smiled at her. "Take your time."

They watched her walk back to the store. The guy said to Mark, "Is that your girlfriend?"

"Yeah. Girlfriend, fiancé, something like that."

"She's hot."

Mark smiled. "Yeah. I think so too."

"Been dating long?"

"We met the day after everything went to hell. Since then we've kind of been doing everything together. We started out in Gillette and rode over here on horses."

"No shit? Are you gonna stay here or keep moving?"

"We've been talking about heading west. Maybe find someplace a little warmer to stay for good."

"No kidding? So let me get this straight. You met this girl a week ago, and now you're engaged and looking for a place to hang permanently?"

"Yeah. Weird, huh?"

"That's awesome, man. I heard her talking to Mr. Thompson. She's kinda laid back, but seemed smart, and wasn't afraid to tell him how things are, you know?"

"Yeah, she's like that."

"So, are you guys gonna head north through Sheridan or are you gonna go south?"

Mark thought about it for a second and said, "Actually, I don't think we've decided yet."

"If you decide to head north, I might tag along, if you don't mind. There was a guy here yesterday who said he came down from Sheridan. He said he lives in Casper and was trying to get home. Anyway, he said there was a train in town when the disaster happened, and there's all kinds of stuff just lying all over the place. But get this: I guess there was some big volleyball tournament at the junior college, and a whole bunch of girls from all over were there when everything went nuts. I'd kinda like to check that out. You know what I mean?"

"Yeah. I hear ya. That train sounds interesting. We might head that way after all."

Megan came back out of the store almost bouncing with joy as she carried the canvas panniers filled with the things she had found. Mark watched her ponytail swing as she moved down the wooden stairs. Just as she stepped onto the asphalt parking lot, a gunshot split the afternoon quiet.

Time slowed almost to the point of standing still. Mark watched in seemingly slow motion as Megan crumpled to the ground on her right side, the canvas bags falling in front of her. A bright red blossom appeared high on the back of her right thigh as she struggled, trying to get the pistol out from underneath her. In part of his brain, he knew he screamed or at least shouted something, but another part was unaware as he pulled his own pistol out of the holster and started moving toward her. He fired blindly one-handed in the direction he thought the shot had come from as he ran. Behind him the crack of the assault rifle rang out and was followed by another and another. In his mind Mark could see the guy in the black t-shirt firing the AR at the unknown shooter. As he reached Megan, she had rolled onto her left side and managed to get her own pistol out and started to aim across the parking lot over the top of the canvas bags. He stopped behind her and started to aim.

The other side of the parking lot was utter chaos. Several people who had been sitting in a small group were now lying

flat on the ground, and those who had been standing were now trying to run and scatter. A man darted toward the right, trying to reach the corner of the store, moving fast with his head low. As if almost by instinct, Mark lined up the front sight of his pistol on the man's side and pulled the trigger. The guy fell face-first on the blacktop, sliding to a stop. Mark noticed a husky woman standing a little farther away and slightly to the left of where the man had started running. She held a gun in her hand. Her brown hair seemed to puff out behind her several times in perfect rhythm with the reports of the guy's rifle before she fell to the ground. As a big man with a bald head pulled a pistol out of his holster, Mark heard Megan's gun click. He turned and fired three times in rapid succession. The guy fell to the ground, wildly thrashing and grabbing and swatting at his chest.

Mark scanned the parking lot, looking for the greasy guy. Several people were obviously dead. A skinny older man with a big gray beard sat alone on the ground with his arms raised over his head. Another guy was trying to pull himself away from the others as he dragged a bloody leg. A thought occurred to Mark as he looked at the store, and he turned around quickly, raising his XD(m) at the corner of the building behind him. Just as the sights lined up, the greasy guy stepped out from the corner of the building. Mark put a neat round hold in the middle of his forehead. He fell to the ground motionless.

All at once, the shooting stopped. From behind him and to the right, Mark heard the hollow metal sound of an empty magazine hitting the parking lot. It was quickly followed by the snap of a new one being inserted into place and the snick of the bolt chambering a new round.

"Goddamn it! That fucking hurts!" Megan shouted.

The sound of her voice snapped Mark's attention from the dead man at the corner of the building back to her. She's been shot!

Mark moved to Megan's side. "Oh my God. Are you okay?"

"Do I look okay to you?" Megan said, holding up her bloody right hand.

"Oh shit. Turn over and let me look at it."

Megan rolled farther onto her left side. The back of her jeans including her butt cheek and most of the back of her right thigh was soaked in blood. Mark could see a linear tear about four-inches long in the middle of the stain. He pulled the knife out of his pocket and said, "I have to cut away some of your jeans, so I can see better."

"Be careful. I don't need a knife wound along with a gunshot wound."

"I will. Just hold still." He slid the knife into the tear in the denim and extended it in both directions. He could see an angry red, three-inch groove open in her skin, about as wide as a pencil and about half as deep. "Wow. It looks like it just skimmed you. It didn't even really go into your leg."

"Well, I seem to be bleeding, and it burns like hell."

From behind them they heard, "I'll go see if Mr. Thompson has a first aid kit or something to help."

Mark looked up to see the guy standing just behind him. "Thanks, man. That would be awesome."

Megan said, "Wait a second. Buddy, I don't even know your name. Why don't you stay here with the rifle and let Mark find the first aid. I don't want somebody getting up and shooting me again, and my gun doesn't seem to work."

"TJ. My name is Travis James Lee, but most people call me TJ."

"Nice to meet you," Mark and Megan said in unison. Megan added, "Thanks for the help."

"No problem. That was awesome."

Mark ran up the stairs and grabbed the handle of the door. He pushed it open and was met by both barrels of the old man's shotgun. Without thinking or a second's hesitation, he grabbed the barrels with his left hand and pushed them to the right as he stepped to the left. The gun roared, blowing a splintered hole in the door the size of a softball. Mark jerked the shotgun forward and out of the man's hands. "What the fuck are you doing, you stupid son of a bitch?"

The old man took a couple of steps backward into the store, saying, "I...I...didn't..."

"You didn't what? Mean to damn near kill me, or make me half deaf?" His right ear was ringing loudly.

"I...I..."

"I know. You said that before. Where's the first aid kits?"

"On the back wall next to the bug juice."

Mark brought the shotgun with him as he walked to the back of the store. He found the first aid kits on a shelf where the man had said and selected a big one.

"That's the Adventure Plus Mountain Pack. That's gonna cost you three hundred dollars."

"Not today," Mark said. "I think you're running a special. It's called a shotgun sale. You damn near blow my head off, and I get any fucking thing I want. Outside. Let's go."

"But I have to stay in here and protect my store."

Mark was about to say something in return when he spotted a box of flashlights like the one he had acquired last night. A second bigger box sitting next to it held the packaging the lights had been in. He asked, "Did any of them work?"

"What?"

Mark pointed at the lights.

"Oh, those. I...ah..."

Mark pointed the shotgun at the man. "Don't lie to me."

"Two of them worked. I had almost a hundred to begin with, but only two worked. I sold one the other day and kept the other one for myself."

"I'll take it. And a handful of batteries. It's called the stupid tax."

"But it's mine."

"No, it was yours; now it's mine."

It took Mark about a half hour with Megan and TJ's help to get the wound cleaned and dressed. After he had washed everything off with antiseptic, the wound didn't seem to bleed much at all. Megan had instructed him on how to apply something called a Telfa pad and tape it in place. Although TJ seemed

to be helpful and generally knowledgeable about taking care of the wound, Mark didn't like the way he was looking at the lower half of Megan's ass and the back of her thigh.

TJ said, "If she's going to ride that horse back into town, you're gonna need some way to hold everything in place, otherwise that little wound will start bleeding again."

Angry that Megan had been shot and frustrated with his abilities, Mark said, "Oh, so now you're an expert in gunshot wounds?"

TJ's tone relaxed as he said, "Easy, man. I'm just trying to help. Actually, yeah, I have done this before. I did eight years and three tours with the Tenth Mountain Division, Third Brigade in Afghanistan."

"Oh. Sorry. This whole thing is just pissing me off."

Megan reached back with her hand and put it on his. "Don't worry. This is no big deal. Not much more than a scratch."

"Yeah, but it could have been. That was too fucking close. I'm getting sick and tired of everything being such a Goddamn struggle and having to fight for everything."

TJ moved around to the front of Megan and sat down on the pavement. "Dude. What you are going through is normal. You were awesome when the shit was flying, and now when it's over, it starts sinking in, and you start getting pissed off. I'd rather have one guy like you with me in Afghanistan than ten guys that freak out. Just chill and ride it out. Remember, we're not the enemy."

Mark was going to say something but decided not to. For a moment there was an awkward silence. Megan broke the spell by saying, "I got it. I know what to do! Mark, I need your help."

She stood up, and he followed her into the store. The owner sat on a stool behind the counter looking at them but didn't say a word. Megan said, "I remember seeing some bicycling shorts when I was looking around before. Where are they?"

The owner grunted and pointed to another room. A small section of the store was dedicated to mountain biking. A small stack of women's biking shorts were stacked next to water bottles, gloves, helmets, and a few other odds and ends.

Megan shuffled through the pile until she found the right size. Standing in the corner next to Mark, she pulled off her boots and her jeans and then, with a little smile, slid off her panties.

Mark whispered, "What the hell are you doing?"

"What?" She grinned at him.

"What? Jesus. You're half naked. You want to fool around now?"

"Normally I would, but we need to get going. I need you to help get these on over that bandage."

They worked together with Mark holding the dressing in place as she pulled up the tight shorts. Although she would have preferred to wear jeans, she found a pair of hiking pants that fit fairly well and put them on.

On the way out of the store, she threw her panties on the counter and said, "Here's a souvenir for you."

Mark opened the shotgun and took out the unspent shell. He laid the gun on the counter and said, "No more stupid shit. The next time the tax will be a lot higher."

Outside, TJ was waiting for them by the horses. He said, "I'm serious about what I was saying about Sheridan. If you guys decide to go, I'd like to ride along. It's always better to have more people. I have all my own stuff."

"Sheridan?" Megan looked at Mark, a little confused. "Are we going to Sheridan?"

Mark said, "I don't know. Maybe. We have to go some way. We can talk about it."

Megan turned to TJ. "Meet us at the Occidental tomorrow night at seven for dinner. We'll buy you dinner and talk about it."

He said, "Sounds good. Any idea when you guys are leaving?"

Megan said, "It will probably depend on how my butt feels in the saddle. Do you have a horse?"

TJ pointed at the four horses still tied to the fence.

She said, "I guess you do."

# 60.

Jack leaned against the fence as he watched the horses of the remuda graze under a slate sky. A warm, humid breeze continued to blow in from the south. He had been alone for most of the afternoon, and it had felt good. In the past he always appreciated his time alone. It gave him a chance to think, to sort things out. In the past week, he'd had very little time to himself. Things had been so hectic and chaotic. Now, although he had offered to help, everybody had told him there was nothing to do at the moment. He used the opportunity to slip away.

Few things relaxed him more than watching horses. If there was something on his mind or something had him concerned, he would find a little time to slip away and watch his herd. The politics of horses fascinated him. In a matter of a few minutes, he could tell who the lead mare was, and after an hour he could just about understand the entire hierarchy. But most importantly, there was something in the peaceful way the horses moved, grazed, and practiced their politics that relaxed him and allowed him to think clearly.

It occurred to him that it had been one week ago that the flare left him stranded in his truck at the side of the road.

Despite the time, it was still hard to comprehend everything that had changed. Life had changed. Every man, woman, and child on the planet had been affected by this catastrophe, and their lives would never be the same. In a matter of a few seconds, everything most people had taken for granted was gone. All of the luxuries of a modern society were wiped out, and they had been thrust back in time. Food, clean water, security, and shelter now had to be considered on a daily basis. Instead of climbing the corporate ladder, keeping up with the Jones, or planning next weekend's entertainment, people were trying to stay alive and figure out how they were going to live through the winter.

Jack sighed. It was too much to think about all at once. Better to take it in small pieces and live one day at a time.

As he thought about the events of the last week, he thought about Ryan. When they had met, he had been initially unimpressed with the boy. The kid was a modern day Peter Pan, a boy stuck in a man's body. He was self-absorbed and lazy. But, he did seem to have changed in the last few days. Jack thought about the conversation when he had asked for a job and smiled. Hearing the kid call him sir had seemed awkward when the word came out of his mouth, as though he had never done it before. He was trying. Got to give the kid credit for that. At least he seemed to be heading in the right direction. Stepping up to volunteer for guard duty last night had been impressive. Hearing the story about how he stood up and shot those riders was downright shocking. The kid might turn out all right after all, if he didn't get himself killed first.

There was also Brooke. He wasn't quite sure what to think of her yet. The girl had issues, but she also had possibilities. On the one hand, she was self-centered, self-absorbed, immature, and spoiled. But on the other hand, she was smarter than what she let on, she had a natural gift with horses, and once she got her head around something, she worked hard. The conversation they had shared in the wagon still bothered him. The girl had some notions about sex that might get her in trouble. In this new world, those ideas and her naïve attitude would be a

bad combination. She could fall into the wrong hands in no time. It occurred to him that she might not have a strong sense of self-worth. What she needed was a good role model, somebody to show her a better way. Jenni would have been perfect. He sighed again. At any rate, he hoped that he could keep her safe on the ranch. Maybe the pride in a good day's work would help.

And then there was Nicole. It wasn't enough that the entire world changed in a matter of a few seconds, but a beautiful woman drops out of the sky, walks into his life, and completely shakes him to his very core. He pictured her smiling, and a warm feeling came over him like it did when he was in high school. He could hear her laugh, and in his mind he could see her face when she had sat on his lap. He started to rewind the events of last night.

"Hey, boss."

The voice surprised Jack. He turned and saw Ryan walking across the lawn toward the fence.

"Whachya up to?"

"Just watchin' horses. What're you up to?"

"Nothin'. It's nice to have a little time off, huh?"

Jack turned back to the horses as Ryan settled against the rail next to him. "Yep. It sure is. Heard you had a little excitement last night." He turned and saw the kid grin.

"Yeah, we did. I did just like you said. They said I killed both those guys. They're calling me a hero."

"Yep. That's what I heard."

They both stood quietly at the fence for a while without speaking. After a few minutes Ryan said, "I don't really feel like a hero."

"What's a hero supposed to feel like?"

"I don't know. I kinda feel like shit."

"Remember when I shot that man in front of the grocery store. You called me a hero. In fact, a lot of people did. Hell, I ain't no hero. I did what I had to do, and you did what you had to do. Trouble is some men lost their lives in the process. We were the guys responsible, and it kinda bothers us. That's

a good thing. Takin' a man's life should never be easy, and I think it should haunt a good man for a while. You should wonder if there weren't some other way things could have gone differently. When you realize there was no other way, that they didn't leave you any other choice, you'll start to feel better, and all the questions in your mind will go away." Jack paused and let the words sink in. "Now, I'm gonna tell you somethin', and I want you to remember it. John Wayne said, 'Courage is bein' scared to death but saddling up anyway.' He was right. You are a hero. You went out there last night knowin' there might be trouble. When it came, you didn't turn and run. You faced it. That's a hero, son. Bein' a hero ain't about killin' those men; it's bein' there to begin with and standin' up when the time came. I'm proud of you."

The two men stood at the fence, watching the horses. When Jack looked over at Ryan, he noticed tears running down his face. He didn't say anything but simply turned back toward the horses. After nearly fifteen minutes, Ryan said in a choked voice, "Thanks. Nobody's ever said that before."

"What? Called you a hero?"

"No. Told me they were proud of me."

At first Jack didn't know what to say. "Well, they should have. You have the right stuff in you." Jack decided to change the subject. "By the way, did Sean tell you that he might be willing to trade horses with you?"

Ryan looked surprised. "No. Why?"

"He kinda wanted to say thanks for the help last night."

"Yeah, but I already got a horse, and I kind of like her."

"She's not a bad little mare; I'll give you that. But I'm not so sure she's ready to haul you up and over the mountains yet. She had a rough go before we set out to come over here, and she hasn't had enough time to recover yet. We put on a lot of miles in the last two days, and a single day off isn't enough."

"Yeah, but she's mine."

"Yes, she is. I ain't gonna tell you what to do, but I am gonna give you some advice. Keep in mind, horses are my business. That little mare of yours is a backyard princess. She's not cut

out for ranch work and long rides. If you take her up in the mountains tomorrow, you might hurt her. If you do get her all the way to my place, I think you'll find she's not big enough to rope off of and doesn't have the muscle mass to trail cows up and down mountains all day. If she stays here, she'll have a good home. That I can guarantee you."

"So just trade her in like a used car? Oh, I don't know."

"I told you what I think. "

"Where is she now?"

Jack pointed to a little, brown horse standing near the edge of the remuda. "She's right over there."

Ryan started to climb the fence.

"Where're ya goin'?"

"I want to talk to her."

"I wouldn't do that if I was you. I've been watchin' these horses for a while. Every herd of horses has a hierarchy, and she's at the bottom. Watch. You can see some of the horses near her flick their ears a little bit, and she'll walk off. It's their way of tellin' her they are the boss. If you go out there and give her attention, she'll get picked on when you leave."

"That's not fair."

"Why don't you go tell all the other horses that. It's just the way they do things. If you want to spend time with her, take a halter and a rope and take her out to the barn. When you're done, turn her out again. She needs to eat." Jack pushed away from the fence. "I better get back before somebody starts lookin' for me. If you want help pickin' out a horse, just ask, or you can talk to Sean. If I don't see you at dinner, remember we are leavin' at first light."

Ryan said, "I'll think about it. Thanks again."

Jack smiled. "You're welcome."

# 61.

Nicole opened her eyes to complete darkness. A sound on the other side of the room made her hold her breath as she listened. With her right hand, she reached under the sheets to where Jack lay and felt nothing. In a quiet voice, she said, "Jack?"

"Sorry I woke you."

"Where are you?"

"Standin' on the other side of the room."

"What time is it?"

"It's about four thirty."

She sat up in bed. "What in the name of God are you doing up?"

"I figured I'd start gettin' things ready to go. We need to be on the road at sunup."

"Yes, but that isn't for several hours yet."

"I have a lot to do. You go ahead and get some sleep. I'll wake you up in a couple of hours."

"You should sleep as well. You'll be exhausted all day."

"Nah. I'll be fine. I had a nap yesterday afternoon, and we turned in early."

"Yes, but we didn't exactly go right to sleep."

"Yep, I do seem to recall that we were up for a while. Don't worry, I'll be fine."

Nicole lay back down and listened as Jack got dressed, walked into the living room, and lit the lantern. She could hear him put on his gun and hat and shut the door after he stepped outside. She heard his boots on the deck outside, and then the casita became quiet again.

In the dark she rolled over and hugged the pillow where Jack had been. She could still smell him, and she smiled. Inside she was confused with so many emotions. She was sad by the loss of her family. Perhaps they had survived, but even if they had, it would be a long time before she would ever be able to see them again. She was worried about the future. There were so many questions left unanswered. Throughout her entire life, she had always had a plan. But now, with everything changed, the future was unknowable. How would they eat? Would they have to fight to survive? Ryan was in a gunfight just last night and had to kill two men. Would this be the way things would be? They still had a long way to travel, and over the mountains no less. Crossing the mountains still worried her. They seemed so big and so high.

But on the other hand, there was Jack. Just the thought of him sent a warm feeling through her entire body, and the majority of her worries seemed to disappear. She pictured the goofy grin he gave her when they first met. He had said, "You see that brown horse over there? That's your ambulance." She wondered if this was the first picture that would always come to her mind when she thought of him. She pictured his face, his hands, his arms, his chest; she could almost feel his arms around her now. Just being near him made her more confident and less concerned about the future. Jack would take care of her.

She thought back throughout her life to what she had considered the ideal man to be like. First and foremost, he would have to be a man, a real man, not some pretty boy Londoner or Wall Street–type. He would have to be confident and strong, but also gentle and kind. He simply must have a sense of

humor, but not crass or dirty. He would have to be intelligent, and she could not tolerate obesity. If a man could not take care of himself, how was he supposed to take care of anyone else? She thought about the qualities of some men she had admired. They all seemed to point to this man. Her man. Jack.

She wondered what it would have been like if they had met before the flare. Would he have been interested in her? Would they have even spoken to one another? She supposed not. A question came to mind. If it were up to her, would she continue to live in the old world with all the comforts she had been accustomed to and her friends and family, or live in this world with Jack. She smiled. She would choose this life without hesitating.

Jack walked to the barn holding the little lantern out in front of him. The wind had shifted to the north and seemed a little colder. A fine, light rain had started not long ago, and he wondered how long it would last. It wasn't enough to soak anything, just enough to make everything wet and sticky. He wondered if there was a cold front moving in.

Dinner last night had been fun. Everybody had gathered in the main dining room and had a wonderful meal. Afterward, people had stayed and talked and laughed. The main topic had been the weird things they had seen or experienced since the flare. It was good that people could laugh and see the humor in something so tragic. To his left he heard a horse chuff in the pasture. "Good mornin', darlin'. Meet me at the gate, and I'll get you some breakfast."

As he walked he thought about the trip over the mountains. Something nagged at him. This little trip shouldn't be very difficult. Hell, they were following the roads, and this was a route he had been over hundreds of times. Nevertheless, he ran through a mental checklist one more time.

About an hour and a half later, he crawled out from under the wagon as he heard the door open. Sean stepped in, carrying a lantern similar to his own. "Whew, buddy! It's darker than

a well digger's butthole out there and just as wet too! Are you sure you want to leave today? We got plenty of room."

"Thanks, but we best be gettin' on toward home. Besides, I don't want to eat up everything you got."

"Nonsense. We got plenty. But I do understand you want to get home. What's it been, a week?"

"Yep. I need to check on Miguel."

"That's what I figured."

"What are you doin' out here this time of day?"

"Oh, I don't know. I thought I might just give that wagon of yours a once over."

Jack smiled. "You're all right, Sean. I just did the same thing myself. I was fixin' to go over the harnesses."

"Get 'em out here. I'll give you a hand."

Jack pulled the harnesses out of the back of the wagon and laid them out. Sean said, "I see you brought your horses in for breakfast. Good idea. Did you get the horse that Ryan traded for?"

Jack looked surprised. "No. I didn't think he was gonna trade. He was kinda in love with that little mare."

"It's his first horse. You remember what that was like. Imagine if you had to trade Marlena off."

"Big difference."

"Not such a big difference."

"Okay, you got a point. What did you two work out?"

"I gave him Hosni."

Jack looked surprised. "Hosni Mubarak? The buckskin?"

"One and the same."

"No shit? That boy must have done some fast talkin'."

"He said you two had a talk, and so he decided to leave the mare with me. He was lookin' for something you'd pick out."

Jack said, "Sean, you don't have to do that. That's a hell of a horse, and we both know it. That kid will never appreciate what you did for him."

"I want to do it. He don't have to know. I think you're doing a good thing helpin' out these strays. If Ryan gets set up right from the start, he might just be a good man to have around.

Besides, a long time ago somebody gave me a chance once. I'm just passin' it on down the road."

"Thanks."

"No sweat. By the way, did you see those jeans that Brooke was wearin' last night? They were so tight if she'd a farted, it would have blown her boots off."

Jack laughed. "Yeah, I noticed."

"Damn, you could see Lincoln smiling on a penny in her pocket."

"We got a little ways to go with Brooke."

"Yeah, you might. But I'll tell you what, I think both them kids are in good hands."

"Thanks. I just hope it's enough."

"It will be."


At quarter after seven, Jack had the wagon loaded and the horses saddled and ready in the barn. Outside the rain had picked up a little, and in the east a cold gray light started to fill the sky. Jared had led Nicole, Brooke, and Ryan up to the gift shop in the main lodge, where he was trying to find hats for them.

"Offer to stay still stands, Doc," Sean said, as he walked out of the tack room with four yellow slickers draped over his arm.

"It's just a little rain," Jack said, as he finished tightening the straps of a scabbard to the front of Ryan's saddle. "It'll probably clear up in a few hours."

"It might. Then again, it might not."

Jack smiled and looked at Sean. "Damn. You're nothin' short of a genius."

"Learned everything I know from you. Took me what, twenty minutes?"

"Sounds about right. Seriously, thanks for everything. I plan to come back this way next spring. I have a couple of bills to settle in Cody and here with you guys. If there is anything you need or anything we can do to help, just send word."

"Doc, you don't owe us a thing. Same thing goes the other way. You're not so far away as we couldn't be over there to give you a hand if need be."

A few minutes later, everyone had come back into the barn. Ryan said, "I don't mind the hat, but I'm not crazy about the little hangy string."

Sean said, "That's called a stampede string. If the wind blows your hat off, it won't go all the way to the ground. Keeps you in the saddle."

"Oh. What's that thing hanging on my saddle?"

Jack said, "It's a scabbard. It's what you keep the rifle in."

"Rifle?"

"Yep." Jack handed the Winchester to Ryan. "Here. You obviously know what you're doin' with it, so I'm gonna have you ride out front. Keep an eye out for anything up ahead we might need to know about. Brooke? Darlin', I'm gonna have you ride behind the wagon. You can keep an eye on our load and the wagon. If you see anything that doesn't look right, just say somethin' before we have trouble. You also might want to keep an eye peeled behind us. We don't need anybody sneakin' through the back door. Any questions?"

Brooke said, "Yeah. Do these slicker thingies come in any other color than yellow? I mean seriously. I look like a school bus."

"Darlin', with your blonde hair and that yellow rain coat, you're a ray of sunshine on a cloudy morning."

She smiled.

Jack said. "All right. Let's get gone."

Jack and Nicole climbed up into the wagon as Ryan and Brooke climbed into their saddles. Brooke said, "Oh, wow. I can feel the warmness of the horse coming up under my coat."

Sean said, "Yep. It's like a built in heater." He walked over to the side of the wagon where Jack sat and said, "Careful out there. If you get up in the mountains and this rain turns to ice, you're gonna be busier than a cucumber in a women's prison. Stay to the side of the road if you can."

"Wasn't it Miguel and I that taught you how to ride in the mountains?"

"Yep. I'm just remindin' you. Sometimes when you get older you start to forget things."

Jack winked at him. "No sweat. I got this. Let's go!"

Jared pulled the double doors of the barn open as Jack snapped the reins and clucked with his tongue. The horses pulled the wagon out into the rainy morning as Ryan and Brooke followed.

# 62.

When they had turned east on Highway 14, Jack handed the reins to Nicole. "Here. You drive."

"Me? I have absolutely no idea how to do this."

"Sure you do. You've been watchin' me since we left Cody, and you know how to ride. It's the same thing, just remote control."

She held the reins in the same way he had, as the horses continued to plod along the road. Ahead Ryan walked along with his collar turned up and his head held low, keeping the rain off his neck. Nicole said, "Sean seemed rather familiar with you. Do you know him well?"

"Sean's pa was an anesthesiologist and a friend of mine back in Texas. He was a good man, but devoted his life to his work instead of his family. Sean went off to school the last year I was there. He started gettin' into a bit of trouble, and his dad was concerned. He talked to me about it a couple of times. Had no idea what to do. Just after we moved up here, Danny dropped over dead in the middle of a case. Sean had a tough time with it. He dropped out of school and found a little more trouble. His mom called me one day out of the blue and started tellin' me what was goin' on. Sean had been caught with drugs and a

stolen car. She needed some help. I worked out a deal with the district attorney's office to let me bring the kid up here and put him to work. He spent three years workin' for me. We butted heads pretty bad for the first two months. Then we started seeing eye to eye."

"What changed?"

"I knocked him on his ass."

"You hit him?"

"Sure as hell did. One morning he started gettin' mouthy. He was testin' the limits, so to speak. I just kept pushin' him until he took a swing. It didn't work out like he planned. It's funny, guys always think they are bigger, tougher, and smarter than they are, until they get knocked on their ass. At that moment they start to become a little more open minded. For Sean it worked out pretty good. He had lots of good men around to show him a better way to go about things. I think every guy gets knocked on his ass a time or too. There's lots of ways for that to happen. Sometimes it's a woman leavin' you, sometimes it's gettin' hit by somebody who cares enough to knock some sense into you. Sometimes it's a lawsuit or three. It doesn't matter what knocks you down; it matters what you learn in the process."

"The same thing most likely applies to everyone, don't you think?"

"I wouldn't doubt it."

"Perhaps even an enormous tragedy such as the flare might even serve to reset and refocus someone's attention on the things that matter most."

"I hadn't thought about that, but I'd say you're right."

She smiled at him. "Of course I'm right."

"Yes, dear."

Ahead ribbons of yellow, red, and dark gray rock lined the sheer stone walls all around them. As they proceeded further into the canyon, the walls became steeper and closer, allowing only enough room in the canyon floor for the roadway and the creek. Jack directed Nicole to the side of the road into a small gravel pull off as he whistled to Ryan.

When Brooke and Ryan were standing next to the wagon, he said, "Let's give the horses a breather before we start heading up. How's everybody doing?"

Brooke said, "I hate it back there. I'm bored out of my mind. There's nobody to talk to. Can I walk up front with Ryan?"

Jack thought about it a little and said, "Sure. I guess that'd be fine."

Ryan asked, "So, what's up ahead?"

"We climb for the next eighteen or twenty miles. There's nothing terribly steep; it's just a long, slow climb. Watch your horse. Make sure they don't get too winded or tired. There's a little overlook area a few miles ahead. We'll stop and let everybody catch their breath. After that, we take it at the horses' pace. As long as they keep doin' okay, we keep goin'."

It was nearly one o'clock when they decided to stop for lunch near a grove of pine trees and a small alpine pond. For the last four hours, they had twisted and turned through the switchbacks of the Bighorns. Only once did he decide to stop, because the horses were looking a little tired after a particularly long stretch of climbing. When they had climbed out of the canyon, and the land around them started to open up, Jack noticed the temperature had dropped considerably, and the wind had picked up a little. For the last couple of hours, he had kept a close eye on the sky as they continued. Nicole had noticed something because she had asked, "Is everything all right?"

"Sure it is. Why're you askin'?"

"Because you have become very quiet. And you seem to be looking around quite a lot."

He had told her that he was just takin' in the scenery, which had led to a conversation about the mountains. Nicole was astonished by the beauty and grandeur around her. He had said, "Darlin', I promise you that someday I will take you to Yellowstone. If you think this is pretty, you ain't seen nothin' yet."

They were finishing the sandwiches that Laurie had packed for them when Brooke looked up and said, "Oh look, it's snowing."

Jack looked up quickly and said, "Damn. Okay, everyone. Lunch is over. Stuff the rest in your pockets. We need to get these horses watered and back on the road as soon as possible."

Brooke said, "But we just got here. Besides, my butt is getting a little tired of that saddle."

Nicole was watching Jack as he had already grabbed the reins of the horses hooked to the wagon and started leading them to the pond. She said, "Brooke, dear, this seems rather important. Perhaps we should do what Jack suggests and discuss it later."

"Fine. But I'm getting kind of sick of this."

Nicole thought for a moment and then said, "Would you like to ride in the wagon for a change? I would be happy to ride your horse."

"That would be awesome."

By the time they started moving again, the rain had completely changed to snow. When Jack climbed up in the wagon, he saw Brooke sitting where Nicole had been. "What the hell are you doin' here?"

Nicole was sitting on Dingo next to the side of the wagon. She said, "It was my idea. I thought a change of pace might be nice."

Jack looked at Brooke for a moment and said, "Fine. But from here on out, any changes need to be run past me first."

Nicole said, "Understood. I apologize if there is any inconvenience."

Jack said, "No problem. Let's go."

After several minutes of riding in the wagon, with only the creek of the leather harnesses and the sound of the horses, Brooke said, "Are you mad?"

Jack said, "I'm not happy."

"Why?"

"Brooke, you signed on as a cowboy. You're workin' for me. Do you remember that?"

"Yeah."

"You're job today was to ride behind the wagon and keep an eye on things, but you didn't like that. I cut you some slack

and let you ride up front with Ryan. Now you don't like that, and you're ridin' in the wagon while Nicole is riding where you are supposed to be. Do you see a problem?"

"Well, first of all, she offered. Secondly, I don't understand why Nicole gets to ride in the wagon while I have to be on the horse the whole time. My butt is not used to sitting like that."

Jack took a deep breath and let it out slowly. "Brooke, I am gonna explain this only one time. Nicole is my..." The word seemed to stick in his throat. "Girlfriend. I have little doubt that I will ask her to marry me, and then she will be my wife. You and Ryan are here because you work for me. You applied for the job, and I gave it to you after explaining what the job entails. Now my future wife is doing your job, and you are sitting here where she should be. Yes, I have a problem with it, and it will not happen again. Are we clear?"

"Oh! My! God! This is so awesome. I should have known that you two would be getting married. You two are so right for each other. I knew the first time I saw you two together. I mean seriously. You both have the same sense of humor and the way you look at each other, I mean it's like you were made for each other. This is totally awesome. Can I be in the wedding? I was in a wedding once where the bridesmaids had to wear these awful dresses. They were plum colored. Seriously. Who picks plum as their wedding colors?"

Jack cut her off. "Brooke. Are we clear?"

"Yes, yes, yes. Of course. I will never let it happen again. Have you thought about a date yet? Oh my God! We have so much to plan and get ready. This is going to be great! Maybe a Christmas wedding. That would be so awesome! Spring weddings are so overdone these days. I mean seriously. How much more cliché can you get?"

"Brooke!"

"What?"

"Stop talking and listen to me. First of all, I ain't even hardly thought about this. Secondly, I haven't asked Nicole. You are *not* to say a word about this to anyone. Do you understand?"

She grinned and in an exaggerated tone said, "I do."

# 63.

The snow started coming down harder as they made their way over Granite Pass and along a flat stretch of road that paralleled Compartment Creek. At first the snow was light with only a few flakes mixed with the steady rain, but soon it all turned to snow and much heavier. Jack noticed it didn't take long before the snow was sticking to the trees, the grass, and even began covering the road. At times it was snowing hard enough he could hardly see Ryan's yellow slicker up ahead of them. He pulled the wagon to a stop and whistled loudly, calling the kid back.

When Nicole and Ryan pulled up alongside the wagon, Jack said, "The road stays pretty flat and might even start heading downhill a little bit. If we can make it a couple more miles, we'll get to Burgess Junction. I think we're gonna change things a bit. If the snow starts covering the road, I don't want to get a wheel hung up in a ditch. Ryan, Nicole, I'm gonna have you two ride on either side of the road near the edges. Stay right in front of the wagon horses. You two can probably see the edges of the road better than I can. I'm gonna stay right between you two, and that way I'll know I'm safe."

Nicole said, "What if we cannot make it to this Burgess place?"

"Then we'll set up camp in the nearest tree line and wait this out."

Brooke said, "You mean we might have to sleep outside? In the snow?"

"It's been done before. We have enough gear. It wouldn't be too bad."

Ryan said, "I could ride up ahead and see how far it is."

"I've driven this road more'n a few times. I know how far it is. More importantly, we need to stick together. It'd be easy to get lost out in this stuff, and I don't want to go looking for somebody."

Nicole said, "How long before we get to the top of the mountains?"

"Did you happen to see that little green sign a couple of miles back that said Granite Pass?"

"Yes, I do seem to recall that."

"That was the top. It's downhill from here."

"But the road is so flat. I don't understand."

"That's what it's like up here. More like a mesa than a mountain. Sorry, no big peak to go over."

Nicole looked around. "I realize this is probably not the best timing, but for the record, it is absolutely beautiful out here."

Jack smiled. The snow was starting to frost the pine trees and cling to the blades of grass on either side of the road. In front of him, Nicole sat on Dingo. A little snow was starting to accumulate on the brim of her hat. Her yellow slicker and the dark mane and tail of the buckskin horse stood out in contrast against the falling snow. Her cheeks were rosy with the cold. He smiled and said, "Yes, it is."

It took them nearly two hours to cover eight miles. Despite the altitude, the road was mostly flat with occasional gentle grades. The wind had stopped, and the snow was falling almost completely vertical, but at times it was coming down so hard

it was difficult to see trees and small patches of forest more than a few yards away from the road. By the time they reached Burgess Junction, there was nearly a foot of new snow on the ground.

Although their pace had slowed considerably, Jack was pleasantly surprised to see how well the wagon and horses were holding up in the weather. The narrow, steel-rimmed wheels seemed to cut through the snow and ride on the road below, but he could imagine that if the snow got much deeper, they would be in trouble. For a short time after the snow began covering the road, the horses slipped occasionally, but soon the wet, heavy snow was deep enough they once again had traction. He kept a close eye on them, but they seemed to be doing fine and appeared unaffected by the climb or the altitude.

On the right-hand side of the road, a large green sign was twisted and bent over. Jack knew the sign indicated the only major intersection along the road and Burgess Junction. He whistled at Nicole and Ryan and pointed for them to follow the fork to the left. Brooke asked, "Are we almost there?"

"Yep. We're close."

"Good. This is like a town, right?"

"Well, kind of."

"But they have stores and stuff, right?"

"They have Bear Lodge and a farm next door. That's about it if I remember correctly."

"A lodge and a farm? That's not exactly a town."

"It is in Wyoming."

Jack looked to his right. The snow had let up enough he could make out the black outline of burned buildings where the farm and stood. The only structure remaining upright was the old grain silo. His heart sank. He didn't know the owners of the farm but had always admired the way they kept things so neat and tidy.

As they pulled into the parking lot of Bear Lodge Resort, Jack's heart sank even further. He nearly felt sick. He had met the owners of the lodge several times, and although he didn't know them well, he knew enough about them to know they

had poured everything into the little resort. When they had purchased it nearly twenty years ago, it was little more than a gas station. Through hard work and unrelenting effort, they had built it into a beautiful mountain resort complete with restaurant, hotel, cabins, and a bar. In the summer they catered to fishermen and horseback riders. In the fall it was the hunters, and in winter they brought in the snowmobiling crowd. Now it was little more than ashes.

Blackened, twisted hulks of steel that once were cars and pickups littered the parking lot. Behind them a few black logs stuck up from their concrete bases and piles of ash, blackened metal, charred stonework, and debris were the only things left. Beyond the remnants of the buildings, he could see that a portion of the forest had burned.

Jack pulled the wagon to a stop and climbed down. The others watched him without saying a word. They could tell from his expression the sight before him was painful. He shook his head as he made his way around the front of the horses and said, "Stay put. I'm gonna look around."

When he had walked around the corner of the building, Brooke said, "Is this where we're supposed to stay?"

Nicole said, "Yes. I think it is."

"So what are we gonna do now?"

"I don't know. Let's just wait and see what Jack says when he returns."

A few seconds later, Nicole jumped and the horses all stepped restlessly when a gunshot boomed from behind what was left of the building. Brooke asked, "What was that?"

Ryan started to swing down from the saddle and said. "It was Jack. I'm going back there. Wait here." He tied his reins to a piece of twisted metal and ran off in the same direction that Jack had left.

"Now what?" Brooke said.

"I think we should wait."

"Yeah, but what if there are some bad guys back there, and they shot Jack. We can't just sit here."

Nicole reached under her slicker and pulled her pistol from the holster. Seeing what she was doing, Brooke reached under the seat and removed the shotgun. Holding it in both hands across her lap, she said, "I think something bad has happened. They should be back by now."

Nicole looked around nervously and said, "Let's just give them a few more minutes, shall we?"

"Yeah, but then what? What are we gonna do?"

"I suppose we should go back there."

"Maybe we should leave. I mean, seriously, if the bad guys are smart enough to get Jack and Ryan, they will definitely get us."

Nicole looked around again. The falling snow made everything very quiet. She thought about calling to Jack, but the sound might alert somebody else they were there. "Let's just stay put for a moment."

Just as she finished speaking to Brooke, Nicole saw movement out of the corner of her eye and turned quickly to see a man step out from the side of the building. Both Nicole and Brooke brought their guns up, pointing them at the figure.

"Whoa!" Jack jumped back behind the corner of the building and yelled, "It's only me. Put them damn things away!" He stepped out tentatively. As he walked to the wagon, he said, "What's got you two so jumpy?"

Nicole said, "We heard the shot and thought something might have happened to you. What took you so long?"

"Coyotes. They were…" He paused. "I shot one and scared the other two off. I found us a place to stay. Let's bring the horses around back. I'll show you."

Jack drove the wagon, and Nicole lead Ryan's horse around the back of the ruined buildings, where the snow lay flat and even across a wide area punctuated by several large trees. He pulled the wagon to a stop and waited as Ryan walked toward them from a pile of debris.

As he approached the wagon, Brooke thought he looked pale. Jack said, "Did you do like I asked?"

Ryan didn't look up as he took his reins from Nicole and said, "Yep."

"Thank you," Jack said and got the horses moving again.

"Wait. What? What did you ask him to do?" Brooke asked Jack.

"A little job for me. Nothin' to worry about."

"But I want to know."

Jack looked at her. "It's obviously somethin' I don't want to talk about right now."

As they made their way north toward the back of the snow-covered lawn, the west side was lined by forest and the east side was bordered by a small lake that wrapped around to the west. Where the tip of the lake and the forest met, a small log cabin was nestled into the trees. Jack pulled the wagon to a stop in front of the small building and said, "I spotted this from the back of the lodge. Thought it might still be standing. This was one of the original buildings up here. They used to rent it as a rustic cabin to people who wanted to know what it was like to live in the old West. Looks like this old technology wasn't bothered by the flare, so it's home to us for a while. If you girls want to start carryin' stuff inside, Ryan and I will take care of the horses."

Jack and Ryan pulled the saddles and harnesses from the horses and lead them along a small gravel drive that ran between the forest's tip and the lake. Behind a little stand of trees, a large, three-sided, wooden building stood open to the east. The interior of the building was stacked to the roof with large, square bales of hay. Ryan asked if the owners of the resort had horses. Jack opened a bale and started spreading hay on the ground for the horses. He said, "Nope. They used it to feed the elk. Up here the snow gets so deep they can't graze, so they head down to lower pastures. If you feed 'em, they'll stick around. When you're bringin' in hunters, it helps to have elk around."

Ryan said, "Oh, I get it. Lay out a feast and then blast Bambi's head off when he wants a snack."

"Nope. They don't start feedin' until late December or January. That's well after elk season is closed. They were tryin'

to keep the herd healthy. When they get all bunched up in the lower pastures, they run out of food, pass disease to each other, and the predators start pickin' 'em off. If they feed 'em, they can keep more elk healthy."

"So now the elk are gonna starve?"

"Not this year. They're smart. They'll just come here to the barn and eat the hay right where it sits. By next year I bet there won't be many left to starve."

Ryan looked at Jack a little confused. "If they make it through this winter, why won't there be many left next year?"

"By next summer the people that are left are gonna be looking for something to eat. They'll start takin' what they want. There aren't exactly a lot of game wardens around to stop 'em."

A look of stark realization came over Ryan's face. "Oh man. So, they will just come up here and start killing elk?"

"A few will. Survival of the fittest. You've seen how everything has changed. Let's say it came down to you and your family starvin' to death or an elk. I hate to break this to you, but you're the ultimate predator, the top of the food chain. What are you gonna do?"

"I'm not sure, but I don't think that killing an elk would be my first choice."

Jack laughed. "You're not hungry enough yet. Come on. Let's head back."

"Hey, don't we have to tie up the horses?"

"They got food and water right here. It's snowin'. Trust me. They'll be here when we come back."

# 64.

Megan lay on her belly in the middle of the bed with an arm tucked under her pillow, snoring lightly as she slept. In the growing darkness, Mark sat in the wooden chair next to the bed, staring at the bandage on the back of Megan's thigh. The longer he stared, the angrier he became.

The ride back to the hotel hadn't been too bad, at least initially. Megan had sat in the saddle off to one side, allowing her butt to hang off. When they were about six blocks from the hotel, she said she couldn't ride anymore, and they walked the rest of the way. Walking was better, but Mark could tell it still hurt.

She had gone up to the room by herself while Mark had unsaddled the horses and turned them out in the lot behind the hotel. He then had to make three trips to haul everything they had acquired up to the room. While he was working, Megan had tried to get undressed and in the process bumped the wound against the sink. When he came back to the room after the last trip, he found her crying in the bathroom.

A little later she had told Mark how to remove the bandage and wash everything out. He had tried to do it as gently as possible, but cleaning the wound hurt like hell, and several times

they had to stop and let Megan rest. After they were done, she wanted to put the bicycling shorts back on, saying they helped with the pain, but they were bloody and a little dirty, so Mark washed them in the tub and hung them on a towel rack to dry. Megan had tried to put on a pair of jeans, but the scraping of the material on her leg was too much. Instead, she wore nothing but her panties and laid on her side or her stomach on the bed.

Once she was at least a little comfortable, he went downstairs and talked to the hotel manager. Across the street and north a couple of blocks, he found a pharmacy with boards covering the front windows and door. Inside he saw piles of merchandise scattered everywhere, and a fat, little man and a tall, heavy-boned woman were trying to fix some shelves under the light of a propane lantern.

Mark said, "Hey. I'm looking for the pharmacist."

The little, fat guy looked up and said, "That's me. What do you want?"

"I need some pain pills and an antibiotic."

"Got a script?"

"A what?"

"A script. You know. A prescription from a doctor."

Mark just looked at him for a moment and then said, "Dude. In case you haven't noticed, things are a little fucked up right now. It's not like I can just call for a doctor's appointment."

"There's a couple of them up at the Johnson County Hospital. I saw them this morning."

Mark said, "Listen, I don't have time for this. My girlfriend got shot earlier. It's not too bad, but she hurts really bad, and we don't want her to get infected."

"Federal and state laws prohibit the dispensing of narcotics and antibiotics without the written prescription of a licensed physician. No script, no drugs."

Mark stood there for a moment and almost turned to go back out the door. Instead, he pulled the XD(m) out of its holster and said, "Okay. Plan B." He stepped forward and pointed the muzzle at the face of the pharmacist. "Listen, I really

didn't want to do this, but I've had a bad day. My girlfriend got shot, and I'm gonna help her out one way or another. Trust me, man. I really won't mind shooting you. I said I want some pain pills and an antibiotic. Are you gonna help me out, or are you just going to be another fucking idiot I have to shoot today?"

The guy rolled from kneeling on the floor to sitting on his ass. He raised his arms up above his shoulders and said, "I'm just trying to follow the law. That's all. I don't want any trouble."

"Dude. There is no law. All that shit went out the window a week ago. Are you going to help or not?"

"I'll help. I'll help."

"Pain pills and an antibiotic. And don't try to give me the wrong stuff, 'cause if I find out you did, I'll hunt you down and kill you."

"No. No. This is easy. Just put the gun away, and I'll get you what you need."

"How about you get me what I need, and then I'll put the gun away."

He started to get up and had to lean on part of the shelving he was working on to hoist himself to his feet. "Where was your girlfriend shot at?"

"Bighorn Mountain Adventure Supply. It's a little store on the west side of town."

"No. I mean what part of her was shot?"

"Oh. The back of her leg, just below her butt."

The man started walking toward the back of the store. "Did the bullet go all the way through, or is it still in her?"

"It just cut through the top of her skin."

"The reason I'm asking is if it hit her and went all the way inside, she really needs to see a doctor. There could be lots of internal damage you can't see from the outside."

"Honestly, I think the bullet just grazed her. She has a gash about three inches long."

"Was it a large caliber or a small one?"

"It must have been pretty big because the cut is almost a half inch across."

"Okay. I see. Well, maybe you can just get by with an anti-biotic. Make sure you keep the wound very clean." He turned his head and called to the woman helping him, "Mary, can you find us some Hibiclens and triple-antibiotic ointment?" As he reached the back counter, he asked Mark, "Do you have bandages?"

"Yeah, we have some, but I should probably get some more."

"Okay, okay, we can help you out with that too. Mary, grab some Kerlex and some 4x4s."

Mark said, "I really need the pain pills."

The pharmacist walked behind a tall counter and was a lit-tle surprised when Mark followed him. "You're not supposed to be back here."

Mark stared at him for a moment and said, "Are you kid-ding me?"

The pharmacist waved a nervous hand quickly and said, "Okay. Is she allergic to anything?"

"Not that I know of."

He walked a few steps back between a couple of shelves and pulled two big bottles down from the shelves. "Well, you better make sure. A drug allergy can be very serious. Is she taking any other medications right now?"

"I don't think so. I haven't seen her take anything."

"Okay. Is she pregnant?"

"No. Definitely not."

He dumped a few pills into a plastic tray and started count-ing them out. "All right. I'm going to give you some hydroco-done. You might know it as Vicodin. Do you know what that is?"

"Yeah. I've taken it before. That should work."

"Tell her to take one pill and wait for an hour. If her pain isn't better, then have her take another one. She can take it every four to six hours as she needs, but don't let her take too many. Never more than eight in a twenty-four-hour period. Do you want me to write that down for you?"

"No. That's all right. I've got it."

He poured some big pink pills into the tray and started counting. "The other pill I'm going to give you is an antibiotic

called Levaquin. It's a good one. She only needs to take it once a day, but make sure she takes it until all the pills are gone. This will prevent an infection in her leg while she's healing. Make sure she doesn't do anything too strenuous while she's taking it because there is a slight risk of tendonitis or even tendon rupture while she's on it."

"Tendon rupture? Jesus. Don't you have anything that won't cause her tendons to rupture?"

"It's only a slight risk, and it was found in a very few athletes who were taking the drug. I never it saw it any of the patients we prescribed it to."

"Would you take it?"

"I have before. Yes."

"How do I know you aren't just filling me full of shit?"

"Look it up if you want to. Here, you can use my books."

"That's all right. I'll trust you."

Mary came back to where they stood and set a pile of things on the counter next to Mark. The little fat guy started putting everything into a plastic bag and said, "Oh. I should tell you that both these drugs have a tendency to slow the bowels down. Make sure she doesn't get constipated."

"Okay. Anything else?"

"Not that I can think of. You can always call us if you have any questions." As soon as the words left his mouth, he realized how silly it sounded. "I mean, you know where we're at. Just ask."

Mark stuck the XD(m) back into its holster on his side and dug into his front pocket. He pulled out three silver coins and set them on the counter. "That's three full ounces of silver. That should cover everything. Look, I'm sorry I had to pull the gun; I never intended to steal anything; I'm just kind of over the edge, you know?"

The guy looked at the coins for a moment and then pushed two of them back to Mark. "One is more than enough. I'm sorry too. I could have been a little more understanding."

Mark said, "Thanks." He picked up the bag and started making his way through the piles of debris toward the front.

When he had almost reached the door, the pharmacist asked, "By the way, would you really have shot me?"

Mark stopped and said, "Earlier today a guy pulled the trigger on a shotgun when the barrel was right next to my head. I still have a headache, so I really didn't want to make a lot of noise in here."

"I see. Well, good luck."

"Thanks again."

Megan had taken two of the Vicodin and the antibiotic as soon as Mark got back and then lay down on the bed. When the pain pills started working and she felt a little better, he changed the bandage and applied the antibiotic ointment. They had talked for a few minutes, and then Megan started feeling tired and lay down again. A few minutes later, she was sound asleep.

Mark sat in the wooden chair and stared at the dressing on her leg. In his mind he replayed the events of the day. He pictured Megan standing on the stair of the hotel and talking to the crowd. He watched her walk out of the hotel, holding the hand of that cute little girl. He saw her smile at him as she sat on her horse and accused him of looking at Stacy's ass. He watched her bounce out of the store in delight, carrying all the treasures she had got for them. He watched her fall to the pavement as the wound on her leg blossomed with her blood.

He wanted to kill that greasy, piece of shit all over again, but this time he wanted to do it slowly and make the bastard suffer. How dare that filthy piece of shit hurt Megan—his Megan. That worthless human trash didn't deserve to be breathing the same air as her.

A stark, hard, cold realization came over him as though he had been slapped. This had been close. Damn close. If that guy had just held the gun a little differently, Megan would be dead. Just a few inches higher and a few inches further forward, and the bullet would have hit her in the stomach. A week ago that would have meant surgery in the very least. Now, surgery wasn't an option. Hell, even though it was just a gash on her leg, it

had been a bitch just getting her back to the hotel. What if the wound had been more serious? An ambulance was out of the question. The thought of Megan being seriously hurt made him feel a little nauseous.

Replaying the events in the parking lot, he remembered Megan having trouble with her gun. He stood up and found the pistol sitting on the small table. He removed the magazine and pulled the slide back, ejecting the round in the chamber. The cartridge looked like all the others. He pulled the trigger, and the gun clicked. I wonder why it didn't fire? He put the round that didn't fire in his pocket and reloaded the gun.

"Hey."

Mark looked over to see Megan looking at him, with her head propped up on her hand.

"Hey, how are you feeling?"

"Fine. I'm just tired. You should go get something to eat."

"Do you want me to get you something?"

"No, not really. Maybe I shouldn't have taken two Vicodin. I feel kinda wiped out. I think I'm just gonna sleep."

"Okay, well, maybe I will get something to eat. Do you need anything? Is there anything I can do?"

She smiled at him. "No. I'm okay."

Mark felt kinda weird sitting by himself at dinner. There was nothing to do but sit and wait for his meal and then eat by himself. Nobody to talk to, no TV in the corner of the room, no newspaper—nothing but his thoughts. Several other people now occupied tables in the restaurant, and he caught several of them glancing over at him as he ate. He noticed a man with gray hair, wearing a nice dark blue sweater, also sat by himself. As Rose brought out a warm piece of apple pie, the older gentleman from the other table pulled out the chair in front of Mark and said, "Noticed you were alone. Mind if I join you?"

Mark said, "Sure. Why not."

The man set his piece of pie on the table, sat, and said, "My name is Peter Christensen." He stuck out his hand.

Mark shook it and introduced himself.

Peter said, "Rose told me you came over from Gillette. Is that right?"

"Yeah. We made the trip on horseback."

"That's what she said. I bet that was a long ride."

"My butt still hurts."

"What are things like over there?"

"Things are just as bad in Gillette, if not worse. At least you still have running water. Huge parts of the town are burned, the hospital was totally wiped out—it was awful."

"I'm kind of curious. Why didn't you just stay there and wait for help?"

"I don't think help is coming. I met a guy at a gun shop on the west side of town and—"

"Red Burton at Wild West Weapons?"

"Yeah, that's the guy. Do you know him?"

"I sure do. I own the gun shop here, or at least I did until about a week ago. We used to work together quite a bit."

"No shit? What happened to your place?"

"Burned to the ground. I recovered a few things, but most of it's gone."

"Oh, Jeez! I'm sorry to hear that."

"Not half as sorry as I am. Guns are worth their weight in gold now. But I'm sorry I interrupted you. You were saying you met Red."

"Yeah, he showed me the compasses and explained that this thing is probably worldwide. He was the one who convinced me that I should head west and find someplace better than Gillette in the winter."

"That's good advice. What's the deal with the compasses?"

"They all seem to point in different directions, or at least they did a week ago."

"No kidding? I'll have to check that out."

Mark put down his fork and then a thought occurred to him. "Hey, you must know a lot about guns, right?"

"I know a little bit."

"Hang on a second. I want to show you something." Mark took off, nearly running upstairs. He quietly opened the door

and retrieved Megan's gun without waking her and then ran back downstairs again. He sat down and put Megan's gun in the middle of the table.

Peter was surprised and said, "Maybe we should take a look at this somewhere else."

Mark looked around the room and saw that the only other table with people held a middle-aged couple, and the man had a gun on his waist. He said, "It's cool. Guns are pretty much everywhere these days. This is my girlfriend's gun. She needed it today, and it didn't work. Just kind of clicked, but nothing happened."

Peter picked up the gun. "This is an STI Legend. Wow, nice gun. Is your girlfriend from Gillette?"

"Yeah, she grew up there."

"Her dad isn't Bill Bennet, is he?"

"Yeah, that's his name."

"I knew Bill. Used to shoot USPSA with him. He's a good guy. I hope nothing happened to him."

"He died at the hospital."

"Sorry to hear that." In a matter of a few seconds, he had the pistol lying in pieces on the table. "Here's your problem. There's no firing pin in it."

Mark looked at the pistol and then up at Peter. "Well, where did it go?"

Peter shook his head. "I have no idea. Maybe Bill had trouble with the old one. He must have taken it out. Doesn't make any difference. This gun will never work without a firing pin."

"Where can I find one?"

"For this gun? About the only place you'll find one is in Georgetown, Texas."

"Texas? I can't go to Texas."

"This is a specialty gun. I doubt a regular 1911 firing pin would work. You might be able to have one made if you knew somebody who had a working lathe and knew a hell of a lot about guns."

"Well, do you know anybody who could sell me a gun?"

"About a week ago I did. Today I'd say you might have some trouble finding one. I do know a few guys in the area who collect guns. They might be willing to part with one if you would be willing to trade for it."

"Sure. Heck yeah. Anything."

Peter wrote down a few names for him.

# 65.

Ryan pushed the door of the cabin open to an incredible sunrise. The sun was just starting to break the horizon in the east, over the top of mountain peaks, and set the sky ablaze with color. Before him the snow was pure, brilliant white and lay perfectly smooth and even. Only the little lake and trees off in the distance disturbed the otherwise unblemished white. "Oh, wow! You guys should come here and take a look at this."

Behind him Jack said, "Sure is pretty, but get that door closed before you let all the warm air out. You'll get to see plenty of it today."

The little cabin had been an incredible find. The entire building was only twelve feet square and made completely out of logs. An old, cast iron stove had been flipped over on its side, but with a little work they had righted it and reattached it to the chimney. Jack had made Ryan light it using a fire flint he carried in his saddlebags. A sleeping loft over the stove had stayed nice and warm, and only once did Ryan have to get up and add wood.

As they started to eat breakfast, Jack said, "You all probably want to dress warm today, but make sure you have layers on

that can come off. It might be a little chilly once we set out, but it usually starts warmin' up as we head down the mountains."

Brooke asked, "How far do we have to go today? 'Cause I'm like getting excited to see where we are going to be living, you know."

Jack said, "We only have about twenty miles, but it's mostly downhill, and a fair bit of it is steep. We're gonna take our time and watch the horses carefully."

Nicole said, "I don't suppose we are going to be going through any small towns, are we?"

"Next town is Dayton, and that's on the other side of the ranch."

"Oh, I see. Not even a small general store or anything such as that."

"Nope. The only general store up here was in the resort, and there's nothing much left of it."

"I see."

Jack looked at her a moment and then asked, "Is there somethin' you need?"

"No, no. I'm quite all right."

He ate a few more bites of his eggs and then said, "If there's somethin' you need, I'll see what I can do about it."

Nicole set her coffee cup down hard. "Well, if you must know, I took my last pill yesterday morning."

For a moment Jack looked embarrassed. Then a thought came to him, and he said, "Just start takin' the next ones today. That'll put things off for a bit."

"Well, you see that's a bit of a problem because I don't have any more."

Ryan asked, "She needs medicine? Are you going to be okay?"

Jack quickly interjected, "No, it's not that. She's just fine. Brooke, do you have any birth control pills?"

Ryan said, "Oh."

Brooke said, "No. I don't take them. I tried them once, but they made me feel a little sick."

Ryan looked up quickly. "You don't take birth control pills?"

Brooke kept eating but said, "No. Why?"

"Why? Because you could get pregnant, that's why."

"I'm not too worried about it. I've never gotten pregnant before."

"Yeah, but just because you haven't gotten pregnant before doesn't mean you won't get pregnant now."

Brooke just waved a hand at him.

Jack watched the whole interaction with a concerned curiosity and slowly shook his head.

Nicole said, "Brooke. I don't suppose you have a..." She looked over at Ryan. "Could I borrow a..."

Brooke said, "Tampon? Sure. But I think I only have one left."

"Ryan, let's go get them horses," Jack said and stood up.

"I'm not quite done with breakfast."

"Then you need to use a shovel. Let's go."

A little more than an hour later, they were loaded up and ready to head out. Jack checked the harnesses, the load, and the breaks one more time and then climbed into the wagon seat. He made a little clicking sound and flicked his wrists, and the horses set off through the snow.

Nicole leaned toward him and asked, "How much snow do you think we got?"

"Close to fifteen inches from what I can figure."

"Will there be snow at your ranch?"

"Hard to tell. Probably not."

"Really, there is that much of a difference in twenty miles?"

"Oh yeah. They can get a lot up here in the winter. In some places they will get over ten feet. We usually get some, but nothing like that."

"Okay, so what I really want to know is do you think there is a chance Brooke could be pregnant?"

He looked at her and said, "I knew that's what you were thinkin' about. Hell yes, there's a chance. Of course there is."

"But she's never gotten pregnant before."

"God only knows why. There could be a million reasons, but the way those two have been at it, I'd say it's probably more'n likely she is pregnant."

"Oh my God."

"That's kinda what I was thinkin'."

They rode quietly for a few minutes, and then Nicole said, "I'm terribly sorry that we can't, you know, be intimate for a while."

Jack said, "I been thinkin' about that. Now don't misunderstand me, but I think that might be just fine. We've been through a hell of a lot this week, and slowin' things down a little might not be such a bad idea. I don't want you to think that gettin' in your pants is the only thing I'm after. I like spending time with you. I like to hear what you think about and all the things you've done. I like the fact that I'm a better man when I'm with you."

"That's a very nice thing to say."

"I wouldn't say it if it wasn't true."

An hour and a half later, they passed a lake on the left side of the road. The snow hung in the tall pine trees surrounding the lake, and the blue water glistened in the morning sun. Nicole said, "Oh my. That has to be one of the most beautiful things I've ever seen."

"That's Lake Sibley. It is gorgeous."

Ahead Ryan and Brooke had stopped. In front of them, a guard rail lay twisted up and stretched across the road. Jack pulled the wagon to a stop, and he and Ryan used a rope tied to Hosni to pull the metal out the way far enough they could pass. Just ahead something large and red stuck up out of the snow in the middle of the road. Jack walked up to it and then back to the wagon.

Nicole asked, "What is that thing up ahead?"

"It's a Coke machine."

"A vending machine?"

"One and the same."

"What is it doing out here?"

"Just lyin' there. The flare must have tossed it here."

"I wonder where it came from."

"No tellin'. There's nothing around for miles."

As they passed it on the right, Nicole said, "Could you stop for a moment." Jack pulled the horses to a stop, and she jumped down. The front door had broken open, and she reached in a retrieved a Diet Coke. She grabbed a second can and then climbed back up in the wagon. "Well, that is certainly handy. Would you care for something to drink?"

"Don't mind if I do."

For the next several hours, they wound their way down the mountains. The more elevation they lost, the less snow they had to travel through. On the left they passed a huge, rocky outcrop with sheer, off-white cliff faces rising out of a snow-covered, grassy hill. "That's Steamboat Point. I always thought it kind of looked like a huge old temple or castle the way those rock walls stand up there like that."

Nicole said, "Funny you should say that. I was thinking the very same thing. Are we getting close yet?"

"We're over halfway, but the next few miles are when we start heading downhill in a hurry."

A few miles ahead, the road hugged a hillside on the left, and to the right an enormous, wide expanse opened before them. Jack steered them into an overlook area and pulled the horses to a stop. "We'll take a little break here for a couple of minutes."

Nicole said, "Oh, Jack. This is absolutely breathtaking. I believe I could almost see all the way to New York."

Jack started digging through his saddlebags in the back of the wagon and said, "I don't know about New York, but you can see Sheridan from here." He pulled a pair of binoculars out of his bag and stepped to the edge of the road.

Nicole asked, "Are you trying to see how much damage occurred in Sheridan?"

Jack ignored her question for a moment and then started laughing. "No, darlin', I wanted to see if my house was still standin'." He laughed again. "Not only is it standin', there's somebody workin' on the roof!"

# 66.

Mark woke up to bright sunlight streaming through the windows. Around the edges of the glass, he could see frost seemingly set on fire by the sun. The air around his face felt cool. He turned over to see how Megan was doing and noticed the other side of the bed was empty. Beyond the bed, the doorway to the bathroom stood open, and he could tell she wasn't in there.

He slipped out of bed, and when his feet hit the wood floor, he shivered. Damn, it's cold in here. He dressed quickly, brushed his teeth, combed his hair, and headed downstairs.

Megan sat alone at one of the tables in the restaurant with a big pad of yellow paper and a cup of coffee. She smiled when she saw him and said, "Hey, sunshine, how are you this morning?"

Mark pulled out the chair across from her and sat down. "Fine. Apparently you're feeling better."

"It's still a little sore, but it's not too bad. I changed the bandage myself this morning, and it looks a lot better. Not nearly so red."

"Good. Did you take a pain pill?"

"No. I don't think I need one."

"But you did take the antibiotic, right?"

"Yes, Mother." She winked at him and smiled.

"I'm just trying to make sure you're all right. You're the best thing I got, and I don't want to lose you."

"Aw. That's nice to say."

"By the way, do you have your gun on you?"

"Of course. Why?"

"Let me see it."

"What? Right here? Now?"

He rolled his eyes. "Yep. Right now." As she handed it to him, he asked, "Did you make sure it was loaded?"

"Yeah. I always do."

"Good." He took the gun from her, pointed it across the room at Rose's back, flicked the safety off, and pulled the trigger. Click.

"Jesus, Mark!" She grabbed the gun from him. "What the hell are you trying to do?"

"Have you shot this gun since you got it from the house?"

"Well, I guess not. Why?"

"Did you happen to notice that it didn't work yesterday when you needed it?"

"Now that you mention it, I think I did try to fire it. What's going on?"

"There is no firing pin in this gun. Your dad must have taken it out."

Megan looked shocked. "You have got to be kidding me."

"Nope. I talked to a guy at dinner last night. He used to own a gun shop just down the street. He was the one who figured out the problem with the firing pin. Anyway, he also told me that it's a special part, and the only way we are going to replace it is if we go to Texas and get a new one from the factory."

"So all this time, I have been carrying a gun that doesn't work. Shit! I might as well of had a rock to throw at somebody."

"If you're making a list of things to do, getting another gun for you should be at the top."

"If the gun shop burned down, that might be a challenge. I can't imagine many people would want to give up their guns. Although, Stacy did say we could have one of hers."

"Yeah, I know she did, but the guy last night gave me a list of guys in town that collect guns. We might be able to find something around here without riding all the way back out to her place."

"You know, it might not be a bad idea for both of us to have the same kind of gun. That way we could use each other's magazines if we needed to."

"You want an XD(m)?"

"I like 1911s. I just know them better. Your Springfield is a good gun, but there are a ton of 1911s out there. It might be easier to find two of those. It would also be easier to find parts if we need them."

"Yeah, that makes sense, but I kind of like this one."

"Keep it if you want. It would make a hell of a backup."

"Okay. Do you think you're up for riding today?"

"I kinda wanted to take it easy, you know. My butt is feeling better, and I'd rather not overdo things if I don't have to."

"Okay. I'll take care of the guns. What's your plan today?"

She said, "Did you happen to notice how cold it was in our room last night?"

"Yeah, I sure did. Just about froze my nuts off getting up this morning."

She smiled. "We can't have that. I don't think the hotel is going to work for us much longer. They don't have any way to heat those rooms. We might need to find something a little more long-term."

"So you want to stay in Buffalo?"

"Buffalo is not too bad. At least they have running water. At best we can only make it about thirty miles a day on horseback. If we left right now, it would probably take us almost two weeks just to get to Cody. That puts us into November. We might want to wait until spring before we start heading west. Besides, if we find the right place around here, we just might want to stick around."

"Makes sense."

"Of course it does. I thought it up."

# 67.

It was midmorning when Mark left the hotel on horseback. He had used a phone book to look up the addresses of the guys Peter had written down for him and then had borrowed a map of Buffalo from the manager at the front desk.

The first house he came to was in a relatively new subdivision on the northwest side of town. As he turned the corner onto the street he was looking for, he knew this was going to be a lost cause. The entire block was nothing more than charred remnants of the homes they used to be. Burned-out hunks of twisted metal sat in driveways and where garages had once been attached to nice little houses.

He rode back into town and then toward the south end. The second address belonged to a stately, Victorian-style, two-story house. He tied Hunter to a broken-down gate in the front yard and knocked on the door. After several minutes an old, white-haired man with glasses and a cigarette hanging out of his mouth opened the door. "Howdy, howdy. What can I do for ya?"

"Hi. Last night I was talking to a guy named Peter Christensen. He told me that you collect guns. I really need a couple for my wife and me. I don't suppose you'd like to sell a couple, would you?"

"Son, you're the fifth person to ask me that. I'll tell you the same thing I told everybody else. You're about three weeks too late. Last summer they diagnosed me with lung cancer, so I sent some of them over to my son in Gillette, and the rest I sold at auction a couple of weeks ago. Thought I needed the money more than I needed the guns. Now I wish I hadn't. I'll tell you what. If you wait around for a month or so, you can have the only one I got left. I'll probably be dead by then."

"Oh, Jeez. Sorry to hear that. I don't suppose you know of anybody that might have a couple extra lying around."

"Peter would know that better than I would. Seems to me there was a young guy on the north end of town that was collecting handguns. You might want to check with Peter for his name."

"I think I already stopped at his place. The whole house was burned to the ground."

"Oh, so I see. Well, I'm afraid I'm not much use then."

"No problem. Thanks for your time, and I hope you feel better."

"Thanks, but that's not likely. Good luck to you, son."

Mark rode away feeling stupid. *I hope you feel better?* How dumb was that. What were you supposed to say to somebody with cancer?

The last address on his list was farther out of town, along a county road that followed Clear Creek toward the mountains. He followed the road for what seemed like a long ways and was about to turn back, when he saw a square, brick post holding a mailbox with the name Cruz on it. He rode up the long, paved drive, which turned to brick pavers almost fifty yards in front of an enormous brick house. The thing seemed out of place and would be better suited around a golf course in Denver. A circular drive led to the front door and surrounded a fountain, which now stood quietly.

At first Mark was intimidated. The house was huge, and whoever lived here obviously had money—and lots of it. He tried to reinforce himself. *Whoever they are, they still wipe*

their ass the same way I do, he thought. He walked up to the door and knocked.

The door opened to a man who looked like he was about sixty. He stood a little taller than Mark, wearing jeans, boots, and a white button-down shirt. He wore bifocals and had black hair with a little gray at the temples. He said, "Hello."

"Hi, I'm Mark." Everything else seemed to stick in his throat. This guy looked familiar somehow.

"Hello, Mark. I'm Delgado Cruz. Most people call me Del. What can I do for you today?"

"Uh, last night I was talking to a guy named Peter Christensen. He helped me with my wife's gun and told me that it couldn't be fixed. He told me you might have a couple of extra guns. I was wondering if I could buy some or trade with you."

"You know Peter, huh? He's a good guy. Why didn't he just sell you one?"

"His store burned down."

"Oh, I see. That's too bad. He worked hard, and it took a long time to build that store. Yeah, I might be able to help you out. Come on in. What did you have in mind?"

"Well, sir, my wife and I would kind of like to have the same kind of guns. You know, so we could share magazines and stuff. She knows a lot about guns and shooting and stuff. She likes 1911s."

"Follow me." He talked as they walked down a long tile hallway. "You're a lucky man. My wife and kids are in Florida at our winter place. I was supposed to go down there last week but got delayed at work. They might as well be on the other side of the moon. I have no way to contact them, and now I have no idea if they are alive."

"I'm sorry to hear that."

"Is that a Springfield you're wearing?"

"Yes, sir. This is an XD(m)."

"That's a good gun. Hard to beat. Are you sure want to get rid of it?"

"Well, maybe. Let's see what kind of a deal we can work out."

"Fair enough." He led them into a large office at the end of the hall. The room was bigger than Mark's entire apartment back in Gillette had been. The walls were covered in rich mahogany, and the ceiling was coffered and at least ten feet high. Huge windows offered a view of the swimming pool and the foothills beyond. In the middle of the room stood a huge, wooden desk with a rich, brown leather top. Behind it stood an enormous book case with several 1911s, standing upright in glass cases. "Have a seat, son."

Mark stepped over to a leather chair in front of the desk. Just as he was about to sit down, he noticed several pictures on the wall behind it. One stopped him cold. The man who was now sitting at the desk was standing with a group of other men in front of the new coal processing plant they had opened a couple of years ago in Gillette. Now he remembered how he knew the name. This guy was the CEO of the mine where he worked.

"Are you looking at my horse?"

Mark glanced to a picture hanging next to the one he had been staring at. A pure black horse stood sideways to the camera with two men shaking hands in front of it. "Yeah. Wow. He sure is something."

"Yes, he is. I got him a couple of years ago from the D-bar-D. Ever heard of them?"

"Ah, well, I'm kinda new to horses."

"I see. Well, they raise and train the best horses I've ever seen. That's Jack Neumann and me, the day I picked up Night. I'll sell just about everything I own if the price is right, but that horse and I will be together until one of us dies."

Mark heard the words the man spoke, but he wasn't listening. He had gone back to the mine. Back to the days of working his ass off and not making ends meet at home. Back to the days of being called "pussy" by the older guys, and the many conversations of talking about how he and all the other guys were working to line the pockets of a few soft, old men.

"Son? Are you with me?"

"Yeah, sorry. I was just thinking about horses."

"I know how that goes. I kinda daydream about good horses myself. I asked if you need holsters for 1911s."

"Oh. Sorry. Yeah, if you have them, that would be great."

"Well, let's see what I have. Hang on a minute."

"Yes, sir."

The guy opened what Mark had thought was a closet door into another room. A few seconds later, he could hear the sound of a propane lantern, and bright light lit up walls covered with guns. Shotguns and rifles of every shape Mark could imagine covered the walls and stood in racks. Pistols—big ones, small ones, revolvers, crazy-looking things—hung on little racks on the walls. Mark thought, I work my ass off and get calls from creditors every goddamn day of the week, and this asshole can afford to live here, have a house in Florida, and collect guns as a hobby.

A few minutes later, Del came out of the closet, carrying two plastic boxes and two leather holsters. He set them on the corner of the desk and sat down in his chair again. He said, "Here. Take a look at these. Tell me what you think."

Mark opened one of the plastic boxes and saw a stainless Colt 1911 very similar to the one he had had taken from the police station in Gillette. "Wow. Looks nice."

"These are both Gold Cups. Sequential serial numbers. If you are lucky enough to still have your wife around, you need to be able to keep her safe. I'll tell you what. I'm going to give these to you. Call it a late wedding gift."

"Wow. Really?"

"Sure. Why not. I've been pretty blessed. I've got extra."

He continued to talk, but Mark's mind had gone back to the mine. He thought about coming home from work covered in black coal dust, about the recent renegotiations of the labor union contract, about the fact he now was going to have to contribute to his retirement, leaving even less money in his check every week. His eyes drifted back to the two 1911s in the glass cases on the book shelf.

"Go ahead. Try one of the holsters on. We need to make sure it will work before you leave. Won't do you much good if it doesn't fit."

Mark stood up and pulled the XD(m) out of his holster. He was about to set it on the corner of the desk, but without ever having a clear thought run through his mind, he pointed the gun at the man in the chair and pulled the trigger. Del's head snapped back as the bullet entered just below his left eye. He slumped in the chair as the back of his head dripped on the floor.

Mark stood in front of the desk for a moment, his ears ringing with the shot inside the building. He stepped around the side of the desk and pushed the dead man and his chair to the side. He reached up onto the shelf and removed the glass top from one of the pistol cases. Inside was a black Colt 1911 with white grips. The sides of the slide were ornately engraved. On one side, a banner of gold bisected with a raring horse was inscribed 1911–2011. On the other side, gold lettering said 100 Years at America's Side. He shoved the pistol into his back pocket and lifted the other glass off the other pistol. Inside this case was an incredible, smoothly polished gun. All of the visible steel had been rounded and highly polished to a mirror, so that it looked almost liquid. Ornate, flowered scrollwork in gold decorated both sides of the slide. The grip was wood and deeply engraved with flowers and the word *Colt*. He picked up the weapon and racked the slide. It moved as though it were on ball bearings. He tried the trigger, and with only the slightest pressure, the hammer dropped with a solid *click*. "Now we're talkin'," he said to nobody in particular.

He moved back to the other side of the desk and looked at both pistols again. These were incredible. Works of art, but the problem was, neither one of them had a magazine with it. He walked into the gun room and held the lantern up. He realized quickly that from where he had sat in the office he could only see a small fraction of this room. There were hundreds of guns in all shapes and sizes. One wall display held more than thirty rifles and had a small wooden plaque below that read M1. Another smaller display held four squatty things that looked kinda half pistol and half rifle. They looked familiar, like he had seen them in a movie. The little plaque read MP5.

A huge gun stood in the middle of the room on a tripod. A belt of ammunition running into the side held cartridges as long as his hand.

On the far side of the room, custom cabinets lined an entire wall. Some cabinets had special racks to display a gun or two, and others had drawers or shelves inside. He started opening doors and found one containing boxes for Colt pistols. There had to be at least thirty boxes. Some were plastic like the ones Del had brought out with the two pistols, and others were fancy blue with a little gold stallion on the cover. He found one that read Diamond Grade, and it matched the pistol he was going to give Megan. He took it and carefully put the pistol inside. Some of the drawers had a little label on the front. After a minute or two of searching, he found a drawer labeled 1911 Magazines. He was about to scoop out a handful but realized he didn't have any place to put all this stuff.

Back in the office, he found a padded camera bag. He dumped the contents out onto the floor and went back into the gun room. He had packed both new guns and eight magazines into the bag when he started thinking about ammunition. There has to be ammunition around here somewhere. He started searching through drawers but came up with nothing but a few orange dummy rounds. He started to think that the guy must have kept the ammunition someplace else, and contemplated searching the entire house, when he heard a noise outside in the back. Grabbing the bag, he ran out of the room and back down the hall. He could see through several large windows in the kitchen toward the back and thought he saw something move. He crept over to the window and carefully looked out toward the mountains. Beyond the pool and standing beside the barn were two guys wearing black hats and denim jackets. They looked as though they were busy with something, but he didn't want to take any chances. He hurried to the front door and out to his horse.

He wanted to run. As he turned Hunter toward the road, it was all he could do not to kick the horse in the side and fly back to town. But, Megan had told him that galloping on a

horse took a lot of practice, and the last thing he wanted to do would be to fall off a running horse and get busted. It killed him, but he kept the horse to a steady walk. Once he turned out of the driveway onto the road, he pushed Hunter up to a trot.

As he rode back to town, Mark started to think. He didn't think anybody saw him, but Peter Christensen had given him the address. If somebody found the old guy dead and two 1911s missing and then started asking questions, Peter Christensen could tell them exactly who did it. They might leave for Sheridan tomorrow after all.

# 68.

It was midafternoon when Jack whistled at Ryan and Brooke and signaled them to turn right onto a gravel road off of Highway 14. They had run out of snow long ago, and the temperature now felt much warmer. Nicole said, "We must be getting close. I'm really quite excited. I finally get to see where you live."

Jack said, "I wouldn't get all cranked up yet. There's no tellin' what we might find. Hell, the whole place might be burned to the ground."

"Oh, stop. You know that's not true."

"Well, we know it's not burned, but we have no idea how much damage has been done. It might be completely unlivable."

"Then we'll just make do, won't we."

"Yes, ma'am. I guess we will."

Jack leaned forward and said, "Easy, darlin'. Easy. We'll get there soon enough." Then he signaled Ryan and Brooke to ride behind the wagon.

Nicole asked, "What was that about?"

"Marlena knows we're almost home. She's pullin' awfully hard, and Lucy is lettin' her do all the work. She probably don't want anybody else to get home before she does."

"How does she know?"

"You'd think they'd get turned around once in a while, but they don't. They always know where the barn is."

A few minutes later, they came around a bend in the road, and a neat, nice-looking, brick ranch–style house sat just off the road nestled into a sparse grove of tall pine trees with a small wooden barn next to it. Both buildings seemed to be completely intact with little or no damage. They hardly noticed the burned up SUV sitting near the end of the drive. Nicole said, "This is positively lovely. The view from the front windows must be breathtaking, and I love the barn—it seems so uniquely American."

Jack drove the wagon on by as he said, "I'll tell Miguel you like it."

"That's not yours?"

"No, ma'am. That's the old place. We lived there for a few years before we built the new house. Now Miguel and his wife call it home. You're right. It is a nice place."

The road followed the contour of a small hill before rising and making a big loop in a grove of tall pine trees. Before them on the left stood a large house built out of heavy logs. Farther on were several smaller buildings, and on the right was a huge barn built to match the house. Everything stood with no apparent damage.

Nicole held her hand to her mouth. "This is where you live? Oh my. This is beautiful."

"Thanks."

Marlena whinnied her arrival as Jack pulled the wagon to a stop in front of the house and set the brake. He jumped down and offered a hand to Nicole to help her out of the wagon. Ryan and Brooke both climbed down from their horses and walked them to where Jack was standing. Brooke said, "Is this it? Is this where you live?"

Ryan said, "Holy shit, man! This is awesome!"

From the direction of the barn, they heard, "Jack? Boss? Is that you?"

Jack yelled, "Miguel! Get over here and say hello."

A small man who looked as though he was in his mid-thir-ties, wearing jeans, cowboy boots, a denim jacket, and a black hat, almost ran from the barn to where they stood. He walked up and hugged Jack hard. When he spoke, he had a Hispanic accent. "I knew it; I knew it. I told Julia you were coming back, but she tell me not to get my hopes up too much. I tell her no matter what, you would make it home."

"So Julia's okay?"

"Yes, yes, she's fine; she's fine."

"Good. I was worried."

"No, no. She's tough. No problem."

"Good. Miguel, there's some people I want you to meet. Miguel Navarro, I'd like you to meet Nicole Meredith, my girlfriend."

The younger man stuck out his hand and then stopped dead when Jack used the word *girlfriend*. He looked up at Jack, who nodded, "Yep, she's with me."

Miguel took her hand and kissed the back of it lightly as he slightly bowed. "Ma'am. I'm honored."

She gave him a little curtsy and said, "I'm honored. Jack speaks very highly of you. *Él habla de ti como un hermano*."

He looked up at her and said, "That is very nice to say. Thank you and welcome."

Jack winked at her and said, "Miguel, this is Brooke Bates and Ryan Miller. They are a couple and friends of mine, but now they work for you. They don't have much experience, but I told 'em we could change that."

Miguel shook both of their hands and said, "Hello, hello. Welcome to the D-bar-D."

Jack said, "Miguel, I'm gonna give these folks the nickel tour, and then I'll come find you in a little bit. We have a lot to talk about."

"Yes, sir." He glanced at Nicole. "We have a lot to talk about."

Jack had shown everybody the house and grounds while Miguel had unhooked the horses and turned them out in a pasture with the other horses. It was almost an hour later when

Jack found Miguel gluing sections of PVC pipe together and laying them in a long, hand-dug trench from the barn to a water tank in a pasture.

"What kind of a project you got goin' here?"

Miguel's head popped up out of the trench, and he smiled. "The steel water line was pulled out of the ground last week. I knew we had to get it fixed, and we had the parts, so I started digging."

"You dug all this by yourself?"

"Yes. It wasn't too bad."

"Well, we sure do need it. I can see that. I tell you what: I'm gonna give you a hand when it comes to fillin' it all back in." He winked as he said it.

"Thanks. With help like that, I don't know what I am going to do with all of my free time." He smiled again and said, "I am very glad to see you, boss. I was very worried."

"I'm glad to see you too. And to tell you the truth, I was a little more than concerned myself. So what happened around here?"

Miguel shook his head. "It's been crazy." He sat down on a pile of dirt, with his feet dangling in the trench. "When I got off the phone with you, Julia was going to turn the horses out. All of a sudden, the lights went out. The emergency light didn't come on, and I thought, 'Oh no. One more thing to fix.' That's when things really went crazy. Lightning started jumping everywhere. I thought the barn was on fire. So I just let both horses go, and we ran outside. That lightning was everywhere, and we could hear a very bad sound like everything was grinding and groaning, you know. I watch my truck. It just flip over on its side. Nothing touched it. It just flip over by itself. I remember thinking that the devil was coming.

"The next thing I knew Julia was crying. She was shaking me and say, 'Wake up, wake up.' When I looked around, the sky was crazy. I thought it was the end of the world." He looked at Jack and smiled. "It almost was. I happened to look over, and all of the horses were out. The whole herd came running straight down the road at us. I had to jump up and get out of

the way, or they would have run us down. That's when Julia started screaming that our house was on fire."

"There was nothing burning around here?"

"No, nothing at all. We could just see yellow flame and smoke down the road coming from our house. We had to run all the way there, and that was when we saw it was Julia's Four-Runner. It was also flipped on its side, but we were lucky: it flipped away from the house. I put most of it out with the hose. We came back up here to collect the horses. By the time we got here, they had settled down and were eating grass in the yard. I put a halter on Soda and led her back to the pasture, but by the time I came out of the barn, she was walking back toward the house. That's when I figured out the fence was down. We just let them graze overnight."

Jack said, "I thought I noticed some new shit in the front yard."

"The next day we fixed the fence and got the horses put away, but I started thinking, 'What about the rest of the fences?' Boss, we got miles of fence down. We're going to have cows in Sheridan before we get all that fixed."

"That's all right. We'll get it worked out. What happened to Tony and Beans?"

"Tony went to Sheridan. I haven't seen him since. Beans went to stay with his mom in Dayton. He was going to help her, you know? Julia and I rode over there a few days ago. Dayton is bad. Burned-up cars are everywhere, and lots of buildings burned too."

"I've seen a lot of that."

"Beans' mom's house was burned up. I don't think they got out."

"Oh, shit. I'm sorry as hell to hear that."

"So what happen to you?"

Jack spent the next twenty minutes telling Miguel what had happened since they spoke on the phone. He told him about meeting Ryan on the road out of Yellowstone and finding Nicole in the airplane wreck. He didn't go into detail about how they met Brooke, but simply said Ryan had met her and invited her

to join them. He told him about the trip out of Cody, about what they had found in Greybull, about the Hideout, and the trip over the mountains."

When he was done, Miguel grinned and said, "Okay, what I really want to know is, what is the story with you and this girl, Nicole?"

Jack smiled back at him. "Yep. Her name is Nicole, and I think she's the one."

"I have to tell you, boss, I didn't expect this. I thought maybe you were going to become a priest."

"I'd get antsy spendin' that much time in church. I guess when you shake everything up, you never know what falls out."

Miguel nodded in agreement. He said, "She is very beautiful."

"I kinda think so too."

"Why the hell is she with you?"

"I ask myself that very question every day."

"Does she know how big of a pain in the ass you are?"

"I figure she's learnin'."

# 69.

Jack set his fork on the edge of his empty plate and pushed it away from him. "Julia, you have no idea how good that home-cooked meal tasted. Thank you." He took another sip of wine and looked around the table. Everybody was smiling. They had come to the end of a long road and been reunited with friends. Throughout dinner the table conversation had been causal and easy. Lots of questions were asked and several dumb jokes had been made, most of them at Jack's expense, but he knew it was all in good fun. Now it was time to transition into a new way of life.

When the conversation lulled, his tone became more serious, and he said, "The way I figure it, for every one of us sittin' here at this table, life has changed. For some of us, that change is pretty big. For others, it's a big change to the way we used to do everything. I'd kinda like to take a few minutes and establish a couple of ground rules, but more importantly, I think we should have a common understanding of where we're all at today, and where we're are all headed from here.

"First of all, I should tell you that the house, the barn, and the pastures behind the barn get water from a spring up on the mountain behind us. I think we should be in pretty good

shape, but if any of you see dirt or contamination in the water, I want you to let me know right away. We would need to get that fixed before winter sets in.

"Secondly, I hate to be so abrupt, especially right after dinner like that, but for those of you that haven't lived in the country before, we aren't connected to a sewer system. Out here we have an aeration septic system. It's a great system and works good when we have power. Without electricity the aeration part of the system doesn't work, so we need to be careful about how much we run through it. Also, other than a little toilet paper, you can't flush anything you can't mash with a fork. Yes, ladies, I'm talkin' to you.

"Third. The propane tank you see outside is big enough to heat this house for about two years, but the problem is the furnace won't work without electricity. When I built this house, we put in two soapstone fireplaces just in case we found ourselves without power for an extended period of time in the winter. Even though it will get damn cold outside, we should be just fine in here, but we are gonna need to be careful about how much wood we burn, and we're already gonna need more than what we got right now. We can't keep the house at eighty degrees and have time to do anything else besides chop wood. What I'm sayin' is: it might be a little cooler than what you're used to. Also, that propane that's heatin' the water is also what we're gonna use to cook with. I'm askin' that you keep the hot water use to a minimum.

"When I was givin' you all a tour this afternoon, I got to lookin' around and thinkin' about things. After dinner tonight we can't just throw the dishes into the dishwasher and be done with it. The washer and dryer don't work anymore. Everything we did as a part of normal livin' changed, and it didn't get easier. I think the responsibility of all the housework belongs to all of us. We *all* have to help out. Trust me, I know that a day's work on this ranch can be long and hard, and at the end of it, you're just about all-in, but we all have to pitch in to keep the rest of the house running as well.

"Miguel, you and Julia are welcome to move in here if it's easier, and I am gonna ask that both of you spend your days up

here. It seems to me that everything would be a lot easier if we have more people to help out."

Nicole said, "Excuse me, but I was just thinking, how are we going to eat? I should think that the quantity of food the six of us would consume in a month should be staggering."

Jack got a funny look on his face. "Food is not an issue." He looked around the table at faces staring back at him questioningly. Only Miguel had a small smile on his face. "When we built this house back a few years ago, I had more than a few doubts about how things were going to go. Like a lot of other people, I was convinced that an economic meltdown was coming. We built a storage room underground as part of the foundation. For a couple of years, starting in, oh, about 2010, we started laying up supplies just in case things went bad. Today we have about twenty-two million calories worth of preserved food put away. That's enough for ten people to eat for a little more than two years at three thousand calories per person per day. We can stretch it longer if we cut the number of calories or supplement it with anything we raise.

"This brings up an issue I think we all need to be clear on. Brooke, Ryan, if you remember, I told you that if you wanted to leave before spring, I would take you to Sheridan. Do you remember that conversation?"

They both nodded in agreement.

"If *anybody* leaves the ranch or happens to talk to anybody outside of our little group here, I'm gonna ask that you don't mention a word of what we have here for food or supplies. If word got out, we'd have people lined up halfway to Sheridan looking for a handout, and our own survival would be in jeopardy. Does everybody understand that?"

They did.

"Last thing that I have—and it's important. Everybody will be armed at all times. When we were back in Cody, Nicole was nice enough to make some predictions for the town leaders about how she thought things in the near future might go. I've been thinkin' about what she said ever since, and I think she's absolutely right. There's gonna be some people takin'

advantage of the fact there is no law. One of 'em might come wanderin' up the road. Might happen in the middle of the day, might be at night. Ryan, you might be out roundin' up cows and some guy comes riding across the grass wavin' at you. We can't be too careful."

Brooke said, "Does that mean I have to sleep with my belt and gun on, because that would be like so uncomfortable. I mean, seriously, how do you even roll over?"

"No, hon. You don't have to wear it when you sleep. You can put it on the table next to you."

"Okay, thanks."

"For those of you that are new to shooting, in the next few weeks, I want to take a little bit of time each day and practice a little. I want you to be able to shoot just as natural as scratchin' your ass.

"In a couple of days, Miguel and I are going to go to Sheridan. I'm makin' a list right now, so if there is anything you need in the next couple of months that we don't have right now, you better make sure it's on the list."

Brooke said, "A couple of months? How would I know what I'm going to need a couple of months from now? No way. I mean, like, Christmas is coming. I don't even know what I want to get anybody yet. Why can't we just make a couple of trips?"

Miguel said, "Sheridan is twenty miles away. It will take at least an entire day to get there and back."

Jack said, "A second trip might not be a couple of months from now. But, it's best to plan for the worst and hope for the best."

# 70.

When Mark got back to the hotel, he found Megan lying on her stomach in the middle of the bed with a paperback in front of her. He said, "Hey, how are you doing?"

"I'm okay. So, did you have any luck finding guns?"

"Maybe."

"Maybe? You either did or you didn't. What's the story?"

Mark pulled the wooden chair up next to the bed in front of her and sat down. He said, "Well, I got to thinking. You know how you keep telling people we're married. Well, what does a girl who's married have?"

Her eyes lit up, and she smiled. "A ring? You got me a *ring*?"

"Whoa whoa whoa! I'm still working on that. What does she get before she gets a wedding ring?"

"I'm not sure. What? Pregnant? I don't know."

"Oh, come on. Sure you know. Think."

"An engagement ring?"

"Okay. You're getting warmer."

"A diamond ring."

"Good. But, since everything is completely fucked up and a regular diamond is really not all that useful, I got you something else."

"Okay. Maybe you should tell me what is going on. I'm completely confused."

Mark pulled the blue box out of the bag and said, "Here. This is what I'm talking about."

She took the box and slid the top off. Inside was the most beautiful 1911 she had ever seen. "Holy shit! Are you freaking kidding me? This is incredible!"

"It's called a Diamond Grade Colt, and I guess it's supposed to be rare. I figured giving you this would be worth a lot more today than a little rock."

"Oh my God. It's awesome! I love it." She held the pistol carefully and looked at it in the fading light. "It's so beautiful."

"I know. That's why I had to have it for you."

She motioned with her finger for him to come closer to her. She wrapped an arm around his neck, pulled him close, and kissed him. "Thank you. This is awesome."

"You're welcome."

"I hope you have a holster for it, because my old one won't fit this, and I want it to hang out so everybody can see it."

"Well, yes, I do have a holster, but the hang it out part... yeah, well, you might not want to do that just yet."

Her expression turned much more serious, and she eyed him suspiciously. "Why?"

"It's a long story and kinda complicated, but I figured we were probably going to be heading up to Sheridan pretty soon anyway, right? Well, as soon as we leave town, it won't be a big deal anymore."

"So how big of a deal is it now?"

"Now? Oh, probably not much."

She looked at the gun again and then wiped off a few fingerprints with the bedspread. When she finally turned to him, she said, "I love the gun, and I love the fact you were thinking about me. I'm not going to tell you what to do or how to do it, but for the record I am going to tell you that whatever you do, make sure you tie up any loose ends. We don't want to have to keep looking over our shoulders. All right?"

"All right."

"Do we need to leave for Sheridan tonight?"

"Nah. We're good."

"Do we need to leave tomorrow?"

"Might not be a bad idea."

She shook her head and smiled. "Okay. I guess I'll be ready. Oh, you did remember we are having dinner with TJ tonight, didn't you?"

"Yeah. I was just going to go get cleaned up a little bit."

"Okay, but Mark…"

"Yeah?"

"You have blood on your shoe."

Mark and Megan had been sitting at the table for about fifteen minutes when TJ came through the door. Megan waved at him, and he walked over and sat down across from Mark. She said, "You're late."

He said, "No, I'm not. You said seven." He looked at his watch. "It's now three minutes to seven."

She sat up straight at the table and said, "Where did you get that?"

"The watch? My dad gave it to me when I was discharged."

"And it works. I mean it actually keeps time?"

"Yeah. Works great. I don't even have to wind it or nothin'."

Mark said, "How does it work without a battery?"

TJ took off the watch and handed it to Megan. "It's a Rolex. It winds itself when you wear it. There's nothing electronic inside at all."

Megan looked at Mark, "A couple of these are next on the list."

He said, "Yeah, that would be nice." In his mind he wondered if Del had been wearing a watch. He thought he had. Damn! If he'd only known then.

Megan handed back the watch and said, "Sorry about the late thing. I guess we were just early. By the way, we both wanted to say thanks for your help yesterday. You really helped us out."

TJ said, "No sweat. I only wish I would have seen the guy pull the gun. I should have been paying attention better."

Mark said, "You were really awesome with that rifle. Very fast."

"When you've carried one as much as I have in the 'Stan, you learn to shoot or get shot."

Megan said, "That's right. Mark told me you were in the military?"

"Yeah. Tenth Mountain Division, Third Brigade. I did a couple of tours. We were definitely in the shit. I was home for a total of three days before all the crazy shit happened."

"So you're originally from here? Were you home when everything went nuts?"

"Yeah, I grew up here. The night it happened, I was on Lake De Smet with a buddy, fishing. One minute we were fishing and laughing and talkin' trash, and the next there was lightning everywhere. All of a sudden, like in a flash, we were underwater. I don't mean just thrown overboard, I mean we were really kinda deep. It all happened so quick. I think the boat got sucked down into the lake, and we went with it. I've always been a pretty good swimmer, so I managed to get to the surface and get my boots and jacket off. The water was damn cold, and swimming to shore just about did me in. I tried like hell to find my friend, but I couldn't see him anywhere. Seriously, I tried everything. I tried to call for help, but nobody was around. Hell, we weren't even supposed to be out on that lake at that time of night. Anyway, I walked to a farm that was about a mile away. I could see what I thought were lights. It turned out to be a car and truck burning like hell in the yard. I stayed close to try and get warm, but that smoke was like so thick and so bad. I used a couple of old boards to start a fire in the driveway a little ways away and used that to warm up and dry off a little bit. After that it was walking home.

"I knew even before I got to town that everything was fucked up, but when I walked down Reservoir Road by the airport as the sun was coming up, it looked like one of the little towns we bombed the shit out of in the 'Stan. Well, you guys know what Buffalo looks like. Anyway, when I made it home, the place had burned. It was bad. Part of me wanted to look, you know? But

another part of me didn't. I knew my mom and dad and both my little brothers were still in there." He paused for a moment, collecting himself, and said, "Anyway, I've just been kinda hangin' out ever since. When I heard about Sheridan, I thought it sounded like a good place to go. Anywhere has to be better than here. Too many memories. Anyway, that's when I started workin' for Mr. Thompson. I knew I needed to get some gear before I headed out. He had what I needed, and I had what he needed, namely, a little security."

Mark said, "Jesus, man. Sorry to hear that. Whatever happened fucked everybody up."

TJ said, "Yeah, it sure did."

Megan said, "So Mark told me that you ran into some guy from Sheridan?"

"Yeah, I did. I guess it was about five or six days ago now. He rode up to the store on a big ranch horse and asked me to watch it while he went inside. Said he'd pay me. So I figured, why the hell not? When he came back out, we got to talking a little bit. He told me he had been working at the Sheridan Hospital, fixing a CAT scanner or something like that, when everything went to hell. Anyway, he had a wife and kids in Casper, and he was going home no matter what—even if it meant he had to walk. I asked him if Sheridan was as bad as Buffalo, and he said the damage on the southwest side of town was pretty bad, but otherwise it was about the same. But get this: there's a train yard in the northeast corner of town, and several trains had been in the yard when everything went crazy. I guess one of the trains was loaded with corn and wheat, and the other one was full of containers from overseas headed to the Midwest. They hadn't even started to open the containers yet. I guess some of the town leaders were also starting to get things organized, at least a little bit. Oh, and he said the water still worked, and some areas still had natural gas, but they had to shut off some of the more damaged areas to get the pressure back up to where it's supposed to be. He even said that if Casper was really bad, he was going to bring his family back to Sheridan. I thought that sounded like a heck of an endorsement."

Megan said, "It sure does. Did he say anything about empty houses or places to stay?"

"No. He didn't mention anything like that, but since it's kinda like it is here, there has to be plenty of empty houses. Sheridan is—what?—thirty-five miles away? I was thinking that if it completely sucked, I could just head back here."

Mark said, "That's only a day on horseback. That's not really that bad."

Megan said, "It's not bad if you don't have a bullet wound in your ass. For me it sounds like a very long day."

TJ said, "We could take it slow. There's no reason we have to do it in a single day. There's probably lots of places we could stay if we had to."

Mark said, "We even have the gear to stay out in the middle of nowhere if we needed to. I think it's a no-brainer."

Megan said, "Okay. We'll do it, but I want to leave early in the morning. That way we don't feel like we have to rush. I might want to take a couple of breaks along the way."

TJ said, "Fair enough. I'm used to getting up early. Four years in the army will do that to you."

Rose came by the table and cleared away their empty plates. The three of them sat and talked, making plans to leave in the morning. When they finally got up from the table, Mark and Megan were saying goodnight to TJ, and someone reached over and grabbed Mark's upper arm.

Mark jumped back in surprise and saw Peter Christensen do the same. Peter said, "Oh, my. Sorry to have frightened you."

Mark looked visibly relieved. "Oh, it's you. No problem. I didn't know you were behind me."

"I noticed you were still wearing your Springfield. No luck finding the 1911s?"

In a smooth, easy voice, Mark said, "No. And it wasn't for a lack of trying. I did meet the old guy in the Victorian home on the south side of town. He said he sold everything or gave it to his kids. The guy's house on the north side of town burned down, and nobody was home at the other place."

Peter said, "Well, shoot. I was hoping you would get to meet Del. He is one of the nicest and most generous guys you'd ever want to know. I figured he might be able to fix you up. Do you know he donated all the money to build the Buffalo Gun Club and gave new rifles to all the Boy Scouts last year? You might want to take another ride back out there. I'm sure he'd be happy to help you."

Mark said, "Well, I would, but I think we are going to be leaving town tomorrow."

"Really? Where are you going?"

Mark thought fast. He didn't want Peter to know where he was going if they started to suspect him of something, but TJ and Megan were looking right at him. "We're thinking about going up to Sheridan, maybe farther."

"Well, good luck to you—all of you."

"Thanks. Take care, Peter."

"You too," he said, and he left.

When they got back to the room, Megan said, "I thought you were going to jump out of your skin when that guy grabbed you."

"Yeah. He was the one who told me about your gun. Kind of scared me."

"Why didn't you tell him we were headed to Casper? You know, throw him off our track."

"Because you and TJ were standing right there."

"We would have backed you up."

"Oh well, it's a little too late now."

# 71.

After dinner Jack lit a fire in the big, stone fireplace, pulled off his boots, and sank into a high-backed leather chair in front of the fire. A sense of comfort and deep peace enveloped him with the radiant heat of the fire. He began to realize how much stress he had been under since the flare, and now, finally safe at home, finally realizing that Miguel and Julia were safe and sound, he could begin to relax. He thought about Annie, and as he pictured her in his mind, some of the stress in his shoulders returned. He hoped she was safe. He wondered what she might be going through and if she was trying to get home.

Making the journey from Illinois to home would be a huge and risky undertaking. Of course he had thought a lot about what the trip would require, both from the perspective of Annie trying to get home and Ryan and Brooke trying to get to their homes in Missouri. He had come to the conclusion that Brooke and Ryan should wait, but the decision had been based on the fact that both those kids were like babes in the woods. Annie was smart. She knew horses, and she knew how to shoot. He didn't think she was naive. But still, twelve hundred miles was a long way to go through a country that was now completely unpredictable.

"Penny for your thoughts."

He turned to see Nicole standing next to him, drying her hands on a dish towel. "They ain't worth that much." He took his feet off the ottoman and said, "Have a seat."

She said, "I was hoping you might like to sit beside me on the couch."

"You know, I think I'd like that."

When they were comfortable, he said, "Thanks for volunteering to do the dishes."

"It was nothing. Julia helped. I like her very much. We seem to have similar perspectives on things."

"That's good."

"Yes, it is. I believe they have decided to continue to stay in their own home at night, but they agree with you it would be much easier to spend their days here. How did it go with Brooke and Ryan and the horses?"

"Miguel seems to think he can teach anybody. I might be a little more skeptical. Brooke is a natural with the horses. Ryan, on the other hand, is not. But, I'll give him credit. He jumps in and tries. I think Brooke looks for ways to get out of doin' much."

Nicole laughed a little. "You already knew that."

"Yeah, I did. Are they downstairs?"

"I believe so, yes."

"Good. I wanted to talk to you. You know, there are a couple of extra bedrooms downstairs. You are more than welcome to anything in this house you want. I want you to be as comfortable as possible."

Nicole quickly sat up straight and looked at Jack. "And just where do you think I will be staying?"

"That's just it. I don't want to be presumptuous, and I don't want you to feel uncomfortable."

"I want to be with you. That's where I will be most comfortable."

"And I want you with me; it's just that I don't want to assume…"

Her expression softened, and she cut him off. "Jack, stop trying to be so careful with my delicate reputation. For the last

time, you are not taking advantage of me in any way. Go ahead, be presumptuous. If I have a problem with it, I'll let you know."

"I want to do what's right."

"Right by whom?"

"Well, right by everybody I guess."

"Oh, I see. Miguel must have told you that you were being completely inappropriate."

"No. Not at all. He's thrilled I met you. He likes you very much."

"Oh, so it must have been Ryan and Brooke. They must have told you how sinful and terrible you are acting."

"Don't be ridiculous."

"Okay. Then who? Who is it that is telling you this might be wrong? Or perhaps I should ask, whose judgment is it you are worried about? Who is it that says a single man and a single woman shouldn't try to find love and happiness?"

"I don't know. Maybe it's just the way I was raised."

She smiled. "I love the fact you are so chivalrous. I think it means you care about me."

"It does and I do. More than you know."

"I should be flattered."

"You should."

After a moment she said, "While we are discussing this, there is a small point I need clarified."

"Sure. What is it?"

"During dinner it became apparent that everybody has a job, except me. What is my role?"

"Anything you want."

"Ah. I see. Back to the same problem. That's very nice. Really, it is, but it doesn't make me feel very included. If I am to be part of your life here and part of this ranch, I need to have responsibilities. Does that make any sense to you?"

Jack sighed. "Yes, it does." He looked at the fire for a moment and said, "Do you really want to know what I'm thinkin'?"

"Yes. Of course I do."

"Well, it's like this. You know that guy at the grocery store back in Cody?"

"The one with the gun?"

"That's the guy. Well, when I saw him, I knew exactly what to do. I had an idea what he was thinkin', and more importantly, I knew what I had to do to resolve the situation no matter how it worked out. But this stuff, this boy-girl stuff with all the subtleties and feelings and things—I'm no good at it. I'm kinda lost.

"I was married for a long time to a good woman I loved very much. When I married her, I thought the promise was until *I* died, so I had planned on being alone for a while yet. After I met you, I had to rethink the whole thing. I decided if it had been me that died I would absolutely want her to be happy, and I think that means finding somebody special to share life with. Jenni would want the same for me. That's the way the woman was made. It was the way she lived her life. We both spent a lot of time and effort trying to make each other happy. So, I'm starting to get my head around all this. I never thought about it before I met you. Never had to.

"So I brought you here, to the home that Jenni and I built together. We haven't known each other all that long, and there's still a lot of things about you I'm learnin'. On the one hand, I'm not entirely sure what you expect. On the other hand, there's half a walk-in closet in my bedroom that's still filled with her clothes. I want you to be happy. I want you to be here with me and share life with me, but I want you to be Nicole. I'm not gonna ask you to do anything you don't want to do. Jenni used to take care of the house, do all the cooking, the cleaning, and wash my dirty clothes. I am perfectly capable of doin' those things. I'm scared to death I might try to shoehorn you into the role my late wife used to have, or a role you don't want. I don't want you to be Jenni. I want you to be you, and I want this relationship between us to be on its own merit."

"All of her things are still hanging in the closet?"

"Yep. Couldn't bring myself to get rid of 'em."

"I think I'm beginning to understand, and I'm more convinced than ever that you are the sweetest man I have ever met. There is something I need to know. I want you to answer this

as honestly as you can. Is bringing me here a dishonor to your late wife?"

He smiled. "You're good at this stuff. I guess that's the question I've been wrestling with. The answer is no—it is not a dishonor at all. She would want me to be happy, and you make me happy."

"Next question. Are you ready to get rid of Jenni's clothing?"

"You know, I think I am."

"Would you like me to help you?"

"Are you good at foldin' things, 'cause I'm not."

Nicole laughed. "Yes, I can fold things."

"Then we're a team."

Several hours later Jack was closing the top of the last box. He stacked it in the corner of the bedroom next to the others. Nicole said, "There. Done at last. That wasn't such a chore, now was it?"

Jack looked up at her. "Nope, but we ain't done yet."

"What could possibly be left? That's the entire closet and the drawers in the bathroom and the wardrobe."

"We need to move your stuff in here."

"Are you certain?"

"Yes, ma'am. Can't have my girl livin' out of a bag."

It only took them ten minutes to put Nicole's few things away. When they were finished, she pulled him close to her and said, "So I suppose we are official now."

"Yes, ma'am, I suppose we are."

She kissed him passionately for several minutes and then ran her hand down the front of his pants. He said, "Whoa. I thought...you know..."

She said, "Just because the rollercoaster is in for repair doesn't mean the entire park is closed."

He blew the lamp out and led her to bed.

# 72.

Mark stood in the cold early light of dawn, holding the reins of his horse and Megan's. Behind him Gus and Ralph, the two mules, stood patiently, and TJ sat quietly on his horse. Mark said, "Fuck this. I'm gonna go get her."

TJ said, "It's cool, man. We got all day."

As Mark started to tie the horses to a bent light post, Megan came out the door of the hotel. She walked toward them carrying a small bag, seemingly without a care in the world. He said, "Where have you been? We've been standing here with our thumbs up our asses for the last half an hour."

She shot him a stern look. "I told you I had a couple of things to finish. Besides, I had to make sure we didn't leave anything."

"Well, can we go now?"

"Take it easy. What's your rush?"

"I'm just tired of freezing my ass off and not getting anywhere."

They climbed up in their saddles, and Mark started his horse moving north through the street, pulling a lead rope to the two mules. TJ fell in beside Megan behind the mules and said, "How are you feeling in the saddle?"

"Oh, okay, I guess. It's not as bad as it was the other day. I put some Vicodin in my saddlebag in case it gets to be too much."

They rode quietly for several minutes. TJ said, "You know, I'm really sorry about the other day. I completely blame myself for you getting shot. I should have been paying much closer attention."

"It wasn't your fault. All of us should have been paying much better attention. It reminds me that things aren't as safe as they used to be."

"That's for sure. I wish it hadn't been you that got hurt."

"Oh well, what do they say? Scars are tattoos with better stories?"

"Yeah, something like that, but a scar back there on you is like a mustache on the Mona Lisa."

TJ couldn't see Megan blush in the weak light. She said, "Aw. Thanks. That's nice to say."

He said, "So Mark told me you two started seeing each other right after everything went nuts?"

"Yeah, it worked out that way. I've been kind of showing him the ropes with horses and guns and stuff. He's a smart guy, but I don't think he spent much time in the country as a kid."

"So, you guys are engaged?"

She smiled. "I wouldn't say we are officially engaged or anything like that. Sometimes I've said we were married or engaged just to make things easier on the people around us, especially at the hotel. Sometimes people are more willing to help if they think you are newlyweds."

"Oh. I see. So, you're originally from around here?"

Megan and TJ continued to talk casually as they made their way out of town and headed north following Interstate 90. They both talked about where they grew up and getting out of the small towns. Megan told him about New York and coming home to be with her dad for his procedure, and TJ talked about serving in the army and his time in Afghanistan. As the sun came up in the east over Lake De Smet, TJ pointed out where he had been when the disaster struck.

Just past the lake, Megan said, "I better ride up and check on Mark. He's been pretty quiet this morning."

"No problem. I'll hang back and keep an eye on the packs."

She gave him a little smile as she kicked Chic up to a trot.

When she rode up alongside Mark, he said, "Sounds like you two were having a great old time back there."

"We were just talking. He was telling me about being in the army, and I told him about New York and stuff. Did you see the lake back there? That's where he was when everything changed. That's a long walk back to town without a shirt or shoes on."

"Yeah. Whatever."

"What's wrong Mark?"

"Nothing."

"It doesn't sound like nothing. It sounds like you are upset about something."

"I'm just pissed off about that stupid town."

"Buffalo? Why?"

"I don't know."

"You're mad at a town? That doesn't make any sense whatsoever."

"Look. I can be mad about any goddamn thing I want. Okay?"

"Okay, okay. Be mad at a town if you want. It just doesn't seem very useful if you ask me."

"I didn't ask you."

"Fine."

They continued to plod along in silence for a while. Megan said, "Do you mind if I ride back and talk to TJ? I don't think he's had many people to talk with since everything got messed up."

"I don't care. Do whatever the fuck you want."

She was about say something but bit her tongue at the last second. An argument wouldn't accomplish anything and would ruin an otherwise nice morning. She pulled Chic to a stop and let the mules pass her by.

Mark was in a black mood. He knew he had treated Megan badly, but at the moment he didn't care. She asked what he was pissed off about, and, in all honesty, he didn't know. He just felt ornery and shitty and didn't feel like talking about it. He had let her believe he was angry about the town they had just left, but, in reality, he really liked Buffalo. He could have easily stayed there. He had pictured finding a little farm or ranch just outside the city limits and setting things up to stay permanently.

He thought about Stacy's place in the foothills. That was perfect. She had everything: a nice little house, a barn with some horses, running water, a little food stashed away. Everything. Well, almost everything. Stacy needed to have a man around. Someone to help around the place, but more importantly, someone to protect her. In his mind he again was looking down the back of her pants as she knelt on the safe door trying to reach inside. She wouldn't have any trouble finding a guy. She was hot, and she had a great personality—even if she did have a kid. He could have had her if he wanted. He was sure of it. He wondered if there was some way he could have had both women, Megan and Stacy. That would have been perfect. In rough times like these, the more help you had around, the better it would be for everybody. Maybe he had missed an opportunity.

He was thinking about what Megan had said about Stacy when Hunter's back foot kicked something that sounded a little different. Mark looked behind him and noticed a flattened aluminum can on the pavement. Out of the corner of his eye, he spotted the white grip of the Colt in the holster beside him. The anger returned.

No, he wasn't pissed at Buffalo. He was pissed that he had to leave Buffalo. That was the truth of the matter.

In his head he replayed the events at the house yesterday. The big fucking house. Hell, the big fucking mansion. The guy had come off nice enough, but that was all part of the act. He probably just came off like that to compensate for all the guilt he felt about taking money from everybody else. That's why he had donated money to the gun club and the Boy Scouts. Big

deal. That little bit was probably nothing more than a drop in the bucket compared to all the money he had stashed away. When that guy went to work, did he work harder than Mark? Hell no. Did he have to put up with all the bullshit Mark did? Hell no. Did he have a girlfriend sitting at home spending every last fucking dime he ever made on bullshit she didn't need and then out fucking some other guy while he was busting his ass at work? No fucking way. Mark pulled the pistol out of the holster and looked at it. It was beautiful and it was his. He deserved it.

He turned the pistol over in his hand, examining the gold inlay and the engraving. He felt the smooth ivory of the grips and the hefty weight in his hands. This gun was beautiful. He liked the way the hammer was pulled back and ready to go. What had Megan told him about carrying a pistol like this? Oh yeah. Cocked and locked. Yep, cocked and locked and ready to fuckin' rock!

It occurred to him that he hadn't shot the pistol yet. In fact, neither one of them had tested these new pistols. That might not be a good idea. Hell, Megan had carried her dad's pistol for several days and had no idea it didn't work until she needed it. Now they were both carrying new pistols that they didn't know would work if they needed them. What if both these guns were nothing more than show pieces—just something that looked pretty and sat on the shelf and were never intended to be fired. The thought scared him. They could be out here in the middle of nowhere, and the only working gun other than whatever TJ had was buried in one of Gus's saddlebags.

Just off the side of the road in the grass lay an old McDonald's drink cup. Mark switched the mules' lead rope to his left hand and brought the pistol up. As he started to aim and squeeze the trigger, he heard Megan yell behind him, "Mark! *No!*"

The gun fired perfectly as the shot rang out in the quiet morning air. In the same instant, Hunter started to rise beneath him. Everything around him moved in slow motion. Hunter was rearing up as the lead rope in his left hand was being pulled backward hard and fast. The rope pulled him

down and toward his left, twisting him in the saddle as Hunter continued to rise up. His right hand dropped the pistol as he reached for the pommel of the saddle. His left hand burned as the rope slid out of his grip. The horse's front legs came down as his back legs started to rise pushing Mark forward as though he was being cracked like a whip. In the next instant, he was airborne, flying forward out of the saddle and nearly over the horse's neck. He just managed to get his right hand out in front of him before he hit the ground.

Megan had been telling TJ about the two guys they encountered between Gillette and Buffalo when she happened to look up and see Mark pointing his gun at something in the ditch. Her first thought was that somebody was trying to get them and fear rose in her. When she realized it was nothing more than a paper drink cup, a new fear rose in her. She tried to yell at Mark not to shoot, but the gun went off before he could react to her.

The loud shot in the otherwise quiet morning sent the horses into a panic. Megan just had enough time to see Hunter starting to buck when she realized that Chic was trying to move fast toward the right. She quickly grabbed the reins and stuck her foot into Chic's side, trying to make her stop, when she saw the mules. They had turned and were now coming directly at them. She let Chic move to the right, out of the way of the oncoming mules, and tried pulling her to a stop. As the mules raced past, she saw TJ being thrown from his horse and hitting the ground.

She spent a moment trying to calm Chic and then climbed down. She started moving toward TJ. "Are you all right?"

"Yeah, I think so. My shoulder is a little sore."

"Does it move?"

"Yeah. I guess so."

She handed Chic's reins to TJ and said, "Here. Hold her. I've got to check on Mark."

She ran up to where Mark was getting up from the pavement. "Are you okay?"

He said, "Oh. Shit."

"Mark? Are you okay?"

He seemed a little dazed. "Ah. Maybe. I think so."

"Does anything hurt?"

"My head. I think I hit it on the ground."

"Here. Let me see." She knelt down in front of him and started running her hands through his hair. She looked at her hands and didn't see any blood, but she did feel a knot starting to rise behind his right ear. "I think you just got a good whack is all. Can you see straight?"

"See? Yeah, I can see just fine. My hand hurts a lot." He held out his left hand and opened it to reveal a half-inch line through his palm and another under his fingertips, where the rope had removed a portion of the skin and left the remainder bright red.

"That's a hell of a rope burn. That's going to hurt for a while. Are you going to be okay if I go try to get the horses back?"

"Yeah, I guess."

Megan walked back to where TJ was now standing and holding Chic. When she got there, he said, "What the fuck was that all about?"

She shook her head. "I have no idea. That had to be the dumbest fucking thing I have ever seen." She looked around. TJ's horse was grazing in the ditch only a few yards from where they stood. Hunter was about two hundred yards up ahead of them and had stopped in the middle of the road. Behind them, Gus and Ralph stood side by side in the median and were starting to crop grass. "You go get your horse. I'm going to try and get the mules without chasing them all the way back to Buffalo. I don't think Hunter will go anywhere once he calms down."

As Megan climbed back in the saddle, she felt the wound on the back of her thigh start to ache. *Damn it!* She had been doing fine, but with all this chaos, she had obviously irritated everything, and now it was starting to hurt. She led Chic into the ditch and then walked down the road past the mules. There she crossed the road to the median and came up behind them.

They didn't seem to pay her much attention, but just kept grazing the long grass. She walked her horse to the front of Gus and leaned over, reaching as far as she could for his lead rope. As she did, the pain in her butt flared up, almost bringing tears to her eyes. She led the mules back to where TJ and his horse stood next to Mark.

She stopped Chic, climbed down, and handed the reins and lead rope to TJ. She stepped in front of Mark. "What the fuck were you thinking!" she screamed.

"What?"

"You fucking *idiot*! That had to be the stupidest thing I have ever seen! What in God's name possessed you to shoot at a paper cup while you were on the back of a horse? Are you brain-dead?"

"I didn't know—"

"What the fuck did you think was going to happen? Did you think that horse was going to hear that huge explosion on his back and just think, 'Oh, I guess the idiot riding me is gonna start shooting stuff. That's okay. I'll just keep walking along.'"

"But, I...I didn't..."

"Shut up! Just shut the hell up. There is nothing you can say that will make a damn bit of sense." Megan walked off in the direction of Hunter.

TJ looked over at Mark. "She seems a little pissed."

"Yeah."

"She kinda has a point. That might not have been the brightest move."

"Yeah, well, I know that now. I didn't even think about it. I mean, they do it all the time in the movies."

TJ worked his shoulder. "When she comes back, I don't know if that would be the first excuse I'd use."

They stood quietly for a moment, watching Megan walk up to Hunter and start leading him back to the group. TJ said, "Hey, is that your gun lying over there?"

Mark walked over and picked up his pistol. A chunk of one of the grip panels was missing, and the side of the slide was

terribly scratched. He emptied the gun and then walked back, feeling terrible.

When Megan returned with Hunter, she said, "We need a break."

# 73.

To the right of where they had stopped in the road was an enormous hay field. Scattered throughout the neatly cut grass were hundreds of giant, round bales of hay. Megan pointed to the field and said, "Let's go see if we can find a nice place to relax for a little bit."

Mark said, "I'm really sorry."

Without looking at him, Megan raised her hand and said, "Stop. Whatever you are going to say—just stop. I don't want to hear it right now."

They walked through the ditch and across a small dirt road into the field. When they had come to a group of the big round bales, she said, "This is as good as it gets."

She dug several pairs of hobbles out of a bag and began to secure the horses. TJ pulled a long corkscrew-like thing out of his bag and twisted it into the ground. He tied his horse to the stake and then helped Megan with the mules. When they were done, Megan dug around in her saddlebag until she found the vial of Vicodin. She popped a tablet in her mouth and washed it down with water. She spread a coat on the ground next to a hay bale and then lay down.

When Megan awoke, it was a little past noon. Mark was sitting on the ground next to her. He said, "Hey. Feeling any better?"

"Yeah. A little."

"Look. I'm sorry. I didn't think."

"I'm sorry too. I shouldn't have said what I did."

"No. You were right. I was stupid. I won't ever do anything like that again."

She looked at him and gave him a little smile. "I gotta know. Why did you do that?"

"I was thinking about your pistol. We didn't know it didn't work until you really needed it. We hadn't tested these. I wanted to be sure they worked."

"Mark. You were sitting right next to me last night when I took both of them apart and put them back together again. Why do you think I did that?"

"I don't know. I just didn't think. I'm sorry."

"Okay. We're good. Where's TJ?"

"He rode off a few minutes ago. He wanted to see what's on the other side of this field. He thought it might be a building or something."

"Let's get the horses ready. When he gets back, we can get moving again."

The rest of the afternoon, they plodded north at the fastest walk Megan felt comfortable pushing the horses. They passed through miles of rolling, grass-covered hills with a jagged line of blue mountains a constant companion on their left.

This time Mark rode drag. There was no way for him to hold the lead rope and his reins at the same time. The wound on his hand hurt like hell, and it seemed to be getting worse. He thought about asking Megan for one of her Vicodin, but his pride wouldn't let him. For the most part, Megan led the group. She had taken one of the exits near Story and led them along a smaller road that paralleled the interstate.

After about an hour, Mark noticed a sign lying along the side of the road. It read Fetterman Monument. TJ had rode

back to see how he was doing, so Mark asked him, "Any idea what that is all about?"

"Oh yeah." He pointed to his right. "That's monument hill. This is where the Battle of the Hundred Slain took place."

"I never heard of that."

"Oh, it's classic. Back in like the 1860s, Lieutenant Colonel Fetterman was leading a group of cavalry through here when he saw a couple of Indians on a hill. The story I heard was that the Indians were insulting the cavalry and shaking their bare asses at them. Well, I guess Fetterman couldn't stand it anymore. He ordered his troops to chase down and kill those Indians. When the cavalry rode over the top of the hill and down the other side, there was somewhere between a thousand and three thousand Indians waiting to pounce on them. The Indians killed every last one of them."

"No shit?"

"No shit. That just shows you, never fall for someone saying stupid shit and calling you names. You never know what they might have waiting out of sight. Also shows what good intel is worth." TJ looked around and said, "Can you imagine what it would have been like trying to battle the Indians out here? Man, they had no radios, no recon, no air support—nothing."

"Kinda like we are now."

"Wow. I never thought about that. You're right. From a technology standpoint, we're not very far away from those guys. Here we are on horseback going from Buffalo to Sheridan. Maybe our guns are a little better, but it's not like we can call in an airstrike. If a bunch of Indians come running over that hill up there, we're pretty much toast."

Mark rubbed the knot behind his ear. "Same thing is true if one of us gets hurt. Can't call anybody to help. There's no medevac helicopter anymore."

"Good point."

"By the way, sorry about your shoulder."

TJ worked it in a circle a couple of times. "No problem. It's just a little sore. It'll be fine in a couple of days. Don't worry about it. We all make mistakes. I should have been paying

closer attention at the store the other day. That guy should have never been able to get that pot shot off at us. If he would have had even a little clue how to shoot, it would have been a completely different outcome."

Mark sighed. "The world is changing. Kind of seems a lot scarier than it did a couple of weeks ago."

The sun was sinking behind the mountains as they got closer to town. Houses were appearing more frequently, and the road was starting to get a little wider. Megan waved at Mark to join them up front. When he rode up beside her, she said, "We need a plan, boys. Any ideas where we should stay for the evening?"

TJ said, "It's been awhile since the last time I was in Sheridan, but I think this road takes us straight downtown."

Mark said, "This might work out pretty good. Maybe we could find a park or something. You know, some place with a little grass to set up the tents for the night."

TJ said, "Eh, I don't know. It's getting dark already, and we have no idea what we're riding into. There could be a thousand Indians in one of those parks. I'd feel better trying to find a vacant house or a field or something else around here we could scout out first. Then, tomorrow morning when it's light, we can send somebody into town to find out what's going on."

Megan said, "Indians?"

TJ said, "Mark and I were talking about the Fetterman Monument earlier today."

"Oh."

Mark said, "I really don't think it's that big of a risk. I mean, seriously, this is still America."

Megan said, "I don't know, Mark. TJ has a point. We have no idea what's been happening in town. For all we know, there could be some guy or even a gang trying to control everything."

"In Sheridan? Give me a break."

TJ said, "It's not likely, but is it really worth the risk? It's only one night."

Megan said, "Okay, so we are not going into town. What now."

Mark waved his arm at the land around them. "If we're not going into town, then anywhere around here should be just fine. Just pick a spot."

TJ said, "We could stay here, but this is one of the main roads that leads into town. Too many people will be using this road. I think it would be better to find something a little off the beaten path."

Mark looked past Megan at TJ and said, "Dude. Seriously. It's not that big of a deal. We can set up a camp anywhere."

"Right. That's why I'm suggesting we just get off this main road. We don't have to go very far away; we just need to get out of the way. It's not very likely anything would happen, but it doesn't make sense to advertise where we are. If you were hungry and cold and just happened to be going past a tent or a cook stove at night, wouldn't you think about trying to take it?"

"Maybe. Whatever. I don't care. Fine. TJ and I are going to take this road up here on the left and ride ahead to find a spot. You can follow along, just stay on the road and don't turn. You'll either run into us, or we'll come back and get you."

Megan said, "I'm not sure I like that part of the plan. So you two are going to ride off and leave me alone with two pack mules loaded with all our stuff?"

TJ said, "We might move a little slower with the mules, but it won't make much of a difference. We really should stick together. There's strength in numbers."

Mark looked forward at the road and said, "Jesus. Whatever. Why did you even bother to ask me if you were going to do whatever you wanted anyway?" He put his heels into the side of Hunter and trotted out in front of them.

Megan waited until Mark was about fifty yards out in front of them. She leaned toward TJ and said, "I'm really sorry about Mark. I don't know what's gotten into him today. He's not usually like this."

"Don't worry about him. He is who he is." TJ let a few moments pass and added, "You know, I was just thinking that I kind of enjoyed this day. It's been fun riding and talking with you."

She turned and smiled at him. "Me too."

It was completely dark before they had both tents set up, the sleeping bags laid out, and the horses put up for the night. Mark had spotted an area just southwest of the airport that had a few small, rolling hills. A small stream ran through the middle of a wide draw with almost two hundred yards of tall grass between the sides. They had found a good spot near the creek that was hidden from the road above. Megan had used the flashlight to help find their gear until they could get a small propane lantern working.

After dinner the three of them sat around the campfire talking when Mark got up and walked over to a bag lying near the tent. "I know what this party needs," he said and pulled out a bottle of Patron Añejo tequila. He sat back down next to Megan, opened the bottle, and took a big drink. "Wow. That is smooth. Might be better with a little lime and some triple sec, but hey, I guess when you're out in the sticks, you gotta rough it."

He passed the bottle to Megan, and she took a small sip. "That is pretty good. Hits the spot."

She handed the bottle to TJ, but he waved it off. "No thanks."

Mark said, "What? You don't drink?"

"Nah. That's not it. It's just that I want to keep my head on straight tonight."

Mark pushed harder, "Ah, come on man. We're relaxing. It's been a long-ass day. You deserve a drink."

"Thanks, but I'm good."

"So, what's the deal, man?"

"I don't know. I've been watching a lot of people over the last week or so when I was working for Mr. Thompson. I shot a few of them too. Things aren't like they used to be, you know? Mark, you even said yourself, things are kinda scary. Sometimes it almost feels like it did back in the 'Stan. I might even sit watch for a while tonight."

Mark took another drink of the tequila. "Dude. You gotta relax a little."

"I will when we have a lot better idea what's going on and who the players are. A couple of walls around me wouldn't hurt either."

Mark offered the bottle to Megan, and she shook her head. "He makes a lot of sense, Mark."

"Fine. Fuck ya then." He took another drink.

Megan said, "Mark, please don't get all shitfaced tonight. Let's just sit here and talk for a while."

"What are you, my fucking mother? Oh wait, she would have been happy to get shitfaced with me." He took another drink and put the top back on the bottle. "Fine! Have it your way." He stood up and threw the bottle as hard as he could out into the darkness. A few seconds later, they heard it thump on the ground. "Fuck you both. I'm going for a walk."

Megan said, "Mark, don't be like that. It's dark out. Just sit down and take it easy."

"Maybe I don't want to sit down. Maybe I've been sitting on my ass all day, and I'm sick of sitting. Maybe I want to stretch my fucking legs. Is that too much or does Mr. Tactical here have some reason that taking a walk might be a security breech?"

She said, "Mark..."

"I'm going for a goddamn walk. I'll be back later." He turned and walked out of camp.

It was several hours later when Mark stood up and started walking back to camp. There was enough moonlight he could easily see the road before him and even a few details of the structures and surrounding countryside he passed. High in the night sky, most of the crazy colors that had obliterated the stars were gone, and now only occasional ribbons of red and green undulated slowly like a vaporous apparition. Most of the anger he had left with was now gone or at least had turned into resignation.

The whole day had been awful. If there was some way to start the whole day over again, he would jump at it in a heartbeat. The worst part was the realization that it was all his fault. If he hadn't been so fucking stupid, this wouldn't be that big

of a deal. If he would have just taken the two Gold Cups the guy offered him, they would still be at the Occidental and having dinner served to them instead of eating reconstituted beef stroganoff out of a bag. If he hadn't gotten the crazy idea to try his new pistol out, his hand wouldn't be hurting like hell, and Megan wouldn't have been so pissed at him. If he had just shut his mouth and listened to TJ, he wouldn't have looked like such a dickhead. Somehow he had to regain face. He had to prove to Megan and TJ he wasn't stupid. He had to show them he could make smart decisions, and he was strong enough to get what they wanted and what they needed.

But, wait a minute, who was this "they" anyway? This had always been the Mark and Megan show until TJ showed up. He was only supposed to be riding with them to Sheridan. Maybe it was about time for TJ to ride off into the sunset. Megan was pretty smart, and she certainly liked to be in control, but hadn't the two of them done just fine up until now? Hadn't the two of them made it from Gillette to Buffalo in one piece? Hell, they had even gotten themselves pretty comfortable in Buffalo, and when they lost a horse, the two of them had figured out a way to get the mules and the gear and everything else they needed.

Tomorrow would be a better day. Tomorrow they would get rid of TJ. They could find out what was going on in Sheridan and start making plans what to do from now on. If there was as much stuff lying around as the guy TJ had met said there was, maybe they would hang out here through the winter. Maybe longer. It all depended on what they could find.

Mark walked at a slow, casual pace on the way back to camp. The night air around him was chilly, and he stuffed his hands into the pockets of his coat. As he walked through the darkness, he tried to picture what the perfect place would look like. Would it be better to live in town and be close to food and supplies they might need, or would it be better to be outside of town and have room for the horses and be a little farther away from other people? Both locations had distinct advantages, and both had disadvantages. It would kind of depend on—

Someone tapped him on the left shoulder. Fear raced through him, as he jerked his hands out of his pockets and spun around, reaching for his pistol. It was gone.

In the darkness someone said, "Shh. Here."

In a panic Mark said in a loud whisper, "What the fuck?" He could just make out the shape of someone standing in front of him but couldn't see enough detail to know who it was. He could see the guy was holding his gun by the barrel with the white grips sticking out toward him.

"Mark, take it easy. It's just me, TJ."

The fear instantly turned into rage. "What the fuck? What the hell are you doing?"

In a voice just above a whisper, TJ said, "Take it easy. I saw somebody coming toward camp in the dark. I had no idea it was you." He handed the gun back to Mark.

"I could have blown your head off. I probably should have."

"That's why I took your gun. Look man, I had no idea it was you."

"Who the fuck do you think it would be?"

"About an hour ago, four people walked down this same road."

"Did you steal their guns and scare the fuck out of them too?"

"They were just talking. Probably just going back to where they live. I didn't think they were a threat."

"But you thought I was a threat. Nice going, Ace."

"Hey. You were one guy alone out here. I had no idea."

"Bullshit. You knew it was me, and you did that just to scare the shit out of me."

TJ laughed a little. "I really didn't. Okay, maybe as soon as I got your gun, I knew. That's why I just tapped you on the shoulder instead of cutting your throat."

His words made Mark think for a second. Could he really have cut his throat? He had no idea TJ had come up behind him, and he never felt a thing when his gun was taken. He thought the guy probably could have. "What the hell are you doing out here?"

"I told you before. I was sitting watch."

"Are you gonna stay out here all night?"

"Nah. I don't think I have to. Probably just until midnight or so. I just want to make sure all the goofballs are off the street. Where did you go?"

"Ah, I was just walking for a while, and then I sat and did some thinking. You know, just some time to clear my head."

"I don't suppose you learned anything while you were out there?"

"You mean like why I've been such a jerk today?"

"Well, that too, I guess, but I was thinking more along the lines of recon. Did you happen to see any people or anything going on?"

"Oh. No. I didn't see anybody."

"Too bad. Dark is a great time to do recon. People in the light have no dark vision. You can see them, but they can't see you."

"Do you ever stop thinking about all this security military stuff?"

"Uncle Sam spent a lot of money training me how to stay alive. It worked for a long time in a bad place. Things around here are more than a little messed up. There's no way I'm going to forget that training now."

And there's no way I'm going to hang around you any longer than I have to, Mark thought. He said, "Yeah, I get that. Did Megan go to bed?"

"She waited up for you for a while, but then she turned in."

"All right. See you in the morning."

"Good night."

Mark walked to the tent thinking about what had just happened. It was pretty cool that TJ could sneak up behind him and take his gun without his even knowing about it. That might be a good trick to know.

He sat on the ground outside the tent and took off his boots. As quietly as he could, he unzipped the tent door and crawled inside. Megan made a little noise and turned onto her side as

she slept. He looked at the curve of her side in the sleeping bag and imagined her skin underneath.

He undressed and unzipped his own sleeping bag all the way. He lay on his side, facing her backside. He ran his hand over her side and along the curve of her hip.

"Ouch! Fuck! What are you doing?"

Mark pulled his hand back as if he had been electrocuted. "Sorry. Is that where you were hurt?"

"Yes, dammit!"

"Oh. I'm sorry. I was just thinking that maybe we could—"

"No way. Not tonight. Don't even think about it."

"But—"

"No. After the way you acted all day, you're lucky I'm even letting you sleep in here."

"All right. Fine. Goodnight."

She didn't answer him.

# 74.

Jack looked around the table. Everybody ate quietly. He said, "Is everything okay?"

Everybody looked up at him. Miguel was the first to answer. "Sure. Everything is fine. Why?"

"'Cause it's quiet enough in here you could hear a mouse fart."

Brooke said, "I'm so tired I can barely lift my fork. Seriously. I'm like going right to bed after dinner."

Ryan simply said, "Me too."

Nicole said, "Julia and I did laundry today. I'm afraid I feel much the same way Brooke does."

Julia said, "I think we need to work out a better system. We about killed ourselves, and we ain't done yet."

Nicole said, "Oh, please don't say that."

Julia shook her head. "No. We only got the clothes done. We still have towels and bedclothes to do."

Jack looked at Brooke and Ryan. "Did Miguel give you two a list?"

Ryan said, "Yeah."

"It looked like you two were busy. What did you all do?"

Ryan said, "Lots."

Brooke added, "We fed all the horses and cleaned all the stalls. I mean, seriously, how much can a horse shit in one night? Then we hauled these giant salt blocks up to some cows on the side of a friggin' mountain. I couldn't believe it. I mean, like the cows didn't even want the salt. Then we had to go check a water tank. Then we came back and started cleaning out all the stuff in that one building that was like half-knocked down."

"Sounds like you had a good day's work."

"Oh my God. We didn't even get halfway done with the list! I wanted to cry."

Jack smiled. "Oh, now don't do that. It all gets a lot easier once you get used to things a bit. I'd say you two did fine for a first day. What do you think, Miguel?"

"I'd say they did good. They work hard and didn't complain. That's very good."

Ryan said, "Oh, she complained. You just weren't around to hear it. I had to listen to it all day."

Brooke whacked him on the arm. "Don't say that. I did not. Well, I might have complained a little bit about the horse I was riding. How come I can't use Dingo?"

Jack said, "All the horses get used. In time you'll have a string of horses you rotate through. Can't wear out the good ones, and can't let the bad ones go soft."

Nicole said, "I didn't see you at all today. What were you up to?"

He pushed his plate back and said, "I rode our north fence line and a good portion of the east. It's bad out there. There's a few areas where the fence is still standin', but there's also whole long sections of it down. I was tryin' to figure out what we can repair and what needs to be replaced. I'm afraid there's a whole lot of fencin' in our future."

Ryan said, "Fencing has got to be better than shoveling out stalls."

"You ain't been fencin' yet. Miguel, what did you find?"

"I took a look at the small tractor like you ask. The wiring is all bad. I took the starter off and most of the windings in the motor are burned. It's no good like it is. I might be able to

re-wire parts of the tractor, but I have to bypass all of the sensors and the dash. Maybe. I also look at the generator. It is very bad. All the wires are burned or melted."

"But you have a list?"

"Yes. Just like you ask, but I don't know, boss. That's a lot to fix."

"What about the Gator?"

"I will look at it tomorrow, but it will probably be the same as the tractor. Maybe."

"Okay. Well, at least we know what we're up against."

Nicole asked, "Are you planning to go into town for repair parts?"

"Maybe in a couple of days. We're still workin' on the list of things we need to try and find. Twenty miles each way is a lot of ground to cover. I'd rather only make that trip once."

A little while later, Jack stood holding Nicole's hand on the deck behind the house. He said, "Used to be you could see a glow on the horizon over there. That glow was Sheridan. After Jenni died, sometimes if I felt kinda lonely, I would come out here and see that glow and know there were still other people in the world."

She said, "Sometimes I would look at the moon and wonder if the man I was going to spend the rest of my life with was looking at the same moon. When you live in London, it was never a question of other people; it was only a matter of the right person."

He smiled. "You're right. I'm glad I found you."

"I am glad you found me too."

# 75.

Mark awoke to the sound of Megan laughing punctuated with little screams and shouts of "No no. Stop it." The sound grated him as he rolled over in the diffuse green light of the tent. He thought, I don't want to get up. But then his eyes opened. Today is TJ's last day, he thought.

Outside he could hear voices and the crackle of a fire. Megan said, "Oh my God! That smells so good! I can't believe you got this." Mark sat up. The air in the tent was chilly and a little stale. He could smell smoke from the fire and probably a little funk from his own sleeping bag, but then a new smell reached him. Bacon. The smell was unmistakable, and it made his stomach twist with anticipation. He dressed quickly and unzipped the tent.

"Hey, sleepyhead," Megan said, as she saw him emerge from the tent. Her voice was light and easy, without any of the anger she'd had last night.

"Hey."

"You're never going to believe what TJ got for us this morning. Bacon! Is that awesome or what?"

"Yeah, awesome." He walked over to where they sat next to the fire. A garbage can lid hung upside down from a makeshift

tripod over the fire, and several pieces of rough-cut bacon lay sizzling inside. "Wow. Where did you get this?"

"I got up early this morning and decided to check things out a little bit. On the way into town, I saw a guy butchering a hog. We talked for a while, and I traded him some advice and ten rounds of .308 ammo for this slab of bacon. Not a bad deal, huh?"

"No. I guess not. What kind of advice?"

"He never butchered a hog before. He was cutting it all wrong and had no idea what he was going to do with all the meat when he was done. I told him how to smoke some of it and salt the rest."

"How the hell do you know that?"

"My dad was a butcher."

"Oh."

Megan said, "Tell him what else you found out."

TJ said, "Well, it turns out there's no Indians."

"Yeah, I kinda figured that."

"Most of the southwest side of town is completely burned out. It's like the north side of Buffalo, where the houses were pretty close together. A couple must have started burning, and the rest just went along with them. Most of downtown is okay. I didn't get that far, but the guy with the hog told me about it. He said there was a lot of structural damage and metal damage, of course, but only a few buildings actually burned. He didn't know much about the west side, but he heard the hospital was still standing, and they were seeing patients there."

"Are they starting to get organized?"

"He said the sheriff and one or two Sheridan cops had gotten a bunch of people together to help. Right now they are concentrating on the rail cars in the northeast part of town. They want to get the grain put away before rain and weather starts to ruin everything."

"So what's our plan?"

TJ flipped the bacon with a fork. "I was kinda thinking about taking a ride around town to see what was going on. If it looks good, I might see if I can help out."

"Help out? Who are you gonna help?"

"The sheriff and the guys trying to get that grain put away."

Mark looked incredulous. "Why would you do that?"

"Why not? I mean, if this is someplace that's worth sticking around, it's worth getting started on the right foot."

"No way. Not me. I spent too long working for somebody else to get rich. I deserve more than that. I'm not doing it again."

"Oh, I see. You were one of those guys."

"What guys?"

"One of the entitled. You thought you deserved more than you got. Am I right?"

"I don't know what the fuck you are talking about."

"Sure you do. You worked at the coal mine, right?"

"Yeah, so?"

"What did you do?"

"I drove a skid steer."

"Did you have an MBA, or even a college degree?"

"No."

"Oh, so maybe some junior college. A welding certificate or something like that?"

"No."

"So why did you deserve more than you got? Look at Megan. She wanted something better, so she got a degree. She worked her ass off to get the job she wanted. Okay, so maybe when she started, it wasn't exactly what she wanted, but she worked hard and put in all the extra hours. She got promoted, got a bigger salary and more benefits. Then she worked even harder and got promoted again. Now she was doing the job she wanted and was making more money because she had more responsibilities. She *earned* her six-figure salary.

"It's kind of the same thing here. The town is chaos right now. Do they *deserve* to eat next spring? Who knows what they deserve or don't deserve. But, I can tell you that if they want to eat next spring, they will have to *earn* it today. They will have to do the work to take care of that grain right now in order to eat later. They will have to work hard to put this town back

together. They will need food, shelter, clean water, and law and order."

"I can tell you one thing: the guy who was in charge of the mine where I worked didn't deserve the millions of dollars he made."

"Really? You know that for a fact, huh? Maybe he inherited the mine from his dad. Maybe he owned the ground that just so happened to have all the coal underneath it. Maybe it was because of his education in finance and business that made it successful. Maybe it was because of all the hard work he did years ago that guys like you had a job in the first place. You have no idea how he got to the position he was in. I can tell you one thing: nobody gets to be in charge of a corporation like that without earning it. The board of directors wouldn't allow it."

"It doesn't make any difference. All that bullshit is over. This is a whole new world. This is survival of the fittest. This is a world where the strong take what they want, and the weak don't survive. This is my world now."

TJ took two pieces of bacon out of the pan and handed them to Megan. He shook his head slowly. "Mark, you can take what you want once or twice, and you might get away with it. But someday, somebody is going to have a problem with your philosophy. Somebody will have a problem with you taking what you don't deserve, and then they will stop you."

"I'd like to see them try."

"You mean like last night?"

"That was bullshit."

"Really? Seems to me, one minute you were walking along, and the next you were disarmed and could've had a knife to your throat." TJ slipped a big combat knife from a scabbard behind his back and used it to stir the remaining bacon in the pan.

"Fuck you. You're not exactly typical."

TJ laughed. "You're right about that. There's lots of guys out there who are smarter than me, a whole hell of a lot of guys sneakier and quieter, and even more guys who will just pick you off a half mile away with a rifle.

"Mark, listen. I think you're right. The world has changed. I think we are at a point where everybody has to choose which side of the line they want to be on. You're either going to be on the side with justice and equality, where the law applies to everybody, or you are going to be on the other side, where it's all about strength, intimidation, coercion, and violence. I've seen that side of the line. That was Afghanistan. Believe me, you don't want that."

"Yeah, and how did that turn out for you?"

"We made huge progress over there. It takes a long time to show people who have never known anything else something better. But this is the American West. People know what freedom is all about. They lived it. In fact, as I recall, back in the crazy Wild West days, most of the gunslingers and outlaws were hung. I bet they will be again."

"You know what? I think I've heard enough of this. In fact, I'm done. Ever since we met you, we have had to listen to your expert opinions on everything. You said you wanted to tag along to Sheridan. Well, guess what, buddy? We're in Sheridan. I think it's about time for you to ride off into the sunset. C'mon, Megan, let's get our stuff together and get out of here."

"I don't know, Mark. I think TJ has a point."

"What? You've got to be kidding me. I can't believe you are buying all the shit he is selling."

"I don't know what happened back in Buffalo, but I do know you wanted to leave in a hurry. I don't want to live where I have to keep looking over my shoulder all the time."

"So what are you saying?"

"I'm saying, I don't want to live like that. I want something better."

"You're either with me, or your with him."

"Mark, don't do this."

"I'm not doing this. You are. So, what's it gonna be?"

"Mark, please…" She started crying.

"What's it gonna be?"

"I can't go with you."

# 76.

After morning chores Miguel had given Brooke a list of things to do with several of the horses. He had been intrigued watching her work with the animals the previous day and wanted to see what she was capable of. All of the tasks required her to bring a horse in the barn where he could keep a close eye on her.

Ryan wasn't a natural with horses, but he could be taught. The question was: what was he good at? Miguel had decided to have Ryan help him with the Gator. Together they had pushed the little diesel utility vehicle into the barn and started examining the wiring.

In the engine compartment, it was obvious that some of the wiring appeared fine, while other portions showed signs of burnt insulation. Miguel said, "Let's take the battery out. I think it will be easier to check the control box without it in our way." He pointed toward a bench along one of the walls. "There is an old ammo can under that bench with some simple tools. Will you bring that here?"

"Sure." Ryan retrieved the drab, olive can and set it on the floor next to the Gator.

"I think this will need a nine-sixteenths-inch wrench."

Ryan popped the top and pulled out a plastic yellow box with two wires sticking out if it and started digging for the wrench. "Here." He handed it to him.

As Miguel started to loosen the bolt on the battery terminal, Ryan picked up the yellow box and asked, "Is this a multimeter?"

"Yes."

"We used one of these in one of my physics classes. Mine was a little different than this one." He twisted the knob in the center of the meter and the LCD glowed green. "Holy shit! This works!"

"What?" Miguel sat up quickly and looked over Ryan's shoulder at the meter. "It does. Check the battery."

Ryan switched the knob to VDC and placed the leads on each of the battery terminals. The meter read 12.86.

"Oh my goodness. This is very good! Very, very good." He clasped Ryan on the shoulder. "Now we can test all this wiring. This will make things so much easier. This is very good."

Ryan said, "The question is: why does it work?" He started digging further in the metal can and found a small flashlight. He clicked the button and a warm yellow glow shone on his foot.

"¡Achalay! This is incredible!"

Brooke walked over from where she was brushing down a horse. "What's going on over here. You two sound like you found a free gift card."

Ryan shone the flashlight at her.

"Oh my God! Are you serious? That is so awesome!"

Miguel said, "We have to tell the boss right now. Brooke, go find him. Tell him this is important. Come quick."

A few minutes later, Jack stepped into the barn, followed by Brooke, Nicole, and Julia. "What's all the excitement? Brooke said you needed me right away, but she wouldn't tell me what the hell was goin' on."

Miguel said, "Show him, Ryan."

Ryan was sitting on the floor next to a metal ammo can. He picked up the flashlight and shone it at Jack.

Everybody cheered.

Jack said, "Oh my. It never hurts to be lucky."

Miguel said, "That's not all. Show him the rest."

Ryan held up the multimeter and twisted the knob. The LCD lit up as though the last ten days had been nothing but a nightmare.

"Well, I'll be dipped," Jack said, taking off his hat and scratching his head. "Now why in the hell do they work when everything else is wrecked?"

Ryan said, "I've been thinking about it. They were both in this metal can. I think it was acting like a Faraday cage."

"A what?"

"A Faraday cage. It's a metal enclosure that blocks electromagnetic radiation. I'm not exactly sure of the specifics of how they work, but I think it's kind of like a hollow conductor. The electromagnetic radiation is conducted around the inside of the box."

"So you're tellin' me that anything in a metal can might have been protected?"

"Maybe. I'm not sure. It might not be that simple."

"But it might be. What about a big shipping container. That's all metal."

"I don't know. Maybe."

"Well, it's sure worth a shot. Miguel, are you thinkin' what I'm thinkin'?"

"Yes sir. C&B."

Ryan asked, "What's that?"

Jack said, "The local implement dealer. They changed things up a few years ago and ran out of room in their building. The keep all their parts locked up in a bunch of Faraday cages out back. I'll fetch the shop manuals and parts lists from the house. Make a list. I think we're goin' to town tomorrow."

# 77.

Mark felt nothing as he rode away from camp. He was numb. It was as though his brain had shut off, and he was operating on some weird autopilot. There was no anger, no jealousy, no sorrow, no heartbreak. Just empty nothing.

He had Hunter and one of the mules. He wasn't sure if it was Ralph or Gus, and he really didn't care. At first he had planned to walk away, but Megan wouldn't let him do that. She made him take the horse and a mule and then made him promise to return Hunter when he had found a horse of his own. She had wanted to give him one of the tents, but he couldn't stand the thought of her and TJ sharing one. She had divided the food and the pistol ammo and most of the camping gear. Occasionally she would come across a seemingly unimportant object or piece of clothing and cry even harder. When she was checking her saddlebags, she found a candle. It was nothing special, just a simple, small, white candle that had come from her home in Gillette. At first she put her face into her hands and sobbed. All at once she threw the candle at him, screaming, "I hate you! I hate you! I fucking hate you! I told you not to do this. Why did you have to do this? Why did you have to turn into such a dick?" He didn't say a word.

When it came time for him to go, he simply got up on the horse, turned it away from her, and rode away, pulling the mule behind him. It just so happened that he had headed east, back the way they had come, but it didn't matter. He didn't have a plan, and any direction, as long as it was away from the two of them, was fine. Behind him he vaguely heard the mule calling for his buddy, but Mark didn't care.

He rode east until he came to Big Horn Avenue, the road they had come in on. He turned left and started following it north toward town for a little while. At Woodland Park, he turned right, heading east again. Ahead, way off in the distance, he could see the interstate cutting through grass-covered hills. When the road ended in a T, he turned left, following Coffeen north toward town again, hoping to find an on-ramp to the freeway. He wasn't sure how far he was from Billings, but he really didn't care.

About a half mile up the road, he passed a tall wood post sign over an entrance drive, reading Sheridan College, a Division of the Northern Wyoming Community College District. As he passed the entrance, he started thinking.

Several blocks farther north, he started passing side streets on his right, which led into a residential area. He turned the horse and slowly made his way along a block lined with several cottonwoods and a few scrubby oak trees. Burned-out cars sat along the edges of the street, and a few sat in driveways. An occasional house had burned, but most stood as they had for years. These homes were nice, but not fancy. They had probably held families just starting out in life or those on the downward side of things. A half a block farther down the road, he found what he was looking for.

Three college-aged girls were in the front yard of a brown, vinyl-sided home near a fire heating a big pot of water. Next to it sat a large, galvanized steel washtub and a pile of laundry. He pulled the horse to a stop. "Excuse me, ladies, are any of you from around here? I need a little help."

A cute blond, wearing a baggy shirt and pink sweatpants, said, "Sorry, we're all from out of town, but we've been here since the big disaster. What do you need?"

Mark jumped down from his horse and stepped around front. "Hi. My name is Mark, and I'm with the sheriff's department. I just got back into town this morning from Gillette. I was over there for a meeting."

Before he could continue, one of the other girls, also a cute blond, stood up. "I'm from Gillette. How did you get here?"

"Well, I rode this horse."

"All that way? Oh my God. How are things? I mean, is it as bad as it is here?"

"Well, yeah, it's pretty bad. From what I've seen of Sheridan so far, I'd say it's about the same."

"You didn't happen to run into some people named Knutsen—Tom and Lucille Knutsen—did you?"

He gave her his best I'm-sorry-but-I-really-care expression. "No. I'm sorry; I didn't. I didn't stay around too long after everything went crazy, and I certainly didn't meet everybody."

"So they might be okay?"

"They might be. I'm sorry; I have no way of knowing."

The other girls walked up and stood next to the first blond as she asked, "You said you needed some help?"

"Well, yeah, I do." Mark took his jacket off and tossed it up onto his saddle. He smiled to himself a little when he noticed the girls looking at his gun. "Like I said, I just got back into town. I had a house a couple of miles west of here, over by the airport. Well, I found out that my house burned down, and I lost everything I have. The guys at work gave me a couple of days off and said there were some empty houses around here. You don't know of any I might be able to borrow, do you?"

"Oh yeah, that's easy." She introduced herself as Katlyn and her friends as Alexa and Hannah. They pointed out several houses in the neighborhood they were sure were unoccupied. They also explained that most of the empty houses closest to the school had been taken by other girls who were in town for the volleyball tournament.

After talking with the girls for nearly a half hour, he learned there were nearly sixty girls in town for the tournament, and they were all bored out of their minds. The girls had learned that he'd had a girlfriend, but she had been transferred to New York for work a couple of months ago, and that he hadn't eaten since last night. By the time he waved goodbye and left, walking down the street, he had plans for dinner and was eating a peanut butter and jelly sandwich. This is too easy. It's like shooting fish in a barrel, he thought.

At the first house he tried, he closed the door as soon as he had opened it. The warm, sickly smell of decay wafted out, making him nauseous. The second house was okay, but it was dirty, and he thought he could do a little better. The third house was a small two-story with a backyard that was completely surrounded by a wooden fence. He found the door locked, but with a little effort and his knife, he soon had the door open. The place smelled okay, which was a good start. He looked around and found the quintessential American home: living room, kitchen, family room, and half bath on the main floor, with two bedrooms and a bath upstairs. The bigger bedroom, obviously the master, had windows that overlooked the front yard, the side, and the backyard. That might be nice if he had to keep an eye on things. Back downstairs he rummaged through the kitchen. There were a few cans of food in a cabinet, but not many, and nothing that looked appetizing. In another cabinet he found some breakfast cereal and a box of crackers and some Easy Cheese. That might make for a nice snack later. In yet another cabinet, he found several bottles of liquor and several cans of Red Bull. That was definitely a bonus. He tried the water and found both hot and cold seemed to be working. Obviously the gas was still on in Sheridan, and the girls had picked the wrong house to live in.

He brought the horses into the backyard, stripped their saddles, and turned them out. In the garage he found a big plastic bucket and used it to provide water for the horses. After hauling the saddle and the pack inside, he sat in a rocker-recliner,

planning to relax for a few minutes. But almost as soon as his butt hit the chair, the weight of the day crushed him.

In his mind the events of the morning began to replay like a bad rerun he couldn't turn off. He heard Megan say, "Mark, don't do this," and "Mark, please," over and over again. He saw her throw the candle at him, and the picture in his mind flashed to a vision of her stepping into the bath, silhouetted by the candles and the Wyoming sunset. He saw her again, standing by the door in the bar at the Occidental with tears in her eyes as she watched him play guitar. He saw her standing naked, except for her goofy boots, in the grass somewhere between Buffalo and Gillette. And he heard her voice, the soft one she used at night, saying his name and whispering little secrets to him. Tears welled up in his eyes and spilled onto his cheeks as the heavy blanket of sorrow and regret enveloped him and felt as though he would smother.

He wanted to take it all back. Take back the stupid argument with TJ. Take back the previous awful day and all the dumb things he had said and done. He wanted to go back to the Occidental, back to where they were happy together. He wanted to go back to the time where he could do things for her. He wanted to be able to change her dressing again and argue with the pharmacist for the drugs she needed and search all over town for a gun for her.

That was when it all changed, wasn't it? It was the stupid guns. He had gone out with the intention of finding the guns that Megan wanted. She said she liked 1911s, so that's what he looked for. That was what he found. The guy at the house had brought out two perfect guns and set them on the corner of his desk. They were solid, reliable, and even had sequential serial numbers. They were everything he needed and more. But he wanted more. No, he *deserved* more. He *deserved* the guns in the cases with the gold and the engraving. These were guns that were bought and paid for by his own hard work at the mine, and he *deserved* them.

Or did he?

He started to remember the argument with TJ, and a little doubt crept into the back of his mind. He thought about the words TJ had used, about the difference between *deserve* and *earn*. He thought about the things TJ had said about the CEO of the mine, about the possibilities. What if the guy had gotten a college degree and worked for a while? What if his father had farmed the land that happened to hold a billion dollars' worth of coal? What if the guy had worked like a dog to build a mine that now employed hundreds of men?

In an instant of perfect clarity, like the flash from the barrel of a gun, he saw the truth. He had murdered Delgado Cruz.

# 78.

It was midafternoon as Jack sat at his desk, frustrated and angry. Piles of papers and legal pads were spread over the top of the desk and the credenza behind him. A wooden filing cabinet had been moved to a spot near the side of the desk, and a drawer stood open supporting several open files and another stack of loose papers.

Miguel knocked lightly on the wall beside the door as he walked in. "Are you busy?"

Jack looked up and over the top of his glasses. "This is worse than doin' taxes. Everything was on the damn computer: cattle records, horse records, inventory—all of it. But, I s'pose there's nothin' that can't wait. What's on your mind?"

"I've been thinking. We are probably ready for this winter with hay and feed, but we are going to need more help."

"Funny you should say that. I was just workin' on the same thing." He leaned back in his chair and held up a legal pad. "From our last count in September, we're expecting nearly four hundred eighty calves and forty-one foals next spring. Nature will handle her end of the bargain, but I have no idea how we're gonna take care of 'em after that. Hell, we still got a hundred head of feeders and twenty heavy culls that were supposed to

go out in a couple of weeks." He shook his head. "Even if we still had Tony and Beans, we'd be shorthanded without trucks, tractors, and everything else we use around here. Oh, and did I mention lights? It'd be nice to be able to get a few things done after sundown without totin' a damn lantern."

"When you go to Sheridan tomorrow, maybe you could find somebody who wants a job?"

"Maybe you could."

"I am not going. I need to stay here. I think you should take Ryan."

Jack studied him for a moment. "Okay, I'll bite. Why?"

"Ryan knows what parts we need, and if you can't find the right ones, he might be able to make another part work. I think he can do it better than me."

"You're puttin' an awful lot of stock into that boy."

"He can do it."

"You didn't see him when we first met."

"Maybe that is good. Maybe I see him how he is now."

Jack thought for a moment about Miguel's words. "All right. I'm in. Who do you want me to hire?"

Miguel smiled. "We need somebody who knows cattle, but it doesn't matter."

"Why's that?"

"Because you will hire somebody you think needs a chance. The only thing I ask is that they know how to ride a horse."

"What? You havin' trouble in the barn?"

"Brooke is good. She will be breakin' colts next spring."

Jack looked genuinely surprised. "I don't know that I've ever heard you that confident in anybody."

"She is very natural. Very good."

"And Ryan?"

"He works very hard. He seems to be very good with mechanical things. But he needs to keep his feet on the ground. He has no balance."

"He rode all the way from Cody."

"Yes, but you probably walk all the way, yes?"

"We did."

Miguel shook his head. "He is very afraid to go faster than a walk."

Jack's face broke into a big grin. "That don't surprise me."

At dinner Jack said, "We're leavin' for Sheridan as early as we can in the mornin'. If anybody needs anything, I'd like to have the list tonight."

Miguel asked, "Do you know all the places you are going in town?"

"I thought we'd better check in and see what's goin' on before we go too far. I gotta hope they're gettin' things organized. Then I thought we'd head over to Big R and see if we can find some barbed wire. I'd like to get as much as we can carry. I figure we can pick up most of the other things we need there as well. We have a couple of other stops to make in town, and then I figured we'd hit the implement dealer on the way out."

"What if you can't find any barbed wire?"

"Then it's timber."

Ryan asked, "Timber?"

Jack said, "You cut down hundreds and hundreds of small pine trees and use 'em to build a fence. It's slow goin', but that's how they did it before barbed wire came along. It would also mean we'd have to cut the size of our pastures, which means fewer cows."

Miguel pointed at Ryan. "That reminds me. See if you can find ignition coil for the chain saws. I think the same part will fit both saws. I will get you the number."

Ryan said. "Will they be at the same place?"

Miguel said, "Oh yeah. We buy almost everything there. They are the biggest dealer in the whole area."

Jack interrupted them. "I'm not exactly sure how long your parts list is, but we all need to be singin' from the same hymnal. If they only have one of any given part, we're not gonna take it unless we got the only thing it fits. There's lots of folks out there that need these parts as much as we do, even if they don't know they might work. I plan to let whoever is in charge know

what Ryan discovered today. Fair is fair, and I intend to be as helpful and neighborly as possible."

Everybody nodded in agreement.

Julia said, "I don't suppose there is any chance they might have a washing machine in one of those magic boxes?"

Jack said, "Probably not, but if Ryan here is as clever as I think he is, it won't matter."

# 79.

The shadows started to draw long on the east wall of the living room. Mark still sat in the chair. Throughout the afternoon he had ridden a rollercoaster of emotions. What started as panic quickly faded into guilt and remorse. At one point he had come close to saddling Hunter and riding as fast as he could to try and find Megan. He wanted to tell her everything and beg her to forgive him. He wanted to tell her how sorry he was and how wrong he was. He was sorry he had put her in danger, and he was sorry that he had been so stupid. But, as the afternoon wore on, a new emotion rose within him. Anger.

Mark tried to think. Okay, so what do I do now? He couldn't stay in the area, at least not in the long-term. It wouldn't be long before word reached town that somebody in Buffalo was looking for him and why. But his original plan was never to end up in Sheridan. He had planned to go farther west from the start. Okay, so maybe he had thought about finding a spot to stay in Buffalo for the winter, but the plan was always to go farther west, and Megan was supposed to go with him.

The problem wasn't the plan. The problem was TJ. If it wasn't for him, they would be riding west together, and everything would be fine. Hell, they would be west of Sheridan

already. TJ had been the one who fucked everything up. Mark remembered the way he had looked at Megan in the parking lot of the store in Buffalo and what he said. He thought about the two of them riding behind the mules yesterday, talking and laughing. What was it TJ had been telling her? Maybe he was filling her head full of all kinds of crazy bullshit. He thought about the way Megan had originally liked the idea of having a drink with him last night, but TJ was the one who changed her mind about that. He thought about TJ handing her the first pieces of bacon this morning. That son of a bitch had been working on his girlfriend right behind his back! The solution to all of this was obvious: he had to get rid of TJ. Once that asshole was gone, Megan would start thinking straight again, and the two of them would be on their way west and on to a better life.

Mark felt energized. There was a solution to this whole mess; he just had to work out the details. He couldn't just walk up to TJ and shoot the bastard, although that idea did have a certain appeal to it. Megan would obviously have an issue with that. So, he had to make it look like an accident, or at least like somebody else did it. That was going to be tough. On the other hand, if he could get Megan alone for a while, maybe he could talk some sense into her. He could tell her what he had figured out. Once she realized everything TJ was telling her was all just bullshit to get into her pants, she would see things clearly. It wouldn't even take that long. He could start out by telling her he was sorry and that he only wanted what was best for her. Then he could tell her he had realized what TJ was doing and felt she should know. Once she understood what TJ was up to, they would be on their way out of town. Too easy.

Mark nearly leaped out of the chair. This was good! Plan A: talk a little sense into Megan, and they were on their way. Plan B: shoot TJ right in his goddamn lying mouth and then leave town. All he had to do was kill a little time this evening, and tomorrow he was out of here. And could there be any better way to kill time than with a bunch of bored coeds? He didn't think so.

Outside, the light was starting to fade. Mark knew what he wanted to do before it got too dark in the house. He opened one of the bags that had been strapped to the mule and dug around until he found his shaving kit. He took off all his clothes, piling them next to the bag, and then climbed the stairs. The light in the bathroom was fading fast, but enough light still came through the small window to let him see himself in the mirror. Not bad, but he could tell things were changing without his normal time in the gym and a little chemical help. He flexed his arms, pecs, and abs. He still had more definition than anyone he had seen since the disaster. Fuck yeah. He was sure of it.

The shower was incredible. When he first stepped into the warm water, he started laughing. He had nearly forgotten how nice it was to simply stand in a stream of hot water. He wondered what Megan was doing now. Was she taking a hot shower? He didn't think so. He let the water pour over his body, washing away the dirt and grime. After he had washed everything, he stepped out and retrieved his razor, shaving cream, toothbrush, and toothpaste and stepped back into the shower. He shaved and brushed his teeth while letting the water run over him. When he finished with those things, he turned up the temperature and continued to luxuriate. He kept adding more hot water until he could barely stand it any longer. When the hot water started to run out, he stepped out and dried off. The mirror in the bathroom had fogged over, so he wiped it with the towel, leaving big streaks across the glass. It was almost too dark to see, but he could tell he looked good. His skin had a pink hue and veins stuck out on his arms and upper chest. Damn good! After he fixed his hair, he checked himself once more in the mirror and headed back downstairs.

He found the flashlight in one of his saddlebags. That had been a big score and a huge rush. He remembered sneaking down the alley and then running up behind the woman. His heart had been pounding so hard with nervous energy. He remembered grabbing the woman and pulling her up against him. He could still feel the warmth of her breath on his hand,

the smell of her hair, and the feel of her butt against his crotch. That was awesome.

He used the flashlight to find the lantern. He set it up on the kitchen table and after a couple of tries got it started. Then he dug around in the pack a little more and found a new pair of black jeans that Megan had gotten for him. He pulled the tags off and slipped them on. The new material was a little scratchy, especially on his junk, but the fit was good. He found a shirt and was about to put it on when he heard a knock at the door. He smiled and left the shirt lying on the pack as he walked to the door.

As he pulled the door open, he noticed Alexa's eyes widen a little as she let them run down his chest and abdomen. "Oh, hey! Sorry. I...ah...didn't know you were getting dressed."

"No problem. Come on in. I just got out of the shower."

"I thought this was the house you found. I mean, we tried to watch where you went, and then when I saw the light inside, I thought this was the one. Wait. What?"

Mark closed the door behind her. "I didn't say anything."

"Yes, you did. Did you say you took a shower?"

"Yeah. You want to smell me? I'm all nice and clean."

"But it was like, cold, right?"

He smiled at her. And here's the bait, he thought. "No. It was as hot as I could stand it. Felt awesome."

"Oh my God! You have to be kidding. We haven't had a shower in like forever. Why do you have hot water?"

"This house has a gas water heater, and maybe it sits at just the right spot on the system. I don't know how long it will work."

"But it still works now, right?"

"Yeah, come here." He led her into the kitchen and stood close to her at the kitchen sink. He turned the water on, took her hand, and held it as he brought it to the stream of running water.

She bounced up and down and squealed with delight as the warm water ran over her hand. "This is *so awesome*! Oh my God. I can't believe you have this. I can't wait to tell everybody about this."

Uh-oh, Mark thought. He said, "Better be careful. I don't know how much gas is left in the system. There might be only enough for one or two more hot showers."

"Oh, wow, yeah. I never thought about that."

Mark decided to take the conversation in a little different direction. "Hey, you want a drink? I don't have any ice, but I can fix you a Red Bull and vodka if you don't mind it warm."

"You have alcohol too? Oh my God! We ran out like a week ago. Yeah, sure. I'll have anything you're having. But, we can't stay here too long. Dinner is gonna be ready in about an hour, and the other girls will start to wonder what's going on if I don't bring you back with me."

Mark was fixing the drinks with his back to her as he spoke. "No problem. We'll have a drink while I finish getting dressed, and then we're on our way. We can bring the rest of the alcohol with us if you want."

"That's an awesome idea. We can have a party tonight."

"Yeah, it'll be fun. Kind of a housewarming party, but at your place instead of mine." He set the drink in front of her as he tasted his own. "It's kind of strong without the ice."

"No problem. I'm sure it's awesome." She took a big drink. "It's perfect."

For the next few minutes, they sat at the kitchen table and talked. Mark asked her where she was going to school and what she was studying. He asked about her family, but when she became a little emotional, he made a mental note not to bring up family at the party tonight. He quickly moved her on to other topics, asking her what they had been up to since the disaster and what her friends were like. When their drinks were gone, he said, "I should get dressed, so we can get going."

She gave him a little smile and said, "I kinda like you like that. Do you work out a lot?"

Mark could tell from the swimming look in her eyes that she was feeling the drink. "I used to. I like to stay fit."

"Oh, for your job."

For a second Mark forgot what he had told them; then it came to him. "Yeah. You never know when you have to overpower somebody."

"Do you have to do that a lot?"

"No, not very often."

She smiled again. "I bet not."

Mark stood up and stepped closer to her. He said, "I've been thinking about the shower."

"So have I."

He squatted down in front of her and stared into her eyes. "I'll make you a deal. Since we don't know how much hot water is left, I'll let you take a nice long hot shower tonight after the party, but you have to bring a friend; you can't tell anybody else, and I get to watch."

"Mark! I'm not a lesbian."

"No. Of course you're not. I didn't think you were. But doing what feels good isn't bad."

She said, "You just want to have a threesome."

"Don't you?"

She nervously laughed a little. "I don't know. I mean, I've thought about it once or twice, but I've never actually done it. I don't know."

Mark stood up. "No problem. You don't have to if you don't want to. I'm sure with sixty girls around I can find two, or even more, that want to have some fun."

She grabbed the loops on his jeans and pulled him back down. "No no no. It's cool. I'll work it out."

"You're sure? Because I'll…"

"No, no. I'm sure. It's cool."

He smiled at her. "I knew I could count on you." He leaned forward and took her face in his hands and kissed her as passionately as he could. When he pulled away, he noticed she had "the look." Her eyes were wide, and her mouth was slightly open. She was hungry and wanted more. She wanted him. This was going to be good.

# 80.

Jack took off his hat and hung it on the rack. He slipped out of his jacket and hung it on the peg below. When he sat on the bench, his backside came down a little harder than he had planned. He pulled both boots off and then just sat for a moment. He was dog tired. The day had been long; he was out in the barn before anybody else was awake, checking on a few things. Right after breakfast he rode several more miles of fence line, trying to determine how bad the damage actually was, and then headed over to inspect the irrigation lines. At least most of those were still in good shape. He had spent most of the afternoon trying to figure out what they had and what they needed to have. Most of the figures didn't work out in his favor.

The biggest problem he kept running into was that he kept thinking the old way: how they had done things for all these years. Now everything was different. They'd have to find a new way to do just about everything. He yawned.

He put his hands on his knees and pressed, helping himself up. As he stepped around the corner, he stopped. At the far end of the living room, Nicole sat on the end of the couch, wrapped in a blanket, reading. The light from the

lantern behind her created a warm glow, framing her head and shoulders. He simply looked at her for a moment. She was beautiful, but the thought that she was here, waiting for him, waiting to find out how his day was, and wanting to tell him about hers, warmed him immeasurably. She looked up, noticed him, and a bright smile lit her face. "There you are. I haven't seen much of you at all today." She bunched the blanket and patted the cushion next to her. "Come sit and talk to me."

"I can't think of a thing I'd like better." He padded halfway across the floor but stopped. "Would you like a glass of wine or somethin'?"

"I'll take a wee bit of whiskey, if you'll join me."

"I think I will." He poured two glasses and sat next to her on the couch. "Whachya readin'?"

"I found this book on large-scale gardening. Some of the techniques they discuss would probably be difficult in this area, but others appear to be quite manageable. If we are to eat anything that does not come out of a can or walk on hoofs next year, we should start preparing things today."

"Damn. You're absolutely right. I should'a thought of that myself. Good thing I got you around."

"So I can think about a garden?"

"No. To keep me humble. What should we be doin' now?"

"We need to prepare the ground now so that we can plant this spring. We really should open the soil and fertilize it."

"Fertilizer I got. A plow, I don't."

"Do you use the granular fertilizer or a liquid?"

"This is more solid."

"Is it pelletized?"

"Nah, I'd say it's more along the lines of round balls."

"Balls, I didn't see that in the book. How big are they?"

"They range in size, but I'd say most are about the size of a small apple."

"An apple? That's entirely too large."

"Horse shit."

"Excuse me."

"Horse shit. I'm talkin' about horse shit. You know, the stuff that falls out the back end of 'em. It's just about the best fertilizer there is, and we have plenty of it."

"Oh. Of course. Why didn't I think of that."

"See there. We make a hell of a team."

"Yes, we do. What about water?"

"Not an issue. I'd say the best place for a garden like you're talkin' about is right at the bottom of the hill behind the house. There's a big white pipe that runs along the west edge of that hay field. It's a gravity-fed irrigation line. We can keep a garden plenty moist."

"So the only real issue is a plow?"

"It is today. We're workin' on it though. What else do you need?"

"Plastic sheeting. Both clear and black. There seems to be an incredible number of uses for that. I noticed several containers of heirloom seeds downstairs. Those will be important, but we could plant hybrids this coming year. There are several other small items that also might be useful."

"I don't s'pose you'd make a list for me."

She smiled. "I'd rather go with you."

"You just love ridin' in that wagon, don't you?"

"I abhor that wagon, and you know it. But I do…" She hesitated for a moment, choosing her words carefully. "I do love you."

"Don't say it if you don't mean it."

"I do mean it. That isn't why I hesitated. I really don't want to frighten you."

"You're not gonna scare me away. You do realize we've only known each other for about two weeks."

"Yes. I am quite aware of that, and I have spent considerable time wondering if this is merely infatuation. I can assure you it is not. This is something much deeper and much more real. I do love you."

He looked deep into her eyes. "Nicole Meredith, I love you."

# 81.

Mark had packed all the liquor and most of the soda into two bags and brought them along to dinner. The meal itself had been an odd assortment of mostly canned foods, but the girls had tried to make it interesting, and for the most part, it had been good. The conversation while they ate was a little awkward, with most of it centered around him and his trip from Gillette to Sheridan. He told them about the guy in the ranch house with part of the metal from the refrigerator wound around and through him and the two guys he shot from the hilltop, but he left out anything to do with Megan. Occasionally in his stories he would catch himself thinking about her and wondering where she was.

After dinner they started mixing drinks, and the conversations seemed to get a lot easier. Six more girls showed up who, he learned, were a team from Casper, and a little later another group of four girls arrived. Mark loved the attention. All of the girls wanted to meet him and talk to him. He was amazed how fast word had traveled that he had information about places other than Sheridan. The whole impromptu party was fairly subdued from Mark's perspective, but as the evening

wore on, the conversations seemed to get louder and involve more laughing.

Mark broke away from a small group of girls he was talking to in a corner of the family room to get himself another drink. When he arrived at the counter where they had fashioned a makeshift bar, one of the girls told him the booze was almost gone. He said, "No problem. I'll find some more."

A tall, big-boned brunette said, "There isn't any more."

Mark smiled at her and gave her a little wink. "There's lots more. You just have to know where to look." He recruited her and a cute little pixie-cut redhead who seemed a little drunk to help. As they put their coats on and moved toward the door, Mark caught Alexa staring at him from across the room. He winked at her and told everybody they would be back in a few minutes.

Outside, in the dark, one of the girls asked, "Where are we going?"

"You'll see." He headed across the street and down a couple of houses to the smelly house he had checked out earlier. At the back door, he said, "You two probably want to stay out here. It stinks pretty bad in there. I think there might be a couple of bodies."

They eagerly agreed to wait, as he opened the door and flipped on his flashlight. One of the girls said, "Oh my God! Where did you get that? We thought everything electrical was ruined."

In the most authoritative voice he could come up with, he said, "This is my duty light. It's disaster resistant." He took a deep breath of clean air and hurried inside. He quickly rummaged through the kitchen, trying to breathe through his bunched-up shirt, which he held to his face. He found an old, half-empty bottle of sherry in the cabinet and nothing else.

Outside and breathing clean air again, he said, "It was worse than I thought, and they didn't really have anything. But don't worry, I know where to go." He led them down the street to the house that had been a little dirty. Mark wondered why he didn't try this one first as he opened the back door and held

it for the girls. Inside, the shadows from the beam of his light danced across the walls and cabinets of the kitchen. He set the light on a counter, so it shined on the ceiling, and said, "Start checking everything."

The big, dark-haired girl said, "Isn't this like stealing?"

Mark grinned at her and said, "It's okay. You're with me, and this is for official use."

"Well, if you say so."

"Yep. I say so."

They started opening cabinets. Mark positioned himself behind the redhead as she squatted in front of the sink. When she stood up, he grabbed her ass and gave it a little squeeze. She gave a quick little moan and backed into him, pushing her butt up against his crotch. Then she bent over.

He grabbed her by the hips and pressed himself against her. His initial reaction was to take her right there. But, he had an idea that if he waited and played this evening out, it would get a lot better. From the other side of the room, the other girl said, "Bingo."

On the floor of a small closet near the door sat two cardboard case boxes. One was filled with Absolut vodka, and the other with Southern Comfort. The shelves above were full of various bottles. Mark said, "The liquor store is now open. Girls, what would you like?" In the end the girls had emptied half of the Absolut case and filled it with an assortment of other bottles. One of the girls offered to carry the flashlight, but Mark said, "We can't shine it outside. You never know who is watching. I'd hate to have somebody try and steal it from us."

When they walked through the door carrying the case, Mark held the big box high above his head and yelled, "Who's your daddy?" All the girls cheered, and the energy in the room increased several notches. Mark cruised around the room, talking to various girls, cracking a few jokes, and checking out various prospects for later. He spotted Alexa waiting in line to use the bathroom and casually worked his way over to her. He leaned against the wall and whispered in her ear. "So, how's it going?"

"Pretty good, but you could help me out a little."

"What do you want me to do?"

"Kiss me like you did before."

"Right here?"

"Yeah. Everybody is watching us. Do it now, and it will make everybody else so jealous."

"If you want them to be jealous, you kiss me."

She wrapped her hands around him and grabbed his ass, pulling him close to her, and kissed him with an open mouth and lots of tongue. Behind them the room quieted a little. Mark pulled away and slapped her on the butt as he walked away.

Several hours later Mark was in the kitchen, talking to the little redhead with a pixie cut. She was weaving a little as she talked to him, and he noticed she was slurring a few of her words. He said, "Hang on. I'll get you something to make you feel a little better." She tried to protest, telling him she didn't need any more to drink, but he insisted. He went to the counter and, with his back to her, opened a can of Red Bull. He poured half the can into another girl's drink and then quickly refilled it with vodka. He brought it to her and said, "Here. This is just a little caffeine and some vitamin B. You'll start feeling better in no time."

Alexa spotted Mark across the room talking to a petite redhead. She didn't know the girl, but she had seen her around a few times. She made her way across the room and pulled him away from the pixie for a moment. She whispered in his ear, "It's all set. If you have a hot shower, we're gonna make it a very hot shower."

"Cool. I'm outta here in a couple of minutes. Meet me at my place as soon as you can."

When Alexa walked away, Mark turned back to the little redhead, "So, you still want to party?"

She nodded.

"Slam that drink and meet me outside like I told you."

Mark made his way around the room, telling everybody he had a great time, but it was time for him to go. He thanked

panties near her hips. He slid them out from underneath her and stepped back to admire his new toy. Very nice. He rolled her over onto her stomach to get a good view of her ass when he heard a knock at the door.

He turned off the flashlight and ran downstairs, grabbing the lantern from the kitchen. He quickly went to the front door and opened it. Alexa stood there alone. She said, "Hey. Look, I'm really sorry. I tried everything, and a couple of the girls were actually really interested. But when it came time to go, everybody bailed out on me. I hope you're not mad."

He said, "I thought you said everything was cool."

"It was! Really, it was! I talked to Brittany, she's from Thermopolis, and she's bi. She was like totally into it, but when I told her I was heading over here, she said she had too much to drink and was feeling sick."

Mark stood to the side, letting her in the house. He closed the door behind her.

She said, "Don't be mad, okay?"

"I'm not mad. I'm just disappointed. You told me you had everything worked out."

"Like I said, it was. What can I do to make it up to you?"

"We'll figure out a few things. C'mon upstairs."

She followed him through the living room toward the stairs and said, "Okay, so, like I'm really nervous. I've never done anything like this before."

He stopped on the first stair. "You've never done anything like what before?"

"Like this. I mean, I've had sex a couple of times before with my old boyfriend, but I just met you today. I've never done anything like this."

He started heading upstairs again. "This is going to be fun. Trust me."

He led her to the bathroom and set the lantern on the counter next of the sink. He put the lid of the toilet down and sat down.

Alexa started laughing.

"What?"

"You can't sit there."

"Why not?"

"It totally looks like you're taking a dump."

"It's just a place to sit."

"Well, can you sit on the floor or something? That would be better."

"Okay, fine." Mark moved past her and sat on the floor near the door. "Is that better?"

"Yeah, but aren't you going to close the door?"

"Why would I close the door?"

"I can't get undressed with the bathroom door open. Just do it, okay?"

"Jesus. Whatever." He moved aside and closed the door. "There. Is that better?"

"Yeah, that's awesome. Thanks." She started to lift her shirt over her head and then stopped. She giggled, "This is so weird."

"Oh for God's sake. What now?"

"It's just that this is kinda weird, you know? I've never had anybody watch me like this before."

Mark sighed and shook his head. "Okay. Pretend I'm not here. Pretend you just came home from class, and you're feeling kinda horny. You go into the bathroom to take a shower and start thinking about a guy at school and getting yourself off. Okay? Does that kind of help you figure out what to do?"

"I don't really do that."

"Just pretend. It's easy."

She pulled her shirt off over her head and then crossed her arms in front of her bra-clad breasts. She turned around, facing the shower, and unzipped her pants and let them slide down her legs and then stepped out of them. The girl had nice legs, but she wore a plain white bra and plain white panties that were larger than anything he had ever seen before. She turned back to face him with her upper arms covering her bra and her hands in front of her crotch. "Oh, I don't know about this."

Mark stood up. "Here. I'll help you." He reached behind her and unfastened her bra. He pulled it over her shoulders while she kept her arms crossed in front of her. Then he knelt

down and pulled her panties down her legs. He was surprised when he looked up. "What the hell? You don't shave?"

"No. I mean, I know most other girls do. I see them in the locker room and stuff, but I never saw a reason why."

"Because it's a lot sexier. That's why. Besides, hair belongs on guys, not on girls."

"I'm sorry. You don't like the way I look." She started to get choked up. "I'm sorry."

"Wait, wait. Come here a minute." Mark moved back to the toilet and sat on the lid. "Come here."

She moved hesitantly toward him.

"Let me see your titties."

She slowly pulled her hands away. Mark smiled. "These are awesome. Do you know how nice your boobs are?"

"One of the girls on my team told me that she wished she had boobs like mine. I guess she liked them."

"They're awesome. Trust me." He played with them a little until she smiled. "Okay, now turn around. I want to see your ass."

Her arms moved back together covering her breasts and her crotch. She said, "I don't know."

"Sure you do. Turn around." He made a little twirling gesture with his finger. She turned around slowly. "That's a great ass. Damn girl! You got it goin' on. Bend over a little." She did, and Mark finally felt himself starting to get hard. He stood up and ran his hand over her backside. It felt good. He pulled his shirt off over his head and quickly took his pants and socks off.

She said, "What are you doing?"

"Turn around and look."

She did and jumped back in surprise. "Oh my God! You're naked. I mean, I thought I was going to take a shower."

"You will. You definitely will before I go anywhere near that bush of yours, but first you're going to give me a little taste."

She looked like a deer in the headlights. "I'm sorry. I don't know what that means."

Mark sat down on the toilet lid and motioned with a finger for her to come to him. She kept one arm across her boobs and the other over her crotch as she moved slowly.

He said, "Kneel down."

She did, but slowly and carefully.

He pointed at his penis and said, "Okay, have at it."

"What?"

"You know. Blow me a little."

"I'm not sure what that means."

"What?" He sat up straight. "Don't tell me you've never given anyone a blowjob before?"

She shook her head. "No."

"It's easy. All you gotta do is start sucking my cock. I'll help you."

"You want me to put it...in my mouth?"

"Yeah. It's great. You'll love it."

"Seriously?"

"Yeah. Come on. It won't wait all night."

"I don't know about this."

"Sure you do." He put a hand behind her head and pulled her toward him. At first she kissed the end of it and then opened her mouth. He pulled her a little harder. "There you go. Just like that."

She looked up at him and said, "Am I supposed to suck it or blow it?"

"You just suck it. *Blowjob* is a figure of speech."

She started again very slowly. He could feel the warmth and wetness of her mouth on him. He said, "There you go. That's it. Now a little faster and a little deeper. There, just like that." He looked down to see the back of her head bobbing up and down slowly over his lap. Finally, they were getting somewhere.

He let her continue that way for another minute or two. She was trying, but it was still very superficial. "Now go a little faster and a lot deeper." As she started to move down on him, he pulled her head toward him and thrust upward with his pelvis. He moved into her mouth fast and hard. The end of his penis struck the back of her throat, and she started to gag and reflexively bit down on him. Both her top teeth and the bottom sank into the soft flesh of his penis. He pulled away quickly, scraping his cock against her teeth. "Ouch! Jesus Christ! What

the fuck are you doing?" He pushed her away hard, and she fell over on the bathroom floor. He looked down and could see a little blood. "You fucking cunt! What the hell did you do that for?"

She started crying. "I don't know. I couldn't help it. I'm sorry." She curled into a fetal position on the floor.

"You don't fucking bite it! Goddammit that hurt! What are you, some kind of retard or something?"

"I'm so sorry. I told you I've never done anything like this before."

Mark grabbed a washcloth from a rail behind the toilet and ran it under the cold water. He wrapped it around his penis, hoping that it would help with the pain. He looked at her lying on the floor crying. "You know what? I've had enough. Get the fuck out of here."

"But I'm so sorry. I didn't know."

"Yeah, I know. You're fucking stupid." He kicked her with the side of his foot. "Get the fuck out of here!"

She was sobbing and holding her side where he had kicked her, but she started to move slowly.

"Faster! Get your shit and get the fuck out of my house. I oughta beat the fuck out of you, you stupid fucking cunt!"

She cowered but moved as fast as she could. She gathered up most of her clothes and started to put them on, but Mark yelled. "I said get the fuck out. *Now!*" She held her clothes up to her and ran out the bathroom door. He thought about following her downstairs, but he hurt too much. He unwrapped his penis and looked at it. It was flaccid and soft. Right in the middle of the shaft, it was swollen, and he could see little teeth marks.

He rinsed out the washcloth and ran it under cold water again. He wrapped himself up and sat in the bathroom for a while. Of all the girls he could have picked out of that party, he had to get the one who didn't have a fucking clue. Awesome.

He sat for a while, and it occurred to him that the little redhead was still in the bedroom. He might be able to salvage the night after all.

A minute later he was standing in the shower with the hot water pouring all over him. He washed everything off and then did it all again. It was as though the smell was stuck in his nose. He couldn't get rid of it. When he got out and dried off, he briefly thought about cleaning up the girl in the bedroom and then fucking her good and hard, but as soon as he opened the door, the smell drifted back to him, and he forgot the idea.

As he lay in the bed of the smaller second bedroom, he thought about the day. He couldn't imagine how any day could be any worse. He had lost his girlfriend, got his dick bit, and got shit on. Tomorrow had to be better. He would have a little talk with Megan, and then everything would be all right.

# 82.

Jack stirred quickly as he added water to the scrambled egg powder. Anything less than top speed, and he was doomed to little chunks in his eggs; he could do without them. Despite his efforts he knew these wouldn't be the best scrambled eggs in the world, but they were far from the worst. On the stove behind him, a percolator began to burble.

He had awoken early and couldn't get back to sleep. Instead of tossing and turning and waking Nicole, he decided to get up and get ready for the day ahead. He had already been to the barn and fed the horses they were going to take to Sheridan. He had also briefly checked the things in the back of the wagon again, making sure he hadn't forgotten anything.

As he sat down to a plate of eggs and coffee, he heard footsteps on the stairs from the basement. Ryan stepped into the kitchen, looking freshly showered and shaved. Jack said, "There's eggs on the stove if you want some."

"Really? Where's Julia?"

Jack was a little confused but said, "It's early. She's probably still at home with Miguel."

"Where'd the eggs come from?"

Jack gave him a look over the top of his coffee as he got ready to defend his efforts in the kitchen.

Ryan laughed. "I'm just kidding."

"You better be, or you might end up hungry."

Ryan fixed himself a plate and some coffee and sat across from Jack. "Is it just you and me today?"

"Nicole is ridin' along with us. She wants to get a few things for a garden."

"Kind of the wrong time of year for that, isn't it?"

"It's things to get ready for next year."

"Oh. Do you want me to ride single alongside the wagon?"

"Nope. We'll drag an extra horse and throw a saddle in the back just in case."

Ryan looked skeptical, "Might not be a bad idea to have somebody able to scout ahead."

Jack thought about this for a moment. "You make a good point, but we should be okay. With a four-horse team and another one walkin' behind, we can keep the horses fresh. I'd like to be back home tonight."

"So, in other words, we're going to hustle all day."

"That's the plan."

They sat for a few minutes in silence as they ate. Jack said, "You know, I been meanin' to tell you, I think both you and Brooke are doin' a hell of a job around here. You've exceeded my expectations."

Ryan smiled. "I bet your expectations were pretty bad."

"Well, when you and I first met, I think we might have had a different view of things. You came from a life of systems. Once you figured out the system and how to make it work for you, you could get ahead. I've spent a lifetime learnin' that hard work and an honest reputation is somethin' to be proud of. Those philosophies are as different as night and day. We ain't been at this long, but it seems to me that you and I are startin' to see eye to eye. You might even be comin' around to my way of thinkin'. I can see it in the job you do."

"I still suck at a lot of things."

"Now, how in the hell do you know that? You've been doin' this for what, all of two weeks? Cut yourself some slack. You're just new is all."

"Miguel doesn't want me around the horses."

"Miguel is just tryin' to figure out what you and Brooke are good at. She's a natural with the horses. That's not good or bad—it's just the way things are. You are good with the electrical and mechanical things. That's pretty obvious. He's tryin' to get you both in your sweet spot."

"I think I get it. I am getting better with my shooting though."

"So I've heard."

"Okay, so, I've been wondering something."

"Shoot."

"Remember when we were in that parking lot at the grocery store, and you shot that guy?"

"Yep."

"How did you get to be that fast? I mean, it was like so quick I hardly saw a thing. One minute you were talking to that guy, and the next you had your gun and shot him."

"I'm not fast at all."

"Yeah you are. I saw it."

Jack put his fork on his empty plate and leaned back in the chair. "What you saw was determination and confidence."

"I don't understand."

"It's kinda like this. When I walked up there, I had a plan in my head. I wanted to talk that man away from the store, or in the very least, get him to put the shotgun down. But, I knew if he made a move—any move at all—it wasn't gonna be good, and I was gonna have to kill him. When he moved, I moved. What you saw was that I didn't hesitate. My decision was already made."

"But that doesn't make you fast."

"It does from your perspective and from the perspective of the man with the shotgun. When you're dealing with a situation that's deadly, it's life-and-death on the line. The instant that little meter in the back of your head flips from talk to shoot,

you shoot. You never hesitate; you never think twice about it; you never have a second doubt. Those few milliseconds will get you, or somebody else, killed."

"But you shot him right between the eyes. How did you do that?"

"I could do it 'cause I've done it thousands of times before. I have no idea how many times I have pulled a trigger; it's been at least a quarter-million times. Practice, practice, practice. Do it over and over, and over again, until it becomes as easy as scratchin' your ass."

"Yeah, but doesn't that waste ammo?"

"Not if you're learnin' somethin'."

"So you don't care if I just blow through a bunch of ammo?"

"Well, these days we have to be careful how much we use. It's not like we can run to the store and pick up some more. But as long as you are really practicin' and not just listenin' to the noise, I'll buy the lead."

"Do we have enough to spare?"

Jack smiled. "I'd say we're pretty well set."

"Should I bring my rifle today?"

"Do you know what you're doin' with it?"

"Yesterday morning I hit a soda bottle at a hundred yards."

"I'd say you'd better bring it."

Light in the east was beginning to stream through the large windows in the great room of the house. Jack offered to do the dishes while Ryan started his morning chores. He was standing at the sink when he heard, "Hey." He turned to see Brooke, with clean wet hair, pulling on her boots. She looked at him for a minute and said, "Are you okay?"

"Sure. Fit as a fiddle. Why do you ask?"

"'Cause I've never seen you do dishes before. I thought maybe you got confused."

"Darlin', I've been doin' dishes since I was half your age."

She smiled. "I thought they ate off of big, flat rocks back then."

She had to duck as the wet dish rag flew through the air at her.

Nicole stepped out of the hallway just in time to see the rag fly. "Don't we have a rule prohibiting the use of artillery before coffee?"

Jack said, "I'm glad you're here. Both them two have been givin' me hell all mornin'."

She smiled. "And I have no doubt you deserved it."

"All I did was make breakfast and do the dishes."

Nicole stepped next to him and put her hand to his forehead. "You don't seem feverish. Perhaps it's something more serious."

"Not you too?"

Brooke said, "That's what I thought. Maybe he had a stroke or something."

Jack said, "I'll give you a stroke."

Brooke laughed and headed out the door. Nicole said, "You were up early. I didn't even hear you get out of bed."

"I didn't want to wake you. There's coffee in the pot, and I'm makin' breakfast. I have scrambled eggs or scrambled eggs?"

"Oh my. He cooks as well. Dr. Neumann, you are an attractive man."

"Thank you, ma'am. If this is all it takes, I'll make breakfast every mornin'."

She took his hand. "Come with me. I think I've decided on something else for breakfast."

# 83.

Jack, Nicole, and Ryan sat on the bench of the wagon. In front of them, four horses stood in their harnesses impatiently waiting to leave. Jack leaned toward Miguel, "*No dejas que hacer nada peligroso los caballos. No puedo reparar hasta que yo vuelva.*"

"Yes, boss, I know. I will watch."

"I know. I'm sorry. I don't need to tell you your business."

"*No hay problema. Ella es como una hija, ¿no?*"

"Yeah. Kinda."

Jack looked behind him in the wagon. "Is everybody sure we got everything?"

They all agreed.

"All right. We're off. See you tonight—tomorrow at the latest." He snapped the reins and clucked with his mouth, and the horses set out down the drive.

After they had gone about a mile, Ryan leaned across and asked Jack, "So what were you telling Miguel?"

"I told him to keep an eye on Brooke. She's got more confidence than ability."

Nicole added, "He also said he couldn't repair anything she broke until he returned. I didn't get the last part though."

Jack said, "Miguel asked me if she was like a daughter. I hadn't thought about it, but I guess she is. Damn kids start to grow on you."

She squeezed his arm. "You are very softhearted. I love that about you."

Ryan said, "Okay, if you two are going to get all mushy, I'm gonna ride in the back."

Jack said, "Nope. No mush. We got places to go and things to do." He pushed the horses up to a trot.

The countryside flew by compared to the speed they had traveled between Cody and the ranch. As they worked their way down through the foothills, houses and small ranchettes started to appear more closely together. The destruction they had become accustomed to in Cody was becoming more apparent and more prevalent. At one point they had to stop and remove a long section of twisted irrigation pipe from the road. At another point they had to detour into the grass to pass two cars that had burned alongside one another, blocking the middle of the road.

As they drew closer to town, Jack pointed to a group of buildings ahead on the left. "That's the implement dealer. We'll spend some time there on the way home." As they passed the dealership, they noticed hundreds of green tractors and trailers and yellow pieces of heavy equipment in the lot. Some were completely destroyed, and others had been moved or flipped over during the event, but still others sat as though nothing had happened. The steel buildings were partially damaged, but behind them Ryan pointed out several steel shipping containers that appeared to be in relatively good shape. Only one lay on its side.

Farther down the road, they passed a large apartment complex that had entirely burned, leaving little but huge piles of black ruins. Only a block away, three greenhouses stood untouched. Nicole said, "It is very nice to see those greenhouses intact. I should think they will come in handy this winter."

A little farther down the road, they approached a large brick building. Jack said, "That's the hospital. Nice to see it's still standing as well. I should probably stop by on the way out of town."

Nicole asked, "Do you think they will try to recruit you as a surgeon?"

"Nah. They don't need me. They got a great bunch of docs around here. Hell, if only half of 'em made it through the flare, they'll have more'n they need. Still, it don't hurt to make sure they're okay."

They followed the same road all the way into town. The destruction and devastation here was similar to what they had seen in Cody. Burned homes, burned cars, twisted metal, and debris scattered everywhere. But, one difference was noticeable: in Sheridan, more people were visible. People were out of their homes and doing things out in the sunshine. Some were moving debris; some were carrying items toward their homes; some were simply sitting on the porch or in a lawn chair observing the happenings in front of them. Jack was pleased to see many of them wave at the wagon as they passed. It told him the mood and spirit of the town he had known for so long was intact and very much alive. He noticed several people were wearing guns, but others weren't. Obviously they felt safe enough not to need them.

Initially they turned north on Main Street and headed up toward the county jail and police department on the north end of town. As they reached the intersection of Main and West 12th, it became obvious that no one was using the police station. The once large, modern building now stood as little more than rubble and burned debris. Jack carefully turned the wagon around in the street, and they headed south.

The county buildings were a collection of yellow brick two- and three-story structures situated near the middle of town, just off Main Street. For the most part, these buildings stood intact, with slight damage. Only one was nearly leveled, with a huge, iron I-beam sticking out of the side and bent almost in half. In front of the largest building, nearly a dozen horses

stood tied to trees, railings, and a small statue. Jack pulled the wagon to a stop in the street in front of the building and set the brake. He said, "Looks like this is where all the action is."

Ryan was amazed. "Holy cow! Look at all the horses."

"Yep. It's the only way to get around now."

Nicole said, "Look at the black horse over there. It has the same mark as all of yours."

Jack looked in the direction she was pointing. "It sure does. Hang on a minute." He walked over to where the horse stood tied to a small tree and looked at it. He walked back with a confused look on his face. "I know that horse. Trouble is it shouldn't be here."

"Why is that?"

"If that's the horse I think it is, it should be in Florida, not in Sheridan."

"Do you think somebody stole it?"

"I doubt it. There's gotta be a story we ain't heard yet."

Ryan asked, "Are we all going in?"

"We can, or you can wait out here if you like. Makes no difference. Might learn somethin' inside."

Just inside the door, two men were piling computers, printers, copiers, and fax machines on a hand cart. Jack wondered if this same process was occurring all over the country. The technology that was once so common and so relied upon was now nothing more than trash. The building had a typical institutional feel, with granite floors and decor from the 1960s. They could hear the echoes of many people engaged in various conversations. They turned left down a large hallway and had to duck under a big metal pipe that hung from the ceiling. Near the end of the building, the hall widened into a large area that had once served as a waiting room. Today it had been converted into a bee hive of activity with several wooden desks arranged into little areas. At each of the desks, it appeared as though a worker was interviewing a citizen.

"Can I help you?"

Jack turned around to see a young man with a black hat similar to his own and a gold badge pinned to the front of his shirt. "Joe? How the heck are ya?"

"Jack! I'll be damned. We thought you'd a stopped by a while ago."

"Had to swing through Cody first."

"Cody? You were in Cody?"

"Yessir. All three of us were. Had a hell of a time gettin' back here."

"I bet you did. Is it as bad over there as what we've got here?"

"Sure is. We're thinkin' this was a global event. Got some ideas what happened as well. Is Deke around?"

"He's been crazy busy, as you can imagine. But, he's supposed to be back any minute. You want to wait for him?"

"If it's only a few minutes, we'll stick around. I got quite a bit to do in town today."

"I'm sure he'll want to talk to you. As soon as I see him, I'll let him know you're here. You can wait over there if you'd like."

"Thanks."

Jack followed Nicole toward an area where roughly twenty wooden chairs were arranged in rows. Most of the seats were already taken, and the people who sat in them seemed to come from a wide section of the population. They found three together in a middle row and sat down. Jack pointed at the seats and said, "Jury chairs. Must a pulled 'em out of the courtrooms. I think they've been around since they founded the county."

Ryan said, "They're not very comfortable."

"They're not supposed to be. Keeps the jurors awake."

In front of them, a young couple sat next to each other. She had pretty, auburn hair just past her shoulders and wore a felt-lined denim jacket. She held in her lap a hat almost exactly like Nicole's. The young man next to her wore a black North Face jacket and had short, brown hair and a nice face. She leaned slightly toward him and said, "Do you have any gum or anything?"

He shook his head and said, "No. Sorry. I can try and find some for you later."

Nicole leaned forward. "Sorry to eavesdrop. I believe I have a mint if you would like?"

The girl turned to face Nicole. She smiled warmly. "That would be awesome."

Nicole pulled a small tin of Altoids from her pocket and handed them to her. When she had taken one, she handed the tin back and said, "Thank you so much. That was really very nice of you."

"You are very welcome."

Jack leaned toward her and said, "So that's your secret. I couldn't figure how you're toothpaste could work all day."

She gave him a wink and said, "I have lots of secrets."

He was about to respond when they heard a deep voice rise above the others in the hallway, "Goddammit! I can only do one thing at a time. You all need to sort the fly shit from the pepper and bring me the important things, otherwise we won't get a damn thing done."

Jack whispered to Nicole, "That'd be Deke."

A minute later they heard, "This is exactly what I'm talkin' about. You should have told me he was here first. You boys handle the bullshit and point me to the bull."

Jack smiled.

Joe, the deputy Jack had talked to earlier, walked quickly to where the three of them sat. He motioned with his hand and said, "Come with me. The sheriff will see you now."

They followed him into an office at the end of the hall. When they walked through the door, a tall, black-haired man with a thick mustache and a neat uniform was reading from a notebook near his desk. He looked up and said, "Jack Neumann, you old son of a bitch. How the hell are ya?"

"I'm not bad, all things considered. You look busy. We won't take much of your time."

"Bullshit. Sit down; let's talk awhile. I could use a few minutes of sanity." He shook his head. "It's been bat-shit crazy

around here. Let's just say that modern law enforcement does not adapt to change well. Who is this with you?"

Jack held out a hand toward Ryan. "This here is Ryan Miller. He's from Missouri." Deke offered his hand, and Ryan shook it. "He found himself stuck outside of Yellowstone. We've been workin' together since the disaster, and now he's one of my hands at the ranch. He's a good man to have around." Jack put an arm around Nicole. "And this is Nicole Meredith. She's with me."

Deke stood without moving for a moment, in utter shock. "You gotta be shittin' me. Sorry 'bout my language, ma'am." He shook her hand and then turned it to look at her wrist. "Jack, you must'a made a deal with the devil, 'cause you aren't good-lookin' enough or smart enough to be with a lady like this, and I don't see no rope burns on her arms." He laughed a little at his own joke.

Jack said, "Ain't that the truth. I ask myself the same thing damn near every day."

"Sit down, sit down." He motioned to a round table in the corner of his office. "Joe said you were in Cody. Is that true?"

"Just west of there when everything hit."

Jack spent the next ten minutes telling the story of meeting Ryan and Nicole and their adventure trying to get home. When he finished, Deke said, "That's amazing. I'm sure glad you're back in one piece. It's been a crazy couple of weeks around here. We still haven't heard much of anything from anywhere else. No contact from the state or the feds. We've just had to make it up as we go. Hell, we still don't even know what happened."

Jack said, "We've got some ideas on that. I think Ryan has it all worked out." He turned to Ryan. "Tell him what you know."

Ryan spent the next few minutes explaining a solar flare and coronal mass ejection to the sheriff. He explained concepts of electromagnetic waves and the relationship of electricity and magnetism and explained how an irregular or non-polarized field could create the damage they'd seen all over northern Wyoming.

The sheriff listened intently and said, "Well, I understood about half what you just said, but I think I got the big parts. Maybe that would explain this." He set a small compass in the middle of the table. The little needle moved and then settled, pointing toward the window behind them. "Ain't that just the damndest thing you ever saw?"

Ryan looked at him questioningly.

The sheriff pointed to the wall behind him and said, "North is that way."

"Oh. Wow. Holy shit! That means the entire magnetic field of the earth has shifted."

Jack shook his head. "That can't be good."

Ryan said, "I'm not sure what it might mean. I'm only guessing, but it might mean more earthquakes and things like that, or it might mean nothing more than learning to use a compass differently." He shrugged his shoulders. "I'm no expert on any of this stuff."

Jack said, "Tell him what you figured out yesterday."

Ryan got a big smile on his face as he picked up the leather bag he had set on the floor next to him. "I was working in the barn with Miguel. He had a bunch of tools in an old, steel ammo can. Anyway, I was looking for a wrench when I found this." He pulled out a small flashlight and turned it on.

The sheriff leaned back in his chair. "Oh my! I don't suppose you want to sell that."

Jack held out his hand to Ryan, and the young man handed him the light. Jack handed it to Deke. "It's yours. You need it more'n we do."

The sheriff took the light and turned it on and off several times. "You have no idea how important this might be. Thank you."

Ryan said, "That's not all. I also found this." He pulled out the multimeter and turned it on. The LCD screen lit up with a blue-green light as the small device ran through a self-test.

"Ain't that just about the damnedest thing. Now, why in the hell do these things work when everything else has gone to hell?"

Ryan explained the concept of a Faraday cage.

Jack said, "I got to thinkin' about it after he explained it to me. Then I started to wonder if a bigger steel box might have the same protective effect. That's when it occurred to me that a shipping container is nothin' more'n a big steel box. We're gonna stop by Sheridan County Implement on the way out of town. They keep parts in those containers out back. If we find the right stuff, we might get a tractor running again, but I thought we'd better run this plan past you first."

The sheriff was leaning back in his chair, trying to take everything in. He said, "Hang on a minute." He stood and walked to the door. He opened it and said to somebody outside, "Go find Charley and tell him to get his ass in here." When he came back to the table, he said, "Charley owns half of that dealership. He's also one of the few remaining county commissioners. I'm sure we'll work out a deal you can't refuse. In fact, I was already thinking about working out some kind of a deal with you."

Jack said, "I'm listenin'."

"We got two trains full of grain all twisted up in the yard on the north end of town. I have a bunch of guys out there now trying to get the bagged up rice, corn, beans, and a bunch of other stuff put up and out of the weather for the people left in town. But, I got a bunch of loose stuff in hoppers we'll never be able to use. I'd be willing to work out a deal to get you that grain for horses and cattle. I need the horses to get around, and we're gonna need the cattle to feed these people."

Jack said, "Maybe we could set up a feedlot outside of town, and then we'll push the cattle to you. Probably be easier."

"Probably would."

"I need to keep enough stock for seed."

The sheriff nodded. "I completely understand. I don't see an end to this anytime soon."

The door opened, and a short, heavyset man with gray hair and a big nose came in. "Joe said you wanted to see me."

"Charley, you know Jack Neumann, don't you?"

"Sure. We've met once or twice. Nice to see you, Jack."

"You too, Charley."

Deke had Ryan show the man the multimeter and explain a Faraday Cage. When he finished, Deke said, "Ryan and Jack thought you might have some electrical parts in those containers behind your buildings out at the dealership. They'd like to get a tractor or two running again and would like to work out a deal for the parts. We were just talking about a deal to get cattle and horses for the town."

Jack added, "We were talkin' about startin' a feedlot. I could bring in yearlings, and you guys could finish 'em with the grain you have. If you have half a train full of grain, you could finish a hell of a lot of cattle."

Charley said, "Where you thinkin' about puttin' this feedlot?"

Deke said, "Don't you have a few acres east of here?"

"I do. There's half a section just outside of town."

Deke said, "I'd say you two are partners in this thing."

Charley said, "I'm in."

Jack said, "Yep. Works for me. But what about you, Deke?"

"Wouldn't be right. If I commandeer the grain for the town, I can't have an interest in it. I'll trade you two the grain for the cattle and horses we'll need."

The three men stood and shook hands. Charley said, "Jack, take whatever you need from the dealership. Don't be afraid to take a part or any of the equipment sitting out front if you need it. I don't see a big call for equipment sales any time soon."

Jack said, "Thanks. I think this will help us a bunch."

Deke said, "Son, do you think this Faraday thing works with all shipping containers?"

Ryan said, "I'm not sure. I think the container needs to be sealed, and they might have to be in contact with the ground, but I'm only guessing. Why?"

"'Cause I got a mile and a half of shipping containers stretched out toward Montana along the north end of town. That was the third train caught up in the disaster. I don't suppose you want a job? I could use somebody who knows a few things about electricity."

Ryan looked shocked. He looked quickly at Jack and then back to the sheriff. "Ah, wow. I don't know." He looked confused and then all at once straightened. He said, "I'd be happy to help, but I already made a commitment. I can't go back on that."

Jack smiled a little. "We'll talk about it."

# 84.

Megan had awoken with the sun, but she didn't feel like getting up. She wondered how long it would take her to die if she stayed in the tent and never left.

Yesterday morning had started out awful. Mark had argued with TJ and then left. Splitting up the things they shared together now seemed like it happened in a fog. She remembered throwing the candle at him and telling him she hated him. She did too. He had promised not to break her heart, and that was exactly what he did. She didn't know what happened. Things had been going so well for them. She was really falling for him, and it was easy too. He was a good guy, and the sex was incredible. Something must have happened back in Buffalo, because that was when everything changed.

But she already knew something happened in Buffalo, didn't she? He had given her the gun, and something about him was different. He didn't want her to wear the gun in public until they left town, and he had pushed for them to leave quickly. She had a suspicion that Mark had taken the guns, probably using force. She had even wondered if he had killed somebody for them. She recalled the single drop of dark blood on the toe of his boot, and a feeling of dread and regret blossomed in her

stomach. If she was honest, she probably helped to foster the idea of using force, but she had never told him to kill somebody. She would never want that. The sad truth was that the pretty gun was great, but it's not what she wanted. She merely wanted them to be safe. She wanted them to get ahead, and, okay, maybe sometimes that meant bending the rules a little, but not like this. She never wanted this.

After Mark had left, she spent the next few hours in her tent. She cried until there were no more tears left in her to cry. In the afternoon she had sat by the fire with TJ. He had tried to console her. He told her that it wasn't her fault, and that the way Mark had been behaving, it was better he was gone. He was going to get them in trouble. Later in the afternoon, he had made dinner and taken care of the horses. He had cleaned up the camp a little and then, without warning, went out in the grass and found the bottle of tequila Mark had thrown the night before. After dinner, he had offered to share a drink with her and had told her funny stories about his family, about growing up as a town kid but working on a nearby ranch, about his time in the army, and about old girlfriends he'd had. At several times he had even made her laugh. Later that night they sat by the fire and talked. Talking to him was so easy. Just before she went to bed, he kissed her. It wasn't a crazy passionate kiss, rather it was a nice, kinda serious kiss. She liked it.

Now, lying in the tent, she hated herself. Mark had only been gone a day, and she had already kissed the guy who was the reason, or at least one of the reasons, he had left. What did that make her? Was she some kind of whore? Was she the kind of girl who had to have a man around? She didn't think so. She had spent a long time in New York without a boyfriend, and that had been just fine. But now times were different. Times were a lot more dangerous than they were a couple of weeks ago. A girl couldn't just be out in the world without knowing she was going to be safe. There were crazy guys out there.

Then again, maybe it was just a friendly kiss. Maybe that's all it was: no big deal, no promises, no commitments. No, she knew better. She had invited the kiss, and if he would have

made any effort to turn up the heat, she would have gone along with it. If he had used his tongue or put a hand on her, she would have had sex with him. She liked him—a lot.

She needed to have a plan. What if Mark came back? What would she say to him? What would she say to TJ? Who would she choose?

Mark was fun. He was passionate, and he did seem to care for her. That's why he went to the pharmacy for her and took care of her and even why he got the guns. But Mark was also moody. Sometimes when he suggested things, he didn't really think them all the way through. Some of his suggestions were even a little dangerous.

TJ, on the other hand, was smart, funny, and reliable. He had come from a good middle-class home and knew how to work. His experience in the army was obviously a plus in times like these. He didn't have the body Mark had. That was obvious, but how important was it? Once she had seen Mark naked a couple of times, she didn't really think about his body much. TJ had a plan to provide a safe future. That was huge. It was a clear and definite plan for now and in the future, not some vague idea of a dream farm away from everyone else.

Her decision was obvious. If Mark came back, she would have to tell him that it was over. She tried to picture the conversation in her mind. It was one thing if Mark made the decision to leave, but it might be entirely different if she told him she was done. He might not take that too well. She remembered how mad he got yesterday. In fact, she had wondered if he might pull his gun on TJ. She thought that if the argument had gotten any more heated or if it had been anybody other than TJ, Mark would have tried something. She needed to be done with him for good.

When she crawled out of the tent, TJ was sitting by the fire. A pot of something that used to be dehydrated was sitting on a rock, keeping warm for her. "Hi."

He said, "Hey there. Did you sleep okay?"

"Yeah, I did."

He smiled at her. His smile was nice. He wasn't a totally hot guy, but he wasn't bad looking either. He had nice eyes. But when he smiled at her, there was something deep in that smile. Something warm and comfortable. Something confident. Something that said, "I have everything under control." She liked that.

He said, "That's good. You needed the rest."

"What time is it?"

He looked at his watch. "It's almost ten thirty."

"Oh wow. Sorry. I know you want to get going. I can be ready in no time."

"Don't worry about it. It's not like we have anything else to do. Sit down and have some breakfast."

She smiled at him. "Thanks." I could get used to this, she thought.

After breakfast she started packing up her things. Several times she ran across something that reminded her of Mark, and it made her sad; but she pressed on, trying to forget him as best she could. When she looked in her bag for the toothpaste, she remembered that she had given it to Mark. She didn't know why they didn't have more than one tube, but now she was stuck. She was about to ask TJ if she could borrow his but noticed that all of his stuff was already packed. She brushed her teeth with just water. It wasn't great, but it would do for now. She just had to remember to try and find some toothpaste later.

When she had brought the horses back to camp, she found that TJ had already rolled up her tent. "You didn't have to do that."

"I know, but it's not like I have a lot of other pressing things at the moment. It's no problem."

"Well, thanks. That was nice."

The two of them packed the mule and saddled the horses. As they rode away, Megan looked back at the little camp beside the creek—for two reasons: she didn't ever want to be as cold and mean as Mark had been, and she wanted to remember this place.

They rode up through the middle of town. The destruction was similar to what they had seen in Buffalo. Several burned-out cars were littered throughout town, and several buildings were burned or damaged. She noticed there were no bodies lying around. Somebody had removed them. Maybe somebody was trying to get things in order around here.

TJ led them to an area downtown, just to the east of Main Street. In front of a large, yellow brick building they noticed seven or eight horses tied to trees in the lawn. Several men were hauling computers and office machines out the front door on a small cart. TJ said, "Looks like this is where all the action is. Let's go check things out."

As they walked inside, Megan thought the building looked a little dated. It had the typical government look she really didn't care for, but thought it was probably functional. Near the end of a large hallway, a deputy asked if they needed help. TJ said, "We're new in town. We'd like to talk to somebody about helping out if we can. We're also going to need a place to stay if possible." The deputy took down their names and told them to have a seat in a waiting area. He assured them that the town could use all the help it could get, and somebody would be right with them.

As they sat together in old, wooden chairs, Megan noticed two men and a woman about her own age come down the hallway. They stopped and spoke to the same deputy. One man looked middle-aged and was clearly familiar with the deputy. The younger man, probably college-aged, kept looking to the older man. Maybe he was the guy's son. The woman was gorgeous. She had dark hair that she had tucked up under an off-white hat that was similar to her own. She noticed the woman slip an arm around the arm of the older man. Probably a stuck-up trophy wife, she thought.

As they sat and waited, the three people she had noticed walked over and sat behind them. Megan started wondering what kind of job they would get. She hoped it wouldn't involve cleaning up dead bodies. She didn't think she could do that. She wouldn't mind working at one of the desks, but she would

rather be outside someplace, at least while it was nice. In a male-dominated culture like the West, she would probably end up at a desk, taking names and addresses or asking what people needed. It occurred to her that she hadn't used toothpaste, and she began to wonder what her breath was like. She leaned over and asked TJ if he had any gum.

It turned out that the woman she thought was a stuck-up trophy wife wasn't stuck-up at all. In fact she was nice. She had a pretty accent that Megan thought was probably English. When the people seated behind them got called up to talk to the loud guy, she watched the woman walk by and happened to notice the gun in her holster. It looked familiar.

# 85.

Deke opened the door to the office, and as they walked out into the lobby area, he asked Jack, "You headed over to the dealership now?"

"Nah. We got a couple of things to do in town. I need to run over to Big R and see if there's any barbed wire that's still useable. I got miles of fence down. We thought we'd swing by the dealership on the way home."

"Sounds reasonable. Any idea when you're gonna be back in town?"

"Not right off. We have so much work we'll be lucky to get back here in a couple of weeks. By the way, you don't happen to know of anybody lookin' for work and a place to stay?"

Deke said, "Not right off. I'm taking all the help I can get myself."

From behind Jack, a young man said, "Excuse me, sir. Did you say you're looking for help?"

Jack turned around to see the young couple who had been seated in front of them. "I sure did."

"Can I ask what kind of help you need and what you're offering?"

Deke said, "That's great. Now you're gonna steal my help."

Jack winked at Deke and then said to the young man, "I have a ranch just west of Sheridan. I think it's a nice place."

Behind him Ryan mouthed the words *very nice* to the couple.

Jack continued, "We run cattle and horses. Honestly, I need help with just about everything. If you can stay on top of a horse and aren't afraid of a little work or gettin' dirty, I can keep you warm and fed. That I can promise you."

The young lady asked, "What is the pay?"

Jack said, "What do you need?"

The young man thought for a moment and said, "We'd like to have a place of our own someday. Maybe a little land to go with it."

"We might be able to work somethin' out. If you two want to come out and take a look, maybe talk a little more, you can meet us at the implement dealer just outside of town on West 5th later this afternoon. We'll probably be there for a couple of hours. It's twenty miles from there to the ranch. If you come on out, I'll buy dinner and put you up for the night. You can decide if you want to stay or ride back to town."

The young man stuck out his hand. "I'm Travis Lee, people call me TJ, and this is Megan Bennett. We'll see you later."

"I'm Jack and this is Nicole and Ryan. That sounds good. We'll see you at the dealership."

Jack was explaining what a feedlot was to Nicole and Ryan as they headed for the door. Just as they were about to step outside, Jack saw a tall man with gray hair wearing a blue sweater, talking to one of the deputies. He stepped over. When their conversation finished, he said, "Peter?"

The man turned around. Surprised, he said, "Jack Neumann. Well, I'll be. How are you?"

"I'm not bad. Not bad at all." He introduced Nicole and Ryan and said, "What are you doing up in Sheridan?"

"I came up here to talk to the sheriff. We had a little trouble back home."

"That can't be good."

"No. No it's not. I hate to be the one to tell you this, because I know you two were good friends, but somebody killed Del."

"What? That can't be. Not Del."

"It's true. Shot him in the head. We've got a pretty good idea who it was, and I have a suspicion he's headed up this way. That's why I wanted to talk to the sheriff. Lots of people back home are pretty upset about this. I'd like to bring him back."

"You fixin' to hang him?"

"If he did it, we will."

Jack shook his head. "I thought I recognized Night out there by the tree. Did you bring him up?"

"Yeah. I don't have a horse, and I'm not the best rider, so the guys at Del's let me borrow him to make the trip."

"I thought Del was supposed to be in Florida this time of year."

"He was, but he got busy with labor talks at the mine. They were trying to work out a plan to prevent laying off half the employees."

Jack shook his head again, "I can't believe somebody would shoot Del. That just don't make sense. Any idea why?"

"Not really. There were a couple of guns missing from the display cases behind his desk, but there were two others sitting right out in the open on the top of the desk. The whole thing just doesn't make any sense."

"It's a damn shame is what it is."

"Yes, it is. I'd like to stand here and catch up with you, but I need to get with the sheriff and get rolling on this thing."

"Yes, you do. I hope you catch that son of a bitch."

"So do I, Jack. So do I."


As they turned to go out the door, Jack happened to look back over his shoulder. TJ had an arm around Megan near the wall, and she looked pale. He stepped over to them and asked, "Are you okay, ma'am?"

TJ said, "She thought she saw her mother over there. Kind of freaked her out."

Jack recalled the months after Jenni had died. There were several times when he thought he had seen her and knew what the young woman must be feeling. "I understand. I'm sorry."

# 86.

Megan was sick of the emotional rollercoaster. For the last two weeks, everything had been up and down, good and bad, wonderful, then terrible. She just wanted it all to end. Life had to be somewhat normal again sometime.

They had just finished talking to the guy with the ranch a few minutes ago. He had offered both of them a job, and it sounded good. Really good. If what he was saying was true, they would have a place to stay, they wouldn't have to worry about food, and they might have a chance to build something. If they didn't like it, they could find something different or just move on. This was a great opportunity, and Megan was excited. This was a chance to move on and away from Mark.

They had been following the rancher and his friends toward the door when Megan spotted the guy from the Occidental. He was the one who had scared the hell out of Mark. His back was turned, and she wouldn't have noticed him if he hadn't been wearing the same clothes he had on the other night. She grabbed TJ's hand and pulled him to the side of the hallway and behind a post. TJ had given her a questioning look, and she whispered to him, "It's the guy from the hotel."

From where they stood, she could hear parts of the conversation quite clearly. Mark had murdered somebody, and they wanted to take him back to Buffalo and hang him. She could make out that the guy who had been killed was shot, and she heard that two guns were missing from display cases. She thought about the gun that now rested in the holster alongside her hip. It was no ordinary 1911. The embellishment and the finish were incredible, and the mechanicals were more smoother and more precise than anything she had ever seen before. This gun was a work of art. This was a gun that belonged in a display case. She remembered Mark giving it to her. He had called it a Diamond Grade and presented it to her like it was a ring. If fact, she had hoped he was going to give her a ring.

She felt lightheaded. This was too much. She felt TJ's arm around her back. Her legs felt weak and shaky, and she wanted to sit down. She knew the rancher came back and asked something. Maybe it was to see if she was okay. TJ had told him something, but her mind couldn't focus. After the rancher left, TJ had moved around to the front of her. He was speaking to her, but she couldn't make out the words. A picture of Mark in Buffalo with a rope around his neck overwhelmed her thoughts. It was too much. This was all too much.

A new sensation began to invade her thoughts. This was warm, wet, and wonderful. It was comforting and protective. All at once, she realized TJ was kissing her. It was more than the kiss they had shared the other night. This was deep and passionate. She felt his tongue invade her mouth, and she welcomed it. She wrapped her arms around him and pulled him close to her. The kiss stopped, but her embrace didn't. She squeezed him as tightly as she could and buried her face into his neck. She smelled the scent of his skin and the feel of the stubble on his neck and cheek. She wanted to be close to him. She wanted him to make this all better.

The tears came, but this time they didn't last very long. Megan held on to TJ and managed to get ahold of herself fairly quickly. He helped her walk outside and over to where the

horses stood tied. As she started to feel a little better, she asked, "Did you hear that in there?"

"Yeah. It was Mark they were talking about, wasn't it?"

"Yeah, it was. I didn't know any of that. I swear."

"I kinda figured that based on the way you reacted."

She smiled. "That's a nice way to say 'freaked out.'"

"You didn't freak out. You were just a little overwhelmed is all."

"I totally freaked out, but that's nice to say. Why did you kiss me?"

"You weren't listening to me, and I really didn't want to slap you. I thought it might get your attention."

"It did, but what would you have done if it didn't?"

"I already thought about that. I was going to bite your lip."

She gave him a little smile. "So you like biting, huh?"

He smiled broadly but didn't answer her question. Instead he asked, "Where do you think Mark went?"

"I have no idea. He could have gone anywhere. He was always talking about going west. He might have left town."

"The reason I'm wondering is because he's obviously dangerous. Do you think he could try and do something to you or me?"

Megan thought about this for a minute and realized she didn't know Mark as well as she thought she had. "I don't know. He had a girlfriend before he met me. He didn't talk about her much at all. He might just move on and try to get away from everything. I think that's more his style."

"Okay. We'll still want to keep an eye out for him just in case, but you're probably right, he probably left town."

# 87.

Jack was quiet as they walked out to the wagon and got ready to leave. Nicole used a soft voice and asked, "The man who was killed, was he a friend of yours?"

"Yeah, he was. He bought a horse from me, and we got to know each other. He and I flew out to a charity auction where we both bought a couple of guns. You're wearin' one of 'em right now. If I recall, I think the proceeds went to fight breast cancer. How's that for ironic? He was a hell of a guy. It's a damn shame that he'd make it through the worst disaster in history, and then some stupid son of a bitch comes along and kills him for no more than a couple of guns. Makes me sick."

They climbed up in the wagon, and Jack said to Ryan, "You're drivin'. Head back to Main and then turn south. I'll tell you where we're headed."

Nicole said, "I'm so sorry for your loss."

As Ryan got the horses moving, Jack said, "It's not my loss. Oh, sure, I'll miss havin' him around, but the real loss is the people in Buffalo. Del was a self-made multi-millionaire. He bought a coal mine that was bankrupt and turned it around. Then he used that money to fund other ventures. As he got older, he started doin' a lot of philanthropy, but he kept most of it local.

He wanted the people of Gillette and Buffalo to benefit from the mine where they worked. He funded a lot of scholarships and educational things, but he also invested in damn near every new business idea that came around, as long as it was local. He was just exactly the kind of man you want to have around to teach the next generation: show 'em what a man is supposed to look like. That's how the world gets to be a better place."

Nicole said, "In other words, give a man a fish, he'll eat for a day, teach a man to fish, he'll eat for a lifetime."

"That's Del in a nutshell."

"I have to say, I was rather impressed with the sheriff when he said he shouldn't be part of this new feedlot venture. I should think most men would be happy to get in on the ground floor of something like that."

"Remember when we were talkin' about million dollar deals on nothin' more than a man's handshake?"

"Yes, I do."

"That's why I came out here. Honor, respect, reputation, honesty—those words mean somethin' to a lot of people around here. I prefer it that way."

"You know, I think I do too."

Ryan said, "I've been thinking. You said you would trade cattle and horses for grain and some of the parts we are going to get today, but nobody said how many. You know, like what if the sheriff comes back to you and says he wants five hundred horses, or that guy says the parts we take are worth a thousand cows, and he wants the cows or the parts back."

"They won't. That's not reasonable. We'll work out details later, but everybody will be reasonable about it."

"So, who says what's reasonable?"

"We all do. We're tryin' to help each other out and help the town in the process. It's all about where you're startin' from. If your idea is to make a big profit off the misfortune or lack of knowledge of others, it won't work. Never does. People are always smarter than what you think they are. If you start somethin' where everybody benefits and everybody wins, you can't hardly go wrong because everybody wants you to succeed."

Ryan was surprised. "No kidding? It seems so simple."

"It is so simple."

"So why did we have all the economic problems that we did?"

"That's a lot more complex, but in the end it was about ma-kin' more than what was reasonable and takin' without givin' back." Jack pointed at a spot just ahead in the street. "Pull the horses up here. I got a little errand to run."

Ryan pulled the horses to a stop. Jack said to him, "Grab that little meter of yours. Nicole, darlin', would you mind wait-in' here for a minute? We won't be long."

"Certainly."

"That shotgun is under the seat if you need it."

"I'm sure I'll be just fine. Hurry back."

Jack turned to Ryan, "Come on. Follow me." He walked down the sidewalk past several stores and then turned right to enter a small shop with boards covering the door and windows. A hand-painted flip sign read Come on in, We're Open!

They walked into the store, and Jack kept walking, heading for the back of the building. As he passed a young lady sitting on a stool near the counter, he said, "Sorry, Stef. We're just passin' through. I need to use your place for camouflage if you don't mind."

She gave him a surprised look and said, "Hi, Jack. It's nice to see you too. I don't mind, but you could at least say hi if you're comin' back through."

"I will," he said, as they headed out the back door.

Ryan said, "Wait. What are we doin?"

Jack didn't slow down at all. Instead he said, "Follow and find out." He turned right again and headed back down the street, passed several stores, and finally walked into a small shop. The sign on the front read Sheridan Jewelers.

Ryan followed him and said, "What are we doing here?"

"I'm makin' things right."

"What?"

Before Jack could answer, a short, busty, middle-aged wom-an stepped out of a back room. She looked at Jack and said, "I know you, don't I?"

He said, "Yes, ma'am. We've done business before, but it was a long time ago. I need a ring."

"We keep everything in the vault these days. I just don't know who I can trust and who I can't. Do you have method of payment? Unfortunately, we cannot accept standard currency."

"Yes, ma'am. I have gold coins."

"That'll work just fine. We are still using the last known spot price, if that's okay with you."

"I'm sure that'll be just fine."

"What kind of ring are you looking for?"

"I want the best engagement ring you got."

Ryan said, "Holy *shit!*" He spun to look at Jack. "Oh my God! You are gonna marry Nicole? Oh, man! This is so *huge!*"

"I'm gonna ask her. It'll be up to her if we get married or not."

"What if she says no?"

"I wouldn't blame her if she did."

Ryan walked in a circle. "This is so crazy! I can't believe you are doing this. You've only known her like—what?—two weeks?"

"It's been a long two weeks."

"And you're sure about this?"

"More sure than anything in a long, long time."

The lady brought out a small, black velvet tray with six rings. Some of them had matching wedding bands. She said, "The two here on the end are the nicest we have. In fact, this one is probably the most well-appointed ring we've ever had in this store."

Jack said, "I don't know. Seems a little complicated. What about this one over here?"

"This is my favorite and the nicest single diamond we have. The center stone is Asscher cut, with baguettes on the side. The total weight is a little over three carats."

"How much are ya askin' for it?"

She took a small piece of paper and wrote down a price. She slid the paper toward him.

"I see. Seems a little spendy given the recent developments in the world."

"Oh, I'm sure we'll get things straightened out in no time."

"No, ma'am. It will be a long time before things get worked out." He took her pen and paper and wrote down a number of his own. "I was thinkin' more along these lines."

He slid the paper back toward her and said, "But you have to size it in the next five minutes."

She looked at him and said, "You can't have that much gold with you right now, do you?"

He pulled a velvet Crown Royal bag out of a small leather case he had brought with him and set it on the glass counter, with the clunk of many small coins inside.

"Oh, I see."

"Ma'am, I have to be on my way in five minutes. With the ring or without it. It's your choice."

"Done. What size do you need it to be?"

Jack pulled a small bar of soap out of the bag. Pressed into the back of the soap was the impression of a ring. He looked at Ryan and said, "She left it on the counter in the bathroom."

Ryan grinned. "That's pretty smart, but are you sure it fits the right finger?"

"She wears the ring I got this from on the same finger but opposite hand. If it don't fit, we'll just have to bring it back another day."

"When are you going to give it to her?"

"When she says yes."

"I mean, when are you going to ask her?"

Jack shrugged his shoulders. "I'm not sure. I guess it'll be when the time's right."

The lady came out from the back of the store. She held up the ring. "What do you think?"

"I think it's beautiful, but it's only half as beautiful as the girl who's gonna be wearin' it."

She gave him a look and said, "Aw. That's nice."

They counted out the gold coins. They had to cut one of the coins into quarters to reach the exact price. He shook the lady's hand, and they headed back out of the store.

As they hustled through the other store, Jack said, "Hey, Stef. How ya doin'?"

She said, "Why are you in such a hurry?"

He said, "I told you. It's camouflage. We can't be caught back here."

"Why? What are you hiding from?"

Jack pulled the little ring box out of his pocket and opened it for her.

"Oh my God, that's incredible! Is that for Annie? Is she home?"

Jack shook his head. "That's for the little gal sittin' out in the wagon. I'm gonna ask her to marry me."

Stef looked blankly at Jack. "No way."

"Yep, I'm afraid it's true."

"I don't believe it."

"Well, I ain't got time to sit here and try to convince you. If you're standin' at the door when we drive by, you'll get a chance to see her. Just please don't say anything. I want it to be a surprise." He started moving toward the door.

"I still think you're lying, Jack Neumann. Nobody even thought you were available."

Just as he was about to open the door, he said, "I didn't either. I guess that's what the right girl can do." He waved as he left.

Nicole said, "Did you get everything accomplished that you wanted?"

Jack smiled. "We sure did. Ryan was a little surprised at the simplicity of everything, but we got it worked out." Before she could start asking questions, he said, "Nicole, it's your turn to drive. Just head back down Main Street another block or so, and then we're gonna follow Coffeen to the left."

"Where is it we are headed?"

"Big R. It's a farm and ranch supply store."

# 88.

Mark awoke with a pounding headache. His eyes were dry and sticky as he tried to open them and focus on the room around him. As he sat up in bed, his stomach rolled over inside him, reminding him he probably drank more than he should have. He wondered what time it was. The shadow on the floor was close to the center of the room, making him think it was probably close to noon.

He remembered the events of last night and started to feel angry all over. Out of all the girls at the party, how could he have picked the one that didn't even know how to suck a cock? Stupid bitch. Then he remembered the little redhead. Maybe she was still in the other bedroom. Maybe he could get a little action after all. He remembered the disgusting mess. Well, maybe he could trade her a hot shower for a little action, or... Well, he could work out the details later, but he was sure he was going to get a little.

He got out of bed, standing naked in the middle of the room. He stretched as he checked himself out in the mirror on the back of a dresser. He looked good. In spite of a hangover and a horrible evening, he looked damn good.

He walked out the door and across the hall into the other bedroom. The little redhead was gone. Evidently she had used the bedspread to wipe herself off. Her shirt, bra, and panties still lay on the floor where he had cut them off her. Oddly enough, her pants, socks, shoes, and jacket were still lying near the closet where he had thrown them. In his mind he pictured her leaving the house in the early morning completely naked with shit stains down her legs. The room still stunk like hell, so he closed the door as he left.

He walked to the bathroom, still thinking about the redhead. Most of the girls he had known didn't mind being naked at home, but they sure didn't like the idea of being naked in public. He knew. He had tried.

He pulled back the shower curtain and looked to see if the shower was wet. Maybe she had taken a shower before she left. It wasn't. He let the water get hot and then stepped inside. As he stood in the water, he thought about a plan for the day. The first thing was to find Megan. He had to talk to her and let her know what TJ was up to. As soon as she understood, they could be on their way. It occurred to him that this might be the last hot shower he would get in quite a while. He decided to enjoy it as long as possible.

He tried to think where Megan might be. Sheridan wasn't a city, but it was still big enough that it might be hard to find somebody if you didn't know where they might be headed. He recalled that TJ had said he wanted to go and see if he could help out. He had said something else about putting away grain before it got rained on. It seemed pretty likely that wherever this grain was Megan and TJ were likely to be close by. The idea of putting a bullet in TJ's face ran through his mind again. It did seem kind of appealing.

Mark leaned back in the shower, letting the water wash the soap out of his hair, when the door to the bathroom closed, and he was plunged into darkness. "What the fuck?" Must have been the wind, he thought. But, that really didn't make much sense. How could there be any wind in the bathroom? He tried to remember if he had left a window open, and he didn't think

he had. He was sure the doors downstairs were closed. He wouldn't have left one of them open. All at once it struck him: the redhead. She hadn't left. She was still here. She was in the house and had shut the door on him in the bathroom, leaving him in the dark. Fucking cunt.

There was no sense in rushing out of the shower. A little light wasn't going to change anything. He finished rinsing off and then stepped out and groped in the dark until he found a towel. He hadn't brought any clean clothes into the bathroom with him. He smiled. He didn't need them. They would just get in the way for what he had planned to do to the redhead.

He fumbled for the doorknob. When he found it, he tried to turn it, but it wouldn't move. Fuck. He twisted again, this time much harder. The knob didn't budge. He didn't think it was locked. Besides, that wouldn't make any sense; a bathroom door should lock from the inside, not the outside. He tried to find a locking knob or button or something. The knob was perfectly smooth. So the little bitch had done something to it on the other side of the door. He couldn't imagine what she possibly could have done to prevent it from turning, but it didn't matter. He could open the door. He stepped back a few paces and then stepped toward the door again, gauging the distance. He stepped back and then moved fast at the door, dropping his shoulder as he was about to make contact. The inner panel of the door caved in, and the entire thing rattled in the frame, but it remained closed. *Fuck.* He made another run at the door. This time the outer panel of the door gave way, shedding a little light inside the bathroom. He used the heel of his hand to beat out the rest of the top half of the door, leaving an inner frame inside the doorframe. He looked out and found an old, chrome chin-up bar wedged between the floor and the doorknob, preventing it from turning. He reached through the hole and twisted the chrome rod until it loosened, and the knob started to turn. He pulled the door open and stepped into the hallway. As he turned to head to the bedroom where he had left his clothes from last night, he stopped dead. Alexa

stood in the middle of the hall with his beautiful 1911 pointed directly at his face.

She said, "Things are a lot more clear in the light of day, aren't they, Mark?"

"Alexa, honey, what are you doing? Let's talk about this."

She smiled. "Honey? Really? You expect me to buy that? I might not know a lot about sex, but I am smart enough to see through your shit."

"We had a little misunderstanding last night. That's all. Let's talk about it."

"No. We're not going to talk about anything. I am going to explain a few things, and then we are leaving. Yes, that means I did find Paige hiding under the bed, you pig. One of the girls from her house came over this morning and was looking for her. I was going to forget the whole thing last night, until I realized you might be doing the same thing, or worse, to somebody else. While you were sleeping, I checked out your bags, and I found your wallet and your employee ID to the mine in Gillette. I also found your other gun, the flashlight, and a little gold and silver. Those are mine now. That's the price you are going to pay for what you did to Paige and I."

"Alexa, please. Let me explain."

Her voice was eerily calm. "There's no explanation necessary. Your actions spoke volumes. You're lucky we aren't going to go the sheriff. I bet he'd be happy to find you a nice cellmate to have sex with. Oh, and one more thing. My daddy used to tell me that it was never okay to take another man's horse, but he didn't say anything about a mule. So, we are taking that and the pack saddle too. I've had enough of this place. I'm going home."

"Alexa, Goddammit!"

She pushed the gun toward him. "Careful. Again, I might not know a lot about sex, but I am a Wyoming girl, and I do know about guns. I can leave a bigger mark on your pecker than what my teeth did last night, so you should think very carefully before you do anything stupid."

"Where is Paige? If she knew how much I helped her out last night, she won't want to do any of this now. She might want to stay with me."

"Do you actually expect me to believe any of that? She did remember you spiked her drink last night. It was also pretty evident that you cut her clothes off and left her naked. She's not sure, but you might have raped her."

"I didn't rape her."

"You did try."

"She was sick. It was nasty."

"That's just it. I was stupid last night. I made a lot of mistakes I shouldn't have. I don't really think you got very far with Paige, but I do know you thought about it. I hope it was your sore dick that prevented it. If I knew for a fact that you raped her, this would be a whole different situation, and you'd be having this conversation with the sheriff. As it is, we're going to let you go with a little fine, but I think you should leave town. Before dark every girl on this end of town will know what you did, and within a week we will spread the story throughout the entire city." She turned away from him and started walking toward the stairs. Just as she was about to start down, she said, "Mark, you are pathetic and stupid. Do you realize if you had just been real and decent and acted like half a man, you could have had every girl at that party last night? Instead, you were acting like a pompous ass and turned half the girls off before the end of your first night here. I kept telling myself you were just a little drunk. I should have known you were just another self-centered, 'me-first' little boy." She walked down the stairs and outside with saying another word.

When he heard the door close, Mark ran downstairs to check on his belongings. The pack saddle was gone and so were the panniers. His food and his cook stove were still there. The XD(m) and the rifle were gone and so was all the ammo. He knew she had the 1911 because he had been staring at it for the last ten minutes. His clothes were still there, and they weren't cut up. That was lucky. He got dressed. Upstairs, he

found three ounces of silver in the pocket of his dirty jeans. At least he had something.

As he looked around at how little he had, he wanted to explode. He wanted to kill the bitch. She had taken everything important, and now he had to figure out a way to get all new stuff before he could leave town. She had even taken the god-damn mule. How was he supposed to replace that? Everything was so fucked up. On the other hand, he was a little glad she didn't shoot him. If she had known that he was actually in the process of fucking the redhead—evidently her name was Paige—when she shit all over him and everything else, she defi-nitely would have shot him. He felt the silver in his pocket. He wondered if it would be enough to buy a gun. If he had a gun, he could get everything else he needed. He was sure of that.

He made himself a little breakfast and decided to get going. He packed up his things as best he could into a small duffle bag he found in one of the closets and then saddled Hunter. He walked back into the house and found his jacket hanging on the back of a kitchen chair. His mind barely registered the fact the jacket felt a little heavy as he swung his arms into the sleeves and found them full of horse shit.

# 89.

Jack had shown Nicole where to park the wagon near the side of the Big R store, where a chain link fence was missing from the fence posts. Several young men sat smoking and talking in lawn chairs just outside the main doors.

When they had driven into the lot, Ryan had noticed the men and leaned over to Jack and said, "Uh-oh. We've seen this before."

Jack said, "Nah. The guy in the center is Chet. He's the manager."

Ryan looked over at him and said, "Seriously, do you know everybody in Wyoming?"

Nicole said, "I was beginning to wonder the same thing."

Jack laughed. "The population of the whole state isn't five hundred fifty thousand. Besides, when you live here and run a cattle ranch, you get to know the manager of the ranch supply store pretty well."

Ryan said, "Yeah, but you know everybody. You know the sheriff, the deputies; you even know people who work in stores downtown."

"Like I said, there just ain't that many people. I think Sheridan is still less than eighteen thousand, and the population

of the entire county is only about twenty-eight. There just ain't that many people to know. When you run a business, you get to know other people who run businesses. Besides, in general, I like people. I have been known to sit and chat for a while."

Nicole feigned surprise, "You? Sit and chat? I can hardly believe that."

"I know, I know, it's a hell of a shock, but it's true."

When Nicole had stopped the wagon and set the brake, they all jumped down. Jack led them to the front of the store, where the men were sitting. As they approached, one of the men said, "Jack, nice to see you. How things at D-bar-D?"

He said, "They're a hell of a mess, Chet. Just about the same as everywhere else, I s'pect."

"Ain't that the truth? What can we help you with?"

"I don't suppose you got any barbed wire that still works?"

"Barbed wire I got plenty of. Fence posts, I don't. Damn things just disappeared right out the lot. One of the guys thought he saw some stuck in the side of the school."

"I'm okay with the posts. The disaster just ripped my fence away. I also need a pile of staples, enough salt blocks to get me through the winter, and a few other things from the store."

"We'll have to take you inside. There ain't a light in the place, and it's a hell of a mess. The other stuff you can find in the lot out back."

Jack said, "I think we'll divide and conquer. Fellas, this is Nicole. She's with me."

All five men jumped to their feet, shook her hand, and said, "Ma'am."

He continued, "I'd appreciate it if one of you could take her in and help her find anything she needs. This here is Ryan. He's from Missouri, but now he works for me. I think he and I'll take the wagon around back and see if we can get the wire we need."

Chet said, "Bobby, Mike, Tracy, go with Jack and give him a hand. He probably wants the ASTM A-21. I'll find the staples and help the lady."

An hour later Jack pulled the wagon up near the front doors of the store. They had loaded twelve eighty-pound spools of barbed wire and six salt blocks in the center of the wagon bed. He could have used a few more of each, but the weight was already near the limit of what the wagon should probably carry. In front of the store was a small pile of seeds, plastic sheeting, and a stack of hand tools including hoes, spades, and rakes. A stack of chemical bottles stood nearby. The guys started loading everything into the wagon.

A few minutes later, Nicole followed Chet out of the store. She was carrying a denim jacket with fleece lining. She showed it to Jack and said, "The girl who was sitting in front of us at the sheriff's office was wearing a jacket like this. I thought it looked wonderfully warm. Would you mind?"

"Of course not. You get anything you need, and I mean anything. You too, Ryan. If you need somethin', now's the time to get it."

Ryan said, "You know, I might take a look around."

"Be my guest, but be quick about it. We got a lot of work yet today."

Jack took the coat from Nicole and put it under the wagon bench, so she could get to it easily on the way home. He started chatting with the guys as Ryan and Nicole shopped with Chet. After a little small talk, he said, "I don't suppose any of you know anybody that's lookin' for some work? I could use a hand or two out at the ranch. I'm offerin' a place to stay, three meals, and more."

None of them did. Mike said, "If we come across somebody, we could send them out your way."

Jack thought about it and said, "Nah, better not do that. It's twenty miles out there, and I'd hate to have somebody ride all that way and then find out I got enough help. Better to find out how I can contact them, and the next time I'm in town, I'll look 'em up."

Mike said, "Ah. Yeah, I understand. Probably not a wise idea to just ride up to somebody's place unannounced anymore."

Jack smiled. "Probably not."

Mike said, "You guys headed home after this?"

"Nope. We gotta stop at the implement dealer. We need some parts."

One of the other guys said, "I hate to tell you this, but parts ain't gonna fix what's broke anymore."

Jack smiled. "Son, I hope you're wrong about that."

A few minutes later, Nicole, Ryan, and Chet came back out of the store. Nicole had a blouse, a pair of work boots, a wool vest, and several pairs of leather gloves. Ryan carried several pairs of gloves and a dark blue box. He asked Jack if he could talk to him a minute. The two stepped behind the wagon. Ryan said, "I've been thinking. I'd like to get something for Brooke, but I really don't have any money right now. Do you think I could borrow a little and then pay you back later?"

Jack put a hand on his shoulder. "Son, I'm not big on borrowing, but I understand what you're tryin' to do, and I understand the fix you're in. Let's just say whatever you got in that box is my gift to you, and you are passin' it along. How's that sound?"

Ryan said, "I'd feel better if I earned it, you know?"

Jack smiled. "The reason I'm giving you a gift is because I see how hard you're workin' to figure things out and do the right thing. I'd say you earned it."

Ryan looked up at him and said, "Thanks."

"You're welcome."

After Jack had settled up with Chet, they climbed up on the wagon and headed north toward the implement dealer.

# 90.

Just as the wagon turned right out of the parking lot, Chet and the others watched a young man riding a red roan gelding enter the parking lot from the south. The guy was wearing a black hat, a gray shirt, and black jeans. He had a small duffle bag strapped to the back of the saddle that looked awkward and half empty. As he drew closer, they could see he was a big guy, well-built and muscular, but he had a nice, clean-shaven face, and when he pulled the horse to a stop, he smiled at them. "Hey, guys. Do you sell guns here?"

Chet said, "Yeah, we sure do."

Mark climbed down from the horse. "I came up from Buffalo yesterday and got robbed along the way. They stole my mule with all my clothes, my tent—just about everything. I had a nice rifle and a pistol—a Springfield XD(m). I don't suppose you have anything like that?"

"Yeah, we have a couple different ones to choose from. But if they stole everything, do you have a way to pay for it or have something to trade?"

Mark pulled three one-ounce coins of solid silver out of his pocket. He said, "I got these. It's all I have left."

Chet shook his head. "Nah, sorry. I can't do that for what you're looking for. I might have a used revolver in your price range."

One of the guys in a lawn chair, sitting behind Chet, said, "Sorry for askin', but if that's all you got, why do you want a gun? Maybe a warm coat, some food, you know, things like that might be a better buy."

Mark said, "After being robbed, there is no way I am going to be defenseless again."

Chet said, "I thought you said you had a gun?"

Mark was a little surprised. Damn, I should have thought of that. "I did. I just couldn't get to it fast enough."

Chet said, "Uh huh. You know, if you're looking for work, there was a guy through here not ten minutes ago. He owns a big ranch west of Sheridan. He needs a few extra hands to get things put back together. He'll put you up, feed you, and probably pay you besides. I've known him quite a while. He's a good guy."

Mark thought for a second. A ranch job might not be a bad gig if he couldn't find Megan right away. "Does he raise cattle?"

"Cattle and horses. His horse operation is famous. They sell horses all over the world."

"No kidding? Yeah, I might be interested. Where is this ranch at? I might just ride out there."

Chet laughed. "I wouldn't do that. Not these days, anyway. I know he's gonna be at Sheridan County Implement this afternoon. I think they're lookin' for parts or something. Otherwise he told us to take down your information, and he'd look you up the next time he came back to town."

"So I gotta see him today? Really? You can't just tell me where his ranch is?"

"That's how he wants to do things, and frankly, I don't blame him. You just never know who might come riding up on you. Ain't that right?"

Mark nodded. "Yeah. It sure is. Where is this implement place at?"

"It's just west of Sheridan. Ride downtown and turn left on Fifth Street. Follow it out past the hospital. If you haven't passed it on your right, you haven't gone far enough. It's a big place. You can't miss it. Jack Neumann is the guy you're looking for. He's with a pretty gal and a younger guy who works for him. They're in a big, green wagon pulled by four horses."

"Okay. Sounds like a pretty good deal. I'll go talk to him. By the way, what did he buy here?"

"Fencing and gardening stuff. Lots of it."

"I suppose he's got credit."

"Nope. Jack don't use credit. He paid for everything when he got it."

"Did he trade for it?"

"Nope. Gold."

"Oh. Yeah, that would probably be helpful. Maybe I'll go try and earn some of it from him."

"Judging by what I know of Jack Neumann, I'd say he probably pays a fair wage."

"Well, I guess I need to get a jacket."

Chet said, "Mike, take our friend inside and help him find a lawyer coat."

Mark looked at him questioningly. "A lawyer coat?"

"Yep. Stays out of your way but covers your ass when you need it."

# 91.

TJ and Megan had a few hours to kill before they needed to meet the rancher and his friends at the implement dealer. TJ suggested they head a couple of blocks north to a park, where they could let the horses graze and they could fix lunch.

On the east end of the park, they found a paved pathway with a map that showed them they could travel west along the path winding through a couple of parks to the road that would lead them to the dealership. They climbed down, loosened their cinches, and walked the horses along the path.

Megan didn't talk much. TJ knew she had a lot on her mind, given everything that had happened in the last couple of days and what she had learned this morning. As they walked he would occasionally make a comment or an observation, but mostly he just gave her some space.

As the pathway followed the park behind several homes, she noticed a picnic table near the edge of a nice little pond. She wandered over, tied Chic and Ralph to a nearby tree, and sat down. TJ tied his horse and sat down next to her.

They sat quietly for several minutes, simply staring at the water. Finally TJ said, "Anything you want to talk about?"

Megan pulled the gun out of her holster and laid it on the table in front of them.

TJ said, "Wow! That is unbelievable! Where did you get that?"

"That"—she pointed at the gun—"is what Mark is gonna be hung for."

TJ picked up the gun and looked it over carefully. He set it back down in front of her and said, "No. That is a gun. It is completely inanimate. It doesn't think; it doesn't move; it doesn't act on its own. It's nothing more than an object. If Mark is to be hung, it's because he made a decision to harm somebody else. This gun, or any other, didn't take that man's life—Mark did."

"Yeah, but he did it because I told him too."

"I don't believe that."

"I told Mark that it would be best if we both had the same type of guns. I like 1911s. My dad had lots of them, and I know how to use them. He went out to find two 1911s for us. That's when he killed that man."

"Megan, what you asked him was perfectly reasonable. You wanted two guns that were similar. There's nothing wrong with that. In fact, that's a very smart thing to do. He went to find them. He had gold and silver, didn't he?"

She nodded.

"He also had another gun to trade, but Mark didn't do that. For whatever reason, he decided to shoot that man. He could have walked away and told you he couldn't find what you wanted. He could have given the man all the silver and gold coins you had. But he didn't. He could have done a thousand things that would have been perfectly acceptable, but he alone decided to murder the man. I think you need to let him be responsible for his own decisions."

"Yeah, but they want to hang him. You heard that guy."

"I know. I'm sorry, but it's his music to face."

"I want to throw the gun in the pond."

"Then do it. It won't solve anything, but if it makes you feel better, go for it."

She said, "It's just a piece of steel, isn't it?"

He nodded. "Yep. It won't care if you throw it in the pond or not. Nothing changes."

"Except if I throw it in the pond, I won't have any way to defend myself."

"That's true."

"So what am I supposed to do?"

"You have to move on. I know it sounds stupid, but it's the best answer I can give you. The phase of your life that was with Mark is over. He made his decisions, and you can't be part of that anymore. The best thing is to leave the past in the past and move forward with your life."

"Working on a ranch?"

"Hey, it's honest, it's good experience, and it's the best option I can come up with. Have you ever spent any time on a ranch?"

"No. Not really. I did the rodeo thing for a summer."

"A ranch is like a big family. Everybody pitches in, and everybody works together for a common goal. It's kind of cool. I liked it a lot as a kid."

"All right. If you say so, I'm up for it. It's something different."

"You'll love it." TJ looked at his watch. "We should keep moving if we want to meet them at the dealership. Can't be late for our interview."

They stood and walked over to the horses. Just as TJ untied his horse, Megan's arms slipped around him. She hugged him tightly and then kissed him. As she looked up into his eyes, she said, "Thanks for making me feel better."

"Any time."

# 92.

As the wagon headed north on Main Street, Nicole sat quietly. Jack and Ryan talked a little, but it was mostly superfluous conversation to pass time. The wagon turned west on 5th and started heading out of town, and still Nicole seemed withdrawn. Her mood bothered Jack, so he turned to her and said, "You seem a little quiet."

"Yes. I am thinking."

"Penny for your thoughts?"

"I wasn't going to say anything, but I realized that it does, in fact, bother me."

"What's that?"

"So it seems we are back to 'she's with me.'"

Jacked sighed and smiled. "I know you think that don't mean much, but around here it does. It's better than sayin' you're my girlfriend."

"Why?"

Jack felt a little nudge in his ribs from Ryan. He ignored it. "Well, 'cause you ain't a girl, and we're more'n friends. So if I say you're my girlfriend, that's like sayin' we have coffee and talk sometimes. If I say 'she's with me,' then everybody knows

we're a couple. Did you see them boys jump up when I told 'em?"

"Yes, I did. I was going to ask you about that."

"They wouldn't have moved any faster if I had said you were my wife. It's their way of showing respect." Jack felt that little nudge again.

"If you wouldn't have said anything, they would consider me fair game?"

"They'd be careful. Very careful. But they might."

"So what if we were married? How would you introduce me then?"

Jack felt the nudge again, only this time it was stronger. "I would introduce you as my wife."

"And would they treat me differently?"

"Probably not. Just like today, they would show you the same respect as they would me, but you don't get all the teasing and bullshit I get to put up with."

"So today you told everybody that I was 'with you.' If I went back to town on my own, what would they do?"

"They'd watch out for you. Make sure you were safe."

"Would things be any different if you had introduced me as your wife?"

Jack felt the little nudge again, and this time he nudged Ryan back with his elbow—hard. The kid wasn't expecting it and nearly fell off the right side of the bench. Jack had to grab the back of his shirt and pull him back up. "Careful, son. There's lots of bumps on the road you're headed down." He turned back to Nicole. "Sorry, darlin'. To answer your question, no they'd probably do the same thing. But I s'pect if I had introduced you as my wife and you wanted to conduct business in my name, they'd probably let you."

"Based on an introduction alone?"

"That's the way things are around here."

As they passed the burned-out apartment buildings, Nicole said, "Oh, didn't you want to stop by the hospital?"

"We'll have to do it another day. We're runnin' out of daylight, and our business at the dealership is more important."

"Yes, but what if they had a patient who needed surgery, and there was no one else available?"

"Then they'd probably be lookin' for me."

She smiled. "Yes, that does make sense."

A few minutes later, they pulled into the parking lot of Sheridan County Implement.

# 93.

As the wagon turned into the lot, Jack could see two horses and a mule tied to the back of a skid steer that lay on its side near the front of the building. "Looks like our applicants made it. Ryan, let's take the wagon around back, so we don't have to haul parts into the next zip code."

Ryan pulled the horses to a stop just behind the back door. He set the brake and tied the reins off on the buckboard. As they looked over the shipping containers, Megan and TJ walked out the back door.

Jack said, "Good afternoon. Glad you could join us."

TJ said, "Thanks. Same to you. I hope you don't mind, but we waited inside. There's a big hole in the west wall over there."

"I don't mind a bit. In fact, let's all go in there, so we can come up with a game plan." Jack grabbed his leather bag from the wagon, and Ryan picked up his small canvas bag with tools and the multimeter.

Inside they all crowded around the parts counter near the back of the store. Jack said, "Okay, we have a list of parts Ryan put together for us. He's already got most of the factory part numbers listed out, so that should make our job a little easier. Charley told me there should be a computer printout hangin'

in a rack with their latest inventory. That should tell us if they have the parts we need and give us the location code. I think Nicole and I'll start makin' two lists of part numbers and locations. Megan, if you and TJ want to find 'em, Ryan will check 'em out with his little gadget before we put 'em in the wagon. How's that sound?"

Ryan said, "Maybe we should check a few electrical things inside the containers first. You know, just random things. If they're bad, there's no sense in looking for the others. If they're good, then it makes sense to dig around."

"The kid's a damn genius."

Ten minutes later Ryan sat on a big box in the back of one of the containers with everybody gathered around. A small round alternator from a lawn and garden tractor sat in his lap next to the multimeter. He connected the leads of the meter to the terminals on the back of the alternator and spun the pulley with his fingers. He looked up and smiled. "It works awesome!"

Megan said, "You mean all the stuff in here still works?"

Jack said, "That's exactly what it means. It also means we might have some equipment running in a few days."

She laughed. "I never thought it would be exciting to get a tractor running. This is wonderful."

# 94.

Mark and the guys at Big R dug through a pile of clothing inside the store for over an hour. They couldn't find anything he liked. Every time they would pull out a coat that seemed to be the right size, he would shake his head and say it looked too "hick." When they did come across something that looked all right, it wouldn't fit or didn't feel right. After a while he started thinking about going back to the house and cleaning up his leather jacket. Maybe the job wouldn't be too bad. He really should've done that in the first place. That black leather fit him great and looked totally badass. The longer they searched and found one farmer coat after another, the more he thought it was only a few blocks to the house and not that much work.

Finally, he left and headed back to the house. He put Hunter in the backyard and tentatively went inside. He wasn't entirely sure the girls might not be waiting for him.

His coat was still lying in the middle of the kitchen floor where he had thrown it. He picked it up and started turning the sleeves inside out as he went to the sink. He needed something to scrape the big chunks off the lining and opened a few drawers looking for a knife or spoon or something. He found a

rubber spatula in a drawer near the corner, and as he looked at the sleeve in his hands, getting ready to start scraping shit, he noticed his XD(m) sitting snugly in its holster on the counter near the toaster. He dropped the jacket and picked up the gun. He couldn't believe it. He ejected the magazine and looked. It was still full. When Alexa had said she had found his other gun, he thought she had meant this one. She must have meant his rifle. This was totally awesome! This was the key to everything else. He wondered briefly how he could have missed it on the counter, but then realized that Alexa missed it as well. He slipped the blade of the holster under his belt and felt the weight of the gun next to him. It felt good. Damn good.

He went back to work on the jacket, but now he didn't seem to mind the job so much. It took him a little over an hour, but he got most of it clean. After scraping off most of the bigger pieces, he washed it several times in the sink. He put it on wet and didn't care. It was time to get out of here.

As he rode down the street, it occurred to him that he could just forget the whole thing. He could leave town and ride away from here and from everything in his past. He could leave the murder in Buffalo, the fucked up girls in Sheridan, and leave Megan to whatever her own future held for her. Now, with a gun, he had options. Now, any and every ranch house or farmhouse along his path was a place to stay. He could follow Alexa out of town and get his stuff back. A mental picture of her lying naked and dead in a ditch somewhere looked pretty good. He thought about Stacy just outside of Buffalo. He could set up with her for a while. That would be awesome. It would be a hell of a lot better than working his ass off on some ranch someplace, probably making another old, soft man rich. The idea did have possibilities...

When he got to the end of the street, he turned right. He headed north toward town without ever really understanding why. Even as he turned west on 5th, he continued to think about skirting around the west side of Buffalo and then shacking up with Stacy for the winter. She had guns, food, water,

shelter—hell!—everything they needed, and she had a great ass as an added bonus. As he passed the hospital, he wondered why he was going to talk about a job on a ranch. Then he smiled. No, he didn't need a job. He had a gun. The guys at the store had told him the rancher had gold. He could make this short and sweet. In and out. Just hand over the gold, mister, he thought, in a cheesy western voice. Nobody needs to get hurt. The thought made him smile. Fuckin' A, man! This was too easy. Get the gold and head out of town. Stay at the first place he found, and then on to Buffalo and Stacy's sweet ass in the morning.

# 95.

Light outside was just starting to fade in the late afternoon as they worked. Nicole and Jack had pored over the computer lists inside the store and had found all of the part locations for Megan and TJ. They were now digging through the containers, trying to find the last of the parts, and Ryan sat near the wagon, testing everything. So far, everything had worked perfectly. Now Jack and Nicole were in the process of trying to find parts Ryan had listed under Generic Repairs on his list. They included things like extra spark plugs and spark plug cables, battery cables, undamaged spools of wire, a soldering iron or the parts to make one, some carburetor parts, chain saw chains, and a few filters. Ryan had also taken the liberty of collecting other parts he decided they needed as they looked for parts on the list. Earlier, when Jack had asked him about several boxes of taillights, several big tractor alternators, and a bunch of batteries, he had said, "Trust me."

Megan walked into the store and asked, "How's it going in here?"

Jack looked up from the computer printout on the counter and said, "Good. We're just about done. We should be wrappin' it before too long. How're you guys doing out back?"

She said, "It's getting so dark in those containers we can't see much. Thankfully things didn't move around very much inside, otherwise it would have been a mess. Ryan said it was because the magnetic field didn't affect the contents of those big boxes. Isn't that weird?"

"Yep, that is weird."

"I'm going out to get a flashlight from my saddlebag. Oh, we found the coils and the controller for the generator. Ryan said he has all the parts to make it work again."

Nicole was looking through a pile of parts and debris on the floor near the door. She said, "I cannot believe we might have electricity again. The simple act of flipping on the lights when you walk into a room seems like a luxury out of a dream."

Jack said, "I am kinda fond of the lights myself, but I'll appreciate a tractor a bit more. It'll save us thousands of hours of work."

Megan said, "I just want a hot shower or bath. It would be so nice to stand in a shower and get really clean again. Just once."

Jack said, "We got that already. Propane at the house works just fine. You'll have that tonight."

"Are you kidding me?"

"No, ma'am. As soon as we get to the house, it's yours."

She smiled and said, "I think I'm going to like this job." Then she walked out the front door.

Nicole said, "I like her. She seems smart, and she knows what she wants."

Jack said, "I do too. Both of 'em have no trouble workin'. That's for sure."

Nicole walked up to Jack and gave him a quick kiss on the cheek. "It's starting to cool off. I'm going to fetch my jacket out back from the wagon. Do you need anything?"

"Nah. I'm all right."

Outside, Megan walked to the side of Chic and began to rummage through the saddlebag. For a brief moment, she started to panic and then relaxed when she found the light. She flicked it on and then off quickly, testing it on the ground

in front of her. She patted the horse on her neck and then grabbed her jacket off the back of her saddle. The evening air was getting cool, and a little shiver ran through her. She put the coat on and then took her hat off briefly to fix her ponytail. Satisfied everything was where it should be, she put her hat back on and headed for the door. She stopped briefly as Chic whinnied loudly behind her. She said, "Don't worry; we won't be long." As the door closed behind her, another horse just beyond the parking lot whinnied back.

# 96.

Mark stood just behind some scrub and trees on the other side of the road from the parking lot of the implement dealership. When he had first ridden up, he had seen the two horses and the mule. At first it didn't even occur to him it might be Megan and TJ. Only when the horse in the lot whinnied and then Hunter whinnied back, did he make the connection. Now the damn things wouldn't shut up. Every five or ten minutes, they would call to each other. He had taken Hunter down the road a little farther and tied him, but it still didn't matter.

He thought the rancher was supposed to be here, but he couldn't see anyone or anything other than the horses and the mule. He thought briefly about sneaking around the back to check things out, but there was probably nothing back there but more tractor crap, and it seemed like kind of a long way. He was just about to sneak up to the store for a closer look when the door opened.

Megan walked out and up to her horse. He couldn't believe it. What were the odds that she would be here? He watched as she dug through her saddlebag. She pulled something out, but he was too far away to see what it was. Then she turned the flashlight on briefly. Of course! It was getting dark, and

they must be planning to wait for the rancher. He wondered if Megan had come up with the same idea he did, namely, to get the guy's gold. She was smart. She had to be thinking the same thing he was.

She picked up her jacket from the back of the saddle and then took her hat off. She hooked it over the pommel of the saddle and then pulled the ponytail out of her hair and shook her hair out. That thick, dark, auburn hair almost seemed to burn in the late afternoon sun. He knew how that hair felt and how it smelled as it fell around his face as she knelt over him and bent to kiss him. God, he missed her!

He watched as she re-did her ponytail and put her hat back on. Then she walked back toward the front door. She had almost reached the door when Chic whinnied. He panicked. If Hunter called back, he was busted. He grabbed and handful of rocks and threw them at his horse's feet. Hunter started to dance. He threw a few more rocks and looked at the door. Megan was almost back inside. He tossed a few more rocks, but Hunter didn't care. He called back to Chic, but by that time the door had closed behind her.

He needed a plan, and he needed it quick. He had to talk to Megan. If he could talk some sense into her, they could figure out something to do with TJ while they waited for the rancher together. Then they could take the gold and get out of town. Things were going to work out awesome! But how was he going to talk to her with TJ getting all up in his shit? He had to figure out what they were doing and where they were inside the building.

He snuck across the street and up behind the horses and the skid steer that lay on its side. He recognized the little loader. It was the same model Bobcat he had run back at the mine. Now it lay dead on its side, and that was fine with him.

# 97.

Ryan had been testing everything they brought to him from the containers. Every single part worked exactly like it was supposed to, or at least as well as he could determine. He was no expert at this electrical stuff, but most of what he was doing was really pretty basic. With every working alternator, circuit board, cable, coil, condenser, and starter he put in the wagon, the more excited he became. This was actually going to work. They should be able to get both the little tractor and the big tractor running again. The little Gator was going to be a breeze to fix. The generator was a lot more difficult, but if they worked at it, they should have all the parts they would need—and a little juice was going to be great! Then it dawned on him: the pump on the freezer and refrigerator were probably bad, and the wiring for the thermostat was probably was shot. Oh well, just more to fix.

When they first started gathering parts out of the containers, he had noticed a red taillight sitting on top of a box. He looked at it carefully and realized that it had LEDs instead of lightbulbs. A half hour later when he was testing one of the alternators, he happened to think of an idea. What if he took an alternator and hooked it to a windmill. The windmill could

turn the alternator and charge a battery. If he used the juice in the battery to power little LED lights, they wouldn't have to run the generator just for lights. Seemed like a good idea.

As he sat and worked, he thought about the light idea some more. He tried to work out all the parts and pieces he would need in his head. He had made a mental checklist and was going over it while he worked when he heard a horse out front whinny. A few seconds later, another horse, this one farther off, whinnied back. That's odd, he thought.

As he continued to work, he thought about the horses. He didn't know that much about them yet, but he did know they didn't make that sound very often. In fact, there were only a couple of times he could remember, and it always seemed to be when one horse was saying hello, or when one horse was lost or wandered too far away from the others. Megan and TJ had two horses and one mule. He remembered seeing them on the way in. They had been tied to some big piece of equipment. The mule didn't make that sound. That was obvious. Maybe one of Megan's horses had gotten loose and wandered away from the other one. The horse out front whinnied again. Then a second one that sounded close to the first called. A third one called back, but this one was farther away. Something wasn't right. Something didn't make sense. There were too many horses making noise. Ryan looked at the horses standing in front of the wagon. All four were at attention with their ears straight up and their eyes trying to look toward the front of the building.

Maybe he was losing his mind, but something was definitely not right here. Ryan thought it might look stupid if he did the wrong thing, but it would be worse if he didn't do anything at all. He stood up, walked to the front of the wagon, and slid his rifle out of the leather scabbard.

# 98.

Mark crouched next to the front door of the storefront of Sheridan County Implement. He couldn't hear anything inside. He pictured Megan and TJ sitting near the back of the store waiting for the rancher to arrive. The inside of the windows had been coated with cheap foil tinting, and the late sun made it hard to see anything inside. He thought about moving to another window to get a better view when a little movement inside caught his eye. He cupped his hands around his eyes and tried to get a better look through the glass.

About ten feet inside the store, Megan stood in the middle of the aisle. She was holding something in front of her, and Mark thought she might be reading the label. He didn't see anyone else. Maybe TJ was out back. That would be perfect.

He snuck to the front door and pulled it open smoothly and slowly and evenly, making little or no sound at all. He stepped inside and caught the door as it started to close behind him. Megan stood about ten feet in front of him. He had been right: she was facing away from him, reading the side of a box. He allowed the door to close quietly and then, as quiet as he could, he moved up behind her. At first, something didn't seem quite right. The jacket was right and the hat was right, but something

about her jeans didn't seem right. She looked like she had gotten taller or lost some weight. Whatever it was, it was working, because her ass looked phenomenal.

She turned a little to the right. Now Mark was certain it was Megan. She had gotten a new holster that was little more than a wide, leather band around the trigger and breech of the pistol. With a good portion of the gun exposed, he could see the highly figured wood grip and polished chrome slide with the gold inlay as it hung against her thigh. There was no doubt—this was the Diamond Grade Colt.

Seeing the gun made Mark remember the moment in the hotel room when he gave it to her. He had thought about proposing. He wanted to. He wanted to offer this gun as a diamond engagement present, but something had stopped him. Maybe it sounded corny to him in his head. She had even given him an excited look when she guessed "ring." He really should've asked her. Maybe in a few days, when they got away from here, he would pop the question; but now, he just needed to talk to her.

Mark knew exactly what to do. He knew because the same thing had happened to him just a couple of nights ago. He quietly slipped behind Megan, grabbed the grips of her pistol with two fingers, and started to slip it out of the holster. But before he could get it all the way out, Megan's hand slammed down on top of his own, and she screamed. But it wasn't Megan.

Mark panicked. He wrapped his left hand around the girl's face and covered her mouth. Her hat fell off, and dark hair spilled out from where it had been. He jerked his other hand holding the pistol up and out of the holster. In front of him, a middle-aged guy with a black hat came flying toward him from the back of the store. Mark said, "Stop right there!" At first he pointed the pistol down the aisle at the man, but then moved it to the side of the woman's head. He yelled, "Don't you fucking move! I swear to God, if you do anything, I'll blow her head off. You get me?"

The man skidded to a stop and stared at him. His eyes were very blue, and he didn't seem to blink. He slowly nodded. "Yep.

I understand. Listen, you don't have to do this. I bet we can work this out."

Mark laughed. "No shit, Sherlock! We're going to work it out just fine, because you are going to do exactly what I say. First of all, I want you to shut the fuck up. Do you understand me?"

"Yeah…"

Mark clicked off the safety and pressed it hard against the girl's head. "Okay. That would be a *no*, you didn't understand. I said shut the fuck up. That means that you don't say anything at all. Get it?"

The man nodded.

Mark looked at the dark-haired girl wrapped in his left arm. She was in a full panic. Tears were running from her eyes, and she was breathing hard through her nose. "See? It's not that hard, is it sweetheart? I guess this asshole over here can be taught." He turned to face the guy again. "Now, asshole, back the fuck up and put your ass up against that counter. Then I want your hands out to the sides on top of the counter. Do you think you can do that, or do I have to draw you a picture? Move!"

Jack backed up and did exactly what the guy asked. He didn't hesitate, and he didn't say anything.

Mark said, "Slowly—and I mean very fucking slowly— take your gun out of the holster by the grip and put it on the ground."

Jack did as he was told.

"Kick it over here."

Jack pushed the gun with his boot so that it slid about half-way between them.

"Now, empty your pockets on the counter. Do it slow and don't try anything, or I'll fucking kill her. You know I will."

Jack pulled a couple of pieces of paper out of his left pocket and set them on the counter behind him. Then he pulled a small, black velvet box out of his right front pocket and set it on the counter.

"Is that it?"

Jack nodded.

"You're the rancher, right? Don't you have some gold?"

Jack shook his head.

Mark turned to Nicole. "Honey, where did you get this gun? Don't you scream and don't you lie to me."

He removed his hand slowly from her mouth. Red marks where his fingers had been started to rise on her right cheek. She said, "Jack gave it to me."

"Okay, pretend for a second I don't know Jack."

"Jack. Right there. That man is Jack."

He waved the barrel of the gun toward Jack. "This guy? The guy at the counter?"

She nodded.

"Okay, asshole. Where did you get the gun?"

"I bought it about seven or eight years ago at a charity auction out east with a friend of mine. I donated it to the firearm museum in Cody, where they had it on display off and on for a couple of years. When we were over there a couple of weeks ago, they gave it back to me, and I gave it to her."

"That's *bullshit!*"

Jack shook his head. "You asked. I told you."

"This is a nice piece. Why'd you give it to her?"

"I'm in love with her."

"Well, ain't that fuckin' sweet. Where's Megan?"

Jack said, "I don't know."

"*Bullshit!* That's her horses outside, and this is her gun. I asked you, where the fuck is Megan?"

"And I told you, I don't know. She might be out back."

"I'm right here." Megan stepped out from behind a shelf that blocked Mark's view of a door. "Mark, let her go."

"Fuck you. I don't think so."

"She's not part of this, and you know it. You came here looking for me, and here I am. Let her go."

"Where's your idiot, pecker-pullin', gaywad fuck-buddy?"

"I'm talking to him, you pussy."

Instantly, Mark was full of blind rage. He wanted to kill her. He screamed, "Fuck you!" And swung the gun toward Megan.

An incredibly loud gunshot rocked the enclosed room. At the same instant, Mark's head flipped backward as blood, brains, and hair sprayed behind him over the front of the store.

Jack ran forward and scooped Nicole up in his arms as Megan screamed and collapsed to her knees. TJ ran in through the back door with his gun drawn. After a quick look around, he secured his weapon and ran to Megan.

Jack moved Nicole to the back and held her while she cried. She said, "I was so frightened. I thought he was going to shoot you, and I couldn't do anything. I'm so sorry."

He said, "There there, darlin'. You did just fine. I was the one to blame. I shoulda had my gun in my hand when he came through the door."

TJ kept asking Megan what happened, but she couldn't talk about it. He held her while she cried.

After several minutes Jack moved everybody outside and away from the smell of gun smoke and blood. As he calmed Nicole, Ryan moved several chairs out of the building and put them around a fire he built from old cardboard boxes and pallets. Once everybody had a chance to calm down, Jack said, "I think we need to talk about this a little bit. I need to understand what happened here. Who was that guy?"

Megan still sniffled but said, "This is all my fault. His name was Mark. He and I met in Gillette, and we kind of started seeing each other. We made our way to Buffalo and stayed there for a while. That's where we met TJ."

TJ took over for her. "Something happened in Buffalo, and until this morning we didn't know what it was. All we knew was that he wanted to leave town fast, and his mood had changed."

Megan said, "He changed. I swear he did. When I met him, he wasn't like this at all. Then he turned into suck a jerk."

Jack stopped her. "Can I see your gun, ma'am?"

She pulled the pistol out of her holster and handed it to him grip-first. Jack took the gun and shook his head. He held it out to show Nicole. She said, "Oh my! That is exactly the same gun I have."

Megan said, "What?"

Nicole showed her pistol.

Jack said, "Delgado Cruz and I bought these at the same time. These are the only two pistols like this in the state of Wyoming, probably in the West. I heard this mornin' that Del was murdered. I guess we know who killed him."

Megan said, "I know. We overheard your conversation with that guy from Buffalo. That's when we found out what he did. I'm so sorry."

Jack bunched his eyebrows in thought. He looked confused and, one at a time, looked at everybody around the fire. He said, "Wait a minute. Who fired the shot?"

At first nobody said anything. Finally Ryan said, "I did."

Jack turned to him, "How'd you know something was wrong? Weren't you out here workin' on things?"

"Yeah, I was. I heard the horses out front, and I knew something wasn't right. I grabbed my rifle and was going to check things out when Megan saw me heading for the door. She followed me, and we heard some of the conversation. The two of us came up with the plan."

Jack said, "What plan?"

Megan said, "I was going to distract him, and then Ryan said he would do the rest."

Jack said, "So you shot him."

"Yes, sir."

"With Nicole standin' right next to him?"

"Yes, sir."

Jack stared at him intently. "You took a hell of risk."

"No, sir. It was an easy shot. The longer we waited, the riskier things were getting."

Jack said, "You're right. I'm proud of you. You did the right thing, and you didn't hesitate. I'm damn glad to have you around, and I thank you for what you did in there."

Ryan said, "Thanks, and you're welcome."

They all sat around the fire for a few minutes without saying anything, everyone lost in their own thoughts. Nicole broke

the silence by asking, "Are we going to try and make it home this evening, or are we going to find somewhere to stay?"

Jack looked up. Thousands of stars shone brightly above, and only faint hints of the ribbons of color swirled occasionally in the sky. Toward the east a nearly full moon was beginning to cast shadows. "We're going home."

Ryan said, "What do we do with the little issue inside?"

Jack said, "Megan, TJ. You both knew Mark. We can't leave him in the store, and it ain't right to just toss him out. If you two give us a hand diggin' a grave, we'll help you lay him to rest."

Megan nodded.

It took all of them nearly an hour and a half to dig a shallow grave and bury Mark in a tree line near the store. When they had thrown the last shovelful of dirt on the grave, TJ bowed his head and prayed. When they looked up, Jack spoke in a deep but quiet tone. "Life is a series of choices. It's the big decisions we make early on that define us and set the course of our lives. We decide what kind of person we want to be. We decide if it's worth the effort to be honorable and respectable. We decide what is important and what is valuable, what should be discarded, and what should be cherished. Sometimes we get it wrong, and our decisions hurt the people we care most about. Then, we get to decide if we are gonna learn the lesson and take it to heart, or not. Doin' the right thing ain't easy, because most of the time, it means you don't get what you want. It's a shame this young man didn't learn all those lessons. Maybe there wasn't anybody to show him."

Half an hour later, they were getting ready to leave. Ryan was finishing the installation of a small switch next to the wagon bench. He flipped it on, and two tractor lights powered by a big battery shined brightly from the front of the buckboard. Jack laughed. "You gotta love technology."

He was adjusting a few things in the back of the wagon to even the load, while Nicole was saddling the single horse for

Ryan. As Jack jumped down from the wagon bed, Megan said, "Well, after everything that's happened, TJ and I thought we should probably head back to town."

He said, "Nonsense. I thought you wanted a job."

"I do. I mean, we do. But you know, with everything that happened, it's all kind of weird."

"Do you want to work, or not?"

"Yeah, we do, but—"

"Megan, honey, you got a choice. You can work hard, be part of our ranch and our family, and build somethin', or you can find somethin' else to do. I don't think you were part of the trouble that boy got into, and if you were, you probably learned an expensive lesson. What do you want to do?"

"I really want to try things at your ranch."

"Then get your ass on that horse."

She smiled. "Are you sure?"

From the bench Ryan said, "Once you get to know Jack, you'll find out he's always sure. Sometimes he's wrong, but he's always sure."

Headlights shown on the four horses as they pulled the wagon out onto the road and turned right. Ryan, Megan, and TJ followed on horseback. Gus the mule and Hunter were tied to the back of the wagon and walked quietly. When they had traveled about a half mile, Nicole said, "I've been meaning to ask you something."

Jack said, "Shoot."

"What was in that little box you pulled out of your pocket."

"I'm not sure I know what you're talkin' about."

"Yes, of course you do. When Mark told you to empty your pockets, you withdrew a small, black box and set it on the counter."

"Did I?"

"Jack. You're not daft. You know precisely what I am referring to."

He smiled.

"May I ask what is in that little box?"

"Are you sure you want to do this now?"

She smiled and slid closer to him on the bench. "Yes. I am quite sure."

"Really sure?"

She was getting very excited. "Yes. I am absolutely certain."

"Here." He handed her the reins of the horses, scooted forward on the bench, and then knelt on the floorboards where his feet had just been. He pulled the little box from his pocket. "Nicole Meredith, I know it's only been a few short weeks since we met, but I've known the entire time that I love you. That feeling has only grown deeper and stronger every day. I would be honored and privileged if I could love you and spend the rest of my life with you. Will you be my wife?" He opened the box.

Tears were freely flowing from her eyes. They streamed down her cheeks and dripped from her chin. "Yes, Jack! A thousand times, yes. I would be honored to be your wife." She grabbed him and hugged him as hard as she could.

When she finally let him go, he asked, "Are you sayin' yes 'cause you love me, or 'cause I'll quite sayin' 'she's with me'?"

"I am saying yes because I am madly in love with you and have been since we met."

"So, how'd you know what was in the box?"

She smiled. "I can't give away all my secrets."

"You might let me in on this one."

"I knew you loved me. That was obvious and has been for some time. But, I also knew it would take you a little while to understand what you felt. You are such a man of principle; if you love me, and I am living in your house, and we are having sex—very good sex, I might add—it would only be a matter of time before you would find it necessary to make an 'honest' woman of me. It's the way you are."

"Did you try to manipulate me?"

"Not at all. It's as you said: it is about the decisions we make. If you would never have asked me, I would stay regardless. That is my decision. I feel actions are more important than titles. I don't need to be your wife to love you and care for you."

"So you think titles are important to me?"

"No. Not in the least. You are not impressed by a man's title, but by his character. Your character dictates that if you love me, you will do everything to honor me. That means giving me your name."

"How'd you get so smart?"

"I've been hanging around you."

They rode quietly for a few minutes. Jack said, "I'm gonna tell you somethin'. It's gonna sound a little weird, but it's the truth. I think this disaster has been one of the best things that ever happened to me. Without it, I never would have met you. I'd still be wanderin' around alone in the dark."

She said, "I feel the same way. I didn't know what was important until everything was taken away, and only the important things were left."

# EPILOGUE

### Saturday, October 27

Jack awoke with a start. He sat up quickly in bed as next to him Nicole said, "Did you hear that?"

He said, "I sure did."

"What was it?"

"I don't know." He was already getting out of bed and trying to find his pants in the dark room. "You might want to get dressed. Probably best to be ready for anything."

As she slipped out of the other side of the bed, Jack managed to find his shirt and then slipped his feet into a pair of leather slippers. He picked up the gun that lay on the bedside table and slipped it into the top of his pants just behind his right hip. Nicole came out of the bathroom wearing a pair of jeans and one of his big flannel shirts. Together they started making their way out of the bedroom and toward the front door.

Jack put his jacket on and, just as he was about to reach for the doorknob, a deep throaty sound outside chugged a few times and then growled to life. Jack looked at Nicole and smiled. "That's the tractor."

"They got it running?"

"They sure did. Let's go see."

He held the lantern in front of them as they made their way across the yard and through the barn. In the back and to the left of the barn was the mechanical shop where Ryan, TJ, and Miguel were working under several battery-powered lights. They were laughing and high-fiving each other as the big, green, four-wheel drive tractor idled in front of them. Jack yelled, "Congratulations!"

Ryan stepped up into the cab and shut the big motor down. He said, "Hard to hear with that damn thing running."

Jack said, "Great job, guys! This is big. This changes everything."

TJ said, "You haven't seen this yet." He sat down in the Gator and twisted the key. The little diesel motor jumped to life, and the lights came on.

Nicole clapped her hands, and Jack shook his head in disbelief. "You guys are amazing!"

Ryan said, "We're starting to figure this stuff out. It turns out that not everything needs to be replaced, and some stuff can be fixed, but everything that has a winding in it seems to be in bad shape. We should have the other tractor running in the morning, and then I'm going to start working on the generator. That might be a lot harder."

"I'm sure you guys'll get it worked out."

"Yeah, I think so too; it's just going to take some time."

Jack looked at his watch. "Y'all realize it's damn-near three thirty?"

Miguel looked surprised. "Oh. That is not too good. We have to get up in a few hours and do chores."

"You guys should sleep in tomorrow. You deserve it."

Nicole said, "I don't suppose you have any plans to repair the washing machine? I realize these are much more important, but doing laundry by hand is really quite a bitch."

Ryan laughed. "Maybe TJ and I will start taking a look at it tomorrow."

Jack winked at him. "I'd say that's probably wise."

## Tuesday, October 30

Nicole stood in the kitchen, kneading bread dough in a big metal bowl. The guys had left early in the morning with both tractors, a trailer, and several spools of barbed wire. Julia had left after breakfast to get a few things done at her own home, and the house was quiet.

Life was starting to develop a rhythm, and that was good thing. Nicole liked the quiet and a pace that felt normal and much more relaxed. As she worked she thought about her mother, her sister, her father, and her upcoming wedding. She wished more than anything that someone from her family could be there. She had always dreamed of a big, white church wedding, of walking down the aisle with her father and having him give her away to the man she would spend the rest of her life with. A wedding in the great room wasn't quite the same, but the reality was, it wasn't about the wedding—it was about the marriage. She realized that the dreams she had were nothing more than pictures of a fantasy. She really didn't care if her father gave her away—hell, he had given their entire family away long ago.

But still…

As things slowed down and life started to seem more normal, everybody on the ranch began to experience small mood changes. It was as though they now had time to start processing all that had happened since the disaster. All they had seen and experienced needed to be dealt with. It needed to be considered and digested and made part of who they were today.

Yesterday morning Brooke had sat at the breakfast table and suddenly started crying. When Nicole had asked if she was okay, she nodded yes, but the tears continued anyway. Later Brooke had told her about having occasional nightmares. Terrible things, like seeing Ryan burned and his body hanging out of a car, or crushed under a twisted length of guardrail alongside a lonely road. They spent a couple of hours talking

about all the things that had happened, and in the end, both of them felt better.

Even Jack, as strong as he seemed, was effected. He didn't say anything, but a couple of nights ago Nicole had awoken to him thrashing in his sleep. He seemed to be running from something or fighting something; she couldn't tell which.

In the quiet of the kitchen, she dealt with her own ghosts. She looked back and carefully thought about various things that had happened. She thought about the bad things they had seen, but she also thought about the good things that she had been a part of. As she carefully considered the entire experience, she decided that Jack was right: the disaster had been the best thing that had ever happened to her.

She divided the dough into several loafs and began placing them into the bread pans when Megan stepped into the kitchen. "Nicole, are you busy? Can we talk?"

She said, "I'm just finishing with this bread for dinner. What's on your mind?"

Megan sat down on one of the wooden stools at the island counter in front of Nicole. "I need to talk to you. I want to tell you how sorry I am for what happened the other day."

Nicole smiled at her. "Megan, there is no need for you to be sorry. In fact, I would go so far as to say what you did probably saved my life."

"It's not that. It's that I should've known better. Mark and I were close. Very close. I knew there was something going on, and I keep wondering if part of what happened was my fault."

Nicole looked at her and said, "I am so sorry you have to go through this. It must be very difficult to look back at a situation and wonder 'what if.' What if things had been different? What if you had said something or done something different? What if you had never met him at all? What you are doing is really quite normal, but you need to understand that it is also quite pointless. The past is behind us. You cannot change a thing, despite how much you may want to. The past is what brings us to where we are today. Are you happy?"

"Well, I don't know. I mean, it's not like I really thought about it. I'm happy that I am here. I'm happy that I'm getting to know TJ; he's a great guy. But I'm sad about what happened. I miss my parents, and I kind of miss Mark."

"That's good. I am not an expert in any of this, and I don't profess to be a psychologist or a counselor, but I think it's good for you to miss Mark. It is normal. You said you were close, so you must have cared about him. No one can simply shut off those feelings all at once, despite what he may have done. I know it's normal to miss your family. I miss mine terribly. Thinking about these things is healthy. Pulling out all of these small painful items and processing them in your mind helps you to understand them. And when we understand them, we can move past them."

Megan said, "I like you. You and I kind of think about things the same way. Can I tell you about Mark and all the things we went through?"

"I'll make us some tea, and then we'll sit by the fire. How does that sound?"

"That sounds great."


### Tuesday, November 20

Jack sat at the end of the kitchen table next to Nicole. She had several pieces of paper in front of her, and they were discussing Nicole's plans for the garden. Ryan sat quietly next to Brooke as they ate breakfast. Julia called from the kitchen, "I have more pancakes if anybody wants them."

Brooke said, "Yeah, I'll take them. These things are awesome!"

Ryan said, "I can't believe how much you can eat. Are you like saving it for later or something?"

"I work hard all day. I need to keep my strength up."

"I know you work, but this is ridiculous. Jack is gonna start charging you for meals if you keep eating like this."

Jack looked up at his name.

Julia brought a plate with three pancakes and a smaller plate with two pieces of toast smothered in peanut butter. As the toast passed in front of Brooke, she quickly turned her head away.

Ryan said, "What's up? You like peanut butter."

She put a hand to her mouth and started to look frightened. She also started to look pale. She said, "Oh my God." And then jumped up from the table and bolted into the bathroom.

Ryan jumped up and ran after her, but she had already closed the door.

Jack said, "Uh-oh."

It was nearly twenty minutes later when Brooke came out of the bathroom. She was pale, and her sweaty hair stuck to the sides of her face. She sat back down at the table but didn't look at the food.

Jack said, "Brooke. When was your last period?"

"Oh my God! We are *so* not talking about this. I thought we had a discussion like this once before. My period is none of your business. Seriously. Nicole, you should keep an eye on him. This is a little bit pervy."

Again, and un-phased, Jack said, "Brooke. When was your last period?"

"I don't know. Okay? It's not like I write this stuff down. Today I'm on the rag, and tomorrow I'm not. I mean, seriously, who cares?"

"Brooke?"

"Okay, so, maybe it was a while ago."

"How long ago?"

"I don't know."

Jack sat, waiting for her.

"Okay. Jesus! It was before I went to Cody. I remember because I got over it a couple of days before I left."

Jack picked up the small calendar Nicole had been using. He flipped through a few pages and said, "First part of July. Probably after the first week. My guess is the eighth."

Nicole sat up straight, and her eyes widened. "Are you saying what I think you are saying?"

Jack nodded.

Brooke said, "What? What are you talking about? What is in July?"

Jack smiled. "Your baby's birthday, darlin'."

## Friday, December 14

It was late afternoon when Nicole sat down on the couch in the great room. She looked around the room at the Christmas decorations she had just hung and smiled. The room was gorgeous. A huge tree stood in front of the windows toward the east, and various wreaths and decorations were now tastefully scattered throughout the room. Pine garland wrapped around the banister of the stairs and along the posts in the wall dividing the great room from the dining room and kitchen.

She had found the boxes marked X-mas in the basement utility room and decided to decorate. Even though she had no lights for the tree and other decorations, she didn't care. The green and red and gold were beautiful and made her feel somehow safe and secure.

Ryan had repaired the generator nearly two weeks ago and had fixed enough wiring in the house to provide lights in the kitchen, dining room, and great room. They had decided to limit the time the generator would run to evening hours only. Although there was a big tank of diesel buried in the ground, it would probably be a long time before they could get it refilled and decided to conserve as much as possible. She knew the lights wouldn't work. Everything, or at least nearly everything, that had a wire and wasn't in a Faraday cage was ruined. She would miss the lights, but she was determined not to let it put a damper on Christmas.

One small, last box sat next to the far wall of the great room near the stairs. She spotted it and remembered bringing it up, but had forgotten to open it. She walked over, sat down on the floor, and started looking through the contents. There were three large Christmas stockings on top, each with

a name: John, Jennifer, and Annie. Below the stockings were several ornaments. Each was unique, and each had writing on it. First Christmas Together. Baby's First Christmas. Charley's First Christmas. Merry Christmas Dr. Neumann! Below them, wrapped in a small piece of tissue paper was a photo. In it, Jack was much younger and had dark black hair. He had his arm around Jenni, and on her lap was a baby in a little, red and white Christmas outfit.

When she first saw the items in the box, it hurt her a little. Hearing Jack talk about his ex-wife was one thing, but to see them together with his arm around her was different. Nicole sat on the floor thinking about things for a few minutes. She hung the ornaments on the tree and put the photo on the mantle above the fireplace. These things were part of Jack's story and his history. They were part of who he was. She loved him—all of him—and that meant she needed to understand and accept his past.

An hour later Jack came through the front door from the barn. When he stepped into the house, he stopped and stared at the room in front of him. "What did you do?"

Nicole was instantly worried. She hadn't talked to him about it; she had just decided to decorate. In fact, with as busy as everyone had been, the topic of Christmas hadn't come up much. "I found the boxes in the basement. I hope you don't mind."

Jack was speechless. He simply stared at the room.

She walked to him and put her hand in his. "Is it okay?"

"Oh, darlin'. It's more than okay." His voice broke a little. "This house hasn't looked like this in a long time. It's beautiful! I can't thank you enough."

"I only wish the lights worked. I am especially fond of those little white lights."

"It'd be nice, but it's plenty beautiful the way it is."

"Can I ask who Charley is?"

"Charley? I'm not sure. I know lots of Charleys."

"Perhaps a Charley close enough that you would have a bulb labeled Charley's First Christmas.'"

"Oh. Charley. He was our dog. A golden retriever. I remember that bulb now. Where did you find that?"

"There was a small box buried behind a few other things in the basement. I also found a photo."

She brought the picture to him.

"Oh my goodness. I forgot about this. Annie's first Christmas. I was pretty young here. I'm sorry; you didn't need to find this."

"No. That's quite all right. I want to put it out. It's part of you and should be part of Christmas here."

He kissed her.


Later, everybody was sitting at the dinner table when they heard a loud rumble off in the distance. It grew in intensity. Jack looked at Miguel, TJ, and Ryan. TJ said, "That's a motorcycle."

Jack asked, "What the hell is it doin' out here?"

Miguel said, "Probably up to nothing too good."

The sound increased in volume. Jack said, "That's gotta be comin' up the road. Grab your guns."

The four men walked outside, each with a rifle. Miguel and TJ walked across the drive near the barn, while Ryan and Jack stood in front of the house. As the sound drew closer, it became more obvious it belonged to a motorcycle, probably a Harley.

After several minutes a black chopper pulled slowly up the drive. Two riders sat on the bike, both of them covered in black leather. The driver wore aviator's goggles, a red bandana over his head, and a gray goatee. The rider wore a black helmet.

The bike came to a stop, and the driver cut the engine. He flipped out the kickstand with his boot and stood up.

Jack said, "I'm gonna have you stay right there until we get to know you a little better."

The guy nodded. "Fair enough. Can't say I blame you, but I don't think you want to shoot me."

"Why's that?"

The guy smiled. "I'm Santa. I brought you a present."

The rider behind him bent forward to remove the helmet. As soon as the helmet started to lift, a light brown, braided

ponytail fell out and onto the black leather jacket. She pulled the rest of the helmet off, and Jack stood looking at his daughter.

"Annie?"

"Daddy!"

"Oh dear Jesus. It's you!" He dropped the rifle he was holding and ran over to her. She stepped off the bike and hugged him.

The rest of the night was filled with introductions and stories. Jack learned that Annie had been out on a farm call as part of her large animal class when the disaster happened. She spent several days trying to get back to campus but then learned everybody at school was trying to get home. She had made it all the way through Iowa on horseback, but then lost the horse to a thief in the middle of the night while she had slept in a barn. It took her several weeks to make it as far as Mitchell, South Dakota, and she began to worry about the weather getting worse. She happened to meet Michael while they were eating at a shelter, and they learned they were both headed to Wyoming. Michael said he had a secret plan, and if she helped him, he would help her get to Sheridan. The secret plan was rewinding the bike's starter and ignition coil with a fine wire in a specific pattern to make them work again. Four days ago they started the bike for the first time.

When Jack introduced everybody around the table, he saved Nicole for last. The idea of introducing her made him nervous, and he didn't want to hurt Annie's feelings so soon after she had gotten home. Finally, she was the only one who hadn't been introduced. Jack said, "You might'a noticed I skipped over Nicole the first time around. That's 'cause I'm not sure how to say this."

Annie started smiling. "Dad, I think you should just say it. She's special, isn't she?"

"She's very special. Annie, this is Nicole Meredith. We met south of Cody at an airplane crash. She and I are engaged."

Annie started laughing. She stood up and walked to where Nicole was seated, and they hugged. She said, "I'm so happy for both of you, but I probably won't be calling you 'Mom.'"

Nicole said, "No, no. I don't think that would be right."

Jack said, "You're not upset?"

"No. Why would I be upset? I've been telling you for years that you need to get out and meet people. Okay, I'm a little surprised. I didn't think you would find somebody so pretty."

"What? You don't think I'm good lookin' enough?"

"No, Dad. It's just, well, you know. Actually, I don't think you're smooth enough."


Tuesday, January 8


By ten in the morning, the gray clouds blanketed the sky, and the first few flakes had started falling. They had gotten a little snow in December, but temperatures had stayed fairly warm, and it had melted away in just a few days. These clouds looked different. They felt different. They felt serious.

By the time the sun started going down behind the mountains, they had nearly sixteen inches of new snow on the ground, and it didn't appear to be tapering off at all. At around midnight, the winds started. The cold wind came out of the north and blew along the Bighorns, piling up the snow they had received earlier.

The next morning Ryan opened the door to go do chores and saw nothing but pure white. Later that morning, Ryan and TJ left the front of the house, with a rope to find their way back if they got lost. They made it to the barn and took care of the animals but could do little else.

When the storm finally blew itself out almost four days later, they had received nearly two feet of snow, but most of it was blown into huge drifts that blocked everything.

Nicole loved every minute of it. It was the first time she had seen a snowstorm. The house was warm and full of activity. Everybody played games and told stories and laughed and

joked around. Best of all, she had Jack to herself. She called it their honeymoon, and they spent the majority of a day in the bedroom.

## Wednesday, May 15

Spring had come early to the Bighorn Mountains. By the middle of May, most of the early flowers were already gone, and the pastures were filled with lush, green grass. The trees were budded out, and activity at the ranch was nearly at a frenzy. The garden was tilled, and the early plants were already in the ground.

At dinner Jack said, "Today's a special day. Anybody know why?"

Everybody looked at him blankly.

"Today is Brooke and Ryan's last day."

Their heads turned quickly toward him.

He said, "If you remember last fall, I told you both that if you work for me until May fifteenth, I would give each of you a horse and all the gear you need to get yourselves back to Missouri. That day is today. Our deal is complete. After dinner if you want to pick out a couple of horses; that'd be fine with me. I want you to know: you both lived up to your end of the bargain very well. I couldn't have asked for better help."

Brooke said, "I can't go anywhere. Look at me. I'm as big as a house! You can't just kick us out like that!"

Ryan put a calming hand on her knee and winked at her. "Sir, thank you. It's been a very enjoyable relationship for both of us as well. I don't think either one of us expected to learn as much as we have. After looking at things, it seems our priorities have changed since we first negotiated our deal. We are not interested in traveling to Missouri at this time. I don't suppose you would be in the position of hiring two experienced hands?"

Jack smiled. "You've learned a lot since we first met."

"Yes, sir, I have."

"Tell you what. I'm not interested in hiring either one of you." He turned and looked at Megan and TJ. "Or either one of you two." He paused for effect and then added, "But I might be interested in takin' you all on as partners. I've been thinking about a lot of things, and I'd kinda like to restructure everything. I'm thinkin' since there isn't any money or any way to pay anybody, and nobody seems bent to leave, we might make this a long-term commitment. Megan, TJ, I know you two want a little place of your own. Brooke and Ryan, you need a place of your own too. I think over the next few days, we should sit down and come up with a plan where there is ownership in it for all of you."

The dinner table was dead quiet.


### Thursday, May 30


Jack and Nicole sat in a diesel Kubota utility vehicle looking at the ranch from high atop Highway 14. They were on their way back home from Cody. Jack had promised himself he would make good on the debts they had incurred last fall, and he intended to do so, but Nicole was not going to let him go alone.

The trip had been much easier in the vehicle. Although it was bumpy and loud, the entire trip from the ranch to Cody took them five hours, and the vehicle never got tired.

They spent the night in Cody and checked on friends. They were pleased to find that the town was doing well. It was organized and clean, and they had little trouble over the winter. They also had several pieces of equipment running and even a couple of pickups, but they were carefully conserving fuel.

When Jack and Nicole stepped into Custom Cowboy, Donna just about fell over in shock. Nicole showed her ring, and Donna hugged and fawned over both of them, calling Nicole "Mrs. Neumann" the entire time. Donna didn't want to take the little stack of gold that Jack put on the counter for her. She kept waving her hand, saying, "This is too much. It was a

gift. Take this away." But in the end they left her with it. As they drove away, Nicole asked, "How much did you give her?"

"Oh, enough to get by."

"Seriously, how much in dollars?"

"Probably close to twelve thousand."

"We didn't spend anywhere close to that last fall."

"No, but it was worth every penny. Besides, Donna is on her own now. She can use all the help she can get."

"You are such a softy."

"That's why you love me."

The entire town of Greybull had nearly burned down. The clean buildings they had seen on the initial trip were gone. There was no one around to tell the story of what had happened.

They stopped at the Hideout and checked on everyone. They were doing well. Several of the guests had left early in the spring, trying to get to the places they called home. After the shootout last fall, they only had one other incident where someone tried to take things by force; but it was a weak attempt, and they had dispatched it quickly. Although, a rider had stopped by several days ago. He had told them about some problems occurring around Casper, where a group of men were raiding farms and ranches.

The trip back over the mountains was beautiful. The warm sun shone, and the skies were crystal clear. Jack stopped at a small mountain lake and pulled two fly rods out of the back of the vehicle. He spent the next few hours showing Nicole how to fish. They had a small picnic in the grass along the shore and made love in the sunshine.

As they lay next to each other, Nicole said, "It's really quite amazing how much my life has changed in a year."

Jack said, "Yep. It's changed for everybody."

She said, "Actually, I'm thinking of more than the flare. I didn't know I was lost. I was searching for something, and until I met you, I had no idea what it was. Our experience together, the entire thing, has shown me something so much deeper and

so much more real than what I previously thought life could offer."

"Maybe it's the clear air."

"No. It's the people. It's you. It's the way people think and act and treat each other. It's the West. I think Sheridan is my eastern limit."

"You think so?"

"I know so. If I should be so lucky, I will never go back to that old way of life again. I think I will live the rest of my life west of Sheridan, and I will be happy."


*January 2, 2011–January 6, 2012*

# AFTERWORD

Thank you for purchasing this book. I hope you got as much enjoyment from reading this story as I did in telling it.

I have been a big fan of post-apocalyptic stories ever since I read Stephen King's *The Stand* nearly thirty years ago. The story was unique in that the disaster *could actually happen*, but the social implications interested me the most. What happens to people when you change everything about the way they live, and you do it in a relatively short period of time?

In recent years technology has invaded and now permeates our lives. It has changed everything from the way we share news and information to the way we communicate with each other. Today, it is just as easy for me to have a conversation with someone on the other side of the planet as it is to talk with my neighbor across the street. It has made us soft. Even the poorest people in the United States and Europe, today live at a standard that is far beyond what the kings of this world had known only a hundred years ago. My thermostat is set at seventy-six because I prefer it a little warm. Seventy-eight is a bit too much if I do anything, and seventy-four is just a bit too chilly if I am sitting at the computer writing. Our televisions get hundreds of channels to provide the entertainment I want, when I want

it. If we're hungry, a snack is usually in the fridge, and if not, we can run down to the store and have a choice of hundreds of tasty, but not necessarily healthy, items in a matter of minutes. I live in the Midwest, and as I sit and type this morning, it is twenty-two degrees and snowing outside. Down the hall in my kitchen right now, there is a bunch of bananas that look perfect. There isn't a bruise or mark on any of them. There is absolutely no natural reason why those bananas should be here in the Midwest cold if it wasn't for technology.

One evening a couple of years ago, I was sitting in a restaurant having dinner. In the booth next to me were two young ladies, and I couldn't help but overhear a great deal of their loud conversation. When the waitress brought their meals, one of the girls looked at the chicken she ordered and said, "Ew! There's *bones* in this!" She was honestly disgusted. I wanted to ask, "Honey, where do you think chicken nuggets come from?" The experience made me realize how far removed from reality we actually live. The other day I was at work, and a group of us were talking; you know how conversations at work go. Somehow the subject of going to the bathroom outside came up, and it quickly became apparent that several of the younger women had never had to relieve themselves outdoors, and most people in the room had never taken a dump outside. Yesterday, when this snowstorm started, I went out to the garage and got in my car. I hit the button and opened the garage door and then drove to work and parked in the underground lot. Not one flake of snow ever touched me.

See what I mean? We're getting soft.

That's what is so fascinating about post-apocalyptic fiction for me. I love the idea of taking people from our world—people we know and interact with who are used to this easy life—and seeing what they do when you shake things up a bit and give them a healthy dose of reality. The other thing I love is that it *could actually happen.*

I read a lot. As I mentioned, I love post-apocalyptic fiction, but I also read action and adventure, thrillers, mysteries, and

I love a good western. To give you an idea of what "a lot" is, last year I read almost eighty books. Most of the stories I read usually fall into the typical Apollonian-Dionysian dichotomy; simply put, good versus evil.

It was about a year and a half ago when I finished reading a book and it occurred to me that most stories follow the good guys around, and then, all of a sudden, the bad guys show up and start shooting up the place. I started to wonder: Where do the bad guys come from? How did they get to be bad? Why do they things they do? Did something happen to them in their past that makes them do these heinous things? As I let those question roll around in my head, I started to realize that people probably don't just wake up one morning and say, "You know, I think I'm gonna shoot me a bunch of people today." In fact, I started to think that most bad guys don't think they are bad guys at all.

When I started this story, it was my intention to illustrate how easy it is to be the bad guy. I suspect that any one of us, given the right (wrong) circumstances, could easily start crossing the fuzzy lines of ethics. Good and evil are not black and white. It is all shades of gray along a continuous spectrum, and at any point along that line, the adjacent shades don't seem so different from where you stand.

Working on a project like this is never done entirely alone. There are many people who help, even though most have no idea that they do.

I'd like to say a special word of thanks to David and Paula Flitner, owners of the Flitner Ranch and The Hideout, and Peter and Marijn De Cabooter, managers and hosts of the The Hideout Ranch in Shell, Wyoming. I have stayed there several times, and it is never easy to leave. It was on an impromptu trip to the Hideout many years ago when I was introduced to the culture and people of Wyoming, and have found myself drawn back ever since. The accommodations are luxurious and comfortable, the food is incredible, but it is the people—their honesty, integrity, and spirit—that make this resort such

a wonderful place to stay. You will arrive as a guest, but you will leave as a friend. The Hideout location is used in this story with permission.

I have long been a fan of Stephen King. I believe I have read nearly everything he has written, and I swear the man could write a story about toenail fungus and I would gladly sit rapt, absorbing every well-written detail.

When I was in the fifth grade, I had a fairly traumatic experience—at least it was traumatic in the mind of a fifth grader. As a result, I never wrote a single creative word until I was forty-five years old. (Shows you what a lousy teacher can do.) In college and graduate school, I only wrote nonfiction, and I was sure to document everything with extraordinary care. I hated the idea of putting something out there that somebody might judge me by.

When I came across *On Writing*, by Stephen King, I wasn't particularly looking for a book like this. But I loved the work Mr. King did on everything else, and as I mentioned above, the man could write about dirt, and it would be good, so I decided to give it a try. This book changed me more than any other. Above all else, he gave me the permission to write. This, from the man whose ability I respect more than any other, was what I needed. He gave me the permission to suck at it, to horse things up, to struggle, and to get it wrong sometimes. By opening the door to the world of writing, he gave me a pastime and outlet like none I have ever known before.

I don't know if I got it right in this story. That's not up to me to decide. It's for you. What I do know is that I have been given a unique opportunity—a gift. I can sit down and let my mind run wild for a while. It's a hell of a ride!

If any of you happen to bump into Mr. King, please extend my heartfelt appreciation and thanks. If you have ever thought about, considered, contemplated, or even had a slight notion to write, please pick a copy of *On Writing*. I hope it changes you the way it did me.

*Dean*